MATHIAS THULMANN: WITCH HUNTER

Witch Hunter

A NAMELESS HORROR stalks the distant district of Klausberg, leaving a trail of bloody destruction in its wake. Can Thulmann and his vicious sidekick Streng solve the Klausner curse and put an end to this reign of terror forever?

Witch Finder

THULMANN AND STRENG travel to Wurtbad to look for a blasphemous book that is rumoured to be hidden there. Shortly after they arrive, plague breaks out, and they find themselves trapped when the town gates are closed to contain the illness. Will cold steel and faith be enough to protect the witch hunter from the disease, foul monsters and magic that haunt the doomed town?

Witch Killer

THULMANN'S HUNT FOR the stolen forbidden tome lead him to a mysterious, isolated town in the wildest reaches of the Empire. Can the witch hunter and his assistant find the book and escape before their souls are trapped forever in this twisted web of evil?

A WARHAMMER ANTHOLOGY

MATHIAS THULMANN: WITCH HUNTER

C. L. Werner

A Black Library Publication

A Choice of Hatreds first published in *Lords of Valour*,
copyright © 2001 Games Workshop Ltd.
Meat Wagon first published in *Swords of the Empire*,
copyright © 2004 Games Workshop Ltd.
Witch Hunter copyright © 2006 Games Workshop Ltd.
Witch Finder copyright © 2007 Games Workshop Ltd.
Witch Killer copyright © 2008 Games Workshop Ltd.

This omnibus edition published in Great Britain in 2008 by
BL Publishing,
Games Workshop Ltd.,
Willow Road, Nottingham,
NG7 2WS, UK.

10 9 8 7 6 5 4 3 2 1

Cover illustration by Andrea Uderzo.
Map by Nuala Kinrade.

ISBN 13: 978 1 84416 554 4
ISBN 10: 1 84416 554 X

Distributed in the US by Simon & Schuster
1230 Avenue of the Americas, New York, NY 10020, US.

See the Black Library on the Internet at
www.blacklibrary.com

Find out more about Games Workshop
and the world of Warhammer at
www.games-workshop.com

Printed and bound in the US.

THIS IS A DARK age, a bloody age, an age of daemons and of sorcery. It is an age of battle and death, and of the world's ending. Amidst all of the fire, flame and fury it is a time, too, of mighty heroes, of bold deeds and great courage.

AT THE HEART of the Old World sprawls the Empire, the largest and most powerful of the human realms. Known for its engineers, sorcerers, traders and soldiers, it is a land of great mountains, mighty rivers, dark forests and vast cities. And from his throne in Altdorf reigns the Emperor Karl Franz, sacred descendant of the founder of these lands, Sigmar, and wielder of his magical warhammer.

BUT THESE ARE far from civilised times. Across the length and breadth of the Old World, from the knightly palaces of Bretonnia to ice-bound Kislev in the far north, come rumblings of war. In the towering Worlds Edge Mountains, the orc tribes are gathering for another assault. Bandits and renegades harry the wild southern lands of the Border Princes. There are rumours of rat-things, the skaven, emerging from the sewers and swamps across the land. And from the northern wildernesses there is the ever-present threat of Chaos, of daemons and beastmen corrupted by the foul powers of the Dark Gods. As the time of battle draws ever near, the Empire needs heroes like never before.

Sea
of
Chaos...

L'Anguille.

Couronne.

The
Wasteland.

Laure
fore

Marienburg.

Arden
forest.

Gisoreux.

Bordeleaux.

Bretonnia

Brionne.

Quenelles.

Grey

Loren
forest

North of Here Lie The
Dreaded Chaos Wastes.

Claus

Erengrad.

"Here Be Trolls..."

Praag.

middle mountains.

Kislev

Kislev.

heim.

Wolfenburg.

Talabheim

The Empire

Udorf.

Karak Kad

Nuln.

The
Moot.

Sylvania.
Dracken
-hof.

Zhufbar.

Averheim.

Black
Water.

Black fire Pass.

rak.
Norn.

CONTENTS

INTRODUCTION

OCTOBER HAS ALWAYS been my favourite month, the season of goblins and ghosts and things that go bump in the night. As a kid growing up, this was the one time of year when I didn't feel like the odd man out, when people didn't crook an eyebrow because you displayed an interest in werewolves and vampires. Shop windows would proudly sport snarling cats and grinning ghouls; supermarkets would add gummi spiders and chocolate eye-balls to their confections; TV stations would pack the wee hours of the morning with everything from *Mad Doctor of Blood Island* to *Tombs of the Blind Dead*. For somebody reared on a diet of horror comics, ghost stories and monster movies, October is simply over much too soon.

It is fitting that I should be writing these words as October once more starts to slip away and all the plastic skeletons and ceramic jack o' lanterns are put aside for next Halloween. The stories which follow these pages are very much the offspring of my life-long attraction to the macabre. I consider them good material to sustain kindred souls in those quiet, bleak hours of the night now that infomercials have put all the horror marathons to rest.

Mathias Thulmann, above all my other characters, holds a special place for me – he provided me with my first foray into the dark corridors of the Black Library. My first submission to the late and exceedingly lamented *Inferno!* magazine was 'A Choice of Hatreds', which had as its major protagonist the Sigmarite witch hunter with the steely eyes and silky voice. The story appealed to Christian Dunn, who was doing much of the editing for *Inferno!* at the time, though before taking on the Herculean feat of editing both that wonderful periodical and its illustrated companion *Warhammer Monthly*. Almost before I understood what was happening, 'A Choice of Hatreds' was slated for publication. At times, events can unfold much quicker than they are anticipated. Soon I had my first gothic fantasy keeping company between a Deff Skwadron strip and an excellent Dan Abnett story. That sense of accomplishment still hasn't worn off.

It would be remiss not to mention the kindness and professionalism of Christian. Under his stewardship, *Inferno!* was a consistently excellent publication and I was well-served to have him editing my early work and pointing out my missteps. While it is all-too obvious what an author's contribution to a finished work has been, the role of an editor is often less recognised. Christian has a keen eye for spotting moments where the pacing of a story could be tightened or perhaps loosened to strike the exact and precise level of tension or drama or horror. I think my obsession with pacing in my stories is very much a product of his influence and I always value his input on a tale.

A writer is often much too close to his work and really needs an extra set of eyes to see the forest through the trees, as it were. Much has been written about editors stifling creativity, the best example being Farnsworth Wright from *Weird Tales* and his often harsh treatment of H P Lovecraft's work, however, I often consider that perhaps it is because of Wright's strict policies that writers such as Lovecraft, Robert E Howard and Clark Ashton Smith are still celebrated today. A less careful editorial touch and the genius of such writers might never have blossomed, lost with so much of the forgettable dreck churned out by a small legion of pulp hacks for less discriminating editors. For holding his writers to a higher standard, there is not enough praise I can give Christian for his tireless work.

The character of Mathias Thulmann grew out of several influences from my formative years. Solomon Kane, the Puritan witch hunter created by the aforementioned Robert E Howard is an obvious inspiration. I first discovered Kane in an old *Dracula Lives* magazine and inspired a quick hunt for copies of the stories he had originally been featured in. Howard is often dismissed as writing only a single type of protagonist, brawny violent types that are disregarded as Conan clones. However, the fanatical and stalwart Kane is about as far from the mould as one can get.

Part of Thulmann was certainly inspired by Kane, but another part was the result of all those old late-night horror movies. The output of studios such as Britain's Hammer and Amicus and the American AIP in the 1960's was an orgy of Gothic terror, with actors such as Peter Cushing and Christopher Lee lending these films a dignity and class that sadly escapes virtually all that has followed after. Filmed on sometimes miniscule budgets and with shooting schedules that could best be described as arduous, these movies nevertheless drip with atmosphere and mood, an almost palpable sense of lurking menace. From flowers wilting beneath a vampire's step to the eerie sight of a rejuvenated skeletal daemon stalking silently into a rain-swept night, these were images to bring chills.

No actor left more of a mark on my psyche than Vincent Price. Growing up, Price was almost the face of Halloween. He'd appear on everything; even the Muppets had him in their Halloween show. With his sinister features, sardonic laugh and cultured voice, Price could bring a shudder simply by reading from the phone book. Nowhere was he better than in *The Conqueror Worm* (the US retitle of Michael Reeves' *Witchfinder General*), portraying a real historical figure, the witch hunter Mathew Hopkins who operated in Suffolk during the English Civil War. Though a witch hunter like Solomon Kane, Hopkins was cut from a much darker, more villainous cloth. Ruthless, manipulative and arrogant, as portrayed by Price, here was a character that was almost the polar opposite of Kane. In creating Mathias Thulmann, I took what, in my admittedly diseased mind, were the most appealing qualities of both characters – some of the arrogance and ruthlessness of Hopkins mixed with the courage and faith of Kane. The result, I think, makes for a decidedly unique sort of protagonist.

After reading this volume, I hope you will agree.

This edition includes for the first time the short story 'Witch Work', a direct tie-in with *Witch Hunter* that was slated for *Inferno!* as a tie-in to the novel. Astute eyes will note that the closing scene from 'Witch Work' was originally part of *Witch Hunter*'s first chapter. With both pieces appearing consecutively, and within the same binding, the reader has been spared a bit of redundancy.

C. L. Werner
October, 29th, 2007

A CHOICE OF HATREDS

ON THE OUTSKIRTS of the small town of Kleinsdorf, a group of raucous men gathered in a fallow field. Before them stood an
inverted anvil upon which a burly man garbed in a heavy blacksmith's apron set a second anvil. The man's bearded face split into
a booming laugh as one of his comrades lit a hemp fuse that slithered between the anvils to reach a small charge of gunpowder. A
hushed silence fell upon the men as the smouldering flame
slowly burned its way to the explosive. Suddenly a tremendous
boom echoed across the barren fields and the uppermost anvil
was thrown into the sky to crash into the ground several yards
away. A great cheer erupted from the group and the blacksmith set
off at a lumbering jog to retrieve the heavy iron projectile, even as
one of his friends prepared another charge.

'It looks like we have chanced into a bit of a celebration, eh,
Mathias?' commented a stout, bearded rider on the road overlooking the anvil-firing party.

The man wore a battered and ill-mended pair of leather
breeches; an equally battered jerkin of studded leather struggled
to contain the man's slight paunch. Greasy, swine-like eyes peered
from either side of a splayed nose while an unkempt beard

clothed his forward-jutting jaw. From a scabbard at his side a broadsword swayed with each step of his horse.

'We come here seeking rest, friend Streng, not to indulge your penchant for debauchery,' replied the second rider. A tall, grim figure, the second man was his companion's senior by at least a decade. Where Streng's attire was shabby and worn, this man's was opulent. Immaculate shiny leather boots rose to the man's knees and his back was enveloped by a heavy black cape lined with the finest ermine. Fine calfskin gauntlets garbed slender-fingered hands while a tunic of red satin embroidered with gold clothed his arms and chest. The wide rounded brim of his leather hat cast a shadow upon the rider's features. Hanging from a dragonskin belt with an enormous silver buckle were a pair of holstered pistols and a slender-bladed longsword.

'You are the one who has taken so many fine vows to Sigmar,' Streng said with a voice that was not quite a sneer. 'I recall taking no such vows.'

Mathias turned to look at his companion and his face emerged from the shadow cast by the brim of his hat. The older man's visage was gaunt, dominated by a narrow, dagger-like nose and the thin moustache that rested between it and the man's slender lips. A grey arrow of beard stabbed out from the man's chin. His eyes were of similar flinty hue but burnt with a strange intensity, a determination and zeal that were at odds with the glacial hue.

'You make no vows to Sigmar, yet you take the Temple's gold easily enough,' Mathias locked eyes with his comrade. Some of the glib disrespect in Streng's manner dissipated as he met that gaze.

'I've not seen many monks with so fine a habit as yours,' Streng said, turning his eyes from his companion.

'It is sometimes wise to remind people that Sigmar rewards service in this life as well as the hereafter.' Mathias looked away from his henchman and stared at the town before them.

A small settlement of some thousand persons, the simple wooden structures were close together, the streets narrow and crooked. Everywhere there was laughter and singing, music from mandolin and fife. A celebratory throng choked the streets, dancing with recklessness born more of joy than drink, at least in this early hour of the festival. Yet, none were so reckless as not to make way for Mathias as he manoeuvred his steed into the narrow streets, nor to make the sign of Sigmar's Hammer with the witch hunter's passing.

'I shall take room at the inn. You find a stable for the horses,' Mathias said as he and Streng rode through the crowd.

'And then?' asked Streng, a lustful gleam in his eyes and a lecherous grin splitting his face.

'I care not what manner of sin you find fit to soil your soul with,' snarled the witch hunter. 'Just see that you are in condition to ride at cock's crow.'

As they talked, the pair did not observe the stealthy figure who watched their exchange from behind a hay-laden wagon. They did not see the same figure emerge from its hiding place with their passing, nor the venomous glare it sent after them.

GUSTAV SIPPED AT the small glass of Tilean wine, listening to the sounds of merriment beyond the walls of his inn. A greedy glint came to the innkeeper's eyes as he thought of the vacant rooms above his head and the drunken men who would fill them before the night was through. The Festival of Wilhelmstag brought many travellers to Kleinsdorf, travellers who would find themselves too drunk or too fatigued to quit the town once the festivities reached their end. Few would be lucid enough to haggle over the 'competitive' fee Gustav charged his annual Wilhelmstag guests.

Gustav again sipped at his wine, silently toasting Wilhelm Hoess and the minotaur lord which had been kind enough to let itself and its horde of Chaos spawn be slaughtered in the streets of Kleinsdorf two centuries past. Even now, the innkeeper could see the gilded skull of the monster atop a pole in the centre of the square outside, torchlight from the celebratory throng below it dancing across the golden surface. Gustav hoped that the minotaur was enjoying the view, for tomorrow the skull would return to a chest in the town hall, there to reside until next Wilhelmstag.

The opening of the inn's front door roused the innkeeper from his thoughts. Gustav smiled.

The first sheep comes to be fleeced, he thought as he scuttled away from the window. But the smile died when Gustav's eyes observed the countenance of his new guest. The high black hat, flowing cape and expensive weapons combined with the stern visage of the man's face told Gustav what this man was even before he saw the burning gleam in those cold grey eyes.

'I am sorry, my lord, but I am afraid that I have no rooms that are free.' Gustav winced as the witch hunter's eyes stared into his own. 'The… the festival. It brings many guests. If you had only come on another night…' the innkeeper stammered.

'Your common room is also filled?' the witch hunter interrupted.

'Why, no,' Gustav said, a nervous tic causing his left eye to twitch uncontrollably.

'Then you may move one of your guests to the common room,' the witch hunter declared. Gustav nodded his agreement even as he inwardly cursed the man. The common room was a long hall at the side of the inn lined with pallets of straw. Even drunkards would be unwilling to pay much for such lodgings.

'You may show me my room,' the witch hunter said, his firm hand grasping Gustav's shoulder and pushing the innkeeper ahead of himself. 'I trust that you have something appropriate for a devoted servant of Sigmar?'

'Yes, my lord,' Gustav said, altering his course away from the closet-like chamber he had thought to give the witch hunter. He led the way up a flight of stairs to one of the larger rooms. The witch hunter peered into the chamber while the innkeeper held the door open.

'No, I think not,' the witch hunter declared. The bearded face moved closer toward Gustav's own and one of the gloved fingers touched the twitching muscle beside the innkeeper's eye.

'Interesting,' Mathias said, not quite under his breath. The innkeeper's eyes grew wide with fright, seeming to see the word 'mutation' forming in the witch hunter's mind.

'A nervous twitch, nothing more,' Gustav muttered, knowing that even so slight a physical defect had put men to the stake in many backwater towns. 'I have a much nicer room, if you would follow me.' Gustav turned, leading the witch hunter to a second flight of stairs.

'Yes, this will do,' Mathias stated when Gustav led him into a large and well-furnished room at the very top of the inn. Gustav smiled and nodded his head nervously.

'It is my honour to serve a noble Templar of Sigmar,' the innkeeper said as he walked to the large oak wardrobe that dominated one corner of the room. Gustav opened the wardrobe and removed his own nightshirt and cap from it.

'I will dine here,' Mathias declared, settling into a large chair and removing his weapon-laden belt. 'A goose and some wine, I think.' The witch hunter stroked his moustache with his thumb and forefinger.

'I will see to it,' the innkeeper said, knowing better than to challenge his most-unwanted guest. Gustav paused a few steps away from the witch hunter. Mathias reached into a pocket in the lining of his tunic and tossed a few coins into the man's hands. Gustav stared stupidly at them for several seconds.

'I did not come for the festival,' explained Mathias, 'so I should not have to pay festival prices.' The witch hunter suddenly cocked his head and stared intently at Gustav's twitching eye.

'I shall see about your supper,' Gustav whimpered as he hurried from the room.

THE STREETS OF Kleinsdorf were alive with rejoicing. Everywhere there was dancing and singing. But all the laughter and joy in the world could not touch the figure that writhed its way through the crowd. The dark, shabby cloak of the man, meant to keep him inconspicuous, was at odds with the bright fabrics and flowers of the revellers and made him stand out all the more. Dozens of times Reinhardt von Lichtberg had been forced to ward away garishly clad townspeople who thought to exorcise this wraith of melancholy in their midst with dance and drink. Reinhardt spat into the dust. A black-hearted murderer had descended upon this place and all these idiots could do was dance and laugh. Well, if things turned out as Reinhardt planned, he too would have cause to dance and laugh. Before they stretched his neck from a gallows.

Hands clasped Reinhardt's shoulders and spun the young man around. So lost in thoughts of revenge was he that he did not even begin to react before warm, moist lips closed about his own. The woman detached herself and stared up into the young man's face.

'I don't believe that I know you,' Reinhardt said as his eyes considered the golden-haired, well-built woman smiling impishly at him and the taste of ale that covered his lips.

'You could,' the woman smiled. 'The Festival of Wilhelmstag is a time for finding new people.'

Reinhardt shook his head. 'I am looking for no one new.' Reinhardt found himself thinking again of Mina and how she had died. And how her murderer would die.

'You have not seen a witch hunter, by any chance?' Reinhardt asked. The woman's smile turned into a full-lipped pout.

'I've met his surrogate,' the girl swore. 'Over at the beer hall, drinking like an orc and carrying on like a Tilean sailor. Mind you, no decent woman had better get near him.' The impish smile returned and the woman pulled scandalously at the torn fringe of her bodice. 'See what the brute did to me.'

Reinhardt grabbed the woman's arms in a vice-like grip.

'Did he say where Mathias Thulmann, the witch hunter, is?' Reinhardt snarled. The coyness left the woman's face as the drunken haze was replaced by something approaching fear.

'The inn, he was taking a room at the inn.' The girl retreated into the safety of the crowd as Reinhardt released her. The nobleman did not even notice her go, his mind already processing the information she had given him. His right hand slid beneath the shabby cloak and closed around the hilt of his sword.

'Soon, Mina,' Reinhardt whispered, 'soon your murderer will discover what suffering is.'

GERHARDT KNAUF HAD never known terror such as he now felt. The wonderful thrill of fear that he enjoyed when engaging in his secret activities was gone. The presence of the witch hunter had driven home the seriousness of discovery in a way that Knauf had never fully comprehended before. The shock and looks of disbelief he had visualised on his neighbours' faces when they realised that the merchant was more than he seemed had become the frenzied visages of a bloodthirsty mob. In his imagination, Knauf could even smell the kindling as it caught flame.

The calf-eyed merchant with his beetle-like brow downed the contents of the tankard resting on the bar before him in a single bolt. Knauf pressed a hand against his mouth, struggling to keep the beer from leaving his body as quickly as it had entered it. The merchant managed to force the bile back into his stomach and let his head sway towards the man sitting beside him.

'Mueller,' croaked Knauf, his thin voice struggling to maintain a semblance of dignity, even as he struggled against fear and inebriation. The heavy set mercenary at his side looked away from the gob of wax he had been whittling into a lewd shape and regarded the merchant.

'You have done jobs for me before,' Knauf continued.

'Aye,' the mercenary cautiously replied, fingering his knife.

'And I have always paid you fairly and promptly,' the merchant added, his head swaying from side to side like some bloated reptile.

'That is true enough,' Mueller said, a smirk on his face. The truth of it was that Knauf was too timid to be miserly when it came to paying the men who protected his wagons. A cross look from Rall, or Gunther, or even from the scarecrow-like Hossbach, and the mercenaries would see an increase in their wages.

'Would you say that we are friends?' Knauf said, reaching for another ceramic tankard of beer. He swallowed only half the tankard's contents this time, spilling most of the remainder when he clumsily set the vessel back upon the table.

'Were you to pay me enough, I would even say that we were brothers,' Mueller replied, struggling to contain the laughter building within his gut. But the condescending sarcasm in the mercenary's voice was lost on the half-drunken Knauf. The merchant caught hold of Mueller's arm and stared into his face with pleading eyes.

'Would you murder for me?' the merchant hissed. This time Mueller did laugh.

'By Ulric's fangs, Gerhardt!' the mercenary swore. 'Who could you possibly hate enough to need killed?' Mueller laughed again and downed his own tankard of beer.

'The witch hunter,' whispered Knauf, his head swaying from side to side to ensure that no one had overheard.

'Have you been reading things you shouldn't?' Mueller asked, only half-seriously. The look of fear in Knauf's eyes killed the joke forming on the mercenary's lips. Mueller rose from his chair and stared down at the merchant.

'Forty gold crowns,' the mercenary declared, waving away the look of joy and hope crawling across Knauf's features. 'And as far as the boys are concerned, you are paying us ten.' Mueller turned away from the table and started to walk into the main room of the beer hall.

'Where are you going?' Knauf called after Mueller in a voice that sounded unusually shrill even for the merchant.

'To get Hossbach and the others,' Mueller said. 'Maybe I'll see if I can't learn something about our friend as well.' The mercenary turned away. He only got a few steps before Knauf's drunken hands were scrabbling at the man's coat.

'How are you going to do that?' Knauf hissed up at him with alarm.

Mueller extracted himself from the merchant's grip. He pointed a finger to the far end of the beer hall where a bawdy song and shrieks of mock indignation marked the crowd gathered in morbid fascination around the man who had rode into Kleinsdorf with the witch hunter.

'How else? I'll speak with his lackey,' Mueller shook his head as Knauf started to protest. 'Leave this to me. Why don't you go home and get my gold ready?' The mercenary did not wait to see if Knauf would follow his suggestion, but continued across the beer hall, liberating a metal stein from a buxom barmaid along the way.

'Sometimes they confess straight away,' Streng was saying as Mueller inconspicuously joined his audience. 'That's the worst of it. There's nothing left to do but string them up, or burn them if they've been particularly bad.' Streng paused to smile at the woman sitting on his knee.

'So how do you go about finding a witch?' Mueller interrupted Streng's carousing. The lout turned to Mueller and regarded him with an irritated sneer.

'I don't. That's the Templar's job. Mathias finds them and then I make them confess. That way everything is above board and the Temple can burn the filthy things without anybody being upset.' Streng turned away from Mueller and returned his attention to his companion.

'So your master has come to Kleinsdorf looking for witches?' Mueller interrupted again.

Streng shook his head and glared at this man who insisted on intruding on his good time.

'Firstly, Mathias Thulmann is not my master. We're partners, him and me, that's what it is. Secondly, we are on our way to Stirland. Lots of witches down in Stirland.' Streng snorted derisively. 'Do you honestly think we'd cross half the Empire to come here?' Streng laughed. 'I wouldn't cross a meadow to come to this rat nest,' he said, before adding, 'present company excepted, of course,' to the locals gathered around him.

As Streng returned his attention to the giggling creature seated on his knee, Mueller extracted himself from the hangers-on and made his way toward the beer hall's exit. The mercenary spied a familiar face in the crowd and waved the man over to him. A young, wiry man with a broken nose and a livid scar across his forearm walked over to Mueller. The mercenary took the flower-festooned hat from the man's head and sent it sailing across the crowded room with a flick of his wrist.

'Go get Gunther and Hossbach,' Mueller snarled. 'I found us some night work.' The angry look on the young man's face disappeared at the mention of work. Rall set off at a brisk jog to find his fellow sellswords. Mueller looked at the crowd around Streng one last time before leaving the beer hall.

The mercenary had found out all that he needed to know. The witch hunter was only passing through Kleinsdorf; he would not be expecting any trouble. Like all the other jobs he had done for Gerhardt Knauf, this one would hardly be difficult enough to be called 'work'.

A CHEER WENT up from the crowd below as a small boy shimmied up the massive pole standing in the centre of the square and thrust a crown of flowers on the gilded skull at its top.

At the moment, Reinhardt von Lichtberg envied the boy his agility. The nobleman was gripping the outer wall of the inn, thirty feet above the square. To an observer, he might have looked like a great brown bat clinging to the wall of a cave. But there were no eyes trained upon Reinhardt, at least not at present. The few revellers who had lifted their heads skyward were watching the boy descend the pole with a good deal less bravado than he had ascended with. Still, the threat of discovery was far too real and Reinhardt was not yet ready to see the inside of a cell.

Slowly, carefully, Reinhardt worked his fingers from one precarious handhold to another. Only a few feet away he could see the window that was his goal. It had been easy to determine which room the murderer occupied; his was the only window from which light shone. Somehow it did not surprise Reinhardt that the witch hunter had taken a room on the inn's top floor. One last trial, one final obstacle before vengeance could be served.

At last he reached the window and Reinhardt stared through the glass, seeing for the first time in six months the man who had destroyed his life. The murderer sat in a wooden chair, a small table set before him. He cut morsels from a large roasted goose, a wicker-shrouded bottle of wine sitting beside it.

Reinhardt watched for a moment as the monster ate, burning the hated image of the man into his memory. He hoped that the meal was a good one, for it would be the witch hunter's last.

WITH AN ANIMAL cry, Reinhardt crashed through the window, broken glass and splintered wood flying across the room. Landing on his feet, the sword at his side was in his hand in less than a heartbeat. To his credit, the witch hunter reacted swiftly, kicking the small table at Reinhardt an instant after he landed in the room while diving in the opposite direction to gain the pistols and longsword that lay upon the bed. But Reinhardt had the speed of youth and the martial training of one who might have been a captain in the Reiksguard on his side. More, he had purpose.

The witch hunter's claw-like hand closed around the grip of his pistol just as cold steel touched his throat. There was a brief pause as Thulmann regarded the blade poised at his neck before releasing his weapon and holding his hands up in surrender. Both arms raised above his head, Mathias Thulmann faced the man with a sword at his throat.

'I fear that you will not find much gold,' Mathias said, his voice low and unafraid.

'You do not remember me, do you?' Reinhardt snarled. 'Or are you going to pretend that your name is not Mathias Thulmann, Templar of Sigmar, witch hunter?'

'That is indeed my name, and my trade,' replied Mathias, his voice unchanged.

'My name is Reinhardt von Lichtberg,' spat the other, pressing the tip of his blade into Mathias's throat until a bead of crimson slid down the steel. 'I am the man who is going to kill you.'

'To avenge your lost love?' the witch hunter mused, a touch of pity seeming to enter his voice. 'You should thank me for restoring her soul to the light of Sigmar.'

'*Thank you?*' Reinhardt bellowed incredulously. The youth fought to keep himself from driving his sword through the witch hunter's flesh. 'Thank you for imprisoning us, torturing us? Thank you for burning Mina at the stake? Thank you for destroying the only thing that made my life worth living?' Reinhardt clenched his fist against the wave of rage that pounded through his body. He shook his head from side to side.

'We were to be married,' the nobleman stated. 'I was to serve the Emperor in his Reiksguard and win glory and fame. Then I would return and she would be waiting for me to make her my wife.' Reinhardt pulled a fat skinning knife from a sheath on his belt. 'You took that from me. You took it all away.' Reinhardt let the light play across the knife in his left hand as he rolled his wrist back and forth. The witch hunter continued to watch him, his eyes hooded, his face betraying no fear or even concern. Reinhardt noted the man's seeming indifference to his fate.

'You will scream,' he swore. 'Before I let you die, Sigmar himself will hear your screams.'

The hand with the knife moved toward the witch hunter's body... And for the second time that evening, Mathias Thulmann had unexpected visitors.

THE DOOR BURST inwards, bludgeoned from its hinges by the ogre-like man who followed the smashed portal into the room. Three other men were close behind the ape-like bruiser. All four of them wore a motley array of piecemeal armour, strips of chainmail fastened to leather tunics, bands of steel woven to a padded hauberk. The only aspect that seemed to link the four men was the look of confusion on their faces.

'The witch hunter was supposed to be alone,' stated Rall, puzzled by the strange scene they had stumbled upon. Reinhardt turned his body toward the mercenaries, keeping his sword at Mathias's throat.

'Which one is he?' asked Rall, clearly not intending the question for either of the men already in the room.

'Why don't we just kill them both?' the scarecrow-thin figure of Hossbach said, stepping toward Reinhardt.

Like a lightning bolt, the skinning knife went flying across the room. Hossbach snarled as he dodged the projectile. The mercenary did not see the sword that flashed away from Thulmann's throat to slice across his armour and split his stomach across its centre. Hossbach toppled against the man who had dealt him the fatal wound. His sword forgotten on the floor, the mercenary clutched at Reinhardt, grabbing for the man's sword arm. Reinhardt kicked the dying man away from him, sending him crashing into the foot of the bed, but Hossbach had delayed him long enough. The brutish fist of Gunther crashed into Reinhardt's face

while his dagger sought to bury itself in the pit of Reinhardt's left
arm. The nobleman managed to grab his attacker's wrist, slowing
the deadly blade's strike. The blade pierced his skin but did not
sink into his heart. His huge opponent let a feral smile form on
his face as he put more strength into the struggle. Slowly, by the
slightest of measures, the dagger continued its lethal passage.

Suddenly the sound of thunder assailed Reinhardt's ears; a
stench like rotten eggs filled his nose. One moment he had been
staring into the triumphant face of his attacker. In the next instant
the mercenary's head was a red ruin. The hand on the dagger slid
away and the mercenary fell to the floor like a felled tree. Reinhardt saw one of the attackers run through the shattered doorway.
The other lay with a gory wound on the side of his head at the feet
of the only other man still standing in the room.'

A plume of grey smoke rose from the barrel of the pistol Mathias Thulmann held in his right hand. The other pistol, its butt
bloody from its impact against the mercenary's skull, was cocked
and pointed at Reinhardt von Lichtberg's own head.

'It seems the last of these yapping curs has not seen fit to remain
with us,' Thulmann said. Although he now held the upper hand,
the witch hunter still possessed the same air of cold indifference.

'Go ahead and kill me, butcher,' Reinhardt swore, his heart afire
with the injustice of it all. To come so close... 'You will be doing
me a service,' he added.

'There are some things you should know before I decide if you
should live or die,' the witch hunter sat down on the bed, motioning Reinhardt to a position from which the pistol could cover him
more easily.

'Have you not wondered what brought me to your father's
estate?' Mathias asked. He saw the slight look of interest surface
amidst Reinhardt's mask of hate. 'I was summoned by Father
Haeften.' Reinhardt started at the mention of the wizened old
priest of Sigmar who led his father's household in their devotions.
It was impossible for him to believe that the kindly soft-spoken
old man could have been responsible for bringing about Mina's
death. The witch hunter continued to speak.

'The father reported that one of his parish was touched by
Chaos,' Thulmann paused, letting the distasteful word linger in
the air. 'A young woman who was with child, whose own mother
bespoke the irregularities that were manifesting beneath her skin.'

Stunned shock claimed Reinhardt. With child. His child.

'Upon my arrival, I examined the woman and discovered that her mother's fears had proven themselves,' Thulmann shook his head sadly. 'Her background was not of a suspicious nature, but the Darkness infects even the most virtuous. It was necessary to question her, to learn the source of her affliction. After several hours, she said your name.'

'Hours of torture!' Reinhardt spat, face twisted into an animal snarl. 'And then you took me so that your creature might "question" me!'

'Yes!' affirmed Thulmann, fire in his voice. 'As the father, the source of her corruption might lie within you, yourself! It was necessary to discover if there were others! Chaos is a contagion, where one is infected others soon fall ill!'

'Yet you released me,' challenged Reinhardt, the shame he felt at his own survival further fuelling the impotent rage roaring through his veins.

'There was no corruption in you,' the witch hunter said, almost softly. 'Nor in the girl, not in her soul at least. It was days later that she confessed the crime that had been the cause of her corruption.' The witch hunter stared into Reinhardt's blazing eyes.

'Do you know a Doktor Weichs?' he asked.

'Freiherr Weichs?' Reinhardt answered. 'My father's physician?'

'Also physician to his household. Your Mina confided a most private problem with Weichs. She was worried that her condition would prevent you from leaving the von Lichtberg estate, from joining the Reiksguard and seeking the honour and glory that were your due.' Weichs gave her a potion of his own creation which he assured her would dissolve the life within her womb as harmlessly as it had formed.'

Mathias Thulmann shook his head again. 'That devil's brew Weichs created was what destroyed your Mina, for it contained warpstone.' The witch hunter paused again, studying Reinhardt. 'I see that you are unfamiliar with the substance. It is the pure essence of Chaos, the black effluent of all the world's evil. In the days before Magnus the Pious, it was thought to possess healing properties, but only a fool or a madman would have anything to do with the stuff in this more enlightened age. Instead of destroying the life in the girl's belly, the warpstone changed it, corrupted woman and child. When I discovered this, I knew you were innocent and had you released.'

'And burned her!' Reinhardt swore.

The witch hunter did not answer the youth but instead kicked the figure lying at his feet.

'There is life in you yet,' Thulmann snarled, looking back at Reinhardt to remind his prisoner that his pistol was yet trained on him. 'Account for yourself, pig! Who sends you to harm a dully-ordained servant of Sigmar?'

Mueller groaned as he rolled onto his side, staring at the witch hunter through a swollen eye. Carefully he put a hand to his split lip and wiped the trickle of blood from his mouth.

'Gerhardt... Knauf,' Mueller said between groans. 'It was Gerhardt Knauf, the merchant. He was afraid you had come to Kleinsdorf seeking him.'

Mathias Thulmann let a grim smile part his lips. 'I am looking for him now,' he stated. The witch hunter smashed the heel of his boot into the grovelling mercenary's neck, crushing the man's windpipe. Mueller uttered a half-gargle, half-gasp and writhed on the floor as he desperately tried to breathe. Thulmann turned away from the dying wretch.

'This Knauf has reasons to see me dead,' Thulmann told Reinhardt, as though the noble had not heard the exchange between witch hunter and mercenary. 'Reasons which lie in the corruption of his mind and soul. If you would avenge your beloved, do so upon one deserving of your wrath, the same sort of filth that destroyed the girl long before I set foot in your father's house.'

Reinhardt glared at the witch hunter. 'I will kill you,' he said in a voice as cold as the grave. Mathias Thulmann sighed and removed a set of manacles from the belt lying on the bed.

'I cannot let you interfere with my holy duty,' the witch hunter said, pressing the barrel of the pistol against Reinhardt's temple. Thulmann closed one of the steel bracelets around the youth's wrist, locking it shut with a deft twist of an iron key. The other half of the manacles he closed around one of the bed posts, trapping the bracelet between the mattress and the wooden globe that topped the post.

'This should ensure that you do not interfere,' Mathias explained as he retrieved the rest of his weapons and stepped over the writhing Mueller.

'I will kill you, Mathias Thulmann,' Reinhardt repeated as the witch hunter left the room. As soon as the cloaked shape was gone, Reinhardt dropped to his knees and stretched his hand toward the ruined body of the mercenary who had almost killed him – and the small hatchet attached to the man's belt.

GERHARDT KNAUF PACED nervously across his bedchamber. It had been nearly an hour and still he had had no word from Mueller.

Not for the first time, the merchant cast his eyes toward the small door at the top of the stairs. The tiny room within was the domain of Knauf's secret vice, the storehouse of all the forbidden and arcane knowledge Knauf had obtained over the years: the grimoire of a centuries-dead Bretonnian witch; the abhorred *Ninth Canticle of Tzeentch*, its mad author's name lost to the ages; a book of incantations designed to bring prosperity, or alternately ruin, by the infamous sorcerer Verlag Duhring. All the black secrets that had given Knauf his power made him better than the ignorant masses that surrounded him, who sneered at his eccentric ways. Before the black arts at his command, brutish men like Mueller were nothing; witch hunters were nothing.

Knauf took another drink from the bottle of wine he had removed from his cellar. The sound of someone pounding on the door of his villa caused the merchant to set his drink down. 'Finally,' he thought.

But the figure that greeted Knauf when he gazed down from his window was not that of Mueller. Instead he saw the scarlet and black garbed form of the mercenary's victim. With a horrified gasp, Knauf withdrew from the window.

'He has come for me,' the merchant shuddered. Mueller and his men had failed and now there was no one to stand between Knauf and the determined witch hunter. Knauf shrieked as he heard a loud explosion from below and the splintering of wood as the door was kicked open. He had only moments in which to save himself from the witch hunter's justice, to avoid the flames that were the price of the knowledge he had sought.

A smile appeared on Knauf's face. The merchant raced for the garret room. If there was no one who would save him from the witch hunter, there was *something* that might.

* * *

MATHIAS THULMANN PAUSED on the threshold of the merchant's villa and holstered the smoking pistol in his hand. One shot from the flintlock weapon had been enough to smash the lock on the door, one kick enough to force open the heavy oak portal. The witch hunter drew his second pistol, the one he had reloaded after the melee at the inn and scanned the darkened foyer. No sign of life greeted Thulmann's gaze and he stepped cautiously into the room, watching for the slightest movement in the darkness.

Suddenly the witch hunter's head snapped around, his eyes fixating upon the stairway leading from the foyer to the chambers above. He could sense the dark energies that were gathering somewhere in the rooms above him. Somewhere in this house, someone was calling upon the Ruinous Powers. Thulmann shifted the pistol to his other hand and drew the silvered blade of his sword, blessed by the Grand Theogonist himself and grimly ascended the stairs.

GERHARDT KNAUF COULD feel the eldritch energies gathering in the air around him as he read from the *Ninth Canticle of Tzeentch*. The power was almost a tangible quantity as it surged from the warlock and gathered at the centre of a ring of lighted candles. A nervous laugh interrupted the arcane litany streaming from Knauf's lips as he saw the first faint glimmer of light appear. Swiftly, the glow grew in size, keeping pace with the increasing speed of the words flying from Knauf's tongue. The crackling nimbus took on a pinkish hue and the first faint suggestion of a shape within the light was visible to him.

No, the warlock realised, there was not a shape within the light; rather, the light was assuming a shape. As the blasphemous litany continued, a broad torso coalesced from which two long, simian arms dangled, each ending in an enormous clawed hand. Two short, thick legs slowly grew away from the torso until they touched the wooden floor. Finally, a head sprouted from between the two arms, growing away from the body so that the head was between its shoulders rather than above them. A gargoyle face appeared, its fanged mouth stretching across the head in a hideous grin. Two swirling pools of orange light stared at the warlock.

The daemon uttered a loathsome sound like the wailing of an infant, a sound hideous in its suggestion of malevolent mirth.

Knauf shuddered and turned his eyes from the frightful thing he had summoned. In so doing, his gaze fell upon his feet and the colour drained away from his face as the horror of what he had done became known to him.

The first thing Knauf had learned, the most important rule he had found repeated again and again in the arcane books he had so long hoarded, was that a sorcerer must always protect himself from that which he would have do his bidding. In his haste to save himself from the witch hunter, to summon this creature of Tzeentch, Knauf had forgotten to draw about himself a protective circle, a barrier that no daemon may cross.

Knauf's mind desperately groped amongst its store of arcane knowledge seeking some enchantment, some spell that would save the warlock from his hideous mistake. Before him, the daemon uttered its loathsome laugh again. Knauf screamed as the pink abomination moved towards him with a curious scuttling motion.

Thoughts of sorcery forgotten, Knauf clenched his eyes and stretched his arm in front of his body, as though to ward away the monstrous horror even as the fiend advanced upon him. The daemon's grotesque hands closed about the warlock's extended arm, bringing new screams from Knauf as the icy touch seared through his veins. Slowly, the daemon raked a single claw down the length of the would-be wizard's arm, a deep wound that sank down to the very bone. Knauf's cries of agony rose still higher as the daemon's fingers probed the wound. Like a child with a piece of fruit, the horror began to peel the flesh from Knauf's arm, the warlock's howl of torment drowned out by the monster's increasing glee.

MATHIAS THULMANN REACHED the garret in time to witness the warlock's demise. No longer amused by the high-pitched wails escaping from Knauf's throat, the pink hands released the skeletal limb they clutched and seized the warlock's shoulders, pulling Knauf's body to the daemon's own. The daemon's giant maw gaped wide and with a formless undulating motion surged up and over Knauf's head and shoulders. The pseudo-corporeal substance of the daemon allowed a horrified Thulmann to see the warlock's features behind the ichorous pink jaws that engulfed it. He could see those still-screaming features twist and mutate as the flesh was quickly dissolved, patches of muscle appearing beneath skin before being stripped away to reveal the bone itself. The hardened witch hunter turned away from the appalling sight.

The daemon's insane gibbering brought Thulmann back to his senses. The witch hunter returned his gaze to the loathsome creature and the fool who had called it from the Realm of Chaos. Atop Gerhardt Knauf's body, a skull dripped the last of the warlock's blood and rivulets of meaty grease; the body beneath had been stripped to the breastbone. The whisper of a scream seemed to echo through the garret as the last shards of the warlock's soul fled into the night. The pink daemon rose from its gory repast and turned its fiery eyes upon the witch hunter.

Thulmann found himself powerless to act as the daemon slowly made its way across the garret room. The preternatural fiend moved in a capering, dance-like manner, its glowing body brilliant in the darkness, sounds of lunatic amusement emanating from its clenched, grinning jaws. The daemon stopped just out of reach of the witch hunter's sword, settling down on its haunches. It trained its fiery eyes on the scarlet-clad Templar, regarding him with an unholy mixture of hatred, humour, and hunger.

Thulmann forced himself to meet that inhuman gaze, to stare into the swirling fires that burned from the pink face, forced himself to match his own faith and determination against the daemon's ageless malevolence. Thulmann could feel the orange light seeping into his mind, clouding his thoughts and numbing his will.

With an oath, the witch hunter tore his eyes from those of the daemon. The horror snarled, no longer amused by the novelty of the witch hunter's defiance.

The daemon launched itself at Thulmann, its mouth still wet with the warlock's blood. Thulmann dodged to his left, the quick action sparing him the brunt of the daemon's assault, but still resulting in the unearthly creature's claws scraping the witch hunter's ribs. Clenching his teeth against the painful wound and the daemon's icy touch, Thulmann lashed out at the beast as it recovered from its charge.

A grip of frozen iron closed around the wrist of Thulmann's sword arm even as the heavy butt of the witch hunter's pistol crashed against the leering head of the horror. The daemon glared into Mathias's face and uttered a sinister laugh. Again, the witch hunter dealt the monster a blow that would have smashed the skull of any mortal creature. As Thulmann brought his arm back to strike again at the grinning daemon, his nightmarish foe swatted the weapon from his hand, sending the pistol hurtling down the stairway.

The daemon's gibbering laughter grew; it leaned forward, its grinning jaws inches from Thulmann's hawk-like nose. The witch hunter pushed against the daemon's frigid shape with his free hand, desperately trying to keep the ethereal jaws at bay, at the same time frenziedly trying to free his sword arm. Thulmann's efforts attracted the daemon's attention and, as if noticing the weapon for the first time, it reached across Thulmann's body to remove the sword from his grasp. Luminous pink claws closed around the steel blade.

The smell of burnt metal assaulted Thulmann's nostrils as the keening wail of the daemon ripped at his ears. As the horror's hand had closed about the witch hunter's blade, the daemon's glowing flesh had started to burn, luminous sparks crackling and dancing from the seared paw. The daemon released its grip on Thulmann and scuttled away from the witch hunter, a new look in its fiery eyes. A look Thulmann recognised even in so inhuman a being: *fear*.

The daemon's left hand still gave off streams of purplish smoke, its very shape throbbing uncontrollably. The daemon looked at its injured paw then returned its attention to its adversary. The daemon could see the growing sense of hope, the first fledgling seed of triumph appearing in the very aura of the witch hunter. The sight incensed the daemon.

Thulmann slowly advanced upon the beast. The witch hunter had gained an advantage, he did not intend to lose it. But he did not reckon upon the creature's supernatural speed, or its feral rage. Before Thulmann had taken more than a few steps towards it, the daemon sprang from the floor as though it had been shot from a cannon. The monster crashed into Thulmann sending both man and fiend plummeting down the stairs.

Mathias Thulmann groggily tried to gain his feet, ears ringing from his violent descent. By some miracle he had managed to retain his sword. It was a fact that further infuriated his monstrous foe. The daemon scuttled toward the witch hunter. Thulmann struck at it, but the attack was a clumsy one, easily dodged by the luminous being. The horror responded by striking him in the chest with a powerful upswing of both its arms. The witch hunter was lifted off his feet, hurled backward by the tremendous force of the daemon's attack. Thulmann landed on the final flight of stairs, tumbling down them to lie broken and battered in the foyer.

At the foot of the stairs, the witch hunter struggled to rise, groping feebly for the sword that had landed beside him. He watched as the giggling pink daemon capered down the stairs, dancing in hideous parody of the revellers of Kleinsdorf. Mathias summoned his last reserves of strength as the daemon descended toward him. With a prayer to Sigmar, the witch hunter struck as the daemon leaped.

A shriek like the tearing of metal rang out as Thulmann's sword sank into the daemon. The blade impaled the horror, its body writhing in agony before bursting apart like a bubble rising from a fetid marsh. A squeal of venomous rage rose from the daemon, shattering the glass in the foyer's solitary window. Tiny sparks of bluish light flew from the point of the daemon's dissolution. Thulmann sank to his knees, thanking Sigmar for his deliverance.

Daemonic laughter broke into Thulmann's prayers. The taste of victory left the witch hunter as he saw the two daemons dance towards him from the darkness of the foyer. They were blue, goblin-sized parodies of the larger daemon Thulmann had vanquished, and they were glaring at him with looks of utter malevolence.

The foremost of the daemons opened its gigantic mouth, revealing the shark-like rows of serrated fangs. The blue horror laughed as it hopped and bounded across the foyer with frightening speed. Holding the sword before him, Thulmann prepared to meet the monster's attack.

Thulmann cried out as a torrent of pain wracked his body. Swift as the first daemon's movements had been, the other had been swifter still, circling the witch hunter as he prepared to meet its companion's attack. Unseen, the blue horror struck at the witch hunter's leg, sinking its fangs through the hard leather boot to worry the calf within. The intense pain made Thulmann drop his weapon, his only thought to seize the creature ravaging his leg.

The blue thing gave a hiccup of mock fright as Thulmann's hands closed around its scintillating form. The witch hunter tore the creature away from his boot and lifted the daemon over his head by its heals, thinking to dash its brains against the floor. In that instant he realised the trickery the beasts had employed. Scuttling across the floor, its over-sized hands dragging the sword by the hilt, was the other daemon. The monsters had taken away his only weapon.

The horror in Thulmann's hands twisted out of his grasp with a disgustingly boneless motion, raking its claws across his left hand as it fell to the floor. Giggling madly, the blue daemon danced away from the witch hunter's wrath, capering just beyond his reach until its companion returned from secreting his sword.

The two monsters circled Thulmann, striking at him from both sides at once, slashing his flesh with their claws before dancing away again. It was a slow, lingering death, like a pack of dogs tormenting a tethered horse because they do not know how to make a clean kill. Thulmann bled from dozens of wounds. Most were only superficial, but the pain caused by their infliction was intense. Every nerve in his body now writhed at the slightest touch from one of the daemons.

Thulmann's eyes fell upon an object lying upon the floor, its metal barrel reflecting the unearthly bodies of his tormentors. The pistol their unholy parent had taken away from him. If it had not discharged or otherwise been fouled by its violent descent, perhaps the witch hunter could find escape from his agony. Trembling with pain, Thulmann reached for the gun.

One of the daemons slashed the man's cheek as he stooped to retrieve the weapon. Dancing away, the creature laughed and brayed. It licked its fanged mouth and turned to rejoin its comrade in their amusement. It did not see the figure emerge from the darkness, nor the brilliant steel blade that reflected the light of its own glowing body.

The second monster sank its teeth into Thulmann's wrist. How dare the human think to spoil its fun? The blue fiend kicked the pistol away, turning to rake its claws through the shredded cloak that covered Thulmann's mangled back. The daemon leapt away in mid-stroke, turning to the source of the sight and sound that had alarmed it. In the darkness, the sparks and spirals of luminous smoke rising from the death of the other blue horror were almost blinding. The beast scrambled toward the being it sensed lurking in the shadows, eager to rend the flesh of this new adversary who had vanquished its other half. A rusted wooden hatchet sailed out of the darkness, smashing into the snarling daemon.

'The sword,' gasped Thulmann, again reaching for his pistol. 'Use the sword.'

The remaining fiend rose swiftly, its fiery eyes blazing. The daemon lunged in the direction from which the attack had come. It was a fatal mistake. The small creature's hands closed upon the naked blade, sparking and sizzling just as its its parent's had. As the blue horror recoiled from its unpleasant surprise, its attacker struck at its head with a sweep of the blade, finishing the daemon in an explosion of sparks and shrieks. Unlike the pink monster, no new horrors were born from the deaths of its lesser offspring.

'You are mine to kill, Thulmann,' a cold voice from the shadows said. 'I'll not lose my vengeance to anyone else, be they man or daemon!' The witch hunter laughed weakly.

'You shall find your task much simpler now, avenger. My wounds prevent me from mounting any manner of capable defence.' A venomous note entered the witch hunter's voice. 'But you would prefer butchery to a fair duel. That is your idea of honour?'

Reinhardt glared at him, tossing the witch hunter's sword to Thulmann. Thulmann shook his head as he gingerly sheathed the weapon with his injured hand.

'I could not hold that blade with these,' Thulmann showed the enraged noble his bleeding palms and wrist, 'much less combat an able swordsman.'

Reinhardt glared at the witch hunter contemptuously. His gaze studied Thulmann before settling upon the holstered pistols on the witch hunter's belt.

'Are you fit enough to use one of those?' the youth snarled.

'Are you skilled enough to use one?' Mathias countered, slowly drawing one of the weapons and sliding it across the floor. Reinhardt stooped and retrieved the firearm.

'When you see hell, you will know,' the youth responded. He waited as the witch hunter lifted himself from the floor and slowly drew the remaining gun. As soon as he felt the witch hunter was ready, the youth's hand pointed at Thulmann and his finger depressed the pistol's trigger. There was a sharp click as the hammer fell upon an already expired cap.

'Never accept a weapon from an enemy,' Thulmann said his voice icy and emotionless. There was a loud explosion of noise as he fired the weapon he had retrieved from the base of the stairs and holstered while Reinhardt still fought the last daemon. Reinhardt was thrown to the floor as the bullet impacted against his shoulder. Thulmann limped toward the fallen noble. The witch hunter trained his eyes upon the man's wound.

'With a decent physician that will heal in a fortnight,' the witch hunter said, turning away from his victim. 'If we meet again, I may not be so restrained,' Thulmann added as he made his way from the house.

Reinhardt von Lichtberg's shout followed the witch hunter into the street.

'I will find you, Mathias Thulmann! If I have to track you to the nethermost pits of the Wastes, you will not escape me! I will find you again, and I will kill you!'

And the people of Kleinsdorf continued to dance and laugh and sing as they celebrated the triumph of light over Chaos.

MEAT WAGON

THE DOOR OF the coaching inn was flung open with a loud bang, causing the denizens of the place to look up with varying degrees of alarm and surprise. The figure framed momentarily in the doorway was a brutish one, a head below average height but nearly twice as broad as most men. A leather hat with a wide brim was scrunched about his head, covering the blonde fuzz that clung to his skull. The brute's face was full and meaty, a bulbous nose crushed in some long-ago brawl looming above an expansive mouth filled with black teeth. In one gloved fist, the man held a coiled whip; the other gripped the edge of the door.

'Coach be leavin' soon,' the harsh voice of the wagoner grunted. 'Suggest you lot get yerselves organised.' With no further word, the hulking drover turned, stomping back out the door and slamming it closed as he left.

'Wretched villain,' muttered one of the seated patrons of the inn's bar-room. He was a middle-aged man, his body on the downward spiral towards obesity. His raiment was rich, more of his fingers burdened with bejeweled rings than without. 'Why I should suffer such disrespect from that creature…'

'Because, like the rest of us, you want to be in Nuln, and you want to be there quickly,' responded the man seated at the table just to the left of the complaining merchant. He was a tall, young, thin man, his striped breeches and double-breasted tunic as refined as the clothes of the merchant, though more restrained in their opulence. The bearded man with the long, gaunt face flipped over two of the small bone cards set upon the table, smiling as he saw the faces of the cards revealed.

'And why are you in such a hurry, might I ask, Feldherrn?' the fat-faced merchant grumbled. 'Surely there are pockets you have not yet picked in Stirland?'

Feldherrn didn't look up, continuing to turn over cards arrayed on the table before him, matching them into pairs and sets. 'I don't hold a knife to anyone's throat. If a man loses the contents of his purse in my company, it is by his own carelessness. But I am sure that taking the silver of those drunkards who crawl into the bottles of vodka you caravan down from Kislev is a much more noble vocation, Steinmetz.' The gambler looked back at the merchant, then turned his gaze to the person seated beside the fat man. Steinmetz's sullen glower at the gambler's words turned into an open scowl as he noted the direction of his antagonist's gaze.

The woman seated beside Steinmetz was pretty, young and frail in build. Her skin displayed the pallor of the north country, the hue of Ostland and the Kislev frontier where the rays of the sun were weak and the hours of night were long. A flush of red coloured her face as the young girl noted the gambler's attention. She smiled slightly, but the smile was quickly banished as Steinmetz gripped her forearm, his chubby fingers pinching her skin.

'Ravna,' the merchant called, his tone sharp. A towering, broad-shouldered man rose from a stool set against the back wall of the room. Unlike the other occupants of the room, this man wore armour, steel back and breast plates encasing his torso and similar ones upon his legs and upper arms. The bodyguard marched toward Steinmetz, one callused hand resting easily on the pommel of the longsword sheathed at his side. Without rising from his own seat, Steinmetz pulled the girl to her feet as Ravna came near. 'Escort Lydia to the coach,' Steinmetz ordered. 'We are to be leaving soon.' With a dismissive flick of his hand, the merchant turned his smirking face back toward Feldherrn. The gambler gave Steinmetz a look that suggested indigestion.

'Indeed, we should all be boarding that travelling termite circus,' rumbled the deep voice of the person seated at the table beside that of Feldherrn. The speaker was a dwarf, just under five feet in height, but broader of shoulder than most full grown men. A long, flowing black beard engulfed his face, only a bulbous nose and a pair of stony grey eyes emerging from the mass of hair. The dwarf tipped the clay stein he had been drinking from, draining the remaining two-thirds of the tankard in a single swallow. With a belch of satisfaction, the dwarf slammed the stein down and returned the rounded steel cap of his helmet to his head.

'Revolting,' complained a voice both rich and husky. It belonged to a woman seated alone, nearer the door. Tall, her features even, too devoid of warmth and softness to properly be termed beautiful, the woman wore a travelling dress of rich green fabric, her gloves and boots trimmed with white ermine. Like the departed bodyguard, she wore a slender bladed sword at her side, but unlike the weapon of Ravna, the woman's sword bore a gilded hilt and there were gems set into the pommel. The woman stared at the dwarf for a moment, then wrinkled her nose in distaste, putting such effort into the grimace that it set her chestnut-hued tresses bouncing about her face.

'I must agree with you, Baroness von Raeder,' Steinmetz's thick tones rolled from the fat man's mouth. 'Quite a disagreeable sight. To travel in the company of such crude creatures is more of a trial even than that loutish coachman. Why we must tolerate their kind in our lands...' The merchant cast a snide, condescending look at the dwarf. 'They should all crawl back into their burrows in the mountains and stop pretending that they are men.' The dwarf glared back, clenching his fists until the knuckles began to whiten.

'Hardly an enlightened statement,' Feldherrn commented, still intent upon his cards. 'When we get to Nuln you might have a look at the walls, or perhaps the sewers. They have stood for centuries, and are as sturdy today as when they were first laid down by Fergrim's ancestors.' The gambler looked up as he finished his speech. Fergrim Ironsharp nodded his head slightly in the gambler's direction.

'The walls and sewers are built,' Steinmetz grumbled. 'We don't need their kind anymore.'

'I understood that Herr Ironsharp was to be an instructor at the engineering school?' the Baroness von Raeder commented.

'That is so,' Fergrim said, turning to face the Baroness. 'By invitation of your master engineers.' The dwarf smiled at the noblewoman. 'I apologise if I offended you, my lady.' The dwarf bowed at the waist and clicked his heels together in the fashion of young officers of the Reiksguard presenting themselves in social situations. The Baroness smiled back at the dwarf engineer. Fergrim jabbed a finger over his shoulder to indicate Steinmetz. 'Don't mind him. He doesn't like my people because we prefer good wholesome beer that puts meat on a person, not the poisonous bear-piss he brings down from the north.' Bowing again, and with a last malicious look at the merchant, Fergrim left the room. Steinmetz mumbled several colourful oaths about the dwarf's tastes under his breath.

'We should be going as well,' Feldherrn declared, rising from his chair and gathering up his cards. 'Our coachmen look to be just the sort of villains who would leave us behind.' The gambler walked towards the door. As he walked near the noblewoman, he extended his arm. 'Shall we repair to your carriage, Baroness?' Her hand lightly resting on Feldherrn's arm, the noblewoman allowed the adventurer to escort her to the waiting coach.

Steinmetz grumbled a few more coloured expressions as they left, waiting a full minute before rising to his own feet and making his own way outside.

The coach stood just before the small roadside inn. It was a large, oak pannelled carriage with two massive stallions hitched to the yoke at its fore. Dark leather curtains enclosed the carriage itself, providing some insulation from the elements for the passengers within. The roof of the coach was laden down by the packs and luggage of the travellers, lashed into place by heavy ropes. A small iron seat had been folded out at the rear of the coach, a similarly tiny ladder allowing Fergrim to ascend to his position behind the carriage. The dwarf cast an appraising eye at several wooden boxes lashed atop the coach, each box bearing a single dwarf rune burned onto its surface, his keen gaze looking for any hint that they had been disturbed. The other passengers were seated within the carriage itself, awaiting the arrival of the merchant, Steinmetz.

At the fore of the weathered, yet serviceable coach, a thin, spindly man sat upon the fur-lined bench within the driver's box.

The man's features were somehow unpleasant, the cast of his face suggesting a furtive and calculating nature. Greasy locks of long dark hair streamed from beneath his feathered hat, disappearing into the collar of his heavy longcoat. The man's skin was dirty, his thin moustaches displaying traces of bread crumbs and dried soup, his clothing grey with dust and flakes of mud. Yet despite his squalid bearing, three shiny earrings, each a wide hoop of gold, tugged at the lobe of his left ear.

The sinister little coachman cast a sullen gaze at the door of the inn, then looked down from his seat to where the massive frame of his brutish partner stood beside the still open door of the carriage.

'How long does that swine think to keep us waiting?' the coachman's thin, weasely voice croaked, the words tinged by just the slightest hint of an accent. The coachman kept his voice low, so that the already embarked passengers would not hear his complaints.

'That prig be thinkin' ta be fashnably late,' the hulking wagoner grinned up at his partner, his paw clenching about the length of whip clasped in his hand.

'It is a real pleasure to have someone of his like among our custom, eh, Herr Ocker?' the coachman hissed, a sly light in his eye.

'Indeed it be, Herr Bersh,' the burly Ocker replied, smiling broadly as Steinmetz strolled casually from the inn, making it a point to display the lack of haste in his stride. 'Indeed it be.'

THE COACH WAS less than an hour out from the inn when there suddenly appeared a figure standing in the road ahead. Bresh and Ocker slowed the coach down, trying to take in the cut of the man who seemed to be waiting for them. The road wardens did not patrol this particular path too frequently and it would not be the first time they would have found themselves forced to drive off a highwayman. But as they drew closer, and more details became apparent, the wagoners found themselves wishing it was a mere brigand awaiting them.

The lone man was dressed opulently: a scarlet shirt trimmed with gold thread, a long black cape trimmed with ermine. A tall, conical hat with a broad round rim rested atop his sharp-featured face. About his waist a dragonskin belt supported a pair of holstered pistols and a sheathed longsword. The man's face was thin, a slender moustache beneath his dagger-like nose, a slight tuft of grey beard upon his chin. The grey eyes of the man were focused intently upon the coachmen, silently commanding them to stop.

'Witch hunter!' swore Bresh, almost under his breath.

'Ride 'im down,' suggested Ocker in a low hiss. But even as the man made the suggestion, a second man appeared on the road. Unlike the witch hunter, he was dressed shabbily, his worn leather armour struggling to contain his powerful build. The other man was mounted, leading a second horse. But it was not these details that attracted Ocker's attention. It was the loaded crossbow in the second man's hands and the murderous twinkle in his eyes that suggested he would dearly love an excuse to use the weapon.

The coach slowed to a stop as Bresh reined in the horses. A muffled protest as to the stop rose from the carriage but the coachman ignored the complaint.

'How can we help you, templar?' Bresh called down in what he hoped was his most affable voice.

The witch hunter's cool eyes washed over the coachman for a moment. 'I have need of passage,' his sharp voice said. 'My horse has thrown a shoe.' Bresh and Ocker looked over to note the second animal being led by the mounted crossbowman. 'It is fortunate that you happened along.' The witch hunter strode towards the side of the coach.

'I would normally be most happy to aid a noble servant of mighty Sigmar...' Bresh began to say. In midsentence, the witch hunter opened the door of the carriage and began to climb in.

'I am very happy to hear it,' the witch hunter observed. 'It would be a much better realm if everyone observed their duties to Sigmar so well.' So saying, the man disappeared into the coach. Ocker began to climb from the box to protest in a more forcible fashion, but a second glance at the witch hunter's mounted companion convinced him to reconsider.

'You can continue now,' the witch hunter said, then withdrew his head back into the carriage. Bresh grumbled and flicked the reins, commanding the horses to gallop forward. The witch hunter's companion fell in behind the coach, still leading the other animal.

'Well, that fixes things,' snarled Bresh in a low voice.

'Khaine take me if'n it do,' swore Ocker. 'That fat pig got more on 'im then we seen sin' Mittherbst! An that dwarf is alwayz fuss'n bout that cargo uv 'is.' The Ostlander twisted his face into a greedy smile. 'I figger that'll turn morn' a few groats.'

'But the witch hunter...' protested Bresh.

'Yer friends 'll deal wiv 'im,' Ocker stated. 'Like dey alwayz done before.'

Within the carriage, the witch hunter took a seat, forcing Baroness von Raeder to shift her position closer toward the gambler Feldherrn. The templar removed his hat and smiled thinly at his fellow passengers.

'My name is Mathias Thulmann,' he said. 'Ordained witch hunter in the service of the most high Temple of Sigmar.' The introduction did little to warm the cool atmosphere within the carriage. Thulmann's next words made the carriage positively icy. 'We have a long ride ahead of us. Perhaps we might pass the time by getting to know each other. Now tell me: who are you, where do you come from and what are you doing?'

IT WAS LATE in the day when the coach emerged from the embrace of the ominous sprawl of the forest. Ahead of the travellers lay a small hollow of rolling land. Once there might have been lush fields and pastures claiming the open ground, but now it was given over to wild grass and squat thorny bushes. Here and there the remains of a stone wall or a lone chimney jutted up from the grass, the only forlorn evidence that this place had once known the hand of man.

As the coach made its way along a narrow, barely visible path that wound its way through the rolling heights and deep depressions in the hollow, a dark cluster of buildings slowly became visible. For a space, the settlement would disappear from view as the wagon's path took it into some low indentation in the valley floor or it rounded some small hillock. But always it became visible once more, visible but indistinct, like a mirage flickering across the horizon. Within the carriage each passenger quietly wondered what breed of men would mark out such a lonely and isolated a spot for their habitation.

Then the coach rounded one final hill and, as if some conjurer had suddenly torn away one last obscuring veil, the town loomed before them. A mass of roofs were visible, rising above a clustered mass of buildings, strewn about like litter. The roofs were in ill repair, timbers sticking through long rotten thatching like broken bones thrust through skin. The empty bell tower of a shrine rose above all else, all the more wretched for its diminished sanctity.

A timber gate stood before the cluster of buildings, the doors open, their panels sagging in their crude iron frames, warped by the forces of wind and rain. A small rectangle of wood dangled from a rusting chain, barely discernible letters burnt into the sign.

'Mureiste? What manner of name is that?' wondered the Baroness as she read the faded letters.

'Sounds like some foreign doggerel,' snorted Steinmetz, grimacing as though from a foul odour.

'It is Sylvanian,' stated the witch hunter, his voice low, filled with suspicion.

'Sylvanian?' gasped Lydia, her eyes going wide with sudden alarm, a delicate hand clutching at her throat. Her skin paled to an even more marble-like hue as the innumerable nightmare tales of horror originating from the blighted former province wormed their way at once to the forefront of her mind. Beside her, the bloated fingers of Steinmetz fumbled to form a crude mark of Sigmar.

'But why in the name of Ranald would we be anywhere near Sylvania?' asked Feldherrn, his own face becoming suspicious.

'Indeed,' observed Thulmann. 'It is a curious road that leads to Nuln in the south-west by taking its travellers north-east.'

The coach continued on into the town. The buildings, seen close up, were indeed as dilapidated as they seemed from afar. Many of the mudbrick hovels had all but collapsed, great holes pitting their walls, thatch roofs fallen in, doors lying amid weeds and brambles. The wooden structures leaned like drunken men, looking as if they might topple onto their sides at any instant. And yet, as ramshackle as they were, to the witch hunter's keen gaze, alarming incongruities presented themselves. Some of the buildings bore marks of crude unskilled repair, dried mud pushed into holes, fresh grass and branches thrown upon a thatched roof. Decayed and forsaken the town of Mureiste might be, but there were signs that it was not abandoned.

The coach came to a stop in what once must have been the town square of Mureiste. At its centre, the remains of a once heroic statue stood upon a weed choked stone pillar. The dreary facades of shops and a two-storied guild-hall considered the decayed champion with dark, gaping windows. One side of the square was dominated by a temple, the bronze hammer icon drooping from its steeple proclaiming it as having once been devoted to Sigmar. Alone among the rotting structures of Mureiste, the temple was constructed from stone, great granite blocks that must have been transported at great expense through forest and hollow.

Bresh shared a knowing look with Ocker, then slid back the small wooden window at the rear of the driver's box to speak to the passengers within the carriage.

'Just a short rest stop,' the coachman assured his passengers. 'This is the last fresh water for some distance. We shall see to the horses, then we'll be on our way again.'

His reassuring smile face faded as he saw the barrel of Thulmann's pistol rise from the compartment and point at his face.

'If either of you scoundrels makes a move to drop from that box,' Thulmann's voice hissed, 'you will have the distinctly unpleasant experience of having your brains blown out of the back of your skull.'

Bresh froze under the witch hunter's threat, the only motion in his entire frame limited to a pleading sidewise glance at his partner. Ocker slowly pulled the wide-mouthed musket from its place at the side of the bench, well beyond the limited vision of those within the carriage.

'I shouldn't do that,' snarled a harsh voice from beside the coach. Ocker's hand froze against the frame of the firearm. He looked over at the mounted ruffian who had accompanied the witch hunter. A heavy crossbow was held in Streng's hands, the bolt aimed at the Ostlander's midsection. 'Breathe in a fashion I dislike and I'll split your belly.'

From his position at the back of the coach, Fergrim Ironsharp stood upon the metal seat, trying to peer over the top of the carriage to see what was unfolding before him. The dwarf craned his neck one way then another trying to see past the barrier of boxes and crates. Then he whipped his neck around, staring at the decayed buildings around the coach. His sharp eyes, excelling at piercing the dark like all of his tunnel dwelling kind, discerned motion within the blackened doorway of an old tanner's shop. Fergrim noticed more motion in the dark recess of an alley, seeing two indistinct figures lurking within the mouth of the shadowy lane. The dwarf licked his suddenly dry mouth. There was something disturbing about those shapes, something unnatural.

'I don't think we're alone,' Fergrim declared, but his words did not reach down into the compartment below. The dwarf continued to watch as the shadowy figures began to multiply. Again he muttered an unheard warning.

Suddenly, from the darkness of a dozen doorways, from the shadows filling alley and lane, horrible shapes loped into the fading light. Each was lean, pale skin stretched tight over lanky limbs and wasted bellies, tattered mockeries of garments draped about loins or cast over shoulders. Long claws tipped each of the creatures' hands, talons more suited to a vulture than anything resembling a man. The faces of each were drawn, the heads bald, long noses perched above wide, fanged mouths. Beady red eyes glared from the pits of each face, burning with an overwhelming hunger. With a low moan-like howl, the loathsome throng began to sprint toward the coach.

'Hashut's bald beard!' screamed Fergrim, ripping his throwing axe from his belt, knuckles whitening over the haft of the blade. This time the dwarf's shout could not fail to be heard and the leather curtains were pushed aside, the occupants of the coach screaming their own cries of horror as they saw the fiendish host emptying from the ruinous streets of Mureiste.

At the front of the coach, Streng looked away from Ocker, the witch hunter's henchman staring in disbelief as the twisted inhabitants of Mureiste howled and wailed in unholy hunger. A slight movement from the driver's box brought Streng whipping around and he fired the bolt from his crossbow just as Ocker was levelling the musket towards him and drawing back the hammer. The bolt smashed into the villain's belly and the Ostlander gave vent to a loud scream of agony. He fell from the driver's box, landing partially underneath the coach. As Ocker's body hit the ground, the musket still held in his hands was discharged by the violent impact with the ground.

The thunderous boom of the firearm caused the stallions to spring into a terrified gallop. The animals sprinted forward, pulling the carriage after them. The rear wheels of the coach passed over the legs of Ocker, and a fresh scream rang from the wagoner's lungs as the bones were pulverised under the tremendous weight. At the rear of the coach, Fergrim was jostled, nearly falling from his seat. The axe fell from the dwarf's hands as his stubby fingers assumed a death-grip on the frame of the roof. Fergrim risked a look over his shoulder, blanching as he saw the first twisted creatures reaching towards him, their claws pawing at the empty air in a desperate effort to rend his flesh.

The speed of the terrified horses soon outdistanced the creatures that had converged upon the rear of the coach. But other twisted monstrosities gathered in the path of the carriage. Atop the driver's box, Bresh was vainly attempting to get some measure of control over his animals. The stallions plowed into the first of the degenerate things, crushing three of them beneath their hooves. Another of the monsters sprang at the wagon, clinging to the panels like a great spider. The beast's twisted face peered in through the window, drool dangling from its jaws. Lydia screamed as the hideous thing's eyes focused upon her.

The Baroness was not so distressed, leaning back in her seat and smashing her boot into the grinning monstrosity's face. The malformed thing howled anew as the violence of the woman's kick caused it to lose its grip on the coach and its body was crushed under the wheels.

Bresh was trying to steer the coach away, out of the blighted village. Everything had gone wrong this time, they should never have come here. He should never have let Ocker talk him into bringing the coach here after they had picked up the witch hunter. As he turned the wagon still once more, he saw yet another lane choked with thin, hungry shapes. Bresh cursed once more, slipping into the seldom used words of his native tongue. They should never have come here before dark. He cursed Ocker once more, and as if summoned up by his words, the coachman saw a pile of bones and blood lying upon the ground, a pile of bones and blood wearing the Ostlander's face. The denizens of Mureiste were indeed hungry this night.

'Make for the temple,' a harsh voice snarled through the window at the back of the box. 'If you don't, we're all dead!' Bresh swore once again, then directed the horses toward the looming stone structure. The stallions were breathing hard now, bleeding from dozens of cuts, filthy black wounds caused by the claws of the deformed monsters. Bresh knew that they would not last much longer. Cracking the whip mercilessly, he drove the failing animals onward, toward the shrine. The animals almost made it.

One of the lead horses failed a dozen yards from the temple, dropping instantly as its heart was stilled by the poison working through its veins. The momentum of the coach and the sudden violent stop caused it to crash onto its side, snapping the yoke, freeing the remaining stallion to drag its dead comrade a few dozen paces before it too staggered and fell. As the coach crashed, a tiny figure was thrown upwards, rocketing ahead of the wagon and crashing into the short flight of steps that led to the rickety wooden doors. The wagon itself continued onward, plowing across the ground, its momentum pushing it forward. Bresh, with an almost inhuman agility, had leaped atop the carriage as it turned over, clutching to the now topmost side, riding the destroyed coach like a child upon a sled.

Fergrim Ironsharp rolled onto his back, groaning loudly, trying to force the sparks to stop dancing before his eyes. As his vision cleared, the dwarf muttered another curse, watching as the mammoth shape of the coach slid towards him. He braced himself for the crushing impact, throwing his forearms behind his face. After a moment, he peered through his arms. A great cloud of dust was billowing all about him, and in the centre of the dust cloud, he could see the shape of the coach, ground to a halt so near to him, that the dwarf could reach out and touch the splintered remains of the driver's box.

ATOP THE COACH, Bresh began to laugh, overwhelmed to have survived the ordeal. The coachman lifted himself, began to slide down to the ground, when a hand closed about his ankle, causing his descent to turn into a fall. The coachman groaned, grasping at his twisted foot. As he turned his eyes upward, he saw the door of the carriage open and the dishevelled form of the witch hunter pull himself from the wreckage. His pistol was gone, but a longsword was gripped purposefully in his hands. Thulmann glared down at the injured Bresh, murder in his eyes.

'Hurry up, Mathias!' shouted a voice from the doorway of the temple. Streng stood at the top of the steps, his crossbow gripped in his hands. 'They've nearly finished fighting over the horses. They'll be on us next!'

Mathias Thulmann dropped to the ground, landing beside Bresh. 'I have half a mind to leave you for the ghouls,' his harsh tones hissed. The witch hunter gripped the front of the coachman's tunic, pulling him painfully to his feet. 'But there is a rope waiting for you,' Thulmann snarled. 'Scum such as you is for hanging.' The witch hunter pushed Bresh ahead of him, following after the coachman's hobbling steps.

Behind them, other figures were slowly, painfully, emerging from the wreckage. First the Baroness, lifted from below by powerful hands. The woman perched atop the coach for a moment, then slid down to the ground, a glance at the nearness of the ghouls lending haste to her feet. Even as the next occupant of the carriage pulled himself through the door, the noblewoman was already sprinting into the temple, skirts lifted about her knees.

By some miracle of fate, none of the occupants of the carriage appeared to have sustained more than bruises. In short order, the other passengers were free of the wreck, the bulky merchant Steinmetz coming last of all, pulled from the compartment by his burly bodyguard, Ravna. The fat-faced vodka seller froze as he saw the lean, hungry figures rising from their dinner of horseflesh. Faces crimson with gore turned in his direction. For a moment, man and ghoul stared at one another in silence. Then the moment passed. The ghoul's gory mouth dropped open, a howl escaping its wasted frame. As though it were a call to arms, the sound brought dozens of the creatures to their feet. Soon a mob of the emaciated fiends was sprinting toward the overturned coach.

'Sigmar's holy hammer,' Steinmetz stammered as his bowels emptied. Ravna tugged at his employer's arm, trying to get him to move. But the obese man was frozen to the spot, eyes fixed on the quickly advancing horde. Finally, the bodyguard pushed Steinmetz from the top of the wreck. The bulky merchant struck the ground with his shoulder, grunting with pain. He looked about him, as if the impact had snapped him back to reality. A girlish wail rose from his lungs and, with a speed which seemed impossible for a man of his decadent build, he ran for the open doors of the temple.

Ravna was right behind the fat man, leaping down from his perch even as the obese man struck earth. The mercenary saw Fergrim sitting at the base of the steps, the dwarf still trying to shake some sense back into his skull after his flight from the back of the coach. Ravna cast a beefy arm about Fergrim's waist, lifting the heavy dwarf from the ground. The bodyguard cast a glance over his shoulder, eyes going wide with horror as he saw a gaunt shape scrabbling over the coach.

'A poor place to gather your thoughts, master engineer,' the mercenary commented, leaping across the steps two at a time in his haste to reach the sanctuary of the temple. A pair of ghouls raced after him, snarling and snapping like feral dogs. As Ravna and his heavy burden reached the top of the steps, one of the ghouls let out a cry of pain, spinning about and crashing back down the stairs, a crossbow bolt lodged in its ribs. The other ghoul clawed at the bodyguard with its talons, ropes of gory drool dangling from its jaws. The claws scraped across Ravna's backplate, scratching the metal but failing to harm the man within. The ghoul was not so fortunate, as a thin sword blade pierced its side. Ravna raced past Feldherrn as the gambler freed his blade from the dying ghoul. Feldherrn cast a single look at the dozen or so other monsters racing toward the steps and hurried after the mercenary.

The wooden doors slammed shut behind Feldherrn, almost in the very face of the foremost of the ghouls. Streng and Baroness von Rader put their full weight into the effort of holding the doors shut. Feldherrn quickly sheathed his own sword and pounced upon the heavy bronze-bound doors just as they began to inch inward. Ravna set Fergrim down on one of the pews that littered the ramshackle chamber of worship. The dwarf snorted as he was set down. The mercenary looked over at the pale figure of Lydia.

'See if you can do anything for him,' Ravna snapped at the girl, racing toward the doors to help hold them against the hungry mob of cannibals outside. He did not spare a second glance at Steinmetz, cowering behind an old podium, muttering a long overdue prayer for absolution of his many moral failings.

The doors threatened to open once again as the weight and frenzy of the ghouls nearly overcame the strength of the four people desperately trying to keep the barrier closed.

'You know, I once escaped from the Reiksfang prison,' Feldherrn said, his voice loud to be heard over the clamour of the ghouls. 'Suddenly having my head separated from my shoulders by Judge Vaulkberg's ogre doesn't seem such a bad way to go.'

Streng adjusted his feet to lend more strength to his upper body even as he chuckled at the gambler's gallows humour. As the professional torturer cast his eyes toward the gambler, he saw a figure in scarlet and black walking toward them from the inner reaches of the hall.

'Lend a hand, Mathias,' the henchman grunted. For reply, the witch hunter drew his remaining pistol. Thulmann advanced upon the embattled doorway. Sighting a hole in the wood, he stuck the barrel of the pistol to it, pulling the trigger. A loud howl of pain sounded from beyond the door and the pressure against the portal faded away almost at once. The witch hunter favoured the four people holding the door with a smile and calmly holstered the smoking weapon.

'That should keep them back for a little while, but I suggest you break up a few of these pews and reinforce that door. When the sun fully sets, I think we can expect them to try again,' Thulmann turned about, his black cape swirling about him. 'Sigmar will understand the need. You'll find some nails in the cleric's cell. There is also a window behind the altar and a side door next to the storeroom. I suggest you barricade those as well before our friends outside remember them.' The witch hunter began to stalk away.

'And just what are you going to be doing?' demanded the Baroness.

'Interrogating my prisoner,' Thulmann replied without turning around.

BRESH WAS TIED hand and foot, lying upon the floor of the old priest's cell at the back of the temple. Thulmann had taken the leather thongs from the saddlebags of Streng's horse, both the henchman's and the witch hunter's animals having been brought into the temple along with the thuggish hireling.

The coachman was struggling against his bonds, trying to worm his wrists free when he heard the dreaded stomp of the witch hunter's boots. Bresh looked up from the floor, flinching slightly as he saw Thulmann's scowling face.

'Not one of your better days, I imagine,' the witch hunter sneered. He made an elaborate show of removing a number of steel needles from a pouch on his belt, then leaned down toward the terrified man. Thulmann favoured the villain with a cruel smile. 'Have you ever heard the old proverb that evil will always reveal itself?' Bresh was sweating now, the salty liquid causing dirt to slip from his face. 'It is only by chance that we happened upon your nasty little racket. My friend and I were trying to find a petty noble whose misdeeds warranted the attention of the Temple. We thought we might be able to pick up his trail again if we followed the stage route he used to escape Carlsbruck.'

Thulmann leaned forward, stabbing one of the needles into the coachman's hand. Bresh snarled in pain, a litany of curses slipping from his lips. The witch hunter nodded his head as the foreign vulgarities continued to stream from the rogue's mouth.

'I thought so,' Thulmann mused. 'You had a certain look about you beneath that grime. I thought at first you might be a Sylvanian under all that filth. Thank you for correcting me.' The witch hunter began to replace the needles into their pouch. 'I was wondering how you two cut-throats managed your vile scheme. The good citizens of Mureiste make a meal of your passengers, and you two divy up their valuables. That is the arrangement, is it not, swine?' Thulmann smashed the toe of his boot into the trussed thief's side.

'You'll never leave this place alive!' swore Bresh, spitting at Thulmann. The witch hunter wiped the spittle from the front of his scarlet and gold shirt, then kicked his captive again.

'You were nervous about me being along for the ride,' Thulmann continued. 'You rushed things. We were supposed to arrive later, after the sun had set, after your other partner was around to keep the ghouls under control.'

'The Master will kill you, witchfinder!'

Thulmann smiled back at Bresh. 'We'll see about that. This was a temple of Sigmar, and unless someone had a chance to desanctify it, it is still holy ground. That gives me an edge over your "master", Strigany.'

Bresh rolled onto his back, sneering at his captor. 'Your Sigmar won't help you! The Master will drain your body and toss the husk to the ghouls!'

Thulmann turned on his heel, striding back into the chamber of worship. 'Keep a happy thought, Strigany. It will make hanging you all the more satisfying.'

Thulmann returned to the main room of the temple. Most of the pews, he found, had been broken apart. He watched for a moment as the dwarf, apparently recovered from his concussion, carted a huge armful of wood towards the front door where the Baroness von Raeder and the gambler Feldherrn were nailing planks in place, reinforcing the portal against a second attack. He could hear more banging coming from the side door within the small storeroom located behind the cleric's cell. Behind him, he could see Streng forcing the remains of a bench against the iron frame of the single window behind the altar. The witch hunter called out to his minion. Streng hastily finished nailing the wood into place and leapt down from the altar which he had been using as a bench.

'I'd prefer a dozen of Morr's Black Guard and maybe a cannon or two,' the warrior said, 'but with a little luck, we might be able to keep them out.'

'I'm afraid that your luck has run out,' the witch hunter responded. Then his eyes caught the bloated shape of Steinmetz seated on an undamaged pew near the column where the horses had been tethered.

'Our merchant friend doesn't help?' Thulmann asked, eyebrows arching.

'I would have forced the issue, but his bodyguard said it was just as well,' Streng answered. 'He said that he'd not trust a nail driven by that pampered trash. He took the fancy girl to help him secure the storeroom door.' Suddenly the import of something the witch hunter had said sank in. Streng gripped his employer's arm. 'Why do you say our luck is done?'

Thulmann fixed his gaze on his henchman. 'Because unless I am much mistaken, in a few moments we are going to be entertaining a vampire.'

OUTSIDE THE OLD temple, the ghouls crowded about the old market square. Hungry eyes stared at the building, drool dribbling from gaping mouths. Several of the twisted deformed men stared at the fast fading sun, their eyes gleaming with expectation. On the steps of the temple, a few ghoul corpses lay where they had fallen. They too would become provender for the hideous denizens of the town, but only after they had been left for a time, after the rot had been allowed to sink into their tainted flesh.

It had been a strange break in the routine when the wagon had arrived early, causing the denizens of Murieste no end of confusion. They had watched and waited. But when it appeared that something was wrong, that perhaps the coach would leave, even the most restrained of their number had panicked and surged forward to claim their portion of the meat. Now, with the travellers trapped within the old shrine, the monsters had settled down to await the night. The intruders might have their loud magic which had exploded the face of one who had been at the front of the pack, but the people of Murieste were not without their own sorcerous resources.

As the long shadows engulfed the town, filling each lane and alleyway, darkness truly fell upon Murieste. The sound of leathern wings beating upon the thin night winds descended from above to thrill the eager ears of the ghouls. The monsters looked skyward with an almost religious fervour, pawing at the earth with their claws and uttering a sound that was not the howl of a jackal nor the chanting of a monk, but something kindred to both.

A shape detached itself from the night, hovering and soaring above the malformed mob. A black shadow swept across the square, circling it twice before coming to land at the base of the old hero's statue. It was a massive, monstrous bat, gigantic fangs jutting from its hideous face like the incisors of a sabre-toothed lion of far away Norsca.

As the creature settled to earth, it wrapped its leathery wings about itself, like a rich burgomaster burrowing into his cloak to keep warm. The talons of the bat slowly grew into muscular legs as it came to stand before the statue. The change that had begun with the legs continued up the animal's body, fur retreating back into pale, lifeless skin, sleek pinions collapsing into powerful arms bulging with muscle and sinew. The face of the bat slowly twisted and rearranged itself into a leering, diabolic countenance. A great gash of a mouth sporting sharp, over-sized teeth dominated a hairless, deformed head. The eyes of the monster, like two scabby pools of blackened blood, stared at the ghoulish throng, fixing the miserable creatures with a pitiless gaze.

At an unspoken word of command, one of the ghouls scuttled forward, cringing before the vampire. The undead beast towered over the comparatively frail cannibal, and reached downward with a clawed hand. The sword-sized talons of the vampire curled about the ghoul's chin, forcing the wretch to meet that merciless stare. The vampire locked its eyes upon those of the ghoul, letting its vision linger, draining the ghoul's memories of the arrival of the coach and all that had transpired after.

The vampire hissed in wrath, pulling its hand away from the ghoul's chin and swiping at the creature's head with its other claw in what looked to be a single impossibly swift motion. The head of the ghoul flew across the square, bouncing from the side of the old guild-hall. The vampire pulled the headless corpse to it, fixing its massive jaw over the spurting stump of the corpse-eater's neck. The vampire sucked the vile-tasting liquid noisily and greedily. It did not pay any notice to the yelps and howls of the ghouls cringing all about the vampire, their pleas for forgiveness and reaffirmations of their devotion.

The vampire let the drained cadaver fall, licking the blood that had coated its chin with a long lupine tongue. It was an abominable feeding, one the vampire was loathe to subject itself to, but it had reason to suspect it would need all the strength it could muster, even such strength as the thin, corrupt blood of a ghoul might bestow. It had seen with the eyes of the slain ghoul the passengers of the coach as they fled into the temple, and the cast of one of them troubled the undead coffin worm greatly. It could recall those long ago years when the great Vampire Counts waged their wars, and the terrible scouring of tomb and grave that had followed when the mortals were again able to hold dominion over Sylvania. It had been a long time since it had cause to fear the stakes of vampire slayers. The corpse-thing cast a wrathful look at the temple. It had no desire to confront such a man in the house of its enemy.

It would just have to send the ghouls in to fetch him out. It was little different than sending hounds to flush a hare from a stand of thorn bushes. The dogs might be injured, but the game would fill the belly just the same.

MATHIAS THULMANN STOOD before the old altar, facing the motley collection of people who had escaped from the sinister plot of the coachmen. The witch hunter studied each of his companions, trying to weigh his impressions of them with what he had learned of them from the idle chatter during the ride to Murieste. They were not the sort of people he would have chosen to stand with. Of them all, he was confident only in Streng to stand his ground, only because the henchman knew how useless it would be to run. The dwarf was another dependable quantity, but he was still somewhat disoriented from his fall. Thulmann felt that the engineer could also be trusted not to break, but how effective a defence he would be able to muster was a question he was much more uncertain of.

Of the others, the witch hunter was more dubious. The Baroness von Raeder seemed a very strong-willed and confident woman, but there was something about her which he did not entirely trust. She seemed a bit too strong-willed, a bit too independent. Such tendencies had led to her being sent away by her husband, and Thulmann wondered where such tendencies might yet lead her.

Feldherrn was a professional gambler, little more than a common thief. Thulmann was not about to place any great store in the courage of a thief. The mercenary, Ravna, was much the same, a man who owed more loyalty to gold than anything else, his loyalty went to the man who promised him further payment, even such a man as Steinmetz, whom the mercenary clearly held in contempt. It was a hold on the man, but Thulmann knew that such a tie might easily be severed when the master of Murieste came for them. A man will risk his life for gold, but he won't give it.

Steinmetz himself was worthless. Thulmann had struck the merchant, trying to knock some courage into the man, but he still slobbered over himself in fear. The merchant's companion was slightly less hysterical, but she was obviously no fighter. In the coming conflict, neither of them could be relied upon to do anything except distract some of the ghouls should the creatures force their way in.

'I've told you all what we are likely to face,' the witch hunter said. Streng had withdrawn several bulbs of garlic from one of the saddlebags and the girl, Lydia, had helped fashion them into makeshift necklaces. Sometimes garlic was useful in his work. The animal familiars of some witches were unnaturally repulsed by them, giving themselves away. Thulmann also knew that common folklore held that vampires detested it as well, and would be kept at bay by the fragrance. Coming from the mouth of a Templar of Sigmar, Thulmann hoped the others would accept the superstition and take heart from their imaginary protection.

'We must hold our ground until dawn, there is no other way out of this. This place is a temple of our mighty Lord Sigmar, bane of the undead, crippler of Black Nagash. The vampire will not dare enter here, for his powers will be weak. But he will send his slaves, and we must defy them. It is not merely our lives which are at risk, but our very souls.' Thulmann doubted that last part. Even if the ghouls did present one of them to their master in anything resembling life, he knew they would strip to the bone whatever the Strigoi left. No chance of coming back from the grave when it is in the bellies of a three score or so ghouls.

Mathias Thulmann pointed a gloved hand at Fergrim Ironsharp and Ravna. 'You two will guard the side door. They didn't attack from that quarter before, but they are better organised now, even if they do not think to exploit it, the vampire probably will.' The dwarf and the bodyguard hastened to their positions, the latter armed with his sword, the dwarf making do with a wood-axe taken from Streng's saddle bags. The witch hunter considered the Baroness for a moment, then turned and pointed at the blocked window. 'Keep a guard on the window. It is unlikely that they will try that way, but be on guard just the same. Any fingers try to pull at those boards, cut them off with your dagger. Above all, cry out. Let us know.' The Baroness stalked past the witch hunter, dagger in her hand.

'I guess that leaves you and me to join your friend at the front door,' sighed Feldherrn.

Thulmann let his eyes pass over Steinmetz and Lydia, then stared at Feldherrn. 'Still think Ranald's luck is with you?' he asked.

'I never put much stock in luck,' Feldherrn replied, walking toward the portal. 'A good gambler finds other ways to prosper.'

The witch hunter joined Streng and Feldherrn at the door. As he stood beside Streng, the man removed his eye from the small knothole Thulmann had fired his pistol through. The henchman was visibly upset, his face ashen. Streng gestured for him to have a look for himself.

Thulmann at once saw what had upset his man. Standing before the old statue was a towering monstrosity, a beast that resembled some ghastly daemon of the Blood God more than it did anything that might once have been numbered amongst men. As he watched, the vampire drew back one of its powerful arms, pointing at the temple with a finger that was tipped by a long black talon. The vampire said something, but the witch hunter did not need to understand the words to understand its meaning.

With a low howl, the ghouls mustered in the square leapt to their feet and scrambled toward the temple.

'Get ready!' Thulmann yelled. 'Here they come!'

THE GHOULS STRUCK the temple doors as a frenzied mass of hungry meat. The heavy portal shook under the impact as if a battering ram had been brought against it. The defenders found themselves forced to put their shoulders against the doors as several of the boards were ripped from the frame by the concentrated force. The rabid howls and snarls of the creatures sounded from the other side of the door, claws digging splinters from the door, eyes peering in. The defenders found themselves hard pressed to keep the door from sagging inward, despite the reinforcement. Thulmann managed to fumble his reloaded pistol from its holster. The witch hunter pressed the weapon against the same knothole. He pressed the trigger and once again there was a howl of pain.

'At least they are consistent,' he commented, holstering the weapon and redoubling his efforts to hold the door.

Streng cursed aloud as a clawed hand wriggled its way through a weakness in the rotten wood. Splinters rained onto his hair as the ghoulish limb scrabbled about in the opening. Filthy black venom trickled from the ghoul's claws. The henchman snarled, bringing his hunting knife against the pale flesh. The ghoul outside screamed as Streng sawed at its wrist. The hand twisted and turned in the hole, but try as it might, it could not be withdrawn. Streng kept at his grisly labour, finally cutting the extremity from the ghoul's arm. The hand flopped to the floor and a piteous wailing could be heard as the maimed creature retreated. No sooner had the first been injured, than another clawed hand was groping through the opening.

'As you said, Mathias, at least they are consistent,' grinned Streng, reaching toward the second hand with his knife.

THE SOUNDS OF the semi-human monsters battering at the doors of the temple sounded in Steinmetz's ears like the booming of cannon. The merchant tried to curl his fat body into a ball, choking on sobs of fear. Terror raced through his body like a debilitating poison. At his side, Lydia placed a delicate hand on Steinmetz's head, stroking his hair, trying to soothe him as she would a frightened babe. Somehow, the intense fear of her employer seemed to lessen her own and she spoke soft words of reassurance and hope into the sobbing man's ears.

At first Steinmetz did not seem to hear Lydia, then a slight flicker of reason fought its way into his eyes. He uncurled himself, his fat hands crushing hers in a desperate, hungry grip. A feverish tremble set the merchant's meaty features twitching. Lydia tried not to look alarmed as Steinmetz stared into her eyes.

'The coachman, Lydia,' Steinmetz hissed.

'Please, don't excite yourself,' Lydia replied, trying to wrest her hands back from the merchant's strong grasp. 'The witch hunter will get us out of this.'

'The coachman brought us here, Lydia,' Steinmetz repeated in a low voice, ignoring her own reply. 'He brought us here. He must know a way out!' Lydia freed her hands and drew away from the merchant in alarm. Steinmetz smiled at her sudden fright. 'If we help him escape, he will help us escape!'

'No, Emil, you can't do such a thing,' protested Lydia. Steinmetz rose to his feet, pulling his arm away from Lydia's attempt to restrain him.

'I'll pay him,' the merchant continued. 'He will accept that. I'll pay him to get us out of here. Just you and me.' Steinmetz faced the girl again, anger flaring in his face as he noted the look of shocked outrage on her features. 'You won't do it?' he snarled. The merchant's meaty hand slapped Lydia's face, knocking her onto her side with the force of the blow. 'Then stay here and die! There are fancy girls enough in Nuln to warm my bed.'

BRESH WAS STILL lying upon the floor of the old priest's cell, straining at his bonds when he heard the fat merchant enter. The coachman went rigid with alarm as he saw the obese man draw a dagger from his boot. Steinmetz stared at him for a moment, but Bresh could not decide what thoughts were squirming about behind those eyes. The merchant waddled forward and Bresh braced himself for the sharp stab of steel.

Instead, he found himself turned onto his side, felt the edge of the weapon slicing through his bonds. Words were dribbling from the merchant's mouth, inane babble about paying the Strigany a king's ransom to get him away from the blighted village, desperate pleas for the coachman to save him from the ghouls howling for his blood, promises to help Bresh escape from the witch hunter. He smiled to himself. There was no fool so gullible as a fool in fear of his life.

Bresh rose to his feet, rubbing at his wrists and knees to try and restore circulation. The Strigany looked up at his benefactor, his features shaping themselves into a mocking smile. He pointed at the knife in Steinmetz's hand.

'Will you help me?' the merchant demanded, but it was but an echo of his former pomposity and arrogance that gave the words their sting.

'Of course,' Bresh smiled. 'I am in your debt now.' He opened his hand, extending it toward Steinmetz. 'The dagger, if you please?'

'Why do you want it?' the merchant asked, voice trembling with suspicion and fear.

'Unless you want to take care of the witch hunter yourself,' Bresh answered. 'We shall have to kill him if we are going to get out of here.' The words had their desired effect and Bresh felt the reassuring weight of the weapon slide into his hand. He briefly entertained the thought of returning it to the merchant, opening the conniving tradesman's belly with his own steel, but Bresh quickly dismissed the idea. It would be much more fun to watch the ghouls dispose of him.

Bresh crept warily back into the shrine. He could see the Baroness, standing atop the altar, her back to him, intent upon the window. She presented a tempting target, but she was not his primary concern. He could also hear the commotion at the store-room door, where Steinmetz had informed him that Ravna and the dwarf were standing guard. It sounded as if a score of ghouls were trying to beat their way through the small door. He turned his eyes forward. The gambler, the witch hunter and the witch hunter's man were holding the larger entryway. Their backs were to the main room as they strove to punish the many black-clawed hands that were clutching at them from numerous holes in the wooden doors.

The Strigany smiled. His master would be greatly pleased if he dealt with the witch hunter, perhaps even forgiving him for bringing the man here in the first place. Bresh knew his master's vile moods and unpredictable temper and knew that anything he could do to strengthen his position would be a matter of life or something worse than death. Bresh tightened his grip upon the dagger and began to move stealthily toward the doors. Behind him, the fat figure of the merchant filled the doorway of the cell, sweating with nervous excitement as he watched the assassin creep across the decrepit hall of worship.

Neither man noticed the small figure that lifted herself from the bench of one of the pews. Lydia watched the Strigany emerge from the priest's cell, saw the dagger in his hand. She followed the course of his furtive steps, noting where they would eventually lead.

'Witch hunter! Behind you!'

MATHIAS THULMANN WHIPPED about as Lydia's scream sounded above the howls and snarls of the ghouls. He saw the Strigany, barely a dozen paces away, the gleaming dagger clutched in his hand. Bresh had turned to see who had betrayed his intentions, losing the opportunity to fall upon the witch hunter's back in one final, swift, murderous rush.

The scrape of steel on leather rasped from Thulmann's side as he drew his longsword. The weapon gleamed in the feeble light filtering downward from the temple's rotting roof. Blessed by no less a personage than the Grand Theogonist of Sigmar himself, the sword was a weapon that could banish daemons and still the black hearts of sorcerers. Thulmann felt it was almost demeaning to force the elegant sword to soil itself with the blood of a mere thief and murderer. But once again, he felt that Sigmar would understand.

Thulmann found the Strigany ready for him, the dagger held outwards and to his side in the manner of a practised knife fighter. Thulmann would have doubted his chances against the man with all things being equal. However, the witch hunter bore no six-inch dagger, but three feet of Reikland steel. It was an advantage none of the Strigany's tricks could overcome.

Bresh managed to twist his midsection away from Thulmann's initial strike, but the witch hunter was too far away for the Strigany to follow through with his attack. Thulmann thrust at the villain's stomach and the Strigany darted to the right, trying to slash the witch hunter's arm before he could recover. But again, the longer reach thwarted the knife fighter's instincts.

'Finish him quickly! They're getting through!' roared Streng. The groan of the doors, the cracking sound of splintering wood grew in volume even as the snarls of the ghouls increased into a

bestial cry of triumph. Bresh smiled, expecting the witch hunter
to be distracted by the calamitous report. He dove inward for
Thulmann's vitals.

The witch hunter stepped away as Bresh flopped to the floor. He
had anticipated the villain to strike, and had met his charge,
bringing the longsword stabbing through the Strigany's throat as
the man leaped forward. Thulmann paused only long enough to
kick the dagger from the dying man's reach before hurrying
toward the doors.

The ghouls had indeed forced a wide gap between the doors
and Streng and Feldherrn were hard pressed to keep them from
opening further. The snarling face and wiry arm of one ghoul
were thrust through the opening, their owner straining to undermine the efforts of his human prey to force the doors back. An
entirely human look of surprise filled the ghoul's face as Thulmann thrust his sword through its eye. The doors slowly inched
backward as Thulmann added his own weight to the efforts of
Streng and Feldherrn.

BRESH COUGHED, A great bubble of blood bursting from the hole
in his throat. But the Strigany smiled a weak and crimson smile.
He could feel his master's rage; it burned within his mind. It did
not concern Bresh overly that his vampiric master was so furious
because it considered Bresh a piece of property that had been
ruined. Only one thought warmed the dying man's soul as it quit
his body.

Now the Master will come and everyone here will die!

It burst through the wooden barricade that filled the window
behind the altar as if it were paper. The hulking shape fell upon
Baroness von Raeder before she could even register the destruction of the barricade. A mammoth hand tipped with sword-claws
ripped her in half, tossing her mangled body across the hall to
crash into a support pillar.

The vampire roared, its screech sharp and piercing. The undead
horror leapt from the altar, springing with panther like agility. The
monster smashed to splinters one of the remaining pews as it
landed. Blood-black eyes glared about the hall, smelling the
hated stench of the living. The vampire hissed, sprinting across
the shrine toward the nearest source of that stench. Steinmetz
tried to scream, but the sound was ripped from his body as the

vampire's claws tore into him, opening him from navel to collar bone, the bulb of garlic flying into the air as it was severed from the crude necklace. The merchant slumped against the wall, organs spilling from his burst ribcage and stomach.

Lydia screamed, the cry attracting the notice of the fiend. The Strigoi turned its head in her direction, but before it could move, a harsh, commanding voice shouted at it. The vampire hissed anew as it regarded its challenger.

'You are quite brave to enter Sigmar's house, filth,' Mathias Thulmann snarled. The witch hunter stepped towards the undead monster, sword gleaming at his side. The vampire's eyes seemed to burn suddenly with an unholy light and there was no mistaking the rage that warped its already twisted features. 'Show me how brave you are, coffin-worm!'

The Strigoi leapt forward. The single hop brought it within reach of the witch hunter, and its claw was already in motion even as it landed. Thulmann managed to dodge the blow by only the narrowest of measures, and the sword-sized talons tore into his cape before gouging the stone floor. And even as the vampire's first attack was avoided, its other hand sought to disembowel him with a crude swipe, blocked at the last instant by the witch hunter's sword. The undead talons smoked where the holy sword had nicked them and the Strigoi drew its bulk back to hiss at its adversary with renewed wrath.

Even as the duel between man and corpse-thing was being fought, the great double doors of the temple at last gave way to the frenzied ghoul mob struggling to get inside. Streng and Feldherrn gave ground before the snarling mass, their every attention given over to defending themselves from the venomous claws and snapping jaws of their adversaries. Behind the first wave of ghouls, dozens more fought amongst themselves to squirm through the doors, the thought of opening them wider eluding their frenzied, ravenous minds.

Thulmann did not wait for the vampire to recover its balance, but thrust at the undead beast, not with his sword, but with his off hand. The crystal flask gripped between his gloved fingers discharged its contents squarely into the vampire's face. The Strigoi howled in pain as the blessed water chewed at its rotten flesh, sizzling and steaming like bacon on a hot iron. The witch hunter darted forward, not allowing the vampire time to consider its injury. The longsword sliced into the vampire's shoulder. Once again, the Strigoi howled in pain, twisting its massive bulk about so as to tear the sword from its flesh even as one of its clawed hands cradled its smoking face. The vampire swiped at Thulmann with its other hand, but the blow was both slow and clumsy. The effect of standing within a holy place was beginning to tell on the corrupt monster, both its strength and speed diminishing rapidly to below mortal levels.

The Strigoi snarled at Thulmann and darted away from the witch hunter, leaping over the heads of startled ghouls, smashing its way through the half-open doors and racing into the night, a trail of putrid smoke drifting in its wake. The ghouls gave voice to a pitiable wail of despair as they saw the vampire flee and began a rout of dismal disorder. Streng and Feldherrn harried the escaping monsters, running several of the degenerate things through the back as they fled.

The witch hunter dropped to his knees, exhaling deeply, thanking Sigmar for the rout of the undead abomination and its followers. But he knew that there were more hours to pass before the dawn and that the vampire would be doubly determined to exterminate them now. Before, they had represented food. Now they represented a threat to the undying horror.

THULMANN TOOK COUNT of the toll the attack had taken. Steinmetz and Baroness von Raeder were dead. The loss of the merchant did not disturb him in the slightest, but the Baroness had represented another pair of eyes and ears that could watch for danger, another blade that could fend off the hungry cannibals. A more telling injury had been dealt at the rear door of the temple. Hearing their vampiric master rampaging within, the ghouls had redoubled their efforts to gain entry, tearing great gashes into the wood. Ravna and Fergrim had kept the pack out, but one of the venom-ladden claws had slashed the wrist of the mercenary. He seemed only slightly dizzy at the moment, and protested loudly that it was no more than a scratch, but the witch hunter knew only too well that the poison of a ghoul's claw was both fast and lethal. He would not last the night.

Mathias Thulmann stood before the remaining survivors. Streng had been set to watch the rear door, Feldherrn peering out of the wreckage that framed the main entrance. There was little hope of defending the doorway after the vampire's brutal exit and the destruction it had delivered upon the doors themselves. As yet, the ghouls had not returned to exploit the indefensible entryway, but Thulmann knew that they would.

'Listen,' the witch hunter spoke. 'We have driven them away, but they will return, more determined than before. The undead thing that rules these wretches cannot afford to let us live to see the dawn. He must return to his crypt when the sun rises and fears that I will find his refuge while he is helpless. It is all or nothing for him, he will offer no quarter.' Thulmann studied each face, noting the expressions of resignation and regret, but finding that fear had passed even from Lydia's pale face. Men who have accepted their own deaths have no place for fear in their hearts.

'When they come again, we must make our stand,' the witch hunter continued, something of a preacher's manners slipping into his tones. 'Here, in this house of Sigmar, we will show this filth how real men die and make them pay a price in misery these wretches will not soon forget.'

A soft clapping punctuated Thulmann's brief speech. Fergrim Ironsharp hopped to his feet. 'And you folk call dwarfs dour?' the engineer chuckled. 'You will forgive me if I am not terribly excited by the proposition of dying to impress a human god, but I think that if I can get back to the coach, I may be able to fix things so we can get out of this graveyard.'

'I don't think the vampire is going to be bribed with your gold,' scoffed Feldherrn from the doorway. 'Indeed, it was probably your "valuable cargo" that made those murderers bring us here in the first place.'

'Gold indeed!' grumbled the dwarf, turning to the gambler. 'If I had a hoard of gold I'd have better uses for it than to take it on holiday to Nuln! I speak of explosives! Five hundred pounds of premium Ironsharp blasting powder!'

The revelation swept about the room like wildfire, exciting each survivor.

'You have an idea of how to exploit these explosives?' asked Thulmann, trying not to let any degree of unwarrented hope creep into his words.

'All I need to do is run a fuse to those boxes and the next time our friends come howling at the door, there won't be enough of them left to feed a crow,' declared Fergrim, puffing himself up proudly. 'Just give me somebody to watch my back, and we'll give that blood-worm a very unpleasant reception!'

IT WAS QUICKLY decided. Streng would remain on guard at the rear door while Feldherrn kept watch inside with Lydia in the event that the vampire again chose to enter through the window. Thulmann emerged from the doorway, his sharp eyes scanning the shadowy town square. The dwarf would have made a better sentry with his excellent night vision, but he had a very different role to play. Ravna, the ghoul venom pulsing through his body now, insisted on accompanying the dwarf. Thulmann noted with some dismay the slow, ungainly steps of the once powerful man.

Fergrim knelt beside the overturned coach, rummaging about amongst the luggage still lashed to the roof. He removed a length of black fuse, traces of gunpowder soaked into the thin line of rope, and then began knocking a hole in the uppermost crate.

Thulmann could hear the sound of many naked feet running in the darkness. He shouted a call of alarm to the dwarf. Fergrim snorted back that he was hurrying. The witch hunter cursed as the sickly grave-stench of the ghouls and their low groans of hunger emerged from the veil of darkness.

'They're closing in, Fergrim,' he said.

The dwarf remained focused upon his task. From the corner of his mouth he swore at the man. 'Perhaps you'd prefer if I made a mistake! We have just one chance at this.' Beside him, Ravna thrust the point of his sword into the ground. Fumbling at his belt, he removed a small tinderbox and a wooden taper. The need for haste had not been lost on the former bodyguard.

The piteous, feral wailing of the ghouls was rising in volume now. Thulmann sighted one of the creatures as it rounded the overturned coach. Aiming quickly, he sent the bullet from his pistol crashing into its skull.

'Grace of Sigmar, dwarf! Move!'

Fergrim finished fixing the fuse to the uppermost box, uncoiling the length of black cord. 'You can't rush a decent job!' the dwarf grumbled. Suddenly the coach shook. Fergrim turned his face upward.

The Strigoi sat perched atop the side of the coach like a crouching panther. The vampire snarled at Thulmann, flexing its claws, promising its enemy a lingering and gruesome death. The witch hunter had emerged from his burrow. Now the advantage was the vampire's.

So intent was the monster on its enemy, that it paid no attention to the much closer prey. Fergrim stared at the undead horror right above his head and slashed at the fuse in his hands, cutting the line much shorter than he had been planning. Suddenly, a powerful grip closed about his belt and the dwarf found himself stumbling backwards falling on the bottom most steps. Even as he started to voice a colourful oath of outrage, the dwarf saw who had thrown him away from the coach, and what he was doing now. Fergrim leaped up the steps and dove onto his face amid the remains of the doorway.

The Strigoi continued to snarl and spit, waiting while more and more of its ghoul minions rounded the overturned coach. Several of the monsters noted the man crouching against the side of the obstacle, just beneath their master and began to close upon him. But even as they did, Ravna stabbed the lit taper into the hole Fergrim had knocked into the uppermost box of powder.

Mathias Thulmann ducked inside the doorway, letting the heavy stone wall of the temple shield him from the explosion. The sound was deafening, like the angry bellow of a wrathful daemon. The temple shook, tiles falling from its roof. Debris, wooden and organic, rushed through the doorway, propelled by a hot wind. As the boom dissipated the sound of painful screams and moans erupted, the stench of cooked meat permeated the air.

Thulmann stepped back through the door. Near his feet, a stout, short form wriggled itself free of the debris that had covered him like a shroud. The dwarf rolled onto his back, grumbling and bemoaning the loss of his valuable supply of powder. Thulmann regarded the devastated scene before the temple. The coach was blown apart, reduced to burning fragments scattered across the square. The firelight illuminated surviving ghouls fleeing back into the shadows, maimed and injured ones slowly crawling away. A score or more were thrown all about, burned, torn and quite dead. The witch hunter quietly saluted the sacrifice of Ravna and prayed that Sigmar would conduct the man's soul to one of the more pleasant gardens within the realm of Morr.

Motion snapped the witch hunter from his thoughts. He could see a massive shape writhing at the base of the now toppled statue. He firmed his grip upon his sword and carefully made his way down the temple steps. He could hear the others behind him, filling the doorway, marvelling at the destruction the blast had caused, but the witch hunter did not turn his eyes from the wounded beast. Now hunter had become prey.

The vampire had been thrown backwards at great force by the explosion. Huge splinters of wood from the coach had been driven through its unclean flesh, piercing it through in a dozen places. The violence of the explosion had tossed the creature as though it were a rag doll, causing it to smash into the eroded statue in the centre of the square. The forgotten hero had struck the ground ahead of the vampire, but had rolled backwards, crushing one of the monster's limbs beneath its weight. The vampire fought to free itself, but the maddening pain of its injuries had reduced its already disordered mind to an animal level. The misshapen fangs worried at the trapped arm, trying to sever it from the Strigoi's body. Suddenly, a familiar scent caused the vampire to snap its head about, pain and imprisonment forgotten.

Mathias Thulmann stared down at the hideous monster as it regarded him with rage-filled eyes of blood. 'When you want to kill someone, do so. Don't talk about it next time.' Thulmann laughed softly as the vampire hissed up at him. 'I forgot. You don't get a next time.'

Thulmann raised his sword above his head in both hands and with a downward thrust, impaled the Strigoi's heart, pinning the undead creature to the clean earth below. The vampire struggled for a moment, then its final breath oozed through its jaws in a dry gargle. Thulmann turned away from the dead monster. The blessed steel would serve as well as a stake until he could decapitate the corpse and dispose of its remains in purifying fire. But such work would wait for the dawn.

Mathias Thulmann turned his horse away from the flickering flames. He patted the steed's neck with a gloved hand and looked over at Streng. 'Well, friend Streng, I do not think we will find our man here. If he did have the misfortune to come this way, he is beyond the reach of the Temple now.' The two men began to walk their animals back toward the gates of Murieste. Behind them, three figures stood beside the pyre, each wearing an angry look.

'What about us?' demanded Feldherrn.

Thulmann turned about in the saddle. He considered each of the people staring at him. Lydia stared back at him with accusing eyes, Fergrim Ironsharp was grumbling into his beard.

'Do what people without horses have done since the days of Most Holy Sigmar,' the witch hunter advised as he turned back around and continued on his way.

'Walk.'

WITCH WORK

THE AIR WAS rank with the smell of decay and death, a morbid
atmosphere that crawled within the murk like a pestilent fog,
staining the rays of moonlight filtering through the thatch roof so
that they became leprous and sickly. The interior of the hovel was
small by any standard, yet into this space had been crammed
enough weird paraphernalia to fill a space ten times as big. Bundles of dried roots and withered weeds drooped from the few
wooden poles that supported the roof, their noxious stench contributing in no small part to the foul air. A set of crude timber
shelves supported a disordered collection of clay jars and pots, a
strange glyph scratched in charcoal upon each to denote whatever
unclean and hideous material might be found within. The rotten
carcasses of dozens of birds swung from leather cords affixed to
the roof beams, ranging from songbirds to water fowl and the
uglier birds found upon battlefields and graveyards – yet all alike
in one way. For not one of the birds was complete, each one was
missing some part – a clawed foot there, a wing here – all vital
ingredients in the practices of the hovel's lone inhabitant.

She was bent and wizened, crushed low by the weight of years
pressing upon her shoulders. A shabby brown shawl was wrapped

about her crooked back; vile grey rags that might once have been a gown billowed about her skeletal limbs. Scraggly wisps of white hair crawled like worms from her head, the blotched skin so thin from time's ravages as to scarcely conceal the bone beneath. Her face was a morass of wrinkles, like the crinkling surface of an autumnal leaf. A sharp nose stabbed out from her face, looming like a hawk's bill above her gash of a mouth. From the sunken pits of her face, two little eyes twinkled with a cold, murderous mirth.

The old woman stared down towards the fire smouldering at her feet. A chill seemed to billow up from those embers, the dread clutch of magic and sorcery, the loathsome touch of powers unclean and unholy. The frigid caress of the supernatural was enough to make even the bravest soldier falter, but the old woman was so accustomed to invoking such forces that she no longer acknowledged the horror of such things. Her toothless mouth cracked open into a ghastly smile as she watched her magic take shape. The eerie fire had changed colour, deepening into a bloody crimson, lighting the interior of the hut as though it were engulfed in flame. Within the fire, tiny figures began to appear: tiled roofs and plaster walls, narrow streets and winding alleys. The old woman could see the tall steeples of cathedrals and temples, the mammoth towers of castles and forts. But her ambitions this night were not devoted to such lofty places. Her business was with a different section of this place. She focused her will and the image began to boil, disintegrating into a crimson fog before reforming into a more concentrated view of the city.

Chanta Favna let a dry hiss of laughter trickle past her lips as the sight manifested itself before her. The merchant district of Wurtbad was one of the most secure places within the river city, surrounded by thick walls thirty feet high and topped with iron spikes. Patrols of city watch and private militia regularly walked the streets, guarding against any would-be thieves who had managed to get over the walls, ensuring that no stranger tarried within the district unless that man had proper business there. For two hundred years, the merchants had been mostly safe from the crime that stalked the rest of Wurtbad, safe from the thieves and murderers who plied their trade in the dead of night. They thought themselves protected from such things within their fortress-like district.

The old witch sneered. Men were so quick to become complacent, to deceive themselves into thinking themselves safe. Her withered hands reached toward the fire, clutching a small wooden doll. The hag smiled as she glanced down at the minnikin. This night the fat, indolent wealthy of Wurtbad would again learn to fear the approach of night, to shudder beneath their bedclothes as they waited out the long hours and prayed to their gods for a hasty dawn.

A new figure appeared within the scene unfolding in the flames. Chanta Favna watched as it tottered over the wall, slipping like a gangly shadow between the iron spikes.

'That's my darling boy!' the witch cackled. 'Over wall and under moon, shade within the night of doom!'

There would be a red sky this night in old Wurtbad, a night of screams and blood and terror. The witch's pulse quickened as she considered the carnage that would soon unfold somewhere within the city. There would be havoc enough to satisfy her for a time, more than enough to remind her patron that his payment had best be as timely and generous as he had promised.

THE TWO RIDERS made their way slowly through the cramped, muddy streets of Wurtbad. The crowd of craftsmen, merchants, beggars and peasant farmers parted grudgingly before their steeds, waiting until the last moment to allow the animals to pass. Half-timber structures loomed to either side of the street, gaudily painted signs swinging from iron chains announcing the goods and services that might be procured within the tall, thin buildings; announcements made more often than not with crude illustrations of shoes and swine rather than written Reik-spiel.

'Good to be back in civilisation, eh Mathias?' one of the riders laughed, his gaze rising to an iron balcony fronting the upper storey of a building some distance down the narrow street and the buxom brunette leaning against it, a much more lively and vivid manner of announcing the establishment's trade. The rider was a short, broad-shouldered man, his body beginning to show the first signs of a paunch as his belly stretched the padded leather tunic that protected his torso. A scraggly growth of beard spread across his unpleasant face, and the disdainful sneer that seemed to perpetually curl the man's lip.

The man's companion was, by contrast, tall and lean, his hair and beard neatly trimmed. He wore a scarlet shirt trimmed with golden thread, fine calfskin gloves clothing his hands as he gripped the reins of his steed. A long black cape trimmed in ermine hung about his shoulders and a wide-brimmed hat of similarly sombre hue covered his head. The face behind the shadow cast by the hat was thin and hawkish, a sharp nose flanked by steely eyes, a slight moustache perching above a thin-lipped mouth. From the man's belt swung a pair of massive pistols and a slender longsword sheathed in dragonskin. The buckle that fronted the rider's belt announced his profession as surely as any of the gaudy signs that swung in the feeble breeze – the twin-tailed comet, holy symbol of Sigmar, patron god of the Empire – the sign of that god's grimmest servants, the witch hunters.

'Foul your soul with whatever debauchery pleases you, Streng,' the witch hunter declared. 'One day you will answer for all the filth you've degraded yourself with.'

'But I'll die happy,' the other man retorted, a lewd smile on his harsh features.

The witch hunter did not bother to continue the conversation, knowing that his disapproval of Streng's vices only made the man take even greater enjoyment from them. Mathias Thulmann had long ago learned that Streng would never rise from the gutter, he was the sort of man who would never be able to do more than live from one day to the next. The future was something that would sort itself out when it came, and the approval or disapproval of any god was a concept far too lofty for a mind like Streng's to ever grasp.

Ironically, it was this quality that made him so capable an assistant for the witch hunter. Streng did not lend his mind to morbid imaginings, did not feed the germ of fear with figments of his own imagining. That was not to say that the man did not succumb to fear; confronted by some unholy daemon of the Ruinous Powers he would feel terror like any other mortal soul, but he was not one who could allow anticipation of such an encounter to unman him before the time of such a confrontation.

'I think we will do better to begin our inquiries with the stage lines, not the bordellos,' Thulmann commented as the two men rode past the establishment that had aroused his henchman's interest. 'From what we know of the character of our quarry, he wouldn't be hanging about a bawdy house.'

'We need to chase a better class of heretic,' grumbled Streng, reluctantly removing his eyes from the shapely woman draped across the iron balcony.

Thulmann nodded in agreement.

'Freiherr Weichs is the most wretched creature we've hunted together,' he agreed. 'He would befoul even that ghoul-warren we found in Murieste. The day that scum hangs, the very air will become less stagnant.' There was passion in the witch hunter's voice, a fire in his tone. The heretic scientist and physician Doktor Freiherr Weichs had been the object of Thulmann's attention for nearly a year. He and Streng had pursued the villain across half the Empire, following his trail from one city to the next. They had come close several times, but always the madman had remained just beyond their reach. Thulmann fairly bristled with frustration at his inability to bring Weichs to ground.

'Suit me fine if we catch that vermin this time,' Streng said, spitting a blob of phlegm into the gutter, narrowly missing the boots of a passing labourer. 'Been some time since I was able to ply my own trade. After all these months, it'll be a pleasure to make Herr Doktor Weichs sing! He'll be admitting to the assassination of Emperor Manfred when I get through with him!'

Thulmann turned his stern gaze on his henchman, draining him of his bravado and sadistic cheer. 'First we have to catch him,' Thulmann reminded his professional torturer.

THE WITCH HUNTER and his companion emerged from the large stone-walled building that acted as the Wurtbad headquarters for the Altdorf-based Cartak coaching house. The Cartak coaching line was one of the largest in the Empire, operating in dozens of towns and cities. They were also know for their scrupulous attention to detail, always recording the names and destinations of their passengers in gigantic record books. But as Thulmann had examined their records, the forlorn hope that something would arouse his suspicion failed to manifest. It had not been entirely a fool's hope, Weichs had been bold enough to use his own name on several occasions and lately had taken a perverse delight in using ciphers for aliases, tweaking the nose of his pursuers. Either the heretic had tired of his little game, or else there had been nothing for Thulmann to find in the Cartak records. The witch hunter had a feeling that the other four coaching houses operating out of Wurtbad would be no more helpful.

As Thulmann strode towards the street, he noticed a company of soldiers dressed in the green and yellow uniform of Stirland approaching. As they came closer, he could see that a golden griffon rampant had been embroidered upon their tunics, marking them as members of Wurtbad's Ministry of Justice. Thulmann watched with mounting interest as it became obvious the soldiers were coming for him. He could hear Streng mutter a colourful curse under his breath. The witch hunter smiled. Under normal circumstances, his companion would have good reason to dread the approach of the city watch, but there had been no opportunity as of yet for Streng to work himself into one of his drunken fits, which raised the question as to what the soldiers did want.

'You are a Sigmarite templar, newly arrived in Wurtbad?' the foremost of the soldiers asked when he and the three men shadowing him were but a few paces away. The stern, almost overtly hostile look on the soldier's face made it clear to Thulmann that the man already knew the answer to his question before he asked it.

'Mathias Thumann,' the witch hunter introduced himself. 'Ordained servant of our most holy lord Sigmar and templar knight of his sovereign temple.' Thulmann put a note of command and superiority in his tone. He'd had problems before with local law enforcers who felt that the presence of a witch hunter was some slight upon their own abilities to maintain order, their own competence in apprehending outlaws and criminals, as though the average watchman was trained to deal with warlocks and daemons. 'Lately of Murieste,' he added with a touch of sardonic wit.

'Kurtus Knoch,' the soldier introduced himself. 'Sergeant of Lord Chief Justice Markoff's personal guard,' he added, putting just as much stress in his own position as Thulmann had when announcing his own. 'My master asks that you meet with him.' The soldier's hard eyes bored into Thulmann's own. 'Now, if it is not too inconvenient.'

The witch hunter gave Knoch a thin smile. 'Your master is arbitrator of the secular law. My business is that of the temple.'

The soldier nodded.

'My master is well aware of the difference,' Knoch told him. 'That is why this is a request rather than an order.' The sergeant's voice trembled with agitation, arousing Thulmann's interest. He and Streng had not been in Wurtbad long enough to have earned this man's ire, nor that of his master. And why would Lord Markoff be interested in a witch hunter from outside the city when there was a permanent chapter house within its walls? Perhaps the reason for Knoch's resentment had something to do with the answer to that question.

'Streng,' Thulmann turned to his henchman. 'Go and secure lodgings for us, then begin making inquiries with some of your usual contacts.' The witch hunter was always amazed at the speed with which Streng was able to insinuate himself with the criminal underworld of any settlement they tarried in, another quality that made the man indispensable. 'With luck, you may learn something useful.'

Streng feigned a servile bow, then retreated down the street.

Thulmann returned his attention to the soldiers.

'I am a busy man, Sergeant Knoch,' Thulmann stated. 'Let us see your master so that we may both of us return to more profitable endeavours.'

THULMANN WAS TAKEN to the monstrous Ministry of Justice, a gigantic, grotesque structure which loomed above the other ministries that had been clustered together within the cramped confines of Wurtbad's bureaucratic district. Knoch led the witch hunter through the marble-floored halls, past the glowering portraits of past Chief Justices and High Magistrates, and to the lavish dining hall that served the current Lord Chief Justice. The room was as immense as everything else about the building, dominated by a long table of Drakwald timber that might have easily served a hundred men. Just now, there was only one chair set before it; dozens more lined the far wall like a phalanx of soldiers.

Lord Chief Justice Igor Markoff was a severe-looking man, his black hair cut short above his beetle-like brow. There was a hungry quality about the man's features and his squinting eyes, not unlike that of a starving wolf. Just now, the object of Markoff's hunger was not the plate of steaming duck on the table but the man his bodyguard had just escorted into his dining room.

'Mathias Thulmann,' Knoch announced without ceremony. The soldier took several steps away from the witch hunter, scowling at the man's back. Markoff set down his knife, dabbing at his mouth with a napkin before rising from his seat.

'So, the stories are true, then,' Markoff said. 'That idiot Meisser has finally decided that he hasn't the faintest clue what is behind our troubles.'

The Lord Chief Justice's tone was harsh and belligerent, tinged with underlying contempt. Thulmann had heard such voices before, from burgomasters and petty nobles across the Empire, men who resented forfeiting even a fraction of their power and authority to the temple, even in times of the most dire need. However, the frustrated fury he saw blazing in Markoff's eyes was something even more familiar to the witch hunter, for it was the same look he saw staring at him in the mirror when his mind contemplated his fruitless hunt for Freiherr Weichs.

'I am afraid that you have my purpose for coming to Wurtbad misconstrued,' Thulmann said. 'I am here pursuing my own investigations. I've not been contacted by the Wurtbad chapter house, either before arriving in your city, or since.'

Thulmann's apology only seemed to irk the magistrate even more. Markoff slammed his fist against the polished surface of the table.

'I should have known that fool Meisser would never ask for help,' Markoff fumed. 'Why should he when no one in Altdorf seems inclined to listen to my complaints? Far be it for the Grand Theogonist and his lapdogs to rein in one of their unruly mongrels!' Markoff lifted his clenched fist, shaking it beneath Thulmann's nose. 'Damn me, but I'll take matters into my own hands! Just let your temple try and burn me for a heretic!'

'You should be very careful about making threats against the servants of Sigmar,' Thulmann warned, feeling his blood growing warm as the Lord Chief Justice voiced his impious remarks.

To his surprise, Markoff did not even blink, but instead snorted disdainfully, before resuming his seat at the table.

'I'll do worse than threats if this cur Meisser continues on as he has,' Markoff stated. 'He has only two dozen men. I have five hundred, and the baron's guard if I need to call upon it.'

Thulmann stared for a moment, at a loss for words. Had he actually heard the Lord Chief Justice of Wurtbad threaten violence against a chapter house of Sigmarite templars? The shock receded after a moment, replaced not with the outrage at such blasphemy Thulmann expected, but a deep curiosity at how matters between the secular and temple authorities could have degenerated to such a point.

'Perhaps I might be able to make your concerns known to the proper authorities if I were to know the particulars of the matter,' the witch hunter told Markoff.

'Particulars of the matter?' Markoff scoffed. He pulled the knife from the roast duck, pointing it at Thulmann. 'Four households slaughtered in two months, slashed to ribbons. This killer doesn't leave bodies, he leaves piles of meat!' Markoff plunged the knife back into his dinner with a savage thrust. 'Nor does this human vermin prey upon the poor and unknown. No, the merchant quarter is his hunting ground! The merchant quarter, a district almost as secure as the baron's own palace!'

Markoff rose again, his body trembling with agitation. 'As if the massacres were not enough, rumour began to build among the superstitious simpletons in the street. They said that no human assassin could manage such horrors, that it was the work of some devilish sending, some daemon beast called up by sorcerers and witches!'

Markoff glared at Thulmann, his face livid with rage.

'That is where your friend comes in! Witches and daemons are the province of Sigmar's temple knights, those who would protect us from the menaces of Old Night. Meisser took over the investigation after the second incident, fumbling about like some backwoods roadwarden. He's arrested fifty-seven people, hung five and burned three! The streets around his chapter house echo with the screams of his prisoners until the first light of dawn!' Markoff's face twisted into an almost bestial snarl. 'And still this murderous maniac has not been stopped! Only two weeks ago there was another incident. The Hassel family, an old and respected house, butchered like swine from the old grey-headed Erik Hassel to Frau Hassel's infant child.'

Thulmann listened to the magistrate's tirade, feeling the fury communicate itself from Markoff to the witch hunter himself. This Meisser, this witch hunter captain, sounded to be as much of a terror to the city as whatever fiend was perpetrating these atrocities. Without having met Meisser, Thulmann could guess his type – brutal and incompetent, perfectly willing to hang and torture the innocent simply to mask his own inability to uncover the real villain. Perhaps there was another reason behind such doings, but Thulmann had seen enough brutality and incompetence wearing the colours of the temple to doubt it.

'Thank you for voicing your concerns, Lord Chief Justice,' Thulmann said, bowing his head to the official. 'Rest assured that I will personally investigate this matter. That is, if you will officially sanction such an investigation.' For the first time since the witch hunter had entered the room, Markoff's hostility abated. He returned to his seat, nodding thoughtfully to himself before speaking.

'Whatever you need from me, you will have,' Markoff declared, a smile crawling onto his face.

THE BATTERED HUMAN body that lay lashed to the top of the wooden table might once have been a woman beneath the dirt, dried blood, singed flesh and blackened bruises. Now, she was like everyone else in the dungeons beneath Wurtbad's chapter house – a condemned heretic, guilty of consorting with the Dark Gods to bring horror and death to the city. There was only the rather irritating formality of wringing a confession from the sorry wretch before she could be legally executed.

Witch Hunter Captain Meisser loomed above the table, his piggish features smiling down at the prisoner with false sympathy. Meisser was an aging man, his body no longer strong and virile, but flabby and wasted beneath his soft embroidered tunic and sleek green hose. His hair had begun to desert him, leaving only a fringe of white about his temples and the back of his head. In some ways, his overall appearance suggested an old hunting hound that had outlived its best days and now desperately clung to what remained of its former power.

'You have been through a terrible trial,' Meisser said, his dry voice echoing about the stark stone walls of the cell. The woman looked up at him, eyes nearly swollen shut, reaching desperately toward the sympathetic tone the witch hunter had allowed to colour his voice. She did not see the knowing smiles that formed on the faces of the two men standing on the other side of the table, the torturers who had reduced her to such a state. They had seen this tactic many times, seen the interrogating witch hunter shore up a prisoner's fading hopes only to smash them like a child's sandcastle.

'You have not confessed to any wrong doing, you have sworn that you are a faithful and devout servant of most holy Sigmar.' Meisser brushed aside a stray lock of matted hair from the woman's face, returning the painful smile that worked its way onto her battered features. 'Perhaps Sigmar has seen fit to gift you with strength enough to resist the ordeals which law dictates we must employ to unmask the heretic and the infidel, the witch and the sorcerer. Still,' Meisser's tone became less insinuating, more careless, as though speaking of trivialities rather than the life of another human being, 'we cannot be entirely certain that you have been truthful with us. You say that you sold herbs and roots to the households in the merchants' quarter, doing so from door-to-door. But how can we be certain that this was your true purpose, that you were not simply using it as a cover for your real activities, a blind to conceal your unholy witchcraft?' Meisser paused for a moment, as though deep in thought. He let the implications of his words sink into the injured wretch strapped to the table.

'What we need is corroboration,' Meisser declaimed, as though the thought were entirely novel and new. He looked again into the red-lined eyes of his prisoner. 'I understand that you have two children.' He let the statement hang in the air, watching as the look in his prisoner's eyes went from one of confusion to one of absolute horror. The woman's body began to tremble, slapping against the wooden table as she began to sob. Meisser waited while the woman's excess of emotion played itself out, until her shuddering body began to lie a little more still upon the table. Meisser cocked his head in his prisoner's direction, then smiled down at the woman. There was no friendliness in his smile now, only a predatory grin.

'What was that you said?' Meisser asked. 'I thought I heard you say something.' The last light flickered out within the woman's eyes, the last gleam of hope draining out of her. She closed her eyes and opened her bruised lips.

'I confess.' The words escaped her in a sob that shook her entire body. Meisser turned away, striding back toward the door of the cell.

'My associates will take down the details of your confession,' he said. 'Please furnish them with whatever they require. We will, of course, need to corroborate them later.' Meisser closed the door on the horrified scream that sounded from the cell as the full level of the witch hunter's ruthless treachery impacted against the prisoner's darkest fears.

Meisser made his way through the maze of darkened bare-stone halls until at last he ascended the wooden stair that would lead him from the dungeons to the chapter house above. There was a great deal of work still to be done. Another confession meant that he would need to arrange a date for another public execution with the Lord Chief Justice and the city burgomasters. That another execution would displease Markoff did not overly bother the witch hunter. The magistrate had no conception of just how deeply the seed of corruption had taken root in his city, and how desperately in need of people like Meisser Wurtbad really was. He'd continue to uncover every witch and heretic in the city before he was through, and when the murders stopped, then even Lord Chief Justice Markoff would be unable to cast derision upon Meisser's methods.

Meisser paused as he walked down the wood-walled hallway of the chapter house. Ahead of him in the corridor he could see Emil, one of his apprentice witch hunters opening the door of Meisser's private study, a tray in his hands. The witch hunter captain snarled under his breath, hurrying forward to confront his underling. No one was admitted into that room unless he himself accompanied them. Emil would not soon forget that rule again once his superior was done with him.

Emil hesitated when he saw Meisser, the colour draining from his face. But it was an even more apprehensive look that he gave to the room itself, lingering but a moment at the threshold before slipping inside. Meisser did not pause to consider his underling's curious actions, but hurried after the man, opening the study door almost as soon as Emil had closed it.

Meisser's study was opulently furnished, a massive desk dominating a room flanked by bookcases crammed with leather-bound folios. A massive portrait of the witch hunter captain himself consumed the wall directly behind the desk. A tall, thin man was standing before the portrait, looking up at it as he drank from a wineglass taken from the tray Emil had carried into the room.

'Rather poor quality,' the thin man commented. 'You should have commissioned an artist to do this rather than trying your own hand with a brush.'

Meisser felt his already aroused anger swell. 'You insolent cur! How dare you!'

The tall man turned around, glaring at Meisser with unrestrained contempt. 'Allow me to introduce myself. Mathias Thulmann, Templar knight of the Order of Sigmar.' Thulmann turned toward where Emil had retreated after bringing him his wine. 'Thank you Brother Emil, that will be all. I would have words with your captain.'

A visibly relieved Emil bowed to each of the men in turn and hurried from the room.

'To what do I owe this visit?' Meisser asked, striving to regain his composure. He fumbled at the tray Emil had left sitting on his desk, pouring wine for himself. 'You have not come from Altdorf, have you?'

'No,' Thulmann replied, stepping away from the portrait and turning a seemingly idle eye upon the shelves of neatly ordered folios. 'Is there any reason you should be expecting a visitor from Altdorf?'

'Why no, none at all,' Meisser responded, taking a deep drink from his glass.

'Then you must have some very influential friends,' Thulmann snapped, spinning about like a cornered wolf. 'The Lord Chief Justice has sent no less than five official protests to the Great Temple calling for your removal! I did not want to believe all that he told me, but since entering this room and reading these,' the witch hunter's hand slammed against the desk where Meisser noticed a number of parchment sheets from his records had been piled, files relating to his investigations into the merchant quarter massacres and the arrests he had made since the first incident.

'These horrors run deeper than they might at first seem,' Meisser sputtered, taking another sip of wine.

'The only thing that runs deeper than it seems is your incompetence!' Thulmann snarled back. 'You've filled your dungeons with innocent men and women on charges so outrageously stupid that it is a wonder the people of this city haven't already ripped down this chapter house and stretched that miserable neck of yours!'

'Now see here!' Meisser retorted. 'You've no authority to speak to me in such a manner! Wurtbad is my posting, my responsibility!' Meisser cringed as Thulmann's hand fell to the sword hanging from his belt.

'You have friends in Altdorf?' Thulmann sneered. 'So do I. You see this sword? It was a gift to me from the Grand Theogonist himself. I would advise against making this a matter to be arbitrated by our superiors.' Thulmann felt a great sense of satisfaction as Meisser wilted before him.

'What would you advise?' the witch hunter captain asked in a haunted, defeated voice.

'First we will free these people you have detained. If they have already confessed, you will strike out their words and burn the confessions,' Thulmann told him. 'Secondly, we will work with Lord Markoff's men in this matter, not exclude them. He has a much larger body of men at his command and we will need them.'

A suspicious curiosity brought words to Meisser's lips. 'Why will we need Markoff's men? If you are thinking to place a permanent guard upon the merchant quarter, it won't work. It's already been tried.'

'You've been too busy arresting herbalists and midwives,' Thulmann chided the other man. 'You've ignored the more obvious facts in the case.' Thulmann's hand slapped against the piled papers on Meisser's desk. 'Each of these massacres occurred during either the first night of Morrslieb waxing full or the first night of Mannslieb falling dark – nights when the powers of evil are at their most powerful. And you have failed to notice another pattern to these crimes.'

'Pattern?' Meisser scoffed. 'There is no pattern to these crimes. They are the work of some daemonic beast spat up from the blackest hell!'

'Perhaps,' conceded Thulmann. 'But if it is a daemon, then someone called it into being. There is a human intelligence behind these attacks. Or do you think a mere beast would select only the households of merchants involved in Wurtbad's river trade?'

'You learned all this just from reading my records of the investigation?' Meisser demanded, his tone incredulous.

'It helps when you do not make up your mind about something before considering every fact,' Thulmann reprimanded the older witch hunter. 'You were so fixated upon the bestial violence of these killings that you did not pause to look for any subtlety behind them. How so inept and pompous a man could ever rise to the become captain of a chapter house is proof enough to me that the Dark Gods are at work in Wurtbad.'

'Then what is our next move?' Meisser asked, his voice struggling to contain the rage that flushed his skin. 'We warn the river traders? Move them to a safer part of the city?'

Thulmann smiled indulgently and shook his head.

'We do neither,' he told Meisser. 'Ask yourself this, who profits the most by these murders, who stands to gain by the slaughter of wealthy ship owners? The answer is, of course, another river trader. We warn these people and we alert the very man who set these atrocities in motion. No, Brother Meisser, the situation calls once more for subtlety. The moon of Mannslieb will grow dark in three days. Until then, we will watch and patrol as before, this time with the aid of Markoff's people. But on the third day, every one of your men will situate himself near the home of a river trader. Because on that day, our killer will strike again.'

TWILIGHT FOUND THE city of Wurtbad gripped by fear as tired labourers and craftsmen hurried to their homes, bolting their doors and windows. There was an almost palpable aura of terror in the streets as the sun began to fade, a despair that would not abate until morning broke. Thulmann had noted the air of dread since his first night within the city walls, but this night, it seemed to him, the fear was even greater, the haste of the townsfolk as they scrambled to their homes just that little bit faster than it had been previous nights.

Torches and oil lamps blazed upon every street corner and in every window in the merchant quarter, lighting up some streets almost as intensely as the noonday sun. Armed patrols of private militia, professional mercenaries and the regular city watch marched along the deserted lanes, the tramp of their boots echoing across the cobbles.

Thulmann turned his eyes to the fading sky, watching as stars began to wink into life, the pale sliver of Morrslieb peeking above the horizon. It would be a long night, a dark night for all the precautions the merchants had taken. But perhaps it would be the last such night the people of Wurtbad would need to suffer through.

'It seems no different from yesterday,' the man standing beside
Thulmann commented. Meisser had forsaken his soft shirts and
patterned tunics for a sturdy suit of leather armour reinforced
with steel, a long-barrelled duelling pistol thrust through the
band of his belt, a heavy broadsword sheathed at his side.

Thulmann rolled his eyes at the comment. Meisser had spared
no opportunity to cast doubt and derision on his rival's every
move, but even for the arrogant, pompous windbag it had been a
stupid remark.

'We will know in the morning if tonight is the same,' Thulmann
replied. 'Until then I suggest that you keep your eyes open.'

Thulmann had positioned himself and a pair of witch hunters
from the chapter house in an alleyway near the home of a merchant named Strasser. Other men were scattered about the
district, teamed with soldiers from the Ministry of Justice and led
by the more capable of Meisser's apprentices. Thulmann had
attached Meisser to his own group, not trusting the man to keep
out of mischief were he let out of Thulmann's sight.

'What do you expect us to look for?' Meisser asked, his tone
surly and petulant.

'We will know it when we see it,' Thulmann said curtly.

One more idiotic quip and he was sorely tempted to have the
man locked in his own dungeons until morning. The thought
brought a smile to the templar's stern features. He was still considering the idea when he saw Streng round a street corner and
jog toward where Thulmann and his group were hidden. Thulmann had placed his underling in command of the men charged
with watching the house of a merchant named Bromberg. If
Streng had taken leave of his post, Thulmann knew that it could
be only to bear very important news.

The bearded warrior came to a halt at the mouth of the alley,
gripping his knees as he caught his breath. Thulmann hurried forward to learn whatever news his henchman had brought.

'We caught someone prowling around Bromberg's house,'
Streng informed his employer. 'Making devil's marks on the walls
he was.'

'It would seem that I owe you an apology,' Meisser commented,
his tone making it sound as though he had just stepped in something foul. 'Night hasn't even fallen and already our plan has
netted us a sorcerer.'

'Perhaps,' Thulmann mused, his suspicions aroused. It was far too easy, and Thulmann had learned the hard way that it was the simple things that were to be trusted the least. 'Let us go see for ourselves.' He turned, ordering Meisser's men to maintain their vigil, then told Streng to lead him to the man he had captured.

THE SCENE BEFORE the home of the merchant Bromberg was anything but the one Thulmann had expected to find. Bromberg's entire household was on the street, arguing violently with the dark-clad witch hunters Streng had left behind. Hunched upon the ground, hands tied against his back, was a miserable-looking man wearing a shabby blue robe. Resting on the ground beside him was a large satchel, it contents spilled onto the cobbles. Thulmann could see several sticks of pigment, a number of brushes and a small chapbook among the debris.

'What is going on here?' Meisser demanded, taking the initiative away from Thulmann before the other witch hunter could seize it. 'Get these people back in their home!' he ordered his men.

'They claim that this man is innocent, captain,' one of the witch hunters spoke, uncertain whether to direct his words at Meisser or Thulmann.

'We caught him making devil's marks on the walls of the house,' Streng growled at the merchant and his family. 'Probably saved all your necks!'

'Doomed us you mean!' a thick-set man Thulmann took to be Bromberg himself snarled back. 'I hired this man to protect my home with his magic!'

'Magic? What heresy is this?' demanded Meisser.

'No heresy,' protested the prisoner, struggling to rise to his feet, but at last resigning from the effort. 'I am a licensed practitioner, a student of the Colleges in Altdorf. I was hired to paint protective runes upon this man's home, to ward away the evil spirits.'

Thulmann listened only partially to the magician's story, turning over the man's effects with the toe of his boot. They seemed to bear out his story, the chapbook proving to be a volume describing certain hex signs employed by the ancient elven mages of fabled Ulthuan. Unsettling, to be sure. Unpleasant, certainly, but nothing heretical.

'You'd hire a mage to protect you from a witch?' Meisser was snarling at Bromberg. 'Why not simply set fire to your house now and be done with it! Arrest these people!'

Thulmann turned away from his examination of the conjurer's effects to countermand Meisser's excessive commands when a shot echoed into the night. Every head turned in the direction from which the sound had originated. Thulmann had given the other witch hunters strict orders to signal if they were in need of help by firing a shot into the sky.

'That came from Strasser's,' the witch hunter said, a dark foreboding clouding his thoughts. Whatever horror was stalking Wurtbad, he was certain that it had chosen now to strike. They'd allowed this foolishness with the hex-dauber to draw them away from where they were needed the most. But perhaps it would not be too late if they were to hurry.

'Come!' Thulmann shouted to Streng and the two apprentice witch hunters. 'We've no time to waste!'

'But the prisoners?' protested Meisser, still waiting for someone to carry out his order to arrest Bromberg's household.

'Leave them,' Thulmann spat. 'You've got a real monster to deal with now!'

THE FRONT DOOR of the Strasser home was open when Thulmann and his party arrived, the heavy oak portal creaking in the chill night breeze. There was no sign of the two men he had left behind, and Thulmann decided that they must have rushed into the Strasser residence when the alarm was raised. The witch hunter cast a warning look to his companions, drawing both of his pistols with a single motion. The other templars nodded their understanding, each man pulling his own weapon. Thulmann looked back towards the house, cautiously making his way to the yawning doorway.

The foyer within seemed unremarkable enough, a slender-legged table laden with a massive clay pot resting against the opposite wall. A gaudily chequered carpet clothed the bare wood floor, and it was this item that immediately caught Thulmann's attention, for it was smouldering beneath an overturned oil lamp. The witch hunter stepped over to the object, Streng and his other companions following close behind. Thulmann knelt to inspect the lamp, discovering that part of the carpet's gaudiness was due to the bright crimson that stained much of its surface.

A sound of shock and disgust brought Thulmann back to his feet. One of Meisser's apprentices was peering into the room that opened to the left of the foyer. The man now recoiled away in horror, fighting to maintain his composure.

Thulmann raced forward to see what had disturbed the witch hunter, maintaining a ready grip on his pistols.

The room inside was a parlour, judging by the numerous chairs and divans. Now it was a slaughterhouse, walls and furnishings dripping with slimy gore. Heaps of human wreckage were strewn about the chamber. Thulmann considered how apt Markoff's words had been. 'This killer does not leave bodies, he leaves meat.'

'I guess this means you were right,' Streng commented from the doorway, scratching at his beard. He looked about the room, his expression indifferent. 'I hope they don't expect us to clean...'

The remainder of Streng's irreverent remark was silenced when a scream rang out from the floor above. Thulmann raced past his henchman back into the hall. With hurried steps, he raced toward the stairway at the end of the corridor, not pausing to see if anyone followed him. As he ran, the scream sounded once more, high pitched and hideous in its conveyance of agony and horror. That a human being was dying an ugly and terrible death, the witch hunter did not doubt for a moment. He only hoped to be quick enough to catch the murderer.

Thulmann reached the wooden stairway, and stared up at the gloom that held dominance in the rooms above. A dark shape toppled out of that darkness and it was only by an effort that Thulmann managed to keep himself from putting a bullet into it. In the slight illumination offered by the stairway, Thulmann could see that it was body wearing the cloak of one of Meisser's men. He could also see the wet, ragged mess that had once been the man's chest, the ruin of a throat that had been torn out. The dying man crashed down the stairs, narrowly missing Thulmann as he jumped out of the way. The dying templar smashed against the balustrade, then rolled to the base of the stair, a scarlet pool spilling from his mangled body as he came to rest.

Thulmann spared only a moment to consider the man's ruin, then sprinted up the remainder of the stairs, taking them three at a time. The unfortunate templar could not have lasted long with such horrible wounds, which meant that his killer was still near at hand.

A sound like tearing cloth greeted the witch hunter as he
reached the upper hallway. Here, the dark was almost complete,
broken only by the fitful light trickling in through the windows.
Thulmann hesitated for a moment, trying to decide from which
direction the sound emanated. He turned toward the room on his
left, kicking the door open.

A spindly figure rose from the floor as the witch hunter entered,
a crumpled heap lying at its feet. It was little more than a shadow,
a black silhouette lit by the feeble light shining through the window, but even so, its inhuman outline chilled the witch hunter's
heart. It was much too thin for even the most emaciated beggar,
much too tall for the lankiest of men. The motions of the thing
were jerky and unnatural, like the death spasm of a slaughtered
beast. It lifted a thin arm and Thulmann could see claws gleaming in the faint light. With an awkward motion, the shadow took
a step towards him.

Thulmann fired his weapons into the ghastly apparition, the
roar of the pistols almost deafening within the confines of the
room. The flash of the muzzles revealed the shadow's leering visage, its spindly body and talons. One bullet smashed through the
thing's shoulder, another tore into its belly. The creature's thin
form jerked and twitched as it was struck, but no cry of pain
sounded from its gash-like mouth, nor did it falter in its gruesome advance. Thulmann noted with horror that the bullet which
had struck the abomination's belly had set something alight, yet
the creature paid its smouldering wound not even the slightest
notice.

More shots rang out and Thulmann became aware for the first
time that he was not alone. Meisser and the two apprentice witch
hunters discharged their weapons into the creature, causing its
skeletal form to twitch and jerk with each impact. Streng lunged
forward, slashing at the monster with his sword. There was the
sound of steel slamming into wood as the blade bit into the creature's leg. Streng freed his weapon only with effort, barely
rearming himself in time to meet the downward swipe of the creature's claw. Sparks glistened in the darkness as steel scraped
against steel and Streng was flung back by the strength of his
enemy's blow.

Then the creature paused, glaring at its attackers from the centre of the room. With a speed that Thulmann would have thought

the abomination incapable of, it turned, sprinted toward the window and leapt through it in an explosion of glass and splintered wood. The witch hunters hurried forward, expecting to find their monstrous foe sprawled in the street below. Instead, they had a fleeting glimpse of a lank-limbed figure scuttling across the rooftops, a twinkle of light flashing out from where the wound in its belly continued to smoulder. Thulmann looked back to the street where a number of Markoff's soldiers and Meisser's apprentices were charging toward the Strasser house. He called down to one of the mounted soldiers.

'You!' Thulmann shouted. 'The killer is escaping across the roofs! Follow it, but don't confront it!' The soldier looked in the direction in which the witch hunter pointed, at once sighting the glow of the creature's burning wound. The man nodded his understanding and set off at a gallop.

'By all the gods,' muttered Meisser, leaning against one of the walls to support his sagging frame. 'What was it?'

Thulmann circled the room, staring at the floor. One of the apprentices had lit a candle, shedding some light upon the carnage that had taken place here. The other apprentice removed his cloak, casting it over the sorry remains the creature had been standing over – all that remained of the other man who had been left behind to watch the house. Thulmann at once noticed the thin, clawed footprints of the creature, picked out in blood upon the floor. They were mismatched, each foot of a different size, and yet as regular in outline as the print left by a man's boot. Scattered about the floor were pieces of burnt straw. Thulmann picked one up, sniffing at its blackened end, unsurprised to detect the smell of gunpowder.

'What in the hell was it?' Meisser repeated, striving to master the hysteria that threatened to overwhelm him.

'Some abomination of the black arts,' Thulmann told him. 'A degenerate derivation of the ancient pagan practices of lost Nehekhara. But where the liche-priests employed stone and precious metal to construct their ushabti, our killer has employed much humbler materials to construct his assassin.' Thulmann looked back out the window, across the silent rooftops. 'And now the puppet is returning to its master.'

* * *

THE HORSEMAN HAD exceeded Thulmann's expectations, maintaining his pursuit of the fleeing apparition beyond the city walls until at last the flickering fire in its belly ceased to burn and he'd lost sight of it. By that time, however, there were other signs for the creature's hunters to follow. The soil outside Wurtbad was soft and rich, easily holding the track of any creature's passage across it. The witch hunters followed the strange clawed prints until at last the trail led them to an overgrown wheat field and the ramshackle hovel that crouched beyond it.

It was nothing much to look at really. Just a tiny little hovel like so many others that might be found beyond the walls of Wurtbad: four walls of timber tilted at an angle by the attentions of time and the elements. The thatch roof was old and ill-maintained, the roofing damp and rotting where it was not missing altogether. Creeper vines and sickly yellow moss clutched at the chinking between the log walls, and the awning of planks that had once shaded the front of the structure now drooped across much of the façade, one its support poles knocked down by some past storm. Indeed, despite everything, the dozen men who had furtively crept through the muddy, overgrown wheat field might have thought they had been led to the wrong place were it not for the thin plume of greasy smoke rising from a hole in the rotten roof and the flicker of light that danced behind the sagging door.

Thulmann went ahead of the rest of the hunters, creeping through the muddy overgrown field until he could study the derelict structure from the very edge of the rampant crop. Thulmann kept a ready hand on the butt of one of his pistols, the other pulling at his thin moustache, a gesture that indicated a mind deep in thought. When he had seen enough, he scrambled back to where the other witch hunters awaited his return.

'You were long enough,' observed one of the men crouching amidst the mud and rot. He was a short man with an unpleasantly cruel face, his features somehow suggesting both a pig and a cur. His hair had begun to desert him, leaving only a fringe of white. He wore a tunic of reinforced leather, stained black and studded with steel. A large duelling pistol was held in his leather-clad hands. The man's fierce eyes glared at the returned watcher, voicing the unstated challenge lurking within his words.

'Perhaps you would prefer that we simply announce ourselves,' sneered the moustached man. 'I am certain that this murderous sorcerer would welcome us with open arms. Perhaps invite us for tea before we take him away to torture and burn.' He turned from the balding man, shaking his head with disgust. 'You've made enough of a mess of things, Meisser. Just do as I tell you and we will free Wurtbad of this horror tonight.'

Meisser's hand clenched about the grip of his pistol making the leather creak. 'See here, Thulmann,' he snarled. 'I command here! Wurtbad is my posting, its protection is my duty, not yours! I'll thank you to remember that,' the piggish man added, his voice boiling with indignation. The other witch hunter rounded on the balding Meisser, a face livid with rage.

'I'll remember four households butchered in their beds while you stumbled about in back alleys arresting mid-wives and herb-sellers,' Thulmann stated, brimming with contempt, thrusting every word like a dagger into the inflated ego of the pompous Meisser. The older witch hunter retreated back several steps before Thulmann's cold fury.

'I'll report this flaunting of my authority!' Meisser warned, eyes round with shock. Suddenly his words were brought up short as the witch hunter felt the sharp prick of steel pressed against his side. He turned his head, finding himself staring into the smiling features of Thulmann's underling. Streng grinned as he pressed the dagger in his hand a little more firmly against Meisser's side.

'You'll do exactly like he tells you,' Streng hissed into Meisser's ear. The balding witch finder looked toward the other men lurking in the muddy field. They were his men, apprentice witch hunters under his command and tutelage. However, not a one of them moved. Meisser might be their commander, but they recognised a fool when they saw one, and none of them were eager to follow a fool into battle.

Meisser licked his lips nervously and nodded his head in defeat.

'Well done, Streng,' Mathias Thulmann told the knife-wielding thug. 'Now if you will kindly relieve Brother Meisser of his pistol in order that I need not worry about a bullet in the back, we'll be on about our business here.' The witch hunter looked around him, gesturing for the apprentices to draw close in order that he might disclose his plan of attack to them.

MATHIAS THULMANN CROUCHED just outside the filthy hovel, listening for any sign that the occupant of the hovel had detected the presence of his party, or the men he had deployed to surround it. He looked back at the five he had chosen to accompany him into the witch's lair.

'I remind each of you,' Thulmann whispered. 'Guard your own lives, but see that the witch is taken alive.' The witch hunter studied each man's face, making certain that his warning was understood. He met the questioning gaze of his henchman, Streng.

'You certain that this is how you want to do it?' Streng asked. 'Wouldn't it be better just to put the place to the torch and have done with it? We'll be burning the heretic eventually anyway.'

'I want to know the reason for these atrocities,' the witch hunter told him. He thought again of the four households, slaughtered down to the last child, each of them the household of one of Wurtbad's most prosperous river merchants. There was something more than simple evil and malevolence at work here. Someone was hoping to profit by these horrors. Greed was one of the simplest motives by which any crime was countenanced. But it had taken a truly sick mind to consider witchcraft as the solution to such ambitions. 'And I would hear who paid to have them done,' Thulmann added.

'Shouldn't you at least send him back to guard the perimeter?' Streng gestured with his head to indicate Meisser. The witch hunter captain of Wurtbad was now equipped with a sword, his confiscated duelling pistol tucked securely under Streng's belt.

'No, I want him with us,' Thulmann commented. 'I wouldn't want Brother Meisser to miss one moment of the excitement.' The witch hunter sighed, drawing his own sword. He pointed his sword at the hovel, and with a shout, the gathered men lunged forward, Streng at their forefront. The burly henchman sent a savage kick smashing into the ramshackle door, tearing it from its rotted leather hinges to crash upon the earthen floor of the hovel. Streng leapt into the room, Thulmann and the other witch hunters right behind him.

The interior of the hut was small, but crammed. Dried bundles of weeds and herbs drooped from the ceiling, dead and eviscerated birds hung from leather straps fastened to every roof beam. A huge pile of bones was heaped against one wall, a collection of foul-smelling jars and pots filling a crude series of shelves beside it. The head and skin of a black cow stared at the intruders with its empty eye-sockets from the hook that fastened it to the support beam that rose from the centre of the hut. Beyond, shapeless masses dangled and drooped, drifting back into the inky recesses of the chamber. A dozen noxious stinks fought to overwhelm the senses of the men, but no more charnel a reek assailed them than that which rose from the small fire-pit and the black iron cauldron that boiled above it. As the attention of the witch hunters was drawn to the only source of light in the gloomy shack, a dark shape rose from beside the cauldron, glaring at the intruders.

It was an old woman, bent backed and shabbily dressed. Straggly white hair hung about her body, drooping as far as her knees. The hag opened her gash-like mouth, letting a trickle of spittle drool from her lips.

'So, my boy was followed after all,' the witch observed, the words escaping her toothless maw in a scratchy hiss. 'But if you think you'll be stoking a fire with these old bones, you're sadly mistaken.'

'Your unholy tricks won't protect you now, old hag,' declared Thulmann, striding toward the witch, sword and pistol both pointed at her breast. 'The judgement of the god you've profaned and mocked is upon you this night!'

The old crone's smile broadened, ghastly in its malevolence.

'Think so, do you?' she cackled. 'But you've forgotten Chanta Favna's darling boy!' From the black interior of the hovel, the sound of creaking wood and groaning iron issued, followed a moment later by the tottering form of the monstrous abomination which the witch hunters had tracked to this, the lair of its creator and controller.

It was so tall that it was forced to stoop under the low ceiling of the hovel. It was rail thin, which was fitting, since just such an object had been used to form its spine. Its body was an old burlap sack stuffed with rubbish and old dried out reeds. Its arms were long sticks, hinged at the shoulder and elbow with iron fittings. Its legs were poles, wooden feet nailed at their ends. The monster's head was an old pumpkin, upon which had been carved a leering and ghastly suggestion of a face. About its neck hung a withered, dried out toad, a talisman that reeked of loathsome and unholy magic. However, it was none of these features which arrested the attention of the men who had moments before challenged the construction's mistress, rather it was the long, sharp claws of steel that tipped each of the scarecrow's slender arms, the bladed hands that still dripped with blood from those it had slaughtered already this night.

Almost before the men could fully register its appearance, the scarecrow was upon them, lashing at them with its murderous swipes of its rickety limbs. One of Meisser's apprentices fell under the monster's steel claws, wriggling on the floor as he tried to push his entrails back into the gaping hole the scarecrow had ripped from his belly. The other witch hunters warded off the butchering sweeps of the automaton's flailing arms, swords crashing against claws of steel. Thulmann fired his pistol into the ghastly pumpkin face, the shot shattering against the sorcery-strengthened shell. Streng tore Meisser's own pistol from his belt, firing at the scarecrow as its bladed hand swept toward the throat of his employer. The shot glanced off the claw, the impact redirecting the flashing talon to chew into the timber wall of the hovel.

Meisser lunged at the scarecrow as it tried to free its hand from the wall, stabbing and slashing at the unnaturally strong substance of its backbone. It seemed impossible that such a ramshackle thing could move with such deadly swiftness. Thulmann moved to aid the witch hunter captain in his efforts, but was dealt a glancing blow that knocked him to the floor. One of Meisser's remaining apprentices shouted a warning to his mentor as the scarecrow freed its trapped arm, but the older witch hunter was too slow in recognising the danger. The scarecrow's claws slashed downward, ripping open Meisser's swordarm. With a scream of anguish, Meisser fell back, his apprentices stepping forward to protect their master. The scarecrow lashed at the swords of the two men, its powerful blows forcing them to give ground before it.

'That's it!' laughed Chanta Favna. 'Kill them all! But do it slow my pet, I want to savour every scream!' The hag's hands were held before her, swaying and jerking in time to the scarecrow's movements. Dangling from those withered claws was an articulated wooden doll, a small manikin that the witch manipulated with deft motions of her scrawny fingers. The severed leg of a toad was fastened about the scarecrow's neck, another also fastened around the midsection of the tiny figure. As the doll moved, so too did her sorcerous construction. From the edges of the battle, Streng noted the old hag's manipulations.

'Mathias!' the bearded henchman called out, deflecting another slash of the scarecrow's claw with a desperate sweep of his sword.

Rising from the floor, half-dazed by the automaton's blow, the witch hunter looked over at his hireling. 'The witch's doll! She's controlling the scarecrow with it!'

Upon hearing Streng's words, the witch's ugly eyes focused upon the recovering Thulmann. She cackled and hissed slippery, inhuman syllables, forcing the witch hunter to meet her transfixing gaze. Chanta Favna placed all of her dark will and malignancy into her hypnotic spell, willing the witch hunter to remain where he was. With her hands, she manipulated the wooden doll. In time to her manipulations, the scarecrow turned away from its hard-pressed opponents, its creaking steps turning back toward Thulmann.

Mathias Thulmann could feel the dread power of the old witch surging through his body, paralysing every nerve, urging him not to rise, commanding him to remain still. He could feel himself struggling to resist her, but it was as if his body was not his own. The witch hunter was dimly aware of the creaking, tottering steps that were closing in upon him, yet such was the numbing power of the witch's magic that he was unable to muster any sense of haste to speed his struggles. Indeed, his entire being seemed to be in a stupor, a stupor not merely of body but of soul as well. Only one part of his being seemed to be clear and distinct. The witch hunter's right hand yet retained its grip upon his sword, the sword that had been given to him in the Great Temple of Sigmar in Altdorf, the sword that had been blessed by the Grand Theogonist Volkmar himself. Thulmann forced himself to focus upon the sword and his hand, and as he did so, the numbing deadness seemed to lessen. He could sense his arm now, then the feeling of warmth and control spread to his shoulder.

Chanta Favna stared in disbelief as the witch hunter began to fend off her viperous gaze. The witch's face grew dark with worry, her manipulation of the manikin a bit hastier and more desperate. She risked a glance to see how her automaton was doing, but found it beset once again by the other witch hunters, their clumsy efforts to destroy it nevertheless managing to impede its progress.

As the witch's attention wavered, Thulmann tore himself from her lingering spell. The witch hunter surged to his feet and sprang at the old woman. 'Enough of your black magic crone!' he cried out. The steel of Thulmann's sword flashed in the flickering light as it swept downward at Chanta Favna. The witch screamed in a howl of pain and despair as the blade bit through her wrists. The scraggly clawed hands of the hag dropped to the floor, the manikin still held in their disembodied clutch. As the doll struck the floor, so too did the scarecrow, tottering for one moment like a puppet struggling to stand after its strings have been severed. The bundle of sticks and straw struck the ground and broke apart, the pumpkin head rolling away from its wooden shoulders.

Mathias Thulmann loomed over Chanta Favna and watched the witch as she pressed the bleeding stumps of her wrists against her body. 'Fetch brands from the crone's fire,' the witch hunter snarled, glancing to see the surviving men from Wurtbad ministering to Meisser's hideous injury. 'See to him later!' he snapped. 'I want this hag's wounds cauterised before she bleeds out. There are questions I would ask her.' The witch stared up at Thulmann's menacing tone.

'I'll tell you nothing you filth! Swine!' The witch managed to forget her own agony to heap maledictions upon the witch hunter.

'Streng, go and fetch the men watching the perimeter,' Thulmann told his henchman, ignoring the curses bubbling from the witch's mouth. 'Tell them to ready some torches. I want this place razed when we leave it.' He turned his attention back to Chanta Favna. One of the men from Wurtbad held her fast while the other pressed a knife he had heated to a red glow against the bleeding stumps of her arms.

'I'll tell you nothing!' the witch managed to scream between painful shrieks. Thulmann considered his prisoner, his face grown cold and expressionless now that the hunt had reached its end.

'They all say that,' he stated in a voice that was not without a note of remorse and regret. 'But in the end, they all talk.' Thulmann turned away from Chanta Favna, and stalked toward the doorway of the witch's hut.

'They all talk,' the witch hunter muttered. 'Even when they have nothing left to say.'

WITCH HUNTER

PROLOGUE

DARK THUNDERHEADS ROLLED across the sky, drowning out the light cast by moon and star, their brooding grey substance taking on the hue of blood where the last feeble rays of a dying sun struck them. Beneath the clouds sprawled a landscape no less sinister and menacing, no less redolent of dark powers and the malevolence of the night. Once, the sprawl of wrack and ruin had been a city, the jewel of Ostermark, a place of such wealth and power as to rival even the great cities of Altdorf and Marienburg, eclipsing even the majesty of the mighty river which flowed beneath its gates and past its streets. But such glories were now a part of its past, destined to never return.

The vibrant cityscape had been crushed and broken, naked beams blackened by fire clawed at the dark sky like lost souls reaching up from the pits of Khaine's hells.

The once teeming streets were now deserted and desolate, choked with rubble and debris and the sorry remains of the unburied dead. Marble fountains spat foul black water into weed-choked basins, stained glass windows stared at muck-ridden lanes from the sagging plaster walls in which they had been set. Everywhere the last remnants of the city's opulence fought a losing war against the decay that crawled from the hungry earth to consume what the night of doom had left behind.

A foul, clammy mist rose from the stagnant waters of the River Stir, crawling down the streets and alleys of the destroyed city, carrying with it the promise of cough, fever and plague. Like everything else around the city, even the mighty Stir had become tainted by the evil of this blighted place, its waters so choked with rubble from collapsed buildings and piers that the flow was almost completely stopped and the once clean waters were now as foul and stagnant as a toad pond.

A bloated black rat the size of a terrier crept from a crack in the only remaining wall of what had once been a resplendent merchant's residence, now was little more than a heap of blackened wood and crumbling plaster.

The whiskers on the rat's mud-spattered face twitched for a moment as the animal tried to separate the multitude of stenches that washed over it, lashing its naked tail as it sniffed out its surrounds. A carrion stench aroused its interest and the oversized rodent scrabbled across the mound of brick and timber, beady red eyes gleaming with hungry anticipation.

Not far from the collapsed debris of the high class home, another pile of wreckage groped at the night sky with talons of masonry and wood. What these ruins had been, none could now say, but they must have belonged to some tall and vast building, as the sprawl of the rubble gave silent testimony. From the height of the mound, a man might be able to see far out across the ruins, or, if some spark of wisdom guided his sight, the broken walls that demarked the limits of what had been a city, signposts to guide the lost back to the sane world beyond the desolation.

A much closer signpost had been placed upon the highest swell of the rubble. A great iron spike, some twelve feet high, perhaps once the support for the bed of a wagon or the hull of a boat, rose from the debris, pointing upwards like an accusing finger. Upon it had been lashed an old carriage wheel, the rich colours of its paint flaking away in the ill air that filled the city.

Lashed to the wheel was a bundle of sorry and ragged remains, the faded debris of a soldier's livery clinging to his pallid bones. Who he had been or what he had done to deserve such a fate, none could say, nor even if he had been alive or dead before earning his seat high above the rubble. The skeleton had long ago been picked clean by crows and ravens, and even the last scraps of meat had been stripped away by the inch-long ants that now infested great sections of the ruins. A scrap of parchment bearing the last vestiges of a wax seal was the only sign of who the unfortunate victim might have been or what he might have done. The grimy rain had faded away whatever account of his misdeeds had once been recorded there and the wind had torn away nearly all that the rain had spared, leaving the skeleton to endure its ignominious end in anonymity.

The bloated rat leapt across the uneven rubble, hopping from one mass of stone to the next, and scrabbled up the base of the iron pole, its curled claws finding an easy purchase on the corroded metal. The rodent perched on the crude wooden sign that some passerby in a moment of morbid humour had affixed to the forgotten gibbet. In dark charcoal letters that rain and fog had yet to devour, the jokester's hand had scrawled: 'Welcome to Mordheim'.

The vermin paid no heed to the bony remains hanging above its head; that meal had been finished long ago. The rat was more interested in the new smell its keen senses had detected, the stench of rotting meat and old blood.

The rat lingered for a moment upon its perch, then leapt back to the ground, scrabbling down the heap of stones then scuttling away down one of the narrow dingy streets. There was a frantic haste to its gait, for this was Mordheim, and even rats knew better than to tempt the Dark Gods by tarrying too long in the open upon the forsaken streets.

Sounds of conflict arose from a square several score yards from where the ghastly welcome sign had been set. Once, perhaps, this had been a place where the good and great of the city might have gathered to compare fashions and gossip, to idle away the day watching ships sailing upon the river. But such frivolity had no place in Mordheim now. The square, like everything else in the city, had been consumed by decay. For every building that leaned sickly against its neighbour to lend it support, three had crumbled, as though some giant hand had pressed upon them from above and pushed them flat.

The square was some forty yards on a side, and within its entire expanse could be found not an inch that had not become tainted and ruined. The small garden that had been lovingly tended in the centre of the square was now choked with weeds, the trunk of the old oak tree that had shaded the flowerbeds warped and twisted. Malevolent faces seemed to stare from the mottled, sickly wood, and though the eager carrion crows gathered in the broken gable roofs that yet faced the square, the desiccated branches of the tree were absent of their croaking black shapes.

The paving stones were cracked and chipped, sickly yellow weeds stabbing upward from beneath them.

The rat crinkled its nose as it sniffed the crimson stain leading into the square, its slimy pink tongue licking at the salty fluid. The greedy vermin sniffed at the air once more, trying to decide if it was too early or too late to follow the trail to a meal. The sound of steel clashing upon steel told the vermin it was still too soon, and with an almost dejected manner, the creature crept back into the sanctity of the rubble-choked gutter.

With a groan, the warrior staggered back, his gloved hand clutching at the crimson seeping from his belly. The soldier looked in disgust at the thing that had dealt him his wound, the crimson gleaming from its dark, rust-pitted blade. His enemy did not seem to notice in the slightest that it had harmed its opponent. That the man yet lived seemed to be its only observation, indeed, if the two pasty orbs that stared emptily from the mouldering ruin of its face were capable of observing anything.

The undead thing took a shambling step towards the soldier, its decayed arm raising its rusted sword once more.

The warrior gritted his teeth against the pain surging from the cut this grave-cheating horror had inflicted upon him, struggling to lift his shield to intercept the zombie's attack. The weight of the shield seemed to have increased and he realised that slow as the zombie's thrust was, his own reactions were slower still. Once again, the rusty sword sank into the soldier's belly. A surge of pain flashed through the man's body like a bolt of fire.

With a savage cry, the soldier swung his hammer around, the heavy steel smashing against the zombie's withered skull.

The undead thing uttered no sound as its brittle bones were crushed and the maggot-infested mire of morbid fluid and greasy pulp that had been its brain was splashed across the grimy cobblestones. Rather, with a quiet acceptance, it crumpled to the ground, as if welcoming this second chance to quit the troublesome world of the living and return to the silent gardens of Morr.

The warrior watched his twice-slain foe crumple, then fell himself upon the debris-ridden ground.

The soldier stared up into the darkening sky, watching as the last feeble rays of the sun turned the ominous clouds as crimson as the fluid leaking from his body.

For a moment, he fancied that it was not the sun that had so transformed the black thunderheads, but the greedy storm gods, sopping up all the blood spilt this day across the foul streets of accursed Mordheim. The warrior clenched his eyes as if to make the image disappear. So close to death, grim storm gods were not the best things to dwell on.

The duel between the soldier and his undead foe over, all sounds of conflict had ended. The ambush had been swift and sudden, felling man and undead thing alike with great speed.

There had been twenty in the soldier's warband, and the pack of rotten creatures that had attacked them had numbered at least as many. Now, the warrior could hear distinctly the moans of wounded comrades and the hideous croaking of crows.

The carrion eaters had grown bold beyond measure in the wretched environs of Mordheim, and did not bother to wait for a body to become still before setting upon it with their cruel beaks and sharp claws. Nor did they retreat any great distance when their mangled meals summoned up the strength to swat at them with maimed arms and bleeding stumps, hopping away only far enough that they might savour the wretched efforts with some assurance of impunity. The birds would then return to their loathsome repast, and no cry of wrath or pain or mercy would cause them to cease their labours.

The soldier clutched at his wound again, this time not to quench the flow of blood, but to encourage it. With the horrible scavengers cawing and croaking all around him, death could not claim him too soon.

The sounds of the crows grew agitated suddenly, and into the soldier's dimming senses came the sound of boots rasping across the unclean cobblestones. The warrior tried to turn his head, to see who was walking towards him, but found the effort beyond him. It did not matter. Whether friend or foe, there was little more that could be done to the veteran swordsman now.

'So,' a cold voice spoke from somewhere near. 'This is how it ends.' The voice was hard and imperious, a slight lisp twisting every consonant into a sneer. It was a voice the soldier had heard before, a voice he knew well.

Though he could not see who was addressing him, the soldier knew who it was. Somehow, it did not surprise him. If anyone could have emerged from the horrible ambush alive and unscathed, that man would have been Witch Hunter Captain Helmuth Klausner.

The boots rasped upon the cobbles once more. Into the warrior's fading vision came a pale face with a square jaw and sunken eyes, nose and chin both cast in such a manner as to make the visage of a devil seem kindly.

Helmuth Klausner leaned down, his gloved hand touching the hole in the man's belly. The soldier grimaced in pain, amazed that such a sensation could still intrude upon the darkness obscuring his other senses. The witch hunter gazed indifferently at the bloody bile coating the fingers of his glove and wiped his hand upon the soldier's tunic.

'All these weeks, all these weeks of cat and mouse, lurking within these unhallowed ruins, and finally it comes to an end.' Helmuth's tone was almost regretful. 'All these long weeks, stalking and hunting, not knowing for certain who was hunter and who was prey. And now,' the witch hunter allowed himself a slight chuckle, 'now it comes to this.' He stared back down at the soldier, and this time even the mask of indifference had fallen away from the wrathful malevolence that blazed behind the witch hunter's eyes. 'Where is he, Otto?' Helmuth demanded, his words so short and rapid that even their normal lisp was clipped. 'You have seen him! He was here!'

Otto stared up into the gruesome countenance of Helmuth Klausner. Once, that face had cowed him, had broken his will with terror and fear. But no longer. He was beyond even the reach of Helmuth Klausner now. The one the witch hunter hunted would see to that. A slight laugh bubbled its way from the dying soldier's throat.

'Damn y-you…' Otto gasped. 'D-damn your… black soul… H-helmuth. May… may t-the Dark Gods… may they k-know you for… for one of their own!'

Helmuth Klausner glared at the dying man as he cursed the witch hunter. A cruel smile split the Templar's harsh features. Swift as a striking serpent he stabbed the soldier deep in his chest with the long silver dagger that he was carrying.

Otto gave voice to a gurgled rattle as life fled him. 'I'll not be seeing them for some time,' Klausner sneered down at the corpse. 'Not until my work is done. You might tell them that when you see them.'

The witch hunter rose from the carcass, his eyes surveying the carnage around him. The ambush had been a costly affair, but he had lost nothing that he could not replace. Swords were more plentiful than grain in the vicinity of Mordheim and hands to wield them cheaper still. His prey might have escaped him this day, but it would not elude him forever. Sooner or later, the light of Sigmar would find the creature he sought, no matter how deep and dark the burrow into which it crept.

Helmuth suddenly became aware of a perceptible chill, a fell odour upon the air. It was a stench of corruption rather than decay or death, the stink of evil, twisted and inhuman.

The crows rose from their loathsome meals, cawing in fright as they retreated into the shadowy garrets of the tumbledown guild-halls. Slowly, the witch hunter turned to face the source of the taint.

It stood within the shadows cast by that great malformed oak, a tall figure clothed in black. The vestment of the creature was ragged and frayed, the once elegant material torn and dirtied, hanging loosely about a figure grown too lean to properly fill it. Thin, pallid hands hung from the sleeves of its robe, the once elegant cuffs shorn away. A large gold ring dominated the finger of one of its hands, held against the shrivelled digit by a crude iron nail, a spike driven through both jewellery and the fingerbone beneath.

Helmuth smiled as he saw the ring, any question as to the identity of his adversary banished at last.

'You,' the shadowy apparition spoke, the sound less like speech and more like the creaking of wood under the attention of a midnight wind, 'and I. Things have ended much as they began, so many years ago.'

The figure strode forward, the pale, sunken face revealed in the fading twilight. The flesh was beginning to flake and peel, blotches of black necrotic skin marring the dead pallor. Great incisors, like the fangs of a rat, pushed apart the shadow's face, spreading apart the bloodless white lips. The only colour in the face was contained in the two fiery eyes that gleamed from the sunken pits that flanked its decaying nose. The eyes stared with a lifetime of hate and fury upon the figure of Helmuth Klausner, burning with a perfection of hatred that no human soul could ever hope to achieve without collapsing under the very strain of containing such malice.

Helmuth Klausner nodded his head slightly at the monster, drawing the sword sheathed at his side. 'Indeed, Sigmar could not allow such a thing as you to profane this world with your puerile mockery of life,' the witch hunter spoke, his tones cold with the extremes of his own fury. 'It is by his grace that I am the one appointed the task of restoring you to the grave you have denied so long.'

The monster stepped toward Helmuth, its pace so fluid that it seemed to glide across the cobbles. 'If there are any gods of justice and vengeance, then it is they who have guided *my* steps. I will have what is mine, I will have restored to me all that you have taken.' The creature's voice was terrible in its subtle violence, its undercurrents of ire and wrath.

'We have talked enough this night, blood-leech. The hour grows late and I have little time to waste trifling with a corpse.' Helmuth Klausner advanced toward the shadowy figure, his sword held before and across his body. The shadow drew its own blade, gliding forward to meet its foe. The dull, subdued tones of an incantation slithered into the quickening night. As they did so, the corpse of Otto began to twitch with an unnatural life...

THUS DID WITCH Hunter Captain Helmuth Klausner, Knight Templar of Sigmar, Protector of the Faith, drive to final and perpetual ruin the thrice-accursed vampire Sibbechai in those dark and fearsome times. Upon the streets of foul benighted Mordheim did he bring the wrath and judgment of Most Holy Sigmar down upon the foul undead abomination.

Or so say the histories written of those distant days...

CHAPTER ONE

THE SHRIEKS OF the old hag echoed within the vast courtyard outside the massive grey-stone fortress at the heart of Wurtbad long after smoke ceased to rise from the pyre. The assemblage of officials and lower nobility who had emerged from the fortress to observe the ghoulish spectacle began to file back through the gaping gateway. The massed crowd of commoners lingered on, watching with rapt attention every curl of smoke that rose from the smouldering remains. It had been they who had felt threatened by the gruesome predations of the crone's monstrosity, and it was with a mixture of relief and satisfaction that they had watched the hag burn.

Burning was an ugly, terrible death and Chanta Favna had been a long time in the dying. Mathias Thulmann had not departed with the rest of the officials, but had stood before the blackened scaffold to the last, lingering until the merest wisp of smoke was no more, his leather gauntlet resting loosely upon the hilt of his sword, his black cape snapping about him in the fiery breeze wafting from the conflagration. The witch hunter had witnessed many such scenes and always they sickened him. A more wretched and loathsome end he could not easily imagine, unless it was to wallow in the depths of villainy and perversion to which such creatures willingly committed themselves.

Yes, the end of a witch was an ugly thing, but ugliness was necessary, a vital part of the grand theatre that was at the very of such executions. There was no question of justice when it came to such things, for whatever evil witches and warlocks had perpetuated was beyond the reach of that within the world of men; there would be a higher authority who would exact retribution upon them. No, the execution of a witch had little enough of punishment to it, a measure of revenge, perhaps, for what that might achieve.

The true purpose of these gruesome displays was for the benefit of those who observed them. The execution of a witch was a cautionary tale brought to life, a terrible parable to evoke horror and repugnance, to make the mind of the commoner shudder and cringe. There were two ways to rule the hearts and minds of men. The noblest of souls could be swayed by love and devotion, but for the rest, for the vast petty masses of humanity, fear was the only thing that could cow them. And fear was a witch hunter's merchandise in trade.

Thulmann studied the crowd of city-dwellers, who were only now beginning to make their way from the courtyard. He watched them depart, fixing upon faces white with horror or glowing with satisfaction. The crowds were always the same, numbering amongst them the appalled and the self-righteous. The witch hunter grimaced as he considered the men and women, the nameless faces of the mob.

Mathias Thulmann strode away from the vast heap of ash and charred timber. The priests of Morr were waiting, spades stabbed into the ground beside them, waiting to conduct the ashes to the unhallowed spot outside the gardens of the dead reserved for sorcerers and heretics. No marker graced the grave of a witch, no mourner wept at the passing of such a creature. A miserable end to a miserable life.

The stocky figure of Streng detached itself from the wall of a cooper's shop facing the square, a partly drained flagon of ale in his grimy fingers. The bearded mercenary took another sip of his devil's brew, then smiled at his employer.

'She took a long time, eh Mathias? I wouldn't have thought the old bird had that much squawk left in her.' Streng gave vent to a short snort of brutal amusement. 'Not after I got through with her at any rate.'

Thulmann strode past his henchman. 'Your skill at wresting the truth from sealed lips is quite notable, Streng, and of great value to me. But for all of that, I find it no less distasteful.' The witch hunter continued on his way, not waiting to see if the thug would follow after him, stalking through the narrow streets of Wurtbad like some grim apparition.

'Keeps you from getting your hands dirty, doesn't it, sir,' the torturer observed, his tone indignant.

'So do the labours of a dung gatherer, yet I hold him in no great regard either.' The witch hunter paused, observing that his path had brought him to the inn where they had lodgings. He reached into the inner pocket of his scarlet tunic, removing a small pouch. Without looking back, he tossed the object to Streng. The pouch landed in the street to the sound of jangling silver. The mercenary reached into the gutter and retrieved his payment.

'Don't think your hands are any cleaner,' Streng told his employer as he counted out the coins into his hand. 'I may break them for you, but you are the one who does the catching. There is just as much blood on your hands as there is on mine.' A wicked leer spread across the ruffian's face. 'I reckon we're more alike than you'd willing to admit.'

Thulmann turned back from the doorway of the inn. 'There is a difference between what you do and what I do, Streng. I do what I do in the service of Lord Sigmar. You do what you do for coin and the base pleasures it can buy you.'

The hireling bristled under the venomous comment.

'If you'll not be needing me further, sir, I'll be retiring to pursue some of those "base pleasures", as you call them.'

'See that you are sober enough to be of some measure of use in the morning,' warned the witch hunter as his henchman retreated along the street.

Without waiting for further comment from the torturer, Mathias Thulmann stalked into the Seven Candles.

The Seven Candles was one of Wurtbad's finest inns, its cellars and pantry among the very best the city had to offer. Its rooms were spacious, its bedding clean, its serving wenches pretty and amiable. Yet despite these qualities, the common room was all but deserted, only a pair of subdued soldiers sitting at the

benches, casting sidelong glances at the sinister witch hunter.
Thulmann did not meet their furtive gaze, knowing well the mixture of guilt and fear he would find in their eyes. He had seen
such looks before. Every man, if he was honest with himself, felt
deep in his heart that he had failed his god in some way. Perhaps
he did not attend services as often as he should, perhaps he did
not pray as often as he might. Had he neglected to tithe a portion
of his silver to the temple, or maybe spoken an impious thought?
Sigmar was a loving god, but also a stern one. Would he readily
forgive such indiscretions? A witch hunter was a living, breathing
reminder that one day all failings would be judged, and perhaps
sooner rather than later.

It was that guilty unease which the witch hunter's presence
evoked that had depopulated the Seven Candles. As the portly
owner of the inn scrambled from behind his counter to fawningly
inquire as to Thulmann's needs, the witch hunter knew the question that was foremost in the innkeeper's mind, the one question
which the little man would never be able to nerve himself enough
to ask. *And when will you be leaving so that my custom will return?*

'Wine and some roast pheasant, if you please innkeeper,' Thulmann addressed the proprietor as the man nervously strode
towards him. 'I will sup in my rooms this evening.' The witch
hunter cast an imperious gaze across the all but vacant common
room. 'The atmosphere here is rather cheerless tonight.'

The innkeeper bobbed his head in acknowledgement of the
witch hunter's demands and hurriedly retreated back into the
kitchen to hasten his cook about preparing the templar's meal.
Thulmann left the man to his labours and ascended the wide
staircase that rose to the private bedrooms above.

Mathias Thulmann, as usual for him, had taken the finest room
in the Seven Candles, relocating the previous occupant to the
local magistrate's dungeon on suspicion of being a mutant. He'd
have the arrogant wine merchant released upon his departure
from Wurtbad, certain that the man would be a much better Sigmarite for his harrowing, and humbling, experience. It was part
and parcel of Thulmann's philosophy that as representatives of
Sigmar's continuing sovereignty over the lives and souls of the
people of the Empire that witch hunters were due every courtesy
and consideration. It was a reminder to every man that to be a
good Sigmarite, sacrifices needed to be made, even if only such

sacrifices as might be extracted from a money belt. Besides, it was well to illustrate to the common man that by devoting themselves completely and fully to Sigmar they would be rewarded, not simply in the next world, but in this one as well. The respect of even the most noble could be any man's if he but had the courage, determination and devotion to prevail.

The witch hunter smiled to himself as he opened the door to his room and sank into the upholstered chair that faced out upon the chamber's view of the clustered rooftops of Wurtbad. After all, one who fought daemons and all the other misshapen abominations that lurked in the black corners of the Empire deserved a few comforts. A comfortable bed, generous provisions and a decent bottle of wine were not really so much to ask of those whose souls it was his sworn duty to protect from the things that would prey upon them.

And yet, no man was infallible. Thulmann considered again the screams of the wretched Chanta Favna as the ancient hag had been greedily consumed by the flames of her pyre. He had nothing but contempt for creatures such as the old witch, they were beneath pity or regret. Exterminating such practitioners of foul and proscribed sorceries was a just and proper thing, a sacred obligation necessary to ensure the continued security of the Empire. But it was not witches and necromancers alone which Thulmann had consigned to the flames. There had been many others, those who did deserve some pity, those who were not unworthy of some measure of sympathy. The evil he fought against was like a malignant plague, striking indiscriminately. The mark of Chaos did not restrict itself to those who invited it into their souls. It could infest even the most innocent, twisting first their bodies then their minds, slowly and insidiously sapping their strength until at last it did corrupt them completely.

Suddenly the source for his ill humour and harsh words to his henchman rose to the forefront of his mind. After the execution, his gaze had lingered upon a face in the crowd that had gathered to watch the destruction of the witch. It had been the face of a woman, soft and comely, filled with fascination and revulsion as she watched the flames consume the murderous crone. But the spectator's face had been more to Mathias Thulmann than a remarkable countenance amidst the crowd, for it had recalled the face of another woman. It had been a window into the past, an unwelcome reminder of another pyre which the witch hunter had lit over a year ago.

Mathias Thulmann could remember every moment of that incident. The report of a taint in the noble house of Von Lichtberg, the swift investigation set into motion upon his arrival, the brutal attentions of Streng as he put the chief suspects to the question. The girl had been the source of that taint, her body infested with a seed of Chaos, a mutant thing that could not be born into a sane world, and a womb that could never be allowed to produce another. She had been innocent of any profane sorceries or heathen witchcraft, innocent of all those twisted deeds and malevolent desires that made it so very easy to perform his duties. No, her only fault had been to heed the advice of a crackpot physician and to love the son of a nobleman. And for that, she had been tortured and finally destroyed.

The witch hunter rose from his chair, the unpleasant memories coming more rapidly now. He'd shown leniency toward the poor girl's lover, the young Baronet Reinhardt von Lichtberg. Knowing him to be free of any taint, he'd ordered the boy to be released. It was a decision that continued to haunt him. He should have had the boy destroyed as well, for he had seen the rage and bloodlust in those young eyes. Indeed, Reinhardt von Lichtberg had pursued the witch hunter across half the province of Stirland, catching up with him in the small village of Kleinsdorf. Their meeting had been a violent one, but again the witch hunter had been lenient, leaving the vengeful youth wounded, but alive, following their encounter. It was a foolish thing to have done. He should have had the boy destroyed for seeking to harm an officer of the Temple. But somehow Thulmann could not bring himself to regret his unwise mercy. Somehow, the knowledge that Reinhardt von Lichtberg was out there somewhere, alive, even if thirsting for the witch hunter's blood, lessened to some degree the lingering sense of guilt Thulmann felt for the regrettable execution of the girl.

There was only one thing that would fully assuage that guilt. For long months now Thulmann had been on the trail of the man responsible for the girl's corruption, the old family physician of the von Lichtbergs, a villain named Freiherr Weichs. Herr Doktor Freiherr Weichs had talked the poor girl into taking a vile concoction of his own devising that he swore to her would dissipate the unborn and unwanted life growing within her belly. But that elixir had been poison, containing the foul substance known as warpstone. Far from destroying the unborn life, it had changed it, and with it the woman herself, polluting her blood with the black filth of mutation and Chaos. Thulmann had sworn an oath to hunt down the physician as he watched the flames devour the girl, and had spent the better part of a year doing just that. Even as Reinhardt von Lichtberg stalked him, so did he stalk the true source of the boy's misery. That trail had led him across three provinces, but at last the witch hunter felt he was drawing near to his quarry.

Mathias Thulmann stared out the window, gazing once more across the rooftops of Wurtbad. Somewhere amidst the bustle and confusion of the city, he would find Doktor Freiherr Weichs. And when he did, he would pile the Doktor's pyre so high they would see the fire even in Altdorf. The incident with Chanta Favna had been a necessary delay in his hunt, but now there would be no further distractions. The man who had hired the witch was in custody and would join her as soon as Meisser finished going through the motions of a trail. The man had thought to control the river trade in Wurtbad through his scheme, now he was going to discover that he'd lost not simply his wealth and position, but his life and very soul by contemplating it.

It did not matter to Thulmann, in the end, that Meisser would take most of the credit for putting an end to the witch and her murderous creation, for unmasking the villain who had made her witchcraft a part of his plotting. That the horror had been brought to an end, that the guilty would meet justice was all that mattered to him. After all, that was all that would matter to Most Holy Sigmar.

Mathias Thulmann looked up from his meal as he heard the soft, subdued sound of knocking at his door. The interruption put the templar in an even blacker mood and it was with an imperious tone that he commanded the supplicant to enter and state his business. The door swung inward and the portly innkeeper darted his head into the room.

'Forgive me, sir, but there is a man here to see you.'

'He can wait until I have finished this mediocre dinner you have seen fit to try and poison me with,' Thulmann snapped back. The innkeeper grew slightly more pale as Thulmann made his displeasure known, horrified that the meal had not been to the witch hunter's liking. Thulmann was certain that their conversation had ended and returned to attacking his plate. When he looked up again, he was surprised to see the man still standing at the door.

'Begging your pardon, sir, but I don't think your visitor is the kind to be kept waiting.' The innkeeper cringed as he saw Thulmann raise a questioning eyebrow.

'You've intrigued me,' the witch hunter stated matter-of-factly. He lifted a napkin to his face and wiped away the residue from his unfinished meal. 'I wonder what sort of man you seem to think is so important that he should take a templar knight of Sigmar away from his humble victuals.'

'He's downstairs,' the heavy-set man stammered. 'Says his name is Lord Sforza Zerndorff.' The innkeeper made the sign of the hammer as he spoke the name. 'Says he's from Altdorf. Says he's a witch hunter like yourself.'

SFORZA ZERNDORFF WAS seated upon one of the benches that rested against either side of the common room's three massive tables. Except for him, there were only two others in the room. But these were no simple off duty watchmen. These were soldiers of a different cast, their liveries black as pitch, massive swords sheathed at their sides, huge pectorals depicting the twin-tailed comet of Sigmar hanging from huge silver chains upon their breasts.

Zerndorff himself was much smaller than his bodyguards, stocky and full in his figure where the two guards were lean and powerful. However, there was no mistaking the strength and authority of the smaller man, his piercing blue eyes considering his surroundings with a haughty air of disdain. Zerndorff idly tapped the polished top of the table with the tip of a small black-hilted dagger as Thulmann strode into the hall.

'Ah, Thulmann,' the dignitary said, his voice conveying irritation. 'I was beginning to think you'd perhaps gone to Altdorf to look for me. Or perhaps my messenger did not deliver my summons promptly?' Zerndorff sent a look of displeasure at the innkeeper who swiftly scuttled away into the kitchens.

'Forgive my delay, Lord Zerndorff,' Thulmann said to the seated dignitary. Zerndorff motioned for the other witch hunter to join him, deciding to ignore the lack of contrition in the manner with which Thulmann voiced his apology.

'I have little time to waste Thulmann,' Zerndorff said, 'so I will cut to the chase. I have need of someone I can trust. As you know, with the rather ugly business that has come forward in the aftermath of Lord Thaddeus Gamow's death, the entire hierarchy of our order has been restructured. There is no longer a position of Lord Protector of the Faith, instead the Grand Theogonist has appointed three Witch Hunter Generals to share authority over the order.' Zerndorff paused, favouring Thulmann with a sly smile of superiority. 'It may be of some small interest to you to know that I have been appointed Witch Hunter General South.'

'Congratulations,' Thulmann told Zerndorff, the hostile emotion boiling within him held in check only by a supreme effort of will.

'Thank you,' Zerndorff replied, nodding. His smile faded away and his expression grew grave. 'I know that we have had our troubles in the past and there is no love lost between us. But I also appreciate that you are a man of conviction, that your faith in Lord Sigmar is absolute and total. This accounts for much these days, much more than any personal animosity that lies between us.'

'I understood that there was something you wished of me,' Thulmann interjected.

'Just so,' Zerndorff answered. 'As you can imagine, the restructuring of the order has not been accomplished without a great deal of bad feeling on the part of those whose power, or ambitions for power, has been compromised as a result of the abolishment of the post of Lord Protector. The Great Temple in Altdorf is a nest of plotters and schemers these days, accusation and rumour as plentiful as sand in the desert of Araby. Everyone seeks to discredit everyone else and even the Grand Theogonist is not without his detractors. Indeed, there are some who try to connect Volkmar with Gamow's heresy, try to say that his restructuring of the order is a heretical plot to weaken the temple and reduce the efficiency of the witch hunters rather than a measure to protect against the possibility of another Gamow.

'You are an honest and loyal man, Mathias, and I trust in your devotion to the temple, even if I question your methods. There is a matter in which I need someone of such conviction, someone I know to be above the petty schemes and plots running rife in Altdorf. Rumours have reached my office, disturbing rumours that give me cause for concern.' The Witch Hunter General's demeanour became somewhat furtive and it was with a slightly lowered voice that he continued.

'You have heard no doubt of the Klausner family?' Zerndorff asked.

'The name is familiar, though I cannot say that the particulars stand out in my mind,' Thulmann replied somewhat warily.

Zerndorff leaned forward, his fingers steepled on top of the table.

'The Klausners are an old and highly respected family,' Zerndorff told him. 'Very devout Sigmarites, and very zealous in their faith. Many of them have been priests and templars over the years, and not a few of them have achieved rather respectable distinction. The family can trace its roots back five hundred years. They were awarded a small holding south of here in 2013, and have lorded over it ever since, their district notable for its very generous tithes of money and crops to the temple. Klausberg, they named it, farm and pasture country, somewhat renowned for the quality of their cattle. The present patriarch of the family and lord of Klausberg, Wilhelm Klausner, is a personal friend of the Grand Theogonist himself.

'You will understand then, why when rumours that something strange and terrible has made its presence known in Klausberg that I was immediately interested.' Zerndorff's voice dripped into an almost conspiratorial whisper. 'Something is killing the people of Klausberg. Something unnatural and unholy, if the tales coming out of there are to be believed.'

'What sort of tales?' Thulmann asked, feeling himself drawn into Zerndorff's theatrics despite his determination not to suffer the man's manipulative tricks.

'Tales of men stolen from their beds in the dead of night,' Zerndorff said, 'only to be found in some field or hollow in the morning, face ripped away, innards spilled about the ground. Tales of young maidens walking home from tending their flocks never to be seen alive again, taken by the daemon beast that stalks unhindered about the land. If we were to trust the frightened gossip that has trickled into the ears of my informants, then this daemon creature has already claimed a hundred lives, adding another corpse to its tally almost every night.'

'Surely an exaggeration,' observed Thulmann.

'Oh, doubtless the stories have grown in the telling,' Zerndorff admitted, a smug smile on his face. 'But even such tales have some truth at their root. Something is going on in Klausberg, something is killing people there. And whatever it is doesn't behave like an animal or an orc or a beastman or any of the other murderous things the people of our troubled land are used to coping with. There is something very unusual about the murders in Klausberg. Given the history of the ruling family, it is not impossible that some sinister enemy of the temple has chosen to wreck havoc upon their lands.'

'I have my own investigations to conduct here in Wurtbad,' Thulmann informed his superior.

Zerndorff shook his head.

'You will have to set all other matters aside,' he told Thulmann. 'Instruct Meisser in what needs to be done. I want you to look into what is going on in Klausberg. I need to know what is happening, the nature of the fiend that is preying upon the lands of the Grand Theogonist's friend. I need to know if this is the opening stroke in some larger plot to discredit or destroy the Grand Theogonist's chief supporters. I have grave concerns that those behind such a plot might be secret disciples of Gamow who may yet operate within the temple. I want you to go there and learn if my fears are well founded.' Zerndorff rose to his feet, retrieving his soft, almost shapeless silk hat from its place on the table.

'I know that I can trust you to not fail the temple in this matter, and to be discreet about whom you inform of your findings,' he said. Zerndorff lingered for a moment as his bodyguard opened the inn door. When one of the soldiers signalled that all was in order, Sforza Zerndorff strode out to the carriage awaiting him outside, without a backward glance.

Mathias Thulmann watched the retreating Witch Hunter General's back, his sullen gaze watching the short man's every step, his manner the same as that of a herd dog keeping a close eye on a prowling wolf. Even after Zerndorff was gone, Thulmann kept an easy hand on the hilt of his sword.

Witch Hunter General South. It was sometimes difficult to maintain faith in justice when it seemed that villainy was rewarded at every turn. Thulmann had worked with Zerndorff long ago, an association which he held no pride in. Zerndorff was a ruthless man, a callous man and above all an ambitious man.

His methods were centred more upon speed and efficiency than they were upon protecting the innocent and punishing the guilty. Zerndorff practised his trade with the same wanton brutality which had characterised the templar knights during the dark days of the Three Emperors. He gave no thought to proving guilt, even less thought to the possibility of executing an innocent man or woman.

For Zerndorff, it was the number and frequency of executions that mattered. Those suspected of some heresy were tried and convicted as soon as their name was made known to him, all else was simply tradition; breaking the suspect on the rack, wringing a confession from their bloody lips, these were nothing more than theatre, placating a secular system of law which Zerndorff felt did not apply to him. He was the sort of man who would cure a crop of weevils by putting it to the torch. Yet this was just the sort of man who had earned the attention of Altdorf, the sort of man who had been promoted to a position that gave him power over a third of the Empire. Thulmann struck his fist into the palm of his hand, cursing the inequity of Zerndorff's good fortune.

That Zerndorff had chosen Thulmann to look into the incidents in Klausberg was, the witch hunter was certain, simply Zerndorff's way of exerting his newly granted authority over his one time associate, of reminding Thulmann of how greatly their positions had changed. That it interfered with Thulmann's own affairs made the matter all the more pleasing to Zerndorff, Thulmann was certain. That the man he hunted might escape once again while Thulmann was on his fool's errand would not have concerned Zerndorff in the slightest. They could always find another witch to burn. Most likely, when he arrived in Klausberg, Thulmann would learn that the incident was nothing more than the work of a pack of wolves or a band of goblins, despite Zerndorff's insistence that it was something more.

The witch hunter paused as he began to consider this light dismissal of Zerndorff's assignment. True, his old rival was a petty and malicious man, but he was also a man who was obsessed with efficiency. If he had made the trip down from Altdorf, there had been more to his journey than trying to put Thulmann in his place. Zerndorff could have simply sent a messenger for something so inconsequential. No, there must be something behind the Witch Hunter General's suspicions, something that Zerndorff expected to profit from by investigating. But what? The Klausners were old friends of the Grand Theogonist. Zerndorff's own familiarity with Volkmar could hardly be considered so amicable. Why then was Zerndorff so interested in the safety of a house that was so supportive of the Grand Theogonist? Did he really think to expose some conspiracy against Volkmar, or did he perhaps hope to gain control of it?

Mathias Thulmann stared once again at the door through which Sforza Zerndorff had departed. What would he find in Klausberg?

THE TINY ROOM was barely five paces wide and only a little greater in depth, its walls of bare black stone illuminated only by the flickering fingers of flame rising from the double-headed candlestick that rested below a small altar. Two doors were set against the walls to left and right of the altar, doors that connected to rooms where warmth and comfort were not considered impious and improper. The air within the cell-like chamber was chill and carried with it the dampness of the outer walls of the old keep.

The small room's sole occupant shuddered in the cold draft, drawing the heavy wool cloak a bit tighter about his scrawny frame. He was far from young and noted the creeping chill far more than any other in his household. Yet he had attended his midnight devotions here, in this small chapel set between the master bedchamber and the one set aside for the lady of the keep, for more than a quarter of a century, and he would never forsake his pious ablutions. Indeed, there were few things that could quiet old Wilhelm Klausner's troubled mind in the long watches of the night sufficiently to allow him to sleep. The calming peace of casting his respectful gaze upon the heavy steel hammer resting upon the altar was one of them. A devout Sigmarite all his life, it did Wilhelm's soul good to think that the patron god of the Empire was looking down upon him.

Wilhelm's hands were thin and pale, blotched and devoid of both strength and substance. The massive gold ring, with its rampant griffon crushing a ravening wolf under its clawed foot, hung loose about the old man's finger, as though the slightest motion might set it sliding from its perch to roll across the bare stone floor. Wilhelm himself was an embodiment of age and infirmity, shoulders stooped beneath the weight of years, face gaunt and lean, eyes withdrawn into their pits, dull and bleary with cataracts. His hair was silver-grey, hanging down about his shoulders in an unkempt nest. It was not time alone that had placed its stamp upon Wilhelm Klausner, but the ultimate effects of a hard life filled with trouble and discord.

The old man lifted his head, his dull eyes considering the altar and its icon. Prayers slipped from Wilhelm's mouth as he repeated over and again a simple catechism he had learned long ago, a plea for protection from the denizens of the Old Night.

Wilhelm's head snapped around from his devotions as he heard the heavy oak door connecting the chapel to his own chambers slowly open.

A man passed through the portal. He was broad of shoulder with a face that was full and plump. His rounded head was all but devoid of hair, only a light fuzz clinging to the back and edges of his skull. His face was sharp despite its fullness, the nose stabbing downward like a dagger. There was a gleam to his soft brown eyes that somehow added to the overall air of cunning that seemed to cling about him like a mantle. He strode forward, his staff clacking against the door as he stepped past it, the large brass buckles upon his boots gleaming as they reflected the feeble light of the candles.

'Forgive the intrusion, my lord,' the steward addressed Wilhelm as the patriarch began to rise. 'I wanted to inform you that I have received word from the village.' The steward paused for a moment, setting the end of his staff against the floor and resting his weight against it. 'It would seem the "the beast" has struck again. Young Bruno Fleischer, body mangled almost beyond identity.' The steward paused again, favouring his master with a look of sympathy. 'I believe that you knew him.'

Wilhelm Klausner gained his feet with a sigh. 'Yes,' he said, the characteristic lisp extending the word. 'I knew him and his father. Very old friends of the family.' The old man cast his gaze to the floor, wringing his hands in despair. 'What have I done that I should invite such horror upon my people?' He looked once more at his steward, his eyes filled with pleading. 'Tell me, Ivar, am I so steeped in wickedness that Sigmar should forsake me? And if I am, why then punish my people and not myself, if the guilt for these things be mine?'

'You have broken with tradition, perhaps that is why this terror stalks the district,' the servant informed his master. 'You should have allowed your sons–'

'No!' the old patriarch snapped, strength suddenly infusing his voice. 'I'll not let my sons walk the same path as me. I love them too well to wish such a curse upon them!'

'A strange way to speak of serving the order of Sigmar's Knights of the Temple,' Ivar commented in a quiet tone. 'One might almost describe it as heretical,' he warned.

'For ten years I played the role demanded of me by tradition. For ten years I travelled this great Empire, searching out the blackest of horrors, things which haunt my mind even now.' Wilhelm Klausner turned to face the altar again. 'I did that out of love for Lord Sigmar. He knows the measure of my devotion. But I'll not condemn my sons to ruin themselves as I have been ruined!'

'To fend off the darkness, there is always a price which must be paid,' cautioned Ivar. 'No good has ever been achieved without the sacrifices of good men.'

'Then let some other suffer that sacrifice!' Wilhelm declared, rounding on his servant once more. 'The Klausners have paid more than their share. I have already lost so much, I'll not lose my sons as well.' The patriarch held his hand before his face, turning the wrinkled, withered thing before his eyes. 'Look at me, Ivar. Anyone would think me your senior. None would believe that you served my father before me. See how the horror I have witnessed has changed me, robbed me of my youth. Well, that is a sacrifice that I have made, and Sigmar is welcome to it. But I'll not send my sons to do the same!'

'That is the tradition of the Klausners,' Ivar reminded his master. 'Back to the time of Helmuth, your family has ever sent its sons to serve among Sigmar's witch finders. It is a long and noble legacy.'

Wilhelm Klausner strode toward the altar, lifting up the candlestick. 'I am not concerned with the nobility of this house, or its legacy,' he told his servant. 'My only concern is for the safety of this family.'

The old man strode past Ivar, through the open doorway that connected the tiny chapel to his own bedchamber.

The steward dutifully followed after his master.

'That also is my concern,' observed Ivar. His master's chamber was opulently furnished, dominated by a gargantuan four-posted bed, its surface piled with pillows and heavy blankets of wool and ermine. A glass-faced curio cabinet loomed against one wall, nestled between a massive wardrobe of stained oak and the yawning face of a hearth. In the far corner, a writing table was set, beside it stood a large bookcase, its overburdened shelves sagging under the weight of dozens of leather-bound tomes. Ivar watched with a slight air of superiority as Wilhelm Klausner let his heavy cloak slip to the floor, the scrawny frame of the old man crawled into his waiting bed. When Wilhelm was fully situated, his servant stepped forward to remove the garment from the floor, draping it loosely over his arm.

'You have served my family well,' the withered man told Ivar. 'And I have always valued your council.'

'Then listen to my words again, my lord,' Ivar said, punctuating them with a stab of his gloved finger. 'There are some who will take your decision in this matter none too lightly. They will see this breaking with tradition as an ill omen, a sign that perhaps those black horrors you speak of may have warped your mind, caused a rot within your soul. Are you so certain that you are so free of enemies that you can allow such thoughts to linger within the temple district in Altdorf?'

'Let my enemies do their worst,' sneered the old man, puffing himself upright amidst his bedding. 'Their yapping will avail them nothing! I still have some influence in Altdorf. My name is not unknown to old Volkmar, or my reputation.'

'I think that is a dangerous assumption to make.' Ivar's voice drifted back into its cautious tone. 'I served your father long before he returned to these lands, and I know how suspicious witch hunters are, seeing a heretic behind every door and an abomination of Chaos in every shadow. Trust not in the ties of old friendships and loyalties when such spectres are invoked.'

'And you would have me destroy my sons to allay the doubts of such verminous fear-mongers?' Wilhelm spat. He shook his head, his face twisted into a distasteful scowl.

'If these murders continue, you will have to do something,' confessed the steward. 'Things cannot go on like this. When it was six or even seven, perhaps we might have been able to handle the matter more quietly. But now...' Ivar shook his head. 'No, such a thing will have been noticed. And the eyes that are drawn to the district of Klausberg will not be those of your friends, my lord. Your enemies will seize upon these occurrences like starving wolves falling upon a scrap of mutton.'

Wilhelm Klausner looked away from his steward, gazing instead out of the window. He considered the cold darkness that clutched and pawed at the glass, the sombre testament of night's black dominion across his lands. What things might even now be crawling under that shroud? What atrocities might they even now be plotting to inflict upon his domain?

'Ivar,' the patriarch's voice sank to a lower, tremulous tone. 'You must not let it come to that. All that I have done has been to draw my enemies away from his place, to protect my family and my people from the unholy things that would do them harm. We cannot fail in this or all has been for nothing!'

The steward strode towards the heavy outer door of the patriarch's chamber. 'Your enemies are already come to Klausberg,' Ivar told his master.

CHAPTER TWO

THE DAY WAS nearly spent when the witch hunter and his henchman reached the village of Klausberg. It was a small settlement,
located almost in the very centre of the rich farmlands that composed the district whose name the village bore and as such it held
a greater importance than its small size would seem to indicate.

The village served as a staging area for the food caravans that
transported the harvests of the district northward to the ever
hungry inhabitants of Wurtbad. At harvest time, the sleepy village
would become a hub of activity, filled to bursting point with merchants and farmers, huntsmen and farriers, each man trying to
outwit the other as they sought to haggle their wares or secure
goods that could be transported the long distance to Wurtbad and
still earn a profit. The sounds of drinking and carousing would
rise from the village's single tavern long into the night as all the
peasant farmers and hunters tried their best to spend the money
they had spent a year earning upon long-denied revelry.

No such sounds emanated from the tavern this day, as the lowering sun cast a burnt orange glow upon the plaster and timber
walls that lined the village's narrow streets. Indeed, save for the
grunting of pigs and the cackle of chickens, the lanes were utterly

silent, the furtive and hastily withdrawn faces that occasionally appeared at the windows of some of the homes serving as the only sign of the villagers themselves.

The two horsemen who navigated the dirty lane that wound its way through the small huddle of buildings proceeded at a wary canter, hands resting against the grip of sword or pistol. If trouble was to manifest itself upon these deserted streets, it would not find these men unprepared.

'As barren as the Count of Stirland's barracks when the gold ran out,' observed the rearmost of the two riders. Streng cast a look over his shoulder, grimacing as he saw another face slip back behind a pair of shutters.

'It would appear that Brother Zerndorff's concerns are justified,' commented his companion. Mathias Thulmann did not look over at his henchman as he spoke, but kept his eyes focused upon the road ahead. He was less unnerved than his mercenary companion by the air of hostility and fear which surrounded them as they passed each dwelling, but he had learned over the course of his career never to completely ignore attitudes of ill will. 'There is most certainly an aura of fear hanging about this place, more than might be occasioned by a pack of wolves or a band of goblins.'

'Yes,' snorted Streng, spitting a glob of phlegm into the dust. 'You'd find a more cheerful welcome in the Chaos Wastes.' The mercenary looked over as another set of shutters slammed shut behind them. 'This lot are jumping at their own shadows.' Streng paused, his leer spreading, a glint appearing in his eyes. 'There is a fair bit of money to be made here, Mathias.'

The witch hunter favoured his underling with a look of contempt. 'We're here to help these people, liberate them from whatever unholy power is at work here, not to fleece them like a couple of Marienburg peddlers!' he snapped, voice laden with disgust.

'All I'm saying is that we might help allay their fears by finding a few witches straight away. A bit of burning would do this town some good,' the henchman persisted.

'Keep that larcenous tongue quiet, Streng,' Thulmann warned. 'Or you might discover that your services are not irreplaceable.'

The bearded mercenary sucked at his teeth as he digested Thulmann's reprimand.

Klausberg's inn loomed ahead at the end of the road upon which they now travelled. The building was surrounded by a low wall of stone, and the courtyard beyond was paved, a small fountain bubbling at its centre.

Thulmann considered the mouldy stone cherub rising above the pool, spitting an endless stream of water from its bulging cheeks. The witch hunter was not unfamiliar with the quality of worldly things and as his practiced eye considered the sculpture, he found himself impressed by the level of skill and artistry that had gone into it. He turned the same appraising gaze upon the façade of the inn itself, noting the quality of its construction.

Clearly Klausberg had been quite prosperous in better times. However, a chill crept down Thulmann's spine as he took note of the sign swaying from the post above the door of the establishment. In worn, faded characters it bore the name 'The Grey Crone' and beneath the crude Reikspiel letters was the image of an old woman, her body bent and twisted by the years.

The witch hunter's thoughts drifted back to Wurtbad and the destruction of the hag Chanta Favna. He made the sign of the hammer, knocking his palm against his saddle to ward away any ill omen.

After waiting for a moment for any sign that a stable boy might scurry out from the large stables attached to one side of the inn, the witch hunter dismounted. Streng followed his master's lead, dropping from his own horse with a grunt. Thulmann handed his underling the reins of his steed.

'The service appears a bit lacking,' he observed. 'Take the horses into the stables. I'll be informing the landlord of that sorry fact.'

The witch hunter strode across the courtyard, his steely stare watching the windows of the inn for any sign of the furtive movement that had shadowed their progress through the village. He paused upon reaching the heavy oak door, banging his gloved hand against the portal. Not waiting for any response, Thulmann proceeded into The Grey Crone.

THE COMMON ROOM that dominated the first floor of the inn was spacious, a cluster of tables strewn about its vastness, a long oak-topped bar running along one wall. Several small groups of peasant farmers were scattered about the tables, nursing steins of beer and jacks of ale.

The men looked up from their hushed, subdued conversations to regard the newcomer, their eyes at once narrowing with suspicion as they failed to recognise Thulmann for one of their own. The witch hunter returned their stares with an expressionless mask, making his way toward the bar. He took especial note of the bunches of garlic and daemonroot that had been nailed to the walls and above the doors and windows, their pungent reek overcoming even the smell of alcohol within the hall.

Thulmann gripped the counter, noting for a moment the age of the wood beneath his fingers, then glanced back at the gawking inhabitants of the inn. Their hushed conversations had died away entirely now, all eyes locked on the scarlet and black-clad stranger.

Presently, the landlord emerged from a little door set behind the bar. He was a short man, hair turning to grey, with large expressive eyes and a cheerful demeanour despite the gloom tugging at his features. As he saw the stranger waiting at his counter, however, a bit of the cheer drained out of him, replaced with an air of severity. He ceased wiping out the metal stein he was holding, setting both vessel and rag upon the bar.

'I suppose you'll be wanting a drink?' the innkeeper asked, his words clipped and his tone surly.

The witch hunter favoured the little man with his most venomous smile, pleased to see some of the anger give way to fear as the innkeeper withered before his gaze. 'If you cannot show your betters deference, I suggest you at least remember to show them respect.'

He turned his stern gaze to encompass the rest of the hall. 'I am Mathias Thulmann, Knight Templar of Most Holy Sigmar, duly ordained witch finder and protector of the faith.' The hostile, sullen faces of the inhabitants of the inn remained the same.

'Aye, we know what you are,' confided the innkeeper. 'But don't expect a witch hunter to find any store of love here.' The innkeeper filled a stein, setting the beer before Thulmann. 'I'll serve you, as that is my duty, but don't expect anything more. Not here. Not in Klausberg.'

Thulmann regarded the pop-eyed man, studying the mixture of fear and hostility he found in those eyes. The innkeeper looked away, rubbing at some invisible stain.

'And why should a witch hunter find cold welcome in Klaus-berg?' Thulmann voiced his demand in a loud, cold voice, causing many of the gawkers to suddenly remember their own drinks. 'Is this some nest of heathens and heretics that the servants of Sig-mar are treated so?'

'No,' the innkeeper replied, shaking his head, a touch of shame in his words as Thulmann cast suspicion on the man's loyalty to his god. 'But there is something, some terrible thing that is killing folks here. And them Klausners,' the man paused, looking in the direction in which the Klausner Keep would lie, 'they do nothing to protect us.'

'Wolf hunts is what they give us,' scoffed one of the farmers. 'Beating forest and field to drive out whatever starveling mongrels hiding there. As if any wolf were the cause of our troubles.'

'What makes you so certain that it isn't a wolf?' Thulmann asked.

'Ever hear tell of any natural wolf sneaking into a man's home, snatching him from his bed and all the while, there beside him his wife lies sleeping?' countered Reikhertz. 'If it's a wolf, then it's no such wolf as should be natural, but some filthy thing of the Powers!' The man rapped his knuckles on the countertop as he made mention of the Dark Gods, hoping to ward away any ill luck that might draw their attention.

'Them Klausners know it too,' commented a straw-haired farmer, his face a mask of dirt. 'They know it and they're afraid, cringing behind their stone walls when night falls, leaving the rest of us to fend for ourselves!'

'Fine lot of witch hunters they be,' sneered another of the farm-ers, spitting at the floor. His bravado died however as Thulmann looked in his direction, and the man wilted back into his seat.

Thulmann turned his attention back to the innkeeper, intending to question him further as to why the villagers felt their lord was doing nothing to end their ordeal, but was interrupted by the open-ing of the inn's door. He watched as three men entered the beer hall.

It was obvious at once that they were distinctly apart from the modest, even shabbily, dressed villagers. Each man sported a leather tunic, breeches and high leather boots that reached to their knees. Each of the men also wore a sword sheathed at his side. The foremost of the men swaggered into the inn, the others following after his lead.

The leader of these newcomers was young, his hair flowing about his head in a primped and pampered mane of pale blond. His features were harsh, his squared jaw set in a look of arrogance and disdain. As he strode into the inn, his head brushed against one of the dangling clusters of garlic cloves. The man spun about angrily, his gloved hand clutching at the bundle of herbs as if it was the throat of an enemy.

'Fools! Idiots!' the man snarled, his words stretched by a slight lisp. The farmers cringed back in their chairs as the man glared at them. 'Heathen nonsense! Yet you cling to such stupidity like frightened children! As if a bunch of foul-smelling weeds had any power against Old Night!'

He hurled the garlic across the room with a grunt of disgust, then looked away from the cowed denizens of the tavern, casting a curious glance over Thulmann as the witch hunter leaned against the counter. He did not voice his curiosity, however, but looked past the witch hunter, favouring the innkeeper with an unpleasant smile.

'And how is Miranda this day, Reikhertz?' the man asked. He glanced about the room. 'I can't see her about. I do trust that she has not taken ill?' The mocking smile twisted a bit more.

'Not at all, m'lord,' stammered Reikhertz.

'Then go and fetch her,' the young man said, his words both a warning and a command. 'The sight of her pretty face… will make that pig's water you peddle a bit more pleasing to me.'

'Your brother won't favour you causing any mischief, Anton,' protested the innkeeper.

'Ah, yes, my brother Gregor,' although his tone did not change, a subtle suggestion of menace exuded from the young man at the mention of his brother. 'Did he perhaps offer you some special service? Perhaps he offered to protect your charming daughter?' Reikhertz licked his lips nervously as Anton spoke his words. 'As if it was me you need protecting from! You should thank all the gods that a Klausner should so much as look at that little cur you sired!'

'But your brother…' persisted the innkeeper, his voice pleading. Anton Klausner slammed his fist against the counter.

'My brother is not here!' he hissed. 'Now fetch that bitch or I'll do it myself!'

'Perhaps the young woman does not favour your company,' a silky voice intruded. Anton Klausner spun around, hand clenched into a fist, glaring at the speaker. Thulmann faced the belligerent youth with a condescending smile. 'If you would learn some manners, you might find the young lady a bit more agreeable.'

'Perhaps I'll teach you a few,' Anton's voice dripped with hostility. He looked over at his two companions, watching as each of the men began to move to place themselves at the witch hunter's back, then favoured Thulmann with his snide grin. 'But first I think I'll teach you to mind your own business.'

Anton aimed a kick at the witch hunter's groin, surprised when the older man anticipated the low blow, stooping and catching his foot in his hands. Thulmann straightened up, tipping Anton Klausner to the floor as he did so. The bully's two companions had been taken by surprise as well and moved to attack the witch hunter from behind when the solid wooden seat of a stool crashed into the face of one of them. The man dropped to the floor, a senseless bleeding heap. Streng swung the battered remains of the stool at the other ruffian, causing the man to retreat back toward the wall.

'Seems to me like this is more my idea of entertainment than yours, Mathias,' laughed Streng. The witch hunter glanced over at his henchman.

'I think I was rather generous, leaving two of them for you,' the witch hunter looked down at Anton Klausner as the young man began to rise, one hand closed about the hilt of his sword. The weapon froze after it had been drawn only a few inches, its owner staring into the cavernous barrel of one of Thulmann's pistols.

'I am Mathias Thulmann, witch finder,' he informed the subdued rouge. 'I have been sent here by Altdorf to investigate the sinister affliction that has been plaguing this district.' Thulmann's silky voice dropped into a threatening tone. 'So you see, this district and what happens here are very much my business.' He motioned for Anton Klausner to stand. The subdued noble glared sullenly at the witch hunter.

'Collect your friend and get out,' Thulmann told him, gesturing with his pistol to the insensible heap lying on the floor. 'And inform your father that I will be paying him a visit shortly.'

The witch hunter watched as the browbeaten bully and his crony pulled their companion off the floor and withdrew from the tavern with their burden. When the door closed behind them, the witch hunter reholstered his pistol. The tables broke out into conversation once more, this time louder and more animated as the farmers discussed the unique and exciting scene they had witnessed. Thulmann turned around as a small glass was set upon the counter near him.

'Thank you,' Reikhertz told him. 'Sigmar's grace be upon you.' Thulmann considered the small glass of schnapps, then gestured at the bottles of wine lined against the wall behind the bar. The innkeeper hastened to meet the witch hunter's wishes. 'That Anton is a bad one, worst of a rotten lot if you ask me,' he said as he returned with Thulmann's wine.

'I shall be seeing that for myself,' the witch hunter informed him as he sipped at his wine. 'In the meantime, I need your best room for myself. You will also make provision for my man here, be it a corner of your common room or a loft in your stable. I'll be dining with the Klausners this evening, so there will be no need for your cook to prepare a good meal. I'll also desire to speak with you when I return, so keep yourself available.'

Reikhertz beamed at the witch hunter. 'Everything will be as you wish. Anything at all that I can do, you have but to ask it.' Thulmann finished his wine and handed the glass back to the grateful innkeeper. He strode away from the counter, noting the admiring looks of the farmers.

'Thank Sigmar you've come,' one of them said. 'Perhaps now there will be an end to these murders.' His declaration caused the rest of the crowd to break into a murmur of agreement and hope. Thulmann walked toward Streng. The bearded mercenary grinned back at him.

'Seems you've won quite a following,' Streng commented. Thulmann nodded in agreement as another voice rose up from the crowd praising his arrival.

'Indeed, that ugly little incident may prove beneficial,' he observed. 'How beneficial I won't know until I've spoken with that young rake's father. Still, the good will of these people is certain to be of some help.' Thulmann looked back at the farmers, toasting his health and boasting of the now swift and certain destruction of the fiend that had been preying upon them. 'Besides, these people could use a little hope in their lives.' He cast a warning look at his henchman. 'Try to control some of your excesses,' he told the professional torturer.

The witch hunter looked over at Reikhertz as the innkeeper served another round of drinks to one of the tables. 'Also, the innkeeper has a daughter. Keep your hands off her.'

The mercenary gasped with feigned injury. 'Don't worry, Mathias, these hands don't go nowhere they haven't been invited first.' Thulmann's shook his head.

'Someday,' he said, 'I hope to find some scrap of virtue in that black pit that acts as your soul.'

'If it comes in a bottle, then someday you probably will,' laughed Streng, walking toward the nearest table and snapping his fingers to gain the innkeeper's attention. Thulmann shook his head and strode out into the darkening streets.

CHAPTER THREE

KLAUSNER KEEP WAS a massive structure looming atop a small hill some distance from the village. The keep was surrounded by unspoilt wilderness, massive trees of incalculable age surrounding it on every side, a swift flowing stream of icy water running about the perimeter of the forest from which the keep rose like an island upon the sea. As the shadows of the trees enveloped his steed, Thulmann could barely discern the twinkling lights emanating from the narrow windows of the keep. The fading gleam of the village had long since been lost.

The witch hunter pondered the isolation of the keep. In most small villages, such a fortification was commonly surrounded by the dwellings of its common folk, the better to exploit the fort's thick stone walls for protection in times of war. Here, however, the village and the keep were distinctly separated, and by more than mere distance. There was every sign that the people of Klausberg avoided the residence of their lords and protectors.

The road to the keep was obviously not heavily travelled and did not branch, but proceeded exclusively and directly to the fortress, indicating that the paths employed by the common folk

of the district detoured at some great distance from the holdings
of the Klausners.

And yet, perhaps it had not always been so. As Thulmann rode
down the path between the trees, he sometimes glimpsed the
tumbled ruin of a wall, the last outline of a building, the faint
impression of a foundation crouched within the shadows of the
trees. He had the impression of old stonework, pitted by time and
weather, heavy with the clutching tendrils of vines.

Were these perhaps the sorry remnants of some past incarna-
tion of Klausberg? Could it be that because the keep had failed to
protect them in the past that the descendants of that long-ago village now dwelt far from the castle? Somehow, the ruins suggested
an antiquity greater than that which would give credence to such
a theory.

Thulmann considered what he knew of the Klausners and their
history. The family first came to prominence during the era of the
Three Emperors in the person of one Helmuth Klausner, a
renowned witch hunter who had been a great scourge of the forces
of darkness and who had been something of a hero during the wars
against the vampire counts of Sylvania. Indeed, the district of Klausberg had been awarded to Helmuth Klausner by no less a personage
than Grand Theogonist Wilhelm III himself in gratitude for the
heroism that marked the witch hunter's accomplishments.

Since that time, the Klausner family had been remarkable in its
devotion to the Temple of Sigmar, many of its sons serving as Sigmarite priests and Templars, following the example of their
ancestor. It was an exemplary history of piety, service and honour,
a record which made the witch hunter question the animosity
and even fear with which the people of the district held the ruling family.

Thulmann knew that a witch hunter's greatest servant was fear,
but it had to be fear tempered by respect. Had the patriarchs of
the Klausner family neglected to recall this important lesson
when they left the service of the temple to govern their own holdings? Certainly the example displayed by the bullying Anton did
not speak well for the manner in which the Klausners conducted
themselves.

Thulmann had travelled beneath the shadows of the trees for
some time before at last the woods opened up and he saw the
keep itself standing before him.

Up close, he began to understand some of the reason the keep was avoided. It was an ugly structure, sprawled atop the small hill like some great bloated black toad. Its walls were high, perhaps forty feet, its battlements craggy and irregular, like the broken teeth of some feral hound.

The central tower rose above the main mass of the structure by another fifty feet, affording it a view that encompassed the entire district. The outer wall of the keep was without windows, its smooth black stone face broken only by the huge door which fronted it. Upon these massive portals of Drakwald timber had been carved the coat of arms that had been the Klausners' for as long as any could remember: the griffon rampant crushing a slavering wolf beneath its heel. The coat of arms was picked out in a golden trim, the only show of colour in the cheerless façade.

Thulmann rode toward the gate, addressing the armoured sentry he found posted there. The guard considered the witch hunter for a moment, holding his pike in an aggressive manner, before withdrawing through the smaller door set into the larger gate. The sentry was gone only a few minutes before the gates swung inward.

The inner courtyard of Klausner Keep was small, scarcely larger than that of The Grey Crone. The witch hunter stared up at the imposing black walls all around him. It was rather like looking up from the bottom of a well, an impression that did nothing to off-set the cheerless air about the place.

Two soldiers with axe-headed pole-arms regarded the witch hunter with stern expressions while a pasty-faced boy scurried out from behind a cluster of barrels to take the reins of Thulmann's steed. The witch hunter dismounted slowly, his eyes once again staring upward at the fast-darkening sky. He corrected himself. Framed by the black walls of the keep, the view was not so much like that seen from the bottom of a well, but from the bottom of a grave.

A bald-headed, round-faced man wearing a heavy black cloak over his dun-coloured tunic and burgundy breeches watched Thulmann arrive from the raised platform that faced the court-yard. He studied the witch hunter for a moment, then detached himself from the doorway in which he had been framed and descended a flight of broad stone steps to the courtyard, accentuating each movement with a flourish of his slender steward's staff.

'Allow me to welcome you to Klausner Keep,' the steward announced as he advanced toward Thulmann. 'I am Ivar Kohl, steward to his lordship, Wilhelm Klausner.' Ivar smiled apologetically. 'His lordship regrets that he could not greet you in person, but his health has not been well of late and his lordship finds the cold night air disagreeable.' The steward smiled again, as false and uncomfortable an expression as Thulmann had ever seen.

'I can sympathise with his lordship,' Thulmann said, his eyes cold, refuting the insincere friendship proffered by the steward. 'There is much in Klausberg that can be considered disagreeable.'

The steward redoubled his efforts to put the witch hunter at ease, his smile growing even broader, his hands extending to either side of his body in a gesture of openness. Thulmann waved aside the steward's words before he could speak them.

'I've not travelled here under threat of nightfall to be turned away by a servant at the threshold,' the witch hunter stated, a commanding note in his silky voice. 'I am here to see your master, and if he cannot come to meet me, then I must go to see him.' Thulmann pointed at Ivar's face as the man's smile slipped away completely. 'Take me to see him now, and without any further delay.'

The steward grimaced as Thulmann voiced his demand, then waved at the stable boy to remove their visitor's horse to the stables. 'If you will follow me,' he said, turning his back to the witch hunter and ascending the small flight of stone steps once more. With a last wary glance at the smothering black walls, Mathias Thulmann headed after the retreating steward.

THE INTERIOR OF Klausner Keep was no less repellent to the witch hunter than its exterior. The cold stone walls closed in upon him, even in the cavern-like main hall that opened upon the courtyard, seeming to exude some malevolent, crushing influence. The sparse furnishings which Thulmann could see within the hall, while excellent specimens of craft and skill and polished to a brilliant finish, had an air of mustiness about them, an indefinable aura of antiquity and age.

The only other items to arrest his attention were hung about the far wall, surrounding completely a monstrous hearth flanked by marble columns. These were portraits, a collection of grim and brooding countenances.

The witch hunter broke away from Ivar Kohl and strode across the vast hall to examine the portraits more closely. The steward took several steps before realising that his guest was no longer with him. Ivar cast a worried look about the hall before sighting the black-clad Thulmann gazing up at the portraits.

'The past scions of the Klausner line?' Thulmann asked as Ivar appeared at his side. The witch hunter was certain that such was the case. There was no mistaking the menacing cast of the eyes, the lantern-like jawline and thin, almost sneering lips. He had seen such a face only a few hours before when he had introduced himself to Anton Klausner.

'Indeed,' nodded Ivar, stretching a gloved hand toward the paintings. 'All the patriarchs of the Klausner family have had their countenances preserved upon canvas and placed here. From Helmuth himself,' Ivar pointed at the massive portrait that hung at the very centre of the collection, almost directly above the hearth, 'to his lordship Wilhelm Klausner,' here the steward punctuated his words by bowing deferentially to a smaller portrait on the very edge of the grouping. Mathias Thulmann studied both paintings, comparing them and the men they represented.

The portraits had all been created by masters. However much Thulmann might despise the keep itself, he had to concede that the Klausners had a deep appreciation and a keen eye for a talented artist.

Each of the paintings seemed more like a reflection of the man who was their subject. Every line, every crease and wrinkle, every expression was there, captured in paint to endure long after the bones of the real men were dust. The look of imperious command was there in every face, the severity and devotion that any witch hunter must possess to perform his always dangerous, often unpleasant calling.

Thulmann stared at the portrait of Helmuth Klausner. He was pictured as a tall man, broad of shoulder, wearing a suit of burnished plate and a wide-brimmed hat. His face bore all the characteristics of the other Klausners, but the look in the man's eyes was even more penetrating. There was stamped the fervent, feverish gaze of a fanatic, so certain and firm in the surety of his purpose as to be beyond all reasoning, unwilling to brook any question.

Even the man's image had a power about him, and Thulmann could feel its echo. Such men became great leaders, heroes of their time, or they were consumed by their own power to become monsters. Thulmann could not decide which legacy the brilliant artist had striven to capture in his intimate study of Helmuth Klausner. The background of the portrait was composed of shadows, clutching, indistinct shapes. Were they cringing away from Helmuth Klausner, or welcoming him as one of their own?

'Nelus, is it not?' Thulmann asked, stabbing a finger at the glowering portrait of Helmuth Klausner. No, the witch hunter decided, there could be no doubt. It was surely the style of the long-dead Tilean master. Truly, the Klausners possessed a true appreciation of art, and were powerful and wealthy enough to bring even a man of such fame as Nelus all the way from Luccini to immortalise them.

'Indeed,' nodded Ivar once more. He gestured back toward the portrait of Wilhelm Klausner. 'His lordship's portrait was done by van Zaentz of Marienburg, some few years before his tragic death.' Thulmann found himself eyeing the more recent painting. It was no idle boast of the steward's, certainly the portrait was crafted by no less skilled a man than the late Marienburger. Thulmann found himself studying the visage of Wilhelm Klausner. There was a strength to the man, a devotion to duty and honour stamped upon his brow, etched into the harsh outlines of his jaw. But there was more. A slight spiderweb of worry pulling at the corners of his mouth, a trace of unease and doubt seeming to drain the conviction from his stern gaze.

Thulmann turned away from the wall of patriarchs, gesturing for Ivar Kohl to lead the way once more. 'A fascinating collection,' the witch hunter declared. 'I am now doubly keen to meet a man blessed enough to have sat for van Zaentz.'

THE MAN TO whom Ivar Kohl led the witch hunter looked more like a withered skeleton than the powerful figure in the portrait. The strong features had grown lean and thin, the once keen eyes blurred and withdrawn. It was only with some effort that Thulmann managed to keep from gawking in amazement at the apparition he faced. Wilhelm Klausner was only a few years older than Thulmann himself, yet the man lying before him looked withered and wizened enough to be the witch hunter's grandfather!

The thin creature who sat propped upon a mound of pillows at the head of a gigantic bed still bore an air of command about him, as he gestured for the servants who had brought him a miserable supper of soup and wine to depart. Then the patriarch of the Klausner family cast a stern and demanding eye upon his steward.

'This is the man who insulted my son,' the harsh words snapped from the old man's lips.

'With respect, your lordship,' Thulmann spoke before the steward could sputter a reply, 'your son is the sort of man who invites trouble upon himself. He is fortunate to be your son, otherwise he might not have fared so well raising his hand against a servant of the Temple.' Wilhelm Klausner matched Thulmann's reproving gaze.

The two men locked eyes for a long moment, as though trying to take each other's measure. Thulmann was struck by the age and tiredness in Klausner's gaze. Here was a man who knew that death was stalking his every breath, who had resigned himself to the brevity left to his days.

Wilhelm Klausner looked away, shaking his head and wringing his hands. 'I know,' he confessed in a subdued tone. 'I have done my best with the boy, done my very best to raise him as a caring father should. But perhaps it is as you say. Perhaps I have overindulged the lad.' He looked again at the witch hunter, this time with a face that was heavy with guilt. 'You see, there is a tradition among the Klausners. The eldest son inherits the title and estates, all that this family has achieved. The other sons frequently resent that, feel that it robs their own lives of any value.'

The patriarch attempted a weak smile. 'Is it any wonder that Anton should display some bitterness, or that he might need to seek ways to relieve that bitterness?'

'Maybe he should take up opera,' Thulmann commented, his voice cold and unsympathetic. A man made himself, and there was nothing that could justify to Thulmann the bullying cruelty he had seen the young Klausner display in the tavern. Cold hostility replaced guilt in the old man's eyes.

It was Ivar Kohl who put an end to the tense moment. 'My lord, may I present Mathias Thulmann of Altdorf,' the steward introduced Klausner's visitor. He pivoted his body to make an expressive bow, his hand extended toward the massive bed. 'His lordship Wilhelm Klausner,' he needlessly told the witch hunter.

'Bechafen, actually,' Thulmann corrected the steward. 'Though I do keep in touch with the Imperial city. It was such a communication that occasioned my coming to Klausberg.'

'Indeed,' said Klausner, his lisp stretching and twisting the word. 'And what do they say in Altdorf that has caused an ordained witch hunter to make the long journey to my humble domain?'

'A great deal,' the witch hunter told him. 'None of it good.'

'I believe that Herr Thulmann has come here to investigate some exaggerated rumours regarding the recent attacks in the district,' explained Kohl.

Wilhelm Klausner lifted his body from the supporting pillows.

'If such is the case, then I fear that you have come all this way for nothing,' the patriarch stated. He shook his head, a grim smile on his face. 'It is some animal, a bit more cunning and fierce than is usual, it is true, but when all is said, still only a wild beast. My hunters will catch it any day now and that will put an end to the matter.'

'They did not seem to think it was something so trivial in Altdorf,' cautioned Thulmann.

'The Klausners are an old family and still hold great influence in some circles,' Ivar Kohl explained. 'And they have not done so without earning their share of enemies, even within the temple. It is only to be expected that such enemies would exploit even the most minor of incidents to try and disgrace the Klausner name.'

'It is a wolf, or perhaps some bloodthirsty wild dog, Herr Thulmann,' reiterated Klausner. 'Nothing more.' He smiled, leaning forward. 'So you see, we have no need of your particular services.'

Thulmann smiled back. Was that what was really behind the patriarch's icy demeanour? Not the fact that Thulmann had put his antagonistic son in his place, but the fact that he did not want a witch hunter operating in his domain, stepping on Klausner's own authority?

There were many magistrates and burgomasters who clung so desperately to their own small measures of power and authority that they deeply resented someone who could take that away from them, however temporarily. But Thulmann had not expected such treatment from Wilhelm Klausner. The man had been a witch hunter himself, surely he would be above such petty and selfish politicking?

'Whether you approve or not,' the witch hunter said, 'I have been ordered by Sforza Zerndorff, Witch Hunter General South, to investigate the deaths that have been occurring in Klausberg.'

The smile faded from Klausner's face and the old man sank back into his pillows. 'If it is simply a wolf, as you say, then my business here will, I am sure, be most brief.' The witch hunter's tone slipped into one of icy challenge. 'Incidentally, just how many people has this wolf of yours killed?'

Wilhelm Klausner gave the witch hunter a sour look, clearly disturbed by the question. Ivar Kohl seemed to choke on his words as they stumbled from his mouth.

'I… they say… some twenty or so,' the steward admitted, his voice rippling with a guilty embarrassment. 'Of course not all of them might have been killed by the same animal,' he added in a weak attempt to salvage the situation.

Thulmann's expression was one of strained incredulity. 'Twenty or so?' Thulmann could not believe the enormous toll, nor the fact that even in trying to be evasive as to an exact count, Kohl would admit to around twenty victims. How high might the actual number be? 'Two phantom man-eaters that you are unable to catch?' he asked. The witch hunter shook his head. 'Perhaps you are trying to catch the wrong kind of killer. They don't seem to share your opinion down in the village. I understand that some of these people were taken from their own homes. Rather bold for an animal, wouldn't you say?'

'Perhaps the victims had a reason to be abroad at a late hour?' Kohl stated. 'Sneaking into a barn for a late night drink, or some clandestine rendezvous. Or maybe the poor fellows heard their animals becoming agitated and decided, unwisely, to see what was upsetting them. Wolves often prowl near livestock, looking for an easy kill. And they say that once a wolf has tasted man-flesh, it prefers human prey above all others.'

'Nevertheless, it might be helpful to have an outsider look into these matters,' the witch hunter told him. He turned his gaze back toward the patriarch. 'I might be able to give you a fresh insight into these killings.'

'If you are determined,' the old man sighed, shaking his head. 'I can assure you that your attention would be better directed elsewhere.' He waved his thin hand, the heavy signet ring gleaming in the flickering light cast by hearth and candle. Ivar Kohl strode toward his master. 'Prepare a room for our guest,' Klausner told him.

It was Thulmann's turn to shake his head. 'That will not be necessary, your lordship,' he told the patriarch. 'I thank you for your generous consideration, but there are questions I need to ask the common folk of Klausberg. It will be easier to conduct my investigations from the inn.' Thulmann nodded at Klausner. 'I am sure you understand,' he added in his silky voice.

'Perfectly,' Klausner replied, his tone cold. The patriarch's face split into a cunning, challenging smile. 'You will of course allow my men to assist you in your hunt. They know this district much better than a stranger such as yourself. I am certain that you will find them invaluable to your investigations.'

'Another generous offer,' Thulmann responded. 'I shall take it under consideration.' He bowed before the bed-ridden patriarch, sweeping his black hat before him. 'I thank you for your time. I will make mention of your kindness in my report to Altdorf. No need to show me out, I know the way,' he said, turning and opening the chamber door before Ivar Kohl could do so for him. The witch hunter stalked away, the heavy oak panel closing behind him. When it had shut completely, the servant spun around to address his master.

'We can't allow him to stay here!' the steward swore. 'He has certainly been sent here to spy on your affairs!' Wilhelm Klausner motioned for Kohl to compose himself.

'We will keep an eye on him,' he told the steward. 'Make certain that he intends this house no mischief.' The old man sighed heavily. 'He may be of use to us, Ivar. Our own hunters haven't been able to track down this fiend. Perhaps the witch hunter can.'

Kohl shook his head, stamping the floor with his staff. 'You can't trust a man like that!'

Wilhelm Klausner sank back down into his pillows, a sly smile reappearing on his tired features.

'Who said anything about trusting him?'

MATHIAS THULMANN STRODE down the wide, empty stairway of the keep, descending toward the vast empty hall and its collection of grim-faced portraits. His meeting with the old patriarch had been a tense affair. The old man was suspicious, and afraid of losing control.

Despite what he had said, Thulmann had read the flickering expressions on the old man's face. He was deeply disturbed by the horror stalking his district, and frustrated by his own inability to put an end to it. That an outsider had come to accentuate his own failure in this matter clearly added to his frustration and guilt over the murders. The witch hunter wondered if the old patriarch could lay aside his wounded pride and desperate clutching at his control over the district in order to put an end to the depredations of this 'beast'.

Thulmann replaced his hat and smiled. Not for a second had he even considered the old patriarch's assertions that the culprit was simply an animal. Wilhelm Klausner had lost his touch, he was no longer liar enough to put conviction in a falsehood he himself did not even slightly believe. No, there was some other agency at work here, an agency every bit as sinister as whatever dread influence had so hideously and prematurely aged the patriarch.

'Are you the witch hunter from Altdorf?' asked a voice from behind Thulmann. He turned to find himself staring at a younger version of the man he had just left. Thulmann's gloved hand dropped to the hilt of his sword, thinking that perhaps he was being called to account for the events at the inn. But, no, as he looked at the man who had spoken to him, he at once realised his mistake.

The face he beheld did not have the cruel twist to its features, the sullen anger in the eyes that had characterised Anton Klausner. This man was of a similar cast, to be sure, with the heavy brow and square jaw of all the Klausners, but there was a firmness and nobility to his countenance, qualities that had long ago faded into an echo in the withered features of Wilhelm Klausner and which had perhaps never made their mark upon the face of his younger son Anton.

'I address Gregor Klausner, do I not?' inquired Thulmann. The fair-haired young nobleman inclined his head.

'You do indeed, sir,' he said. Some of the keenness and affability drained from him and his demeanour became apologetic. 'I must apologise for my brother...'

Thulmann raised his hand, waving away the young man's words of contrition. 'Your father has already made his apologies,' he informed Gregor.

'Anton is rather temperamental,' explained Gregor. 'I have tried to curb his excesses, but sadly, I fear that he seldom listens to my counsel.'

'Your father should take matters in hand,' Thulmann advised. A guilty look came upon Gregor, suggesting to Thulmann that the eldest son of Wilhelm Klausner had voiced such opinions to the old patriarch on several occasions. Gregor quickly regained his composure and began to usher the witch hunter down the remainder of the staircase.

'It is very good that you have come,' the young man told Thulmann as they walked.

'His lordship does not seem to view things in quite such a way,' the witch hunter replied. 'I am sure he would rather settle things his own way. However long it might take,' he added.

'My father is a very independent man, very set in his ways and firm in his beliefs,' Gregor stated as they reached the bottom of the stairs and began to walk across the vast entry hall. The footsteps of the two men echoed upon the polished floor as they walked, their voices rising to the vaulted ceiling high overhead. 'But his methods are not working. We need new ideas, a new approach to putting an end to this fiend.'

'There are only so many ways to catch a wolf,' Thulmann said. Gregor clenched his fist in silent rage.

'It is not a wolf,' he swore in a low voice. 'You won't find a man, woman or child in this district who believes that, no matter how many times my father tells them it is so. Though it would be easier to believe it was some manner of beast! To contemplate that a human being could sink into such depravity sickens the soul.'

'You are certain that there is a human agency behind this then?' Thulmann asked, pausing to study Gregor in the light cast by the hall's mammoth fireplace. There was outrage, a thirst for justice about the man. Unlike his brother, it appeared that Gregor valued and cared for the people of Klausberg and their misery was something that offended him deeply.

'Several of the victims have been stolen from their beds, from behind locked doors,' Gregor said. 'What beast can open a lock? What wolf ignores swine in their pen to steal a maid from her room in her cottage?'

Thulmann nodded as he heard the conviction and emotion in Gregor's voice. There was a possibility that the young man had been sent by his father to spy upon the intruding witch hunter, but Thulmann was a good judge of character and though he had only just met the man, he felt that Gregor would be a poor choice for such duplicity.

'I am staying at The Grey Crone,' he told Gregor. 'It would help me a great deal if you would meet with me there. You have, no doubt, a great insight into your father's methods of hunting this fiend and why they have failed. Once I know what not to do, I should have a better idea of how to proceed and perhaps some inkling as to the nature of this fiend we seek.'

The young Klausner gripped Thulmann's gloved hand in a firm grasp. 'If you will give me time to fetch a cloak and have a horse saddled, I will go with you now.' The enthusiasm fell from his voice and it was with a grim expression that he continued. 'Even now, I fear that this malignant power may be working its evil.'

DARKNESS, BLACK AS pitch, cold as ice. That was what greeted the blinking eyes of Tuomas Skimmel as he sat bolt upright in his bed. The farmer cast his frantic gaze about, trying desperately to penetrate the gloom. Not even the shadows of the room's furnishings could be discerned, so complete was the blackness. The farmer gasped as he released the breath that had caught in his throat, immediately cringing as the hiss thundered in his straining senses.

What was it? What had broken his slumber? Had it been a sound? The creak of a floor-board, the rustle of a rat as it crawled through the walls of Skimmel's cottage? Perhaps it had been the icy touch of a draft whispering between the cracks in the walls, or the touch of a moth as it flittered about the room? Maybe it had been nothing more than his own mind, already overburdened with anxiety.

The fiend had struck the cottage three miles away only last week. It had been reason enough for Skimmel to send his wife and sons to stay with his mother in the village. But someone had to remain behind, to feed and look after the cattle. Skimmel's wife had considered him very brave to decide to stay alone at their home, but right now, Skimmel was more inclined to agree with her second assessment of his actions as they had made their painful goodbyes. She had said that it was foolish to stay with the fiend still abroad, and doubly foolish to do so alone.

Skimmel continued to sit frozen with fear. He could see nothing, hear nothing. He couldn't even smell anything unusual. Yet he knew. He knew that there was something in the darkness, something horrible and malevolent. Perhaps it was standing beside him, jaws stretched inches from his face.

Any moment he might feel its hot breath blasting his face, smell the stink of rotting flesh trapped between its fangs. Perhaps it was watching him even now, waiting for him to move, waiting for him to betray the fact that he was awake and aware.

An uncontrollable tremble began to worm its way through Skimmel's body. The farmer tried to fight the spasm, tried to crush it back down, keep it from overwhelming him, from betraying him.

The monster would see, it would see his legs as they shivered, it would see the goosepimples prickling his skin. It would see and it would know and it would pounce. The farmer gasped again, then gulped back another breath. Even breathing was difficult now. His body would not inhale unless he concentrated on it, and if he concentrated on breathing, then his limbs would start trembling even more fiercely.

What was that? The farmer turned his eyes without moving his head. He'd heard something, seen something in the corner of the room.

He tried to tell himself it was a mouse or a rat he had heard, tried to tell himself that the shape slowly appearing out of the darkness was nothing more than an old coat thrown across a chair. He tried to tell himself all of this as tears bled from his eyes, as the trembling of his limbs began to shake his bed.

The shape in the corner moved. Skimmel opened his mouth to scream, but no sound would escape from his paralysed throat. The trembling grew still more fierce and slowly, against his will, the farmer rose from his bed. The shape gestured to him with an outstretched hand, then it receded back into the darkness.

A CROOKED MOCKERY of a man stepped out from the humble cottage of Tuomas Skimmel. He wore a heavy cassock, grey and threadbare, trimmed in black wolf-hair about the sleeves and neck. The robed figure stared back into the gloom of the cottage and gestured once again with his thin, spidery hand. The flesh upon that hand was pale, marked by an almost leprous tinge.

At the man's gesture, Tuomas Skimmel emerged, eyes wide with terror, marching in stiff-legged-steps.

The necromancer smiled. His face was sallow, and the features were almost ferret-like in their suggestion of a malicious and scheming cunning.

Ropes of ratty brown hair dripped down into the necromancer's face as he exerted his will upon his victim. Carandini savoured the delicious terror he saw in Skimmel's eyes, enjoying it as a healthy mind might relish a glass of wine or a beautiful painting. He could just as easily have subdued the man's mind with his spell, but the necromancer preferred to watch his victim's agonies. He loathed the lowing, unthinking masses of mankind, but there was an especial hatred for the men of the Empire.

Indeed, such a man had nearly ended the necromancer's life in the Tilean city of Miragliano several years ago, an injury not easily forgotten. It was satisfying to Carandini that his knowledge of the black arts had grown tremendously since then.

The necromancer looked away from his enthralled, helpless victim, staring at the night-claimed landscape around them. He would need to be taken through the woods, led some two miles to where the ritual would take place.

Carandini pointed toward the distant trees, and watched his slave awkwardly march off into the night. How much greater would the man's terror become when he came to understand the full horror that was planned for him? He wondered idly if perhaps his heart might burst from fright when he beheld the awful aspect of Carandini's ally.

Yes, the necromancer thought as he followed after his victim, my knowledge of the black arts has grown, but it is still not enough. With the help of his ally, however, that situation would change. Carandini smiled as he considered his ambitions and their fulfilment. When he had his prize, then he would no longer fear death, whatever shape it wore. Rather, death would fear him.

Carandini hastened his steps, urging his slave to greater effort. The night was old and he was eager to complete tonight's sacrifice.

CHAPTER FOUR

THE LONG WATCHES of the night brought with them ethereal landscapes of grey worlds and fantastic visions. In the cold and chill hours, dream and nightmare clawed at the sleeping minds of men, filling their thoughts with curious sights and unquiet memories...

The sickly sweet smell of spoiled fruit and rotting cabbage surrounded the witch hunter. The darkness within the old warehouse was almost like a living thing, tangible, reaching toward him with groping claws, clinging to his clothes like some soupy vapour.

The old dry floorboards beneath his feet creaked as he made his way through the dust and filth. Plague had done its deadly work in this part of Bechafen two years before, few had been willing to return to the devastated neighbourhood with the memory of disease and death still fresh in their minds. But someone had not been so timid, and their footprints shone out from the dust as the witch hunter's light fell upon them. The hunter firmed his grip upon his sword, bracing himself. His quarry was very near now.

'So you did manage to keep my trail?' a cold, sneering voice rose from the darkness. The witch hunter froze, his eyes trying to pierce the clutching veil of blackness all around him. He directed his lantern toward the voice, casting the speaker into full visibility. He was a tall man, his black hair fading into a steel-like hue, his once aristocratic features beginning to sag and droop as age began to pick the meat from beneath his skin. He wore a bright red robe about his thin frame, the long garment hanging from him like a shroud. There were markings upon the hem of the garment, upon the sleeves and edges of its long cowl. These were picked out in gold and silver and azure hues, and they were no such symbols as any healthy mind should contemplate.

The sorcerer's empty eyes blazed into a fiery life as they considered the man who had come so far and risked so much to force this confrontation. 'I congratulate you upon your determination. Perhaps you are not quite the fool I had thought you to be.'

The witch hunter fought the uncertainty crawling through him. He had seen what this man could do, he had seen first-hand the awful, devastating power at his command. There was no question that the abominations he served were all too real, and there was no question that they had bestowed their dark gifts upon the sorcerer. The witch hunter had seen armoured knights cooked by eldritch flame in the blink of an eye. He had seen a steel gate break free from its frame of stone at a simple gesture and word from the warlock. And he had seen the unspeakable manner in which those who had died in the infernal rituals conducted by this madman to honour his foul gods had perished.

Who was he to challenge such awful power? What madness made him think he was the equal of a sorcerer?

Mathias Thulmann stared again at the visage of his foe. His face was twisted with contempt, as though it was the witch hunter and not the murderous heretic who was the deviant.

It was a face made all the more terrible for its echo of Thulmann's own. For Erasmus Kleib was the witch hunter's uncle, though madness and lust for power had long ago stripped Kleib of all that was decent and noble, leaving only a power hungry husk enslaved to the will of insane gods.

'You have no chance against me, boy,' Kleib spoke, his thin moustache curling as his face contorted into a sneer. 'You've only survived this long because I have allowed it. Some lingering trace of familial courtesy,' he gave a dismissive wave of his lean hand.

Thulmann shuddered as he considered the sorcerer's words. Could it be true? Had he indeed been able to come so far solely because of the madman's whim? He thought of his companions, his friends and comrades-in-arms. Dead, all of them, their bodies lying in graves strewn about Ostland. Even his mentor, the renowned witch hunter captain Frederick Greiber, his throat ripped out by some black and winged horror upon the road from Wolfenburg. Doubt worked its way into Thulmann's face.

The sorcerer laughed, a short and hollow sound.

'That's right, boy,' he snickered. 'All of it, all the misery and fear, all the suffering and sorrow. All of it was needless, all of it was worthless.' The sorcerer studied the back of his hand for a moment, then looked once more at the witch hunter. 'If you ask nicely, however, I might be persuaded to allow you to leave this place.' Erasmus Kleib smiled, a look of malevolence and triumph. 'But you should be quick in your begging. I find myself becoming tired of this little game.'

The witch hunter found himself stepping back, the tip of his sword beginning to dip down toward the ground.

Despair, the rancid clutch of failure, coursed through his veins. It had all been madness, and now that madness would cost him his life. Somehow, the thought disturbed him but not for the reasons he had always imagined that it would. It was not death itself which he feared, but the thought that Erasmus Kleib would continue on after him; that once he was dead the sorcerer would continue to kill and commit atrocity after atrocity. It was the thought that Kleib would go unpunished that fuelled his fear.

One of the first lessons Thulmann had learned from Frederick Greiber suddenly came to his mind. A witch hunter did not meet the works of Chaos with wizardry of his own. He did not challenge the Dark Gods with weapons as steeped in depravity and wickedness as they. No, a witch hunter's weapons were courage and determination, to never allow fear and horror to take command of his heart, to never allow doubt and regret to weaken his resolve. He must trust completely and fully in Sigmar, armour himself in a shield of faith that would shine out into the darkness, that would challenge the terror of the night.

He must say, 'I am a servant of Sigmar, and his judgement is upon you,' and know that the strength of their god would be within him at such times. He must have faith, a faith strong enough to banish all doubt.

'No,' the witch hunter snarled, lifting his sword again. 'It is the grace of Sigmar that has brought me here. It is his determination that I shall be the one to visit his justice upon you, Erasmus Kleib, Butcher of Bechafen! And, though I perish in the doing of it, I shall see that you answer for your crimes!'

The sorcerer's face swelled with wrath. 'I see that I was mistaken,' he hissed in cold tones of subdued fury. He swept his arms wide, spreading his heavy crimson cloak about him. 'You are an idiot after all. Perhaps I shall one day answer to your puny godling's ineffectual concepts of justice, but not for some considerable time. There is much work that I have yet to complete for my own masters.' Erasmus Kleib looked at the shadows to either side of him. Thulmann could hear something moving in the shadow, the sound of claws scrabbling across rotten timber, the furtive patter of naked feet, low whispers of amusement rasping through inhuman jaws.

The witch hunter threw open his lantern to its full, illuminating the warehouse. He recoiled in disgust as he saw what the light revealed. Inhuman forms scuttled toward him from every side, shapes with crooked backs, slender limbs and long naked tails. They wore tunics of leather and loin wraps of filthy cloth, and their flesh was covered in a dingy brown fur where it was not marked by grey scars and crusty scabs.

The faces of the creatures were long and hound-like, protruding from beneath their leather helmets and cloth hoods. Beady red eyes gleamed from the faces of the Chaos-vermin, and massive incisors protruded from the tips of their muzzles.

Erasmus Kleib laughed as his inhuman allies scuttled forward to subdue the witch hunter. Thulmann could hear their chittering laughter as they gnashed their jaws and gestured with their rusty-edged weapons.

'Witch hunter! Witch hunter!' the monsters chanted in their squeaking voices. The sound of their naked feet became a dull tattoo upon the floor. 'Witch hunter! Witch hunter!' they hissed as they stalked closer still, the reek of their mangy fur heavy in the air. 'Witch hunter!' they laughed, the sharp report of their feet once again slapping against the floor.

MATHIAS THULMANN AWOKE with a start, hands flashing at once to the sword and pistol resting beside him on the bed. It took him only a moment to register his surroundings, to recall that he was not in Bechafen, but in Klausberg. He wriggled his body to free it of the bed clothes that had twisted about him like a cocoon during his restless slumber, then patted at his face with the edge of one of the blankets, wiping away the cold sweat.

Dreams and nightmares. However firm his faith, however devout and complete his conviction, Thulmann seldom escaped their grasp for very long. He was only surprised that it had been the shade of Erasmus Kleib that had haunted him this night.

He'd encountered things far fouler and more horrific even than his degenerate uncle and his loathsome allies, things that made even Kleib's most heinous acts seem nothing more than the mischief of an unruly child.

Perhaps there was a reason behind the invasion of his nightmares by the dead sorcerer? There were some who said that dreams held portents of the future within them, if one but had the wit and wisdom to discern their meaning. Of course, such thought was well within the realm of astrologers, wizards and other persons of dubious morality and piety. Still, the witch hunter sometimes wondered if there might not be some truth in their beliefs for all their heresy. Were not dreams the method with which grim Morr communicated with his dour priesthood? And if Morr, the god of death, should deign to guide his servants in such a manner, who could say with certainty that mighty Sigmar, protector of man, might not use similar methods?

'Witch hunter!' came a muffled voice, accompanied by the sharp report of bare flesh striking against hard wood. Thulmann cast aside his ponderings as the sounds from his nightmare echoed through his room atop The Grey Crone. He rose swiftly from his bed, sword and pistol held in a firm grasp, and walked to the door before the person outside could knock once more.

'I've had men put to the question for a fortnight for disturbing me at such a Sigmar-forsaken hour!' Thulmann snapped as he threw the door open, frightening the colour from the already nervous Reikhertz. The innkeeper jumped back, crashing against the solid wooden wall of the hallway.

The witch hunter kept his angry glare fixed upon Reikhertz, his pistol held at the ready in his hand. 'It is courting heresy to disturb the sleep of an ordained servant of Sigmar.' Thulmann paused as Reikhertz began to mumble unintelligibly. 'Well, out with it man! What foolishness makes you court heresy before the cock has crowed!'

Reikhertz fought to compose himself, training his bulging eyes on the witch hunter. 'Fo... forgive... the... the intrusion... I... I... I m-meant n-no offence, noble... noble...'

Thulmann rolled his eyes, lowering his pistol and stepping out into the corridor. 'Despite the early hour, I begin to doubt if we will finish this conversation before the sun has again set.'

Like a mask, Thulmann discarded the anger he had assumed upon throwing open the door of his room. There was a time to intimidate commoners, to instil in them the proper deference and fear which his station demanded. But now was not one of them. Thulmann slipped into the quiet, concerned voice of a father confessor, his eyes gleaming now not with hostility, but a keen interest in what the innkeeper had to say.

'It is clear that something of importance has happened,' he told Reikhertz, his tone now friendly and calming. 'I would hear whatever tidings you bear.'

Reikhertz swallowed hard, then nervously began to smooth the front of his woollen nightshirt. 'Please, begging your pardon, sir,' the shivering innkeeper said. 'But there has been another killing.'

Thulmann's expression grew grave. He nodded his head toward Reikhertz. 'Like the others?' was all the witch hunter said.

'Mangled and ripped apart,' the innkeeper confirmed. 'Old Hans found him, returning from frog-catching out by the bog-ponds. He thinks it might have been Skimmel, one of the district's cattle-herds.' Reikhertz looked down at the floor, fear creeping into his voice. 'He can't be certain though. There isn't enough left to be sure.'

'How is Lord Klausner attending to the incident?' Thulmann asked.

'Hans came here straight away,' Reikhertz answered. 'The Klausners haven't been told yet. Not that they would do anything about it in any event,' the innkeeper added, spitting at the floor.

'Send him to the keep just the same,' Thulmann told Reikhertz. 'If nothing else, I should like to see first-hand how Lord Klausner conducts his investigations into these killings. Then I may know better how not to conduct my own.' Thulmann paused for a moment, considering his next words. 'Tell this Hans to be certain that Gregor Klausner is informed and that I would appreciate his assistance. His knowledge of this district could prove quite useful.'

Reikhertz bowed to the witch hunter. 'Shall I have your horses saddled?' he asked.

'Yes, I'll be only a few moments,' Thulmann sighed. 'Breakfast will have to wait until I return. I expect you to see that it makes amends for my disturbed sleep.' The witch hunter dismissed the innkeeper with a gesture of his hand and Reikhertz hastened off down the hall. Thulmann turned and stalked toward the door that opened upon Streng's room.

'Streng!' he shouted, pounding on the closed portal. 'Rouse yourself you filthy drunkard! The killer has struck again and we ride in five minutes!' Thulmann lingered long enough to hear the thump of a body striking the floor and the sharp squeal of young woman, followed upon by muttered oaths and curses in Streng's sullen tones.

GREGOR KLAUSNER MET Thulmann and the still surly Streng shortly after the witch hunter had begun his ride toward the keep. Thulmann was once again struck by the competence of the younger Klausner.

Despite his naturally suspicious nature, the Templar had to admit that there was quite a bit of merit in the young Gregor. Their conversation of the previous night had revealed to Thulmann that Gregor Klausner was the polar opposite of the brash and bullying Anton.

Gregor had an eye for detail, a genuine passion for knowledge and, more importantly, a very high degree of personal morality and honour. Many times, in explaining to Thulmann the events of the past weeks, the pent-up frustration at his personal inability to relieve the suffering of the district came to the fore, breaking through his otherwise steely composure.

There had been another moment when Thulmann had observed Gregor's composure falter. When Reikhertz's daughter had brought them ale and wine, a look that had passed between the two young people. Reikhertz had quickly ushered his daughter from the room, casting a venomous look at Gregor, even more hostile than the one with which he had favoured Streng and the plump town whore he had managed to dredge up while Thulmann was away at the keep. It had been a tense moment, and Thulmann wondered at its import.

Gregor favoured Reikhertz's daughter, a situation which the innkeeper was perfectly willing to exploit in matters of protection, but also a situation which he did not condone. Suddenly Anton's behaviour of the previous night could be viewed in a new light.

Had Thulmann intruded upon a random act of bullying and arrogance, or was there something more? Anton probably knew that his brother favoured the pretty Miranda. As the younger son of old Wilhelm Klausner, the witch hunter wondered just how much Anton might resent his situation and that of his older brother.

'If it was any colder I'd be pissing ice,' snarled Streng, clapping his gloved hands against his fur-covered shoulders.

Thulmann cast a withering glance at the grousing sell-sword. 'We are about Sigmar's business. Perhaps if you considered that, your faith might keep you warm.'

'I'd prefer a set of warm sheets and the body of a hot woman,' the bearded ruffian grumbled. Thulmann ignored his complaints and turned to face Gregor Klausner. The young lord was dressed in a heavy fur coat, his head encased within the bushy mass of a bear-skin hat cut in the Kislevite fashion. Thulmann noted that both a sword and a holstered pistol hung from Gregor's belt. The witch hunter smiled. Gregor had his wits about him, even in such a lonely hour, preparing himself against not only the cold, but the unknown. There were many noblemen in Altdorf who would not have displayed such common sense and intelligence.

'This hollow that the frog-catcher described,' the witch hunter said. 'I trust that you know where it is?'

Gregor extended his hand, pointing toward a series of distant wheat fields. 'If we cut across those fields, we can come upon it from firm ground. The bog-ponds lie to the west of the woods, and south of it is an expanse of rough ground that some of the cattlemen use as pasture.'

The younger Klausner nodded at the witch hunter. 'We can make better time going across the fields than using the road. Besides, that is the route which Anton and my father's men will take.' Gregor's hard features spread in a grin. 'I rather imagine that you'd like a look at the body without my father looking over your shoulder.'

'I've made no mention of such intention,' the witch hunter told him, though there was no reproach in his tone. He motioned for Gregor to lead the way. 'The fields, then?'

The noble rode off, Thulmann and Streng following close behind him. A sharp mind, that one, thought the witch hunter. He'd possibly have made a good witch hunter himself. Indeed, given his family legacy, Thulmann wondered why he hadn't taken up such a vocation.

As they rode across the desolate fields of harvested grain, Thulmann reflected upon some of the things Gregor Klausner had told him the night before. Among the first of his revelations had been the fact that the current string of killings had not been the first to plague the district. There had been similar killings in the time of his grandfather, and his great grandfather, as any grey-hair in the town would relate in a subdued whisper if Thulmann cared to question them.

It was only by the tireless vigilance and selfless heroism of the Klausners that this horror had been driven back time and again and the lands protected from its marauding evil, or so the family tradition had it.

However, there was something more, something that disturbed even the most garrulous of the village elders. The deaths were different this time, bloodier and more savage than any of the previous ones. And it seemed that this nameless fiend was even more hungry for blood now than in the past, for all of the elders said that it had settled for far less death in their day.

Thulmann considered once more Wilhelm Klausner's insistence that the thing preying upon his district was merely an extremely clever wolf. In light of the grim tradition held by the villagers, Thulmann did not see how Klausner could honestly believe in such a theory. A wolf that had preyed upon the same district for over a hundred years? Working its mayhem in brief orgies of bloodlust and then slinking back into the wilds to wait decades before striking once again?

The old man might have been organising wolf hunts, but he could not honestly believe that what was haunting his lands was any normal animal. The old patriarch must surely be lying. Perhaps the old landholder was fearful of the scandal that might arise should knowledge of his family's grim curse become widespread. Perhaps he merely refused to believe that he might be unable to stop whatever fiend was behind his district's misfortune, and so refused to see his unknown enemy as a possibly supernatural being.

No, Wilhelm Klausner had been a witch hunter himself, he would be beyond such foolishness. He would have seen for himself the power of the Dark, seen with his own eyes some of the nameless things that haunt the night.

Thulmann wondered just who Wilhelm Klausner was trying to deceive about the nature of these tragedies. After a long career confronting such horrors, retiring to the comfort of his ancestral home, perhaps Klausner was no longer able to accept such manifestations of evil.

Perhaps he needed to cling to some belief that having survived his years as a Templar of Sigmar, he had likewise escaped from the dread clutch of Old Night. Perhaps he could not cope with the idea that such evil might stalk him again, rearing its foul visage within his own lands.

Maybe he clung to the notion that his enemy was a normal, clean animal, not some dread beast touched by the corrupting hand of Chaos, or some daemon emissary of the beyond. The one Wilhelm Klausner was trying to convince might just be the old patriarch himself.

CHAPTER FIVE

THE CAWING OF crows announced that they had arrived at their destination. The three men dismounted on the very edge of the last of the fields, just where the level ground dripped away into a small wooded trench. As the witch hunter and his companions descended the dew-slicked slope, the stench of blood made itself known to them.

Thulmann could see a shape strewn about a stretch of open ground beneath the twisted, gnarled boughs of the hollow, alive with cawing, hopping scavenger birds. Several of them cocked their heads as the men advanced, favouring them with irritated looks. Streng set up a loud yell that caused the scavengers to take wing and scatter into the morning mist.

'Hopefully they haven't made too much of a mess,' Thulmann commented, striding ahead of his companions. The object that had so fascinated the crows had indeed once been a man, though the frog-catcher could easily be forgiven his inability to render the corpse a positive identity.

The arms and legs were the only parts that looked to be unmarked. The chest was a gaping wound, looking as if it had been torn open by a bear. The head was in even worse shape, little more than a mass of peeled meat resting atop the corpse's shoulders.

'Pretty sight, that one,' observed Streng, a bit of colour showing beneath his dirty beard. The witch hunter agreed. Death, horrible and unnatural, was part and parcel of the witch hunter's trade, yet seldom had Thulmann seen evidence of such unholy brutality. Gregor Klausner, unused to such sights grew pale, lifting a gloved hand to his mouth as the bile churned in his stomach.

Streng began to circle the body as Thulmann strode towards it. The mercenary stared at the ground, cursing colourfully when he found no sign of tracks. 'Ground's clean, Mathias,' he reported. 'Not a sniff of either a paw, claw or shoe.'

Thulmann bent over the corpse, casting a practiced eye upon the body. He glanced up, staring at Gregor Klausner. 'Rather savage work, even for a wolf, don't you think?'

'My father is convinced that these deaths are the work of some beast,' Gregor replied, speaking through his hand. He risked removing it and gestured at the mutilated body. 'Surely only a beast would be capable of such a frenzied act.'

'You've never seen a norse berserk,' Thulmann said. 'But this is not the work of some frenzied, maniacal bloodlust.' The witch hunter's voice grew as cold as the chill morning air. 'No, this was a very deliberate act. Deliberate and unholy. Evil has come to Klausberg, and it is fouler than any I have ever come upon.'

Gregor Klausner watched intently as Thulmann picked a long stick from the ground and began to indicate marks upon the savaged body. The noble felt his breakfast begin to churn in protest. Streng noticed the young man's discomfort and chuckled.

'Observe the lack of blood, either upon the body or the ground,' the witch hunter said. He gestured with the stick, indicating a heavily stained streak that spread away from the body. 'Except here, here alone does blood stain the ground. Note its direction. If we were to imagine it as an arrow, it should point to the south and the east. There is importance in that fact, for it is our first sign that this was a deliberate and carefully orchestrated atrocity.'

The witch hunter gestured with the stick again, this time indicating a large wound in the side of the body's neck. 'A deep, swift stab into the artery, allowing the blood to spray outward from the body. The wound is triangular, which tells us something more, for few are those who employ triple-edged blades.'

'Then you are saying a man did this?' Gregor Klausner could barely restrain the shock and outrage in his voice. Thulmann nodded grimly to the young noble.

'Oh yes, a man who wishes with all his foul, polluted soul, to become something more, no matter how abominable the price.' The witch hunter stabbed his stick again at the body. 'Observe, the mutilation of the face and skull, a feeble attempt to hide what was actually done to this man. Note the massive injuries done to the chest, the ribs peeled back to expose the inner organs.' Thulmann pointed at the messy remains of the corpse's left breast. 'Yet, what is this? Something missing, and a tidbit far too heavy to have been claimed by even the most gluttonous crow, and cut away much too cleanly to be the work of a fox or weasel.' The witch hunter discarded his stick, backing away from the body.

'There can be no doubt,' he informed Gregor. 'This is the work of a necromancer. The savage blood-letting, arranged that the precious humour might point toward the south-east, a blood offering to the profane Father of Undeath. The wound itself, delivered by a triple-edged blade, the tool of the foul elves of Naggaroth, from whom legend says the Black One learned his dark arts. Had the head not been so badly mutilated, we would no doubt find that the brain of this unfortunate had been removed, ripped from his skull by barbed hooks inserted up each nostril. The heart, too, taken, ripped from his still warm body that his vile murderer might work his loathsome sorcery.'

The young noble turned away, spilling his breakfast against the side of a tree.

Streng laughed at the sight, subduing his amusement only when he noticed the sharp look Thulmann directed at him. Gregor rose from his sickness, wiping the last of the vomit from his lips. He smiled in embarrassment, then, reasoning that his belly was already empty, stared directly at the human wreckage that had provoked him.

Gregor Klausner shook his head, trying to absorb the villainy the witch hunter had just described. It was almost impossible for him to believe that a man could lower himself to such acts of degeneracy and wickedness. Yet, there was no doubting the conviction and certainty in the witch hunter's words.

'Why?' was all Gregor could say. 'Why would any man commit such an outrage? What could he hope to accomplish by working such an atrocity?'

Thulmann's expression became troubled. 'If I knew that, I should be a great deal…'

'Riders,' interrupted Streng, drawing his sword. The witch hunter turned, his hand loosely resting upon the wooden stock of his pistol.

Horsemen thundered down the hollow, brush and fallen branches cracking beneath the hooves of their steeds. There were a dozen of them, hard men wearing heavy coats over their suits of sturdy leather armour. They favoured Thulmann's party with looks that bespoke obvious annoyance, seemingly more interested in the witch hunter's party than they were in the mangled thing that lay sprawled upon the ground near them.

Thulmann was somewhat surprised, however, when one of the horsemen forced his way to the fore of the group. He was wrapped up in the mass of an immense bear-skin cloak, the fur of its collar rising so high as to cover his cheeks. A rounded hat of ermine was crunched down about his ears. Even so, what little flesh of his face was left exposed was pale and tinged with blue and there was a trembling shiver to his lean frame.

'You should have waited for me and my men,' the lisping voice of Wilhelm Klausner hissed from his shivering lips. 'As lord of this district, propriety would dictate that you allow me to conduct you about my lands.' Wilhelm Klausner cast a disapproving eye on his son Gregor, who averted his eyes in a shame-faced fashion. 'But then, there are quite a few people, I find, who are not bound by the laws of propriety.'

'With all respect, your lordship,' Thulmann bowed slightly to the old patriarch. 'I felt that it was important I see the body at once, before it was disturbed.'

Wilhelm chose to ignore the suggestion in the witch hunter's tone. 'I can hardly imagine that such a sorry spectacle might have anything important to tell,' the old man stated. 'If you have seen the work of a wolf once, that is enough.'

'But it isn't a wolf,' protested Gregor, fire in his voice. 'There is something else at work here, something evil.' Gregor noted his father's unchanging expression. The young Klausner stepped forward, gesturing at the maimed corpse of Skimmel. 'This was not the work of a wolf, or any other beast!' Gregor declared. 'Just listen to this man, father, he will tell you! He will show you how wrong you are!'

Wilhelm Klausner looked away from his son, casting a sceptical glance to where Mathias Thulmann stood, his gloved hand still resting upon the grip of one of the pistols holstered on his belt. 'I am certain that the witch hunter has been quite convincing in his observations.' The old man smiled thinly, the faint whisper of a laugh hissing from his throat.

'But you forget that I too was once a witch finder. I know only too well how that grim calling preys upon the mind and soul, twisting them until one sees evil everywhere and a monster lurking within every shadow. Were I to give free rein to such morbid fancy, I myself could gaze upon those savaged bones and spin speculations just as wild and horrifying as those this good fellow has no doubt been relating.'

Wilhelm Klausner clenched a bony fist, shaking it at his son. 'But such sick imaginings would not be true. You should be wary in what you listen to, and what you choose to believe.'

The witch hunter studied the old patriarch. There was something new about him, something lurking just beneath the surface, something that might drive a man to any act of desperation or folly.

There was fear in Wilhelm this morning, carefully hidden, yet no less prodigious than that which might fill a witch's eye as she lay upon the rack. It was something more than the fear and suspicion his own presence might account, nor had it been evoked by the bloody corpse strewn about the ground.

No, there was something else that occasioned the old man's terror, something that had not manifested itself until he had laid eyes upon his son Gregor. A quick glance told Thulmann that whatever fear was bubbling up within Wilhelm Klauser was absent from the countenances of his companions, even the glowering Anton and the obviously discomfited Ivar Kohl.

Mathias Thulmann stepped toward the mounted men, noting at once that several of the old patriarch's troop let their hands slide toward the hilts of their swords. The Templar chose to ignore the menacing motions, instead focusing his attention firmly upon Wilhelm Klausner. 'With all respect, your lordship, it seems you have forgotten the lessons you should have learned in your prior calling. The world is far less pleasant than we might have it. There are times when evil is everywhere, there are times when monsters do lurk in the shadows.'

'Not here,' swore the old man. 'Not in Klausberg. You are allowed to operate within my lands only by my indulgence. Do not give me cause to revoke it.'

'I will linger in this district until this unholy butcher is brought to ground,' Thulmann's silky voice intoned. 'Your sovereignty extends to secular matters, but I am an agent of the Temple and beyond your will to command. It is by my indulgence that I have so far chosen to respect your authority and try to operate within your auspices. In future, I shall reconsider such courtesies.'

Wilhelm Klausner's lips twisted into a snarl, swiftly punctuated by a snort of disdain. 'Chase your phantoms from here to hell for all I care!' The patriarch glared again at his eldest son. 'Come along, Gregor, leave this man to his shadow-hunting.' The old man extended his hand toward his son, indicating that he should join the company of riders. The angry expression melted from Wilhelm's face, replaced by a look of shock when Gregor remained unmoving.

'I cannot, father,' the young noble said, his voice a mixture of defiance and regret. 'I think that Herr Thulmann is correct in this matter. Look for yourself, father! These horrible acts are not the work of a simple wolf. There is something evil, unclean about these deaths! Why can't you understand that? Perhaps it really is the curse the villagers speak of.'

Wilhelm Klausner doubled over in his saddle, overtaken by a fit of violent coughing. Two riders moved in to support the old man and prevent him from falling from his steed. After a moment, Wilhelm straightened his body, waving aside the supporting arms of his steward Ivar Kohl and his younger son Anton. The patriarch locked eyes with Gregor. 'I would not have believed you to give credit to such contemptible legends,' Wilhelm sneered. Another fit of coughing wracked the old man's body. He looked over at his steward.

'The keep, Ivar,' the old man said weakly. 'Leave these fools to their foolishness.' As the steward helped Wilhelm turn his horse, the old man gripped the arm of his younger son.

'I leave the hunt in your hands, Anton,' he said in a rasping whisper. 'Do not fail me.'

'I shall not,' declared Anton, his words sharp and strong. He watched as Ivar led his father's horse away, then turned his gaze back upon Mathias Thulmann and Gregor. There was an air of triumph and superiority about the younger Klausner now, his cruel face scarred by a victorious leer.

'You heard my father,' Anton said. 'I am now master of this hunt. If you will remain, then you shall do as I say. Otherwise you shall pursue your foolishness elsewhere and leave this matter to men of true quality.'

Mathias Thulmann tipped his hat to the gloating huntmaster. 'I think there will not be much to discover once you and your mob have finished trampling every inch of ground in the hollow, and to follow your lead would be more foolishness than I care to contemplate at present.' The witch hunter turned, motioning for Streng and Gregor to return to their horses. Anton Klausner watched the trio depart, his face darkening with rage at the Templar's disparaging remarks.

'Witch hunter, I've not dismissed you!' Anton Klausner spat. Thulmann froze in his ascent up the slope.

'There are very few men who speak to me in such a tone,' the witch hunter told him, not deigning to turn around. 'You are not one of them.' Thulmann continued his climb. 'I suggest that you remember that,' he added darkly.

Anton Klausner fumed as he watched the three men ride off, the colour growing ever more vibrant in his face. 'Come along, you scum!' the lordling snapped as he jerked his horse's head around. 'I want that animal's head on a spear before nightfall. Then we'll see which of Wilhelm Klausner's sons is the fool!'

CHAPTER SIX

MATHIAS THULMANN AND his companions sat astride their horses, staring back down at the hollow from the vantage of the overlooking fields. The Templar shook his head and sighed in disgust.

'Superstition, ignorance and fear are the greatest armour the Dark Gods ever crafted for themselves,' he commented. 'Against the folly of the human soul, even the might and glory of Sigmar is hard pressed to persevere.'

'I am certain that my father can be shown that he is wrong,' Gregor Klausner told Thulmann, a defensive quality in his voice. Clearly the implication that the three failings he had spoken were to be found in abundance in the Klausner patriarch had offended Gregor. Even from a man like the witch hunter, he was not about to hear ill spoken about his father.

'There are none so blind as those who refuse to open their eyes,' observed Thulmann. He lifted his hand to forestall the angry protest that rose to Gregor's lips. 'It would aid me immeasurably if your father could be brought to accept the true nature of the horror that has visited itself upon this community, but I fear that no amount of evidence will sway him. He refuses to accept this thing not because he disbelieves, but because he knows it to be true.'

'That cannot be!' snapped Gregor. 'My father is a virtuous and courageous man! He served the temple for ten years as a witch finder! He is no coward!'

'I did not say that he was,' Thulmann's voice drifted into the low and silky tones that so often caused condemned heretics to confide in their seemingly sympathetic accuser. 'Not in the sense you mean. But courage and virtue have their limits, and I think that Wilhelm Klausner long ago met and surpassed his own. When he put aside the mantle of a witch hunter, I think he also imagined that he had put aside the duties demanded of one who takes up that calling. Now, perhaps, he cannot bring himself to call upon the man he once was, cannot bring himself to do what needs to be done.'

Gregor grew quiet as the witch hunter spoke, considering the Templar's words, much of his anger dripping out of him as doubt flooded in to take its place.

Thulmann noted the exchange of emotions, considering how close his suppositions about the elder Klausner might have come to hitting the mark.

'Shall we scout around the edges of the hollow, Mathias?' Streng inquired, jabbing a meaty thumb back toward the trees. 'Maybe pick up the heretic's trail?'

'No, I don't think that will serve any good,' the witch hunter replied. 'We seek a man, not the animal of Wilhelm Klausner's fancy. And even a madman knows the value of a decent path. No, if there was a trail to be found, the hooves of Anton Klausner and his thugs will have destroyed it.'

'Then how do we proceed?' Gregor Klausner asked.

Mathias Thulmann was quiet for some time, considering what little he had learned since coming to Klausberg. A decision reached, he stared once more at Gregor. 'I think we might uncover much if we were to perhaps delve a bit deeper into this curse the villagers speak of. There might be something to learn, something that might put a name to this fiend we hunt.'

Gregor Klausner nodded his head. 'There are extensive records of my family's history kept in the keep. If there is any truth to the curse, then it will be in those records, if it is to be found anywhere.' The nobleman grew silent, a distant look entering his eyes, and he turned a suddenly grim face back upon the witch hunter. 'But first, I think there is something you should see,' he said.

THE FOREBODING WOODS that bordered upon Klausner Keep had been frightful, shadowy apparitions when Thulmann had first seen them upon his twilight ride to the fortress. In broad daylight, they were no less unsavoury and disquieting. The trees were twisted, gnarled things, as though the trunks were writhing in silent torment. The bark was discoloured in leprous splotches, the leaves more often coloured a sickly yellow than a healthy green.

Streng reached out his hand to inspect one of the branches that overhung their path, only to have the wood crumble away into a reeking dust as he touched it.

'They call it "the blight", and have done so for as long as any can remember,' explained Gregor as Streng tried to wipe the filth from his hand, only to have the piece of bark he was employing for the task crumble away in a similar fashion.

'Are many trees so afflicted?' Thulmann asked.

'No, only those near the keep. My father believes that it is some deficiency in the soil,' Gregor stated.

'Strange that there should be such a patch of unwholesome ground at the very centre of all these productive fields and orchards,' observed Thulmann. He suddenly brought his horse to a halt, nearly causing the trailing Streng to crash his own steed into Thulmann's animal.

The witch hunter dismounted and strode into the bushes beside the path, the bracken crumbling softly beneath his booted feet. He extended his hand, brushing a twisted clutch of brambles away from an object partly buried in the diseased loam. It was a section of slender stonework, possibly once part of a column or pillar. The witch hunter studied it intently for some time, his hand slowly running along the fine curves and sharp angles.

'Elves lived here once,' Thulmann stated.

'There are quite a few such ruins still scattered about these woods,' Gregor told him. 'Though many of them have long since been broken up and used by the villagers and farmers to construct their homes.'

The witch hunter rose from the broken column, striding back toward the path, a new sense of unease about his bearing. The elves were a strange and fey race, mysterious in their ways and

deeds. They were a magical people as well, tapping the unnatural winds of magic with a skill unknown to mere men, a
proficiency which men of Thulmann's calling often took as certain evidence of the corruption inherent in the elder race. They
were a people not to be trusted, as the ancient dwarfs had
learned at great cost, and their ruins were haunted places, echoing with the lingering traces of the enchantments worked by
their long dead builders.

Thulmann wondered if there might not be some manner of
connection between the existence of these ruins and the affliction
that Gregor had named 'the blight'. Indeed, the witch hunter
could only conjecture whether 'the blight' might not itself be a
symptom of the greater affliction now plaguing the district.

'So old Helmuth Klausner built his fortress upon the bones of
the elves,' Thulmann said, his gaze straying in the direction of the
keep, which loomed unseen somewhere beyond the overhanging
trees. 'I wonder if he truly appreciated what he was doing.'

'DRINK THIS,' THE woman spoke in a stern voice, lifting the bowl
of steaming broth to the old man's mouth. Wilhelm Klausner
screwed his jaw tight and turned his head in protest.

'I'll have none of that,' the woman scolded him. She was
younger than the old man who lay muffled within the mass of
blankets and furs piled atop his bed, her long red hair just showing the first hint of silver. She was pretty, a woman who might
once have claimed beauty before the hand of time had begun to
caress her plump, robust frame. Her cheerful visage and ruddy,
healthy glow of her skin were the utter antithesis of the withered,
gaunt apparition who grumbled at her from his cavern of bedding.

An observer would never have guessed that Ilsa was two years
her husband's senior.

'This soup will warm the chill that you let sink into those stubborn old bones of yours,' Ilsa said, her round cheeks lifting in a
smile. Her husband turned his head to face her.

'Am I master in this house or not?' he growled, his lisp stretching the words into a hiss. 'Damnation woman, if I don't want to
drink your concoction, then let me be!'

Ilsa cocked her head at Wilhelm's vituperative outburst.
'Indeed, and I suppose it was I who told you to go racing out into

the morning frost like a starving halfling.' She lifted the bowl to the old man's face once more. 'Now you drink this, unless you like having ice-water in your veins.'

'Her ladyship is right,' conceded Ivar Kohl. The steward was leaning against the side of the hearth, nursing the fire with an iron poker. He had shed the heavy furs from his morning ride, replacing them with his black livery and robe.

'You see,' beamed Ilsa Klausner triumphantly, 'even nasty old Ivar thinks you should do what's good for you.' With a sour look at his servant, Wilhelm opened his mouth and allowed his wife to feed him. Ilsa persisted until the bowl had been drained down to its final dregs.

'Satisfied?' Wilhelm grunted as his wife withdrew the empty bowl. He did not have time to await a reaction, however, but at once doubled over as a fit of coughing seized him. Ilsa reached forward, a concerned look on her face.

'Whatever possessed you to go rushing out into the cold like that?' she asked, trying to soothe away the coughing with her tender caress. She glanced back at the steward. 'You are smarter than this Ivar!' she snapped. 'He's not a young man any more!'

'His lordship can still present a very fearsome figure when his anger is upon him,' protested Ivar. 'And your husband was most determined about his course of action this morning. I doubt even you would have stopped him.' Ilsa turned her attention back toward her husband as the fit subsided.

'You are too good to me, Ilsa,' the old man said, his gnarled hand touching her cheek. 'All the gods smiled upon me when they put you in my life.' Wilhelm drew his wife's hand to his lips, then sank back into his mound of pillows. 'I can imagine no greater treasure in this world than the love of a woman like you. You, and Gregor and Anton,' the patriarch smiled as he spoke the names. 'The house of Klausner can never have been more fully blessed.'

Ilsa rose from her husband's sick bed, discreetly wiping a tear from her eye. 'Listen to you prattle on like some hen-pecked cuckold. Now you sit still and rest.' She turned a stern gaze upon Ivar Kohl. 'He needs his sleep,' she told him.

'Ivar, stay a moment,' Wilhelm called out, his voice a tired rasp. 'There are a few things I wish to go over with you.'

Ilsa favoured both men with a reproving look.

'As you will have it, but only a moment,' she declared. 'Then you get some rest,' she ordered her husband, wagging a scolding finger at him. Ivar Kohl watched her withdraw, closing the door after her.

'Has she gone?' inquired the patriarch. His steward listened at the door for a moment, then nodded his head. The old man waved at Ivar, beckoning him to the side of the bed.

'This witch hunter is a menace,' Wilhelm told his servant.

Ivar Kohl shrugged. 'Perhaps, but it is just possible that he might discover who did kill that unfortunate wretch we found in the hollow,' the steward told Wilhelm.

The old man reached out, grabbing Ivar's arm.

'I don't care about that!' he hissed. 'You've seen Gregor! He is fascinated by that man and what he is, tagging after him like an eager puppy.'

'It is only natural,' explained Ivar. 'He is a Klausner after all. The trade is in his blood. Now, if you would only allow him to go to Altdorf...'

Wilhelm's clutch on his steward's arm tightened, bringing a gasp of pain from the man. 'I've told you, I'll not see my sons robbed of their life and happiness as I was! While I still draw breath, they'll not!'

Kohl gasped in relief as Wilhelm's strength failed and the old man sagged back into his pillows, releasing his grip. The steward tried to smooth the rumpled sleeve of his shirt.

'You've done all in your power to steer him away from that path,' admitted Ivar. 'But you cannot defy fate. Perhaps Gregor is meant to...'

'I'll defy the gods themselves,' Wilhelm stated, his voice barely a whisper, 'if it will keep my family from harm.' He laughed weakly, holding his withered hands before him. 'Once I thought I could save the entire Empire from the clutch of Old Night with these hands. Now I only want to protect my own.'

'You shall,' the steward assured him. Wilhelm swung his head around to look at Ivar once more.

'I will!' the old man exclaimed. 'This witch hunter, he must be kept away from Gregor.'

Ivar Kohl nodded in sympathy, but spread his hands in a gesture of helplessness. 'There is only so much we can do,' the steward told him. 'He is an officer of the temple. Even you have no authority over him.'

'I want him kept away from my son,' the old patriarch repeated, his gnarled hand closing into a fist at his side.

MATHIAS THULMANN STOOD before the object Gregor had led him to. It was some distance from the path, almost completely covered by the grasping, sickly weeds. It had taken little time to clear them away however, the fragile things crumbling at the touch, a cold breeze sweeping away the filmy dust.

The witch finder discovered that the chest-high diamond-shaped plinth was no elven relic, but something of much more recent construction, and cut by human hands. Indeed, with his knowledge and eye for quality in works of art, Thulmann could readily appreciate the skill and craftsmanship that had gone into it. The black marble plinth was topped by a small stylised griffon clutching a heavy warhammer in its upraised claw, one of the many symbols of the cult of Sigmar, one that had been quite popular two centuries past. Beneath the statue was a bronze plaque. Thulmann read the inscription.

'The sacrifices of forgotten martyrs are remembered always,' the witch hunter read aloud.

'Hmmph,' sneered Streng, spitting into the brambles. 'Looks like this thing was pretty well forgotten for all its fancy words. Otherwise you can bet your boot some enterprising wretch would have turned that fancy plaque into bread and ale.'

'The people of this district are a very superstitious sort,' explained Gregor. 'They would not desecrate such a shrine even if they did know of it. I only discovered it when hunting hares several years ago. It was apparently constructed by my great-grandfather, to commemorate the deaths in the village that had preceded the demise of his own father. I wanted you to see this, to show you that in the past, my family has not always regarded the curse with scorn.'

Thulmann looked away from the plinth, his eyes wandering across the landscape around them. 'These trees are old,' he stated. 'Even two hundred years ago they would have been large.'

'What's that have to do with anything?' Streng asked, not following his employer's train of thought. Thulmann stared at the brutal mercenary.

'Why place a monument, especially one that has obviously been constructed at such great expense, where no one could see it?' the witch hunter elaborated. He turned his gaze toward Gregor. 'Unless of course it was not meant to be seen. Perhaps your ancestor felt guilt for the deaths he associated with the family curse, felt an obligation to honour what he considered their sacrifice, but at the same time was ashamed to display that obligation openly.' The Templar turned away from the plinth and his thoughts.

'I need to examine these records you have mentioned,' he told Gregor.

CHAPTER SEVEN

THE BROODING MASS of Klausner Keep seemed to swallow Thulmann and his companions as they rode through the black gates. Once again, the witch hunter had the impression of some vast and noxious toad squatting atop the hill, surrounded on all sides by a wretched and diseased forest and the crumbling relics of an elder age. Even in daylight, the unpleasantness of the small courtyard and the black stone walls was not lessened.

Gregor Klausner conducted the witch hunter and his henchman into the vast entry hall, leaving the horses to be tended by servants. The young noble turned to speak with Thulmann as he led the way.

'The library is located on the northern face of the keep. The records we want to examine will be found there,' he explained. The young noble turned as he saw the black-clad shape of Ivar Kohl descending the broad staircase. 'Excuse me please,' he told the witch hunter.

Ivar Kohl regarded Thulmann with an oily look, a false smile forcing itself to his features. He continued to descend the stairway as Gregor hurried toward him. 'Master Gregor,' the steward addressed the noble. 'I trust that your morning has been... productive.'

'My father, Ivar, how is he?'

The steward adopted a posture not unlike that of a lecturer delivering a dissertation. 'Well,' Ivar began, 'your father is not a young man. I am afraid that the excitement and tragedy of the scene in the hollow has upset him greatly. And the chill of this morning has disordered his humours. He is not so resistant to the caprices of temperature as he once was,' Ivar stated regretfully.

'I should go to him,' Gregor declared. The grin on Ivar's face spread, becoming a touch more genuine. He reached out and gripped the noble's shoulder.

'Yes, you should,' agreed the steward. 'Your father is resting at the moment, but I am certain that seeing you would do him more good than any amount of sleep.'

Gregor nodded. He looked back toward Thulmann and Streng. 'I shall only be a moment, I wish to check upon my father.' He looked back toward the steward. 'Ivar, please conduct Herr Thulmann and his associate to the library. I shall join them shortly.'

'Ivar, conduct those men out of my home,' a harsh, commanding voice spoke from the top of the stairs. All eyes turned upon the gaunt, sickly figure that stood there, lean frame swaddled in a heavy cloak. Wilhelm Klausner glared down at the witch hunter for a moment, then swung his gaze upon his son. 'In fact, you can see them out of my district. I don't want them here, scaring the peasants and filling their heads with all sorts of morbid nonsense.'

Ivar Kohl took a reluctant step toward the witch hunter, but a sharp glance from Thulmann froze the servant. Thulmann advanced to the base of the stairway, looking past Gregor at the skeletal figure of his father.

'There is still evil abroad in these lands, your lordship,' Thulmann said, his silky voice rippling with menace. 'While it is, there is work for me to do here.'

'Then you refuse to accept my wishes?' the old patriarch snarled. 'That is unwise.'

'Father,' interrupted Gregor, climbing the stairs to stand beside his sire. 'Herr Thulmann has come here to help.'

'He's come here to undermine my authority!' corrected Wilhelm, his lisping voice rising with his anger. 'Come here to twist this entire district against me with his bogey stories and shadow-chasing. But I'll not have it!' The old man shook his thin hand at

Thulmann. 'You forget just who I am, witch finder. I am no petty burghomeister to be bullied and frightened by your tricks. I am not without my own influence, and I shall bring it to bear upon you if you continue to defy me. The elector count himself has dined within these walls, and I have sat to supper with two emperors. Need I remind you that the Grand Theogonist is one of my oldest and dearest friends?' Wilhelm laughed, a low dry rattle that slithered from his throat. 'Defy me and you will wind up burned at the stake yourself as an apostate!'

Thulmann stood his ground, meeting the patriarch's challenging gaze. 'There is a monster at work in your district, Klausner. I will leave when it is ash and blackened bone and not before. No threat from you will change that.'

Wilhelm Klausner's face twisted into an animalistic snarl, but before the patriarch could give voice to the invective boiling up within him, another fit of coughing wracked his body. Wilhelm crumpled into the arms of his son, allowing Gregor to conduct him back to his room. Thulmann watched the two Klausners withdraw, then faced Ivar Kohl once more.

'His lordship is not quite himself,' the steward apologised. 'These killings and his unwise venture this morning have disturbed his thoughts.'

'I will conduct my inquiries in the village today,' Thulmann told the servant. 'Perhaps when I return I will find his lordship in a more conciliatory mood.'

'That would be for the best,' Ivar Kohl nodded his head enthusiastically. 'I am sure that when this sickness passes you will find his lordship much more agreeable.' Thulmann lifted a warning finger.

'Cooperative or not,' he said, 'I will be back. You might relay that information to your master.' Turning on his heel, the witch hunter stalked from the hall. Streng paused to snort derisively as he passed the steward, then followed his employer into the courtyard.

Ivar Kohl watched the door close behind the two men, the false pleasantry slipping from his face, his usual mask of cunning rising to take its place. Sick or not, Wilhelm Klausner was correct, the witch hunter was a menace. Possibly one that might have to be attended to in a more direct manner. Still, while the perpetrator of last night's atrocity was still abroad, the witch hunter might have his uses. There was no reason to act in a hasty and irreversible fashion.

Not yet, at least.

UPON HIS RETURN to the inn, Mathias Thulmann found the common room of The Grey Crone crammed with people. As the witch hunter strode through the door, the excited murmur of the crowd died away and every face in the building turned in his direction.

The witch hunter scrutinised the crowd, seeing old men stooped with age and young, burly lads just beginning to grow their beards. They were garbed in simple homespun or furs, or else in modest fabrics such as might be found clinging to the frame of merchants and traders in any town in the Empire. It was a cross-section of Klausberg that faced Thulmann, men from the lowest classes and men from what passed for the wealthy elite of the village. They were men who under normal circumstances would not have deigned to walk the same side of the street as one another. But these were not normal times, and a grim and dreadful common purpose had united them and brought them here.

Streng muscled his way past the witch hunter, the thug's hand dropping to the hilt of his sword. The mercenary did a quick count of the sullen, expectant faces looking at them. 'Aren't you the popular one?' he muttered to his employer from the corner of his mouth.

Streng discreetly removed his hand from his weapon. In a louder voice he said: 'I don't know about you, Mathias, but I could do with some ale to wash away the chill from our ride this morning.' Streng left his master's side and strolled toward the counter where Reikhertz stood wiping his hands upon his apron.

'It seems your custom has improved, friend Reikhertz,' Thulmann said in his silky voice. The familiar tone nearly caused the innkeeper to drop the flagon he was handing to Streng.

Reikhertz cast a nervous glance at the mob.

'Can I help with something perhaps?' the witch hunter asked the foremost of the men, a rotund fellow with brightly striped breeches of white and red and a bronze-buttoned leather vest. Thulmann's tone was imperious and the surly merchant retreated from his gaze. The witch hunter turned his attention to the man standing beside the merchant. He was tall and black-bearded, his bare arms rippling with muscle. Thulmann guessed that the man was a blacksmith.

'Aye,' the man said, 'you can start by telling us what you and those damn Klausners intend to do to stop these murders!' With every word, the mob surged uneasily, their courage bolstered as their spokesman gave voice to the source of their fear and outrage. Thulmann did not speak at once, but stepped toward the bar, leaning his back against the hard wooden surface, adopting a practiced pose of unconcern and inoffensiveness.

'A glass of wine, if you would, Reikhertz,' the witch hunter told the innkeeper. 'Red, and in a glass, if that is achievable.' Thulmann turned around, taking his time to answer the smith's question, allowing the crowd's mood to simmer.

He needed these people angry. Anger was a poor cousin to courage, but it would suit his purposes. These people were afraid of the thing that was preying upon them, and that fear might keep their lips closed when Thulmann needed them at their most active.

'For my part,' the witch hunter said, nodding to Reikhertz as the nervous man set his wine down on the counter and scuttled away, 'I intend to bring a halt to these atrocities.'

'And what about his lordship?' an angry voice snarled from the back of the crowd. Thulmann took his time to answer, sipping at his wine. Beside him, an increasingly uneasy Streng watched the discontent grow within the crowd.

'As for his lordship,' Thulmann commented, setting his glass down once more, 'he is convinced that a wolf is preying upon his district.' The statement brought an incredulous murmur from the gathering. 'In fact, one of his sons is leading a hunting party to look for the animal even as we speak.' The murmur grew into an angry roar.

'Sure you know what you're doing?' Streng asked in a low whisper.

'Rest easy and continue drowning your wits,' Thulmann told his underling.

'Klausner plays games!' growled the smith, his deep voice roaring above the crowd. 'He plays games while our people die!'

'Yes!' shouted a second voice. 'He's safe behind his walls with his family, while our brothers and sons, wives and daughters are dying!' Thulmann listened to the fury swell within the mob, waiting for his opportunity.

'Our people die!' snarled a third man. 'Our blood to feed the damn Klausners and their curse!'

'The Klausner curse,' Thulmann's voice rose above the crowd, projected to the very back of the room, a trick often employed by actors upon the stage and taught to every Templar and priest of Sigmar. The crowd grew silent again, staring once more at the man whom they had come here to confront. 'I have heard much of this curse, but know little,' the witch hunter continued when he saw that he had the attention of the room. 'I have seen for myself the remains of one of this fiend's victims, a cattleman named Skimmel who was found in the early hours of this morning.' The news brought a shocked gasp from some in the crowd who had not given full credence to the rumours that had already been circulating about the village. 'His lordship thinks these crimes are the work of a wolf. I know better. I must know more.'

Thulmann strode away from the bar, stepping to the fore of the crowd, his keen gaze sweeping across the faces filling the room. 'You, the good folk of Klausberg are the ones to whom I must turn if we are to put an end to these atrocities and bring this insidious fiend to justice. You must tell me all that you have seen, all that you have heard.' Thulmann let his lean features spread into a grim smile. 'Together, if we keep our faith in Sigmar, we will overcome this evil.'

The witch hunter's quick, impassioned words had their effect, and a new murmur, this one of excitement and cautious hope, rippled through the room. Thulmann smiled as he watched his handiwork take root. Now he needed to cultivate it and force what he had planted to bear fruit.

A small, mousy man broke away from the crowd, nervously approaching the witch hunter.

'I can help you, master witch finder,' the little man said, wringing his hat between his hands. 'You see, I have seen the daemon for myself,' the little man confessed when he was aware that he had Thulmann's attention.

At the bar, Streng overheard the little man's story. He grumbled into his ale and drained the last dregs from his flagon. 'There are times when I truly regret deserting the army,' he mused. 'I have a bad feeling that this is going to be one of them.'

* * *

'I'M SORRY, SIR, but I be closing early. You'll have to come back tomorrow,' the butcher informed the man who had just slipped into his tiny shop. The rebuked customer stood in the doorway of the shop, a perplexed look contorting his pale features. He brushed a ratty string of oily hair from his face as the butcher rounded the counter, tossing his stained apron on the floor.

He glanced about the shoddy interior, staring with keen interest at the bisected pig carcasses hanging from hooks fixed to the ceiling, at the barrel of dismembered chicken refuse that would be later ground into meal for hogs, dogs and the least discriminatory of the town's human denizens. The smell of blood and the buzzing of flies occupied the visitor's other senses.

'It will only take a moment,' he told the butcher. 'Some sausage and a bit of pig's blood to boil it in.' The butcher shook his head, hastening toward the door and hurrying the robed man before him as though he were a wayward duckling.

'No time, my friend,' the butcher told him. The big man paused, his eyes narrowing as he looked more closely at his guest. 'I don't think I've seen you here before,' he commented with an accusing voice.

'Humble means,' the pasty faced man returned, shrugging his shoulders in apology and resignation. 'I fear I cannot often afford decent meat but must make do with what I can provide for myself.' He froze for a moment, staring at a haunch of meat resting on a wooden platter, trying to decide what exactly it had come from. The crawling blanket of flies that clothed a fair portion of it did little to aid his study.

The butcher snorted with distaste. 'Poacher, eh? Lord Klausner will catch you soon enough, rabbit-catcher, and then you'll be for it.' The man laughed grimly. 'He might even try and lay the terror on your head if you're not careful. He'd be just as happy to put the blame on a two-legged wolf as a four-legged one.'

The customer chuckled nervously. 'That would certainly be an unpleasant turn of events,' he muttered. His speech trailed away as he stared at a cow head lying atop a wooden box, its lifeless eyes staring back at him, its thick tongue protruding from its dead mouth. 'All the more reason for me to procure some of your provender,' the man said hastily as he saw the butcher advancing toward him. The big man was not moved, pushing his ill-featured patron back out the door.

'Sorry friend,' the butcher mumbled, turning to lock the door to his shop. 'Afraid you'll have to live on rabbit a bit longer. Big doings at the inn, and I'll not miss a moment of it.'

'Is that so,' the pale man asked, glancing in the direction of The Grey Crone. There was indeed a steady stream of traffic flowing into the building. He tried to recollect his sketchy knowledge of Imperial holidays. 'The Festival of St. Ulfgar?' he asked as the butcher completed his task.

'No indeed!' the butcher scoffed. 'The witch hunter is there, taking statements from any who will give them.' The butcher turned, walking quickly in the direction of the inn. 'Finally, somebody's going to put an end to these killings,' he called back as he raced away.

Carandini scowled as he heard the villager's words, quickly sheathing the triple-edged dagger he had been holding beneath the voluminous sleeve of his tattered grey cassock.

He had feared something like this. Things had been stalemated for several weeks now, but the arrival of this witch hunter would give a new strength to the enemy. The necromancer scuttled off down the nearest alley, trying to remain inconspicuous. Strangers were common enough in Klausberg, even under the current pall, but he wanted to take no chances. This close to achieving everything he had ever hoped for, he was even more paranoid than usual about putting his own neck in jeopardy.

The necromancer hastened to where he had tethered his sickly mule and rode off to bring the ill news to his confederate.

NIGHT HAD FALLEN by the time Carandini returned to his lair, a small and abandoned shack five miles outside the village. Even so, the necromancer was obliged to wait for nearly an hour before his ally put in his appearance. Carandini turned away from his small fire as he heard the swish of clothing behind him. The necromancer could barely make out the white face that rose above his confederate's black clothing, even with his supernaturally keen night sight. Carandini rose to his feet, wiping the dirt and soot from the front of his cassock.

'Forgive my tardiness,' the shadow said. Carandini could just make out the movement of the speaker's mouth within the smoky darkness that surrounded him. 'I was unavoidably delayed.'

'You have not been discovered?' demanded Carandini, his hand closing about the small vial he had sewn within the lining of his cloak.

'I am not so reckless as to jeopardise all that we have worked for,' the shadow hissed, his powerful tones redolent with resentment. 'There is nothing in this world or the next more important than the prize we will claim.'

'A permanent and lasting end to both of us is something that I should hold of greater importance!' Carandini snapped. 'It might be of interest to you to know that a witch hunter has come to Klausberg. You must be more cautious than ever! If it is even suspected…'

'I have known about the witch hunter's arrival for two days now,' the other told him. 'I watched him ride from the keep the first night he was here.' Carandini rounded on his companion, fury swelling within him, forgetting for a moment even the habitual loathing and fear which his ally caused in his heart.

'You knew about him and said nothing!' the necromancer shouted incredulously.

'Would you have informed me were our positions reversed?' the shadow asked calmly, his deeply accented voice twisted with a cruel mirth.

Carandini scowled and retreated back toward the fire. There was truth in his ally's words, Carandini would indeed have kept the information to himself, in hopes that he might find some way to use the witch hunter against his associate when the time came.

It did not disturb Carandini that his companion did not trust him, neither of them were such fools as to trust one another any more than a miser would trust a dwarf with his money-belt. They were useful to one another right now, but once that usefulness had run its course, their fragile alliance would come to an end, and the one who struck first would most likely also be the one to triumph. No, their mutual capacity for treachery was something of an unspoken understanding between them; what disturbed Carandini was the felicity with which his associate had predicted what shape his plots might assume when that time came.

'Do not brood so,' the shadow hissed. 'There are ways that we might turn this man's arrival to our advantage.' Carandini looked up sharply, his face twisted with suspicion. 'Our mutual advantage,' the shape added.

'Being burned at the stake is not something I should find advantageous,' spat Carandini. 'And I dare say that it would not do yourself any great amount of good.'

'We can arrange something to dispose of this man, certainly,' the shadow hissed, slowly circling the fire. 'If he hunts a beast, then perhaps we should let him find a beast. But consider this,' the voice dropped into a slithering whisper. 'We might do better than simply kill him. We might direct his attention to where it will serve us best. The enemy of our enemy,' the figure grew quiet as he considered his idea.

'His presence here interferes with our plans,' stated the necromancer. 'I had to abandon my choice for the next ritual because of his presence in the town.'

'The rituals will proceed,' the shadow assured Carandini. 'Nothing can be allowed to prevent them. You will simply have to find another viable sacrifice. However, it is wise to plan for every contingency.'

EMIL GUNDOLF SLOWLY picked his way through the trees, lips pursed as he whistled a low, mournful tune. He had walked this way countless times, yet never had his spirits been so low, his fears so great. Evil was abroad in Klausberg, striking everywhere, striking anyone. It was dangerous to be abroad at night.

He cast a nervous look over his shoulder, staring at the now distant light twinkling from his home. He could be at home now, safe and warm beside his wife and children.

The thought of his wife and daughters caused the forester to grip his axe a bit more securely. He fastened the top button of his coat and strode onward. Whatever fiend was abroad, it could be no more deadly than an empty belly, of that Gundolf was certain. And if the blight really had spread from the Klausner estate into Franz Beicher's timber, then Gundolf could expect a very summary dismissal from Beicher when the merchant discovered that his logging grounds had become corrupted.

Warmed by such grim pragmatism, Emil Gundolf continued to whistle and walk through the maze of rail-thin trunks.

He did not see his attackers, for they set upon him in darkness and silence from behind.

A heavy hood was slipped over his head before Gundolf could even open his mouth to scream, and powerful hands tore his axe from him.

The forester struggled as he was pushed and pulled, striving to overcome the tremendous strength of his captors. He soon realised that he was no match for those that held him, but Gundolf had no delusions regarding what his fate would be if he allowed them to drag him away.

Every step he tried to stamp the feet of his attackers, tried to smash an elbow or a shoulder into the face or stomach of one of his unseen adversaries. Sometimes he was rewarded by a grunt of pain or a muttered curse, sometimes the grip upon him would lessen slightly. But never enough, never would his captors weaken enough to allow him to slip their clutches.

Emil Gundolf thought of his wife, his tiny twin daughters, waiting nervously beside the hearth, waiting for him to return. Within the cloying darkness of the suffocating hood the forester shouted, screamed in impotent anguish, but the mask smothered the sounds. Tears welled up in his eyes, dampening the cold leather.

After some time, his captors brought him to a halt. Gundolf was gasping for breath beneath the hood, fighting to pull every scrap of air through the heavy leather. Sightless, with his arms now bound at his sides, he was unable to brace himself when his captors threw him to the ground. Gundolf groaned as his foes kicked and rolled his body into position upon the cold damp earth.

'That will do,' a cold voice spoke from somewhere above him. The last thing Emil Gundolf heard was the sound of his wool shirt being cut open and the wet flop of his guts as they spilled from his torn belly.

CHAPTER EIGHT

MATHIAS THULMANN SAT before the small table that rested within his room at The Grey Crone, staring intently at the old map of the district he had acquired from the village scribe. It was a crude thing, and now bore the irregular splotches and blemishes the witch hunter had daubed onto it.

Each splotch was accompanied by a number, and each number accompanied an entry in the cloth-bound chapbook in which Thulmann had written all the information he had gained from the villagers. He rubbed his eyes, cursing once again the ethereal weapons of the Dark Gods: ignorance, superstition and fear. They had certainly been working overtime upon the people of Klausberg. The peasant farmers, tradesmen and rugged foresters were jumping at every shadow, cringing at every sound in the night, certain that the perpetrator of these vile crimes (which they had named the Klausner daemon) was near. Thulmann had hoped to learn something of value. Perhaps he had, but separating it from all the chaff of panic and superstition was going to be a monumental task.

He read one of the entries in his chapbook, sipping at a glass of wine from the bottle Reikhertz had provided him with. It was a perfect example of the confused nonsense that he was coming up against in his inquiries. A swineherd had gone out at night to investigate the agitated sounds of his hogs. Turning from the swine pens, he had nearly expired from fright when he had seen the evil eyes of a daemon glaring at him from the dark loft of his barn.

A few quick questions about the daemonic eyes and their size in relation to the dimensions of the loft, had convinced Thulmann that they were not nearly so large nor so extraordinary as the man had imagined them.

The witch hunter drew a line through the record. The swineherd's account was almost certainly a case of mistaken identity, in this instance a harmless owl transformed by shadow and fear into some emissary of the Ruinous Powers, one of many accounts Thulmann was finding himself drawing marks through.

It was a strange paradox. On the one hand he had Wilhelm Klausner, who, for reasons of his own, refused to admit the possibility of the unnatural no matter the evidence that might be presented. On the other hand he had the people of Klausberg, who were seeing a ghoul behind every tree and a blood-hungry fiend under every haycart.

Thulmann looked again at his map. There were several marks that were made not in the blue paint with which he had denoted the peasants' accounts, but in bright red. These denoted incidents that could not be disputed, incidents that were without a doubt the work of the witch hunter's quarry. For at each of those sites, some forsaken soul had met a gruesome and hideous death.

The witch hunter counted them again, shaking his head at the enormity of the horror that had struck this community. Twenty-seven. Twenty-seven red marks. Twenty-seven lives ended by this unholy marauder.

Thulmann studied the locations of the victims, trying to decide if there was any pattern to the fiend's carnage. But there was nothing. North of the village, east of the village, south, west. In woods and in fields, pasture and bog, it seemed to make no difference.

Thulmann sighed in frustration at the turn his thoughts had taken. Klausner's mythical wolf would have chosen some sort of hunting ground, its methods and actions betraying its simple brute intellect. If the enemy were a simple beast, it should have displayed such character from the beginning, stalking a particular sort of prey and only under particular conditions. But this fiend must be something else. Thulmann wondered if the killer's disordered mind still clung to any sort of purpose, or had the killings themselves become all the purpose they needed? Those who dabbled in the black arts did so at the peril of not only their immortal soul, but their very ability to reason.

Once again, Thulmann found himself considering the foul Erasmus Kleib. He had all too readily dismissed the sorcerer as a madman, falling into the same trap that had caused his mentor to underestimate their foe, at the cost of his life.

Kleib had been a twisted and evil man, but he had not been truly insane. He had been all too aware of the horror and perversion of what he did; he had appreciated in the full that his actions were lawless and murderous. That great intellect, that powerful mind had been twisted, tainted, but it had not been broken. It was not the base cunning of a madman that had allowed Erasmus Kleib to remain at large, committing his atrocities, for so many years, but the wicked application of that tremendous intellect. It had been all too easy to call him a madman, as if that would excuse his seduction to the ways of evil.

Thulmann considered if he might not be doing the same with the Klausberg fiend. He removed a thin volume, bound in leather, from an oilskin pouch that rested upon the covers of his bed. Speaking a quick prayer for guidance to his patron god Sigmar, he opened the slender tome.

It was a simple thing, employed by many witch hunters. Upon the pages of the slender book were drawn many of the symbols and signs employed by those who practised the darker aspects of wizardry. The more potent sigils and scripts employed to create the full designs were absent, but enough were present to allow the witch hunter to recognise such symbols should he encounter them. It was a book Thulmann consulted only with reluctance, for even such reduced emblems of sorcery disquieted him, but there were times when its usefulness could not be denied.

He flicked slowly through the worn pages, trying to match one of the patterns he saw there to the arrangement of crimson splotches upon his map.

A sharp knock upon the door roused him from his tedious labour. The witch hunter rubbed at his eyes again, slipping the thin volume back into its sheath.

After hours of study, Thulmann decided that his sudden inspiration was an unlikely one. Whatever foul ritual his nameless foe was perpetrating, the sites of the killings did not seem to be a part of it. None of the symbols he had tried to impress upon the map had fit, no matter how complex. There were always other murders, other deaths that did not conform to whatever pattern Thulmann tried to establish.

A sudden chill crawled along the witch hunter's spine. Unless the fiend were crafty enough to slay simply to break such a pattern. If that were the case, it would truly take the hand of Sigmar to outguess the monster.

Thulmann sipped at his glass of wine, grown warm from his neglect, as he walked across the room and opened the door. He half expected to see Reikhertz the innkeeper, following his established custom of inquiring as to the witch hunter's needs before seeking his own bed. Instead, Thulmann was surprised to find Streng standing there. An uneasy alarm crept into him. It would have taken no mean matter to make the mercenary leave his drinking and gambling after their collection of statements had been completed.

'Seems you need to update that doodle of yours,' Streng said, a wicked grin on his face. 'Reikhertz just let a very distressed fellow in. Insists he needs to speak to the witch hunter.'

Thulmann set his glass down with a groan. 'My ears are fairly bleeding already with the imaginings of these people. If I have one more hell-hound described to me by some oaf who wouldn't know a troll from a fox with the mange, I swear that the lout will be introduced to a tall tree and a short drop.'

Streng scratched his scraggly beard. 'Not that sort of thing he wants to see you about,' the mercenary informed him. 'Seems this fellow had a brother. A brother who went out tonight and never came back.'

Thulmann stared intently at his henchman, his irritation forgotten. 'Go on,' he told him.

'Well, this fellow gets worried when his brother doesn't come back. So he leaves his brother's wife and children safely locked up in the house and goes out looking for him.' The mercenary looked over at the map sprawled across the table. 'You better stock up on red paint,' Streng nodded toward the table. Thulmann reached behind him, snatching up his weapons belt from where it lay draped over the bed frame. Pausing to grab up his hat and cloak, he joined Streng in the hallway.

'Have the Klausners been informed?' he asked in a low voice.

'Not by our man,' Streng told him. 'But in a village this size, you can bet that they have more than a few eyes and ears.'

Thulmann strode toward the stairs. 'Then we'd better be quick. I'd like a little time to examine the surroundings before Wilhelm's men arrive to run us off,' the witch hunter said as he descended the stairs.

THE MOONS OF Mannsleib and Morrsleib were low in the darkened sky as the witch hunter and his party made their way through the maze of thin, pole-like trees. He had taken a reluctant Reikhertz along with them, as well as the brother of the slain man to act as their guide.

The brother, one Fritz Gundolf, had been no less reluctant than the squeamish Reikhertz to accompany Thulmann on his gruesome expedition. It had taken an exertion of his authority and a few thinly veiled threats to impel Fritz to lead them to his brother's remains. Having seen the mutilated body once, Fritz was visibly horrified at the prospect of revisiting the horrid scene, taking long pulls from the squat clay bottle of ale Reikhertz had provided him with, trying to bolster his courage and numb his fear.

A chill wind whipped Thulmann's cloak about as he followed the light cast by the lanterns borne by Reikhertz and Streng, desiccated leaves swirling about his every step.

He glanced about him, remarking once more upon the remoteness of the area. They were so close to the heart of the district, and yet to the witch hunter, it felt every bit as lonely here as on the slopes of the Grey Mountains or the haunted domains near the dreaded Drakwald Forest.

There was an ugly reason for this, one which Fritz Gundolf had repeated to him. The Klausners might be the lords and masters of the district, but they were not well-loved and their black-stoned keep and its surrounding forest were openly shunned by the common folk. It had been the rather diminished value of the land adjoining that of the Klausners that had prompted the Gundolfs' employer, a Klausberg lumber merchant, to purchase the property.

Only the lure of money could give any of the people of Klausberg reason enough to linger so near the ill-favoured family's holdings.

What had the Klausners done to earn such enmity, the witch hunter wondered? True, the younger son, Anton, was a vicious and foul-tempered brute, but Wilhelm Klausner himself seemed a fairly considerate lord, his inability to put a stop to the murders notwithstanding, and Gregor Klausner was a bright and honourable man, one who had a deep commitment and affection for the people of the district.

The villagers and farmers could certainly have done much worse by way of rulers. Why then the resentment and fear? Was it some legacy from the Klausners' careers as witch hunters?

Thulmann knew only too well the fear and nervous suspicion a witch hunter evoked in all he encountered. But was that enough to explain the stigma that clung to the Klausners, or was it something more? Time and again over the course of the night, Thulmann had heard hushed voices speak of the dread curse that hovered about the patriarchs of the Klausner line, the horrible thing that would ravage the land until it bore the elder Klausner's soul back with it to the blackest pits of the Dark Gods.

Ahead of him, the lanterns came to a halt. Thulmann advanced, joining his companions. Streng and Reikhertz were looking at Fritz. The forester was turned around, his back facing the direction in which they had been travelling.

The trembling man took another pull from his bottle, spilling the fiery liquor about his shirt. With his other hand, he stabbed a finger at the trees behind him.

'That way,' the man choked as the alcohol stung his throat. 'Emil is in there! And ain't nothing you can do to make me go no further!' he swore, staring at the witch hunter with a mixture of terror and defiance. Thulmann nodded, drawing one of his pistols from its holster.

'Very well, friend Gundolf,' his silky voice spoke. 'But you will remain fixed to this spot.' He wagged the barrel of his gun at the subdued peasant. 'I warn you, even in poor light I am an excellent shot.'

Thulmann stalked ahead and gestured for Streng and Reikhertz to accompany him. A part of him disliked threatening the forester, he had after all done his duty and had already displayed a commendable degree of fortitude by returning to this place despite the possibility that whatever had killed his brother might still be abroad. Yet another part of him understood that only by keeping Fritz more afraid of him than whatever had killed his brother would Thulmann keep the man from fleeing back to his hovel as soon as the witch hunter was out of sight. It was an unfair and brutal sort of efficiency, but that did not lessen its effectiveness.

The smell of blood and excrement announced the body long before the light from the lanterns revealed it. Thulmann deftly relieved Reikhertz of his lantern as the innkeeper withdrew to vomit beside one of the spindly trees.

The form sprawled across the grass had spilled its guts in an entirely different fashion.

Thulmann stepped closer, holding his lantern high to reveal as much of the sorry form and its surroundings as he could. Once again, blood stained very little of the ground, most of it splashed across the ground in the familiar south-easterly direction. The body itself was hideously mangled, but the witch hunter had some idea what he was looking at, and what he was looking for.

A cursory glance showed Thulmann that the forester's belly had been slashed open, his intestines and stomach removed and placed on the ground beside the corpse's left boot. Further mutilation had occurred in the chest, the ribcage again cut open and spread.

This time it was not the heart that had been removed, but the lungs. The witch hunter's mind swept back to an incident three years before, in a small town just outside Talabheim where a fledgling daemonologist and necromancer named Anatol Drexel had practised his foul arts. One of his rituals had been to expunge the 'breath of life' from a corpse by puncturing its lungs.

According to blasphemous texts written by no less terrible a personage than the infamous Doom Lord of Middenheim, doing so would make the corpse ideal for a sort of grisly pseudo-resurrection as one of the undead. But if that was what had been done here, why had the perpetrator of this atrocity left the body behind, where it was certain to be discovered?

'This wolf is getting pretty damn artsy, eh Mathias?' Streng chuckled with morbid humour. He looked away from his employer, delivering a gruesome description of the corpse for

Reikhertz's benefit. Thulmann ignored the renewed sound of retching and leaned down, inspecting the corpse a little more closely.

Once again, the blood had been drained from the body, but this time the bloodletting had not been achieved by a stab into the jugular vein, but by the more crude method of slitting the victim's throat. The witch hunter looked again at the spread of the blood on the ground. This was not the precise spray-effect that had marked the site of Skimmel's death, but the more sloppy effect of liquid discharged from a bowl.

The witch hunter stood back, studying the scene in its entirety. There had been less care made with this murder, the ritual fashion was there, but it was less efficient, less precise. There had been no attempt at further mutilation to obscure the intentions of the culprit, and the bloodletting had been crude compared to the single deep stab that had ended Skimmel's life.

There was an overall suggestion of haste and carelessness about this killing. Thulmann considered what this might mean. Was the killer losing patience with whatever sorcery he was trying to work, or perhaps there was an element of timing to his magic, and the time left to him was growing short?

Perhaps the fiend he sought was becoming frightened, worried that he might be caught now that an outsider was investigating the killings. But such a conclusion would mean that the fiend did not fear the Klausners, who had been hunting him now for over a month. Thulmann wondered if he dare follow that notion where it might lead him.

'Our wolf has a friend,' Streng interrupted. Thulmann looked over at his henchman. Streng was pointing his foot at an impression on the ground. 'Boots, and rather fine ones,' the mercenary commented. 'Much better than that poor dead bastard is wearing,' he added with a nod of his head toward the feet of the corpse. Thulmann did not need to shift his gaze to recall that Gundolf had been wearing a set of badly patched fur boots.

The mercenary moved about, setting his foot beside another impression in the ground. Unlike the first, this mark was somewhat smaller than Streng's foot, though it was likewise the mark of a heeled boot, not unlike a cavalryman's. 'Might even be a third one,' the henchman told Thulmann. He gestured toward a deep mark beside one of the trees. 'Of course, it is only a partial and the man might have slipped when he made it, which would have stretched it a bit.'

Thulmann nodded in approval. 'The Count of Ostland lost a good scout when you deserted,' he observed. 'Though I imagine that the longevity of his sergeants has improved in your absence.'

The witch hunter began to stalk the area, inspecting the ground for footprints. 'A good deal of tracks coming from that way,' he pointed the barrel of his pistol in the direction that they themselves had come.

'Aye,' agreed Streng. 'That's how they brought the sorry bugger here. He must have tried to dig his feet in every step of the way to judge by the marks.'

Thulmann circled the area again, inspecting the ground for further clues. After several minutes, he straightened, shaking his head in disgust. 'They may have been sloppy in everything else,' he hissed, 'but they made certain to leave no sign of where they went after committing their little atrocity.'

'We might find something when the sun comes up,' suggested Streng.

The witch hunter shook his head.

'We are on borrowed time already,' he told his underling. 'I think it is asking too much of even Sigmar to be free of Klausner's meddling that long.' A sudden idea caused the witch hunter to break into a sly smile. 'Of course, we might avail ourselves of his hospitality while he concerns himself with this occurrence.'

Thulmann considered his idea a bit more, letting a slight laugh slip from his mouth. 'We might even find him rather accommodating if he thinks he is keeping us from discovering this spectacle.' Thulmann cast one last look at Gundolf's body, then motioned for Streng to withdraw.

'Let's fetch Reikhertz and send him on his way, and tell that man Fritz to keep a close tongue.' Thulmann smiled again. 'It wouldn't do for his lordship to know we've been here. Not until I'm ready, at least.'

CHAPTER NINE

THE WITCH HUNTER found Klausner Keep in a great deal of agitation as he and Streng rode their steeds toward the imposing structure. Every window seemed to have been lit up, blazing with light and making it look as if the black toad of the keep had suddenly opened a chaotic multitude of eyes. The mouth formed by the gates of the keep yawned wide, and Thulmann could see riders galloping from the fortress, half their number holding aloft flickering torches that betrayed their advance. The horsemen thundered down the path, the hooves of their steeds flinging mud and pulped leaves in every direction.

Thulmann watched them advance with an elaborate calmness. Beside him, Streng caressed the stock of his crossbow.

The foremost rider pulled his horse savagely to a stop only a dozen feet or so from where Thulmann and Streng's horses stood beside the road. The sudden halt brought the rest of the company to a disordered stop, men and mounts grunting in protest. Anton Klausner curled his lip as he considered the witch hunter.

'Such unpleasant things one finds upon the roads after dark,' the young lord said, his smouldering eyes locking with Thulmann's. 'I should have expected to find you occupied elsewhere.'

Anton's expression turned into a look of suspicion as much as contempt. 'Or were you unaware of the latest killing?'

'I am well aware that the fiend has struck again,' Thulmann returned, choosing to ignore the rogue's baiting tone. 'And you might have found me investigating the matter had my guide not deserted me.'

'And you thought to conscript a new one from the keep?' Anton Klausner's smile was every bit as unfriendly as an orc's. 'Somehow, I don't think you will find my father eager to bend on his knee to please you. We are well capable of catching a simple wolf.'

'You've done a fine job of it so far,' observed Streng, shifting his position so that the bolt of his weapon was aimed at the brash noble. Anton Klausner gave the henchman a murderous look.

'Your pet vermin is speaking out of turn, witch finder,' he hissed. 'Keep him in line lest I be forced to teach him some respect.'

'You are welcome to try,' Thulmann told him, his silky voice remaining level. 'Of course, he isn't so restrained as I am when it comes to putting swaggering hotheads in their place.' Anton Klausner's hand shot to the hilt of his sword. Thulmann could hear the nervous muttering of some of the other horsemen, uncertain whether they should aid their master, uneasy about raising arms against an agent of the temple.

'Stop it at once! This bickering is pointless!' Ivar Kohl manoeuvred his steed between the two men. He glared for a moment at Anton, who reluctantly let his hand slip from his weapon.

'You must forgive Master Anton's rudeness, Herr Thulmann,' the steward said, his face displaying the false pleasantry it habitually slipped into. 'The news of this latest tragedy has shocked and disturbed his lordship, indeed all of us, greatly.'

'I am certain that it has,' Thulmann stated, keeping his eyes on the scowling Anton. 'In fact, it was on this point that I journeyed to the keep. I wish to discuss with his lordship how we might bury our differences of opinion in this matter and combine our resources.'

'You will find that my father is indisposed,' Anton said, fairly spitting the words. Kohl cast another hostile look at the young noble. When he turned his attention back to Thulmann, he was once again displaying his oily smile.

'It is true that his lordship is still very weak, but I think that he would receive a man such as yourself,' Kohl told the witch hunter.

'It is a pity that you were unable to verify this tragic account. I am certain that the patriarch would be most anxious to hear any news about this matter.'

'As I have said,' Thulmann informed the steward, 'my guide let his fear get the better of him. No matter, I doubt if we would be able to find anything in the dark in any event.'

Ivar Kohl nodded his head, chortling with enthusiastic agreement. 'Oh doubtless, doubtless. Nothing more foolish than crashing into trees in the pitch of night. Still,' Kohl shrugged his shoulders, a gesture that somehow reminded Thulmann of an over-eager vulture, 'the simple folk of this district would not be so understanding. They would take any delay on the part of his lordship in this matter as a sign that he was disinterested and unconcerned. So, for us, I fear, this foolish venture is unavoidable.'

Kohl turned his gaze back on Anton Klausner, gesturing with a sidewise motion of his head that the young noble should get his men moving again.

'I do hope that you and his lordship can come to an agreement,' Kohl told the witch hunter as Anton's men began to gallop off down the path.

The steward turned his own horse around. 'Rest assured, Herr Thulmann, we will send word back to the keep in the unlikely event that we discover anything.' With a slight wave of his hand, Kohl joined Anton and the pair set off in pursuit of the departed soldiers.

'There goes a man who is quite pleased with himself,' commented Thulmann as he and Streng continued their own journey. 'A man who is trying to be deceitful is always the easiest to deceive.'

The witch hunter reflected upon the exchange as they continued to ride. Clearly the steward Kohl had been the one in command, a certain sign that Wilhelm Klausner did not trust his son Anton with the task of beating Thulmann to the location of Gundolf's body, even to mollify his son's inflated ego.

He could appreciate the elder Klausner's position: he could ill afford to let an outsider solve these crimes, and was desperate to maintain his edge over Thulmann. At best, to allow such a situation to occur would certainly cause his perception of power and authority in the district to diminish greatly. At worst, perhaps the patriarch feared the unearthing of some old legacy of the Klausner clan, some evidence that the curse was more than a simple fable. No doubt Kohl had orders to rearrange the murder scene when he came upon it, to mislead or confuse the Templar's own investigations. Perhaps it might even resemble the work of a wolf by the time Kohl was finished with things.

Thulmann also pondered the absence of Gregor in the hastily assembled hunting party. By all accounts, Gregor was the more intelligent and capable of Wilhelm's two sons, and certainly Thulmann's own impression of the young noble did not contradict such an evaluation.

Why then had Wilhelm sent Anton rather than Gregor? Was there some motive behind the patriarch's decision, or had Gregor refused to be a party to Wilhelm's deceptions and intrigues? The young man did have a very deep-seated sense of honour, one that might be very easily offended by Wilhelm's plotting.

Certainly, Gregor had displayed a much more helpful attitude than his father and seemed just as eager to end this menace to the people of Klausberg as the witch hunter himself. Such feelings would not lend themselves well to old Wilhelm's desperate and selfish attempts to maintain his authority.

Thulmann decided that when he reached the keep, he would speak with the young Gregor openly about what he had learned from his study of Gundolf's corpse. Sharing such intelligence with the young noble might further ingratiate Thulmann into Gregor's confidence, and the witch hunter was in desperate need of at least one ally at the keep.

WILHELM KLAUSNER WAS indeed indisposed when Thulmann arrived at the keep. The servant had conducted the witch hunter and his henchman to a small parlour in which he had found the patriarch's wife seated in a high-backed chair knitting a shawl with a pair of long iron needles. The woman smiled when she saw the witch hunter, apologising profusely for her husband's inability to receive visitors. He had not been in the best of health lately and recent events had not improved the situation at all.

'I am afraid that you are to blame for some of the worry he feels,' Ilsa Klausner told him. 'These terrible killings have been distressing him horribly, sapping his strength. But I think it was your arrival that really weakened him,' she confessed. 'He has lost his old self-confidence. I think he takes your arrival here to mean that others have lost confidence in him as well.'

'I am not here to usurp his lordship,' Thulmann said, seating his lean form in the chair opposite the lady. 'My only concern is to learn what is behind these outrages and put an end to them.'

Ilsa Klausner bent forward, severing a strand of wool with her teeth. 'I understand that, Herr Thulmann. But you must understand, protecting this district is my husband's duty, and one he takes very seriously. I am afraid that he takes your being here as something between an insult and a challenge.' The woman smiled, setting aside her handiwork. 'I know that a person should not speak so openly with a man in your profession, you are so unaccustomed to people speaking their mind. But that is how I see things between yourself and my husband.'

The sound of boots clicking upon the tiles of the floor caused Ilsa to look away from the witch hunter. Thulmann followed the woman's gaze, not entirely surprised to find Gregor stepping into the room.

'Ernst said that we had guests,' Gregor said as he walked toward his mother's chair. He leaned forward, allowing the older woman to kiss his cheek. Straightening, he bowed his head toward Thulmann. 'I am sorry that you have again been cheated of a decent night's sleep, Herr Thulmann.'

'It is another quality of the insidious practices of the forces of darkness that they must wait for the most uncharitable hours in which to work their devilry,' the witch hunter said. 'One becomes accustomed to irregular hours.' Thulmann's eyes narrowed. 'Of course I was rather surprised not to find you with your brother. We passed him and his men on the road coming here.'

Gregor and his mother shared an awkward look for a moment. Ilsa was the first to look away and speak. 'My son did want to go. He insisted, but my husband forbade him,' she stated. 'My husband is a very cautious man and he felt it would be far too reckless to jeopardise both of his sons upon such a potentially dangerous excursion.'

'It is just as well that you did remain at the keep,' Thulmann told the young noble. Gregor Klausner's expression became one of cautious interest. 'You see, there were some things which I wanted to discuss with you. I have learned quite a bit since we parted ways, but I feel that I need a man of your insight to evaluate the facts I have collected.'

Ilsa started to rise from her chair. 'That means, I suppose, that you have men's business to discuss,' she said. Gregor motioned for her to sit down.

'No need to leave, mother,' he said. 'When Herr Thulmann was here last, he expressed a wish to see the family records. I think that we can have our discussion there just as easily as here.' Gregor turned his head back towards the witch hunter. 'Herr Thulmann, shall we withdraw to the library then?' He extended his hand to indicate the open doorway through which he had made his own entrance.

The witch hunter nodded and rose from his chair. He bowed again to Ilsa Klausner.

'Give my regards to your husband,' the witch hunter said. The woman smiled up at him as she returned to her knitting.

'Assuredly,' she told Thulmann. 'But not until you have finished your business with my son,' she added with a conspiratorial wink. Thulmann marvelled at her for a moment, then followed Gregor from the room.

THE LIBRARY WAS a large room, dominating one corner of the keep. It might once have been a barracks of some sort. Thulmann could still see the remains of wooden beams sunken into the perimeter walls of the room, the last remnants of walkways and ladders that had once provided archers with access points to the narrow windows set some fifteen feet above the floor.

Now the vast hall had been fully converted, mammoth wooden bookcases filling the centre of the room. Each was at least ten feet in height, and at least three feet in depth. Doubled upon one another, sometimes in ranks four and five long, the cases made a maze of the old chamber. Each was filled almost to bursting with thin folios and monstrously bloated tomes, mounds of cylindrical scroll-cases and stacks of unbound parchment and paper.

The musty odour of rotting wood and mould was thick and heavy about the hall. Thulmann smiled to himself as he was conducted into the room. How many times had he stood in rooms exactly like this stalking some obscure shred of knowledge? For every second of terror spent confronting some loathsome visitation of the Ruinous Powers how many hours had he spent rummaging about in some dusty old library?

'Your mother is quite a remarkable woman,' Thulmann told the young noble. Gregor looked away from lighting a number of candles fixed into the claws of a candelabra shaped like a wrought-iron sea monster standing at the centre of a small desk.

'That she is,' Gregor admitted. 'She has a sharp mind and a proud spirit, and isn't afraid to let anyone know it. When my father went away to serve the temple, Ivar Kohl tried to run the estate his own way, as he had when my grandfather left, but my mother wouldn't let him. She had her own ideas, and was not about to let Kohl push her around.'

Gregor chuckled as he slipped into his recollections. 'I have to say, even old Ivar would have to confess that she ran things very well until my father returned.'

Thulmann only partly heard what Gregor was saying, his attention instead fixed upon the large map of the district hanging upon one of the walls. The witch hunter could see more detail was present in this work than the one back in his rooms at The Grey Crone.

He stared at it for some moments, studying its every line, imagining red splotches upon its surface. There had to be a key, something that would make these killings take up some semblance of reason. It was like one of the cryptograms such groups like the Pallisades played with. Once the code was discovered, the message would stand revealed. But what was the code? And what was the hideous message it concealed?

The witch hunter looked away from the map, staring intently at Gregor. 'I need your help,' he told the noble. 'You are aware that another life was taken this night. I have seen the body, and it was not the work of any brute beast. My associate,' Thulmann indicated Streng, who had slouched down into a heavy chair and was studiously inspecting a portfolio of exotic Bretonnian woodcuts, 'found tracks this time. Footprints of at least two men.'

Gregor considered Thulmann's statement, striding back and forth behind the desk as he turned them over in his mind. 'Then it is not one fiend we are seeking, but some dark conspiracy!' he exclaimed.

'The secret, I feel, is somehow tied into your family history,' the witch hunter told him. He waved his arm to encompass the towering bookcases behind him. 'Somewhere in these records may be the clue we need to learn the nature of this fiend.' The witch hunter clenched his fist. 'And once I have put a name to this pestilence, then I may be able to guess its intentions, and predict where it will strike next.'

'And destroy him,' Gregor stated.

'And destroy him,' the witch hunter concurred.

CRUEL EYES STUDIED the two-storey, half-timber structure. The night was nearly spent, the moons already retreating toward the horizon. There was not much time left in which to act, but Carandini was nothing if not a careful man. He wanted to give the poison every chance to work its course.

A few of the brutish farmers had been quite large, and it might take the poison a little longer to run its course through bodies so laden down with meat and muscle.

The necromancer looked at the rotting thing beside him. He had long ago lost any sense of horror at the many appearances assumed by death. In fact, to him there was nothing quite so wondrous as watching that almost mystical transformation as a living body became a corpse, to see the corruption work its way through the flesh, as tissue withered and bones broke through the weakened flesh.

The necromancer smiled at the stiff, still figure. His pale hand patted some of the mould from the front of its tunic, stopping when the rotted cloth began to fall apart. Dismayed, Carandini instead concentrated on stuffing the creature's dangling eye back into its socket. He found the organ reluctant to return to its place however, popping free whenever he removed his hand.

Annoyed, Carandini produced his dagger and pounded the greasy, staring object into the zombie's skull with the hilt of the weapon.

Turning from his gruesome maintenance, the necromancer stared keenly at the house once more. He had come upon it shortly after dark, creeping across the farmyard to the brick-lined well that stood before the house. The poison had gone in, and he had slunk back to the shadows. It had been hard not to laugh when the wife of one of the farmers had emerged to retrieve a bucket of water from the well.

The woman could not imagine how astounding they would find this evening's gruel. Indeed, they would never eat anything else ever again.

Carandini motioned for the creature beside him and the five others like it to advance. The necromancer followed after his loathsome creations. He would allow his zombies to enter the structure ahead of him, let them discover if anyone still lived. After all, a knife in the ribs or a hatchet in the head would not do them any great deal of harm. Nothing that couldn't be made right by a few incantations and a little baby's fat.

The walking corpses stalked towards the door, their movements stiff and silent and began to batter on the heavy door with their decaying fists.

The necromancer watched the windows of the house. If anyone was still inside, they could not fail to hear the commotion. However, no light appeared in any of the windows, and the only sound to rise from the structure was the howling of a dog. Carandini smiled. If he ever tired of trying to unlock the secrets of death, he might make a successful career as a professional poisoner back in his native Tilea.

After a few minutes, the relentless pounding of the zombies caused the door to collapse inward with a resounding crash. Carandini heard the frightened yip and the angry snarl of a dog as his undead slaves marched inside. The necromancer waited a few moments more to follow after them, then with swift, scuttling steps, made his way into the residence.

The main room of the farmhouse was a shambles, furniture tipped over, part of a rug pushed into the embers in the fire-pit where the covering was now slowly smouldering.

Carandini strode towards the hearth and pulled the rug from the fire, stamping out the fledgling flames with his boots. It would hardly do for the place to burn down. The necromancer looked up from his task, his weasel-like face grinning as he spied the large iron pot that had fallen to the floor. As he had known, there was some still-warm gruel at the bottom of the pot.

Another thing that the Tileans despised about the people of the Empire – their predictability. They were so disgustingly easy to predict, their thoughts regimented and unimaginative. It was no wonder that all the great thinkers and artisans were Tilean born and bred. The necromancer smiled again – as his scheming ally would learn soon enough for himself.

Carandini made his way from the living room, throwing aside the heavy fur curtain that separated a niche at the rear of the room. He peered into the gloomy space beyond, staring at the simple straw mattress, at the filthy fur blankets, at the two bodies lying sprawled upon the floor.

Carandini pursed his lips and tutted as he saw the corpses. 'Must have been something they ate,' he muttered, wiping a stringy lock of hair from his face.

The necromancer went back into the living room, this time following the small hallway, finding another tiny room at its terminus. The hanging here had already been torn down, and the necromancer could see two gaunt figures standing above the straw bed. He shuffled into the chamber, oblivious to the reeking corpse-things, and smiled down at the two bodies curled upon the bed.

There was no need to feel for any sign of warmth or pulse, the purpling tinge of the corpses told the necromancer that his poison had done its work. He looked at each of the stationary corpse things. They did not glance at him, but remained motionless, their colourless eyes focused on the wall.

'Take these into the other room,' Carandini told his slaves. There was no real need to speak to them, it was the exertion of the necromancer's will that caused the zombies to obey his commands, but there were times when Carandini slipped into his old habits.

The corpse-creatures bent forward, almost in perfect synchronisation, and pulled the two bodies from the bed. Carandini did not linger to see his slaves complete their task, but slipped back into the hall, climbing the stairs that led to the upper floor of the dwelling.

At the top of the stairs he found another of his zombie slaves, this one standing idle over the body of a very fat and very old woman. A small dog dangled from the monster's arm, worrying the rotted flesh viciously. The zombie was oblivious to the damage being inflicted upon it, its vacant stare contemplating the floor.

As Carandini came forward, he extended his will. The zombie lifted its free arm and brought its skeletal fist smashing down into the skull of the dog. The animal gave a muffled yelp, then fell to the floor, its weight snapping the arm it had been worrying like a twig. Carandini stared down at the dead animal, then looked up at his rotting creation. A look of annoyance crawled across his features. The necromancer pulled his dagger and grabbed something dangling from the zombie's face. With one deft stroke, he cut the veins connecting the recalcitrant eye to the creature's skull and tossed the disagreeable organ down the stairs.

'Take that,' the necromancer ordered, pointing at the old woman's body with his knife, 'below.' Once more he did not wait for his creation to obey, but continued down the narrow hall. A sudden sound made the necromancer pause. It did not sound like one of his creations blundering about, he thought. Carandini paused then hurried into a room at the far end of the hallway.

He found another of his creatures here, its skull-like face looking blankly at the wall. The bed was actually equipped with an iron frame, though the bedding itself was the usual pile of straw covered by furs and blankets. Two bodies were sprawled here, but they did not interest Carandini as much as the others had. No, it was the tiny shape nestled between them, the tiny little shape that sobbed with a fear its small mind could not fully appreciate.

The child's eyes were locked on the grisly shape of the zombie, not even looking away when the necromancer glided towards the bed.

'Oh,' Carandini said, his voice soft. 'You poor little thing,' he reached forward, picking the child from between his dead parents. The boy began to cry as the necromancer held him. 'You have been a bad little thing, haven't you?' the necromancer said. He exerted his will, causing the zombie to pull the child's father from the bed. He could hear the other two zombies pulling bodies from one of the other bedrooms. The child hid his face in the fur of Carandini's cassock, and the necromancer gently patted his back.

'You really should have eaten your gruel like a good little boy,' Carandini told him, striding from the room ahead of the overladen zombie. He paused in the hallway, shifting his grip on the boy and removing a small object from a pouch on his belt. His associate's contingency was a small thing, and something of an enigma to Carandini. He was not entirely sure how it would benefit them to have the witch hunter discover it here, but such had been his confederate's directions when he had given it to Carandini.

The necromancer let the small object fall to the floor with a metallic ping.

Carandini walked ahead of his zombies, willing them to bring the bodies into the living room. It would be much easier to perform the ritual over all the bodies at once. The little boy began to cry again in the necromancer's arms.

Carandini set him down, smiling at the dirty-faced blond child. The child's face was dripping with tears and a thin stream of snot dangled from his nose.

'Now then,' the necromancer said, 'don't cry so.' His eyes lit up, and he let a false enthusiasm spring into his tone. 'You know, I might have something for you if you're good and quiet.' He took a few dried berries and a tiny glass vial from a pouch on his belt.

So utterly predictable, these men of the Empire, Carandini thought as the boy stuffed the berries into his mouth. That was why his confederate's ploy was unnecessary. Because the witch hunter would not be escaping the trap Carandini had set for him.

CHAPTER TEN

THE WITCH HUNTER shut the heavy wood-bound volume closed with a crash, pushing it across the table from him in disgust. He reached to his face, pulling away the tiny pair of pince-nez reading glasses he had adopted upon beginning his labour and rubbed his eyes, then snatched up the cup of now-cold tea a servant had brought to the library some hours ago.

The witch hunter made a sour face as the drink chilled his lips, cursing once more whatever thrice-damned sadist had constructed Klausner Keep. He could imagine a Kislevite kossar catching a cold within the gloomy damp of the fortress, with its infinite drafts and omnipresent chill. It had been a steady struggle to keep warm, and several times he had pondered casting some particularly uninformative volume into the hearth to augment the sparse heat being generated there. It had been a tedious vigil, delving into the massive collection of portfolios, books and uncollected manuscripts through the small hours of the morning and on until now, somewhere beyond the dreary walls, the sun was at its full height.

The sound caused the head resting on the other side of the table to shoot up, Gregor Klausner sputtering in surprise. The young noble cast an ashamed look over at the witch hunter.

'I am sorry, Herr Thulmann,' he said, trying to stifle a yawn. 'I must have dozed off for a moment.'

'Yes,' sighed Thulmann, pulling another massive old history toward him and flinging the cover open. 'You did,' he said, eyes locked upon the coarse yellow paper, 'about four hours ago.'

Gregor looked at the witch hunter, his face incredulous. 'Four hours?' He reached toward one of the cups, recoiling when he discovered that the tea had gone cold. 'Did I miss anything?'

The witch hunter kept his eyes on the pages before him. 'Streng ran out of questionable wood cuts about the time you took your nap and left, most likely to avail himself of the wine cellar or a chamber maid, whichever he happened upon first. Then about an hour ago Ivar Kohl returned, quite pleased with himself, though that quickly passed when I told him I wouldn't be needing to see the scene of the latest murder since I had already been there.'

'I should have thought he'd have told my father and had you removed from the keep,' commented Gregor.

'Perhaps he was too tired,' Thulmann answered, an uncertain quality to his voice. 'Of course, with somebody as duplicitous as your father's steward, I doubt his motives are quite so simple. Still, he's let me alone.'

Gregor rose from his chair, walking around the table to glance down at the book Thulmann was perusing. The young noble's brow knitted as he tried to decipher the scrawl.

'The career of Gustav Klausner, head of your line about three hundred years ago,' the witch hunter informed him. 'Volume eight of sixteen,' he added in a weary grumble.

'Have you found anything that might be of help?'

Thulmann looked up from the book, closing the ponderous volume. An ironic smile tugged at his face. He lifted a thick pile of parchment sheets from the tabletop. 'My notes,' he informed Gregor. 'Your family has quite a colourful history, as you might imagine.' He let the papers drop back to the table, rubbing his eyes again. Gregor leaned forward and read what the witch hunter had written.

'Renzo Helder, Hierophant of Nuln; Detlef-Erich von Engelstoss, the Ghoul-lord; Faustine Kurtz, the Black Witch…'

'It reads like a roll-call of the chamber of horrors in Marienburg,' the witch hunter told him. He pointed his finger at the volumes strewn about the table and the nearby floor. 'One could hardly accuse your ancestors of being idle.'

Thulmann took his notes from Gregor, leafing through them. 'I've tried to eliminate a lot of the chaff. We know that the foul art of necromancy is involved, so I have concentrated my efforts on that arena, eliminating such villains as...' Thulmann glanced over the top sheet, picking one of the names he had written down and then crossed out, 'Grey Seer Kripsnik. One of your father's investigations. Then there are the ones whom we know to be dead,' he rummaged through the notes again, choosing another name he had drawn a line through. 'For instance, Giselbrandt Vogheim, one of the disciples of the late and unlamented Great Enchanter. They still have his skull on public display at the temple of Morr in Carroburg.' The witch hunter shook his head and sighed. 'Even so, there are fifty-seven names on my little list.'

'Surely we could eliminate the older names,' observed Gregor. He gave voice to a soft laugh as he picked up the heavy tome Thulmann had been perusing. 'I mean, is it really necessary to go back three hundred years to put a name to our fiend?'

'It might be,' Thulmann informed him, his voice carrying a sense of deadly seriousness. 'The filthy art of necromancy has at its heart a twisted search for immortality, and it is a testament to the power and twisted genius of some who practise that art that they can extend their lives well beyond the span granted to them by the gods. Some can even bind their spirits to their bodies after death and motivate their own corpses into a gruesome parody of life.' Thulmann smiled thinly at the young noble. 'Who can say how long such a creature might harbour a grudge, and your ancestors have certainly crossed the path of more than a few of them.' He lifted the notes again.

'For instance, your grandfather was responsible for bringing down the profane Nehekharan vulture god cult established by the deranged wizard Tefnakht in Averheim. While he did succeed in bringing Sigmar's justice to the sorcerer, he himself was not satisfied that all of Tefnakht's followers had been captured. Your great grandfather made battle with a creature calling itself Khanzhik Vasalov somewhere near the Kislev border. His account relates that he took all the necessary precautions in disposing of the creature, but one can never be entirely certain with vampires.'

The witch hunter ruffled through his notes again. 'We might even go so far back as the progenitor of your line, Helmuth Klausner, who relates that he destroyed a vampire calling itself

Sibbechai in the cursed city of Mordheim over five hundred years ago.' Thulmann set the pages down.

'Even your father has his share of skeletons in his history,' he told Gregor. 'He tracked down the vile Enoch Silber in Helmsgart, although that loathsome individual escaped before he could be burned at the stake for his crimes.'

Thulmann paused, recalling his own encounter with the insane 'Corpse Collector' in the catacombs beneath Talabheim. The witch hunter still shuddered at the recollection of the madman's collection of 'bits and pieces', each crawling or screaming with an unnatural vitality. Silber was not Thulmann's best choice, being far too demented for the care and craft he had seen exhibited by the mind behind the Klausberg crimes, yet he was not a possibility the witch hunter wanted to dismiss out of hand. 'Then we have his encounter with the necromancer Dragan Radic, who was discovered looting old barrow mounds in Sylvania. There is an interesting fact that escaped your father, although he hung Radic, there have been recent reports of the necromancer being seen in the Ostermark.'

Thulmann shook his head again. 'Any one of these disgusting creatures might be behind your district's affliction. Or none of them, I have only just scratched the surface of your family's history. As you well know, it was common practice for all the Klausner men to offer their service to the temple.'

Gregor turned away. 'Yes,' he sighed, 'a tradition which my father has broken with. He has forbidden either of us to follow that tradition. He fears that by serving the temple we will somehow invite great tragedy upon ourselves.'

When Gregor turned back around he found the witch hunter staring at him intently. 'For myself, I would like to serve, to become a champion of Sigmar and purge this land of the forces of the Old Night. It would somehow give me a sense of worth, make me feel that I truly deserve to inherit the family fortune and the right to wear the name of Klausner.'

'And your brother?' Thulmann said, his voice low.

'I think he resents my father's edict even more than I,' Gregor told him. 'Anton has always lived his life under a shadow. Mine, I am afraid. He's lived his life knowing that everything he saw, everything he touched, would one day be inherited by me. I imagine that makes him feel somehow less important than me, as if he didn't matter as much. Becoming a witch hunter would have given him purpose, made him feel that he had worth and value.'

'And yet, if anything, your brother is more eager to please your father than you are,' Thulmann pointed out. Gregor conceded the issue.

'Yes, and he has always done so,' he said. 'Anton has always tried to impress my father, in whatever way he can. He might not like my father's edict, but he would never question him about it.'

The door of the library suddenly swung inward, causing both men to turn around in alarm, Thulmann's hand sliding toward the pistol resting beside his papers on the table. Standing in the doorway was a grimy, flush-faced man wearing a tunic of studded leather over his stained breeches and shirt. Streng grinned through his unkempt beard.

'Sorry to disturb you, Mathias,' he said, hooking his thumbs in his belt. 'Thought you might be interested to know that our friend struck again last night.' Streng's smile grew broader as he elaborated. 'It seems our foe is getting bolder. They wiped out an entire household this time.'

'What?' exclaimed Gregor, shock and fury filling his voice. Thulmann motioned for the young noble to be silent.

'Where did this happen?' the witch hunter asked. 'And how did you come to hear of it?'

'Not far from here,' the mercenary answered. 'Only a short ride. Heard about it from one of his,' Streng pointed a finger at the young Klausner, 'brother's bully boys.'

'Well, that answers our questions about why Kohl was content to leave me here,' Thulmann said in disgust. 'They must have discovered this atrocity last night.'

'Could be,' agreed Streng. 'But shouldn't we go and have a look anyway?' There was a note of enthusiasm in the thug's voice.

'Kohl might have overlooked something of value,' Thulmann said after a moment of thought. 'In any event, we shall be no worse off than we are now.' He looked over at Gregor Klausner. 'I imagine that you want to come as well?'

'Try and stop me,' Gregor told him, the lisp stretching his words. Thulmann studied the determination, the smouldering outrage in the young noble.

'Then let us be on our way,' Thulmann said.

* * *

BENEATH THE SHELTER of the few rotting beams that were the last
remains of the old cottage's roof, Carandini sat, his gleaming eyes
focused upon the grisly object he had set upon the ground. It was
a noxious thing, a large preserved hand.

The withered claw was wrapped round with dirty grey-green
cloth, upon which the faintest outlines of script could still be
seen. It was old almost beyond belief; the man to whom it had
belonged in life had been born well before even Sigmar had
walked the lands of men. There was the blackest of sorcery about
the claw, both in the fell magics that had preserved it down
through the ages and the lingering power of the spirit of the man
to whom it had originally belonged. Mighty had the vanquished
tomb king Nehb-ka-menthu been in life, and some of that power
remained in his severed hand.

Carandini stirred from his half-sleep as the claw began to
twitch. The necromancer leaned forward, staring intently as the
limb began to move.

The spirit of Nehb-ka-menthu was still tethered to his hand,
trapped between the worlds of death and life, even that of unlife.
It could see far beyond the mortal world, even into the ancient
past or the unwritten future at times. And what that spirit saw, the
hand could relate.

Carandini had dipped the fingers of the claw in ink before setting the ethereal spirit of the old tomb king to watch over the
farm house he had visited the previous night. It would watch and
wait, reporting all those who came and went.

The necromancer stared as the claw began to scratch its picture-
script upon the sheets of human skin that Carandini had set
beside it on the ground. The necromancer was attentive to remove
each sheet as they filled up with the claw's observations, so that
the ghoulish oracle might have a fresh page upon which to write.

Carandini smiled as he read the hieroglyphs. The prey was
almost in the trap.

CHAPTER ELEVEN

THE HOUSE WAS fairly nondescript on the outside, like so many other half-timbered structures that dotted the countryside throughout the Empire. A small number of log outbuildings and a barn with a thatched roof completed the small compound. The log fence that surrounded the buildings had clearly been neglected, tied together by bundles of rope and twine in places where the ground had given way, sagging forward in awkward angles in others.

As Thulmann's party rode toward the small farm, the witch hunter spied a half-dozen horses tethered to a hitching rail between the buildings. A number of men exited the structure as the witch hunter approached. At their head was Anton Klausner.

'You have the nose of a vulture,' Anton said as the witch hunter rode through the gate. 'We only just found this place ourselves.'

'Then you must have spent a fair time riding circles around this place,' Thulmann stated, having seen the poached earth left behind by the hooves of Anton's men's horses. Whatever tracks there might have been to follow, Anton and his men had obliterated them, trying to impair the witch hunter's own hunt. Clearly, the tracking skills of Anton's group had not yielded any great success, leading the frustrated nobleman back to the farmstead.

'How bad is it?' Gregor asked, his face drawn with concern. Anton sneered up at his brother.

'Not a man, woman or child left alive,' he declared. 'He even killed the Brustholz's little dog. This is certain to stir up the village this time. They might even turn on our friend the witch hunter,' Anton hissed. 'People are so very fond of... dogs.' The brute chuckled, gesturing for his followers to mount.

'I grow tired of what passes for your wit,' Thulmann warned the brash ruffian as he climbed into his saddle. 'And I'll not tolerate any further interference from yourself and Kohl.'

'It is you who is interfering,' Anton snapped coldly. 'This is my father's land and it is his job to defend it!'

'These lands are still a part of Sigmar's Empire,' Thulmann retorted in a voice every bit as devoid of warmth. 'You and your father might remember that.'

'When the messenger my father dispatched to Altdorf speaks with your superiors, it is you who will be reminded of your place,' Anton warned. He whipped his horse's head about with a savage tug of the reins and spurred his steed into a gallop. His comrades quickly followed his example, thundering out of the gates in his wake. Thulmann watched the horsemen disappear down the muddy path.

'You know,' Streng commented, looking askance at Gregor, 'I am really starting to not like your brother.'

Mathias Thulmann dismounted, tying his horse's reins to a fence. The witch hunter cast his gaze across the compound. There was no sign of life, not even a single chicken or goose. He would have expected the animals to remain, bound by habit to the place despite the death of their owners. However, if these deaths were indeed the work of the fiend he sought, then perhaps the animals had sensed the unnatural nature of the events and been frightened into flight.

He knew that it was not uncommon for dogs to sense the workings of sorcery, and not unheard of for lower animals to also be disturbed by lingering traces of magic.

Thulmann withdrew one of his pistols from its holster as Gregor and Streng dismounted. He looked over at the two men, his eyes lost in shadow beneath the brim of his hat. 'Be on your guard,' he cautioned them. 'There is something not right here.'

Gregor nodded his own understanding, checking that his sword was loose in its scabbard. Streng simply grinned, pulling his crossbow from its sheath on his saddle.

'Expecting trouble?' the warrior asked, an eager note to his speech.

'Just keep an eye open,' Thulmann told him, striding toward the house.

THE FRONT DOOR had been battered from its hinges, lying upon the earthen floor just inside the threshold. It was a fitting precursor to the scene of destruction and horror that occupied the room beyond. Furnishings, meagre and fragile to begin with, had been toppled and destroyed, wooden tables and chairs crushed and shattered in a mindless rage, clay pots and jars broken to shards that crunched underfoot as the witch hunter strode into the room. But it was the sight at the centre of the room that arrested their attention.

The bodies had been piled like cordwood, stacked in a precise and cold manner that was utterly at odds with the reckless destruction that surrounded them. All wore their nightshirts, their exposed skin pale and tinged with a sickening purple hue. Vacant eyes stared out from rigid faces that were locked in the last grimace of some agony, their hands contorted into frozen claws.

There were ten in all. Anton Klausner had been right, the fiend had spared neither woman nor child.

'The bastard,' Gregor swore as he laid eyes upon the evidence of mass murder. 'There is no end fitting enough for such scum!' He smashed his fist against the wall in impotent fury.

'Rest assured, we shall find this monster, and bring it down,' Thulmann told him. He slowly circled the mound, staring intently at the bodies.

'Well, it seems Anton and his lads didn't do too fine a job of searching this hovel,' Streng stated with a macabre humour. The mercenary lifted a clay bottle from the floor, holding it to his ear so he could hear its contents slosh about. 'Any wagers on whether it is ale, mead or beer?' he asked.

'You should include poison on your list of liquors,' Thulmann said. Streng arrested the bottle's advance a hand's breadth from his lips. With a nervous look, the mercenary lowered the bottle, dropping it to the floor with a crash.

'Is that how this was done?' asked Gregor, struggling to maintain his calm. These might not have been mighty nobles or great scholars, but they had been people, good hard-working Klausbergers. To see them slaughtered in such a cold and ruthless fashion offended every sensibility in the young man's body and filled his heart with a fiery need for revenge.

'There are no marks of violence that I can see,' the witch hunter informed him. 'Apart from some scratches that are hardly of enough import to have caused death. Indeed, I rather suspect that they were caused after death, when, for whatever reason, the fiend decided to construct this morbid testament to his evil.' Thulmann turned away in disgust from the piled dead. 'No, our killer employed some foul venom to work this evil, or else some sending of the blackest magic.'

Gregor shuddered at the possibility. To kill without a sword or weapon of any sort, to simply mutter an incantation, make a few gestures and then invoke death. It was a horrible thing to contemplate.

Thulmann began to inspect the room, looking for any clues as to the motivation and purpose for this last atrocity. There had been something more to this act; it had broken entirely with the pattern set by the other murders. No lone woodsman, no solitary farmer lured from his home in the dead of night, rather an entire household slaughtered under their own roof!

Did it bespeak some final sacrifice, an end to the fiend's blasphemous rituals? Or perhaps these people had not been so innocent as they seemed. The villain he sought had associates, and perhaps it was they the witch hunter now gazed upon, given a treacherous reward by their unholy master. Whatever the truth, Thulmann held out a vain hope that some clue might yet linger within the charnel house, something left behind by the perpetrator of this act and not discovered by Anton Klausner and his men.

'Search the floor above,' Thulmann told Gregor and Streng as he peered into the little sleeping nook set to one side of the room. 'Look for anything out of the ordinary.'

Streng nodded in understanding, patting Gregor's shoulder and motioning for the noble to follow him.

The two men climbed the stairs, the rickety steps swaying beneath Streng's heavy tread. The mercenary paused at the top of the stairs. He stared down at a tiny crumpled shape, turning it over with his foot, then bending down to extract the rotting object clenched in its jaws. It was a human forearm, the flesh so decayed and rotten that in places the bone peered through. A large section had been stripped completely bare by the dog's fangs.

'Rather unusual toy for anybody's dog, don't you think?' Streng said, letting the loathsome object fall. The mercenary continued on, ducking into one of the side rooms.

Gregor stared down at the rotted limb. His mind cringed as he considered how it might have come to be in such a place. For the first time, something of the true nature of the man they hunted impressed itself upon him and Gregor appreciated in full the horrible power arrayed against them.

As the noble began to turn away from his fascinated study of the rotted arm, his eyes caught a slight glitter upon the floor. He took a few steps and bent forward to retrieve the small metal object.

When he saw what he had picked up, he stared at it as though he held a lethal serpent in his grasp. Gregor's limbs began to shake, shivering with a palsy of terror. He could feel his stomach churning, his bile fighting to purge itself from his body. The noble's vision began to blur, refusing to accept the thing his eyes beheld.

It was a ring, a simple band of gold. Its face bore a shield-like device, upon which had been etched two figures. One was a griffon rampant, and beneath its clawed foot it crushed the shape of a slavering wolf. Gregor closed his fist around the object, refusing to accept the importance of what he had discovered. How often had he gazed upon this ring? How often had he seen it, clinging to his father's frail fingers?

'Come along now,' Streng's voice intruded upon Gregor's terrified thoughts. The noble snapped out of his fear, stamping it down as he forced control back into his frame. The mercenary looked at Gregor with a glint of suspicion in his eye. 'Find anything?' he asked.

'No,' stated Gregor, discreetly slipping the ring into his pocket. 'Shall we try the other room?' he asked.

'If it's as small as this one, I think I can manage on my own,' Streng told him. 'You go down and see if Mathias needs any help.'

* * *

GREGOR STEPPED DOWN into the central room of the cottage, gripping the creaking banister with a hand that had not entirely ceased trembling. He looked over to find the witch hunter emerging from the back room, a bit of mouldy cloth impaled upon a long iron needle gripped in his hand.

'I found this back there,' Thulmann told him. 'Rather shabby even for a peasant, wouldn't you say? Stinks worse of death than those over there do.' The witch hunter shook the offensive scrap from the end of the needle. 'It's my guess that our friend did not work alone when he did this, and his assistants were of a most unusual sort.'

'We found an arm bone upstairs,' Gregor told the witch hunter, 'clutched in the jaws of a little dog. It looked like it had been a month in the grave.' The noble's expression suddenly changed, his eyes going wide with alarm, his mouth dropping open with shock. A gasp emptied his lungs and it was with a trembling hand that he pointed at the witch hunter.

Thulmann spun around to see what had drained the colour from Gregor's face. He sprang back as he saw the pile of corpses begin to twitch, as the topmost of them began to lift itself with awkward movements. The rigid expression locked upon the dead woman's face did not change, nor did any sound issue from her frozen mouth, but a ghastly intent emanated from her dull eyes.

'Zombie,' the witch hunter hissed in a mixture of alarm and loathing. He lifted his pistol, bringing it to bear upon the animated corpse. It crawled from the pile, falling to the floor with a heavy thud, then awkwardly began to gain its feet once more, ignorant of the ankles that had snapped beneath its ungainly descent.

'Streng!' Thulmann called out as the rest of the slain family began to stir.

The witch hunter pushed Gregor toward the door. 'It's a trap! Get the horses!' he ordered the young noble. The harsh commands snapped Gregor from his horrified paralysis and he raced out into the yard, only to be brought up short a few feet from the collapsed doorway.

Six stumbling, shambling shapes had emerged from the barn, bits of hay still clinging to their rotted, dripping frames. They must have lain hidden beneath the hay when Anton had made his search, only to emerge now to close the trap. Gregor met the empty, vacant stare of the skull-faced horrors, then withdrew back into the house.

'No good!' he told Thulmann. The witch hunter had backed up nearly to the stairway, the shuffling zombies slowly closing in upon him. 'There are more outside!'

The witch hunter snarled under his breath, firing his pistol into the nearest of the corpse-creatures, exploding its skull. The thing took another stumbling step forward, then collapsed, tripping up two of its fellow abominations. 'Damn it Streng!' Thulmann called out.

The mercenary appeared at the head of the stairway, his crossbow gripped in his hands. He took in the situation with a calm, chilling detachment, then aimed his weapon. The bolt smashed through the arm of one of the decaying horrors that was now stalking through the front door, pinning the rotting limb to the wall.

'I shouldn't stay down there if I were you, Mathias,' the mercenary said. Gregor and the witch hunter followed his example, slowly ascending the rickety stair. The silent, stumbling figures shuffled after them.

'An excellent suggestion,' Thulmann commented, drawing his second pistol and firing over Gregor's shoulder into the rigid face of the foremost of the monsters. The bullet tore through its skull, exploding from the back of its head in a spray of greasy brain matter. The zombie sagged to its side, flopping on the floor like a fish out of water.

Thulmann slammed the smoking pistol back into its holster, swiftly retreating up the stairs. Gregor followed in his wake, slashing with his sword to keep the undead horrors at bay. His sword ripped and tore at the clutching arms that reached out toward him, tearing the lifeless flesh, spilling rank and gluey blood.

'Mathias,' Streng called down as he reloaded his crossbow. 'Probably a bad time to point this out, but there's no way down from here.' The mercenary aimed and fired, the bolt punching harmlessly through the chest of one of the undead monstrosities.

'What about the windows?' Thulmann snapped, reaching forward and pulling Gregor back as the clawing hand of a zombie nearly fixed upon the young noble's arm. Thulmann lashed out with a sidewise slash of his longsword, bisecting the putrid creature's face. The zombie stumbled back, arresting the advance of its fellows, then began to lumber forward once more, teeth dripping from its injury.

'No good. They're too narrow for a fox to slip through,' Streng snarled in disgust. 'Made to keep thieves out.'

'They also serve to keep us in. I fear I underestimated terribly the cunning of our enemy. It seems he isn't adverse to playing the hunter himself.' Thulmann suddenly noticed a shudder pass through the oncoming horde.

For a brief moment, they were still, but it quickly passed. The witch hunter did not have long to wonder about the cause. The controlling influence of the zombie master had isolated one of the monsters from its fellows, guiding it toward the piled mass of straw and bedding that was heaped in one corner of the room below.

Thulmann watched in fascinated horror as the monster fumbled at its pocket, removing a small tinderbox. With dull, idiot movements, the rotten fingers began to work the mechanism.

'Streng, shoot the one in the corner over there!' Thulmann cried out. The mercenary aimed and fired, the bolt punching through the corpse-creature's neck and burying itself in the monster's shoulder. The zombie did not so much as flinch. Thulmann swore. Below him, Gregor sliced the clutching hand from one of the creatures, a bubble of black blood oozing from the stump.

'We could use an idea right now,' the noble said. 'Maybe push through them after their friend gets its fire started and they start to retreat?'

Thulmann shook his head, his sword crunching into the collarbone of the zombie that had slipped into the space vacated by the one Gregor had maimed. The zombie pitched sideways, breaking through the banister and crashing to the floor below. No sooner had it hit the ground then the corpse began to pick itself up, broken rails protruding from its chest.

'They won't retreat,' the witch hunter stated. 'These things are simply a mockery of life, enslaved completely to the will of the one who called them from their graves. They will keep pursuing even as the entire building comes down around us!'

Streng fired another bolt into the zombie down below. The thing crumpled as its knee exploded, pitching forward into the flickering flames that were beginning to rise from the heap. The mercenary gave voice to a colourful curse as the burning creature rose, its skin and clothing afire. Its task completed, the burning automaton limped across the room to join its fellows.

'Wait a moment!' exclaimed Gregor as he watched the flames rise. 'If we can't go down, perhaps we can go up!' Thulmann glanced overhead, observing that the roof was simply thatch thrown over wooden beams.

'Streng!' he cried. 'Find something to stand on and knock a hole in this roof! We'll keep these creatures at bay.'

The mercenary hurried off, slipping into one of the rooms. Thulmann and Gregor could hear the mercenary tip some heavy object over, then the sound of him savaging the ceiling with his sword. The two men continued to back up the stairs, the undead horrors shambling after them in eerie silence. Below, one entire side of the room had become engulfed in fire, the flames quickly spreading through the dry wood and even dryer thatching of the roof.

'He'd better hurry,' Gregor grunted as he slashed at the zombie reaching toward him. The creature stumbled back, its arm dangling uselessly from its cloven shoulder.

A shout from the side room caused both men to turn their heads. 'You go first,' Thulmann ordered Gregor. The noble opened his lips to protest, but the expression in Thulmann's eyes brooked no question.

The noble slashed once more at the zombies climbing the stairway, then turned and raced toward the room. He found that Streng had tipped over a heavy wooden wardrobe, the most lavish furnishing they had yet seen in the hovel. Overhead, sunlight shone through a large hole that had been cut through the thatching.

Gregor sheathed his blade, then climbed atop the wardrobe. Stretching his arms, he jumped toward the opening, catching the beams that edged the hole and pulling himself up onto the roof.

Gregor paused for a moment, looking around him for any sign of Streng, but he could not see the mercenary. Smoke was rising from a section of the roof only twenty feet away, and he could see tiny fingers of fire peeping between the thatching. He looked back down into the hole.

'Herr Thulmann!' he shouted. 'There is not much time!' He waited, watching the room beneath the hole, with many a nervous glance at the creeping smoke and flame. Suddenly, a shadow

moved across the floor. The eager, hopeful look on Gregor's face
faded however, when a purple-skinned figure shuffled into view,
surveying the room with sidewise swings of its torso.

The zombie paused for a moment, then lifted its head, staring
straight up at Gregor with its dull, vacant eyes. The noble cringed
back as the monster reached up toward him. Cursing, Gregor slid
down towards the low end of the roof, lowering himself from its
edge with his hands and dropping to the ground.

'Nice to see that you made it,' Streng called out to him. Gregor
turned about to see the mercenary seated on the back of his horse,
the reins for Gregor's and Thulmann's own steeds clutched in his
meaty hands.

'Nice of you to wait,' Gregor snapped. The bearded mercenary
chuckled.

'I risk my neck only when it might serve a purpose,' Streng told
him. 'I didn't see any way that dropping back down would help
the situation.'

'But your master! He's still in there!' As Gregor spoke the words,
a look of regret came upon Streng. 'We have to go back for him!'
exclaimed the young noble.

'Back into that?' Streng said, his voice sombre. Gregor turned to
regard the cottage. The lower floor was almost entirely engulfed in
fire now, the plaster peeling away as the flames devoured the
beams beneath them. Thick black smoke billowed upwards into
the sky, turning the afternoon into twilight. The noble stared
down at the ground, shaking his head.

'I vow that I will not rest until this fiend is made to pay for his
crimes,' Gregor swore.

'A commendable oath,' a silky voice told him. Both Gregor and
Streng turned their heads to see the witch hunter emerging from
the billowing smoke. His hat was gone, his thin face stained by
soot and the long cloak upon his back was torn, but otherwise he
looked none the worse for his ordeal.

'I thought they had you,' stated Gregor. Thulmann nodded to
the young noble.

'I will admit that there was a moment when I thought the same,'
he confessed. 'Some reckless desperation seemed to come upon
them and they pressed me harder than before. One of them even
slipped past me. I was forced to turn my back to them and trust
to the grace of Sigmar to preserve me as I raced toward the

opening friend Streng provided us with.' The witch hunter shook his head as he recollected his near escape. 'I dropped down on the other side of the building, somewhat alarmed not to find you two awaiting me.'

Thulmann turned and regarded the blazing structure. A figure could be briefly seen shambling towards the doorway, its body wreathed in flame. But even as it staggered forward, its knees buckled and it fell to be consumed by the fire. 'It seems our enemy desires to swap the roles of hunter and prey,' Thulmann told his companions. 'This might mean he's worried that I might be close to guessing his purpose and thwarting whatever diabolical plan he has in his mind.'

The witch hunter climbed into the saddle of his horse. 'We proceed with care now,' he cautioned. 'For our enemy has become doubly dangerous.'

CARANDINI GLARED AT the scrabbling mummy's claw, hissing with rage as he read the inscription upon the page. The necromancer rose to his feet, pounding his fist into his hand.

'Did you truly think it would be so easy?' the low voice of his confederate spoke to him from the deep shadows at the back of the ruin. The necromancer turned around with a start, visibly flinching from his surprise. He tried to recover his composure, determined to show no weakness before his nebulous ally.

'I had not expected you,' he said. 'Not so... soon. Are you certain that it is safe to be out?'

'My being here is not without some slight danger,' the shadow conceded. 'But no more than I am willing to risk.' The voice grew stern. 'Certainly less dangerous than your failure to kill the witch hunter.'

'My plan was flawless,' spat Carandini, glaring into the shadows. 'There was no way he could have escaped!'

'And yet, to judge by your reaction, he has,' observed the necromancer's associate. Carandini scowled, pulling his ratty hair from his face.

'I suppose that you could do better?' he challenged. He cringed back as the dry, rasping laughter of his ally echoed through the ruin.

'I can and I shall, little man,' the shadow told him. Carandini could feel the air grow cold, the chill touch of the tomb caress his face as his ally began to call the foulest of powers into his body. The necromancer fancied he could see a ghostly green glow burning from the eyes of his confederate. The necromancer watched in rapt fascination, promising himself that one day such power would be his.

'It is done,' the shadow spoke as the glow began to fade and the temperature began to creep back.

'What is done?' Carandini asked, a keen quality to his voice.

'What needed doing,' the shadow declared. 'I have called upon my own resources to salvage this situation from your bungling. The witch hunter will never reach the keep alive. My hounds shall see to it.'

CHAPTER TWELVE

FROM AN OVERLOOKING rise, the witch hunter watched as the flames devoured the last of the cottage, his keen gaze alert for any sign of unnatural movement among the rubble. He'd always read that creatures such as those that had attacked him in the house were amongst the lowest and simplest of the undead, and that destruction by fire would be sufficient to end their unholy existence. But Thulmann was a cautious man and waited until the smoke began to lessen. Satisfied, he holstered the pistol he had been reloading and turned toward his companions.

'Shall we withdraw and inform his lordship that his district is now lessened by one farm?' he asked Gregor. The young noble's face was grim, his eyes filled with a distant melancholy. Thulmann could imagine the man's thoughts: one's first encounter with the restless dead was always a profoundly disturbing experience. He guessed that Gregor was at that point where he was questioning the power and wisdom of Sigmar to allow such profane things to walk the earth. Thulmann himself had faced a similar dilemma when he had first seen the power of the necromancer's arts in a crypt beneath Wolfenburg over a decade ago.

'Lead the way, Streng,' Thulmann told his henchman. 'I want to be back at the keep in time for his lordship to invite us to dinner.'

Streng grinned at the comment, urging his steed to turn around and gallop off in the direction of Klausner Keep. Gregor extracted himself somewhat from his brooding thoughts and followed Streng's lead.

Thulmann studied the man for a moment. In the face of such unholy visitations, it was all very well to question the power of the gods, the witch hunter thought, so long as one drew the correct conclusion. Anything else was the first step on the path of heresy. Thulmann hoped that Gregor would reach the right conclusion.

THEY WERE RIDING along a path that wound through a tangle of woods that bordered on the area where Thulmann had found the ruined remains of Emil Gundolf the forester. That fact, and the growing darkness, made the witch hunter's skin crawl with a sense of unease. There was no doubt it was a cheerless, friendless region.

The moon overhead bathed everything in a disconcerting grey illumination, fighting a hopeless struggle against the ascendant shadows. Even the crickets had fallen quiet and the only sound that accompanied the clop of horse hooves was the rustle of wind-blown leaves blowing between the trees. Thulmann patted the neck of his white steed as the horse gave a nicker of fright.

Ahead of him, he saw Streng's steed come to an abrupt stop. The mercenary swatted the animal with the end of the reins, but the horse remained resolute, whickering in protest as Streng tried to urge it forward. 'Something's gotten into him,' Streng said, looking back to his master.

Thulmann did not reply, instead looking past the mercenary at the gaunt shape that had ghosted out of the trees and was now standing in the centre of the road, as if in challenge. It was large, the size of a yearling calf, its shoulders broad, its frame squat.

Despite the encroaching gloom, Thulmann could make out its lupine outline, could catch the gleam of bared fangs. However, more hideous than the wolf-like creature was the stink that emanated from it, a foul and carrion reek.

The eyes of the creature regarding them glowed with an unholy light, like glittering pools of green pus.

'What in the name of Holy Sigmar?' marvelled Gregor. Thulmann paid him no mind, his head snapping around as he heard a twig snap among the trees. Three more pairs of glowing eyes stared back at him from the darkness. A swift glance to the other side of the road showed four more creatures creeping between the trunks.

'Ride for your life!' the witch hunter shouted, digging his spurs into his mount's flanks. His charger thundered down the path, smashing into the snarling creature that stood in its way. Thulmann heard the snap of breaking bones as his steed rode down the wolf, but did not hear the creature give voice to any sound of pain.

He glanced back to observe Streng and Gregor riding hard after him, the broken remains of the first wolf snapping at them as they passed, pulling itself after them with its front legs, leaving its broken midsection to drag along the ground behind it. More successful were the half score of sleek shadows that erupted from the trees, loping after them with swift, tireless bounds.

Thulmann ripped one of his pistols from its holster and fired back into the pursuing pack. The bullet caught one of the wolves dead on, throwing its body upwards. It was a killing shot, but the witch hunter did not expect the eerie blue flame that erupted from the wound, nor the long drawn-out howl that emanated not from the wolf, but from the wisp of grey smoke that spilled from its injury.

The other members of the pack paid no attention to their companion's demise, loping after the three men without breaking their stride.

'By all the hells!' shouted Gregor. 'What are they?'

'More creatures of the necromancer!' Thulmann called back. 'We must outrun them,' he added. 'I only have two silver bullets, and I've used one already.'

The riders continued to barrel down the path, their hellish pursuers close behind them. The heavy breath of the terrified horses resounded in Thulmann's ears, but from the sleek shadows loping after them there came not the slightest sound. He turned his head to check their position, horrified to find that the pack was only about a horse length from catching up to them. And they were gaining. He looked ahead, spying a fork in the road.

'The left path!' shouted Gregor. 'If we can just keep ahead of them, a little longer we can reach the keep!'

Almost in unison, the men turned their animals toward the left. The sudden manoeuvre spoiled the leap of one of the wolves as it pounced for Thulmann's steed. The black-furred brute struck the ground, rolling hard. Yet the creature was hardly phased by its ineffective leap, gaining its feet almost at once and loping after the rest of the pack.

They were now travelling through the relatively healthy trees that bordered on the region afflicted by what Gregor had called 'the blight'. The trees here were older, their trunks gnarled, their branches thick. They cast their shadows upon the road, covering it with darkness.

The fleeing riders had to trust to the instinct of their steeds, and the straightness of the path. Thulmann prayed that no branches had fallen since the road was last cleared, so nothing might lie upon the path to trip their steeds. If any of the horses should stumble at such breakneck speed, their rider could be killed by the fall.

The horses were gasping now, their strength and vitality waning from the long chase and the terror the wolves evoked in their hearts. They could not sustain the pace much longer. Behind them, the tireless wolves maintained their unnatural, unwavering stride. Thulmann drew his second pistol, firing another bullet into the pack. There was a flash of blue fire, another long, unearthly howl. At least there would be one less when the pack caught them.

A new sound suddenly intruded upon the nightmarish chase, the soft babble of flowing water. Thulmann recalled the road that led to Klausner Keep. A small stream wound through the diseased woods; the sound had to be coming from that. If so, they could only be five or ten minutes' ride from the safety of the fortress. Could the horses maintain such a cruel pace for that long?

'By the light and glory of Holy Sigmar, bane of the unlight, I abjure you!' Thulmann shouted back at the pack.

It was an incantation from the rites of exorcism as practised by some of the Templars of his order. Of course, there were all manner of preparations and paraphernalia that were needed to complement the ritual, things the current situation did not really lend itself to. Still, perhaps it might cause the unholy things to flinch back, recoil in fear for a moment. Every last second might save them now.

The wolves did arrest their pursuit, the sleek shadows coming to a stop in the middle of the path. For the space of a heartbeat, it seemed that the simple prayer had broken the strength and will of the unholy pack. But the illusion swiftly faded, for as the next second came to pass feral snarls and wheezing growls hissed from the gaunt frames. With a redoubled savagery, the undead wolves bounded towards their prey once more.

'Nice going,' Streng commented, rolling his eyes. 'Now they are mad.'

'They were already going to kill us,' Thulmann retorted, trying to urge his tiring horse to greater effort. The small wooden bridge that spanned the stream was ahead of them, the witch hunter could see its black mass separating the gleam of the slow-moving water. 'We are close now!' he shouted.

The three men thundered across the span, the hooves of their animals flying across the wooden surface. They had no intention of stopping on the other side, but a startling occurrence caused them to pull their steeds to a halt.

An icy chill seemed to surround them, and a peculiar odour, like singed hair. There was a bright flash of light and a sound not unlike the crack of lightning. An agonised howl punctuated these events, and when Thulmann looked back towards the bridge, he could see a shape lying upon it, grey smoke rising from its still form. The rest of the wolf pack was glaring at him with their glowing green eyes as they paced back and forth along the far bank.

Thulmann dismounted, pulling his sword from its scabbard.

'You sure that's wise?' Streng called to him as Thulmann strode toward the bridge. The witch hunter did not hear him, too perplexed by what he had just felt and witnessed.

It was lighter here, a break in the trees allowing the light of Mannslieb to illuminate the scene. Now the witch hunter could see the full horror of the things that had stalked them through the woods. They were monstrously oversized wolves, almost as large as the extinct great Sylvanian wolf, and certainly more vile. Their flesh clung to their bones like wet paper, their pelts were mangy, the black fur missing in clumps and patches. The patches of naked flesh were clearly necrotic, the pale bodies of maggots crawling about in the meat.

The faces of the animals were likewise decayed, their muzzles bare and skeletal. Their gleaming eyes were utterly ethereal;

Thulmann could detect no sign of any physical eye behind their fire. The monstrous hounds glared back at their observer, snarling and growling in frustrated bloodlust.

The witch hunter turned his attention to the wolf lying on the bridge. It was rapidly decaying, even as he watched it, the skin peeling away and the fur withering. It was as if all the years the ghoulish creature had cheated its grave had been thrust upon it. Soon, there was only a pile of bone, and even these began to crumble in upon themselves.

'Truly you are blessed by Sigmar,' Gregor said, his voice subdued by the awe of their miraculous escape. The witch hunter shook his head.

'No, this is not the work of Sigmar,' he said, a haunted quality to his words. 'I have heard old folk fables that claim the restless dead cannot cross moving water. But never have I read or encountered anything that would give such legends credence.'

'Well, there is your proof,' said Gregor, pointing at the dwindling remains on the bridge.

Thulmann again shook his head.

'No, there is something fouler than legend at work here,' he declared. 'Can you not feel it all around you? A crawling in your skin, a greasiness in your breath, the chill of the crypt slithering across your bones? It is the stink of decay and corruption.' Thulmann could see by Gregor's reaction to his words that the young noble had indeed felt the same sickening sensations.

'What does it mean?' he asked in a sombre tone.

Thulmann looked back across the stream at the pacing pack. 'The same force that gave those obscenities their mockeries of life,' he said. 'I have seen abominations destroyed in just such a manner, in the madhouse of Enoch Silber's unholy experiments. A necromancer takes pains to preserve himself from that which he calls from the tomb.'

Gregor Klausner recoiled from the witch hunter's statement. 'But that can't be,' he protested.

'It can and it is,' stated Thulmann flatly, his eyes cold and stern as they looked into Gregor's. Both men turned as Streng rode towards them.

'Seems like that lot want another chance at us,' the mercenary swore. He hefted his crossbow, grinning at the witch hunter. 'Think this would do any good?' he asked.

'Not any appreciable damage,' Thulmann told him. 'Holes punched through dead flesh have little effect. But I have something here that they won't shrug off so easily.' Thulmann removed his powder flask from his belt and a silver ball from his cartridge case. The pack stopped their pacing, fixing him with their luminous gaze. The creatures gave voice to a final snarl of anger then fell back, slinking into the night.

'Our friend has quite a mixed bag of tricks,' commented Streng as he watched the wolves disappear into the darkness. Thulmann turned his own gaze back upon the stream.

'Yes,' he said in a low whisper. 'A mixed bag indeed.'

MATHIAS THULMANN THREW open the front door of the main ʼ the keep. His cloak was torn, his clothes stained by soot an his boots covered in mud and the greasy pseudo-blood o bies he had battled at the Brustholz farm. However, it of cold, cruel menace upon his face that caused the se met his party at the door to race away in search of

Thulmann ignored the departed servant's await the steward, and began to climb the st the hall. Gregor Klausner followed after th strode toward the blazing fire set beneath the Klausner patriarchs, turning when ing to warm the numbness from his

'What the devil do you think y Kohl's heavy voice. The steward glaring up at the witch hunter a

'I am going to have word snapped, not bothering to lo tered a colourful curse and b

'His lordship is sleeping,'

'In that case, I will wake looking back. Ivar Kohl's the stairs ahead of the

'I said that his lord extending his arm to

The witch hunter have my man bre Thulmann's voice, Ko ing as they tried to form

'Perhaps I should speak with him,' Gregor said when they stood outside the door of his father's room.

'No,' Thulmann told the young noble. 'It is time your father heard the situation laid out before him in no uncertain terms. He will face reality this time, and Sigmar take his precious ego!' The witch hunter knocked once upon the heavy wooden portal, then flung it open.

Wilhelm Klausner was resting in his bed, his frail body nestled amidst its mound of pillows and furs. His wife sat beside him on the edge of the mattress, feeding her husband a bowl of medicinal broth. Both of them gave a start when the witch hunter strode into the chamber.

'What is the meaning of this!' rasped Wilhelm, raising his body from the bed. 'How dare you!'

'He forced his way past me,' explained Kohl, squeezing his way to the room behind Gregor. 'I'll have him removed at once.'

'Think about leaving this room, and I'll snap you in chains,' snapped Thulmann. 'I've had enough of your plotting and scheming. Any more of it and I will put you somewhere where you can't interfere.'

'arrogant dog!' hissed Wilhelm, his wrinkled face contorting to a mask of fury. 'I'll have you know I've made them aware heavy-handed posturing in Altdorf.' He wagged his emaciated finger at the witch hunter. 'I am the authority here, and messenger returns from seeing the Grand Theogonist, receive a most forceful reminder of that fact!'

'please,' protested Gregor, stepping towards the bed.

cast a pained look of disappointment and contempt at

'expected my own son to side against me,' he stated.

restraining hand on her husband's shoulder, but he expect disappointment from Anton, but this as keenly as the knife stabbed into my heart.'

is doing something to put a stop to the horror your district,' Thulmann informed the sickly filthy, rotting object upon the bed. It was the hand of one of the Brustholz zombies. Wilhelm in horror at the loathsome object.

twice this night by things that by all rights in their graves,' stated the witch hunter. stholz farm was a trap, a cunning trap laid for me by the insidious fiend who has conceived these atrocities. No sooner had your son and myself arrived than the slaughtered family took to their feet in a ghastly parody of life, motivated by the murderous will of their killer. We were attacked again on the road here, hunted by wolves, your lordship. Wolves that feel no pain and have bale-fires instead of eyes.'

Wilhelm Klausner began to tremble, a confused look coming upon his face. 'Can this be?' he gasped.

'Yes, it is, father,' Gregor told him. 'I was there, I saw these horrors for myself.'

'We were saved from the devil dogs by a most unusual phenomenon,' Thulmann said, his silky voice carrying a hint of challenge. 'The wolves were unable to pursue us across the stream that borders your estate. Indeed, the one that did so dropped dead instantly, crumbling into dust as we watched it. Most unusual, wouldn't you say?'

Ivar Kohl blanched at the implication in the witch hunter's voice. It was with a visible effort that he regained some measure of calm. 'Any peasant can tell you that the unquiet dead are unable to cross running water,' he stated. As the steward spoke Gregor stared at his father and shuddered, his hand seeking out the ring he had secreted in his pocket.

Thulmann swung his unremitting gaze on the steward. 'Something destroyed the monster,' he stated. 'Something more tangible than peasant superstitions.'

'There are a great many elf ruins on my lands,' Wilhelm said. The witch hunter turned back toward him, impressed by the even, level quality to the man's words. 'Perhaps it was some lingering enchantment of the elder race that preserved you and destroyed the wolf?'

'Perhaps,' Thulmann conceded, though the dubious quality in his voice said that he was far from convinced. 'Or perhaps there is another reason.' The witch hunter stalked toward the door. 'I will finish my consultation of your family records, then you will provide me with an escort back to the village. I don't have the time to continue placating your pride, Lord Klausner. Cooperate with my needs and we will rid your lands of this menace.'

The witch hunter looked over at Ivar Kohl and smiled thinly. 'Wherever it might hide itself,' he added.

* * *

GREGOR KLAUSNER REMAINED behind in his father's room after the witch hunter had withdrawn. Ivar Kohl was not long in making his own excuses, hurrying away like some mammoth spider slinking back into a dark corner. Gregor walked over to his mother, asking her to leave him alone with the patriarch.

The woman nodded her head, kissing her son and withdrawing to her own room, telling Wilhelm to call out if he needed anything.

Gregor smiled at his mother's statement. Even with an entire household at her beck and call, she preferred to see to her husband herself.

'Gregor,' Wilhelm said, clutching his son's arm. 'Dear Gregor, can you really appreciate the horror of what you involve yourself in?'

'I have seen it for myself, father,' Gregor said, his tone defensive. 'And I have fought it with courage.'

'Courage?' Wilhelm chuckled scornfully. 'Do you think you know the meaning of that word? I pray you never have cause to discover what real terror is!' He stabbed a warning finger at his son's chest. 'But if you continue on the path you walk now, you will! I tell you again, Gregor, have nothing more to do with that man!'

Gregor did not hear his father's words, however, for he had been frozen to the spot when the old man's claw had reached toward him. There, upon his thin, spindly finger, was a gold ring, the device of a rampant griffon and a slavering wolf impressed upon its device. Gregor clenched the hand in his pocket, feeling the object there dig at his palm. It was impossible, the young noble thought. The ring in his pocket was the same as the ring on his father's hand.

'You can't begin to understand what is going on here,' Wilhelm continued. 'I pray that you never need to.' He pulled his son downward so that he could stare up into Gregor's eyes. The old man's face was moist when he spoke. 'Leave the witch hunter to his business, Gregor. Stay out of it.'

'I can't,' Gregor told him, pulling away. 'These atrocities must end. Our people cannot go on suffering, not knowing which night death will come to them.'

Wilhelm sagged back into his bed, defeated.

'If that is your decision,' he said, his voice empty and hollow. He looked over at his son, and this time there was no mistaking the trickle of tears. 'Whatever happens, know that I love you. Know that everything I have ever done has been to protect this family.'

'I know that,' Gregor assured him. He walked away from his father's bed, back out into the corridor. He needed time to think, to consider the enigma that preyed upon his mind. He was not sure whether to feel relieved or alarmed by the discovery that his father's ring was still upon his hand. And that conflict of emotion worried him even more.

Wilhelm watched his son depart and shook his head.

'Forgive me,' he whispered.

THE BLACK-ROBED figure smiled down at the bound form stretched out beneath his feet. The captive tried to scream, but the heavy linen gag stuffed into his mouth muffled the sound.

'I'm afraid that it is too late for that to do any good,' the robed man said, a regretful tone in his voice. He gazed upward, studying the sky. The great bloated mass of Mannsleib filled the night, but it was not with the greater moon that the stargazer was concerned. He was awaiting the emergence of Mannslieb's smaller brother, the dim, darkling moon Morrslieb, sometimes called the 'moon of sorcery'. There was a truth to such fables, for the influence of Morrsleib was beneficial to enchantments and wizardry.

A cold wind caused the clawing tree branches above them to sway, the crawl of dead leaves upon the ground melding with the creak of the wooden limbs. The stargazer looked back down at the bound man.

'Not so very long now,' he told him, removing the gleaming blade from its sheath on his belt.

THE LONELY HOWL of a dog echoed through the blackness, like the mournful wail of a lost soul. The analogy was not at all improper, the man with the blade thought. This was the hour of lost souls, when the restless dead were at their most powerful. The blasphemous writings of Kadon, the high priest of thrice-accursed Morgheim, claimed that it was at this hour, when the watches of the night were at their longest, that the Supreme Necromancer had raised the first corpse from its grave.

There was a great, unholy power at such times, a power made all the more potent still by the emergence of Morrsleib from behind its brother.

The sorcerer looked again at his chosen sacrifice, savouring for a moment the fear he saw crawling through the man's eyes. Oh yes, he could feel the power, feel its dread influence clawing at his spine. He knows what is going to happen, the part he is to play. A magical ritual was not so very unlike a theatrical production, the sorcerer considered. The success of the performance depended on much the same things: the quality of the props, the location of the theatre. And of course the selection of the actors. Was the wizard truly skilled enough to do justice to the performance demanded of him? Was the fair-skinned sacrifice really so fair, his blood really so rich and vibrant as it seemed?

We shall soon find out, the sorcerer thought, as he watched Morrsleib appear overhead.

THE KNIFE STABBED quickly, sinking deep into the sacrifice's neck. A spasm of thrashing and trembling gripped the man's body as life spilled from his frame. The robed figure above him wiped the crimson from his blade, sliding it back into its sheath. It had played its part. Now it was time to close the circle, complete the ritual.

'BY THE THREE thousand torments of Nagashizzar do I defile,' the crisp, clipped tones of the sorcerer sounded. The gruesome object clutched in his hand began to crawl with maggots. The man's lip curled in pleasure as he saw the loathsome worms, then dropped the organ to the ground where they could continue their cannibalistic work.

'By the four names of power do I desecrate,' the man hissed again, this time holding the bisected eyes of his victim. The organs began to decay, dripping into a watery filth that sizzled upon the ground and yellowed the grass.

'By the might of He Who Was, He Who Is, He Who Shall Be Again, do I destroy!' The sorcerer cast the stringy material he had removed from the sacrifice's skull into the brass brazier resting before him. The smoke that arose from his offering seemed to swell with the ghastly impression of a death's head.

THE MAN IN black robes hurled the organs from him, wiping his hands in disgust on a heavy strip of leather. The wet, gleaming things collapsed upon the ground beside the body's foot. He bent down toward the corpse again and cut a lung from the man's chest. With the organ clenched in his fist, he called out into the night.

'To Phakth do I give the breath of life,' the man cried out. 'That he might speed upon the wings of justice and undo the works of wickedness.' He bent down, extracting the other lung.

'To Ptra do I give the breath of life! That his glory might shine out into the darkness and banish the dominion of night.'

The black-robed figure returned his attention to the corpse, cutting the body once more. He rose with another piece of the corpse.

'To the watcher at the gate, Djaf the jackal...'

CARANDINI CONSIDERED THE wretched ruin of his victim. He flicked his wet, sticky hair from his face. Invoking the dread powers always excited him. He never felt more alive than when he was working the fell sorcery of death. The necromancer turned toward his associate, who had remained silent throughout the ritual.

'It is done?' he asked.

'It is done,' the necromancer assured him, a proud quality to his voice.

'It had better work this time!' the shadowy figure warned. Carandini fingered the vial secreted in his cassock.

'I have told you before,' he said. 'We must wear them out. They can't keep up with us forever.' Carandini favoured his confederate with a superior smile. 'I should think you'd have learned patience after all this time.'

THE BLACK-ROBED man stared down at the ruin of his sacrifice. There was nothing more to be done, the ancient ritual was complete. However, there was another part to it, something that had been added much later. The robed figure fell to his knees, hands closing about each other. He bowed his head, shutting his eyes so that he might not see the blood staining the ground.

'May Lord Sigmar forgive the doubts and fears of the flesh and honour the sacrifice of this noble martyr, who has died that evil may not prevail,' the man said. Slowly he rose to his feet, motioning for his associates to rejoin him. His thoughts turned away from the gruesome act he had committed, the ancient pagan rite he had performed. Instead, he considered the troublesome witch hunter. Things were swiftly coming to a head, their enemy must strike soon. The witch hunter was an unnecessary complication.

One that would have to be removed.

His face set into an expression of grim determination, Ivar Kohl removed his robes and made his way back to the keep.

CHAPTER THIRTEEN

MATHIAS THULMANN SCARCELY looked up as Reikhertz crept into his room, a plate of steaming sausage and boiled cabbage held before him. The odour was enough for the witch hunter, his brow lifting in surprise.

'I had thought you to be a more devout Sigmarite than that,' he commented, still regarding the map laid out upon the table. His words caused the innkeeper to freeze.

'Your pardon, sir?' he muttered, his voice a nervous squeak.

'You expect a servant of Holy Sigmar to fortify himself on that?' Thulmann asked. 'Take it away,' he added in disgust. The innkeeper flinched away at first, then began to bristle as he considered the witch hunter's high-handed tone. Before he fully knew what he was doing, the innkeeper's mouth was open once more.

'Look here, just what sort of food do you think I can afford to keep feeding you?' he snapped. 'I've yet to see any sort of coin from you, not that I've asked for any,' he hastily added when he saw Thulmann look up. 'I am just saying that this isn't the Nine Crowns in Nuln. I can't afford to keep feeding you better than I do myself.'

Thulmann regarded Reikhertz with an angry gaze, his finger stroking the thin moustache on his upper lip. Eventually, he reached into the pocket of his scarlet vest and withdrew a pair of gold crowns, which he tossed to Reikhertz. The innkeeper caught the coins with his free hand, his face dropping into an expression of stunned marvel.

'I ask no man to sacrifice more than he can afford,' Thulmann told him, a note of apology in his voice. 'There are times, however, when I forget that not every man is as privileged as I. You've been most helpful, friend Reikhertz, a true servant of Sigmar.' The witch hunter pointed to the coins gripped in the man's hand. 'Take that, go and get us a lamb, the best spices you can round up in this village and see that it is enough to feed both an innkeeper and a Templar.'

Thulmann smiled. 'Whatever is left, I am sure you can find a use for.' He looked back to the map, focusing on the marks he had made upon it.

Reikhertz stood in the doorway a moment, considering the sudden change that had come upon the witch hunter. He strode forward. 'Please don't misunderstand,' he told Thulmann. 'We really do appreciate how you are helping us. I know, everybody in the village knows, that you are doing your best to…'

'But my best isn't good enough,' sighed Thulmann, leaning back in his chair. 'Oh, I am making progress, but so is this fiend I am hunting. He grows more bold, more desperate every hour. And it is your people who pay the price for every day I fail to–'

'You sound as if you're giving up,' Reikhertz interrupted. 'If that's the case, then I'll be giving these coins back to you and ask you to kindly leave my house.' The emotion in the man's voice brought a smile to the witch hunter's tired face.

'No, friend Reikhertz,' Thulmann said. 'I'll not rest until this animal is made to pay for his crimes. But it is a frustrating hunt,' he pounded his fist against the map. 'I know that the key lies in the murders themselves, each one is a part of some ghastly whole. If I could only find the pattern, I would know what this monster is up to and where he may strike next.'

Reikhertz withdrew toward the door. 'You sound like a man who's lost and can't see the forest through the trees,' he observed. 'Maybe what you need to do is stand back and try to see things a different way.' The innkeeper stepped aside hurriedly as Streng pushed his way past him, a beer stein gripped in his grimy paw. There was a twisted grin on his face.

'Drinking again, and at so early an hour?' commented Thulmann, disapproval dripping from his voice.

'Still drinking, Mathias,' the mercenary shot back. 'I have to stop for it to be "again"'.

'Well, this might sober your sodden brain,' Thulmann said, rising to his feet. 'From now on, we pay for what friend Reikhertz is gracious enough to provide us with.' The witch hunter smiled as his henchman's expression grew grave. 'That includes anything from his cellars.'

'As you say, Mathias,' the thug said in a surly tone. He cast an angry look over at Reikhertz, then turned back to his employer.

'Might interest you to know that our friend has been busy again,' the mercenary reported. 'A fellow has just come in – says he's found another body. Wanted me to report it to the witch hunter.'

'What?' gasped Reikhertz. 'Another murder? Who?'

'Farmer named Weiss, apparently,' Streng told him. 'Same as that second fellow we found, Mathias. Didn't take the time to try and hide who it was, just did his business and went his way. Mind you, the fellow downstairs didn't stay around to note too many of the particulars.'

Thulmann snatched up the map from the table. Reikhertz was leaning against the wall, a pained expression on his face. 'Old Weiss,' he muttered in solemn reflection. 'Used to drown cats by the old mill when he was in his cups, but a good man just the same.'

'Where did this take place?' Thulmann demanded, thrusting the map under Streng's nose. The mercenary stared at the map for a moment, brow knitted in concentration as he struggled to read the names marked on it.

'A dry stream bed near someplace called Dagger's Reach,' he said. Reikhertz walked over, taking the map from Thulmann and pointing out the relevant feature, a jagged fang of rock situated amidst a tangle of fields and wood. The witch hunter spun about, removing a heavy brush from a pot of pigment resting on his table. He daubed a bright crimson mark where Reikhertz had indicated.

The witch hunter sat down again, studying the map intently, trying to perceive how this new atrocity might fit into any of the patterns he had been trying to impose upon the murders. After a few moments he pounded the table in frustration.

'There is a pattern,' he swore. 'I know there is! I am just too much a fool to see it.' For the umpteenth time, he began to draw lines between the murder sites with a stick of chalk, snarling every time they did not merge into anything resembling even the most esoteric shape.

Reikhertz and Streng watched Thulmann work with bewildered interest.

'My credit good for one more stein?' Streng asked the innkeeper from the corner of his mouth.

'I'll join you,' the innkeeper told him. Both men turned, only to find that the hallway was blocked. Gregor Klausner, wearing a bicorn hat and a heavy grey cloak trimmed in rabbit fur, stared back at them. Reikhertz only spared a brief glance at the young noblemen, then locked eyes with the plump young woman with her arm about Gregor's waist.

'Back to your work!' he snapped at his daughter. Miranda withdrew her arm, setting it on her hip.

'Gregor wanted to see the witch hunter on a most urgent matter,' she snapped back. Father and daughter glared at one another for a moment. It was the daughter who looked away first.

'You see that they ain't helping themselves to my ale down there,' Reikhertz told her in a stern voice. Without another word, Miranda retreated back down the hall.

'It really was my fault,' apologised Gregor. 'Don't be too hard on Miranda.'

Reikhertz transferred his glare to the lord. 'You're the son of Lord Klausner, and that puts certain obligations upon me, certain privileges custom dictates I extend to you.' Anger flared up in his voice and he jabbed a finger toward Gregor. 'But those privileges don't extend to the person of my daughter.' Reikhertz started to stalk out into the hallway. Gregor caught him by the arm.

'I've been nothing but proper and honourable with your daughter,' he told the innkeeper. Reikhertz brushed the young noble's hand away as though it were a noxious insect.

'I appreciate what you've done for us,' the innkeeper told him. 'But you're a Klausner all the same. Being the best of a bad breed doesn't make you any more decent.' Reikhertz took a deep breath. 'You know my father was killed by your family. Not an easy thing to forgive or forget.'

'That is a fact that might have been worthy of knowing,' interrupted Thulmann. Unobserved by the other men, he had risen from his table to listen to the tense conversation.

'You'd heard enough stories like it the other night,' Reikhertz told him. 'It is not something I like to talk about,' he added.

Thulmann looked at him expectantly and the innkeeper continued in a subdued voice. 'It was near on twenty winters ago, I was only a boy, but I can recall every detail. His,' he pointed toward Gregor, 'grandfather was dying, health fading quite fast. Then the daemon came. My father was one of its last victims.'

Thulmann nodded his head in grim appreciation of the tragedy Reikhertz had alluded to. A sudden flare of inspiration filled his eyes. 'Do you know where your father was found?' he asked, gesturing for Reikhertz to come over to the table. Soon all four men were staring down at Thulmann's heavily marked map of the district.

'It was over near the old crossroads that lead to...' the innkeeper's voice caught in his throat. His finger had been following the road, but when he reached the site he wished to indicate, he found a bright crimson splotch. 'But you've already marked the spot,' he muttered. 'How did you know?'

Thulmann shook his head. 'I didn't. That mark shows where a herb grower named Jannes was killed. This is very important, Reikhertz. You say your father was the last of the daemon's victims?'

Reikhertz shook his head. 'No, there was a midwife, Lucina Oberst. She died a few nights after my father. She was the last. But I don't remember exactly where they found her. Someplace near...' he looked away as he saw still another crimson splotch where he had been about to point. 'What does this mean?'

Gregor looked away from the map, grasping the importance of what they had chanced upon. 'There were six victims back then,' he told Thulmann.

'Yes, and I would wager that each of them died at a spot already marked on my map,' the witch hunter declared. 'Thirty years and the killer strikes in the exact same places.'

'But it has never been this bloodthirsty before,' protested Gregor. 'They haven't killed six this time, they've killed twenty-nine times, if we discount the massacre at the Brustholz farm.'

Thulmann nodded. 'Yes, that atrocity was a trap designed to dispose of me, not a part of whatever foul ritual these other murders are a part of.' He began drawing lines between the first six murders, snarling in disgust when they did not match up. Then he noticed a curious fact. Both of the marks that Reikhertz had indicated, also murders from three decades ago, were not among the first six killings.

'Reikhertz, the other murders thirty years ago, do you recall where the bodies were found?' The innkeeper leaned down again. 'I remember. It's the sort of thing a person doesn't forget.' He pointed out the scenes, each, not surprisingly, already marked in red. Thulmann saw that only three of them were included in the earliest killings. Realisation began to dawn on him. He drew a connection not between the current killings, but those long ago, finding himself staring at a hexagonal shape. Then he looked back to the other murder sites he had bypassed in drawing his shape.

A sudden understanding filled him as he began to draw the connecting lines between these. A pentagon was soon described upon the map.

The witch hunter leaned back in something approaching triumph. 'There is a connection, a pattern,' he declared. 'I did not see it because there is not one here, but two. The hexagon, the squared circle employed by mystics to protect them from daemons and other malign supernatural forces.'

'The dire wolf at the bridge!' exclaimed Gregor. Thulmann nodded.

'Then we have this other figure,' the witch hunter indicated the pentagon. The murder sites used to form it were spaced much more widely, completely enclosing the first shape. 'The pentagon is employed by daemonologists and necromancers to invoke the forces of death and ruin, to summon and bind the blackest currents of sorcery.' Thulmann's voice grew contemplative. 'Not one ritual, but two. One designed to protect, the other...' He stared at the multitude of other marks upon his map, those that had not yet been fitted into a pattern. Gregor noted the witch hunter's area of study.

'You can add another mark to your map,' he told Thulmann in a sombre voice.

'There's a man trying to reach the bottom of a cask of ale downstairs who already told us,' Streng interjected.

'Then you already know that Otto the frog catcher was killed last night?' Gregor asked. The other three men in the room stared at him.

'No,' sputtered Reikhertz. 'They said it was Weiss,' the innkeeper seated himself on the edge of Thulmann's bed, shaking his head in disbelief. The witch hunter grabbed Gregor.

'Where was the man found?' he demanded, his words clipped by his excitement. The young noble tapped the surface of the old parchment, indicating a spot some distance from the place where Weiss had been found.

'This horror compounds itself,' Thulmann commented as he marked the spot. 'Two murders in one night. This man Otto, what condition was his body in?'

'A terrible sight. One of Anton's men found him and said that he only knew it was Otto because his frog bag was lying nearby.' Thulmann leapt to his feet when Gregor had related his information.

'Go to the shrine of Morr and bring back the priest,' Thulmann ordered Streng. The mercenary grinned, handing his stein to Reikhertz and departing at a brisk jog.

'The priest?' asked Gregor.

'I need to know exactly how each of these,' the witch hunter gestured at the marks on his map, 'died. You see, there is not one fiend plaguing Klausberg this time. There are two.'

AFTER THE DOUR mortuary priest had left, Thulmann smiled in triumph at the white chalk lines that swarmed across his map, describing a number of hexagons and pentagons. He looked over at the expectant faces of Gregor and Streng. Reikhertz, disturbed enough by the grim business, had withdrawn to meet his afternoon custom in the tavern down below.

'Two,' Thulmann repeated. 'Two necromancers at work.' He gestured at the complex network of pentagons and the solid ring of hexagons. 'One conducts the rituals that form this hexagon. He is less cautious about his craft, taking no pains to hide the nature of his ceremonies. The other plies his trade farther afield, mutilating the bodies when he is finished with them. His handiwork composes this pentagon.'

The witch hunter gave a sigh. 'But the question remains, what is the purpose of these atrocities, and why have they become so much greater than those in the past? Unless...' Thulmann glanced over at Gregor. 'Perhaps these unholy degenerates are not working in concert with one another, but rather seek to undo each other's rituals.' He stabbed a finger at the map again. 'The killings that form the pentagon, from the beginning they were not the same as what was done thirty years ago. Something new, something outside the established pattern. Perhaps something meant to break that pattern?'

'Then finding the one won't yield up the other,' groaned Gregor.

'Removing one of these predators may expose the other, if we can take the fiend alive,' Thulmann told him. 'If these sorcerers are at odds, then they must know something of one another. More than we know about them, in any event.' He looked back at the map, staring at the only partially formed figures he had drawn. 'The pentagon needs two more points to close the current pattern,' he said. 'But the hexagon is nearly complete. Only one more red mark to seal it. If the pattern holds, the fifth and sixth sacrifices that compose the six-sided circle will occur on coincident nights.'

'That would mean the killer will strike again tonight!' exclaimed Gregor. Thulmann smiled grimly.

'Yes, but this time we know where his ritual will take place,' the witch hunter told him. 'And we will be ready for him.'

'I'll alert my father, gather some soldiers from the keep,' Gregor stated, turning to leave the room.

'That would be unwise,' Thulmann's sharp tone brought the young noble to a halt.

Gregor turned slowly, a questioning look on his face. The witch hunter gestured for him to look at the map again. 'The hexagon, the protective circle, do you see what lies at its heart?' Gregor's eyes widened with shock as he saw Klausner Keep lying perfectly within the hexagonal pattern. It could be no coincidence that the keep lay at the very centre of the figure, there was some dark purpose at work.

Gregor pondered once more the sickeningly familiar ring he had discovered amidst the carnage of the Brustholz farm. If the keep was at the centre of this web of horror, then most assuredly Wilhelm Klausner was the centre, the cornerstone, of the keep. But what possible reason could there be that might drag his father into such gruesome and horrific occurrences?

'I fear that the man we hunt is not unknown within the halls of your household.' Thulmann rose to his feet, gathering up the hat Reikhertz had procured to replace the one he had lost to the burning farmhouse and the heavy leather belt from which dripped his pistols and sword.

'No, we will keep what we have learned to ourselves,' Thulmann declared. 'Then we may be sure that our quarry will not be expecting us.'

'Just the three of us then?' asked Gregor. Thulmann nodded.

'Right and justice are with us, Gregor,' the witch hunter stated. 'They are all the reinforcements we shall require.' Streng gave his employer a sarcastic grin. Thulmann turned on him, his voice sharp. 'You doubt the might of Sigmar?' he snapped. Streng shook his head.

'Not at all,' the thug said. 'I just respect it more when it is wearing plate mail and the colours of the Reiksguard.'

A HALF-DOZEN MEN were scattered about The Grey Crone's common room when Thulmann and his companions descended the stairs. The witch hunter paid them little heed, striding toward the bar where Reikhertz was busy serving a large man with a bald head and a massive moustache.

'We'll be needing our horses, friend Reikhertz,' the witch hunter said. The innkeeper paused and nodded to the Templar. The heavy-set man he was serving turned around, looking over Thulmann with a sour look on his rugged features.

'The man was serving me, witch finder,' he snarled. Thulmann gave a thin smile in return and turned to walk away. 'I was talking to you, witch finder,' the ruffian called after him, stalking away from the counter.

'But I was not talking to you,' Thulmann retorted with a dismissive voice. The bald man dipped his head in a slight mockery of a bow.

'Of course not, you only talk to wretched old ladies,' he sneered. 'Talk 'em into saying all sorts of silly things so you can burn 'em and hang 'em and whatever else tickles your fancies.'

Thulmann's eyes narrowed, his face slipping into a mask of sullen anger and indignation. He shook his hand toward his assailant.

'As a duly appointed servant of Holy Sigmar,' Thulmann warned him, 'I can tell you that your words flirt with heresy. Since you are obviously drunk, I am prepared to be lenient and ignore your impious remarks.'

'Oh, is that so?' snorted the ruffian. His hand slid to his belt, pulling it around so that the sword sheathed at his side was in ready reach. 'I'm not some poor defenceless woman that you can beat and abuse. You'll find me a much colder vintage than that.'

'I suggest you go home and sleep away these bottled spirits that so affect you,' Thulmann told him. There was a sharpness to the witch hunter's words now, and a crueller glint in his eyes than there had been moments before. 'Before I begin to take offence to your belligerence.'

The swordsman laughed, looking about the room, his face lifted in amusement. From the base of the stairs, Streng and Gregor watched the situation unfold. Streng gripped the young noble's arm to prevent him from interceding in the coming confrontation.

'I can't tell you how much it frightens me that I might cause you offence,' the swordsman snickered. He leaned forward, his face a hand's breath from Thulmann's own. 'Tell me, would it offend you if I were to say your precious Sigmar isn't fit to lick the piss from Ulric's boots?'

The witch hunter leapt back, meeting the swordsman's dancing blade with his own sword. His attacker seemed shocked by the older man's speed, but quickly regained his composure, pressing his attack. The other patrons in the room scattered, chairs clattering to the floor, leather jacks and clay steins spilling ale and beer as the men gripping them rose hurriedly, giving the two combatants ample room to fight.

'Blasphemy and heresy,' the witch hunter snarled above their crossed steel. 'You had best hope that my sword finishes you, friend.' The swordsman's eyes displayed a flicker of fright at the cruelty stamped upon Thulmann's words. He withdrew a pace, the witch hunter at once capitalising upon the opening and pressing his own counter attack.

The clash of steel rang through the common room as the blades of the two combatants flashed, struck and parried.

The bald swordsman's earlier bravado began to fade, and his movements degenerated into ever more frantic and desperate swings. By contrast, Thulmann worked his blade with a cold, judgmental manner, parrying his opponent's every move with a delicate turn of wrist and waist.

The swordsman cried out in alarm as Thulmann's blade penetrated his defences and slashed his shoulder. 'I hope the sight of your own blood does not offend you,' the witch hunter said, his voice rippling with a sadistic mockery. 'You'll see a fair deal more of it before I finish with you.'

The swordsman cast a desperate look behind Thulmann, then redoubled his frantic efforts at defence. As the man fell back before Thulmann's advancing blade, a scream of agony sounded from the back of the room.

Streng wiped the blood from his knife on the grimy surface of his breeches even as his victim clutched at the wound in his neck. The heavy pistol fell from the rat-faced man's hand, and a moment later, the backshooter joined his weapon on the floor, body shuddering in its death agonies.

Seeing his comrade down, Thulmann's opponent directed a wild swing at the witch hunter's head, trying to slip past the witch hunter as he reacted to the erratic attack. Thulmann deftly ducked the wild swing and slashed his sword along the man's ribs. The swordsman staggered away, slamming into the base of the counter as he slipped to the floor.

The witch hunter strode toward him with slow, deliberate steps. His enemy lifted his blade in a last attempt at defence, but his fading strength was unequal to the task and the heavy length of steel clattered to the floor.

Thulmann sneered down into the man's pained features, then stooped down over his body, rummaging in the man's pockets.

'They meant to kill you,' exclaimed Gregor, rushing to the witch hunter's side.

'Yes,' Thulmann said, rising from the wounded swordsman, holding the small leather bag he had withdrawn from the man's tunic. 'They were paid to,' he kicked the leg of the bald man. 'This scum was supposed to keep me occupied while his associate put a bullet in my back. Isn't that so, swine?' By way of answer, the swordsman gave voice to a dull groan of pain.

Thulmann looked back toward Gregor. 'I think you will find that the Klausner treasury is missing a few gold crowns.' Thulmann's eyes hardened into chips of ice. The witch hunter reflected upon the pattern he had discovered, upon the situation of Klausner Keep at the very centre of the web, and upon Gregor Klausner's timely arrival. Had he come to relay information, or to find out how much the witch hunter already knew? Thulmann gave voice to the suspicion his instincts forced to the fore of his thoughts. 'Are you certain you came here alone?'

Gregor pulled back in shock. 'You don't mean to think that I…'

'Let's ask this vermin,' the witch hunter replied. But when he turned to speak to the wounded man, he found that it was too late. His blow had punctured one of the man's lungs. The only thing that would be coming from his mouth now was a thin trickle of blood. 'Heathen wretch,' Thulmann hissed. 'He might have held on a few moments more.'

'The other one's dead too,' Streng informed him.

'My thanks, friend Streng,' the witch hunter replied. 'To show my gratitude, you may keep the money you removed from his person.' The mercenary nodded, clearly not entirely pleased that his employer had guessed about the second bag of gold.

'I swear to you, Herr Thulmann,' protested Gregor. 'I never laid eyes upon these men before. On my faith in Sigmar, I swear it.'

'He may be right about that,' observed Reikhertz, peering over the counter at the dead man slumped against his bar. The innkeeper's face wrinkled in annoyance as he saw the blood spreading across the floor boards. 'These two were caravan guards. Came in with the last wagon train from Wurtbad.'

The name of the city gave Thulmann pause. Could it be that these men had nothing to do with the Klausners and Klausberg? Had they perhaps been hired by the same man who had employed the witch Chanta Favna to slaughter his business rivals? It was not entirely impossible that the merchant might not have some means of working his revenge even from a dungeon cell. Still, his instinct told him that the man who had paid these assassins was much nearer at hand.

'Perhaps things are as you say, Master Klausner,' Thulmann said, his voice uncertain. 'In any event, you know too much for me not to trust you a little longer.' The witch hunter's face slipped into a thin smile. 'We will find out tonight if that trust is misplaced.'

Fuming from the witch hunter's words, Gregor could only nod his head in understanding. Thulmann indicated the door, motioning for the young noble to precede him. Streng paused to remove a brass buckle from the dead man lying against the counter, then produced a knife to cut away the bronze buttons from his tunic. A sharp growl from Thulmann caused the mercenary to rise from his ghoulish labour, stuffing the few trinkets he had looted into a pocket. Slamming his knife back into its sheath, the mercenary hurried after Thulmann.

When they had gone, Reikhertz came around the counter to study the dead man a little more closely. His face again wrinkled in annoyance.

'Nasty...,' he muttered. He turned and shouted to his remaining patrons. 'Right, that's nasty. Help me clean it away now!'

IVAR KOHL STALKED the corridors of Klausner Keep, his face dark and brooding. His spies in the village had reported that the two sell-swords had failed in their task to kill the witch hunter. The steward hissed in anger as he considered how disastrous things could have become had either of them lived long enough to say who had paid them to murder the Templar. Perhaps Sigmar truly was lending his aid to Kohl's purposes.

Of course, the survival of the witch hunter might also be taken as a token of divine intervention. Bruno Fleischer had been quite an accomplished blade in his own rights, and Kohl had been quite confident in the swordsman's ability to despatch the Templar, especially with a second man to stack the odds in Fleischer's favour. The steward cursed again. It was bad enough that things had become so complicated and drawn-out. The meddling of a witch hunter was the last thing he needed, especially since it seemed he might be coming close to guessing the truth.

The steward strode into the kitchens, ignoring the servants who scurried out of his way, knowing better than to cross the grim Kohl in his current mood. Ivar Kohl soon faded past them, his black livery melding with the shadows that hung heavy about the short hallway that led to the wine cellar.

There was no question about it: the witch hunter was a threat, and a pronounced one. He would have to be dealt with. Kohl would arrange a more certain course of action, perhaps send for a professional assassin rather than trust again to the capabilities of ex-soldiers.

Kohl found himself within the dingy confines of the cellar. Ranks of wine racks filed away off into the gloom while mammoth casks and barrels of beer loomed against the walls. The steward strode toward one of the beer barrels, its surface covered in cobwebs.

He slid his fingers into the tiny groove just under the steel rim of the barrel, depressing the tiny stud he found there. The top of the barrel slid back, exposing a small compartment within. Kohl reached down and withdrew the heavy black robe and gleaming gold-hilted knife he found there.

Threat or no, the steward considered, the witch hunter would have to wait. Tonight's ritual would complete the pattern and close the circle. It was too important to put off, and any delay would undo all that had already been done. Ivar Kohl shuddered as he considered the horror of such a disaster. No, nothing could be allowed to stop the ceremony.

He spoke a short prayer to Sigmar that no more rituals would be needed after this one, that it would be the last.

CHAPTER FOURTEEN

DARKNESS HUNG HEAVY across the land. Clouds, thick and dark, had been blown down from the north, casting a pall across the gleaming face of Mannsleib. The moon could only be dimly seen behind the cloud cover, a dull glow behind the dark, nebulous shapes, flaring brilliantly during the infrequent breaks between the clouds. The same chill wind crawled about the ground, causing leaves to skitter and trees to sway.

It was a night made for horrors, when even the most sceptical city dweller might ponder the darker mysteries of the world and pause before every shadow, jump at every unseen sound.

Through the darkness, two shapes crept from shadow to shadow, pushing a third before them. Wet, wailing sounds could dimly be heard shuddering from the leading figure, her white dress standing out brilliantly against the landscape when she chanced to linger between shadows. Her body was young and shapely, a thing of delicate curves and slender smooth-skinned limbs. She was shivering beneath the thin covering of white homespun, damp with the sweat of fear.

The woman's steps were awkward and ungainly despite the gracefulness of her form, and it was with groans of pain that she

stumbled and fell, her choking sobs muffled by the filthy linen
sack that had been thrown over her head.

Her name was Deithild, one of five daughters of Reimar Stoss,
one of Klausberg's numerous shepherds. In her twenty years of
life, she had never experienced much that had been remarkable or
exciting, and her ambitions did not extend beyond the prospect
of a dreary marriage to seal some business dealing of her father's.
The terror that had been stalking the district had been the first discordant note in her life, breaking up the harmony and pattern of
her days.

Now, instead of taking turns to tend the flocks, her father took
the entire household with him, determined that the horror stalking the land would not glut itself upon his valuable animals. This
night, however, Deithild had begged away from helping her sisters, claiming illness with such conviction that even her
suspicious father had not pressed the issue.

However, instead of long hours of restful slumber, the young
woman had found herself awakened in the middle of the night.
The terror that had been prowling Klausberg had reached out to
claim her, snatching her not from the chill of her father's pastures,
but from the supposed safety of her own bed.

'Pick up the pace, bitch,' snarled one of the brutish men following her, his leathery hand jerking sharply on the rope that bound
Deithild's hands behind her back. The woman wailed into her
cruel hood as she was forced back to her feet by the painful pressure working on her arms.

The two men wore rough leather breeches, tunics of wool and
crude boots of hide and fur. Swords hung from their hips and
one of the men fingered the stock of a pistol holstered across his
belly. Their faces reflected the simplicity of the minds behind
them.

They were men who took a sadistic delight in the labours which
they were sometimes called upon to perform, the sort of
unscrupulous men that might be found in the service of any
noble family, much like an ill-tempered guard dog, creatures tolerated purely for their usefulness.

These men had made themselves very useful over the past few
weeks. Certainly, their nocturnal labours had been greatly different from their usual duties – the beating of peasants who refused
to pay their tax, torching the wagons of merchants that thought to

escape paying Lord Klausner for the privilege of passing through his lands. Still, the escalation of their brutality did not disturb the two unduly. Certainly these nocturnal sojourns for Ivar Kohl paid much better than any tasks they had before been charged with before. For men without conscience, that was enough.

Deithild was leaning against a tree, trying to gather breath between her terrified sobs. The brute holding the rope jerked her around, spilling the girl to the ground. His companion gave a short bark of amusement.

'Now you've gone and got her all dirty,' he laughed.

'Pick the wench up. Kohl will skin us if we're late,' the other snarled. His companion stepped forward, his hairy hands grabbing a hold of Deithild's arms. He paused in lifting her, moving one hand to slide down the length of her leg. The captive tried to wriggle out of his clutch, but her strength was not equal to the task.

'Shame to waste a fine cut of meat like this on Kohl,' the brute holding the girl commented. He laid his neck on the woman's shoulder, blowing his hot breath through the sacking. 'What say you? If you're be nice to us, maybe we'll let you go.'

'Enough of that!' snapped the man holding onto the rope. 'We don't have time to bounce the wench. Kohl's expecting us.' The other kidnapper licked the bare shoulder of their captive before withdrawing.

'It just seems like a waste, that's all,' the thug said. He looked back at the bound woman, raising his voice so that she could hear every word. 'I mean taking her out there, to him. To be cut up like something at a butcher's shop.' Deithild fell to her knees again, shuddering and sobbing, wailing with horror. The man holding the rope gave it a savage tug, pulling her back up.

'She faints and you're carrying her,' growled the brute holding the rope. His companion laughed again.

IVAR KOHL STOOD beneath the shadows cast by the broken stone wall. It was a curious thing, the steward thought. The blocks did not seem to have been mortared but rather fit into one another with such precision that nothing more was needed to hold them in place. Most likely some old elf trick, the steward shrugged. There were many mysteries surrounding the elder race. He doubted if men would ever uncover them all.

The steward cast a nervous eye overhead, licking his lips nervously as he saw the darkening clouds. This was a problem he did not need. The emergence of Morrsleib had to be timed correctly for the ritual to have its full effect. Kohl did not want to trust to any diminishment of the power of the ancient rite. For a moment, he almost wished he knew some sorcerous tricks that would banish storms.

The steward smiled at the thought, chiding himself for such weakness. *That way lies heresy*, he told himself.

Kohl cast a sour glance at the man standing beside him, then looked away when he heard the faint sounds of someone making their way through the woods. He retreated a bit deeper into the shadow, but as he listened further, he could hear the now familiar muffled sobs and wails of a sacrifice as the doomed soul was led to the place of ritual by his thugs.

A fanatic gleam flared up in the steward's eyes. He looked again at the figure standing beside him, nodding his head. The man helped Kohl into his black robe, then handed the steward a golden dagger.

'Pray to Sigmar that this is the last,' Kohl said, striding out into the clearing to greet the approaching figures. He could see his men leading their charge forward. A sickly smile crept onto Kohl's features. Sigmar forgive him, but a part of him hoped it wouldn't be.

'STAY WITH THE horses,' Thulmann said, his voice sharp and cold. Gregor Klausner glared back at the witch hunter.

'I tell you again that I had nothing to do with those men at the inn,' he said for what felt like the hundredth time that night. As before, his declaration did not impress the Templar.

'We will soon find out, won't we?' There was no mistaking the tone of menace in Thulmann's words. They stood within the trees bordering the Klausner estate, gazing down upon the clearing where the witch hunter had predicted that the next ritual would take place. The witch hunter had brought them here directly after the events at The Grey Crone, secreting them among the trees. All three men had shared watch duty, waiting until their insidious quarry showed himself. Gregor had begged the witch hunter to spring as soon as they had seen the two men lurking at the edges of the clearing, but Thulmann had called for them to maintain their vigil, awaiting the arrival of the other conspirators and their victim.

'Streng,' the witch hunter hissed. The bearded mercenary looked up at him from where he crouched close to the ground. 'Master Klausner is remaining here. Kindly relieve him of his armaments.' The witch hunter smiled thinly at the young noble. 'Purely so you might not be tempted into any injudicious actions,' he explained. Gregor scowled as he lifted his arms and allowed Streng to remove his sword belt and pistol.

'Nothing personal, you understand,' Streng told him. The mercenary cast an appraising eye over the sword he held. 'Of course,' he considered, a greedy glint in his eyes, 'if you are a heretic I'll get to keep these.' He grinned back at Gregor. 'Nothing personal of course.'

'An end to your chatter, man,' snapped Thulmann, drawing both his pistols. 'We've work to do.'

Gregor Klausner watched the two men slip into the darkness, slinking toward the clearing where they could now see three figures approaching. Gregor knew they had to be the other heretics and their captive. A cold determination swelled up within him. He stepped away from the horses, removing the tiny pocket pistol Streng had not known about. It was an old thing, a relic captured by some long dead Klausner during a crusade in Araby. Since that time, it had served the Klausners well. It would do so again this night.

Of that, Gregor was determined.

SWEAT BEADED KOHL's brow as he stepped toward the approaching men. This would be the one, he could feel it. This would be the one that would put an end to the horror. It had to be. It had to work this time. Kohl fingered the hilt of the dagger nervously as he advanced.

A sharp crack and boom intruded upon the silence. Kohl crumpled to the ground as his knee exploded, bursting apart as though an ogre had smashed it with a hammer. The ceremonial dagger flew out of his grasp, skittering off into the dark. Kohl winced in agony, rolling onto his back, fighting to keep from blacking out from the pain surging through him.

He could see a man emerging from the trees, black cloak billowing about him, his face hidden in the shadow cast by the brim of his hat. Smoke rose from the pistol gripped in his left hand. He pointed with the other into the gloom. Ivar Kohl felt disgust and rage swell over his pain. The witch hunter! He should have known.

'Draw your steel, you sons of blaspheming slatterns!' Thulmann roared, his voice burning with outrage and challenge. The pistol in his hand roared in turn, spitting flame and smoke. The ruffian holding the rope that bound the captive woman gave a cry of agony. He released his grip, falling to the ground and rolling in agony as he clutched the weeping crimson mask that had moments before been his face. The woman dropped to her knees, screaming in terror into the sack that covered her head. The other brute turned to run.

'Going somewhere, friend?' hissed Streng, emerging from the trees opposite Thulmann and plunging Gregor's sword into the fleeing villain's stomach. The man gasped, hands flying to his injury, trying to staunch the stream of blood and bile.

Streng smashed him aside with the engraved hilt of the sword, knocking him to the ground. The mercenary lifted the pistol gripped in his other hand, sighting across the clearing at the dark-garbed man who emerged from the trees. The pistol cracked and roared, the impact of the bullet spinning the man as he ran toward Thulmann, a cavalry sabre clenched in his fist. Kohl's assistant cried out as he fell.

Thulmann strode toward Ivar Kohl's prone body, holstering his pistols and drawing his sword. A look of indignation, wrath and disgust pulled at the witch hunter's features.

He glared down at Kohl. If he was surprised to see the steward's face underneath the black robes, Thulmann did not let it show. He pricked the injured man's throat with the point of his blade. Kohl's eyes grew wide with horror. Thulmann smiled down at him coldly.

'Oh no,' his silky voice had a quality of malevolent mirth about it. 'You don't die so easily, or so quickly.'

Across the clearing, Streng removed the linen sack from the sobbing Deithild's head. He paused to admire the cast of her pretty features, then busied himself undoing the knots that bound her hands.

He fumbled with the knot for some time, one dirty paw clutching at the woman's chest, ostensibly to support her. The mercenary looked up at her, a lewd smile on his crude features. 'Sorry about that,' he told her, doing nothing to remove the groping fingers. 'Everything's going to be all right. Isn't nobody going to hurt you while I have anything to say about it.'

As he freed her hands, Streng braced himself for a slap to his jaw. Instead, such was the woman's relief at her rescue that she wrapped around Streng's neck, crushing him in a fierce hug, her face buried in his grimy tunic as she sobbed with relief.

Streng smiled above her embrace. 'Very nice to see you feel this way about me,' he grinned.

Mathias Thulmann set his heel on Kohl's chest, pinning the injured steward to the ground, then inspected the man's wound. His leg was pumping a steady stream of blood; already a small puddle of it was congealing around the man. Thulmann swore under his breath, sheathing his sword and pulling a laced handkerchief from his vest.

'It won't do to have you bleed out on me, Master Kohl. Not until you've answered a few questions.'

'I'll tell you nothing!' Kohl snarled through his pain. The witch hunter tore the piece of fabric, then wound it around the steward's bleeding stump. He smiled in cruel mockery at the heretic as he pulled the makeshift tourniquet tight.

'Yes,' he chuckled grimly, 'I do believe I have heard that one before.'

'Thulmann!' Gregor's voice shouted from the night. Thulmann turned his head to see the young noble emerging from the trees, a small pistol clutched in his hand. Before the witch hunter could react, the gun gave a sharp bark and yellow fire, grey smoke and lead death erupting from its barrel. The echo of the discharge was almost immediately drowned out by a burbling wail of anguish.

The witch hunter turned his head in the direction of the sound. The man Streng had earlier shot was lying in a spreading pool of gore, a dark depression in the middle of his forehead. The man's dead hand was closed around a dagger.

'Friend Streng,' Thulmann called out. The mercenary was looking over at his employer, having extracted himself from the thankful embrace of the young woman as soon as he had heard the pistol shot. 'Your slovenly marksmanship will cost you five gold crowns,' the witch hunter declared. The mercenary shrugged his shoulders, turning his attention back to Deithild's gratitude.

Thulmann looked over at Gregor. 'Thankfully your own was much better,' he said, smiling. The young noble nodded his head in acknowledgement of both the spoken compliment and the unspoken apology.

Gregor Klausner stared in horror and loathing at the prostrate form of his father's steward. Anger, the righteous indignation of a man who had sworn to put an end to the horrible crimes committed against the good folk of Klausberg, boiled within him. But the emotion was subdued by the sick horror that drained the colour from Gregor's skin, that gnawed at the pit of his stomach and his soul.

Ivar Kohl, a man he had known all his life, a man who had in many ways acted as his father's surrogate when Wilhelm Klausner had gone away to serve the temple of Sigmar. A stern and unpleasant individual, one who Gregor had feared more than respected as a boy, who he had tolerated more than liked as a man. But to see Kohl unmasked before him as the perpetrator of such heinous acts of heresy and wickedness was a thing beyond belief. Yet the evidence, the unquestionable evidence of his own eyes, was laid out before him.

The young noble thought once more of the ring hidden in his pocket, that talisman of the Klausner line. The sickness swelled as he desperately tried to tell himself that his fears were impossible. How could his own father be a party to such crimes? Yet why else would his oldest and most trusted servant be lying upon the ground, the witch hunter's bullet in his leg? How else could a Klausner ring have come to be lying upon the floor of the Brustholz farm?

'What are you going to do with him?' Gregor pointed down at the figure of Ivar Kohl. The subdued steward glared back at him. Thulmann pulled the wounded man to his feet, ignoring the cries of pain the steward uttered as his weight pressed against the wound.

'As a duly appointed representative of Sigmar's Holy Order of Witch Hunters, it is within my authority to question my prisoners in any provincial or municipal structure I deem suits my needs,' the witch hunter told him. 'I am sure that Herr Kohl will not object greatly if we escort him home.' The witch hunter looked away, shouting over to Streng. 'What about those two?'

'They're done for,' Streng replied, casting a sideways look at each of the wounded men squirming upon the ground. 'The one you shot won't last another five minutes. The one I stuck is spilling his belly, might take him a few hours to finish bleeding out.' The mercenary spat at the writhing man. 'A load better than the vermin rates,' he snarled, much to the approval of the woman who still held him in a fierce embrace.

'Well, see that they are both finished and hurry it up,' the witch hunter snarled. 'We're going to take Master Kohl here back to the keep. There will be work for you to do when we get there.'

Streng's face split in a bloodthirsty grin.

CHAPTER FIFTEEN

THE WITCH HUNTER's boots clicked across the floor of the keep's entry hall. He cast an imperious gaze across the dimly lit room, then focused his attention back on the frightened servant who had admitted him and his party. The man kept looking over at the sagging, bleeding figure of Ivar Kohl with an expression that was a mixture of shock, wonder and even a fair degree of satisfaction. The steward was not well loved by his staff.

'Gregor,' the witch hunter spoke. 'Escort Streng and my prisoner down to the cellar you spoke of.' During their ride back to the keep, Gregor Klausner had related that his great grandfather, a morbid and intensely zealous man who had expired in the act of scourging himself with a steel whip in his later years, had maintained a gruesome reminder of his years as a witch hunter. Beneath the wine cellars, in a sub level, he had built a torture chamber, equipping it with all the vicious implements of his trade. It was an ugly little room, and though it had never been used, it still seemed to echo with the sounds of screams. Thulmann had smiled grimly, commenting, 'Sigmar provides.'

The two men carried their injured captive away. Streng sneered into the semi-conscious heretic's ear. 'Many's the time you went past that room, I'll wager,' the mercenary laughed. 'Didn't ever think you'd be visiting it yourself though?' Pushing their near insensible prisoner, the two men disappeared down one of the corridors opening onto the great hall. The shocked servant watched the men leave.

'You,' Thulmann's silky voice snapped, causing the servant to spin around. 'Take this girl to the kitchens. Get her some food, some decent clothes and a bit of good wine to burn the chill from her bones.' The witch hunter gestured and the servant took the hand of the pale, trembling girl who lingered upon the threshold. Deithild pulled away in fright.

'It's alright, child,' Thulmann's soothing tones told her. 'This man will take you somewhere warm and get you something to eat.' He fixed the man with a warning look. 'No harm will come to you.' Deithild reluctantly allowed herself to be led away, pausing before Thulmann to return his cloak, which the Templar had thrown about her when they had left the site of Kohl's abortive ceremony.

The witch hunter smiled in return, watching the rescued woman be taken away. As soon as she was out of sight, the smile dropped into something unfriendly and filled with anger. Thulmann lifted his gaze toward the stairs.

It was time for a reckoning.

MATHIAS THULMANN GLARED across the bed chamber, his wrath fixed upon the withered man nestled within the mammoth bed. The witch hunter's face twitched in barely restrained fury. He pointed a gloved finger at the chambermaid who was fluffing pillows in a corner of the room.

'Leave us,' he snarled. The tone in his voice caused the girl to set down her work and hurry from the room with only a single, worried glance to her bed-ridden master. 'Now,' the witch hunter added in a hiss when she did not move fast enough.

Thulmann's anger was matched by that of the aged Wilhelm Klausner. 'How dare you?' the old man growled. 'I'll not put up with this nonsense any longer!' He reached his hand for the bell rope beside him, tugging it furiously. Distantly, the jangle of the bell could be heard sounding somewhere within the keep below.

'You'll find your steward is otherwise occupied,' Thulmann informed the patriarch. 'He is with my man, down in your torture chamber, your lordship.' The scorn in his voice was like the edge of a knife. Wilhelm Klausner flinched away, his already pallid skin losing yet more of its colour.

'Oh yes, your lordship,' Thulmann pressed, noting the old man's anxiety. 'The fiend that has been preying upon your district has been unmasked at last.' The witch hunter's hand closed about the hilt of his sword, the knuckles whitening beneath his glove. 'By Sigmar, you are more of a monster than any of the vermin you sent to the stake!' he spat. The violence in his words caused Wilhelm to regain much of his composure, the old man rising up to the Templar's challenge.

'Who do you think you are to speak to me in such a fashion, in my own home?'

Thulmann began to pace, his hand opening and closing about the hilt of his sword. He stalked past the small writing table situated near the corner of the room, its surface pitted by age beneath its sheen, a well-worn Book of Sigmar dominating its surface.

Above the table, fixed to the wall was a wooden plaque upon which had been fixed the seal of Sigmar, the sigil of the twin-tailed comet that was given to every witch hunter. Thulmann scowled as he considered that it had once been worn by the patriarch. It was a struggle for the witch hunter not to rip it from its fixture. 'I have not dragged the story in its full from Kohl,' he snarled, turning away from the offending plaque. 'But be certain that I shall. My man is a hedonist, a thug and a drunkard, but when it comes to the art of torture, he is a prodigy. What little I did glean from his semi-coherent ramblings already turns my stomach. Preying upon your own people! Offering them up in pagan sacrifice in return for some sorcerous protection!'

'You dare!' shouted Wilhelm, his entire body trembling from the emotion swelling up within him. 'I deny these filthy allegations! How dare you accuse me, I, who have served the temple and the Empire with devout loyalty my entire life!' The old man's withered claw rose, swiping at the air. 'Get out of my house!' he roared.

'You have no authority here, your lordship!' spat Thulmann, stalking forward like some great beast. 'This farce is at an end!' he added with a snarl. 'All you deny is the glory and might of Holy Sigmar!' The door began to open behind him, a liveried servant moving to enter in answer to Wilhelm's summons. The witch hunter grabbed the handle, slamming the portal shut in the man's face.

'You, a servant of Sigmar,' the witch hunter sneered, voice dripping with venomous contempt. 'Be thankful that I was in time to stop your steward from completing the obscenity he contemplated this night. It will be one less crime to answer for when you stand before Sigmar and are judged for your blasphemies.'

The Templar stalked past the foot of the bed once more, passing before the old man's massive wardrobe and a glass-faced cupboard that held musty relics from Wilhelm's time of service to the temple.

Wilhelm Klausner seemed to wilt as he heard Thulmann's words. He lifted a trembling hand to his mouth. 'You... you stopped...' A look of absolute terror came upon him and he gave voice to a rattling sob that seemed to surge from the very pits of his soul. 'Now we are doomed,' the old man groaned.

'You were doomed and damned when you chose to forsake the might of Sigmar and put your faith in profane sorceries to preserve you from evil,' the witch hunter rebuked him. The door behind him opened once again. This time it was no servant, but a livid Anton Klausner who stood outside. The younger Klausner stepped into the room, his face contorted with his own indignant fury.

'What the devil are you...' The young noble's words were cut off as he spoke. Thulmann's gloved hand shot from the hilt of his blade, striking Anton across the face with the back of his hand with such force that the young man was thrown to the floor, falling beside the hearth. Thulmann glared down into Anton's face as the boy reached for his own weapon.

'Draw that blade but an inch,' the witch hunter growled, 'and I shall paint that wall with your life's blood, be you guilty of your father's heresies or no.' The cold, chill manner in which Thulmann spoke his threat caused Anton to back down, the young Klausner daubing at the thin trickle of blood dripping from the corner of his mouth.

The boy turned his gaze from the glowering witch hunter to the withered old man on his sick bed.

Anton stared in bewilderment at the expression on his father's face. Written upon that aged visage was misery and defeat and shame, emotions Anton had never before seen exhibited by his always stern and stalwart father. More, there was the agonised appeal in old Wilhelm's eyes, the desperate cry for pity and understanding and forgiveness.

Anton felt contempt boil within his heart. After all these years, long years of trying to prove his value to the old man, and now it was his father who showed himself to be of no value. Wilhelm Klausner had given everything to his eldest son. To Anton, he had given only his name, and Anton had taken great pride in that name and in the long history of honour and tradition that graced it. The name of Klausner was what made him important, made him better than the swineherds and farmers. He could clearly see the guilt in his father's face, more evident even than the old man's shame and fear.

Wilhelm Klausner had given Anton his name, and now he was taking even that away from him, staining it with such crimes that he had drawn the attention of an outlander witch hunter.

The youth bared his teeth in a feral snarl, picking himself from the floor and storming from the room, slamming the door behind him. Thulmann again fixed Wilhelm with his harsh gaze.

'I know not how deep this heresy runs,' he spat, 'but I will find out! I will learn the root of this madness that has infected you and your household and I will burn it from the face of the Empire!'

ANTON KLAUSNER SMASHED his fist against the hard stone wall, giving voice to an inarticulate howl of animal rage. How dare that old man! How dare he! Anton would not have believed anything the witch hunter said, anything that anyone said. But he had seen the truth in his father's eyes, the dismal guilt and self-loathing, the resignation to a long-deferred doom.

The youth howled again. He would not cry, he would not shed a tear for the old bastard.

Anton looked below to see Gregor racing up the steps, taking them two at a time. The other Klausner son had finished conducting Streng and his prisoner to the old dungeon and was now desperate to reach his father, to hear for himself Wilhelm's reaction to the witch hunter's accusations.

Despite the firm conviction that gripped Thulmann, and Gregor's own disturbing discovery of the family ring at the Brustholz farm, the young noble could not bring himself to believe his father guilty of participating in such an unholy conspiracy.

'What has happened?' Gregor called out to Anton as he approached his brother, seeing the violent distress on Anton's face, the blood trickling from his bruised mouth and savaged hand.

Anton's gaze was as cold as the winds of Kislev. 'Ruin,' Anton answered. 'Ruin has come upon us. Your witch hunter friend has destroyed us.' Anton's face twisted about into a grim sneer. 'Oh, maybe you,' he laughed without mirth. 'You'll still get the title and the lands and the power! But all I had was the name, the name of Klausner and the legacy of honour and valour that accompanied it!' He clenched his bruised fist. 'It's being stripped away! The witch hunter won't leave that! When he is finished, there will be no honour left!'

'He is with father?' Gregor asked. The murderous hatred in Anton's eyes caused him to recoil.

'That sick old heretic bastard up there is no father of mine,' he spat, storming past Gregor, shouting for his ruffian cronies. Gregor watched his brother, shaking his head, then continued on to his father's room.

GREGOR FOUND THE witch hunter pacing across his father's room, his body trembling with every step, his hand clenching and unclenching about the hilt of his sword. The old man on the bed seemed even more shrunken and withered than before, looking like a pile of old, tired bones. Something had been taken from his father, some vital spark, and its absence had diminished the old man hideously.

Thulmann turned on Gregor as the young noble entered. The Templar's face retained its mask of grim judgement and for a moment, Gregor actually thought that he was going to draw his sword.

'This does not concern you, Gregor,' the witch hunter told him. 'If there is one man in this entire district who is innocent of this heresy, it is you.' Thulmann closed his eyes, a tiny fraction of his rage escaping him in a sigh. 'Your marksmanship earlier this evening proved that.' When he opened his eyes, the intensity flared up again. 'Leave this room.'

The young noble stood his ground. 'He is my father,' Gregor said. The words caused Wilhelm's face to twist in pain and an agonised groan to hiss from his wasted body.

'He is a heretic and a murderer,' Thulmann snarled. 'He knew about his steward's blasphemous practices. At best, he turned a blind eye to them. At worst, he condoned these profane rites.'

Or orchestrated them, Gregor thought, his eyes turning toward the Klausner coat of arms fixed above the hearth and considering the ring that bore that heraldry still secreted in his pocket. He looked again at his father. The old man lowered his eyes, as though too ashamed to face his son. Gregor shook his head. 'Whatever he has done,' he repeated. 'He is my father.'

'Whatever he has done,' echoed Thulmann. He sneered at the patriarch. 'And what have you done? To what depths of obscenity have you sunk? How many people have you seduced into this loathsome sorcery?' He shook his fist at the old man. 'I will have my answers,' he warned. 'By the temple, I'll have my answers, if I have to rip them from you with whip and knife!'

Gregor clutched at the witch hunter's arm. 'You would not dare!' he gasped in horror.

Thulmann's expression grew grave. He could sympathise with the young noble's emotions, the affection and love he had always known for his father were not so easy to banish. Still, for the sake of all those who had been so ruthlessly slaughtered, he would not be dissuaded from that which needed to be done.

'I'll have my answers,' he repeated coldly. 'Leave now.' The witch hunter stabbed his finger at the door. 'Now!' he snarled. Gregor strode instead to the small side door that led to his father's private chapel.

'You are wrong,' he said, his voice heavy with doubt even as he said the words. 'My father couldn't...'

'He has,' Thulmann spat, glaring once more at the wretched creature on the bed. 'Look at the guilt gnawing at him, the shame of his unmasking. Wilhelm Klausner, witch hunter,' Thulmann snorted in contempt. 'Wilhelm Klausner, necromancer and sorcerer is nearer the truth.' He looked at Gregor, studying the younger man's face. 'You know that I'm right.'

Gregor swallowed the lump that swelled in his throat. 'I will pray for you. Pray that Sigmar will rid you of these hideous delusions that beset you.'

'Pray instead for your father's black soul, that Sigmar might show it some of the mercy this animal never showed his victims,' the witch hunter retorted.

'Do not harm him,' Gregor warned. 'I will be able to hear all that occurs in this room.' Wilhelm clenched his teeth in agony as he heard his son's words. The witch hunter merely nodded.

'I will not do him injury,' Thulmann said in a chill hiss. 'Not until he ceases to answer my questions. When that time comes, you can help me destroy this legacy of evil, or you can become a victim of it. That choice I leave to you.'

Gregor said nothing more, but left the room, slamming the chapel door behind him.

'Don't harm him,' Wilhelm implored in a dry rasp.

Thulmann stared down his nose at the wasted old man. 'My sons are innocent of the evil I have been guilty of. I would not let it touch them.'

The witch hunter smiled back, an expression as cruel and malevolent as any that had ever been cast in stone upon the Great Temple's gargoyles.

'Convince me,' Thulmann commanded.

CHAPTER SIXTEEN

ANTON KLAUSNER AND his three closest cronies galloped down the winding path through the blighted woods that surrounded Klausner Keep.

The young noble's mind brooded upon the drama he had left unfolding in the fortress behind him. He refused to accept the events, lashing his steed to greater effort as anger welled up within him.

The horror that had been preying upon the countryside was no doing of his father, it simply could not be. What end would it serve? These killings did nothing but weaken the power and authority of the Klausners within their own district. No, this outlander witch hunter had some other motive behind his accusations, some conjuration of the family's enemies. He had twisted the old man's feeble mind into believing these falsehoods, into accepting them as the truth.

Such were the lies Anton told himself. He did not care overmuch if his father really was guilty of that which he had been accused, nor did he really find himself disturbed by the thought of the old man ending his life screaming upon a rack or tied to a stake.

All his life, Anton had tried to measure up to the old man's ideals, and yet, when he had become old enough, when he was at last man enough to go forth and earn his own legacy of honour and accomplishment, the spiteful old tyrant had denied him the opportunity. Gregor, dear Gregor, the elder son, would inherit the title and the lands and the power.

What would Anton have if he did not go out and win it for himself? Nothing, only the name of Klausner and the aged heritage of tradition and honour that was a part of that name. Now even that was going to be taken from him. Anton was not going to allow such a thing to happen.

Anton glanced aside at his men. They would show this witch hunter. They would go out and find a more expedient culprit for the murders, find him and bring his mangled body back to the keep, show this outlander swine how wild and baseless his mad accusations were. He would pull his father out of the pit of dishonour and scandal he had dug for himself and which the miserable, thoughtless fool was seemingly resigned to.

Anton sneered as he imagined the old man's gratitude. Perhaps then he would see his younger son's worth and value. All the young noble need do now was settle on which miserable wretch from the village he would say was responsible for the murders.

The horses thundered across the tiny bridge that spanned the stream where Thulmann and Gregor had had their remarkable escape from the undead wolves. There was still a darkened stain, like a burned outline, upon the wooden surface where the wolf had been destroyed. Anton paid the crossing no notice, intent upon his own dark thoughts. However, when the horse of one of his comrades gave a sharp whinny of terror, the young man gazed around him in alarm.

They had ridden into the narrow pathway that snaked its course among the sickened trees and crumbling elf ruins, where not so long ago Anton's own brother had been beset by the restless dead.

Dead things stirred once more upon the edge of the blighted wood, prowling the borderlands of the Klausner domain. Anton could see them shambling out from behind the trees in a rotting, mouldering horde. Limbs picked clean of flesh groped toward the riders as grinning skulls opened their jaws in soundless howls of battle. Rusted swords and crumbling axes lashed out.

Anton could see that one of his friends was down already, his horse gutted by a corroded axe. Three of the skeletal horrors loomed over the thrown rider, their weapons rising and falling like the hammers of clockwork bell-ringers. The screams of the man weakened, then stopped.

'Holy Sigmar!' Anton shouted in terror. The youth tore his sword from its scabbard. One of his friends tried to ride through the horde as they began to converge upon the path ahead. The man's steed slammed into the rotting figures, bowling the first few ranks aside as though they were tenpins. But as it plunged deeper into the host, the charge lost its impetus, the horse was slowed by the clutching hands and by the rusted blades that tore at its legs and flanks. A ghastly wail like the sound of a soul tossed into the Pit exploded from the rider's lungs as the skeletons pulled down his weakened steed, and he disappeared beneath the bodies of his foes.

Anton Klausner lashed out desperately as the skeletons continued to pour from the trees, his sword smashing into bleached skulls and decayed shoulders.

Sometimes, his blows would splinter the bone, crashing into the fleshless horrors with such force that their animated bodies would come apart, falling into a jumble of shattered bone and rotten armour. Other times, he would only succeed in causing a crack in the sorcerously reanimated bone, and the unfeeling monster would continue to press forward, requiring repeated blows to finally arrest its advance.

Anton struck to the left and right, his blows finding targets wherever he turned. In the span of only a few seconds, he brought down five of the undead abominations, and still they came at him, neither noticing nor caring about the fate of their comrades. There seemed no end to the monsters. To every side, Anton could see only the grinning, fleshless heads of things newly called from their graves.

Beside him, his last companion finally faltered, flinging his sword into the face of one of his skeletal attackers and jerking the head of his horse so sharply that he nearly overturned the animal. The skeletons rushed upon him, even as he spurred his mount to flee.

The horse galloped away, seven of the undead monsters clinging to it, either by means of their claw-like hands or the rusty blades they had buried in the animal's flesh. The terrified animal raced across the bridge, carrying its horrible cargo along with it. The skeletons held firm, however, and soon dragged the faltering brute down by means of their continued attacks. Not so very far from the scorched timber that marked the dire wolf's destruction, the undead warriors hacked Anton's friend to bits.

Anton did not see his comrade die, however. Beset on all sides, at last several of the monsters penetrated his own desperate defence. His horse gave vent to a sound that was almost eerily human as it was dragged down.

Anton tried to fend off the blows that followed as his horse struck the ground, and he along with it, but grasping claws ripped his sword from his hand. The young noble looked up, his vision filled with the grinning, eyeless countenances of his unnatural enemies. Rusty swords and crumbling spears were raised above him, poised to strike.

'No,' Carandini's voice slithered from the night. The necromancer pushed his way through the mouldering ranks of his soldiers, his children of the grave. 'This one does not die so easily.' He stared down at Anton, a greasy smile working itself upon his face. 'I think that my friend will want to see this one.' Carandini snapped his fingers and the skeletal warriors seized Anton Klausner, dragging the screaming man from beneath his horse.

Carandini followed behind the skeletons as they carried their prisoner into the darkness.

'Oh yes,' the necromancer hissed. 'I am most certain that he will be pleased to see you.'

GREGOR CLOSED THE door behind him, lingering for a moment just beyond the threshold. He could hear the angry voice of the witch hunter shouting in the room he had just left, haranguing his father once more. Much softer, almost inaudible, were the old patriarch's subdued responses. Gregor fought to keep the emotion from his face. He needed to be strong now, not give way to the hopeless despair that gnawed at him. There was a way out of this horror, there had to be.

The young noble's face dropped as he fingered the ring in his pocket. He considered the possibility, nay, the probability that his father truly was guilty of all the witch hunter accused him of. The thought had preyed upon Gregor for days now, and it was one that even his love for the old man could not fend off.

The ring old Wilhelm had worn afterwards could have been a copy. Tradition held it that the patriarch's ring was the same one worn by Helmuth Klausner five hundred years ago, handed down from father to son along with the title and lands. But who was to say that it was the same ring? There could have been any number of copies made over the years, perhaps with the originals buried in the vaults with the men who had worn them in life. If such was the case, Wilhelm would have known this and had one of these rings taken from the old graves when he discovered that his own had been lost.

Gregor knew what he must do. He must help the witch hunter. He must do his duty to the Empire, to Sigmar and help discover the source of this horror that had overwhelmed his father's mind. But Gregor also knew what helping the witch hunter would mean; he knew what fate Thulmann would put his father to.

On the road back to the keep, Streng had taken a sadistic pleasure in describing the atrocities he would visit upon Kohl, gleefully illustrating for the wounded steward how flesh might be scraped from bone without the victim losing consciousness.

Gregor knew that Thulmann would not spare his father from similar torments simply because of his position or his former role as a witch hunter himself. He had seen the outrage, the fury in Thulmann's eyes. He took the descent of a former witch hunter into such vileness as a personal affront, a slight upon the temple itself.

Thulmann would not rest until every life taken by Wilhelm and Kohl had been avenged through torment. Gregor felt sorrow and regret for the lives that had been lost. For Kohl, he could summon not even the shadow of pity, but his father, how could he leave the old man to such a miserable end?

Gregor turned, walking toward the altar. He needed to pray, needed to beg at the shrine of his god that the madness that had risen up to devour his world could be pushed back, that all could go back to what it had been. He stopped when he saw a figure crouched before the altar, its form covered in a long black cloak. The shape moved its head, the hood falling away from a head of greying hair.

Ilsa Klausner smiled at her son, a pained expression that spoke more than Gregor wanted to hear.

'How long have you been here?' Gregor managed to ask after a few moments.

'Long enough,' his mother responded, her voice old and dry. 'Long enough to know that it has all come to an end.' She looked toward the door through which Gregor had only moments before passed. Her face was moist with the shimmer of tears. 'You knew?' Gregor gasped. 'You knew about this all the time?' A new horror squirmed through Gregor's soul. The woman shook her head.

'No,' she told him. 'I did not know. I did not know because I did not want to know. I loved your father. I still do and always shall, whatever that may cost me.' She looked deep into her son's eyes. 'And know this, Gregor, above all else, he loved us. We were his light, his life, his soul. Whatever he did in his life, he did it because he wanted to protect us, to keep his family safe. That was all that mattered to him. Whatever he has done, it was not toward some selfish end. It was to keep us safe.'

Gregor extended his hand, leaning against the wall to support a body that had suddenly grown weak. He had just begun to resign himself to the fact that his father was a monster, a bloodthirsty beast who preyed upon the countryside with his unholy hunger. Now his mother had bolstered his doubts and rekindled his fears.

'I think, whatever he has done, whatever secret he and Ivar shared, it is a very old secret.' Her eyes hardened even as her voice grew quiet. 'Remember, Ivar was your grandfather's steward before he served your father. And Ivar's grandfather was steward before him…'

Gregor's eyes grew wide with shock as he considered the path to which her mother's frightful statement might lead. He thought again of the old monument buried, hidden, within the blighted woods. He thought of the old legends, stretching back into the mists of time. The Klausner daemon. How aptly had it been named, for it was not a daemon that sought to prey upon the Klausners, but the Klausners themselves who were the daemon.

'You should go to him,' Gregor said in a soft voice. 'Before… Before the witch hunter…' Ilsa Klausner shook her head.

'He would not endure the shame of it,' she told him. 'And, may Sigmar forgive me, I could not see that sort of pain in his eyes.'

Gregor thought of the crushed, degraded and humiliated creature that had gazed upon him from his sick bed and knew that his mother was right.

'Then all we can do is pray,' the young noble said, dropping to his knees beside his mother. 'All we can do is pray that Sigmar will take my father's misguided soul before the witch hunter begins his work.'

'A FAMILY SECRET then?' Thulmann's sharp words lashed out like the barbed end of a whip. 'Some unspeakable pact between your ancestors and the Dark Gods?' The witch hunter slammed his hand against the polished headboard with a violent thump. 'Speak damn you! I will know how far back this profane taint extends itself! I've seen the hidden monument on your property! I've heard the legends they whisper in the village! Tell me when this nightmare began! Confess, man, and lessen the taint that has swallowed your soul!'

Wilhelm turned his eyes toward the ceiling. They were dull, almost lifeless, filled with a terrible weariness. His lips trembled as if stricken with palsy. When he spoke, it was in a rasping croak. 'The ritual was never meant to go so far,' he said, almost imploring his accuser to believe him. 'Ever before, it had only taken six to complete the circle.' He could see the fiery gleam burning in Thulmann's gaze and hastened to explain further. 'The circle was meant to protect, to safeguard the keep and the lands around it. Nothing more!'

'You sent six innocent souls to their graves and you call that nothing!' snapped the witch hunter.

Wilhelm drew himself back, a fragment of his old strength surging into him.

'Six peasants, six dullard farmers and swineherds who could not even write their own names. Six sorry specimens of humanity to preserve the line of Klausner, to produce sons who would carry on the fight to the enemy, who would serve the temple as its sword and hammer.'

Wilhelm's voice trembled with the violence in his words. It was an echo of the argument he had heard Ivar Kohl use upon him many times, an echo of the last words he had heard uttered by his own father upon his deathbed. It was an argument that even now, Wilhelm fought desperately to believe.

'I notice that you have forbidden your own sons to carry on that tradition,' Thulmann sneered. 'Reconsidering the hypocrisy of your heritage? Deciding to embrace your pagan beliefs in full perhaps? Does that explain why so many have died, to proclaim your loyalty to your new masters?'

Anguished horror filled Wilhelm's face, the horror of a guilty man desperate to explain the motives behind his crime or desperate to have them believed.

'No! I have never allowed my sons to know of this hideous legacy! I would not let them be destroyed and damned as I have been! That is why I forbade them to serve the temple, and why I took measures to ensure that the ritual need never be performed again! I could never allow them to become what I have become.' The patriarch's words drifted off into a miserable sob.

'But something went wrong,' Thulmann snapped, not giving the old man a second to compose himself. 'Something went wrong and it was not six who had to die. Nor seven. Nor eight,' with each statement, the old man covered his ears and moaned in horror. 'What were you hoping to accomplish! What went wrong with your profane rites this time!'

Wilhelm's eyes had become black pits of despair. 'The enemy had some new trick, some powers it had never had before. Only the blood from half the deaths stains my hands, the others were the work of… it. It performed its own rites, its own dark sorcery, and those rites undid the power of Kohl's rituals. With every new murder, the circle of protection began to weaken. Ivar had to kill again and again just to maintain the circle's power.' The old man looked at Thulmann again, and the fear the witch hunter saw there was of such intensity that even he had never seen its like. 'You stopped him tonight,' the old man's finger shook as he pointed at Thulmann. 'The circle is broken now, and it will come and kill us all.'

'What will come?' Thulmann demanded, the hair on the back of his neck prickling with foreboding.

'The enemy that has haunted my line since the very beginning,' the old man replied. His voice dropped into a horrified hiss as he spoke the name, the strength seeming to drain out of him once more as the syllables left his lips.

'Sibbechai.'

ANTON KLAUSNER WAS thrown to the ground, his arm tearing itself open upon the jagged rubble. The youth ignored the pain, however, scrambling behind a crumbling block of stone. He stared in fear at the silent, skeletal shapes that had carried him through the woods to this place, their fleshless claws clutching his arms and legs with grips as strong and chill as the glacial ice of Norsca. The cold wind pulled at the lingering scraps of rotting leather and links of chain armour that clung to their limbs and ribs.

The animated corpses did not return his gaze, did not appear to still notice the captive they had brought here.

Anton's hand closed about a mass of fallen masonry. If he could strike quickly, before the weird, unnatural spark that motivated the dead warriors asserted itself once more, perhaps he could destroy his captors or at least give some account of himself before they hacked him to ribbons as they had his friends.

There were only four of them, the others had stayed behind, patrolling the section of road where Anton had been ambushed. Even so, it was bad odds, one weaponless man against four undying things from beyond the grave. They were odds that gave Anton pause, made him delay before leaping into a reckless and desperate fight. The decision to act or not was soon taken from him.

The already cold atmosphere of the ruined cottage suddenly became even colder. Anton shuddered, shocked to see his breath forming into icy mist before him.

A foul, revolting stench swelled about the ruin, the stink of something long dead, something necrotic and decayed, something rife with a corruption even more loathsome than his silent captors. Fear gnawed at the very depths of Anton's soul, a fear so profound, so complete and all-consuming that his stomach purged itself without warning and a warm foulness dampened his legs.

Tears coursed down Anton's face and the block of masonry fell from his shaking hands. His breath stopped, even his heart seemed to slow.

It was there, the young noble knew, in the darkness behind him, lurking within the shadows cast by the few remnants of the building's roof. It was something horrible and foul, something of such unholy terror that the mere sight of it would destroy him.

Anton began to weep freely now, the sounds harkening back to the crib, back to the multitude of childhood phantoms and fiends that had prowled the nursery until his cries had brought his nanny running with a lantern to chase them away again. He would not look at it, he would not see it. He would close his eyes and hide his head and wait for nanny to chase it away. Whatever happened, he would not turn. He would not look at it.

Anton Klausner shifted his position, turning his body to face the darkness. Despite his terrified conviction, an urge had come upon him, a command that seemed to burn into his brain, a compulsion that did not originate from his own mind but from another's. His eyes grew wider and wider until they seemed that they might pop and the only sound that now came from him was an inarticulate whimper.

A part of the darkness glided forward, moving more like a wisp of smoke than any mortal's step. The shape was tall and thin and decayed. It wore a long black robe about its reed-like shape, a robe with a leather collar that looked as though it had been stitched together from the wings of bats. Chains and leather cords dripped from the garment, each string ending in some morbid talisman. Here, a cord of severed human and inhuman ears, there the tiny pickled hand of an unborn infant. Upon the hem of the garment the picture-writing of long-dead Khemri had been stitched in golden thread.

The arms of the figure were long and cadaverous, the hands protruding from the sleeves of the robe. They were thin and desiccated, the skin grey, corrupt and rotten. Long nails, like the talons of a vulture, tipped each of the fingers, the enamel hardened into a shiny brown surface that resembled the back of a corpse beetle.

The apparition's head was shrunken and withered, little more than a skull with a thin covering of grey, leathery skin wrapped about it, its bald pate covered by a rounded cap of black velvet from which grinned the skeletal face of a dead bat. Long, pointed ears flanked either side of the misshapen head, looking as though they had been cut from the head of a wolf and stitched onto the monster's skull. The face of the creature was that of a death's head, the nose fallen away long ago, the eyes withdrawn into their pits, lips pulled back from the over-sized jaw. The teeth alone carried with them a hint of vitality, shining like polished ivory, the eye-teeth grown into ghastly, rat-like incisors.

The vampire's smouldering eyes suddenly gleamed with a terrible and unclean vigour. The creature stretched forth its hand and Anton could do nothing except obey the unspoken summons.

The youth took a slow, shambling step toward the ancient monster. The vampire closed its eyes, hiding their unnatural light, and its shrunken chest drew a deep breath.

'A Klausner,' the thing's voice hissed like leaves crawling across a grave. 'I will never forget the smell of that blood, no matter how many lifetimes have fallen into dust.' The vampire's eyes blinked back into unholy life. Its corpse-face stared at Anton, the leathery flesh pulling back into a malevolent grin. 'The hour has indeed grown dark,' it observed.

The vampire shifted its gaze to consider the man who had approached from behind the unmoving skeletons.

'A most rare gift,' Carandini said, bowing his head slightly in deference to his ally. 'Something to display my commitment to our common purpose.' The necromancer smiled ingenuously, not caring that the undead monster might read his expression. 'Something to display my loyalty,' he added in what was only marginally a servile tone.

'One that is appreciated,' the vampire said, its withered face puckering into a sneer. 'What other things have you observed this day?' it asked, the hollow voice brimming with suspicion.

'The witch hunter has stopped the Klausner's ritual,' Carandini told the vampire. 'Without any new blood to bolster it, the protective circle will collapse. We shall be able to proceed very soon.'

The necromancer smiled as he added the lie to the truth. The witch hunter had indeed stopped the ritual, but that event's debilitating effect upon the wards had been much quicker and more profound than he wished his confederate to know. Carandini had seen with his own eyes his skeleton warriors carried across the stream that marked the boundary, the line over which the restless dead could not normally cross. He had seen, too, those same skeletons unharmed by that passage.

The vampire smiled back at Carandini. It knew that it could not trust the mortal, any more than any of the living could be trusted. It knew what Carandini had seen, ripping the images from Anton Klausner's mind. The circle was already down. The necromancer's usefulness was at an end.

The monster fought down the urge to destroy the sneering, scheming wizard. Did he dare to think that his feeble deceptions would trick Sibbechai, that his transparent manipulations would trap the vampire? Did he think that the vampire would fall upon the Klausner pup like some blood-hungry von Carstein, slaking its thirst for vengeance upon this sorry mortal while the necromancer stole past the defeated wards and made off with the real treasure?

'How shall we proceed?' the vampire asked. The necromancer smiled back at him.

'In a day or so, the wards will lose their power. Then we can strike,' he replied.

'Perhaps they are already weakened,' the vampire said, voicing the thing they both knew to be the true. 'I am not so easily dissuaded as one of your battlefield relics,' the monster observed, enjoying the flare of anger that worked itself onto Carandini's face as he heard Sibbechai diminish the necromancer's powers.

'I would remind you that your curs could not cross the wards either,' the necromancer retorted. 'I would also remind you that you did not know the secret rites that would weaken those same wards.' The necromancer smiled coldly at the vampire. 'For all your knowledge,' he added with another sneer. 'Besides, even if you could cross, there is the problem of gaining entry to the keep. Something one of your kind should find difficult.'

The vampire grinned back, an expression as much of menace as of triumph. The scheming idiot had solved that problem on his own, though he did not see it. Sibbechai shifted its gaze to the trembling, transfixed Anton. Carandini followed the gesture and what little colour there was in his pasty skin faded. Sibbechai let the necromancer's understanding of what he had done sink in.

'A very fine gift,' the vampire hissed. It closed its eyes, picking into the tangle of thoughts and emotions crawling within Anton's soul. Sibbechai opened its eyes again, releasing a fraction of its control over the youth. There was an irony, a deep irony to what the vampire had in mind now, though it had long ago ceased to be human enough to appreciate it. The vampire tilted its arm, exposing its wrist. With the talons on its other hand, it slashed through the rotten skin. Thin black filth oozed up from the injury.

'I offer you what your father has denied you,' Sibbechai told the youth. 'I offer you purpose. I shall raise you above the peasant cattle. You shall become an aristocrat of the night, and mighty shall be your name. Men will tremble in fear of you and your power shall know no end.'

The vampire's face twisted in macabre mirth as it read the crude, simple desires and the smouldering resentments of the young noble. 'I shall help you to avenge the dishonour your father has brought upon you and he will know the power and strength of your will before he dies.' The vampire released the rest of its control over Anton Klausner. The youth shook, trembling still with the unnatural terror which the vampire's presence evoked. But he stood his ground, for all his shivering, for all the fear in his eyes.

'Drink,' Sibbechai said, lifting its bleeding wrist. 'Drink and all that I have promised will be yours.' *In so much as you shall be my slave until I tire of you.*

The vampire sneered as he saw the youth struggle with his decision. It already knew how Anton would decide, knowing the young noble's mind better than he knew it himself. Anton lowered his head, his warm lips touching the cold, clammy skin of the vampire. He sucked at the dark liquid drooling from the monster's wound. Sibbechai let only the smallest portion pass Anton's lips before wrenching its arm away.

'We share the same blood,' the vampire hissed, watching as Anton staggered and fell, overcome by the power now racing through his body. The vampire looked over at Carandini, studying the necromancer's anxious face. 'Be not dismayed, necromancer. I shall go myself. You may remain behind, where it is safe.'

'I would happily accompany you,' Carandini protested, hands toying with the cuffs of his cassock.

'Your newly found valour,' Sibbechai shook its head, its voice rumbling with a dangerous mirth. 'Why does it fill me with such...' the vampire paused as though struggling to find the right word. 'Uneasiness?' it said at last.

'No, you shall stay here,' Sibbechai proclaimed. 'I shall go.' Its voice slipped into a malevolent whisper. 'I shall reclaim that which is mine!'

CHAPTER SEVENTEEN

'SIBBECHAI.' THULMANN REPEATED the name. He cast his thoughts back to his study of the Klausner family records. It was the name of the vampire that Helmuth Klausner had hunted to the cursed city Mordheim and destroyed five hundred years ago. The witch hunter knew that a vampire's destruction was sometimes a nebulous thing and that at certain times, and by certain rites of such horror that they defied the most morbid imagination, such creatures could be called back from the realm of the dead. He also knew that a vampire was like a dragon: age did not diminish its potency but rather increased its power and malevolence.

What might this creature Sibbechai have become after five hundred years?

Wilhelm dipped his head in a solemn nod. 'Yes,' the patriarch said. 'The great shadow that has haunted my family from the very beginning. A vampire sorcerer, a monster of loathsome and awful power. One of that most obscene of the profane breeds of vampire – a necrarch.' The old man spoke the last word only as a frightened whisper. Thulmann made the sign of the hammer as he heard the evil name spoken.

A necrarch. Vampires were an unclean, loathsome kind of being, lurking among the people of the Empire like wolves prowling among sheep. Except during certain times of decadent permissiveness on the part of past aristocrats and nobility, it had been the witch hunters' duty to root out these monsters and destroy them.

Many were their breeds and diverse were their powers, but above them all, there was one kind that was feared even by the servants of Sigmar: the vampire sorcerers known as the necrarchs, a foul kindred of undead wizards who looked upon the living not simply as prey, but as subjects for their unholy experiments.

There was a foul and abhorrent tome, kept under lock and key in the lowest vaults of Altdorf's Great Cathedral, a book of such vile evil that only the most pure and devout of Sigmar's servants were allowed even to see it. The *Liber Mortis* of the mad necromancer Vanhel.

Thulmann had been permitted access to the *Liber Mortis*, allowed to study fifteen pages of its ghastly text for the space of two hours, a brutish, illiterate temple guard standing at his shoulder, watching him for any sign of corruption. Even now there were times when Vanhel's spidery script would boil up within the witch hunter's mind, disturbing his slumber, robbing his food of its taste and perfume of its scent.

It was a poison of the soul, a tainted knowledge that corrupted all who contemplated it. A glimpse had been enough, perhaps even too much. But in that glimpse, Thulmann had read of the necrarchs, of their foul nature and their abominable ambitions. Vanhel himself had been frightened of them, calling them the 'Disciples of the Accursed'. He related the foul prophecy of the progenitor of their bloodline, W'soran, a prophecy that the necrarchs hoped to fulfil. For, like the Great Necromancer himself, the necrarchs dreamed of a world that was still and quiet and cold.

Other vampires sought power over the living, in one way or another. The necrarchs sought a way to destroy all life, to scour the world of every living thing and leave it as a shadow peopled only by the restless dead.

If this Sibbechai was one of the filthy breed of the necrarchs, then the Klausners had good reason to know fear.

'It was long ago, in the Time of the Three Emperors,' Wilhelm continued. 'The land was rife with war and ruin. Plague was everywhere. In those days, the name of Klausner was not so well known, they were just another family of merchants. Then plague came to the town of Gruebelhof.' Wilhelm looked at the witch hunter, and it was a look of pain, the mark of a man who was about to confess some great shame. 'The plague struck down most of the Klausner line, laying low the old and the young, wiping away in an instant almost three generations. The priests and healers could do nothing, even when one among the priesthood bore the same name.

'Helmuth watched in horror as the plague devoured his family. At last, only his brother Hessrich and Hessrich's wife and daughter remained. Hessrich was determined to save his family, and did not intend to leave their survival in the hands of the gods. He had learned a few heathen practices from an old witch who dwelled outside the village, petty magic that might make his family resist the plague. Hessrich saw the potency of the hag's spell and he left Gruebelhof in search of a sorcery mightier still, a sorcery that would make his family immune to the disease.

'In his absence, the heathen rites practised by Hessrich's wife were discovered by their neighbours. She was denounced as a witch, put in irons and cast into jail. Helmuth pleaded desperately to save them, but he was powerless before the will of the townspeople and his brother's wife and their young daughter were burnt at the stake.'

Wilhelm paused, licking his lips nervously as he considered the next part of the tale. 'The smoke was still rising from their pyre when Hessrich returned. He had found the knowledge he had sought. He had travelled to a shunned and haunted tower and been captured by the thing that dwelt there. Despite his terror, Hessrich had pled with his captor to release him so he might find the magic he needed to save his family. In its twisted humour, the vampire had offered not only to release him, but to give him the knowledge he needed as well. All Hessrich had to do was drink the vile liquid that coursed through the monster's veins and be inducted into its unclean brotherhood. Hessrich died in that nameless tower, transformed into one of the undead. The newborn monster took a name of power, discarding forever the name of Klausner. Its new name was Sibbechai and it was a man no longer.

'Sibbechai's rage was great and terrible when it learned what had been done, for the salvation of Hessrich's family had been the only lingering shred of humanity left in the creature. It massacred over half of the already plague-wracked town before the priests were able to drive it away. Amid the carnage wrought by the thing that had been his brother, Helmuth swore a grim oath to atone for the horrors of Sibbechai and not to rest until the vampire had been destroyed.

'Across the Empire he hunted the beast, stalking it through lands haunted by war and disease, until at last, the monster came to the cursed ruin that had been the great city of Mordheim. It was there that Helmuth confronted the monster and terrible was their battle. After hours of combat, Helmuth fell and the vampire leapt after him in a frenzied madness of bloodlust and hate. In its violent pounce, the monster did not see the broken spear gripped in Helmuth's hands. It impaled itself upon the weapon and with a final shriek of malevolence and profanity, it died.'

'But the monster did not stay dead,' observed Thulmann, listening intently to every nuance in Wilhelm's tale. Wilhelm shook his head.

'Helmuth was too fatigued from his battle to destroy the remains properly and he was compelled to leave the shunned ruins. It took him three days to gather together a strong enough force of fellow witch hunters and mercenary hirelings to return. When he did, they found no trace of the vampire's body.

'Helmuth prayed that some foul beast, some nameless creature of Chaos from the Cursed Pit had devoured Sibbechai's remains. But it was not so. Within a year, as he scoured the Empire, purging it of sorcerers and mutants, Helmuth learned that the vampire had survived. It eluded his efforts to track it down, lingering just beyond his reach, a vengeful spectre waiting to strike at him whenever he let down his guard.

'So it has ever been for the Klausners,' Wilhelm continued. 'The men of the Klausner line have always tried to hunt down this loathsome beast, but never have they succeeded in destroying it. Over the centuries, many of the descendants of Helmuth have fallen victim to the vampire Sibbechai and the threat of the fiend's undying lust for vengeance has never diminished.'

Thulmann was quiet for a moment as he reflected upon the old man's story, pacing the room as he contemplated the tale. At length, he spun about, his voice snapping like a whip. 'But this does not explain the foul necromancy your family is guilty of. You have told me the reason for it, but not its cause! To save yourselves from the vampire, yes, but how did this abominable practice come to be? How did corruption burrow its way into the pious legacy of the Klausners?'

'It has been with us from the beginning,' Wilhelm relented. 'It was Helmuth who first performed the ritual of protection, so the family he made for himself after the era of the Three Emperors might not be claimed by his undead enemy. And the ritual has been handed down ever since, tied into the title and legacy. At the end of his life, each father inducts his eldest son into the secret.'

'And have you told Gregor yet?' the witch hunter demanded. The old man wilted back into his covers, a long sigh shuddering from his chest.

'No,' he protested. 'I have told you I would not let this evil touch my sons. That is why I forbade them to become witch hunters, forbade them to continue the hunt for Sibbechai. I felt that if the vampire was let alone, if the monster was not hounded and if... other measures... were taken, it would have no reason to menace this house any longer.' Wilhelm's eyes shone with a desperate eagerness. 'Don't you see? This was to be the last time there would be any reason to perform the ritual! I was going to bring the shameful tradition to an end!'

'By making peace with an undead monster who lusts after the death of the world?' Thulmann sneered. His eyes narrowed as he fixed upon the subject Wilhelm was trying to avoid. 'How did Helmuth learn this loathsome ritual? What was the source of his knowledge?' The old patriarch looked away, refusing to speak.

'I will find out,' the witch hunter's voice was like steel. 'Either now, or after my man has torn your old body into an open wound!'

THE BURNING EMBERS of Sibbechai's eyes flared within the darkness, tiny pinpricks of malice floating amid the shadows of the night. The vampire strode between the rotting trees, its unnatural vision allowing it to navigate flawlessly through the pitch black that had fallen across the land as the moons once again were consumed by the brooding clouds overhead.

The vampire stared at the sombre sky, its face twitching with the faint echoes of memory. It had been on just such a night, so very long ago, that it had nearly been destroyed, that it had been cheated of its vengeance. Sibbechai had long ago ceased to believe in such things as fate and destiny, but there was something terribly fitting that the hour of its long-denied victory should mirror that of its ignoble defeat.

The vampire rotated its skull-like head, watching the wretched thrall it had created from Anton Klausner. There was still much of the man within the thrall, it had not been dead long enough yet for the thoughts and cares of life to fade. Sibbechai struggled to remember what it had been like to have such vibrant emotions surging within it, struggled to try and capture the faintest trace of the man it had once been. It could remember the events, remember the places it had walked when alive, the people it had known, the things it had done. But the vampire could no longer feel the emotions that had been attached to those places and persons. It knew that it had loved a woman and a tiny baby girl, but it recalled that fact with distance and coldness, as though it had been another who had felt such things.

Sibbechai could remember leaving the village, and finding the haunted tower where it was said a sorcerer lived. It could still see the corpse-visage of the thing that had killed the man Hessrich Klausner and put in his place the vampire Sibbechai. The vampire could remember too the horror and loathing it had felt for its condition in those days and weeks after it had been transformed, only its lingering love for its family keeping it from going mad.

That link was severed when Sibbechai had returned to its village, severed by flame and fire. Severed by Helmuth Klausner, the man who had been its brother.

The vampire looked again at Anton Klausner, and the skull-like face peeled back in a gruesome smile. So very like Helmuth this one was, bristling with ambition and petty jealousy, filled with cruelty and brutality. Helmuth Klausner, the man who had lusted after his brother's wife, who had bristled with resentment and envy every time he saw Hessrich's family pass him upon the street. Helmuth Klausner who, to indulge his bitterness and innate cruelty had become a witch hunter and begun a vicious purge of the township, all in the name of cleansing it of the wickedness that had drawn the plague there.

When it had returned to the town, Sibbechai had been stunned that Helmuth's cruelty had dared to claim even his own family, imprisoning and torturing his own niece and stepsister and then condemning them both as witches to be burned at the stake. The vampire was not so naïve now. All life was treacherous and cruel, self-serving and unpredictable.

Helmuth and his followers had managed to overcome the vampire, for in those days, Sibbechai did not fully understand the power of what it had become, nor was it so detached from the emotions that had flowed through it in life as to be inured to the grief that wracked its dead heart.

Rather than destroying the vampire outright, Helmuth had decided to imprison and study it. It was a foolish decision, for he underestimated how powerful the undead monster was and when the sun again set, Sibbechai had escaped the jail with ease. But the witch hunter had captured more than just the vampire, he had also taken from it the thing it had stolen from the tower of the elder necrarch, the thing it had hoped would save its family from the plague.

Sibbechai clenched its bony fist, the old withered flesh creaking as the knuckles cracked. It would reclaim that tome, that grimoire of ancient secrets and profane lore. It had read and understood enough of the book to know the power that was contained within its pages. That power would belong to Sibbechai again.

The vampire stared once more through the darkness, peering past the twisted trees. It exerted its malignant will and the Anton-thing turned its eyes upon the necrarch.

'As you command,' the thrall hissed.

The vampire strode out from amongst the shadowy boughs, stalking across the path, ignoring the dismembered corpses that only hours ago had been its friends and comrades. The vampire walked toward the small bridge and the stream it spanned.

Anton hesitated for a moment as it reached the bridge, new senses warning the fledgling vampire of the faint echoes of power that yet coursed about the barrier. Then he stepped out onto the wooden planks, striding with purposeful steps across the span. From the blackness of the wood, Sibbechai smiled.

The protective circle was no more. The power that had guarded the Klausners for centuries had been banished. Now nothing would stop Sibbechai from reclaiming its own.

Not the dead.
Not the living.

CARANDINI SAT UPON the cold, wasted ground within the ruins of
the farmhouse, his eyes narrowed as the intellect behind them
slithered through the twisted corridors of his mind.

Events were proceeding swiftly, threatening to slip beyond the
necromancer's ability to control. Now, so close to all that he
hoped for, so close to the knowledge that he desired, things were
at their most dangerous.

The vampire was becoming reckless, something that Carandini
had not anticipated. He had expected the monster to be shrewd,
certainly, and he understood that Sibbechai was not so foolish as
to trust the necromancer any more than he trusted it. But he had
not imagined that a creature who had waited centuries might
become impatient when the goal was so very near at hand.

Sibbechai had set off on its own, to confront the Klausners and
the outlander witch hunter in person. Carandini was at a loss to
understand such a foolish action. He would have stayed safe
within the darkest depths of the forest and sent wave after wave
of reanimated warriors to assault the keep, not setting foot inside
until he was certain that no living thing remained within its walls.
That was the way to be sure. The vampire's way courted calamity.

Perhaps it was true what was whispered about the bloodline of
the necrarchs, that all of that unholy brotherhood were insane, or
perhaps there was indeed a cleverness in Sibbechai's insanity. Perhaps the monster was not so contemptuous of Carandini's
powers as it tried to appear. Perhaps it feared the inevitable confrontation between them when victory was at last theirs.

The necromancer smiled as he considered this pleasant thought,
that his knowledge of the black arts was enough to impress one of
the undying necrarchs. Maybe the vampire felt it had good reason to
put itself at risk, intending to seize the prize and escape with it before
Carandini could react to the monster's treachery, perhaps even leaving the necromancer behind to contend with the witch hunter,
should the vampire leave the man alive.

Quite clever, in its way, if such had been the vampire's purpose.
There was only one problem with Sibbechai's plan. Sibbechai was
a vampire, and as such needed a place of sanctuary when the sun
bathed the land in its golden rays.

Oh, the creature had taken such pains to keep its lair hidden and secret from Carandini, but the necromancer had discovered the cave with Sibbechai's casket all the same. Carandini had continued to 'search' for the vampire's refuge ever since to deceive the monster into thinking its secret was still safe. For who continues to look for something they have already found?

Oh yes, Sibbechai would attempt some treachery, of that Carandini was most certain. But the vampire would have a rather interesting surprise when it slunk back into its cavern to hide from the sun and rejuvenate its unclean vitality within its casket.

The necromancer was quite pleased with his plotting. It was rather like a game of regicide, only as a mortal man, Carandini had a slight edge over his supernatural opponent. For a man was not bound by the same rules as a vampire. Carandini stared out into the night, chuckling as he imagined Sibbechai's reaction when it saw what had been left in its coffin.

A sudden movement in the shadows caused the necromancer to stand. Only eyes as unnaturally attuned to the night as Carandini's could detect the low, slinking shapes that crept about the fringe of the ruined farmhouse walls.

The necromancer hissed under his breath, fumbling about within the secret pockets of his gown. It seemed that the vampire had not been derelict in making its own treacherous plans. Carandini cursed his overconfidence. He should have prepared for something of this sort, should have brought the entire host of his animated soldiers back with him instead of the feeble quartet that had taken hold of Anton Klausner.

The low, grisly snarls of Sibbechai's rotting wolves sounded from the darkness. Even as Carandini willed his skeleton warriors into action, mangy lupine shapes lunged at them from the night. The wolves smashed the slow-moving skeletons to the ground, ignoring the fleshless talons that tore at their maggot-ridden flesh as their jaws worried and savaged the brittle bleached bone of their foes.

Carandini cursed again, spinning about just as another wolf lunged out of the night, the black-furred beast streaking toward him. The necromancer flung a foul grey powder into the zombie animal's face, causing the wolf's muzzle to disintegrate into a steaming white ash. The wolf crashed to the ground, its body shuddering as the powder continued to eat its way down the length of the creature.

The necromancer cast more of the powder into the second wolf that lunged for him. The creature's leg crumbled, spilling it to the ground in a writhing pile of fur and swollen entrails. The other dire wolves rose from the mangled remains of Carandini's warriors. There would be no help from that quarter for the necromancer. His hand sifted the bottom of the small elf-skin pouch that held the consuming dust.

Carandini's face twisted into a look of horror as he considered how much powder remained as opposed to the number of Sibbechai's wolves that now began to circle him with hackles raised. He did not find the calculation to be a favourable one.

The monstrous wolves prowled about the embattled necromancer, their rotting muzzles scrunched into feral, hungry visages. The lights that shone in their wasted eye sockets gleamed from the black shadows of their skulking forms. Warily they paced, awaiting the ideal moment to pounce. The necromancer stared back at them with cold resignation.

The hollow, deathly howl of the pack leader sounded in the darkness and like a midnight wave crashing upon the bow of a ship, the wolves leapt upon their prey.

CHAPTER EIGHTEEN

'THE VAMPIRE'S GRIMOIRE,' Thulmann proclaimed as the idea came to him. He saw shock flare up in Wilhelm's eyes and knew that he had struck upon the truth. The witch hunter considered how much sense his guess made. Helmuth Klausner had captured his vampire brother, a vampire that was of the sorcerous necrarch breed. It made sense that he would have seized whatever book of spells the monster carried, spells, perhaps, that it had hoped to use to protect its family from the plague. It also explained something else that had been nagging at the witch hunter.

Wilhelm had tried to describe the vampire's motive as being a centuries-long quest for revenge. With another of the polluted breeds of the vampire, Thulmann might have believed the old man. It was known that while vampires did not feel emotion the same way as living men, they were still capable of many of the baser emotions like hate, lust, envy and spite. But a necrarch was something different. In them, even the most base of emotion seemed diminished, if not absent altogether.

No, they were motivated by something colder and less human even than hate. The necrarchs only cared about their sorcery, their store of profane knowledge. The quest for supreme mastery of the black arts was the one thing that drove their inhuman hearts, even as it consumed their minds and souls.

Revenge would not have kept a necrarch haunting the Klausners. But the repossession of some tome of blasphemous knowledge might.

'Helmuth kept the vampire's spell book,' Thulmann declared again. Fury swelled up within him as he recalled his own sickening glimpse into the *Liber Mortis*. 'Sigmar's Blood! How far into the pit of heresy and evil does this family's madness run!'

Wilhelm shook his head with what strength remained to him, an imploring look on his wrinkled features. 'He never sought to become some nightmare of sorcerous power,' the old man gasped. 'No, he sought to use the works of the enemy against itself! To fight fire with fire! To use the foul magic that had destroyed his brother in the service of Sigmar, to scour the Empire of the filth that festered within it!'

'Your ancestor was a heretic and a warlock!' spat the witch hunter, violence in his eyes. 'Recall the scriptures: "Suffer not the necromancer, shun his works. By smoke and by fire shall they be consumed and blessed shall be the land whose sorcerers are ash." So said Sigmar in his wisdom. Your ancestor would have done well to heed the voice of his god.'

'He served Sigmar,' Wilhelm growled. 'As have all the Klausners!'

'Even Hessrich?' Thulmann directed his comment like a sword. 'Whatever lies Helmuth told himself to justify his purposes, he was heretic and worse. Better men than him have paved the road of their damnation with the noblest of intentions. But it was damnation awaiting them just the same.' The witch hunter's voice trailed off, the image of Lord Thaddeus Gamow suddenly springing into his mind and the horror that exalted figure had caused. He broke from his recollection, glaring down into the old patriarch's eyes.

'I want what the vampire has tried to take from this fortress for five hundred years,' he told the old man. 'I want the book!' Wilhelm sank back into his pillows, a sad smile on his face.

'I cannot give it to you,' Wilhelm said.

Thulmann pounded his fist against one of the posts that supported the bed's canopy.

'Unrepentant wretch,' the witch hunter hissed. 'Is it not enough that this book has been allowed to taint and corrupt this family for hundreds of years? Is it not enough that it has drawn unspeakable evil to these lands like moths to a flame? End this horror! Give me the book so I can destroy it and put an end to this nightmare!'

The smile remained on the old man's face as he shook his head. 'Some things are not destroyed so easily,' he said. 'Even if I could, I cannot help you.'

Thulmann sprang forward, his gloved hand pointing accusingly into the patriarch's face. 'Cannot? Or will not?'

'Whichever you like,' Wilhelm sighed. 'It is the same.'

Thulmann turned away from the old man, pacing the room once again like a caged lion. 'I will find out,' he said. 'I *will* find out.' He turned to face the old man again. 'I will not hesitate to put you to torment if you refuse to confess all to me and renounce this filth that has tainted your legacy!'

A part of Thulmann desperately hoped it would not come to that. The old man would have to die for his crimes, there was no getting around that, but the thought of putting this man, who had once been a hero of the temple, a champion against the dark, the thought of putting such a man to torture sickened Thulmann.

Then there was Gregor to consider. Despite all he had learned, Thulmann was still certain of the young man's nobility and character. He would spare Gregor as much misery as he could. The execution would be hard enough, the youth did not need this as well.

The witch hunter shook his head in disbelief as the old man still refused to speak. 'I give you until I return to reconsider your position,' he said. 'Fortunately, I have another prisoner at my disposal.' Thulmann's voice slipped into a threatening growl. 'If you still pray to Sigmar, pray he tells me what I want to hear.'

THULMANN STALKED ACROSS the room, knocking upon the door that connected to the small chapel. He swung the door inward, only slightly surprised to find two figures kneeling before the altar instead of one.

'Lady Klausner,' the witch hunter said, dipping his head, yet keeping one wary eye on the room behind him and the old figure lying upon the bed. 'I did not mean to interrupt your prayers.'

'Sigmar knows what I would ask of him,' Ilsa Klausner returned. 'I am sure he would welcome a respite from hearing an old woman pleading over and again for the same thing.' The woman rose to her feet, looking squarely into the witch hunter's eyes. 'Tell me, will it be quick?'

A look of regret came on the witch hunter and there was a touch of genuine pain in his eyes. 'That I cannot say.' He turned his head to look back at the bed ridden patriarch. 'It depends on him. There is much that must be done this night.'

Ilsa nodded her head in understanding. 'Then I should prepare some tea,' she said. 'Would you like some tea, Herr Thulmann? I promise not to poison it, should that thought have occurred to you.'

The witch hunter smiled thinly and shook his head. 'I am afraid that I can only allow myself to trust one Klausner right now,' he apologised. 'I am sure that you can understand my position, given the circumstances.'

'Well,' sighed Ilsa Klausner. 'I think I will find some tea for myself then.' A suggestion of fear and anxiety crept past her air of resignation as she started to leave. 'That is, if I am still free to do so?'

Thulmann motioned for her to proceed. 'I need to speak with your son,' he told her. 'There is something I need him to help me with,' he added as he saw the fear swell up in Ilsa's eyes. The woman cast a lingering look at her son, then retreated through the small door that connected the chapel with her own room.

'There really is no hope, is there?' Gregor said when she had left.

'For your father,' the witch hunter replied. 'No. He is guilty of such crimes that his life must be forfeit.'

'And for the rest of us?' Gregor asked, a tremor in his voice. He had heard the dark tales that were sometimes whispered, tales about overzealous witch hunters who, having found one member of a family guilty of sorcery had then scoured the length and breadth of the Empire to destroy the entire line.

'He claims that only he and his servant knew what was going on,' Thulmann said. 'I believe him, in that much at least.' He placed a reassuring hand on Gregor's shoulder. 'A man is not damned by the sins of his father, he must damn himself. Two of the most famous members of the Order of Witch Hunters were Johann van Hal and Helmut van Hal, both of them direct descendants of the infamous necromancer Frederick van Hal.'

Thulmann paused for a moment, recalling the skeleton swinging from his own family tree, the black sorcerer Erasmus Kleib.

Like the van Hals, the existence of such a foul taint upon his lineage helped to strengthen his spirit and resolve, fill him with a consuming need to atone for the misdeeds of his wicked relation.

Gregor's face was contemplative for a moment as he too considered the witch hunter's words, appearing to find some reassurance for himself in them. He had hoped for some reassurance for his father's fate. 'Must he... must he be put to the torment?' Gregor asked in a subdued, fearful whisper.

'Unless I can pry the secrets he refuses to relate from Kohl,' the witch hunter sighed. 'I have to go below and see if Streng has broken Kohl's determination yet. I need someone to remain here and watch the patriarch.'

'You would trust me with such a task?' marvelled Gregor.

'You are intelligent enough to know that you would not be doing the old man any service by helping him escape. He would be hunted across the land like an animal, and his soul would assuredly be damned to the darkness.' Thulmann smiled grimly. 'Besides, I have seen the strength in you, the honour and courage that makes me think the taint that has attached itself to your line does not run deep. You would never be able to help a murderer escape justice, to let innocent blood go unavenged.'

Gregor watched as the witch hunter stalked away. A part of him was proud that Thulmann trusted him enough to bestow such an important duty upon him, that childish part that still believed in honour and duty, that still looked with wonder and awe upon the great deeds of the Templars. The other part of him seethed with silent rage as it watched the witch hunter leave, so certain that he could trust his evaluation of Gregor's character. The part that saw past the codes of honour and devotion and obligation. The part that saw one brutal, simple fact.

His father was going to die. Slowly or quickly, his father would die.

THE DOORMAN MAINTAINED his position within the massive entry hall, watching from the shadows as the witch hunter descended the stairs and made his way down the corridor that led to the cellars. The Templar was going to join his henchman, no doubt. The doorman did not envy Ivar Kohl when the witch hunter arrived.

It had been a strange and fear-fraught night. The dramatic entrance of Gregor Klausner and the witch hunter's entourage, a

bleeding Ivar Kohl in tow. The horrific story told by the shep-
herdess the men had rescued from Kohl. Then there had come the
raised voices emanating from Lord Klausner's room, the ghastly
accusations of the witch hunter echoing down from the heights of
the keep. The doorman wondered where it would all lead.

He was certain that things would grow worse before they
became better.

The sound of the heavy iron door ring pounding against the
massive wooden portal brought the servant out of his gloomy
reflections. He strode across the hall, swinging the heavy wooden
panel inward. He was somewhat surprised to see Anton Klausner
on the other side. As the doorman held the portal open, Anton
stepped inside, without any of the swearing or slapping that had
characterised his exit earlier. The younger son of his lordship had
left the keep only a few hours before, brimming with anger and
outrage. The night air seemed to have done the young Klausner a
great deal of good, for it had certainly cooled his temper, though
his skin was very pale. The young man must be frozen to the
bone, thought the servant.

'Welcome back, Master Anton,' the doorman said. Before he
could elaborate, the pale young man turned, staring back into the
blackness of the courtyard with an intense gaze.

'Enter this house freely and of your own accord,' Anton said into
the night. The doorman glanced outside, trying to determine who
the noble was addressing. Darkness and shadow seemed to
become solid, just beyond the threshold. The doorman flinched
away from the sudden chill, from the charnel stench, but it was
already too late. A thin, almost skeletal hand shot out from the
darkness and with one deft motion broke the man's neck like a
twig.

The shadow glided over the twitching corpse of the servant.
Anton bowed before its advance, following in the apparition's
wake. Sibbechai paid the vampiric slave no further mind. The
thrall had achieved its chief purpose. There were strange limitations to the power of the undead, one of these being that they
could not cross the threshold of a dwelling unless first invited by
one of its occupants. The corpse-face of the vampire smiled as it
again considered how the necromancer's scheme had turned
against him. Sibbechai wondered how long it had taken the
wolves to finish its erstwhile ally.

'There,' Anton hissed, pointing a pale hand to the stairs. 'The Klausner is up there.'

Sibbechai's smile grew wider, the grotesque fangs gleaming in the flickering light cast by the hearth. Soon, all that had been taken from it would be restored.

CHAPTER NINETEEN

THE WITCH HUNTER'S cloak billowed after him as he swept down the narrow stairway that burrowed into the basement levels of the keep. Thulmann's mood was as black as the garment he wore.

The revelation that the Klausners had never been the pure and pious champions of the temple that legend and history proclaimed rested ill upon the witch hunter's heart. If such a noble lineage as the Klausners could be so grotesquely tainted, then there truly was no saying how far corruption had sunk its fangs into the fabric of Imperial society.

Despite Thulmann's reassuring words to Gregor, the taint of his family was more ghastly and hideous than anything Thulmann had ever heard of. This was no case of a lone madman profaning the name of his family by his misdeeds. This was a tradition of horror and heresy that stretched back hundreds of years, back to the very foundation of the line. Van Hal had been but a single man, Klausner was a dynasty, the entire honour of its name nothing but carefully maintained illusion. Whatever lies they told themselves, however they might justify their sorcerous heresy, the Klausners were every bit the filth they hunted in the name of Sigmar.

Perhaps Gregor could redeem the name, reinvent the line? Certainly it would fall to him, because Thulmann did not see Anton rising to such a thankless task. It would take many lifetimes to atone for the crimes of their ancestors, many generations to wash away the evils of the past.

First though, this foul tome of sorcery that had tempted Helmuth Klausner to his fall had to be destroyed. Thulmann could not allow such a profane work to exist.

He thought again of the spidery script of van Hal crawled across the pages of the *Liber Mortis*, the taint of madness dripping from every word. He would sleep better knowing such a work had been purged from the face of the world. It might not be within his power to decide the fate of the *Liber Mortis*, but it was within his power to destroy the grimoire of Sibbechai. There could be no redemption for the House of Klausner while the source of their corruption remained intact.

The witch hunter's steps carried him to the heavy iron door that closed off the old torture chamber from the rest of the cellars. It was something of a testament to the erratic eccentricity and morbidity that had infected the Klausner patriarchs that such a room, devoted to such a purpose, should be situated here, where servants would constantly be passing by it as they hurried about their duties, rather than hidden away in some dark corner.

Torture was a vital tool of the witch hunters, fear of torment was something that had broken many a witch and set many a sorcerer into flight, thereby revealing himself. But it was still a despicable tool, for all its necessity, and one that the Templars did not display for all to see. The location of this room was exactly that, the open flaunting of what the long dead patriarch had been and what he had done.

A groan sounded from beyond the door, followed by a harsh snarl in Streng's brutal tones. Thulmann lifted his gloved hand, banging on the cold iron surface of the door. 'Sigmar protects,' the witch hunter said. It was an arranged code between himself and his henchman to indicate that all was well and that he should open the door.

Thulmann knew that he was taking a risk by conducting his investigation here, but he also knew that it was the quickest way to unmask the conspiracy at work, to flush out the rats who had been associated with the heresy.

The witch hunter did not care overmuch for his own safety. His life and death were almost inconsequential things to him. He had left a sealed report of his discoveries with Reikhertz back in the village, instructing the innkeeper to ride to Wurtbad and deliver the report to the temple of Sigmar there should Thulmann fail to return by dawn. He was certain that the simple tradesman would follow his instructions, and the report would soon come to the attention of Sforza Zerndorff.

His own death would not help the Klausners, Thulmann concluded grimly. Just the opposite, they would be trading the surgeon's knife for the headsman's axe, for Zerndorff would not be so careful about trifling matters of innocence and guilt. If the Witch Hunter General South read that report, he would come with a small army and blast Klausner Keep into rubble.

Streng pulled the door inward, a glowing iron rod clenched in his upraised hand, ready to dash the brains from any unwanted visitor who might be accompanying the witch hunter.

The mercenary stepped back when he saw that Thulmann was alone. The witch hunter slipped past him, his icy gaze considering the dank, miserable room he had entered.

It was like stepping into the study of a Solkanite inquisitor. Iron manacles hung from steel staples fixed to two of the walls. A massive fire pit had been hacked into the stone floor, a large bellows looming beside it to ensure that the flames would be as hot as the breath of a daemon. Gibbets and small iron cages that seemed too small to hold a human body no matter how contorted hung from the beams overhead.

A dusty wooden rack held a grisly assortment of pincers, tongs, bone saws and even a few implements that Thulmann did not recognise and whose use the witch hunter was not too eager to contemplate. A gigantic iron sarcophagus dominated one corner, its surface morbidly cast into the image of a praying abbess.

Thulmann had employed such 'iron sisters' before; sometimes the mere sight of such an instrument of slow and agonising death was enough to break the will of a heretic. Beside the iron sister sat the cruel framework of a Tilean boot, a ghastly device that made a slow and exacting art of breaking every bone in the foot of its victim.

Ivar Kohl was bound to a long wooden table that dominated the very centre of the chamber. The steward's hands were locked into an iron bar, his feet bound likewise at the other end of the table. Thick ropes connected the iron bars to the pulleys that were fixed to either end of the table.

The rack, a fiendish invention concocted by some long forgotten sadist; a loathsome device, but one that was as necessary to Thulmann's trade as the sword and the pistol.

The man bound to the table did not react as the witch hunter stared down at him. Kohl's face was pale, beads of sweat dripping from his brow, jaws clenched against the steady and persistent pain. Thulmann glanced down at the man's injured leg, noting with some alarm a faint trace of crimson splattered upon the surface of the table.

The steward was already weak from his wound, and might not be able to withstand being put to the question for long.

'Has he said anything?' Thulmann snapped as Streng shut the iron cell door with a metal crash.

'I've only had him an hour,' protested the mercenary. 'Haven't even pricked his skin or scraped his bones yet.' Streng grinned down with sadistic anticipation at his prisoner. 'Don't worry, he'll be talking soon enough.' The grin grew wider. 'But not too soon I hope,' he added.

'I care not about your bloodthirsty amusement,' Thulmann snapped at his underling. 'Get this wretch talking!'

'I was about to introduce Herr Kohl to my little friend here,' Streng gloated, brandishing the red hot iron and ignoring his employer's reprimand. 'He'll be singing like one of the divas of Altdorf's theatre district in a few moments,' he added boastfully. The shape stretched upon the rack whimpered pitifully as Streng drew closer.

Thulmann lifted his hand, motioning for the torturer to hold back.

'My associate is very eager to be about his work,' the witch hunter said, his silky voice frigid with menace. 'Give me a reason to keep him off you and I shall. All you need do is tell me exactly what I want to hear.' Kohl groaned as he heard Thulmann speak his threat. The steward's eyes were open now, staring with wretchedness and defeat at his captors. Thulmann fully appreciated the resignation in that broken gaze.

'I know that you were taught these profane rituals by your master,' the witch hunter stated. 'He has confessed as much to me.'

Thulmann smiled as he heard the captive groan again as whatever hope he had that Wilhelm Klausner might be able to save him was dashed. 'Though it took me some time to get that much from him,' the witch hunter said. He smiled as he continued. 'He was most adamant that he knew nothing of what you were up to. Perfectly willing, eager even, to place all the blame for these heretical acts upon your head.'

Kohl growled, then sobbed in agony as he heard Thulmann describe the patriarch's betrayal of his servant. It was of no importance to Thulmann that he had told a lie. The greatest obstacle facing him would be Kohl's loyalty to his master. Once that was destroyed, the steward would be only too willing to tell Thulmann whatever he knew.

'Lord Klausner would not...' Kohl sputtered through his broken, swollen lips. The witch hunter pounced upon the steward's desperate protest.

'Your master is concerned with saving his own neck now,' Thulmann told the steward. 'He is perfectly willing to paint every person in this household as a heretic if he thinks it might keep his own neck from the noose. Or him from sharing your position on the rack,' the witch hunter added with a slight maliciousness.

'I have served him faithfully,' Kohl cried. 'All that I did was as my masters ordered.'

Thulmann chuckled grimly, his gloved hands running along the length of a set of grotesquely oversized tongs. 'I seem to recall an epitaph of that sort,' he mused. After a pause, he gasped in mock recollection. 'Oh yes, Macherat, the captain of Vlad von Carstein's Sylvanian guard. I think they inscribed that on the ten-foot stake they impaled him on. Took the swine a week to die, so they say.' Thulmann stared coldly at the prone man. 'But I imagine that you will be more forthcoming than Macherat was.'

Kohl screwed his eyes shut, unable to maintain the witch hunter's intense stare. 'Lord Klausner gave me a parchment upon which he had transcribed the rites he wanted me to perform. He said that they were meant to protect his family, to hold back the forces of Old Night.'

Thulmann nodded his head as he digested his captive's words. 'So old Wilhelm never showed you any book, any record of spellcraft? He only gave you this parchment, written in his own hand?' Thulmann began to pace across the chamber. 'Tell me, is this how Wilhelm's father instructed you in performing this ritual as well?'

The witch hunter watched as the remaining colour in Kohl's face drained away. Clearly the steward was not very comfortable with Thulmann knowing of his involvement with the earlier crimes. The time for soft words and false kindness was over. The witch hunter stormed across the torture chamber, slamming both hands down upon the surface of the rack.

'I know full well the extent of your evil, Ivar Kohl!' Thulmann spat. 'And you will answer for every atrocity that has blackened your loathsome soul! But first you will tell me how you learned these obscene practices and then you will tell me where it is!'

'Where what is?' the steward's broken voice squeaked. The witch hunter leaned down, his face only inches from that of his prisoner.

'The grimoire,' Thulmann hissed. 'The source of all this evil. Helmuth Klausner's tome of sorcery.'

GREGOR STOOD BESIDE the door of his father's chamber, staring in silence at the old, withered figure of the patriarch. The old man stared back, his gaze filled with such shame that Gregor knew the witch hunter would not have to kill his father now. With the ugly secret revealed, everything Wilhelm had been was gone.

No one would remember the hero who had hunted the darkest corners of the Empire in his pursuit of the enemies of man. No one would remember the gracious ruler who kept his lands safe and prosperous. Perhaps no one would even remember his all-consuming love for hearth and home, his limitless devotion to his family.

'I am so terribly sorry,' the old man croaked at last. 'I never appreciated how this could affect you and Anton. I never thought that my crimes might shame you. The risk to myself I never gave a thought, but I would not have allowed you to be hurt by my deeds.' There was an imploring quality in Wilhelm's voice. 'Please understand that. I would never have allowed any harm to come to either of you. Everything I have done has been to keep you safe.'

Gregor detached himself from the wall. 'I do understand, father,' he said as he walked toward the bed. 'But you must understand something. You must understand that it was not your place to take all those lives, no matter what you hoped to achieve, no matter who you hoped to protect. No good can come from such a thing. Can't you see that?' A moan of despair rattled from the aged frame of the patriarch.

'Now,' he said. 'Now I understand. I could not before, or perhaps I simply would not. Kohl explained to me the dark secret of our family, and your grandfather, upon his deathbed, told me what must be done to keep our line from harm. I recoiled in horror as they revealed these things to me. I did know it was evil, but I persuaded myself that it was a necessary evil.'

Wilhelm grasped his son's hand, the old man's withered claw closing about Gregor's fingers with a strength that surprised his son.

'You must get away from here!' the old man told him. 'When the sun rises you must gather your mother and Anton and leave this place.'

Wilhelm's face flared with anger as he saw the questioning look on Gregor's face. 'Don't question me in this! If you ever honoured and loved me, obey me this last time! It is not safe here any longer. I thought it would not come, that it would leave us alone if we left it alone.' A haunted, miserable light crept into the old man's watery eyes.

'You cannot placate evil,' he told his son. 'You must hunt it down and destroy it, never tolerate it to thrive, never suffer it to live. That has been the great crime of our family. We feared to face our enemy, and hid ourselves behind spells and walls crafted from innocent blood. But the walls are gone now,' Wilhelm cautioned. 'There is nothing to keep it away now. That is why you must leave.'

'What is coming, father?' Gregor asked, his curiosity kindled. Wilhelm lifted his withered frame from the bed, his wrinkled face peering into that of his son.

'Death,' the old man hissed in a voice that was more shudder than speech. The heads of both men spun around as a loud crack roared through the room. The heavy oak door exploded inward, slamming against the floor as its twisted hinges rattled across the chamber.

A chill froze the room and with the cold came a stink of graves and blackening blood. The flickering candles dimmed as a shadowy shape billowed across the threshold, two pits of corpse-fire glowing from its darkness veiled face.

Gregor could feel the terror stab into the very core of his being like a dagger of ice. He could feel the breath in his lungs freeze, feel the blood in his veins congeal, the strength in his knees crumple.

The young noble found his gaze riveted to the embers that smouldered from the face of the dark shadow, transfixed like a small bird beholding the approach of a serpent. On the bed behind him, Wilhelm gave name to the unholy visitation.

'Sibbechai,' his voice shivered. The burning eyes of the shadow turned towards him and the dark shape drifted forward, the feeble light in the room illuminating its rotten flesh, mouldering raiment and skeletal figure. The skull-face of the vampire curled into a malevolent sneer, the withered face pulling back from the gleaming rodent-like fangs.

As the vampire surged forward, the motion caused such a wave of horror in Gregor that he found his terrified paralysis overcome. The youth tore his sabre from its sheath, the sound of steel rasping against leather somehow invigorating him with its simple normalcy.

The vampire didn't even glance in his direction; its burning eyes instead transfixed Wilhelm Klausner. The undead creature reached a withered claw towards the bed.

'You won't have him!' Gregor shouted, lunging toward the monster, his steel held before his body like the lance of a knight. In his terror, the young noble had reverted to base instinct, all his martial skill forgotten.

The crude attack did not fall upon its intended target. As Gregor lunged, a powerful grip closed about his neck, lifting him from the ground. Anton's cold hand ripped Gregor's sword from his grasp as if he were plucking a toy away from a child.

Anton stared into his brother's face, his ghoulish eyes filled with contempt and triumph. With a sweep of his arm, Anton hurled his brother across the room, Gregor's body slamming into the wall with such force that the plaster cracked and rained about him as he fell.

Anton Klausner grinned at his fallen sibling, the thrall's cold flesh pulling away from the monster's gleaming fangs. The beast took a step towards the stunned man, but the horrified gasp that sounded from the patriarch's bed caused him to pause, turning to face his mortal father with a look of bitter victory.

'Anton!' the patriarch sobbed. 'Not Anton...' The corpse-lights burning in the face of Sibbechai flickered with amusement as the old man's agonised wail crawled through the room.

'Yes,' the Anton-thing hissed. 'It is I, your second son. Your reserve in case anything should happen to your darling heir.' The malevolence in the vampire's voice struck the old man like physical blows. 'The son you denied purpose. The son who received nothing from you except his name, until you stripped even that from him.' Anton turned his gaze, gesturing toward the malignant shadow beside him. 'But I have found a new father. One who has promised me purpose. One who has promised me power.' The thrall's hand closed about the bed post, his unnatural strength causing the wood to splinter. 'Let me show you that power, old man!'

An inarticulate snarl from the Sibbechai brought Anton up short. The vampire thrall turned towards its master, cringing before the elder necrarch's displeasure liked a whipped cur. Sibbechai waved its claw, gesturing for its slave to withdraw. Then its smouldering gaze returned to the wizened patriarch.

'You have something that belongs to me,' Sibbechai's words bubbled from its putrid mouth. 'I will have it returned.'

'Rot in the grave you have so long cheated!' Wilhelm shouted, his voice cracking with fury. What the vampire had done to Anton had caused such wrath to well up within him that even the necrarch's aura of fear was not enough to subdue it. The vampire watched with amused interest as the old man rose from his bed. 'You'll get nothing from me!'

With a speed that belied belief, the undead monster surged forward, its cold hand grasping the bottom of Wilhelm's chin, forcing the old man's head back at such a violent angle that it seemed his back would snap. The vampire's lifeless, decaying breath washed over Wilhelm's face as it glared down at him.

'I tire of these games,' Sibbechai said. 'You will tell me what I want to know or I will kill every living thing in this district and drown you in their blood. Then I will force life back into your swollen corpse and repeat the process.' The vampire's fingers twisted, the claw-like nails tearing Wilhelm's skin.

Sibbechai's eyes glowed more intensely as it saw the old man's blood weeping down the front of his nightshirt. 'Tell me where it is, Helmuth's *Das Buch die Unholden*. Your end can be quick, or it can be longer than you are possible of imagining.'

'Sigmar rot you, carrion worm,' Wilhelm managed to snarl. The vampire forced the old man's head back still further and Wilhelm could feel the strength and anger flowing through its clutch, threatening to overcome the control of the vampire's malicious intellect.

'You will tell me where it is, you weak-willed fool,' Sibbechai promised. The vampire's gaze shifted as a figure struck at it from behind. Once again, its slave Anton intercepted Gregor's attack, catching the naked steel in its bare hand. Instead of cleaving through the vampire's cold flesh, however, Gregor felt the blow resonate back up his arms. It was as if he had just struck a granite wall. Anton twisted his hand, snapping the blade he held, then lunged at the man who had been his brother. Sibbechai's foul visage spread into a smile as it saw the patriarch's eyes go wide with a miserable despair.

The vampire released its hold on the old man, spinning about and ripping Anton from Gregor's chest. The thrall slunk away, staring at its master with resentment and terror. Sibbechai locked its arm about Gregor's neck, lifting the young noble back to his feet. The vampire spun him around so that Wilhelm could see his older son's face. Sibbechai's lips drew back in a savage grin.

'Perhaps you do not value your own life,' it hissed. 'But what of your son's?' Sibbechai laughed as it saw the anguish that wracked the old man. The vampire pulled at Gregor's hair, forcing his head to tilt and expose his neck. A thin line of black fluid, like stagnant water, dripped from the vampire's fangs. 'Nothing to say?' its malicious voice rasped.

'Tell this monster nothing!' pleaded Gregor. Sibbechai forced the youth's head back even further, stopping his words with a pulse of pain.

'Be quiet boy,' the undead thing snarled into Gregor's ear. 'This does not concern you. This is an arrangement between...' the vampire's voice dropped, its tones slithering with a mocking scorn, 'gentlemen.'

Sibbechai raised its voice once more, directing its attention back toward the old man. 'But will you do it, Lord Klausner? Will you save your boy from death? Or will you watch him die?' The vampire uttered another snort of tittering laughter. 'Or perhaps worse than death,' it threatened. Wilhelm could see the vampire slice its palm with one of its long nails, could see the black blood of the monster begin to weep from the injury. Sibbechai began to move its hand toward Gregor's lips...

'Anything!' the old man cried. He began to lunge for the vampire, but was held fast by the interceding figure of Anton. Wilhelm struggled feebly in the grasp of his undead son, watching as the fiendish figure of Sibbechai threatened Gregor with the same fate. 'I'll do anything, just release my son!'

Sibbechai gazed at the old man for a moment, its corpse-face studying that of Wilhelm Klausner. 'Where is the book?' it hissed.

'I will take you to it,' Wilhelm offered. 'Just release Gregor.' The vampire seemed to consider the old man's offer, then inclined its head ever so slightly.

'Your father is a wise man,' its rotting voice purred into Gregor's ear. Its hand closed about Gregor's face, flinging him across the room. The youth crashed against his father's heavy oak wardrobe. For the second time, Gregor fell to the floor but this time did not rise.

Sibbechai smiled at Wilhelm, displaying its rat-like fangs. 'If you play false with me,' it warned, 'we shall return here and you will watch me do all that I have promised. Perhaps I shall even leave the slaughter of your household in the capable hands of your sons.' Sibbechai surged forward, one diseased talon pressing against Wilhelm's cheek. 'Where is the book?'

'In the cemetery,' the old man choked. His eyes were fixed upon the unmoving figure of Gregor. A grim determination filled him.

'I will take you to where it is kept,' he said.

'THE DARK GODS will feast on your soul, you filthy maggot!' Mathias Thulmann growled into Ivar Kohl's bloodied face. 'Damn you, confess your iniquities! Repent your evil ways!' Kohl's head sagged weakly against the surface of the rack, a trickle of blood dripping from his mouth. The witch hunter's gloved hand lashed out, striking the man's face once more. 'Do one decent thing with your wicked life! Help me to destroy this evil, to wipe its taint from this family forever!'

Thulmann had been interrogating the unrepentant steward for the better part of an hour, his questioning growing more intense and enraged with every passing moment. Every ploy he had tried to break Kohl's resolve, every trick and deception had failed. Just when the steward's will seemed to break, the man would dredge up some new strength from some black corner of his being.

The loyalty of Kohl would have been commendable in a healthy mind, but the witch hunter found the presence of such a virtue in the murdering sack of filth laid out before him whipping up his fury like lamp-oil thrown upon a fire. It might take days to break the man, and there was a dread gnawing at the witch hunter, a foreboding of doom that told him he did not have days, perhaps not even hours, to wrest the hiding place of Helmuth Klausner's book of spells from the steward.

Words began to sputter from Kohl's broken lips. Thulmann leaned down, hoping to hear the heretic's whispers. Instead, the steward spat a mouthful of blood into the witch hunter's face. A satisfied smile flickered on the captive's battered visage.

Thulmann pulled away, wiping at the filth with a silk handkerchief. He glared down at the man, then looked over at Streng. The mercenary was grinning at his employer, openly enjoying Thulmann's discomfort and growing frustration.

'Got you, did he?' Streng chuckled. The witch hunter paid the jibe no attention but gestured toward the brazier of hot coals and the three irons that were nuzzled within them.

'This vermin will talk,' Thulmann swore. Streng dutifully retrieved one of the irons, its tip smoking and glowing from the heat.

'I'm not so sure that is a good idea,' the torturer commented. 'You might be better leaving him be for a time.' Thulmann snatched the cruel implement from his henchman.

'When I want your advice, I'll ask for it,' he snapped. The witch hunter moved the heated iron toward Ivar Kohl. Yet as he did so, the already tormented man's body shuddered, seeming to collapse upon itself. Thulmann dropped the iron to the floor, grabbing the front of Kohl's robe.

'The book!' the witch hunter snarled into the heretic's face. 'Helmuth Klausner's grimoire! Tell me where it is!'

Streng strode past Thulmann, staring intently at their prisoner. At length, he reached out and turned the man's head, finding no resistance. Streng wiped his hand on the remains of Kohl's robe then stepped back.

'You'll have to speak louder if you expect him to hear you now,' the mercenary observed with a shrug. 'Or maybe send for the priest of Morr again.' The witch hunter swallowed an enraged curse. Streng grinned over at him. 'I told you to hold back a little.'

Thulmann turned away from the dead man, crushing his fist into his palm. He knew that Streng was right, it had been the overwhelming need for haste that brewed within him that had caused this. He had pressed Kohl beyond what the man's already weakened frame could endure. Now there was only one place he could go to learn what he needed to know.

'We'll start on the old man then, eh?' asked Streng, not able to hide the brutal anticipation in his voice. Thulmann sighed with resignation and bowed his head.

'Yes,' he said. 'Wilhelm Klausner is the only one now who can tell me what I need to know.'

The witch hunter turned, stalking across the chamber and opening the iron door. As the door opened, a terrible scream echoed down from above. Thulmann glanced over at his henchman, then raced back up the stairway, his sword in one hand, a pistol clenched in the other.

The nagging foreboding that had been haunting him was surging through his mind now as the screams were repeated, echoing down the cellar stairs. The sounds spurred Thulmann on, and soon the Templar was leaping up the steps three at a time. Even so, he knew that he would not be in time to thwart whatever dark doings were afoot.

The witch hunter sprinted down the empty corridors of the keep, running towards the sound of frantic voices and frightened sobs. Then something else made itself known to him, a chill that plucked at his skin, a foul carrion stench that assailed his nostrils. The nagging foreboding that had haunted Thulmann exploded into tragic reality. He soon found himself standing in the main hall, his pistol sweeping about the chamber as he entered it.

A mob of terrified servants was huddled near the roaring fireplace, as though seeking protection from the stern-faced Klausner patriarchs captured in pain hanging from the wall behind them. Even a cursory glance told the witch hunter that every man and woman among them was trembling with fear.

Upon the polished floor of the hall, he could see three bodies lying in crumpled heaps, servants who had tried to stop whatever foulness had visited the keep this night. Pools of blood glimmered in the flickering light cast by the hall's torches.

'They took him!' a woman's voice shrieked. Thulmann turned toward the speaker, surprised to find that the terrified words came from the normally calm, precise and collected Ilsa Klausner. The noblewoman pointed her shivering hand toward the main door. Thulmann's gaze regarded the portal, finding that the heavy oak door had nearly been wrenched from its fittings.

'Who did they take?' the witch hunter asked, his sharp tone lashing at the frightened mob like a stream of ice water. He already knew what the answer would be.

'His lordship,' a blond-haired groom muttered, his voice a feeble croak.

'They were monsters!' a young chambermaid gasped. 'They weren't human!'

The girl's words brought a gaggle of hysterical confirmations to her claim, as each witness struggled to be heard over the others. Above the babble, the witch hunter heard something that at once arrested his attention.

'Anton? Who said that one of these intruders was young Klausner?' the witch hunter demanded. A pair of burly manservants stepped away from the crowd.

'We saw him when Rudi and Karl tried to stop him,' one of the men said. 'It was the young master. But he was wild and his strength was that of a daemon!'

'It was not my son,' Ilsa Klausner swore as she came forward. 'Whatever it was, it was no longer my son behind its eyes.' She fixed Thulmann with her wretched gaze. 'I know enough of my husband's former profession to recognise one of the undead when I see it. It was a vampire, like the thing it was with.'

Thulmann spun around as a shape rushed at him from behind. It was only by chance that he did not fire his pistol and explode the skull of the man who ran towards him down the corridor. Streng drew his bulk to a sudden stop, exhaling sharply as he considered how near he had come to getting killed by his master.

'Tardy as ever,' the witch hunter sneered, replacing the pistol in its holster.

'Miss all the fun, did I?' Streng asked, still visibly shaken.

'The vampire was here,' Thulmann told him. 'It came and took the old man. Anton was with it, which is how it gained entry to this place. The boy is a monster now as well.' A sudden thought occurred to the witch hunter. He lifted his eyes toward the upper floor, then pointed at Ilsa Klausner. 'I left Gregor with his father,' he told her. Ilsa lifted her hand to her mouth to stifle her horrified gasp. 'Go and see to him, if he yet lives!'

Thulmann ignored the noblewoman as she raced up the stairway, several of her servants hurrying after her. He glared at the remaining staff. 'Did any of you see where they went?' he demanded. A grimy, dirt-covered man hesitantly raised his hand. The witch hunter fixed him with a harsh and impatient look.

'I was outside, in the courtyard,' the man sputtered. 'I saw the... the things...'

'Where did they go?' the witch hunter snapped.

'It... it looked like his lordship was leading the others... leading them toward the... toward the cemetery.'

The witch hunter turned away, the gardener's recollections no longer of any interest to him. He nodded toward Streng. 'Come along, you'll earn your gold tonight,' he said. The mercenary jogged alongside Thulmann as the witch hunter crossed the ravaged hall with long strides.

It was not long before they were outside within the courtyard, staring at the human debris strewn about the open gate. It seemed that the vampire had been quite thorough about slaughtering all who had witnessed its arrival, from gate guards to stable boys. Streng swallowed nervously as he realised that the injuries he saw had been done without benefit of a trebuchet or cannon. Thulmann was more disconcerted by the fact that the monster had shown no interest in disposing of those who had seen it leave.

'Where are we going?' the mercenary asked. Thulmann did not look at him, but continued striding toward the open gate.

'The only place Wilhelm could be taking them,' he said. 'The place where all of this started.'

CHAPTER TWENTY

MIST ROLLED ACROSS the graves, coiling about the headstones, clutching at faded and forgotten names with wispy tendrils of nothingness. From the wasted boughs of an old dead oak, an owl called out into the night while from the dried-out brambles that clustered about the walls of the cemetery a chorus of toads croaked and chirped.

All sound died away as three figures approached the gate, the aura of dread and malevolence exuding from the group crawling across the graveyard like the icy breath of Morr himself. The toads huddled against the ground, their warty skins burrowing into the soft soil, desperate to hide from the dread that clawed at their tiny amphibian minds. The owl gave one last cry, then took to wing, intent on continuing its mournful song in some less forsaken place.

The vampire struck the wrought iron gates with its hand, snapping the chain that lashed them together and throwing them open. Its smouldering eyes glared into the pale, perspiring visage of Wilhelm Klausner. The vampire's lips pulled away from its fangs.

'Here?' it scoffed.

'Where better than amongst the dead?' the old patriarch retorted, pushing past Sibbechai, his frail frame shivering from weakness and the cold that had set into his bones. The vampire followed close on the old man's heels, the thing that had been Anton Klausner striding silently behind them both.

Wilhelm tottered his way amongst the graves, sometimes lingering to consider a name, to recall a face or some fragment of family history.

Whatever the witch hunter had said, the Klausners had accomplished a great deal of good over the years, more than enough to atone for the ritual they had handed down from father to son. They were a noble line, with pure intentions and a fervent devotion to Sigmar.

The fact that in five hundred years not a single Klausner had used *Das Buch die Unholden* beyond employing the ritual of protection was mute testament to the fact that the family was not corrupt and tainted, not driven by the nameless promises of black magic and blacker gods. The fact that they had kept the profane tome from the clutches of creatures like Sibbechai for hundreds of years was justification for what they had done. It had to be.

The patriarch glanced behind him, finding the hideous shadow of the necrarch beside him, its gaze smouldering into his own. 'Where?' it hissed. The old patriarch pointed toward the massive marble crypt that stood at the very centre of the graveyard.

'Helmuth's mausoleum,' Wilhelm said, trying to regain his breath, the nocturnal excursion quickly depleting his thin reserves of strength. 'It was entombed with him and has never left the crypt.' The vampire's claw pushed the old man forward.

'For the sake of your family, I hope that is so,' snarled Sibbechai. 'I have had a very long time to consider how best to destroy this family. Some of the notions that have occurred to me are most inventive.'

The patriarch did not answer the vampire's threat, but continued to walk towards the old tomb. As he climbed the short flight of steps set before the squat marble structure, Sibbechai came towards him, hissing a warning into the man's ear. Then the vampire swept its claw through the cold night air, motioning for Anton to precede them. The vampiric thrall strode forward, exerting its increased strength upon the heavy stone doors. Slowly, the portal began to slide inward.

A foul, damp smell billowed out of the darkness within the crypt. Sibbechai's eyes glowed with an eager and desperate hunger.

'Take me to it,' the creature snarled, pushing Wilhelm forward once more. The old man stumbled up the steps, his eyes watering with regret and shame as he saw the sneering face of what had been his son waiting on the threshold to greet him. Anton snorted derisively as its father passed.

Wilhelm fumbled about within the darkness of the crypt until he found the lantern and tinder that had been left there. He was under no delusion that his monstrous companions could not see him in the shadows. They would allow the lantern only because they still needed the old man to guide them, but they would not suffer it to allow Wilhelm an advantage. As soon as the old man had the lamp lit, Sibbechai muttered an inarticulate snarl and Anton ripped the lamp from his hands, shoving its father against the wall.

'Lead the way, old one,' the Anton-thing snapped. Wilhelm nodded weakly, sickened by the empty, soulless sound of the vampire's voice. With slow, reluctant steps, he strode toward the flight of marble steps that burrowed downward from the small square anteroom. The two vampires filed after him.

The steps descended some twenty feet beneath the cemetery. Niches cut into the walls held the shrouded remains of past Klausner patriarchs. There were even a few empty niches that would have served Wilhelm and Gregor, had things proceeded along the path they had always followed. The fact was not lost on Anton, and Wilhelm could hear the vampire's snarl of envious wrath as they passed the empty places.

The corpses became less complete the deeper they descended, as the hand of time came to rest ever more heavily. Many were now nothing more than fragments of bone and cloth, cobwebs and dust. The stink of slow decay and grave mould managed to make itself known even above the stench of Sibbechai's rotten flesh.

A centipede scurried away from the light, creeping back into the crack that had snaked its way down the smooth marble surface. A rat gave a sharp squeak of fright as Sibbechai's unholy presence offended its senses, the rodent scrabbling at the walls in its desperate attempt to flee before falling dead from fear as the vampire's shadow fell upon it.

Ahead, at the bottom of the stairway, a small chamber opened. Wilhelm paused as he stared up at the name carved into the archway, the name of the man who had brought doom and dishonour upon the generations who had followed after him. Then he continued onward, into the clammy darkness of Helmuth's tomb.

The light of Anton's lantern fought to illuminate the tiny chamber, its beams flickering upon the massive stone sarcophagus that filled the centre of the room. Upon the lid of the sarcophagus had been sculpted a life-size image of Helmuth Klausner, depicted in the prime of life, wearing his armour and prayer beads, hands folded across his chest, the witch hunter's sword laid out atop his body with the blade pointing at his feet and the pommel upon his lips.

Sibbechai surged forward, the witch-lights in its face glaring down at the sarcophagus. It had been many centuries since it had last set eyes upon that face, but it was a face that the vampire would not forget should a thousand years come to pass. The vampire stared at the cold stone features, remembering them warm and coursing with a life every bit as perverse as its own...

THE CHILL OF black sorcery set the brooding crows flying into the darkening night above the cursed rubble of Mordheim, croaking their fright at the icy clutch of necromancy in the air about them. The old, crumbling facades of the buildings seemed to become still more decrepit as the years tugged at their decaying structures, hurried along by the foul magic swirling about the ruins.

Dead things twitched, rigid arms began to flex their rotting muscles and sightless eyes snapped open in decomposing faces. The mangled dead began to stir once more, their spirits dragged back from oblivion to provide a shallow mockery of life to the shells they had worn only moments before.

Sibbechai's corrupt visage contorted into a mask of scorn and contempt. 'More sorcery, Helmuth?' the vampire hissed. 'Is there no limit to your hypocrisy?'

The witch hunter captain continued to mumble his conjurations, allowing the zombie monsters to shuffle and shamble their way between himself and his undead enemy. 'The tools of your loathsome kind can be made to serve the cause of Light,' Helmuth Klausner snarled. 'By such perversions is this great land threatened and by such perversions shall every last witch and wizard be driven from the Empire!'

The vampire paid only partial attention to the witch hunter's words, watching as the zombie creatures of the madman closed in upon it. The monster's face twisted with wry amusement. 'Is this the best you can do?' Sibbechai laughed. 'I find your efforts insulting.'

Sibbechai launched its lean form forward, the vampire's clawed hands lashing out, tearing the head from the shoulders of the nearest zombie as easily as a child pulling wings from a fly. The necrarch snarled a word of power and the next zombie toppled, crumbling into dust before it even finished falling to the blood-soaked cobbles. Sibbechai spun about, gesturing with its clawed hand, sending another blast of dark magic searing into a pair of the shuffling corpses, the unholy power turning both cadaver-things into walking torches.

The vampire was spinning about to smash its way through the last of Helmuth's zombies when sharp, blinding pain surged through its body. The vampire stared down with revulsion as a pustulent mass spread across its chest, a green morass of goo alive with maggots and filth. The vampire ripped the robe from its withered body, hurling the tainted garment into the face of an approaching zombie, the creature shambling onward a few moments before the writhing corruption ate through its skull and consumed its festering brain.

Helmuth Klausner snarled as he saw the vampire's inhumanly quick reflexes react to the pestilential spell the witch hunter had directed at it. Klausner had travelled far to uncover and destroy the corrupted festival, had nearly been killed by the loathsome and bloated priest of Nurgle who had acted as the carnival's master. He had done so because he had imagined that the spellcraft of such a sorcerer might prove of great use against the restless dead. Fortunately, there was more than one way to burn a bat.

The witch hunter pulled his heavy blackpowder pistol from its holster of blackened leather. The vampire saw the man's reaction, the undead abomination not even deigning to consider such a crude device any threat. Sibbechai ripped through another pair of zombies, finding its path to Helmuth unhindered.

Helmuth returned the corpse-thing's stare, the fanatic zeal in his veins countering the aura of supernatural malice exuding from the vampire's eyes. With calm deliberation, Helmuth lifted the pistol, whispering the slithering words he had extracted from the mangled body of a wizard in Averheim, the words of an ancient and pre-human spell of guiding. The pistol cracked and roared as Helmuth depressed the trigger, foul black powder smoke blowing back into his face and causing his eyes to tear.

The vampire darted aside as the witch hunter's crude weapon fired. It had fought many men who employed the smelly, unreliable firearms before and had learned that even on the rare occasions when their bullets did strike, they could do the monster no lasting harm.

But Sibbechai had not reckoned upon the sorcerous augmentation of the witch hunter's marksmanship, nor the uniqueness of the shot he had loaded into his weapon. The golden ball smashed into the vampire's shoulder, spinning the necrarch around and slamming it to the ground. Sibbechai snarled in agony and disbelief as it tried to lift itself from the broken cobbles.

A strange paralysis seemed to spread from its injury, making even its wasted limbs seem as heavy as stone. The witch hunter laughed, slipping his smoking weapon back into its holster.

'Surprised, monster?' he sneered down at the struggling vampire. 'I've learned a few new tricks since last our paths crossed.'

The witch hunter's boot cracked Sibbechai's face, smashing the vampire's rotting nose and spraying filthy black blood about the ground. 'I employ a rather unique shot now, graciously provided by a Solkanite inquisitor I encountered in Nuln. Poor misguided fellow, he seemed determined that I was a servant of the Dark Gods, a depraved sorcerer. Can you imagine that?'

Helmuth kicked the vampire again before stepping away. A thoughtful expression flickered across his face. 'I killed him of course. I found that his golden mask, melted down and treated with certain prayers, had a certain amount of usefulness to a man of my calling.' The witch hunter glared down at his foe. 'But you've discovered that for yourself, haven't you?'

Helmuth Klausner called out, his lisping voice a deep and commanding boom. From the dirty shadows where they had hidden themselves, the witch hunter's followers appeared. They were, for the most part, miserable and dirty creatures, their clothing almost as tattered and ruined as the grave cloth hanging from the corpses of Klausner's zombies.

These men were the bitter, the desolate and the dispossessed, men to whom the light of existence had winked out, whose families and livelihoods had been consumed by plague, famine and war. They were men from whom everything had been taken except the hate that boiled within them, that kept their hearts warm and their blood hot.

They were men who had been only too eager to listen to the witch hunter, to join him on his crusade to purge the Empire by spell, fire and sword. They were men who did not question the hypocrisy of one who burned a witch after stealing her secrets, nor the heresy that seemed so obvious when the man they followed sent lifeless abominations given vitality and motion through the black arts to contend with the mortal attendants of a vampire. They had put aside such questions. They were no longer needed.

Helmuth Klausner gave them something more important than any moral debate, he gave them a way to lash out, a way to make their hate fulfil itself. Klausner made these men something nobler than simple murderers and thugs, and to question the correctness of his methods was to question the righteousness of the barbarities they performed on his command.

The dirty-faced rabble of warriors and zealots glared at the carnage strewn all about their leader, at the mangled zombies and the still-dripping bodies of those of Sibbechai's fold who had yet to breathe their last. Several of the thugs drew daggers and set to hastening the demise of the wounded men.

One among them, an elderly man with hollow cheeks and steel-grey hair, the soiled white vestment of a priest of Sigmar still fluttering about his spindly form, strode towards the still moving monster at Helmuth's feet.

Walther stared down at the vampire, trembling as he saw the necrarch's unholy orbs look back at him. The old priest stood his ground, however, lifting the long wooden shaft he carried, its end carved into a sharpened point.

The priest began to pray in a soft and solemn voice, calling upon his god to guide his hand. Sibbechai stared back, an air of resignation and something that might even have been expectancy seeming to enter the foul creature's face.

Walther leaned back, then made to drive the stake into the vampire's chest, the full weight of the priest's body behind it. He found his strike foiled, however, as a strong hand closed about the other end of the stake, thwarting its descent. Walther turned his head, finding himself looking into the cold eyes of Helmuth Klausner.

'No,' the witch hunter told him. 'I have hunted this filth too long to let the end be so quick for him.' Helmuth smiled malignantly at the paralysed vampire. 'There are things I need from him before I finish with him.'

Sibbechai felt a flash of rage boil up within its old, cold heart, a ghostly return of the emotions that had run through it before the vampire curse had completely consumed its humanity. By a supreme effort, the vampire lifted its head, mouth dropping open in a snarl of inhuman savagery. 'You have already taken everything!' the vampire spat. 'My wife! My daughter! My life! There is nothing left, finish it and be damned!'

The witch hunter's features spread into an expression of loathsome and ghastly amusement. 'Oh yes, dear brother, I most certainly have! I have taken from you everything that you won with your miserable sorcery, everything you tricked and cheated the gods of fortune into tossing into your lap. Your life, your inheritance of our father's trade contracts, his farms and businesses, awarded to you by the few minutes your sorcerer's gods made you my elder! And your lovely wife and daughter,' the witch hunter's lip twisted into a sneer. 'She should have been my wife! My child! Only by your heathen magic did you prevail, did you turn her affection for me into hate!'

'No magic in this world or the next could have done that any better than the cruelty and malice in your heart, Helmuth,' the vampire hissed. 'How could she love such a thing as you, a thing of bitterness and envy, coveting everything that was not your own and hating those you could not look down upon. Is it any wonder that a man such as you should rise above the fears of your neighbours, to rise above that fear in order to prey upon it?'

The vampire's eyes gleamed with contempt. 'Tell me, Helmuth, did any priest ordain you to torture and burn innocent women and children, or did Sigmar himself call down to you and tell you to become a monster?'

Wrath blazed up in the witch hunter's face for a moment, but swiftly faded into a cold and malicious spite. Helmuth sneered down at the vampire. 'Oh, I did more than torture that slut you chose to pollute our name,' the witch hunter declared, a note of pride in his voice. 'I waited until you had gone, of course, to confer with your sorcerer friends. Then I denounced her, her and her daughter. Denounced them as witches before the whole town.'

The witch hunter chuckled with sinister mirth. 'You know, not one of them spoke a word in her defence. That rabble you so loved and helped with your heathen magics, your elf lore and pagan prayers. Not one of them dared to defy me, for they saw that justice was within me. And before justice, no unclean thing can prevail!'

The vampire struggled against the power that pressed upon its limbs, struggled to rise and rend the gloating figure of its hated enemy. But it was a struggle the monster could not win. Helmuth watched Sibbechai's desperate movements for a time, then continued his tormenting.

'I am impressed,' the witch hunter mused in a thoughtful tone. 'I had imagined that all the humanity would have burned itself out of that rotting carcass of yours some time ago. Don't tell me that there is still enough of my...' the witch hunter paused, putting such an emphasis on the next word that it seemed to explode from his mouth, '*little* brother that he still feels some connection with that slut of his? Would it anger him to know that the favours she chose to deny me and bestow upon you are not unknown to me now?' The witch hunter laughed again as he saw the enraged vampire struggle once more to rise. Walther cast a nervous look at the vampire, then at his leader, uncertain which of the two was the greater menace.

'She was most forthcoming,' Helmuth continued. 'One might even say eager. I spent many a happy night before I tired of her incessant begging and pleading.' The witch hunter shook his head. 'I can't understand why you were so devoted to that boring cow. But, it might lift your spirits to know that they died together.'

Helmuth laughed. 'A single pyre is so much more economical,' he stated. Sibbechai growled, the creature's immobile claws scratching deep into the cobbles. A stern expression came upon the witch hunter.

'Don't deceive yourself, monster,' he snarled. 'You are no longer my brother Hessrich! You did not drive me from Gruebelhof, pursue me across the Empire, follow me into this place of horror and madness simply to avenge that carrion.'

The witch hunter pulled open a heavy leather satchel that hung from a strap across his chest. From it he removed a mass of paper and parchment, held together by an array of string and leather cords.

Helmuth brandished it before the vampire, watching with satisfaction as Sibbechai's eyes narrowed with lust and desire. 'Yes,' Helmuth cooed. 'The book you brought back to Gruebelhof after your *accident*. Of course, I have added to it since then, added to it with the rites and spells of a dozen sorcerers, the hexes and charms of a score of witches. But this is no longer some coffin-worm's grimoire, nor some magister's tome of profane lore! This is *Das Buch die Unholden*, Helmuth Klausner's book of unholy things, his weapon against the powers of Old Night! I shall not use this vile tome as you would, vampire! I shall use it to give glory and honour to Sigmar, to destroy those who would mock and profane his holy name!'

Helmuth drew a deep breath, calming himself after his tirade. The witch hunter glanced aside, finding that his minions were staring at him. He gestured at the vampire. 'Seize it!' he snapped. 'Bind it!'

The witch hunter smiled as he watched his men overcome their hesitance and fall upon the vampire, winding chains of silver about its withered limbs. Iron spikes were driven into the cobbles, the chains wrapped round them. The men strained at their task, extending the vampire's limbs, forcing the monster to spread itself upon the ground.

The witch hunter nodded in satisfaction as he saw his followers complete their labour, retreating back in revulsion and fear as the vampire snarled up at them.

'Such a work,' Helmuth said, rubbing his hand across the weathered pages, 'should have a proper setting, don't you think? I have seen for myself that necromancers choose to enshrine their despicable secrets within covers of human skin. It should only be fitting then to entomb my great work within the hide of one of the loathsome monsters that threatens Sigmar's noble Empire.' Helmuth turned away, pointing to one of the most brutal looking of his henchmen, a grizzled bear of a man dressed in furs and mud. 'Skin it,' he ordered the warrior.

Walther grabbed the arm of his leader, flinching away when he saw the look of anger in his master's eyes. 'You can't do such a thing!' he protested. 'That sorry creature was your brother! Whatever it has become, surely you can extend it some small measure of mercy?'

The priest understood that the monster needed to be destroyed, but the savage horror of what Helmuth intended sickened him even more than anything else he had been witness to since joining up with the witch hunter. 'Even the most pious of Sigmar's champions can show pity. Destroy it, yes, but not this way.'

Helmuth Klausner's voice was like the cackle of one of the Dark Gods. 'Destroy it?' he laughed. 'I am rather hoping that it does not die. Some of the nosferatu are capable of suffering hideous injuries before meeting their end. I hope to amuse myself with this creature for quite some time.' The witch hunter laughed again as he saw the skinner cut away the tatters of Sibbechai's robe. The crescent-shaped knife sank into the vampire's rotten skin, flaying it from the flesh beneath.

A low howl of anguish rose from the undead creature.

'Destroy it?' Helmuth gave the priest an incredulous look. 'I've not even started with it yet!'

IT WAS IN the long dark hours when all was quiet and still that Walther crept his way toward the place where the vampire had been left.

It had taken many hours for Helmuth's men to fall asleep, revelling in their leader's victory. The witch hunter himself had retired to his own room within a half-collapsed tavern, there to consult his tome of sorcery. There had been no one to watch Walther go, no guard to prevent his departure. Yet it had taken many hours more for the old priest to justify what he intended, struggling to overcome beliefs that had been branded into his soul and the last lingering traces of faith and loyalty some dark part of him still felt towards Helmuth Klausner.

The witch hunter was mad. Walther had known it for quite some time, if he was fully honest with himself. It was only now, however, that he had the courage to accept the fact.

He had followed Helmuth for two years, at first believing that the witch hunter's plan to drive the pawns of the Ruinous Powers from the Empire by employing their own profane arts against them. He had believed because he knew the nature of those wizards and warlocks he had seen, selfish men who pursued their

338 . *C.L Werner*

own interests, whether knowledge or power, with a reckless abandon, contemptuous of the gods and their fellow man. But Helmuth had been different, a man who had within him a great and zealous devotion to Sigmar.

Walther had believed in the witch hunter, believed his claims that a righteous man could bend the twisted powers of sorcery and use it in the name of justice and good.

Walther could only shake his head at his former naiveté. He had watched the foul knowledge Helmuth had collected consume the witch hunter, twisting him into the very likeness of those he hunted. He had watched as the corrupt power devoured the witch hunter a bit more every day.

What might he become if left to continue as he was? Would the evil of his outrages be any less for being consecrated to Sigmar? Or did it make them worse, fouler even than the devotions of depraved Chaos cultists and witches?

The old priest had seen far too much of Helmuth's black power, knew only too well the profane forces the witch hunter could command. It terrified him, for all his faith in Sigmar. He knew that he could not challenge Helmuth on his own. He did not have the courage or the faith. He worried that at the last moment, some fragment of his former loyalty to the man would assert itself and stay his hand, delay the fatal blow. Then the witch hunter would destroy him, and Walther shuddered as he considered how inventive the man would be when dealing with one who had betrayed him.

Walther stared at the unmoving figure that lay sprawled upon the street, arms and legs made fast to iron spikes driven deep into the cobbles.

He hesitated, trembling as he recalled the monster's screams. Perhaps it was already dead, perhaps he had risked discovery and damnation for nothing. No man could have survived what Helmuth had put the vampire through, no mortal could have endured such pain for hours on end. And even if it yet lived, how could it possibly have strength enough left within it to help him?

The old priest closed his eyes, whispering a prayer to Sigmar that he might have guidance, that he might be shown what to do. When Walther opened his eyes, he felt an impulse to run, to flee the accursed and damned rubble of Mordheim. The old priest turned to do just that, but a slight change in the vampire's shad-owy figure caused him to hesitate.

Two glowing eyes were staring at him from the vampire's man-gled form, shining out at him with a cold wrath. Walther stared back, feeling the faint traces of the monster's aura of fear prickle his skin and crawl along his spine. Sibbechai lived, and Helmuth might still be stopped. The priest walked toward the silent shad-owy mass, feeling his stomach turn as he saw what remained of the vampire, a dry mass of bare meat and muscle, like the carcass of a dried-out toad. Sibbechai stared up at the priest, its stripped face incapable of any sort of expression.

'Come to finish my brother's labours?' a dry voice wheezed from the vampire's mouth. Despite the horror of its mutilated tones, Walther could detect a hopeful ring to Sibbechai's words.

The priest noticed for the first time that he held his long wooden stake at the ready, poised to thrust it into the vampire's chest. He smiled weakly, lowering his weapon. 'No,' he said at length. 'Only Sigmar can grant you peace,' he added with a note of genuine sympathy and regret.

'If Sigmar has chosen a man such as Helmuth Klausner as the instrument of his will, then I pity man,' Sibbechai sighed. The vampire stared intently at the expression that came upon Walther's face. 'You know what he is, I can see it in your eyes. I am a monster,' Sibbechai stated, 'but how much more so is my brother? He clothes his horror within the cloak of justice and beneath the banner of righteousness, but is he truly so different from what I have become?' The vampire might have smiled had it understood how directly and precisely it had read the troubling doubts boiling within the old priest's mind.

'Helmuth Klausner serves the Empire, serves holy Sigmar,' the priest declared as he fought to regain his composure. 'He turns the powers of the enemy against themselves, fighting the fires of corruption with their own flame.' The vampire hissed with bitter laughter.

'Is that so? Your noble champion serves Sigmar?' Sibbechai's mangled form shuddered with the force of its anguished mirth. 'Then tell me why I find him here? I did not follow your master to Mordheim, I waited for him. I knew he would come here, come here to harvest the wyrdstone. To use it to attempt a thing no sor-cerer or necromancer has ever dared to contemplate.'

The vampire itself seemed to shiver with fear as it thought about the dark purpose that had drawn Helmuth Klausner to Mordheim. The old priest turned pale at the mention of wyrdstone, for the witch hunter had indeed been gathering as many of the greenish-black shards of rock as he could find. But unlike the mercenary rabble who conducted their own wyrdstone hunts through the ruins, Walther knew that Helmuth had no patron waiting to buy the stones from him.

'Helmuth seeks only to cleanse this land of its pollution, to drive corruption from the Empire,' Walther insisted, fighting against his own doubts and fears.

'In his diseased way, that is what he hopes to do,' Sibbechai said. 'He would burn the field to save the crop.' The vampire's hiss dropped into a whisper. 'I know what it is that he stole from me, I know the ancient secrets he learned from my book!'

'You do not frighten me,' Walther swore at the monster, brandishing once more the wooden stake. The vampire shook its head slightly, all the movement it could manage.

'Then you are a fool,' it told him. 'For your master has had time enough to decipher that book, to unlock its most terrible lore. I tell you, Helmuth Klausner came to Mordheim with one purpose: he means to recreate the Great Ritual of Nagash!'

The wooden stake fell from the priest's hands, clattering upon the cobbles. Walther recoiled in horror as he heard the vampire whisper the ancient and blighted name of the First Necromancer, the undying father of the undead.

He staggered as the enormity of what Sibbechai had suggested struck him. The Great Ritual, a dark fable that was still whispered on winter nights, an event of such atrocity and infamy that its echoes still resonated through the souls of men, a story that was still remembered by men who had never even heard of the lands where it had unfolded.

The Great Ritual, the apocalyptic spell by which Nagash had destroyed the kingdoms of Nehekhara and transformed them for all time into the Land of the Dead, the spell through which he had slain every man, woman, child and beast then resurrected them as soulless abominations to walk the barren wastes until the ending of the world. Walther felt sickened even by the possibility that such knowledge had not been purged from all existence with Sigmar's smiting of the Black One.

'I heard Helmuth,' Walther snarled at the vampire. 'You hunted him here to reclaim your filthy book. You intend to work this abominable spell yourself!'

'I waited because I knew that he must come here,' Sibbechai corrected the old priest. 'I came here to avenge the outrages he committed upon my wife and daughter.' The vampire's voice seethed with rage as it spoke. 'I have hunted Helmuth all these years for revenge, not for some tome of cursed and blasphemous knowledge!'

The priest glared down at the monster, considering its words. At last Walther nodded to himself, drawing a dagger from his belt. 'You will help me to stop Helmuth if I release you?' the old priest asked, his voice quivering from the disgust he felt at what he was doing. The vampire nodded its head as much as it could. 'When it is finished, you understand that I cannot let you live,' the priest added.

'When Helmuth is dead,' Sibbechai told him, 'there will no longer be any reason for me to live. I will not hinder you from doing what must be done.'

The priest leaned downward, gripping one of the silver chains. He pressed the edge of his dagger against it, then hesitated, staring at the vampire once more. 'How can I be certain that you will honour your word?' he demanded.

'I swear by Sigmar, who I worshipped when I yet drew breath,' the vampire told him. Then, in a softer, pitiable voice it added, 'But if that does not bind me to you, then I shall swear upon the souls of my wife and child that I shall work no harm upon you.' Walther bowed his head, accepting the conviction and misery in the vampire's tones. He set to sawing through the silver links.

'The bullet,' Sibbechai hissed. 'It drains me of strength. Cut it from me first, or I can be of no use to you. If I am too weak to help you, you must leave the chains, leave me to Helmuth.' A growl of hate rumbled up from the vampire. 'Only promise me that even without my help, you will strike down the heretic!'

Walther rose from attacking the chain. He stared into the vampire's ruined face, seeing for the first time not a soulless monster, but a cursed and tormented man. He nodded his head, feeling a new strength flow through him. 'I promise it. I promise on my faith in holy Sigmar that Helmuth Klausner will answer for all he has done.' The priest knelt beside Sibbechai, staring now at the gory hole that had bored and burned its way into the meat of the vampire's shoulder. He looked over at Sibbechai's face. 'I suspect this is going to hurt,' he commented.

The vampire clenched its jaws against the agony that flashed through its ravaged body as Walther's knife probed into the wound.

It was some minutes later when Walther rose from his gruesome labour. The lack of blood had somehow added to the horror of the operation as the vampire's collapsed veins shed not a drop of fluid as the priest's blade worried its way past them. The priest held the gold bullet before his face, wondering how so small a thing might bring low so dreadful a being as a vampire.

The priest's face contorted with an ironic smile. This dreadful being was now his only ally against a man he had once called friend and mentor. Strange indeed were the twisted paths of fate.

'It is done,' he said, tossing the bullet away. 'Do you feel any change?' The question died unanswered as Walther turned back towards the vampire.

Sibbechai had leapt to its feet the instant the old priest's attention had wavered, ripping the iron spikes from the cobbles with inhuman strength. Sibbechai whipped one of the silver chains dangling from his wrists towards Walther, the heavy iron spike fixed to the end of the chain length smashing into the side of the priest's skull.

The man fell to the cobbles and in an instant the vampire was upon him, strangling the life from the old man with one of the chains, ignoring the burning wracking pain that sizzled into it every time the naked meat of its palms touched the metal. In a brutally short time, the priest's body grew slack. Sibbechai let the man's corpse slump into the street, Walther's neck nearly cut clean through by the action of the chain upon his flesh. The vampire stared hungrily at the puddles of blood that had already drained out from the corpse. It fell on its hands and knees and began to lap the crimson liquid from the filthy cobbles.

There really had been no hope that the fool's plan might have worked, the vampire told itself. It was too weak to confront Helmuth Klausner so soon, and even if they had accomplished some miraculous victory over the deranged witch hunter, Sibbechai doubted if it would have been able to escape with the book afterwards. That was what mattered. Not Helmuth's death, not some noble attempt to thwart the witch hunter's insane schemes.

The transcription of the Great Ritual was fragmentary, Helmuth's hopes of recreating it were nothing more than delusions. Far greater minds than his had tried and failed. Nor was revenge enough to spur the vampire to such foolish and suicidal action, though the old priest had been quite willing to believe it would.

No, Sibbechai decided, all that mattered was regaining that which had been stolen from it. It would take some time to heal the injuries done to it this day by Helmuth, but it would recover. And then it would reclaim its property, if not from its brother, then another. The book was all that mattered.

As the vampire reached that decision, and slipped back into the shadows of the night, a tiny voice deep inside it, a part of it that had grown steadily weaker and quieter, screamed as it faded into darkness…

SIBBECHAI ROSE FROM its study of the sarcophagus, withdrawing from its reverie. The vampire's claw scratched a jagged line down the unblemished stone face. 'How did he die?' it asked, not looking away from the disfigured sculpture.

'He was old,' Wilhelm Klausner said. 'Very old. He had lived a full and prosperous life, commended and decorated by the Grand Theogonist himself. He was given this district by the Elector Count of Stirland.'

The patriarch swallowed as he considered the haunted legend that had been handed down from generation to generation, the cautionary parable that warned against using *Das Buch die Unholden* for more than protection. 'As I said, he was very old. He took to keeping himself in his room, not even allowing his son to see him. The flicker of candlelight could be seen from his window at all hours. It was thought that he was trying to prepare for his death, to set his affairs in order or to leave a complete record of his deeds. Then one dark night, the keep was awakened by the sound of a pistol shot. Helmuth's door was broken down when he did not answer. Smoke rose from the pistol that lay upon the floor, and beside it lay the first Lord Klausner. He had put a golden bullet through his brain.

'He'd not been writing,' Wilhelm went on. 'He had been reading, reading from that accursed tome. He was afraid of death and knew that in that blasphemous body of profane knowledge he could find a way to defy death. A ghastly, abominable way, but a way. In the end, he triumphed against the temptation,' there was a note of pride in Wilhelm's tone. 'He chose to destroy himself rather than succumb to the lure of unlife.'

Sibbechai's filthy voice bubbled with a grim laughter. 'He could have been no more a monster dead than alive,' it hissed, a faint trace of faded emotion echoing through its twisted mind. For a moment, the monster idly considered whether the bullet its brother had ended his life with had been the same one that had nearly caused its own demise amidst the corruption of Mordheim. 'Long may he rot.'

The vampire turned its gaze about the remainder of the room, its head freezing in place as it sighted the large stone lectern that rested in front of the rear wall. The necrarch made a low cackle, like a starving man who has discovered a scrap of bread.

'At last,' its loathsome voice croaked. 'After all this time, it is mine again. Flesh of my flesh!' The skeletal apparition rounded the lectern, its grisly visage lifted into a mask of morbid rapture.

The smile fell away, supplanted on the corpse-creature's visage by an expression of such malevolence that might chill the spirit of a god. Sibbechai glared across the crypt at Wilhelm Klausner, seeing the glimmer of proud triumph that shone in the old man's eyes. The vampire's claws gripped the lectern, toppling the heavy stone pedestal to the floor.

The necrarch's thin lips pulled back in a howl of frustrated fury. Its fist slammed into the wall, crumbling the marble. Wilhelm Klausner fled, placing the stone sarcophagus between himself and the vampire. Anton withdrew several paces up the darkened stairs. Sibbechai's howl of anguish lingered as the vampire punched the marble wall again and again. Then its wrath turned toward Klausner.

'Where is it?' Sibbechai raged. 'It was here! What have you done with it?' Wilhelm cowered before the furious monster, watching as the embers of its eyes seemed to glow white-hot. The vampire's thin figure grew rigid, then it lunged for the old man, hurling itself across the small room.

The crack and roar of a pistol thundered above even the snarls of the vampire. Sibbechai's body was punched in mid-air, dashed against the wall as a bullet smashed into the vampire's breast.

Anton turned his head, lips drawing back in a savage snarl as he saw the two men descending the stairway.

A look almost as rapturous as that which had come upon Sibbechai when the monster had reached out to claim *Das Buch die Unholden* filled Wilhelm Klausner's features as he saw Mathias Thulmann stalking down the darkened stairs.

'Doom and judgement are upon you!' the witch hunter shouted. 'This night, Sibbechai of the necrarchs, you atone for your crimes of sorcery, heresy and outrage upon the Empire!'

ANTON KLAUSNER HURLED himself at the witch hunter, hands curled into claws, face contorted into an animalistic leer. Streng fired his crossbow into the rushing monster, the bolt smashing into its ribs. The Anton-thing stopped, uttering a menacing chuckle as he tore the missile from his body, not so much as a drop of blood weeping from the wound.

'You can't hurt me!' he spat. 'So what do your little toys matter?' Anton watched with grim amusement as Thulmann pointed his second pistol at the monster. Before the witch hunter could fire, the vampire lunged up the dozen steps that separated them. Anton's claw forced Thulmann's hand upward, causing the witch hunter to fire his shot into the ceiling.

The vampire's other claw closed about the Templar's neck, forcing Thulmann's head back, exposing the warm pulse throbbing at his throat. Anton distended his jaw, exposing the chisel-like fangs.

Suddenly the vampire's face twisted in pain. Anton released his grip, retreating several steps. He held his hand against the bleeding wound that punctured his side, staring in shock as he saw the blood staining his pale claw. Mathias Thulmann firmed the grip upon his sword, stalking downward.

A look of fear pulling at his features, Streng drew his own blade, but was careful to keep well behind the avenging figure of his employer. Having seen the vampire already demonstrate its invulnerability to honest steel, the mercenary was resolved to allow the witch hunter to attend to it with his priest's tricks and Sigmarite mummery.

'Yes, you bleed, blood-worm!' the witch hunter spat. 'This is the sword of Sigmar, blessed by the Grand Theogonist himself. You are not the first unclean abomination to feel its kiss,' Thulmann told the vampire. 'Nor will you be the last,' he promised.

The sneer Anton had worn in life slithered onto its cold flesh as the thrall drew its own sword. 'It seems we shall finish that fight we started in The Grey Crone, old man,' he hissed. 'But I should warn you, I am not the same man I was a few days ago.'

With no further word of warning, the undead creature launched itself at Thulmann. The witch hunter's blade clashed against Anton's sword and so began the deadly game of lunge, parry and strike.

WILHELM WATCHED IN horrified fascination as what had been his son attacked the witch hunter. The blades of man and thrall were a blur of flickering steel, the ring of weapon against weapon echoing through the crypt, rebounding from the dripping walls. They were evenly matched, it seemed. The cold, calculating skill of a seasoned swordsman, a man who had learned his art from accomplished masters, was behind the witch hunter's blade. But behind Anton's was the savage strength of the undead and the feral swiftness of a thing from beyond the grave. It was hard to tell which would prove the deciding quality, but Wilhelm prayed with all his being that it would be Thulmann's sword that emerged victorious and granted to Anton the death that was now the only thing that could redeem the boy from the horror that had claimed him.

As the patriarch continued to watch the duel, he saw Anton's tireless strength begin to take its toll. The vampire could put its full power behind every sweep and still muster the same power for its next blow.

The witch hunter did not have such supernatural reserves to call upon. More and more of Anton's blows were slipping past the Templar's guard, delivering painful slashes to arm and thigh. The witch hunter had managed to avoid any of the vampire's more telling attacks, but Wilhelm knew that his luck could not endure forever.

The old patriarch reached out his hand to the cold stone lid of the sarcophagus, grasping the sword that lay upon the image of Helmuth Klausner. The chill grip of the sword felt like ice in the old man's hand.

He turned to lend his own meagre aid to the struggle, but even as he did so, a different sort of ice closed upon his left hand. Wilhelm gasped in pain as the vice-like grip of Sibbechai's clutching claw crushed the old man's bones.

'The book,' the ghastly vampire hissed. Its chest wept a thin black tar from where the witch hunter's blessed bullet had slammed into it. But after five hundred years, Sibbechai was not so easily defeated. Even a bullet of pure silver, blessed in the Great Cathedral of Sigmar, was capable of little more than stunning the monster. Where Helmuth Klausner's bullet had almost fatally paralysed the necrarch, Mathias Thulmann's had only immobilised it for a few minutes. The vampire's fangs gleamed as it exerted its strength and broke every bone in Wilhelm Klausner's hand.

'Where is my book?' Sibbechai hissed again, depraved madness blazing within its grotesque gaze.

The old patriarch crumpled before the might of the vampire, falling to his knees before it. Sibbechai closed its hand still more tightly, grinding the shattered bones against each other. The incredible pain caused Wilhelm to drop his ancestor's sword, the heavy weapon clattering upon the marble floor. He glared defiantly at the undead monstrosity.

'Where you will never find it!' he snarled. Maddened by rage, Sibbechai flung Wilhelm against the side of the sarcophagus with such force that the snapping of the old man's back could be heard even above the clash of swords echoing from the entrance. The vampire roared at the broken man, its rat-like fangs bared.

'Living or dead,' Sibbechai shouted, 'you will tell me!'

THULMANN DESPERATELY PARRIED the flash of Anton's blade, knocking the blow aside, feeling the power of the assault shudder up his arms. The witch hunter risked a quick glance at his henchman. Streng nodded in understanding, removing a small vial of coloured glass from a pouch on his belt.

With a grimace of uncertainty and dread Streng rushed forward, flinging the contents of the small glass vial ahead of him. The liquid splashed across the left side of the vampire.

Anton uttered a shriek of agony as his flesh began to steam and his skin began to bubble. The thrall dropped his sword, pawing at his steaming face. Thulmann did not hesitate, rearing back and putting his force into a brutal slash that severed the thrall's hands and caused its head to leap from its shoulders. The decapitated monster slumped against the wall even as its head bounced into the crypt below.

The witch hunter drew a deep breath, trying to regain his strength.

'You're going to get yourself killed playing with things like that,' Streng grumbled as he kicked Anton's body away from the wall.

'I wanted to save the Tears of Shallya for the other one,' Thulmann wheezed. The witch hunter collected himself, sprinting down the remaining steps with his sword held before him.

He found the necrarch leaning over Wilhelm's broken body, a great gash torn into the vampire's wrist.

Tarry black blood oozed from the wound. At the sound of the witch hunter's approach, the vampire's grotesque face turned upon him. Thulmann could feel the ageless malignancy of the monster clutch at him, seeking to drain his courage and resolve.

The witch hunter blinked away the momentary confusion. He had been here before, this place of doubt and despair, facing the black sorcery of Erasmus Kleib, the strength of his will his only defence against the dark sorcery of his foe, faith in Sigmar his only armour. He had not failed then and he would not fail now.

Thulmann forced his foot forward, forced his sword to rise. Words came pouring from his lips and it was only after they were spoken that he realised he was reciting a prayer of protection. The vampire twisted its body away from the broken figure of Wilhelm, surprise showing on its corpse-like face.

'I have killed more of your kind than I can count,' mocked Sibbechai. 'If you go away now, I might forget this pathetic display.' The witch hunter took another step forward.

'This sword has put an end to one blood-worm this night,' he retorted. 'It is hungry for another.'

Sibbechai drew back, its face contorting with fury. The smouldering embers of the vampire's eyes bored into the witch hunter's, probing for any trace of fear, any sign of weakness. Finding none, the vampire uttered a disgusted hiss.

'I should show you the foolishness of such a boast,' Sibbechai said. 'But I will concede that there is a slim chance that you could cause me harm with such a trinket.' The vampire gestured toward the toppled lectern, waiting for Thulmann to shift his gaze. When the witch hunter did not, it continued in an arrogant tone. 'There is nothing here to give me cause to entertain such a risk. The gods of fortune are fickle, after all.' The shadows darkened around

Sibbechai as the vampire crept back toward the wall. 'But know that to every dawn a night must fall.'

Thulmann lunged forward, realising that while he had avoided the more obvious ploy of having his attention diverted, he had not escaped the subtle, disarming tone in Sibbechai's voice. As the vampire's soft hissing speech had crawled through the witch hunter's mind, he had let his guard down. Now, the darkness swelled and billowed about the creature, summoned from the shadows of the crypt.

Thulmann slashed at the pillar of darkness. In reaction to his stroke, a grisly shape fluttered past his head, a gaunt bat with ebony wings, leathery hide stretched tight over a skull-like face. Its tittering laughter bounced about the crypt.

The bat circled the chamber twice, then flew up the stairway, easily avoiding Streng as the mercenary swung at it with his crossbow. The thug shouted after the fleeing nightbird, raining every curse in his colourful vocabulary upon the creature.

THULMANN TURNED AWAY, walking to where Wilhelm Klausner's broken body had crumpled. Blood stained the old man's face, thick and dark with bile. Heretic or misguided servant of Sigmar, the old patriarch would answer to an authority higher than any to whom Thulmann could have sent him. As the witch hunter stared down at him, the old man's lips began to move. Thulmann leaned down to hear Wilhelm's feeble voice.

'Tha... thank you,' the patriarch whispered. 'Thank... you for... saving... Anton...'

'He is at peace now,' Thulmann assured the dying man.

'What... of... Gregor?' Wilhelm asked, voice cracking with despair.

'Your son will live,' Thulmann replied, not knowing if it was the truth or a lie, but praying that it was the truth he spoke. The statement brought a flicker of contentment to the dying man's face.

'It was all for them,' Wilhelm said, tears boiling up in his eyes. 'I did it all for them... destroyed the tradition, put an end to it all.' He looked at the witch hunter, his eyes filled with a deep shame. 'I... I know it should... should have been for Sigmar... for the poor people... but it was... for them.'

Thulmann stared intently at the old man, trying to discern his meaning.

'The… the ritual,' Wilhelm explained, coughing another quantity of bloody spray. 'There were never… six. There… were seven. The spell needed to feed… needed to feed. It fed on the trees… the life of the trees. But it needed a man to focus it… it needed to suck the vitality from a man.' Wilhelm's words drowned into another fit of coughing. Thulmann considered the old patriarch's words. It explained much, the so-called 'blight', the premature ageing of Wilhelm himself, all to feed some ancient pagan spell. And Wilhelm determined to prevent his sons from being consumed by the ghastly tradition as he had been consumed.

The old man lifted his heard, a pleading, intense energy filling his face. 'Sibbechai did not… did not get… the book.' Wilhelm closed his eyes against the pain that surged through him. 'Couldn't keep… it… here. I couldn't… destroy… it. Sent it away… to Wurtbad. Look… look for… the book… in Wurtbad. It's there.' The old man's head sagged downward, toward his chest. 'Forgive…' he hissed as the death rattle bubbled up from the back of his throat.

Thulmann put his fingers to the old man's face, shutting his eyes. The witch hunter stared down at the crumpled figure, uncertain how he should feel. The man's mixture of virtue and heresy was a puzzle the witch hunter doubted he would ever be able to accept or understand.

'He may have been a murdering heretic bastard,' Streng commented in his gruff tones, 'but he died like a champion.' The mercenary gestured at the room around them. 'We burn the bodies here, Mathias?' he asked.

Thulmann stared once more at the broken form of Wilhelm Klausner, the man who had defied gods and monsters for the sake of his sons, who had risked even his immortal soul to ensure their welfare and safety. The witch hunter glanced over at the corrupted remains of Anton. He almost felt sorry that the old man had seen his dreams die before him.

'No,' Thulmann told his waiting henchman. 'We will carry them out of here and burn them in the open. Somewhere clean.'

EPILOGUE

Two RIDERS SLOWLY made their way down the road that snaked away from the township of Klausberg, winding between small hills and fields of wheat. Eventually it would join up with the much larger main road that would return them to the city of Wurtbad.

The foremost of the two riders was quiet, his face hidden beneath the wide brim of his hat, his thoughts turned inward, contemplating things and decisions he did not wish to speak. The witch hunter's companion continued to grumble into his beard, bristling under the chill of the morning air.

'We might at least have waited for the frost to clear,' Streng groused. 'Why the haste, Mathias? You could make your report in a week and no one would complain.'

The witch hunter did not regard his henchman, his eyes studying instead the slopes of the hills, the clusters of rock and tree that huddled about and upon them and the cold breeze that slithered around them. 'I should think you'd be eager to fill your pockets with the temple's gold,' Thulmann returned, a note of reproach in his tone. As usual, Streng chose to ignore the witch hunter's distaste for his openly mercenary motivations.

'Aye, it'll be nice to have full pockets again,' the mercenary observed. 'Though we could have turned a better coin,' Streng added with a sullen grunt. Thulmann turned about in his saddle, fixing the man with a stern look.

'What larcenous drivel are your spouting?' Thulmann demanded.

'I was only remarking that we could have had a bit more coin for our efforts,' Streng said. 'Five gold for old man Klausner, another seven for his vampire son, and another nine for Kohl and his lads.' A greedy gleam twinkled in the mercenary's eyes. 'We could have done a bit better is all I was considering.'

'Speak plainly,' Thulmann snapped. 'I tire of your insinuations.'

'Well,' grinned Streng, leaning back in his saddle. 'That vampire did attack Gregor Klausner, and now the boy is sick. Might have gotten another seven gold if we'd waited around.' Thulmann shook his head in disgust, returning to his contemplation of the countryside.

'There was nothing about him to suggest that the vampire's taint flows through his veins,' the witch hunter stated. 'The violence of the creature's attack and the death of his father, coupled with the hideous truth about his family's legacy would naturally have undermined his health.' Thulmann's voice grew sombre. 'There are monsters enough in this world without you inventing more.'

'I rather did like the feel of his sword,' pressed Streng. 'Fine blade. Hated giving it back to him. If he'd been a vampire or involved in his father's heresy...'

'You can have half of my payment,' Thulmann snarled, 'if it will quiet that scheming tongue.' It was an old argument between the two men. The materialistic, hedonistic Streng saw ample opportunity to exploit the office of witch hunter for petty gain and was always quick to give voice to his suggestions.

Thulmann knew that there was no lack of men who did just that, exploiting the power and respect demanded by their profession toward their own selfish ends. It was a sore point with Thulmann, because it was a temptation that he was never entirely convinced he himself had not yielded to.

'Keep your filthy money, Mathias,' Streng sighed. 'You know me better than that.' There was a note of genuine injury and offence in the mercenary's tone. After a moment he regained his composure. 'Back to Wurtbad then, eh?' he asked.

Thulmann nodded, straightening in the saddle as new thoughts occurred to him. 'There is some chance that we may yet pick up Weichs's trail, and I'll not let that man slip through my fingers if there is even the remotest chance of catching him.' There was a venom in the witch hunter's voice, as he recalled the nefarious doctor and his disfiguring, corrupting experiments with warp-stone.

He'd hunted the man for many years, and been forced to kill far too many of his tainted victims. Then there was the matter of Helmuth Klausner's book of unholy lore. With his dying breath Wilhelm Klausner had confessed that he had entrusted the tome to someone in that city. It might take quite a bit of investigation to discover who the old man had trusted enough to leave the book with. The fact that the vampire Sibbechai was still at large and still hunting for the book was enough to make the witch hunter doubly keen on tracking it down and destroying it.

The thought of the uses to which a necrarch would put such a blasphemous work caused Thulmann to urge his horse into a gallop, and soon he was many lengths ahead of his henchman.

'Ah well,' grumbled Streng, urging his own horse to greater effort. 'There's wine and wenches enough in Wurtbad, I suppose.'

GREGOR KLAUSNER LAY upon his bed, heavy fur blankets wrapped about him, his head propped upon pillows. He could hear the soft, concerned voice of his mother giving directions to her servants to attend her son. He could feel the soft towel that wiped away the feverish sweat beading upon his brow, and smell the heavy pungent aroma of the medicinal herbs smouldering in the urn beside his bed. But it was with a detached, almost unreal way that he perceived these things. It was like his mind was outside his body, observing it from afar.

His thoughts brooded upon the deaths of his brother and father, slaughtered by the filthy monster that had invaded their home and profaned their name. The ghost that had so haunted the Klausner line that for fear of its wrath, generations of noble Klausner men had practised a filthy and unspeakable ritual. The vampire had very nearly slaked its thirst for vengeance, but it had made one mistake. It had not finished what it had started with Gregor Klausner.

The young noble could still taste Sibbechai's vile blood upon his mouth, a few drops of filth forced upon his lips when the vampire had hurled him aside after threatening his father.

His father had led the monster away trying to save him, but the truth was that the vampire had already done its worst. The thought of the creature's cruel treachery brought a groan of anger from Gregor's feverish lips. At once, soft warm hands caressed his cheeks, trying to soothe his pain.

Somewhere within the back of his mind, Gregor was laughing. Why did they try? Couldn't they see? Didn't they know?

The witch hunter had known or at least suspected, which was why he had made his departure with such awkwardness and haste. He had known what he would have to do if his suspicions proved themselves. He'd left, hoping against hope that Gregor would recover, that his lust for life would drive out the filth that clawed at his soul.

But Gregor had no lust for life. Only one thing mattered now. He had to find and destroy the creature that had damned him and his family.. He had to track down and destroy the vampire Sibbechai, for there was no one else left to do so and no other way to redeem the name of Klausner. Gregor could sense the vampire's presence, sense the creature as it fled through the early morning back to its refuge. There was a link between them now, a tether of corruption that bound them together.

Gregor would follow that bond, follow it back to its source and force Sibbechai to answer for all its monstrous sins. Before he could allow his own tainted existence to be put to an end, Gregor would see the necrarch destroyed.

The young noble sank back, staring up at the shadowy forms of his mother and their servants, ignoring the bright gleaming lines that burned within the grey and indistinct shapes, ignoring the warm flowing blood that called out to him. Gregor cried as he wondered how long he would be able to deny that call.

The shadows within the gloomy, dank cavern grew even darker, as though the nebulous pockets of blackness were striving to become things of solidity and form. The chill of the forsaken and blighted place sank into an almost icy atmosphere and the rank stink of the place became unspeakable in its foulness. The small wooded hill had been a barrow once, burial mound to the naked half-intelligent savages who had wandered the lands of the Empire in the aeons before Sigmar's birth. There was a power to such places of ancient death, and that grim power seeped into the stones and earth, making animals snarl and men avert their gaze. Such shunned places called out to their own, shining like black beacons to the creatures of night and horror.

A shape emerged from the shadows. Tall and thin, its body draped in a grim black robe, ghoulish adornments dripping from its garb. The vampire Sibbechai turned its head, its fiery eyes narrowing with disgust at the faint flicker of dawn that danced about the small opening to its refuge.

Unlike many of its diseased kind, the necrarch could endure the sun for limited periods, provided that the proper enchantments were invoked. But it did so at great peril, for the creature would lose much of its strength, and the ravages of the purifying rays of the sun could not be fended off completely. The sun was forever the bane of Sibbechai's kind, dispelling the night with which the vampire shrouded itself, providing the monsters with no shadows in which to hide but revealing them for what they truly were.

The necrarch hissed its anger. It had been cheated once again, cheated when it was so very close to achieving what had been denied it for so very long. But it would endure and it would prevail. It was only a matter of time now, and time was one thing that Sibbechai had an in abundance.

The vampire's withered face spread into a malevolent grimace as it considered the events that had unfolded in Helmuth's tomb. Its pet had been destroyed, which was irritating. But far worse had been the humiliation of being forced to retreat from that mortal swordsman.

Still, even so slight a risk as the witch hunter had posed was to be avoided when there was yet so much to accomplish. The vampire could afford to swallow its pride; there would be ample opportunity to claim restitution from the man's mangled bones in the future, when their meeting would be under circumstances of Sibbechai's choosing.

The vampire strode back into the gloomy tomb, its gaze fixed upon the large coffin of polished Drakwald timber that rested against the far wall. It was one of a matched set of twenty that Sibbechai had commissioned long ago. Its black surface was edged in gold, the griffon and wolf emblem of the Klausners worked upon the sides and the top of the lid.

The flawless wood had been polished to a sharp shine, so that even the tiny embers of Sibbechai's eyes shone back at the vampire from the walls of its casket. The vampire still smiled at the ingenuity of the device, the cunning lock it had taken a dwarf craftsman the better of a decade to design. It had been the dwarf's finest work, a perfection of craftsmanship that the fellow had never exceeded. The insidious traps in the lock were themselves tiny masterpieces: needles that would stab at the flesh of any would-be trespasser, delivering a lethal dose of a most unkindly poison, a small glass vial that would shatter and release a mephitic vapour, safeguards that had ensured the sanctity of the vampire's slumber for many years.

Sibbechai removed the iron key from the chain that hung about its neck, leaning down toward the dwarf lock then stepped away hissing in rage. The lock had been destroyed, nor by any simple, crude means. The ancient device had been reduced to a glob of molten metal clinging to the singed side of the coffin.

The vampire uttered a savage snarl of rage, its claw lashing out to rip the heavy lid of its coffin from its hinges. The panel of Drakwald timber crashed against the wall of the tomb and Sibbechai glared down at the velvet-lined bed of its coffin. The necrarch hissed again and flinched away as it saw the silver icon resting there.

'I thought it might be prudent to make certain changes in the décor,' a malicious voice called out from the darkness.

Sibbechai spun around, glaring at the shadows. The sneering face of Carandini greeted him. The necromancer had been waiting for his treacherous ally for some time, veiling himself in a cloak of sorcerous shadow that even the necrarch's unnatural gaze had not penetrated.

'Get rid of it!' Sibbechai demanded.

The necromancer laughed back at it.

'Patience,' he scolded the monster. 'Patience. You act as though a few minutes were a matter of life and death. Or undeath,' Carandini smiled, casting a sidewise look at the growing glow clawing at the mouth of the barrow.

'Take it away!' the vampire repeated, its words more snarl than speech. Carandini smiled back at the monster, apparently unconcerned by the creature's barely restrained fury.

'If I am to help you,' the necromancer observed, 'then you should help me.' The mocking smile fell away and the man was at once as serious as the grave. 'Hand over the book,' he told it. 'I could of course dig it out of your ashes after the sun has done its work, but I'd rather not risk the book coming to any harm.'

Sibbechai glowered at the necromancer, jaws clenching and unclenching. He lunged toward the gloating sorcerer, but flinched away as Carandini held up an identical icon. The vampire paced before Carandini like some caged beast, averting its gaze every time it chanced to glance at the silver hammer clutched in the necromancer's hand.

'You really should at least try to be helpful,' Carandini said. 'Otherwise I think things are going to go rather badly.' The necromancer laughed as Sibbechai again reached for him, then recoiled from the hurtful aura of the Sigmarite relic. 'One of the benefits of being a man in my position, vampire, is that one can enjoy the benefits of both worlds, that of the living and that of the dead.'

'I don't have the book,' the vampire snarled as it retreated before Carandini's holy symbol once more. 'It wasn't there.'

A blank look fell upon Carandini's features. The necromancer pushed a wisp of ratty hair from his pale face, then sighed in disappointment. 'I suppose we really have nothing more to discuss then. I must confess, however, that after your little trick with the wolves, I will find a great deal of enjoyment in watching you shrivel into a cinder.'

Sibbechai snarled at the man, more infuriated by the contempt with which Carandini dismissed the vampire's attempt to kill its partner than anything else. Its pride had been injured enough this night. Yet Sibbechai knew that if its pride did not suffer still one more time, then it would shortly discover the grave it had defied for so long.

'I know where the book is,' the vampire growled. Carandini's expression shifted between amusement and doubt as he heard the monster speak.

'Really?' the necromancer snickered. 'Why does this sound like something I've heard before?'

'The old man knew I was coming for it,' Sibbechai explained. 'He had it removed, gave it to a friend.' Sibbechai considered the fragmentary memories and images the necrarch had ripped from the dying man's mind, the secrets which by his very determination to keep from the vampire had risen to the forefront of Wilhelm's thoughts.

'And where might that be?' Carandini asked. Sibbechai looked away from the man, pointing once more at the casket.

'We bargain for that information,' the vampire snarled. 'Take that filthy thing away!'

The necromancer studied his undead adversary, pondering just how far he could trust the monster. It could not possibly be dealing false with him. It would know that he would search it as soon as it slipped back into its grave, and slipped into the half-sleep of its kind.

Sibbechai could be under no delusion as to what the necromancer would do to it if he found the book hidden away nearby.

A sly smile on his face, the necromancer strode across the cave, careful to keep the holy icon between himself and the vampire.

Still facing the necrarch, he put his hand into the open coffin, fumbling about until he grasped the Sigmarite symbol. Carandini held both symbols before him, staring in open challenge at the vampire. Sibbechai covered its eyes with one clawed hand. The glow of dawn was strong at the mouth of the barrow now, and the necromancer could see that the vampire's movements were growing slower and more ungainly by the second.

'What is your bargain?' the necromancer asked, a tone of mirth in his voice.

'I know where the book has been taken,' Sibbechai replied in a desperate hiss. 'We can still share its secrets!'

Carandini was silent for a moment, pursing his lips as he considered the vampire's offer. Sibbechai fidgeted before him, the vampire's body twitching and twisting with anxiety. 'Are you proposing a return to our earlier arrangement?' the necromancer's tone was incredulous. 'Just forget everything that has happened and let bygones be bygones? Is that what you are offering?'

'Yes,' hissed Sibbechai, a dry sound that seemed to wrack its lean frame. The necromancer smiled and stepped away. The vampire did not speak, but at once leapt forward, scrabbling into its coffin like a rat racing back into its hole. Carandini stepped away from the casket, smiling at the undead monster's refuge.

'That sounds agreeable,' the necromancer laughed, though he knew the vampire could not truly hear him. He patted the bottle of sacred water secreted within his robes. He was almost sorry that he wouldn't get a chance to use it now, but the possibility that the vampire was telling the truth was a bit too important to indulge his petty ambitions for revenge. *Das Buch die Unholden* was a prize that would more than compensate him for his near death beneath the fangs of Sibbechai's wolves.

Still, there were a few experiments that Carandini knew of that required the fangs and claws of a vampire to perform. The necromancer had been looking forward to attempting a few of them.

Of course, there was no reason he could not return to them after Sibbechai led him to the book. One could never quite tell what a new day would bring.

Carandini walked from the barrow, out into the cold morning air, an evil dream shining behind his eyes.

WITCH FINDER

PROLOGUE

GREY CLOUDS HOVERED above the tiled rooftops of the city, stretching across the horizon like a gigantic shroud. A chill wind stirred the air, an unseasonably early harbinger of the coming winter. From the brick chimneys of every house and hovel, thin serpents of smoke slithered upwards, adding to the already dingy atmosphere, blotting out the sun's feeble efforts to smile down upon the streets of Wurtbad.

The narrow lanes that wound their way between the sprawl of the city were subdued, despite the masses of grim-faced men and women. With winter threatening an early advent, the people of Wurtbad were eager to gather provisions for the harsh months ahead. Bakeries and wine shops bustled with commerce, and rang out with the clink of coins changing hands. But there was little conversation. Each tradesman's eye was narrowed with suspicion and fear. Cloves of garlic, pots filled with fragrant flowers and parchment seals marked with prayers to Shallya, goddess of healing and mercy, marked most doorways. The threat of winter was still some distance away. But the threat of plague was already upon Wurtbad.

The disease had appeared in the harbour districts first, the miserable little ghettos to which dockhands and labourers slunk back once their day's toil was at an end. Foul black boils festered upon the victim's skin until, at last, they burst open, weeping brown pus. The sick and dying would linger for weeks, their bodies becoming ever more grotesquely infected until there was no nourishment left in their wasted frames to sustain the disease. Then they expired. It was an ugly, loathsome death, of a kind that the city's doktors and scholars, even the temples of Shallya and Morr, had never witnessed before. But it was not all the victims had to bear. To the terrifying stigma of the disease was added the horror of the unknown.

Sinister shapes stalked the streets now. Strange figures born from the city's despair. One such apparition prowled that part of the city that had been given over to brothels and taverns. The stranger wore a heavy brown topcoat about his tall, elongated frame. On his head sat a wide-brimmed hat, it was battered and twisted, stained by the tainted rain from the smoke-befouled clouds. His gloved hands held a long, steel-handled walking cane and a dingy leather satchel. But his most distinctive feature was the mask that shielded his face from the elements – a mask of oiled leather with a long, bird-like beak, stretching out from beneath the shadow of his hat. Its smoky lenses were glazed, like the eyes of a vulture, hiding the human orbs that peered from behind them. The faint smell of lilac suggested itself as the stranger passed, seeming to exude from the bird-like bill.

The stranger was a plague doktor, one of the only men in Wurtbad with the courage to venture into the homes of those brought low by the blight. One of the only men greedy enough to make their suffering his business.

He reached the end of an alleyway, his steps frightening a starving cur from where it hid beneath a staircase. His mask turned upward, his eyes studying the red slash painted upon the doorway above the steps – the sign that the Blight had struck. Without hesitation, the plague doktor ascended the stairs, rapping upon the portal with the steel crown of his cane.

Shuffling steps told of movement, and the portal shuddered inward as its warped frame was pulled inside. The grimy face at the door considered the strange apparition with an expression between hope and terror. The plague doktor did not wait to be admitted, forcing the occupant to retreat before him. The interior was dingy and decrepit, dirt and debris piled against its cracked plaster walls. A small corridor branched off from the foyer while a rickety wooden staircase wound its way upward.

'Who is sick here?' All humanity in the doktor's voice was smothered by layers of leather and sheepskin.

'Four floors up,' the concierge was quick to reply, stabbing a finger at the ceiling. The doktor's mask rose to follow the gesture, then fixed its lifeless lenses on the grimy little man. The concierge loudly swallowed the knot in his throat.

'This is the third visit I have paid to your household,' the doktor stated. 'Infection has perhaps taken hold.'

'She's no kin of mine!' the concierge protested hastily. 'A common whore, like the others!' His cry was desperate, as though denying any relationship with the infected woman might spare him from the disease itself.

'You will show me to her room.' The concierge's face grew more pallid beneath its layers of grime as he hurried after the visitor. 'I should like to examine everyone who resides here,' the plague doktor said. 'If the blight has appeared here three times, others are likely infected.'

'Is that really necessary?' the concierge gasped.

'It is not you who pays the cost,' the doktor consoled the little man, seemingly oblivious to the reason for his concern. 'And it would be better than contracting the blight yourself.' The concierge nearly tripped on the stairs as he forgot which foot he was using.

'That – that isn't – I couldn't…' the concierge stuttered. The doktor paused on the stairway. He looked down from the upper step as though he was one of the gargoyles crouched upon the cathedral of Sigmar.

'Do not discount the possibility,' the doktor asserted. 'After you have shown me to the woman's room, I suggest you retire to your own. I shall examine you when I am done.' His leather glove creaked as he made firm his grip upon his cane. 'All it will cost is a little time, and a little silver.'

The concierge swallowed again, and hurried to conduct the visitor to his appointment.

'REMOVE YOUR CLOTHING,' the muffled voice intoned from behind the mask. Vira Staubkammer raised a slender hand to her breast, her fingers lighting upon the strings that dripped from her bodice.

The plague doktor did not seem to notice, his gaze swept the room, studying its dingy squalor. Shabby excuses for a wardrobe and dressing table were visibly crumbling. There was a reek of dirty straw from the small bed-frame, its mattress supported by sagging ropes.

The woman might once have been considered possessed of beauty, but long years of squalor and shame had cheapened its bloom. Her mouth was too accustomed to false laughter and hollow pleasure, her eyes were pits of emptiness that had seen far too much ugliness in her short life. What remained in her shapely figure, in her long dark hair, was only the illusion of what stirred longing in the blood of men. But it was enough to suit her needs; enough to serve men who would pay for the tattered reflection of that which they desired.

'I am not accustomed to this,' said Vira, her voice struggling to assume its normal bold haughtiness. 'I am paid to remove my clothes. *I* have never paid for the privilege of removing them myself.'

'You should change your bedding,' the plague doktor said, completing his inspection of her room. He strode past the young whore as she opened her bodice, exposing the pale flesh beneath. Oblivious to her partial nudity, he set his bag down upon the table. 'All sorts of ill humors can gather in such squalor.' He removed a set of gruesome picks and bone-scrapers. Vira blanched as she saw the ugly instruments, her face turning almost as white as her bodice. The mask turned to regard her once more. Vira quivered before its vulture-like eyes. She would have been more at ease to see lust, despair, even hate, in the man's face, but the mask betrayed not the slightest hint of emotion.

'Extend your arms,' the plague doktor ordered. 'Hold them to either side.'

'It is only a cough,' Vira protested even as she obeyed. 'I was out late… a friend who was too eager to wait to reach indoors. It will pass.'

'Perhaps,' the muffled voice mused. Vira shuddered as the man strode from the table, a long, needle-like lance in his gloved clutch. The plague doktor circled her slowly, as though he really were a vulture circling some carrion before feeding upon it. The lilac scent exuding from the mask's leather beak filled her lungs. Vira cringed as the cold tip of the lance touched her skin, prodding her to raise her armpit. From the corner of her eye, she could see the mask nod up and down. What had he seen, she wondered?

'I fear that Herr Kemper is something akin to a biddy,' Vira said, silently cursing the prying concierge who saw fit to send for this man. It was only a minor cold, she was certain of that. That it could be anything more was too horrible to contemplate.

The plague doktor strode back toward the table. Vira watched with relief as he began to drop the sinister instruments back into his bag. The vulture-like mask turned toward her once more. 'Lower your arms and restore your clothes.' Vira breathed an audible sigh of relief, hurrying to comply.

'I am well then?' she dared to ask, unable to hold back the relief. The doktor removed a small bottle from his bag.

'Perhaps,' he repeated. 'There is no outward sign of the blight about you, but this cough disturbs me. It may signify an imbalance among your humors.' He held the tiny bottle in his gloved hand.

Vira felt a wave of unease as the plague doktor approached, beyond even her earlier trepidation. Her eyes fixed on the clouded glass clutched in his hand. 'What is that?' she asked.

'Medicinal vapours,' came the answer. 'They will restore the harmony of your body's humors. You should have a rag at hand, I fear. And I do hope you did not spend too much for your breakfast.'

The young woman suppressed a cough and smiled nervously. 'What must I do?'

Although she could not see his face, she seemed to sense the plague doktor smiling as he pulled the clay stopper from the bottle.

'Just breathe deeply,' he told her. 'The vapours will do the rest.'

THE PLAGUE DOKTOR slipped into the shadows of an alley beside the brooding brickwork of the Black Sleep tavern. In the darkness he removed his outer garments, carefully folding his topcoat and hat before slipping them into his bag. He undid the small bronze clasp that held his mask against his face, inhaling deeply as he freed himself of the lilac odour. The pomander within the bill of his mask would need replacement when next he went abroad, but it was a small expense when weighed against the great work in which he was engaged.

It was a lean, elderly man who emerged from the alleyway, tapping on the cobblestones with his steel-tipped cane, frosty white hair standing out in the flickering lamplight. The old man smiled politely as a pair of burly ruffians emerged from the Black Sleep, stepping aside with an elaborate gesture as they swaggered into the night. His mouth pulled into a quiet sneer as he watched them fade. He would not have to linger amongst such squalor for long. Very soon his work would be completed and his name ranked amongst the immortals, as the greatest mind of his time

The old man paid little heed to the Black Sleep, his eyes not dwelling on the boisterous crowd inside the tavern. He strode away from the bierkeller, toward a small stairway set against the wall nearest the bar. Lingering for a moment, ensuring that he was not observed, he slipped down the stairs.

He soon found himself within the Black Sleep's cellar, surrounded by casks of ale, beer and wine. The old man cast one more cautious glance over his shoulder. Satisfied that he was still alone, he walked to one of the casks, sliding his body into the narrow space between the huge barrel and the cellar wall, then worked his way along until he reached a narrow gap. A length of black cloth hung against the wall. He lifted it and entered the crude, burrow-like tunnel it concealed. Hesitating for one moment, he lit a tiny lantern he found resting within a niche in the earthen wall of the tunnel.

He had not proceeded far before he was greeted by a diminutive figure bearing a lantern similar to his own. The old man peered down at the small shape, noting with amusement its awkward, spider-like gait. The lamplight performed further malevolent tricks on the little creature's disordered features.

'Your work went well, herr doktor?' the gargoyle's shrill voice enquired.

'As well as might be expected,' the old man replied. 'I treated a half-dozen this day. I shall send our friends to collect two of them. They will make rather interesting subjects for my studies.'

The old man handed his bag to his minion, the tiny creature nodding his malformed head. It was a gruesome combination, he thought, a head large enough for a full-grown man rising from the shoulders of a halfling. But one could never be certain of what exact form his studies would take – nor, indeed, of what shape the objects of his studies might choose to manifest themselves in. At least he had been able to prove that halflings were not completely immune to what ignorant men called 'Chaos'. And poor little Lobo has proving a most enthusiastic servant, since he believed only the great Herr Doktor Freiherr Weichs could ever cure his affliction.

A sound in the darkness caused Doktor Weichs to turn about, his feverish eyes peering into the shadows. As the scuttling noise repeated itself, the doktor slowly lowered his lantern. His new friends were not over-fond of the light, nor was it was wise to upset them. A trickle of fear ran down Weichs's spine. The kind of stark, mortal terror that even the Templars of Sigmar had failed to wring from his corrupt soul. The stink of mangy fur, the reek of sewer filth, exuded from the dark. Once again, Weichs heard the scrabbling of claws on the earthen floor of the tunnel, the soft chittering of inhuman whispers. They weren't supposed to be here. Skilk was supposed to keep them away!

Weichs cringed as he sensed something drawing near. Red eyes gleamed from the shadows, reflecting the dim light from his lantern. Beside him, Lobo emitted a moan of fright. The scientist fought to compose himself. He knew these creatures had senses far beyond those of a man, that they could smell fear dripping from a human body. They were drawn to any sign of weakness, any taint of frailty. The doktor remembered the bag he had given to Lobo. That was what had drawn them. It was the odour within. He should have known. Should have expected. Should have prepared for them.

The red eyes were not looking at him now; they had shifted and turned toward Lobo and the bag. Weichs gained an impression of whiskers twitching in the dark, of a rodent's muzzle sniffing at the air. Of furred lips pulling back, exposing inch-long incisors. Beyond the first set of eyes, he now saw others gleaming within the tunnel.

'You are most punctual,' Weichs stated, his voice echoing loud. The red eyes instantly turned back upon him. 'I had not expected you so soon.' He fought to keep his timbre calm, struggled to impose a note of command. 'Grey Seer Skilk is fortunate to be served by such capable and noble followers.' Weichs noted the eyes flinch as he spoke the name of Skilk, his sense of smell registering the unpleasant musky odour that exuded from the shadows. If they didn't understand anything else he said, at least the vermin had recognised the name of their inhuman priest.

'I need you to collect two more subjects…' Weichs held up his hand, displaying two fingers. He knew from previous experience that the creatures could see far better in the dark than even a dwarf. They would not fail to notice the gesture, any more than they would miss the lilac scent that led them to their victims. Again, the chittering gnawed at the shadows, making the doktor's flesh crawl as their ghastly voices clawed at his ears.

'Yes-yes,' a sharp voice hissed from the darkness. 'Man-meat find-take. Grey seer like-like!' Slowly the gleaming eyes withdrew back into the darkness. Weichs heard the sound of verminous paws pattering their way down the tunnel. The scientist lifted the lantern again, throwing its door wide open, revelling in the warm comfort of its illumination.

'Back to the laboratory, Lobo,' he ordered. The halfling nodded his oversized head, limping back down the tunnel, struggling with the doktor's heavy bag. Weichs watched him for a moment, then cast a nervous glance after the retreating red eyes, suppressing another shudder. His dealings with the skaven always filled him with dread. He could see their envy and hatred of the entire human race burning in their eyes.

Weichs fought back his loathing. It was immaterial what he felt, or what the skaven felt. All that mattered was his work. He needed a safe place to conduct his studies. Skilk had provided that. He needed subjects for his experiments. Skilk was able to provide that, also. But most of all, he needed warpstone, and that too was in Skilk's power to provide.

Yes indeed, the world would soon come to know the name of Doktor Freiherr Weichs.

One way or another…

CHAPTER ONE

THE SUN SLOWLY sank into the west, its last rays smouldering like a dying ember behind the gaps in the grey clouds. Night would soon fall upon the land, strengthening the shadows and heralding the supremacy of darkness. Travellers upon the road would hurry to find sanctuary, however mean and humble, to huddle about warm fires and hide behind locked doors, praying that the horrors of Old Night would pass them by. The eyes of such men were ever on the lookout for the flickering lantern of a roadside inn or coaching house, seeking the welcoming watchlight as keenly as they did the approach of some denizen of the dark.

No such eager hope turned the heads of the two men now riding slowly down the old dirt road. They had seen too often the dread shapes within which Old Night clothed itself. Their fears could never hope to conjure an apparition as frightful as those that walked the corridors of memory. And they had seen that there was no safety from darkness behind locked doors or beside roaring hearths.

The foremost of the two horsemen was a squat, stocky figure, his bulk straining at the weathered mass of a leather tunic reinforced with steel studs. A simple scabbard, the surface scarred where some marking had been crudely removed, swung from his hip. The sword held within was unremarkable, like any that might have been issued to the Empire's many armies. Like the crossbow holstered on the saddle of the rider's horse, it was the simple but effective tool of a professional soldier.

But the rider no longer considered himself as such. Still, old habits, like bad habits, were difficult for Streng to be rid of. The bearded mercenary lifted the fur waterskin hanging from a strap across his chest and took a deep swallow of something far more vibrant than water. Streng grunted appreciatively, letting the skin fall, the liquid within sloshing noisily as it slapped against his hip.

He preferred beer. It was a much more sociable drink, and it took a vast quantity to put him down. Vodka was a much harsher spirit, and overindulging in its favours could result in assorted aches and bruises, a visit to the local dungeon, or a bill for damages. Still, his time campaigning in the north had taught Streng one unassailable fact – there was nothing better to chase away the cold of winter than a bottle of good Kislevite. He only wished he'd been able to liberate more of it from the wine cellar of the Grey Crone back in Klausberg. Of course, the innkeeper would have noticed the disappearance of more than two bottles. Reikhertz had been a decent enough host, and Streng would have hated to bash his skull in over something as minor as a few bottles of vodka.

He sucked at his teeth, growing thoughtful. There would be a fair bit of coin coming his way when they reached Wurtbad. The Temple of Sigmar's gold was more honest than most he had earned during his brutal life, but it spent just as quickly. The mercenary smiled. He should manage a week of drinking, gambling, whoring and fighting when he reached the city. Assuming, of course, that he stayed one step ahead of the watch. And allowing that his employer didn't have other plans. Streng cast a sour look at the rider following in his wake.

The witch hunter was a black shadow upon the back of his white steed. His cloak whipped about him in the wind that blew from the north, his face hidden beneath the brim of his tall hat. The weapons that hung from the templar's belt were more extravagant than those borne by Streng: a pair of pistols with their dark-stained grips inlaid with gold; a silvered longsword with a gilded pommel sheathed in a dragonskin scabbard. But then, everything about the witch hunter was meant to provoke the onlooker. To evoke feelings of respect and pious terror.

Streng looked away, hawking the aftertaste of the vodka from his mouth and spitting it into the dust. From the arch of his companion's shoulders, the way his chin sagged toward his chest, Streng could tell he was deep in thought. He could well imagine the paths down which those thoughts roamed. For he himself had travelled with Mathias Thulmann, templar of the Order of Sigmar, far too long to deceive himself that his employer's mind was considering cold tankards of ale and hot-blooded tavern wenches.

Well, perhaps Streng might be able to indulge those vices for a day or two. At least when they reached Wurtbad, and before the witch hunter had need of his services again.

'PLEASE.' THE BEGGING voice gnawed at Thulmann's mind, as fresh in his memory as the dark day in which the words had been spoken. 'She is just a child!' The witch hunter could still smell the sorry stench of pig dung and spoiled cabbage, the ugly odour of decay and poverty. 'For Sigmar's sake, my lord, show mercy!'

Thulmann's calfskin gloves tightened their grip on the reins of his steed. How many times had he thought back to that loathsome, black day in Silbermund? How many pleasant moments had that same recollection reached out to kill? The memory was burned into his brain like the brand of some malevolent daemon, forever festering there until he answered the final call of Morr, lord of death.

'For Sigmar's sake, I cannot let her live.' The words had tasted like wormwood as he spoke them, spitting them from his mouth as though they would choke him. The woman had fallen to her knees then, sobbing, wailing, washing the filth from his horse's hooves with her tears.

How many ugly little villages had he travelled through, always one step behind the thrice-accursed heretic he was in pursuit of? And how many times had he arrived too late to bring his quarry to ground? Too late to find anything but the monster's handiwork, like the calling card of a daemon. Thulmann knew that it was no coincidence. His quarry was taunting him, mocking his efforts. Daring the witch hunter to make good the chase.

He thought again of the little girl. How long had she lived? Six summers? Seven? Surely she had seen no more than eight. The child had been kicked by a mule, her tiny leg snapped and broken. It was feared she would never heal, for the break was too complex for the poor farmers of Silbermund to set. The little girl was destined to be a cripple – if she survived at all. But then, one of the gods had smiled down on the village when a traveller chanced to tarry awhile. He was a healer, a man of medicine. His promise was that he would look upon the child, and help her if he could.

Oh yes, the gods had indeed smiled upon Silbermund. The Dark Gods.

Thulmann could see the faces of the farmers, glaring at him from every corner of the square, hate boiling in their eyes. No, they would not challenge him. For they knew it had to be done. But how they hated him for it. And how he had grown to hate himself. Even the girl's father could not challenge him, but instead stood slumped against the wall of the blacksmith's shop. His gaze staring into nothingness. His face twisted in pain.

There were some heretic philosophers and mystics who dared claim that Chaos did not embody the force of evil. They said that it was like fire or water – a worldly force, a force of nature neither good nor evil. Was water evil when the banks of the Reik swelled and drowned a village? Was fire evil when it escaped the hearth and laid waste to the most part of an entire town? Such was their argument. And such men were more dangerous than the vermin who bowed and grovelled before the Dark Gods themselves, for they cloaked their degeneracy behind words like 'reason' and 'science'. They did not fear the judgement of Sigmar because they saw no evil in what they did, even when that evil glared back at them from the darkness of their deeds.

Herr Doktor Freiherr Weichs. That name haunted Thulmann, mocking him from the shadows. He had first learned of this deranged physician from a Sigmarite priest named Haeften. Weichs had been employed by the Baron von Lichtberg to act as physician to his house. It was an appointment that ended in a hideous tragedy.

One of the village girls had been with child, a child sired by the baron's son. To avoid complications, the foolish girl had turned to Weichs, begged him to find a way to undo what had been done.

The doktor, may all the gods damn his soul, had prescribed a potion he promised would dissolve the seedling life as harmlessly as it had been created. But that potion had not contained hope. It had contained the seeds of mutation. Of death. The girl's own mother reported what had happened to the village priest, when it became clear to see that the life growing within her belly was no clean thing, but a spawn of darkness.

Haeften had, in turn, informed the temple and they had sent Thulmann to assess the matter. It took some time to determine the cause of the girl's condition. At first, he had thought the seed of the mutation might lie with the father, and so had put Reinhardt von Lichtberg to the test as well as Mina Kurtz. But later, much later, Mina had confessed her shame. Confessed what she had asked Weichs to do. But by then it was too late. The heretic had seen which way the wind was blowing and fled. Thulmann tarried only long enough to dispose of Mina Kurtz, and the unclean life within her. He then set out on the trail of the man truly responsible for the girl's destruction.

THULMANN REMEMBERED CLOSING his ears to the sounds of wailing that filled the air. He had looked toward the pile of wood heaped in the centre of the square; at the stake rising above it; at the tiny form lashed to it. There was a faction of the Order of Sigmar who held that suffering was needed to purge the soul of any who were tainted by Chaos. Sforza Zerndorff was one such man, the late Lord Protector Thaddeus Gamow had been another. They claimed it was necessary to wrench every last scream from a heretic before extinction. For only thus could the witch hunter ensure the soul of the condemned might be pure enough to enter the sight of Sigmar on passing through the Gates of Morr.

The witch hunter stared at the tiny figure. At the little girl slumped against the pole. What crime had tainted this child's soul? She was surely guiltless – a victim of heresy, not a heretic herself. It would take a cruel, calloused soul like Zerndorff not to see that. If a child had to be tortured for the greater glory of Sigmar, then he was not the same god that Thulmann worshipped and served.

Thulmann had commanded the innkeeper to produce his strongest grog, and then had Streng feed it to the child until she fell into a drunkard's stupor. He hoped that it was enough, that she would not regain her senses when the flames did their work.

A child's broken leg. Thulmann wondered at the corrupt mind that could seize upon such misery and exploit it. That could subject a small child to his abominable experiments. Weichs had set the child's leg, then wrapped it in a poultice which, he assured the girl's parents, would speed the healing and ensure the bone would not knit crookedly. Then he had left, words of gratitude following him as he departed the village. Two days later, Thulmann had arrived in Silbermund and asked the villagers if a stranger, a tall elderly man who might be presenting himself as a doctor, had passed their way. His enquiries led him to the child.

The witch hunter shuddered as he remembered that moment – just as he recalled so many similar moments. He'd voiced a prayer to Sigmar that even Weichs would not be so depraved, that he had spared the girl his inhuman attentions. Then, slowly, he had cut the poultice away from her leg. There had been screams then, the girl's parents wailing in horror. Thulmann himself turned pale. He had seen worse things, but never on the body of a child. Coarse black hair covered the flesh beneath the poultice, an unclean growth like the fur of a fly. The contagion was spreading, too, already beginning to creep upwards toward her knee. The fur was an outward sign of the infection, but what other changes might be happening inside, within the girl's mind and soul? Perhaps the cruel mutation would so completely consume her that she would become no more than an animal, loping off into the woods to join the foul beastman tribes, a lust for human flesh gnawing at her belly.

Thulmann spoke prayers to Sigmar as he cast the iron brand into the pile of burning wooden fagots, but truly did not know if he meant them for the little girl or for himself. The flames had burned quickly, fiercely. The witch hunter had ordered most of the village's store of lamp oil dumped upon the tinder. He doubted if even one of the fire wizards of the bright magic college could evoke fire so swiftly. Yet, even so, it seemed to take an eternity to burn. Thulmann had forced himself to watch, refusing to look away, and once more swore the same oath he had made at each such pyre – that he would find Herr Doktor Weichs and make him pay for his crimes.

* * *

THE TRAIL HAD led to Wurtbad. Weichs was known to have been in the city, before he became embroiled in the strange and sinister murders that led to the arrest and execution of the witch Chanta Favna. But the trail was cold now. Ordered by Sforza Zerndorff, newly appointed Witch Hunter General South, Thulmann had been forced to abandon his hunt to investigate the dire events unfolding in the village of Klausberg.

Thulmann forgot the mad doktor for a moment, turning his thoughts to more recent events. Even if Weichs was no longer in Wurtbad, the witch hunter had business there. He had learned that an unspeakable tome of profane knowledge had been hidden in the city, a blasphemous grimoire titled *Das Buch die Unholden*. The foul tome had been the dark secret of the Klausner family and had ultimately brought about their doom.

The book had drawn the interest of a powerful vampire lord, a creature named Sibbechai, one of the ghastly necrarch bloodline. Thulmann did not think the death of old Wilhelm Klausner would be enough to kill the vampire's coveting of the book. For the necrarchs were a breed of vampire sorcerer, existing only to increase their knowledge of the arcane, determined to one day exterminate all living things and create a world of the restless dead. It was vital that the witch hunter should find it first and destroy it. The implications of such a tome in the clutches of a necrarch were too ghastly to contemplate.

Thulmann's mind turned to the fate of the last son of the house of Klausner. Sibbechai the vampire had attacked young Gregor Klausner, left him for dead in the ruin of his father's chambers. When the witch hunter had left, Gregor was still bedridden from his ordeal, but recovering.

Recovering? Thulmann did not want to think about how swift, or how likely, that recovery would be. It had been one of the reasons that drove his hasty departure from Klausberg, more so than the desperate hope of finding Doktor Weichs or the compelling need to destroy *Das Buch die Unholden*. Gregor Klausner had been a noble, courageous man, a comrade who had helped Thulmann to uncover the horror plaguing Klausberg – even though the trail led back to his own house. Gregor had saved Thulmann's life, a debt the witch hunter knew he could never repay. For all signs indicated that Gregor had been exposed to the poison of the vampire. If he had remained any longer, Thulmann would have had no choice but to acknowledge those signs, and to do what had to be done.

There were already too many ugly memories haunting his sleep. Thulmann cursed himself for such selfish weakness, but he would spare himself the destruction and dismemberment of Gregor Klausner if he could. He would return to Wurtbad, make his report to his superiors in the Order of Sigmar, then have Meisser send one of his men to investigate Gregor's condition. Perhaps he would make a full and clean recovery. Thulmann had known men among the Templars who had staved off the infection of a vampire's bite through their faith in Sigmar, and sheer strength of will. Both qualities were strong in Gregor. But, if they were not strong enough, then whomsoever was sent by Meisser would have to deal with the fate of Gregor Klausner.

THE WIND MOANED outside the black walls of Klausner Keep, like the spectral wailing of ghosts. Red-rimmed eyes turned toward the narrow window, discomfited by the sinister sound. There was enough misery and dread within the ancient black-stoned fortress without the elements contributing their own efforts. The woman's soft hands rose, wiping the moisture from her eyes. Miranda had been sitting beside the enormous iron-framed bed for most of the day, maintaining her quiet vigil. At times, she had been joined by Lady Ilsa Klausner, dressed in her black widow's garb, her face drawn and wasted. There was no comfort or solace in her brief visits. She had buried a husband and one son already, and the icy hopelessness that filled her gaze told Miranda she expected to bury another son before much longer.

Miranda choked back another sob. Surely, the gods could not be so cruel as to take away her Gregor? Her brave and noble Gregor. Her kindly nobleman who took an interest in the welfare of even the lowliest peasant of Klausberg. Who had risked his life to do what was right. Surely, the gods would not punish him for possessing the courage to confront the inhuman forces that preyed on the good people of Klausberg?

The young woman sighed. Gregor was dying. He had not taken food for two days now, and had not moved so much as a finger in the last twelve hours. The only sign of life lay in the faint rise and fall of his chest and in the slight rasp of air escaping his mouth. She shook her head in despair, helpless to stop the decline of her beloved, helpless to stop her hopes and dreams from fading into the shadows that reached out to claim him. Miranda gave up her contemplation of the darkening landscape outside the window. Her eyes fell once more on the silent, statuesque figure of Gregor.

He remained perfectly still, but Miranda sensed that something had changed. It took only a moment to realise her beloved nobleman's eyes had been closed before. Now they were open, staring vacantly at the ceiling. She gasped in astonishment, hurrying to the side of his bed.

'Gregor! Gregor!' she cried, reaching out and clasping her stricken lover's hand. The pale flesh was cold, utterly devoid of warmth. Miranda's face contorted with sympathetic pain as she rubbed her own hands against Gregor's, striving to force the warmth of her own body into his.

Gregor Klausner gazed up at the ceiling, his eyes registering only a colourless expanse. Slowly he began to register the presence of the young woman at his side. The warm hands stroking his icy arm. Gregor turned his face toward her. He could perceive the room as a colourless background of light and shadow, the rich tapestries and polished wooden furnishings robbed of their vibrancy. Miranda herself was only a grey shadow, indistinct, as though his eyes could not focus upon her. But most alarming of all were the vivid pulses of crimson that shone from within, a network of rivers coursing through the apparition. Gregor closed his eyes and clenched his teeth.

He had thought it a symptom of his fever – this unreal, unholy delirium that made shadows of the living. He had believed the entrancing light flowing through those shadows a perverse dream, a foul imagining brought on by his injuries and his sickness. Now he knew it was not. He could see the blood burning within Miranda's body. See it flowing beneath her shadowy form. He could feel the warmth of it reaching out to his chilled flesh, smell its aroma caressing his face. His mouth writhed with anticipation, filling with the phantom taste of salty crimson wine rushing down his parched throat.

Gregor ripped his hand from Miranda's caress, sitting bolt upright in his bed. She reached out toward him, but Gregor recoiled as if from a viper, raising his hands to ward her off.

'Gregor!' the young woman cried again. Emotion clawed at his heart, his face twisting with an agony he had never believed possible. Again Miranda reached for him, forcing Gregor to slip from the bed onto the floor. Miranda hesitated, waiting as her beloved nobleman raised himself. But as he did so he stepped away from the bed, towards the stone wall behind him.

'Stay back, Miranda!' Gregor snarled, summoning up every last ounce of authority. His words arrested her as she made to rise from the bed. 'For Sigmar's sake, stay away!' he added in a piteous tone. The sound stabbed into the young woman, her face contorting in anguish.

'Why Gregor? What is it? What is wrong?' She began to rise once more. Gregor waved her back with a violent gesture.

'Please!' he cried. 'I don't want to hurt you!' As Miranda took one single step toward him, a worried smile formed on her face. Gregor retreated before her approach.

'But you… you would not injure me!' she insisted. 'What is this nonsense that you speak?'

'The vampire, Miranda, the vampire!' Gregor wailed. His back was to the wall now, he could retreat no further. 'It touched me! Its poison is within me!' Miranda froze, her face growing pale as the horror of Gregor's words bore down upon her.

'No,' she dismissed his hysteria. 'That isn't true. You've just been sick. Unwell. The burden of your father's death…'

Gregor buried his face in his hands, his body shuddering as deep sobs wracked his form. 'It is true, Miranda. Hideously, loathsomely true. I am poisoned, corrupted. There is no future for us…'

He looked up at her, watching as the tears rolled down her shadowy face. 'I release you, my sweet. Find a good man. Make a life for yourself. I can give you nothing now.' Gregor turned away, unable to gaze upon her any longer, unable to bear the unspeakable hunger growing within him. 'Only death.' With one fluid motion, Gregor leaped forward, crashing through the glass window, falling into the black of night.

Miranda screamed, racing to the shattered glass and twisted iron fittings. She stared out into the darkness, looking for any sign of Gregor's body. She steeled herself to find it crushed at the base of the keep's wall. But nothing met her gaze, only a few shards of glass twinkling in the moonlight as the clouds briefly released Mannslieb from their grasp.

Miranda withdrew back into the room, weeping, her mind struggling to accept what she had seen and heard. She was startled when Lady Ilsa Klausner appeared, taking her into a motherly embrace.

'He's gone,' was all Miranda could manage to say.

'I know,' Lady Ilsa tried to console her. 'I know. My son died three days ago.'

WITHERED FLESH STRETCHED into a grotesque leer, a look of feral, inhuman triumph. Crimson eyes narrowed with satisfaction, the flaming orbs burning a little brighter from the pits of the vampire's face. It had taken many days, far longer than it expected, but at last its call had been answered. The taint it had placed in young Gregor Klausner's blood had at last begun to consume him. The strength and defiance of the boy's spirit had surprised the necrarch, for a time it had even worried that Gregor might be able to resist its power, to overcome its venom and sink into a mortal, permanent death.

But the ancient will of Sibbechai had been greater, more than sufficient to devour the man's soul. It was good that there had been such strength within the last of the Klausners. Sibbechai had need of such strength. By the use of its arcane arts, the vampire would add it to its own reserves of power. It was akin to those practices of mortal wizards, who studied light magic and employed small retinues of acolytes to aid them in focusing and empowering their spells. It was so foolish to think that dark magic might not profit by similar means. Of course, there was some danger. The necrarch was not certain of control over its newly created spawn. If Gregor Klausner had not become its slave, then he would certainly try to avenge himself on the vampire. And the magical link between them would work both ways – Sibbecahi would always be able to sense its new progeny, but perhaps Gregor would be able to follow that same bond back to his unclean father of darkness.

The necrarch lifted a shrivelled hand, its black, necrotic flesh clinging to the bones like wet parchment. It pushed upon the heavy wooden lid of its casket, forcing the panel to the floor with a resounding crash. Sibbechai exerted a small measure of power, causing its body to pivot upwards as though fixed on unseen hinges. It was a vain employment of the vampire's black arts, but Sibbechai knew such displays would keep its unwanted ally nervous and uneasy. It did not want the miserable mortal wizard to enjoy a moment's peace while he stood in the presence of one who was a master of the necromantic arts, centuries before the wizard was even a gleam in his father's eye.

Sibbechai's skeletal face considered the dank shadows of its new lair which was a small barrow mound just beyond the district of Klausberg. The vampire's unnatural vision pierced the darkness, exposing every crack in the walls, every pebble lying upon the floor. The figure of a man stood revealed, standing between the vampire and the barrow's opening. Thin and scraggly, his slight figure huddled within the fur-trimmed mass of a heavy cassock, ratty black hair falling about his pale, leprous face. Scrawny hands scratched at the sleeves of his necromancer's robe, and Sibbechai smiled again at the mortal's unease, exposing its chisel-like fangs. The necromancer took a step back, one spidery hand slipping within the sleeve of his grey robe. Then the wizard seemed to collect himself, glaring angrily at the vampire.

'The maggot crawls from its hole, does it?' Carandini's spiteful voice lashed at the vampire. 'I grow weary of waiting, leech. Three days and three nights I have stood here while you rested within your coffin. I will wait no longer!' The necromancer's hand emerged from within his robes, a small, silver twin-tailed comet icon dangling from the slender chain twined about his fingers. Sibbechai recoiled from the holy symbol, but its mocking smile did not wither. It had seen the fear within the mortal's eyes, however bold his words. The necromancer was fearful that he had made a mistake. Fearful that he had allowed the vampire too much time.

'Put that obscenity away,' Sibbechai's hissed. 'As you grow weary of waiting, I grow weary of your childish theatrics.' The vampire turned its head, watching as Carandini returned the tiny icon to a pocket within his robes. Sibbechai responded by stepping down from its coffin, its tattered black robe hanging shroud-like about its spindly frame.

'Your waiting is at an end, necromancer,' Sibbechai pronounced. 'I am recovered from my ordeal, ready to resume the quest we share.' The vampire studied Carandini's pale features. No, the necromancer could not conceal his doubt and fear. But killing him now might not be so easy, a frightened wizard was still a wizard, after all, and even a frightened man may speak a Word of Power. Besides, the recovery of the grimoire had already taken several unexpected turns. The mortal might possibly come in useful, if fate held any more in store. For the time being, it was better to let Carandini live and believe their tenuous alliance still held.

'Where has the book been taken?' Carandini asked. Sibbechai had bargained with the necromancer for its life with the abhorrent *Das Buch die Unholden*. Claiming that it knew where the book had been hidden by the late Wilhelm Klausner, it swore an oath that even the vampire feared to break. Now the necromancer was anxious to have his side of the bargain fulfilled.

'Klausner sent the book to Wurtbad,' Sibbechai said. 'For some reason, he had decided it was no longer safe in Klausberg.' The vampire displayed its lethal fangs, reminding Carandini what the reason for Klausner's desperate action had been.

'Where in Wurtbad?' the necromancer demanded. Sibbechai shook its head, lifting a claw-like finger.

'You are far too eager,' the necrarch said. 'Was it not you who extolled the virtues of patience?' There was venom in the vampire's voice as it remembered the taunting words spoken by Carandini as he kept the vampire from its coffin, as dawn began to break. 'You will discover where in the city when I feel the time is right.'

Carandini's glare was murderous. He could barely restrain his anger at the undead sorcerer. 'How then shall we proceed?' he said at last.

'We shall journey together to Wurtbad, you and I,' Sibbechai hissed. 'It will take two days to reach the city and I shall rest more easily with so devoted a comrade to watch over me during the hours of day. After all, if any harm came to me, you would never know where the grimoire is located. I should think that a poor mortal, whose years are so dreadfully few, would take great pains to avoid losing his chance at eternal life.

'For now, however, you shall need to find us transport to the city. Something big enough for my–' the vampire gestured with its claw towards the heavy wooden casket, '–baggage. And you might bring me back something to fortify myself with. The younger the better. Young blood is so much more sustaining.'

Carandini gave the vampire a last sour glance, then crept back into the gloom. Sibbechai watched the necromancer depart. It would be able to trust the man, for now at least. He would be

useful in getting to Wurtbad – Sibbechai had not spoken falsely
when it praised the boon of a guardian to watch over it while it
slept. It had spoken rather less truthfully about the need to feed.
The necrarchs were not slaves to their thirst in the way that other
breeds of vampire were. They learned, over time, to subdue and
deny their hunger. The oldest of the breed rarely fed at all. But let
the necromancer believe Sibbechai to be a slave to its thirst.
Carandini might hope to exploit that as a weakness, and when he
did, the necromancer would be unpleasantly surprised.

For, in the end, only one of them would possess the dark secrets
of *Das Buch die Unholden*. Sibbechai had no doubt which of them
it would be.

THE HEAVY OAK door slowly creaked inward as a slender shape crossed
the threshold. The shadow paused, ears straining at the darkness for
any sign her stealthy approach had been betrayed by the door's rusty
hinges. The only sound that answered was a deep rumble of snoring
from the large bed that dominated the tiny chamber. The woman's
expression transformed from nervous caution to savage, bestial hate.
She waited, savouring the moment, letting her eyes become accustomed to the gloom that surrounded her.

The small rooms above the Hound and Hare were owned by the
bloated parasite that ran the tavern itself. He rented them by the
hour to his patrons, the wealthy merchants and ancient aristocrats who composed Wurtbad's elite, offering them privacy for
their night games. Of course, later he would expect a tithe from
whichever whore had plied her trade in one of the squalid little
rooms, an iron cudgel ensuring his demands were always met
promptly and in the correct amount.

Carefully, the woman began to cross the small room. She had
removed her boots, so that her footsteps might not betray her,
ignoring the wooden splinters that the floor stabbed into her
naked feet. Beside the anguish that wrenched at her heart, the sliv-
ers of wood were nothing. She glided toward the bed, like some
night hag conjured from a fable, glaring at the two figures
sprawled among the fur blankets. The woman only gave a scant
glance to the lithe shape lying on the left side of the bed – the
strumpet who had replaced her seemed of little consequence. Her
interest was focused upon the bed's other occupant. The man
who had betrayed her.

Manfred Gelt was a wealthy river trader, one of the richest in Wurtbad. It was a boast she had heard oft spoken, but Manfred had the money to back his claim, throwing it away in buckets during his visits. The best wines, the finest minstrels, the richest meals. Even the squalid little rooms above the Hound and Hare, rented not for a few hours but for an entire evening. Manfred was a man who did not like to be rushed in his pleasures.

He had spoken such pretty words to her, such enticing words. Manfred visited her exclusively for three months, promising to one day raise her from the squalor, to make an honest and respectable woman of her. He bought her gifts, putting some substance to his fine words. The woman had heard such fantastic stories before, from every drunken sailor and melancholy soldier she had entertained through the years. But Manfred's stories were different, for he had made her believe. For the first time in her short, hopeless life, she had dared to hope for better things.

The woman glared hatefully at the familiar face snoring upon the pillow, his fat little hands clutched against his breast. She should have known better. Manfred's ardour had started to cool, until at last his roving eye found a prettier face. Yes, she should have known it would end in such a manner, but the woman could not help but feel betrayed.

She leaned down over the bed, a stray beam of moonlight shining through the shuttered window revealing her pale arm and the foul, black boils that defaced it. The woman bent her head towards his slumbering face, lips parting into a hateful sneer. Slowly, she edged closer until her lips were crushed against those of the man she had so stupidly allowed herself to love. As she withdrew, the slumbering merchant sputtered, the pattern of his snoring interrupted. The woman froze for an instant, wondering if he would awaken, then her eyes narrowed, deciding she did not care. What could he do to her now? She was already dead.

Spitefully, the woman spat into the merchant's open mouth, willing the contagion that pulsed through her body to enter her betrayer. Manfred stirred but did not awaken. With a last hateful look at him, Vira Staubkammer slipped back into the shadows. The sound of a creaking door broke through the silent darkness once more. Then the only sounds in the small room were the rumbling snores of the river merchant.

* * *

'YOUR EVENING WAS productive, excellency?' the liveried servant enquired, his arm extended to receive his master's cloak. The first rays of dawn shone down upon the streets of Wurtbad, as the sounds of the city began to stir.

'Most productive,' his corpulent master replied, his meaty jowls lifting into a lewd grin. 'Positively decadent, one might say.' He stalked past his servant, striding into the massive hall. His imperious gaze swept across the tiled floors, the marble columns and the panelled walls, secure in his knowledge that he was master of all he surveyed. 'I should have been born an Arabyan sheik, Fritz, then I should not be bothered with appearances.'

'Of course, my lord,' Fritz replied, hurrying after his master. A pair of soldiers dressed in uniforms of green and white flanked the two men, following them into the enormous hall. Fritz's master noted their approach, dismissing the two warriors with a wave of his fleshy hand.

'So tiresome, these swordsmen,' he proclaimed.

'They are only obeying their orders, my lord,' Fritz responded. 'After all, it is their sworn duty to protect your person and keep you from harm.'

'Perhaps,' sighed his master. 'But they are so terribly common. I should replace them with something much more daring. Some ogres from the Middle Mountains, perhaps, or a company of Sartosan pirates!' The obese figure's laughter faded into a dry, wracking cough. Fritz hurried forward, but his master shook his concerned servant away.

'You should be more cautious,' Fritz said, his voice heavy with worry. The brothels were a breeding ground for all manner of diseases. Every time his master went abroad he courted sickness.

'It is only a trifle, Fritz,' the fat man declared. 'A chill, nothing more.

So saying, Baron Friedo von Gotz, cousin to the Elector Count Graf Alberich Haupt-Anderssen of Stirland, governor of the city of Wurtbad and all its provinces, ascended the marble stairs, withdrawing to his chambers for a few hours of rest before the tedium of his office beset him for another day. As he departed, Fritz could hear the baron's boots echoing upon the tile floor, the steps occasionally punctuated by the sound of coughing.

CHAPTER TWO

CATHAYAN SILKS CLOTHED the enormous bed, its frame carved from pale Estalian wood. Its engraved surfaces depicted mermen and other fabulous beasts of the sea cavorting in a most unsettling pattern of intertwined tentacles and finned tails. Velvet drapes hung from the canopy of the bed, pulled back and bound to the pillar-like bedposts by silken cords. Sprawled amid the opulence was a gigantic mound of humanity. Silk sheets concealed his nudity, his sausage-like fingers depleting a platter of soft-skinned grapes with the rapacity of a Norse berserker in a convent. But even as he indulged his hunger, the eyes that stared from his bloated face were apprehensive, drifting helplessly across the visages of the men who surrounded him.

'Well?' Baron Friedo von Gotz demanded at last, his voice quivering in anticipation of an answer. The trio of physicians glanced toward each of their confederates, praying that one of the others would take the initiative. The aged individual hovering on the left of the bed, as feebly thin as the baron was indulgent, was the first to blink, clearing his throat with a nervous croak.

'Well,' Doktor Kleist began, seeming to parrot the baron's uncomfortable tone. 'After a careful examination, we must accept that… That they are certainly boils, your excellency.' Kleist's hands spread outwards in a gesture of helplessness. Baron von Gotz growled and sputtered.

'Of course, there are many things that could mean, my lord,' the physician to the baron's right hastily squeaked, trying to forestall the nobleman's distemper. He was a bloated creature himself, as though in emulation of his aristocratic master. His girth strained at the velveteen waistcoat that encompassed his frame. Doktor Gehring felt the baron's hopeful gaze sweep back upon him. 'I should like to lance the pustules again and inspect the humor that is exuded by the wound.' The baron nearly choked on the fistful of grapes he was cramming into his face.

'Filthy leech!' he snapped. 'You've had enough of my blood this morning, you'll get no more.' He swung his attention to the doktor who had yet to speak. He was older than either of the others, his head bereft of hair, his garments simple and devoid of ornamentation. Doktor Stuber maintained a neurotic fastidiousness, keeping his entire body clean-shaven in order to provide no breeding ground for lice and fleas, drinking vinegar every morning in order to thin his blood and prevent it from overwhelming his heart. Popular legend had it that Stuber would burn his clothing after wear, refused to eat any meat unless he inspected the animal before it was slaughtered, and would boil his hands after touching another person to remove any taint of disease. Even now, Stuber was wringing his slender hands before him, as though trying to scrape the contagion from his fingers. Baron von Gotz regretted allowing the physician to speak as soon as his pallid mouth snapped open.

'They could be communal sores,' Stuber stated, with the self-righteousness of a street-corner prophet. 'I have warned his excellency against dallying among the rabble. They are a breeding ground for all sorts of filth.' Stuber visibly shuddered.

'I suggest your attitude become more helpful, herr doktor,' the baron warned, as Stuber's pale features faded to grey. 'I have plenty of room in the dungeons for malcontents. It is wrong to keep a hound in the kennel, he must be free to prowl and hunt.' The fat man's face broadened into a vain smirk. 'After all, even a fine woman like the baroness is not able to fulfil a robust appetite like mine.'

In truth, Friedo's wife had not allowed him to lay a hand on her since he'd bloated into 'something more often seen in a stockyard than a palace'. But Stuber's words gave the baron pause. Was that all that was wrong? Was it simply the mark of some unsightly social disease? Such a minor ailment might seem as welcome as a visit from the Emperor amidst the blight that hung over Wurtbad.

'That may indeed be all it is.' All heads turned toward the speaker, a tall, slender man who had been sitting in one of the leather-backed chairs scattered throughout the bedchamber. He was younger than the physicians, his face dominated by the massive black beard that tumbled down to his chest. A round cap topped his head, the border embroidered with a scrolling gold leaf that matched the rich colouring of his flowing robes. A tall staff of the same metal rested against the wall, rushing into his open hand as he rose from his seat, gesturing toward it. The three doktors grumbled and muttered, unimpressed by the wizard's flaunting of his sorcery. He noted their distaste and smiled, having as little use for them as they for him. It was time to undermine these fawning sycophants. They had misread their patient. Baron von Gotz was not interested in platitudes and placebos this morning. He was frightened, as they knew he had good reason to be, though none was willing to confirm his fears. For no doktor could offer hope to the baron. That was the sole province of the wizard, who would use it to win favour with his patron.

'It may be all,' the wizard repeated. 'But can we afford to take that risk?' The question cut the fragile feelings of the physicians like a knife.

'And does Magister Furchtegott have some insight that he wishes to share with us?' Doktor Gehring demanded. 'Perhaps boil a few frog-legs into a broth and mumble a few elven words over it?' The comment brought chuckles from his fellow doktors, but the wizard was pleased to note the baron was not laughing. 'The solution to this problem requires scientific method, not arcane rites of dubious merit.' Though Gehring laced his words with scorn and derision, there was no hiding the uncertainty that undermined them. If the wizard's star were to rise, he could well guess at whose expense it would be.

'There are certain rites and spells that have great facility in healing.' Furchtegott's tone was precise and certain. 'Even working their magic against such noxious maladies as Stir blight.' The name of the dread disease chilled the air. The wizard was pleased to note the gleam of desperate hope rekindled in the baron's eyes.

'Forgive me, magister,' Gehring scoffed, 'I was unaware that you had any facility with medicine. I had always understood that the only wizards who made a practice of healing were those of the light order, not the mystics of the gold order.' But the doktor's sneer became an expression of alarm, when he saw the keen interest in the nobleman's eyes.

'Furchtegott, tell me what you need to work your spells,' the baron implored. The doktors began to sputter protestations, but the nobleman waved them away with an angry gesture.

'I shall need some rather expensive material components and, of course, the gracious indulgence of yourself, my dear baron.' Furchtegott struggled not to let the sense of triumph welling up within him become too obvious, though he was not entirely successful.

'Whatever you need, you shall have,' the nobleman swore.

'Oh yes,' the wizard thought, 'I am most certain of that.' Once he had cured the baron of this corruption of the flesh, Furchtegott would play the nobleman's gratitude for all it was worth. He would become the most powerful wizard in Wurtbad – possibly even in the entire eastern half of the Empire. He would have the ruler of a mighty city eating from his hand. Even the powerful Supreme Patriarch of Altdorf could not boast that same degree of autonomy and political influence. With the ruler of Wurtbad under his thumb, Furchtegott would be able to spend the wealth of an entire city to expand both his magical library and his knowledge, far beyond what he had been taught by the gold college in Altdorf.

But a moment of worry tugged at the wizard, his eyes lingering on the ugly boil just visible beneath the folds of fat dripping from the baron's chin. There was the small matter of curing the plague, something even the Temple of Shallya and all of the city's physicians had been unable to manage. Still, they did not possess the genius of Furchtegott. And they were trying to cure an entire city. Furchtegott needed to cure only one man.

True, the healing arts were not the central focus of a school of magic centred on the enchanted properties of gold, the most royal of metals, but Furchtegott had ideas about how to rectify this omission. There were not so many mystics and mages within Wurtbad that the court wizard of Baron Friedo did not know them all by name. Many of them he counted as his only friends in the sprawling metropolis. Many nights had they discussed theories on the nature of magic, many times had they swapped pieces of occult knowledge.

Furchtegott conjured up one name in particular, an old wizard who no longer plied his trade but had relegated himself to the role of scholar and sage. Even if he no longer channelled the ethereal winds of magic through his old bones, he still owned a most impressive library. And there was one book, in particular, that Furchtegott recalled with a keen interest.

Hopefully, the old sage would allow his friend to borrow the tome. But if destiny decreed otherwise, Furchtegott was certain the baron's authority could make any such request quite compelling.

THE SPRAWL OF Wurtbad was a dark blemish upon the horizon, the first indication to Thulmann that the city was near. However, the witch hunter's attention was directed toward the more immediate activity unfolding upon the road ahead. Several dozen labourers in coarse woolen tunics were busily constructing a small watchtower from timbers they unloaded from wagons. Other men struggled to roll huge stones into the road, the beginnings of what promised to be a formidable obstruction. A large number of armed men were milling about, some of them sharpening their swords, others finding themselves a patch of shade to sit in. Thulmann was mildly alarmed to note that the uniforms they wore were not the colours of some petty baron or count, banishing his supposition that this was some minor noble's attempt to create a toll road. The rough uniforms were the green and yellow of Stirland's standing army, the uniform of the elector count's own troops.

Overseeing the operation was a mounted officer, his powerful build encased within a suit of steel plate. He watched the work crew with a keen interest, while also casting worried glances in the direction of Wurtbad. One of his soldiers, a rangy youth with a quiver of arrows hanging from his hip, rushed over and directed his attention to the two riders now approaching him.

'What do you make of this?' Streng asked, the words slipping from the corner of his mouth.

'No doubt we are about to find out,' Thulmann replied in the same subdued tone. He noted the sound of Streng moving in his saddle. Without turning his eyes from the approaching officer, he instructed his henchman to leave the crossbow where it was. 'Stirland is not a wealthy province. You can wager that any soldier armed with a bow brought it with him when he was inducted, and knows how to use it. I'd rather not end my days as a pin cushion, and I dare say a dozen arrows in your gut may prove an impediment to your drinking.'

The officer rode forward as the archers drew their bows. The raiment of a witch hunter was quite distinct. Thulmann knew there was no question that the officer had recognised him for what he was. It was why the man was riding forward to parlay, rather than chasing them off with a volley of arrows, though it seemed he was keeping that option open to him.

'Good day, templar,' the officer greeted Thulmann, halting the grey gelding he rode at several horselengths from the witch hunter.

'Good day, captain,' the witch hunter replied, noting the oak leaf badges upon the collar over the soldier's breastplate that displayed his rank. 'You look to be very busy here.' The officer's face grew solemn.

'Plague,' he said, letting the menacing word linger on the air. 'I fear that if you have business in Wurtbad you will not be able to pursue it. By order of the elector count, the city is under quarantine. No one goes in. No one comes out.'

Thulmann fixed the officer with a stare that had caused many a warlock or heretic cultist to break out in cold sweat. 'I am on the temple's business. I must go to the city to complete my holy work. You do your uniform credit by your efficiency, but I must ask that you let us pass.'

The officer shook his head. 'Did you not hear me? The city is infested with the plague. Graf Haupt-Anderssen does not want the contagion infesting the rest of the province, if it is not already too late. He has nearly two thousand men setting a cordon around the city and the river patrol is keeping ships away from the port.'

'I fear no pestilence,' Thulmann retorted. 'I am upon Sigmar's business. Surely the will of a god overrides the edict of a mere man, even if he is an elector count.'

'My apologies, templar, but I have my orders.' There was a tone of genuine regret in the officer's voice. 'I can let no one pass through the cordon.'

'Looks to me like you haven't finished setting up your cordon,' Streng piped up, pointing to where the work crews struggled to erect the tower and block the road. The officer shook his head. Sighing, he reached an autonomous decision.

'As you are going *into* the city, and you are a templar, I will not block your path. But I advise against it. The disease is decimating Wurtbad, they say. Hundreds are dead already, and it will only get worse. Especially once food becomes scarce and winter sets in.'

'Nevertheless, that is where my duty takes me,' Thulmann insisted. The officer moved his horse to one side of the road, waving back to his troops to allow the witch hunter to pass.

'A word of warning, templar,' the officer said. 'Once you pass my post, there is no return. My orders are quite clear. Even Sigmar himself will not find his way out of the city until the elector count lifts the quarantine.'

'I DIDN'T LIKE all that talk about plague,' Streng confessed once they were out of sight of the guard's post. 'Are you certain this is a good idea?' Thulmann gave his henchman a cold smile.

'Have faith, Streng,' the witch hunter told him. 'Sigmar protects his servants, perhaps he can spare some protection for you as well. And if that is not comfort enough, consider that, as a result of our activities in Klausberg, you'll be liberating some of the gold from the treasury at Meisser's chapter house.'

'Thin bit of good that will do me if all the whores have plague,' the mercenary grumbled. 'I was in Wissenbad when the Red Pox hit it. After a few months the beer was so scarce that two crowns could hardly buy a pint.' Streng leaned over in his saddle, spitting into the brush beside the road as though to rid himself of the memory. 'We should have gone back to Klausberg and laid low until the plague was done with Wurtbad.'

'We don't have the leisure to waste that much time,' Thulmann said. 'You seem to forget that we are still on the hunt.'

'Weichs?' The witch hunter nodded his head. 'I don't think he'd be fool enough to linger in a city infested by the plague,' Streng snapped back.

'Quite the contrary, the good doktor would probably find the pestilence a perfect cover for his own twisted activities,' Thulmann declared. 'He'd find any number of willing subjects for his experiments if he offered them a cure for the plague. Besides, we have other business in Wurtbad besides picking up the trail of Freiherr Weichs.'

'The book?' Streng sucked at his teeth, considering the unholy tome that brought ruin to the Klausner family. 'It's been safe in Wurtbad this long, surely a few months won't change matters.'

'You forget, the vampire is looking for it too,' Thulmann stated. 'He knows now that the Klausners no longer have it in their keeping. We can't take the chance that Sibbechai may find it before us, and a little thing like a plague isn't enough to keep him away from Wurtbad if he learns the book is there.'

'So where do we begin?' Streng demanded. It appeared there would not be one single night of drunken debauchery before getting back to work.

'You start by securing lodgings for us,' Thulmann told him. 'Don't skimp on stables for the horses. With plague abroad, I want them kept somewhere they are not likely to be slaughtered for their meat by an enterprising stablemaster. Then you will arrange for me to occupy my old rooms at the Seven Candles. I am sure the innkeeper will be pleased to see us back so soon.'

'And what will you be doing while I'm running your errands?' Streng said in a surly tone.

'Our first priority must be to locate Helmuth Klausner's spell book. Towards that end, I think it will be prudent if I visit our friend Captain Meisser. Even an incompetent fool like him must keep a record of licensed wizards operating in the city. The man we are looking for should be on that list.

'At least if he is still *in* the city,' Thulmann added.

FRITZ GOTTER LEANED a bandaged hand against the cold, stone wall as a wracking cough shook his body. The baker lifted his other hand to his mouth when the spasm had passed, hoping not to find blood trickling from it. His hope was in vain. The disease was chewing up his innards as surely as it was disfiguring his flesh. Thankfully it hadn't reached his face yet, allowing him to conceal his malady from his patrons. It was doubtful if anyone would buy bread from a baker whose face was covered in Stir blight boils.

The sickly baker descended the short flight of stairs to the cellar where he kept his supplies. With the quarantine in effect, no more ships were coming into the harbour, no supplies to feed

Wurtbad's teeming masses. The demand for food was already rising as people began to stockpile rations against the winter. The quarantine was like tossing oil onto a fire. There was a great deal of money to be made – money that Fritz Gotter could use to pay for the plague doktor's regular visits.

Gotter sniffed at the tunic he wore beneath his apron, wincing at the smell. It still carried the lilac perfume scent left by the dokter after his visit. Gotter disliked the smell, it made him feel like a three-shilling tart down by the harbour. Still, it was a minor inconvenience when balanced against the prospect of a slow and horrible death.

The baker paused on the bottom step, allowing his eyes to adjust to the gloom. He could see the stacks of flour heaped in one corner, a few barrels of honey sitting beside them.

The sound of furtive scurrying made his face twist with disgust. The damnable rats were back. The filthy things were too shrewd to waste their time with Gotter's sawdust-ridden bread. No, they went straight for the flour, and never managed to stumble into the many traps the baker had set out for them. Sometimes it seemed to Gotter that the vermin were almost human in their intelligence.

He picked an old table leg from a small pile of junk beside the stairway, slapping the improvised cudgel into the palm of his hand. He had troubles enough without rats eating away at his income. But there would soon be a few less of the vermin to bother him.

The baker began to creep across the cellar, straining to prevent even the softest noise betraying his approach. He knew that even in the dim light streaming down from the stairway, he'd be perfectly visible to the thieving rodents. His only chance to catch them would be if they remained occupied with their stolen supper. Gotter glanced down at the floor to ensure there was no clutter underfoot to stumble on. As he did so, the colour drained from his sickly face. A thin coating of dust covered the floor, remnants of the cheap mix that went into his bread. Something had disturbed that dust. There were tracks on the floor, the clawed footmarks of rats, only larger. Much larger.

Gotter peered into the darkness in the corners of his cellar, conjuring up shapes without form or distinction. His mind raced with horrors recollected from childhood, frightful stories told to terrify the unruly child. 'Be a good boy, Fritz,' his mother used to say. 'Or the underfolk will come and take you away.' The baker shuddered, tears rising unbidden to his eyes, blurring his gaze even as they darted from side to side, straining to see every inch of the cellar.

The faint scurrying persisted, and Gotter was certain he could smell something that was not flour nor sawdust nor the mustiness of the room. The stench of mangy fur, of rank verminous breath, of rotting meat caught between sharp fangs. A cough began to gather in his chest. The baker fought to contain the spasm, his eyes on those hideous tracks.

'Sigmar preserve me,' he prayed. 'I'll never take advantage of anyone that lives again. I'll make honest bread with real flour. Just let me make it back to the stairs. Don't let them see me.'

Even as the thought crossed his mind, there was movement among the shadows of the flour stacks. Red eyes gleamed out from the darkness, seeming to peer straight into Gotter's soul. The baker fought to move, tried to turn and flee back up the stairs, but the only response from his paralysed body was the trickle of urine that spilled down his leg.

The shadow began to slink forward. More red eyes winked into existence, glaring at him from the darkness. The cough he had been suppressing wheezed from his mouth in a choking rattle, its strength diminished by the terror surging through his mind. The shape became more distinct as it emerged into the dim light. Gotter tried to look away, tried to shut his eyes, but his body refused to obey even so small a command.

It was the size of a man. Its outlines suggested the basic human form. Tattered scraps of leather and filthy cloth clung to its shape after the fashion of a tunic and kilt. But it was not a man. Unclean brown fur covered most of its form, save where it faded to a mangy white upon its belly and throat. The hands were tipped with sharp claws, like obscene talons. From the creature's hindquarters, a long, naked tail twitched and writhed. Its face was pulled into a long muzzle, whiskers surrounding its nose, huge incisors protruding from its mouth. The red eyes considered him with pitiless malevolence, a spite beyond human comprehension.

The monster stalked forward, its movements cautious. Gotter almost gave a nervous laugh as he noticed the faint white powder staining the creature's muzzle, realising what had been stealing his grain and flour. But his paralysed body was too rebellious to embrace the onset of madness. The skaven raised its face, sniffing at the air. The monster gave voice to a sound part hiss and part squeak. Other lurking shadows skittered forward, revealing themselves as the creature's noxious kin. The first skaven scuttled right up to Gotter, its muzzle sniffing at his clothes. As the ratman hissed, two more of the monsters hurried forward.

A black paw pulled the table leg from Gotter's grasp, while other inhuman hands closed upon his shoulders and arms. Their touch snapped the baker from his paralysis. Gotter kicked and struggled in their grasp, a wretched moan quivering past his lips. But the skaven were unmoved, pulling him into the darkness. The sound of grinding stone rumbled through the cellar. Gotter watched in horror as a portion of the wall fell inward, revealing the black opening of a tunnel.

'Take-take,' the first skaven chittered. 'Doktor-man like-like. Grey seer like-like. Reward much-much.' The other rat-men laughed at their leader's pronouncement. Gotter joined their hideous merriment as his mind broke. The skaven, undisturbed by his madness, carried him forth into the tunnel.

'Fritz has been a bad boy, mummy,' Gotter giggled as the blackness loomed toward him. 'And now the underfolk have come to take him away!'

The baker's laughter faded as the door slowly closed behind him.

CHAPTER THREE

THE SUN RETREATED before the encroaching darkness, relinquishing its dominion like a vanquished prince. Shadows gathered about the narrow streets of Wurtbad, bringing with them the cold chill of autumnal night. People hurried back into the shelter of their homes, abandoning their streets to those bold enough to challenge the dark or rich enough to hire bodyguards. For night brought out the city's predators, its thieves and cutpurses, murderers and housebreakers. The night was their time and decent folk best stayed behind locked doors. With the plague abroad, the ranks of the desperate, the killers and looters, was swollen by wretched men looking not for the price of ale, but the price of bread. The city watch now patrolled in mobs of a dozen and more, and even they kept mostly to the well-lit streets, perfectly willing to allow the human scum to ply their nefarious trades in the side streets and back alleys.

A different sort of scum gathered in the shadows of an old guildhall. Seven men, their garb heavy to ward off the chill of night and black to blend into the shadows, traced patterns into the dust with their feet. They were old hands at villainy – cutthroats, kidnappers and worse. Their catalogue of sin was enough to shame Khaine, the lord of murder, down in his fiery hells. Yet even these men were uneasy, their shreds of conscience sickened by the acts perpetrated upon their own people these last weeks, and the deeds their hated master would still have them do. But the will to survive was stronger, a shackle their loathsome master had wrapped about each of their necks. A bond not one of the seven had either the courage or the decency to break.

The sound of a trapdoor slamming shut startled them. It brought the rogues around to face the archway that yawned at the rear of the meeting hall, behind the rotting remains of a wooden lectern. It was a portal that opened upon shadow, leading back into the old offices and storerooms of the guild. Now it led to the passageway that connected this place to the lair of their master. The thieves cast nervous looks at one another, some fingering the daggers and swords they wore beneath their cloaks. Their unease did not lessen as a tall, thin figure emerged from the darkness. The elderly man wore a heavy brown coat about his emaciated frame, a massive hat covering his head. The thieves bowed their heads slightly as their master stepped into the grey moonlight seeping through the guildhall's grimy windows.

'You are all here,' Doktor Weichs pronounced. 'Forgive my delay, but it is unfashionable for a gentleman to be punctual. As gentlemen yourselves, I am sure you understand,' he added with a withering sneer.

'You have brought it?' one of the thieves almost pleaded, his voice cracking. The other men remained silent, but the question was foremost in their own minds.

'Of course,' Weichs smiled, stepping toward the battered lectern from which the long dead guildmaster once conducted meetings. The doktor's gloved hand removed seven small clay bottles from his coat, setting each upon the pedestal. The man who had spoken took a step forward. The doktor shot him a stern glance. Chastised, the thief retreated, wiping his moist hands upon his cloak.

Weichs studied the desperate yearning within the feverish gazes of the men. He locked eyes with each of them, fairly daring them to rush forward and take for himself that which each needed, to quench the longing that burned within their veins. Finally, Weichs stepped back, waving his hand towards the podium. Like a pack of starving curs, the thieves rushed forward, shoving and pushing one another as they took up the bottles and hastily downed their contents.

When the last bottle had been emptied, Weichs clapped his hands together. A shadow detached itself from the darkness of the archway. Smaller than Weichs, its hunched shoulders were covered by a filthy black robe, its head by a black cowl. It walked with an unsettling motion that suggested the inhuman, an odour of decay clung to it like an unholy aura. From the front of the cowl, a rat-like muzzle protruded, its chisel fangs exposed. Hands covered in mangy brown fur hung from the sleeves of the robe, gripping the wooden box the creature held before it. The thieves backed away as the monster advanced, setting the box down beside the lectern.

'A fresh supply of medicine for you,' Doktor Weichs told his men. 'A fresh supply of medicine for Wurtbad.' Flashes of guilt flickered across the faces of the thieves.

'You know what to do,' Weichs said. The thieves nodded solemnly, hastily producing leather gloves from their pockets. From the linen bags they carried, the men removed strange leather masks. One of the thieves produced a tinderbox and each man came to him to light a hemp match. Another thief handed out small cloth knots that smelled faintly of lilac. Each thief lit the cloth, the smell of lilac intensifying as the fabric smouldered, then dropped the pomanders down the narrow beaks of their masks. With the scent of lilac filling the meeting hall, human faces disappeared behind bird-like visages.

Doktor Freiherr Weichs uttered a sardonic laugh as his plague doktors came forward, removing the bottles of poison the skaven had brought. Each man took one and placed it in the bag he had brought with him. They would spread out, filtering through the city like daemonic messengers. Heralds of hope to the terrified people of Wurtbad, all the while carrying the very doom that those same people feared. There was a sick irony behind such a deceit, such as only a man like Weichs could appreciate.

Of course, there was an even more subtle irony behind his hold over the men. They had been poisoned by Weichs soon after he arrived in Wurtbad, with a foul mixture of crushed warpstone and weirdroot in their beer and ale. A combination almost guaranteed to cause mutation, if it did not bring instant death. Weichs had happily informed these thieves and murderers of what was happening to their bodies, and why. He had told them the only way to protect themselves from total degeneration was with the potions only he could provide. There was no other choice. They had to become his slaves, if they did not wish to become monsters. Weichs chuckled again. There was an even more poetic irony in that the 'medicine' that held them to his will was nothing more than a smaller dose of the very concoction that poisoned them. His plague doktors worked to help him secure subjects for his experiments, little suspecting that they themselves were just part of one grand experiment.

The old man's features disappeared behind those of a bird of prey. The plague doktor reached down into the wooden box, removing the last of the black glass bottles. He turned the grey lenses of his mask upon the rat-man lingering nearby. 'I shall need six tonight,' Weichs stated, lifting his hands and displaying the appropriate number of fingers. The skaven chittered in its own vile language, holding up its malformed hands to display six clawed talons in response. Doktor Weichs turned away, marching from the guildhall with a deliberately unhurried pace.

The skaven's malicious gaze followed the plague doktor's departure. The creature laughed. It had not been deceived. It had smelled the fear beneath the man's calm demeanour. Trickles of saliva dripped from the creature's mouth. Perhaps the time would soon come when Skilk had no further use for the doktor-man.

Hungry thoughts crawled through its mind, the scent of lilac in its nose. The skaven scurried back into the welcoming darkness.

THE WITCH HUNTER and his companion rode in silence toward the city, sensing the grim atmosphere that hung all about them. Despair clung to the walls of Wurtbad, the unspoken dread that hangs over any community haunted by pestilence. The first sign of the corruption was outside the city walls, the great pit that yawned open in what had once been a wheat field. The plague pit had been filled with naked bodies, black robed priests of Morr chanting sombre prayers to sanctify the dead as they were hastily thrown in. Barrels of quicklime edged the pit, the priests tossing shovels of the powdery substance upon each body as it settled. Lit by flickering torches bound to tall poles, there was something spectral about the ghastly sight.

More sinister still had been the two silent, armour-clad warriors who stood guard over the priests and the plague pit. Encased in plate mail crafted from obsidian, they wore a hooded tabard not unlike the robes of the priests. They were the Black Guard, templars of Morr, god of death. Warriors who did not concern themselves with the living, only with the sanctity of the dead. The mere presence of such fearsome knights kept even the most distraught mother from reclaiming the body of her child from the plague pit, and their deadly reputation kept opportunistic grave robbers from plying their trade.

Within the city, the streets seemed even more desolate than Thulmann had remembered them. Sewage and waste had begun to accumulate in the gutters, a sure sign that the dunggatherers and muckrakers were no longer active. The witch hunter shook his head as he wrinkled his nose at the stench. He had seen enough over the years to know that doktors and physicians were right to claim filth was a breeding ground for disease, and that sanitation was the best safeguard against pestilence. Altdorf's elaborate network of sewers had been constructed because of such concerns, as had those of Nuln. But Wurtbad, once the glittering prize of one of the poorest realms of the Empire, had no such system. Living in squalor, the men and women who cleaned the streets were among those hardest hit by the plague.

'Watch what you're stepping in!' Streng snarled at his mount, slapping its neck in irritation as the hoof squashed against the dirty cobbles. The bearded mercenary displaced his irritation from the animal and back to his employer.

'We were better off in that ghoul-nest Murieste,' the thug spat. 'They'll have to drown this place to get rid of the stink!' Thulmann gave his henchman a tired stare.

'Persevere,' the witch hunter told him. He turned his gaze back around, staring at the street sign the two riders had just passed. A clutch of shadowy figures lurked within the mouth of an alleyway. As Thulmann rode beneath one of the street lamps, and they saw what kind of a man they were shadowing, the ruffians slipped back into the darkness. 'If foul odours are the worst trial we face here, then Sigmar is being exceedingly kind.' Thulmann stared upwards at another street sign. With a slight pull on the reins he brought his steed to a halt.

'We part company here,' the witch hunter said. 'I must go and see Meisser. You go to secure lodgings at the Seven Candles.' Thulmann did not wait for Streng to reply, but carefully turned his horse about. Streng watched his employer ride off, listening to his mount's hooves upon the cobbles.

The mercenary's hand dropped to the purse swinging from his belt. There were still a few pieces of silver in the worn leather pouch. Enough for at least one night of debauchery. A lewd grin began to work its way onto Streng's face. Let Thulmann find his own rooms, the thug decided, he had his own priorities.

Streng looked at the shop signs swaying in the cold breeze, studying the pictures they bore. The ex-soldier had little skill with letters, but an excellent eye for detail and a prodigious knack for building maps within his head. By the signs, he recognised a chandler, a cobbler and a knife maker all in a row. That meant he was in the Griefweg neighbourhood. If he continued along this street, it would eventually connect with Stahlstrasse, and its overabundance of taverns, brothels and gambling dens.

The Seven Candles could wait. Right now, Streng decided he needed ale, a wench – and more ale.

IT HAD BEEN almost ridiculously easy to slip past the guards on the city walls. With his pallid features, dark attire and the air of morbidity that hovered about him, the soldiers at the east gate had taken Carandini for one of the priests of Morr, returned from dumping corpses in the vast plague pit beyond the city walls. The rickety old cart and the stench of death emanating from the wooden box it carried only added to that illusion. Not that the soldiers would have been able to stop him in any event. Carandini was bringing something much worse than plague to Wurtbad, something that would have destroyed the guards as swiftly and ruthlessly as it had their fellows who maintained the quarantine.

The necromancer shuddered as he recalled the ease with which Sibbechai had killed them.

As the cart rumbled through the silent streets, Carandini heard the soft creak of the box opening and closing behind him. The chill of the night air increased, the reek of death became still more distinct. A grotesque shadow rose above the necromancer, then settled beside him on the seat of the cart.

'North,' the vampire voice rasped. Carandini stared at the monster, trying to read some expression in the fires that shone from the sockets of the ghoulish face.

'That takes us to the waterfront,' the necromancer protested. 'We will not find what we seek there.' Despite a lifetime spent delving into the black arts and the morbid rites of necromancy, despite years of forcing the simulacrum of life into rotting corpses, Carandini winced as the vampire's desiccated lips pulled back, exposing its over-sized fangs.

'First we find a safe place to hide my resting place,' the necrarch hissed. 'I would not want to secure the treasure after so many centuries only to be destroyed by the rising sun.' There was an unspoken threat behind Sibbechai's words. Carandini wondered if the monster intended to turn on him even before they had secured the book.

'Why the waterfront?' Carandini asked, trying to discern the vampire's intent.

'I hear much,' Sibbechai replied, 'even within a wooden box. The soldiers at the gate spoke of plague in the dockyards. The living avoid such places when they can. There will be many buildings abandoned by their cowardly owners. Plenty of places to hide.' A dry laugh, like the death rattle of a man choking upon his own blood, bubbled from the vampire's withered throat.

'Fear not, necromancer,' Sibbechai spat, 'once my grave is safely concealed, we shall find this wizard. Then we shall recover my book.'

THE CHAPTER HOUSE of the Order of Sigmar, headquarters of the witch hunters of Wurtbad and its surrounding districts, was exactly as Thulmann had first seen it several weeks previously. It was a squat, two-storey building with a gabled roof and a plaster icon of the twin-tailed comet looming above the main door, with no sign of the subtle decay and neglect that had started to gnaw at some of the surrounding streets. Leave it to Meisser to ensure the street in front of the chapter house was swept, the gutters mucked out and the walls scrubbed clean, Thulmann told himself. The man should have been a bureaucrat. An entire city rotting away around him, yet he found time to worry about dirty walls and muddy gutters.

A man like Meisser should never have risen to the rank of witch hunter captain. It was a hurried posting, whereby a heretic had been replaced by a lord protector who had himself been a heretic. Thulmann knew there was a faction within the Order of Sigmar that strove to redeem the late Lord Thaddeus Gamow's name, but charges of heresy rang a little too true. Indeed, posting a bullying, incompetent and ineffectual swine like Meisser to such an important rank in one of the Empire's larger cities was hardly the decision a capable lord protector would make. At best, it was an almost criminally stupid decision, at worst an act of sabotage, blackening the reputation of the Order by presenting a back-alley racketeer as its public face in Wurtbad. Thulmann wondered how many such suspect decisions Gamow had made. Certainly enough to make the Grand Theogonist believe the heresy rumours, and Volkmar was not a man to reach a decision without weighing all the evidence.

Still, perhaps there was something providential in Meisser's promotion. He was weak-willed and easily dominated, the kind of man who preferred to let others fight his battles for him. Although Meisser was witch hunter captain of Wurtbad, Thulmann had assumed command of his investigation of the scarecrow murders after deflating his pomposity with a few threats. Like all brutal, incompetent men who were given power only to abuse it, Meisser lived in terror of his superiors and of losing his prestigious position. Thulmann had exploited that fear before. He would do so again to find *Das Buch die Unholden*.

One thing Thulmann had to credit Meisser for was his excellent record keeping. It seemed every detail of every confession ever extracted during his tenure had been saved, to judge by Thulmann's previous inspection. A man with such a rat-trap mind could not fail to have a listing of licensed wizards and mystics among his documents. Wilhelm Klausner might have entrusted the unholy book to just about anyone, but something told Thulmann that his confidant was a practitioner of the arcane arts. There was nothing solid to lead him to such a conviction, only an idea that could not be rooted, however he tried to rationalise it away.

A wizard? Would Klausner really have entrusted a wizard with something as dreadfully potent as this grimoire was supposed to be? No witch hunter trusted those who dabbled in magic, for all magic was born of Chaos, the great enemy of Sigmar and of the Empire. Licensed wizards were barely tolerated but deemed a necessary evil by some, heavily monitored where possible, watched for the first hint of corruption. But Klausner had himself been corrupted, meddling with powers far more sinister than anything a student of the colleges of magic was permitted to call upon. Yes, such a man could very well have given *Das Buch die Unholden* to a wizard, reasoning that only such a man could keep it safe from Sibbechai.

Thulmann extracted himself from his thoughts, reining his horse before the main door of the chapter house. He dismounted, striding to the door, his gloved hand pounding on the stained oak. After a moment, an elderly servant opened the door, staring suspiciously until he recognised the Sigmarite emblems on Thulmann's hat and clothing.

'I've come to indulge Captain Meisser's hospitality,' Thulmann stated, stepping across the threshold. The old servant, Eldred, could not quite hide the smile fighting to appear on his face. After rescuing Meisser's investigation and bringing Chanta Favna to trial, Thulmann had become something of a hero in Wurtbad – not least to the men of the chapter house, who felt he had salvaged their honour along with the investigation.

'Welcome back, Brother Mathias,' the old man said, bowing his head. 'I'll have a boy take your horse to the stable.' The servant reached for Thulmann's hat and cloak, but the witch hunter waved him away. It was, perhaps, a little indulgent of him, but he wanted to present as imposing a presence as he could when he once again set eyes on Meisser.

'You'll find Captain Meisser in his study,' the old man told him. This time the smile couldn't be resisted. 'He has company already. A lady friend,' the servant grinned, hurrying away to arrange the care of Thulmann's steed.

Thulmann looked down the hallway that would conduct him to Meisser's study. A lady friend? Meisser had a decided lack of concern for the plague ravaging his city. Even for a heretic like Gamow, it was an act of audacity to promote such a reptile to the rank of captain.

Thulmann did not bother to announce himself, but simply pushed open the door of the study. The room was opulently furnished, dominated by the massive wooden desk that sprawled

across its centre. Bookcases crammed with folios and loosely
bound documents sat at each flank. There had been at least one
change to the décor. On the wall behind the desk had once hung
a portrait of Meisser himself, which Thulmann had gently
mocked upon his last visit. The witch hunter smiled to see that
Meisser had had the painting removed.

There had been one other change. Meisser was not alone. Seated
behind the desk was a striking young woman, her flaxen hair
gathered about her face like the halo of a saint. A glass of wine
rested among the clutter of documents across the surface of the
desk. The deskwork commanded her complete attention and she
did not look up as Thulmann made his entrance. The fawning figure that hovered about her, fetching documents from the shelves,
did, however. Meisser looked despondent as he recognised his
unexpected visitor.

'Br–Brother Mathias,' Meisser sputtered. 'I– we did not expect
you to return so soon.' Meisser's words caused the woman to look
up from her work. Her piercing gaze focused upon the visitor, a
faint smile appearing on her face.

'Mathias Thulmann,' her soft voice observed. 'This is indeed an
honour.' Thulmann removed his hat, handing the garment to
Meisser. Meisser stared at it for a moment, before carefully setting
it down in an unoccupied chair.

'It appears you have me at a disadvantage,' Thulmann silkily
confessed. 'You seem to know me, but I can't remember our having met. I am certain I would not forget such an event.'

The woman rose from behind the desk. She was tall, with clothes
more suited to a young rake out prowling the taverns than a woman
of her station. Yet the incongruity did nothing to diminish her qualities. Knee-high boots and red leather breeches clung to her long,
lean legs. A shirt of soft white fabric, its sleeves sporting the extravagant frills currently in fashion among the nobility, rose above the
silver-trimmed belt that circled her slender waist. Above the shirt,
she wore a black leather vest, the straps unbuckled where the garment constrained the swell of her breast. About her neck hung a
brooch set in snakeskin, the rampant griffin insignia of Igor Markoff
engraved upon the gleaming bauble. A heart-shaped face rose above
the circle of snakeskin, framed by locks of flaxen hair.

Like a startled spider, Meisser scuttled out of the woman's way.
She extended a delicate hand to Thulmann. 'Silja Markoff,' she

introduced herself. 'I am the Lord High Justice's daughter,' she added when she saw his eyes grow thoughtful. 'You did a great service for my father by exposing the witch Favna.'

Thulmann lifted her hand to his lips. 'I did only what was expected of me,' he said. 'What my oaths have demanded I do.' A thin smile appeared on his hawkish face. 'So, tell me, what brings Silja Markoff to be entertained by the esteemed Captain Meisser at so lonely an hour?'

Seizing the opportunity, Meisser's nervous voice slipped in before she could compose an answer. 'I have decided to coordinate my current investigation with the Ministry of Justice. Lady Markoff is helping me examine the methods and procedures practised by my men. The Ministry is somewhat concerned that we are being more zealous than efficient in our work.'

Thulmann was quietly impressed. It was the closest to an admission of incompetence he had ever heard from Meisser. The witch hunter turned his attention back to Lady Markoff. She must have had a very powerful personality to crush Meisser's arrogance so thoroughly. He could well understand why Markoff's daughter could also be his most trusted and capable agent.

'Captain Meisser is convinced that the plague afflicting Wurtbad is not a natural phenomenon,' Silja stated, tossing one solitary crumb of comfort. 'In the event that he is correct, my father wants to assist in his investigation. To that end, I have been examining the records of his investigation so far. Pointing out his errors,' she shot the witch hunter captain a scornful glare, 'and his excesses.'

Thulmann could well imagine. Unable to uncover Chanta Favna and her sorcerous assassin, Meisser had resorted to torturing and executing anyone even rumoured to be a witch, condemning far too many innocent men, women and children to death. It seemed Meisser was making just as little progress with the plague and had resorted to his old tactics of deception. Thulmann's face mirrored the disgust in Silja's eyes.

'That explains my presence,' she said. 'What brings you back to our city, Brother Mathias, at so inopportune a time?'

'My investigation in Klausberg has led me back to Wurtbad,' Thulmann declared simply. 'I had hoped the chapter house might be able to assist me in my labours.'

'Of course,' Meisser replied, far too hastily for Thulmann's liking. The man's motivation was as transparent as the lens of his spectacles. His own brutal investigation had degenerated into such a fiasco that the Ministry of Justice was taking control of it. Meisser now saw a chance of redemption by insinuating himself into Thulmann's work. 'Anything the chapter house can do for you, you have but to ask it.' His servile smile was nauseating. Thulmann was happy that Streng wasn't present. The mercenary would have wasted no time wiping that look from Meisser's face.

'You can help me,' Thulmann said. 'The man I am looking for is probably a licensed wizard.' Meisser nodded his head like an agreeable idiot. 'I want to go over the records of every one of them residing in Wurtbad.' The smile faded from Meisser's face. There were not many wizards in the city, but they were powerful men, and not just in the field of magic and sorcery. They also wielded considerable influence as advisors and helpmates to the big guilds and trading houses. Even Baron von Gotz had a wizard among his court. Hunting down and bringing to justice lone witches and warlocks was one thing, but Meisser was not terribly eager to begin harassing real wizards. The thought of the political scandal the mystics might bring crashing down about his ears made the prospect of fighting Chanta Favna's blade-handed scarecrow seem pleasant by comparison.

'I shall get the documents you require,' Meisser said, his enthusiasm already curling up and dying inside him. The witch hunter captain rummaged about the shelves of the bookcases for several minutes. He returned with a bundle of parchment sheets bound by string.

'We have complete histories of each wizard, at which of the schools of magic he studied, who his instructors were, and his accomplishments after being released from the colleges of magic. We need to know, of course, who it is we are dealing with, should one of these men become corrupted by the dark forces they study and turn renegade.' Thulmann waved Meisser aside, grabbing the stack of papers.

The witch hunter smiled as he read the topmost document. Sigmar was truly going out of his way to assist him. Some names had been crossed out with thick black strokes as the wizards they represented had died or moved out of the city. But one name stood out and Thulmann knew it was the one he was looking for.

'Wolfram Kohl,' Thulmann read. Wilhelm Klausner's steward and accomplice in his acts of heresy had been a man named Ivar

Kohl. It couldn't be a coincidence. The witch hunter handed the stack of documents back to Meisser, his finger resting on the name. 'I want to know everything that you know about this man.'

STRENG LED HIS prize away from the Splintered Skull tavern, his arm wrapped about her waist. The mercenary greeted the few men who crossed their path with a predatory scowl that made them increase their pace. He studied the shop signs swaying in the cold night breeze. Getting his bearings, the thug turned his companion toward a narrow alley that opened onto the street. The woman hesitated.

'Just what kind of tart do you take me for?' her shrill, girlish voice demanded. 'I ain't no animal to be rutted in some gutter!'

'I'll wager you've done worse,' the mercenary chuckled, his hand dropping from her shoulders to deliver a playful swat to her flank. The harlot squealed in surprise. 'Worry not. I know a place where the rooms are cheap and the fleas are small.' Streng slapped the woman's backside again. 'Now move your arse along before I lose my patience!' he growled. The woman squeaked in mock fright and hurried into the alleyway. Streng chuckled, following her into the darkness. Their laughter died, however, when his companion uttered a gasp of alarm, then a grunt of pain. Streng hurried forward, drawing his sword from its sheath.

Around the dark corner of the alley, he found the woman sprawled on the cobbles, curled into a foetal position, her arms cradling her chest. Standing over her was a man in a ragged black coat. Streng recognised him as the weak-looking young man who had been entertaining the woman in the Splintered Skull, before Streng had appropriated her. A muddy boot kicked at the woman's back before he turned to face Streng.

'We'll finish our talk in a moment, strumpet,' the rogue snapped. 'After I have words with your lover man.' Streng glared at his foe, taking a few careful steps to place the corner of the alleyway within easy reach. It was all well and good to fight for the honour of a lady, but Streng didn't think his companion had all that much honour – nor was she much of a lady. If Black Coat decided to produce a pistol from his pocket, a quick dive and an even faster sprint would see Streng back on the main street.

'Grew some bollocks, I see,' Streng snarled. Black Coat's face split in a hateful glare. The man's hand fell to his side and Streng braced himself to dive. He almost sighed with relief when he saw his enemy pull a sword from its sheath.

'I don't brawl with scum,' Black Coat announced. 'I kill them.' A murderous smile twisted Streng's features.

'Funny,' Streng growled, 'I've always try to follow the same rule.'

CHAPTER FOUR

A DARK FIGURE detached itself from the shadows, slinking across a black alley to conceal itself in an arched doorway. The heavily cloaked man cast a furtive sidelong gaze back along whence that he came, flicking a stray lock of greasy hair from his pallid, sickly face. Satisfied that he was unobserved, he gave his attention to the ironbound oak door looming beside him. Pale hands fumbled in the innards of a leather satchel, producing a desiccated claw bound in mouldering wrappings.

Strange, unclean words belonging to a tongue known only to the blackest sorcerers slithered from the necromancer's lips. Carandini's eyes blazed in the shadows as the unholy power passed through him. The claw, the dismembered hand of the tomb king Nehb-ka-Menthu, began to scratch at the oak, digging runes and hexes into the wood. Carandini smiled as he read the ancient hieroglyphs. The wizard's house was indeed protected by wards, but they were weak and feeble, wasted by neglect. How very different from the protective spells the Klausners had woven about their own home. In some ways, the necromancer almost felt insulted, that final victory should be bestowed upon him with such ease.

The claw grew still, and Carandini restored it to his bag. More words dripped from his tongue and the hieroglyphs scratched upon the door flared suddenly into flame. A moment passed and the flames were gone, leaving behind blackened outlines of the symbols. The necromancer removed a small packet of grey powder from one of the pockets concealed within his heavy cassock. The mummy's hand had done its work, calling upon the dread sorcery of the long-dead Nehekhara. The feeble wards placed upon the house were no more.

Carandini cast the powder upon the bronze lock that glared from the side of the door. The necrotic powder worked its fell magic, devouring the metal and the wood surrounding it, corroding both surfaces as though the weight of a thousand centuries had aged them in an instant. The necromancer pushed open the door as the foul, black residue of the lock dripped to the ground.

He stepped across the threshold, into the small parlour that connected the dreary side entrance to the inner chambers of the house. Carandini enjoyed the faint, musty smell of old books and piled dust. The smell of scholarship. For a sorcerer, he believed, it was the smell of treasure.

Thoughts of avarice and power withered within the crooked corridors of Carandini's mind, as another smell overwhelmed the mustiness. The odour of death and decay pounded his senses, his pale skin prickling with goosebumps as an unnatural chill crawled up his flesh. Even the feeble light cast by the streetlamp outside seemed to grow dimmer. Without turning around, Carandini knew there was something standing behind him. Just across the threshold, something tall and gaunt and unholy.

'Do not think to cheat me, necromancer,' Sibbechai's rasping voice snarled. Carandini turned upon his partner, his smug smile fighting against his unease.

'Such a strange peculiarity,' he mused. 'The great Sibbechai, lord of sorcery and the black arts. A centuries-old vampire with the strength of ten men in his withered arms. Yet you stand helpless to enter a simple dwelling.' His smile grew as he considered the curse that was part of the necrarch's taint. So strong was the hate of life within the necrarchs that the creatures were incapable of entering any structure that man made his home.

Some said the curse had been placed upon the vampiric sorcerers by the gods themselves, that the necrarchs might be thwarted in their diseased schemes. Others held that the power that bound them came from a far fouler source – the accursed one, the supreme necromancer, Nagash the Black, that his undying slaves might never again linger among the living and be distracted from their profane studies. That no seed of sympathy might somehow take root within the putrid remnants of their hearts. Whatever its source, no vampire sorcerer could cross any man's threshold unless first invited by one who was already inside.

'Reconsider this folly, mortal,' the vampire warned, its smouldering eyes glowing in the dark. Carandini's bravado flickered as the corpse-like visage snarled at him. Sibbechai's burning eyes seared into the necromancer's brain, driving foreign thoughts into his mind. 'Invite me across,' Sibbechai repeated.

For a moment, Carandini's body trembled, struggling to resist the command that thundered inside his skull. Slowly, the Tilean's lips parted. Against his will, words began to wheeze from his mouth. He tried to force them back down, but they were spoken before they could be stopped. 'Enter this house freely, and of your own accord.'

Like a weary moth, Carandini crumpled to the floor, hands clutching at his throbbing head. The gaunt shadow that had been framed in the doorway swept across the threshold, the vampire lingering only to give its duplicitous companion a further command.

'Wait outside and keep watch,' Sibbechai hissed. Carandini turned his face to glare at the monster. The vampire bared its fangs in a bestial snarl. 'Beware, necromancer. Your usefulness is now diminished. Soon you may be at the end of it.'

Carandini managed to linger long enough to watch the vampire pass through the far door and into the hallway beyond. Then, compelled by the necrarch's will, he crept back into the street.

The necromancer's thoughts were black. His hand continually closed about the tiny bottle of holy water sewn into the sleeve of his cassock. It would have been much easier to take the book from Wolfram Kohl, both for himself and for the doomed wizard. Now they would both have to face the vampire. After Sibbechai's recent display, Carandini was less certain than ever about his chances against the necrarch.

* * *

MATHIAS THULMANN STALKED the deserted night streets like a
hound that scents the nearness of its prey. Wolfram Kohl. Brother
of Ivar Kohl. Student of the amethyst college in Altdorf. Amethyst,
that school of wizardry closest of all to the forces of dark magic
and necromancy. The witch hunter had thought Wilhelm Klausner an idiot to entrust a potent work like *Das Buch die Unholden*
to a wizard, but he must have been mad to entrust it to one who
was practically a necromancer already.

How many years had Kohl been in possession of the forbidden
text? How many years had the wizard spent studying its abominable rites and blasphemous incantations? According to
Meisser's records, Kohl had suddenly stopped practising the
arcane arts five years ago. Amethyst wizards were in high demand,
for their profane spells could call upon the spirits of the dead to
communicate with the living. For the bereaved, one last moment
with a departed loved one was worth any price. When he turned
his back on his art, the wizard ended a very profitable series of
séances. Thulmann knew even wizards placed some value on gold
– if only to fund their arcane studies. Wolfram Kohl must have
had a good reason to quit his trade. Was it to devote himself body
and soul to studying Helmuth Klausner's unholy spellbook?

Thulmann kept one eye on the men following him through the
lonely streets. Bearding a wizard in his lair was always a dangerous proposition. Supernatural powers could give the wizard prior
warning of a witch hunter's approach, while an infinite number
of spells and wards could be called upon to protect him and bring
harm to his enemies. Not a few witch hunters refused to pursue
such a course without a wizard of their own, to fight magic with
magic. It was particularly common in Altdorf, where the colleges
of magic and their students were readily available. Thulmann had
always found such tactics unconscionable. Even more so now, for
it was alarmingly similar to the heresy that had consumed the
Klausner line. He preferred to put trust in his courage, and faith
in the grace of Sigmar, not the unclean spells of conjurers.

Even so, he would have felt better with more men. After discovering the existence of Wolfram Kohl, Thulmann had ordered
Meisser to round up every available witch hunter. But only five
could offer their services, the others strewn about the city conducting investigations on Meisser's behalf. Two were not
unknown to Thulmann, his comrades in arms at the conclusion

of the scarecrow murders, who had helped to surround the hovel of Chanta Favna. He could be certain they would stand firm if his worst fears about Kohl proved well founded. There were two apprentices who seemed cut from the same cloth, but then he had seen expensive equipment and exhaustive training shatter before the powers of Old Night too many times. The last was the elderly warrior priest Father Kunz, attached to the witch hunters by the Wurtbad temple of Sigmar.

His sixth conscript from the chapter house was less agreeable. It was only natural that Witch Hunter Captain Meisser should volunteer to assist. Indeed, the wily Meisser had suggested that matters may become politically difficult for the visiting witch hunter, should he refuse. The balding Meisser, with his piggish eyes, was an indifferent swordsman – doubtless even more so with one arm still injured from his encounter with Chanta Favna's automaton. Still, Thulmann was somewhat relieved by the offer, if only because it seemed Meisser was more concerned for Thulmann's welfare than he himself.

The reason for Meisser's concern walked with all the dignity of an emissary from the royal court of Bretonnia, her hobnail boots scratching on the cobbles as she unerringly picked out the cleanest places to set her feet. Silja Markoff had insisted upon accompanying the witch hunters, stating that her role as liaison between the Ministry of Justice and the Order of Sigmar demanded no less. Thulmann was of a mind to refuse, but swiftly relented when he considered the politics involved. He was in no mind to play games with the ministry when his quarry was so close at hand. Besides, Silja Markoff had brought her bodyguards with her. Thulmann recognised that two highly-trained soldiers from the Ministry of Justice may well have their uses.

A sharp curse made Thulmann turn around. A faint smile flickered on his face as he saw Silja wipe something from her boot. It seemed her unerring footwork had at last deserted her. The witch hunter sighed as he watched the woman discard her soiled handkerchief. When they arrived at their ultimate destination, he hoped she at least would have the good sense to stay out of the way.

'You are wise to keep an eye on her,' Meisser whispered from beside him. 'She's trying to weaken the order here in Wurtbad, to subvert our authority on behalf of her father.'

Thulmann arched an eyebrow, staring intently at Meisser's swinish face. There was no mistaking the innate cunning he saw there. 'Indeed,' he mused. 'She's told you as much, has she?'

'Actions speak more loudly than words,' Meisser stated. 'She's been a thorn in my side ever since the quarantine was established. Getting in the way. Hindering the investigation.' His tone became indignant. 'As though secular authority has any power over our order.' Meisser's clammy hand gripped Thulmann's arm, pulling him closer. The witch hunter looked back to see the suspicious, disapproving look that Silja directed at them.

'You might not know it, Mathias,' Meisser confided, 'but you are very highly thought of in certain circles. Our uncovering of the witch and her scarecrow impressed not a few of Wurtbad's notables.' Thulmann fought to control his disgust as Meisser referred to *their* tracking down of the witch. It had been Thulmann who discovered the fiend behind that series of ghastly murders. Left to his own devices, Meisser would have continued torturing and executing innocents until the return of Sigmar. 'Not a few regard you as some sort of hero.' Again, the cunning gleam entered Meisser's eyes. 'Now, if you were to protest this unprecedented intrusion into our order's affairs, I am certain some action would be taken.'

'So that's it,' thought Thulmann. 'Get me to fight your battles for you.' He detached Meisser's hand and stepped away. 'Captain Meisser, I've not been back in Wurtbad long, but it seems that there are a great many people here who feel the city needs to be protected from the Order of Sigmar.' His withering hiss of contempt silenced any retort. 'But who, Captain Meisser, is going to protect the Order of Sigmar from *you*?'

As Thulmann left the insulted captain to brood on his scorn, he took a backward glance at Silja Markoff. She nodded respectfully at the witch hunter as their eyes met. Thulmann returned the gesture.

He looked out on the city's horizon to the distant artisans' quarter. Wolfram Kohl's house would be found there, and his quest to destroy *Das Buch die Unholden* would soon reach its conclusion. After so much darkness, so much doubt, the prospects were finally starting to look brighter.

THINGS WERE STARTING to look very bleak, the mercenary decided, as he beat back the blade of his enemy. Streng's relief that the young tough he'd insulted had equipped himself with a sword rather than a pistol, had quickly evaporated on his discovery that the rogue was more than proficient. Streng's left arm bled from where Black Coat's sword had glanced off his flesh. The cut in his side was deeper. Streng knew that if he didn't stem the blood seeping through his armour, it would not be long before he had no strength to lift his own blade.

'Where's your glib tongue now?' Black Coat was sneering, parrying Streng's retort with an insulting degree of ease. 'Isn't it funny how all the bravado drains out of a man once he starts to soil his breeches?'

Streng growled at his antagonist, his sword managing to slip past his enemy's guard and scrape along his forearm. Black Coat gasped in pain, flinching and transferring his blade to his uninjured hand. Streng grunted with satisfaction. Black Coat might be skilled, but he was no veteran duellist. He was allowing his overconfidence to make him sloppy, his sword making flashy attacks that left gaps in his defence.

'Don't like the sight of blood, eh?' jeered Streng, mustering his strength in the brief respite his enemy had allowed. Black Coat's face contorted into a look of such intense rage that Streng was reminded of a Norse berserker. With a bestial snarl, the youth leapt to the attack once more.

Streng blocked it with his own blade, letting Black Coat's charge carry him forward, so that the faces of both men were scant inches from each other. Streng hawked phlegm into his mouth and spat the foulness in his adversary's face. Black Coat recoiled in disgust, momentarily blinded as he wiped the spit from his eyes. He still managed to block Streng's retaliation, the mercenary's sword ringing as it crashed against Black Coat's parrying blade. But the attack was only a feint. With a savage kick, Streng's heavy boot smashed into Black Coat's knee, breaking the joint with an ugly popping sound.

Black Coat spilled to the cobbles like a sack of grain, a dry shriek ripping through his lungs. Streng was on him in an instant, his boot attacking the side of the youth's neck, choking the scream as it snapped. Black Coat's body writhed in silent pain until Streng's sword slashed downward into his spine. The mercenary had seen far too many mortally wounded men muster enough strength to finish off their killer. The thug's cold eyes watched as the spasms that wracked Black Coat's broken frame gradually subsided. Only when they had stopped did Streng let his sword drop, hands clutching at the gash in his side.

With a moan of pain, he crashed to the street. The mercenary tore a strip from his undershirt, prodding it into the gap that Black Coat's sword had slashed through his leather armour. The cut wasn't deep, it had missed any vital organs, but it could prove no less fatal if he did not stem the loss of blood. He'd have to get the harlot to help him, to send her for a chirurgeon. Streng turned his face back to where he had seen Black Coat kicking the woman. He groaned in disgust, but not surprise. The whore had not lingered to see who would emerge victorious from the back alley duel. She was probably already spending Streng's money in some tavern.

'Well,' Streng spat at the corpse lying beside him. 'The way I see it, you owe me a debt.' The thug grunted in pain as he rolled onto his side and crawled over to Black Coat's body. Bloodied hands pawed through the dead man's clothing. Streng grinned as he removed a small purse, its contents jingling with coins. He was less certain about the purpose of the leather mask he found hidden under the black coat – a long, hook-nosed object that reeked of lilac. Streng tossed it aside and continued his search, removing a small linen bag from the dead man's belt. It contained a bottle. The smile that greeted the discovery of the money pouch echoed across the thug's harsh features. But as he removed the bottle from its wrapping, the smile faded. The dark glass vessel was empty, but it was not this that alarmed Streng. There was an air about it, a taint that Streng had experienced many times since pledging his service to the witch hunter. It was the stench of sorcery, the cold chill of black magic.

Streng hastily replaced the bottle within its wrapping. The witch hunter would want to examine it, to know more about the man who had carried such a talisman. The mercenary pawed once more at the corpse. He recoiled in horror as his probing hand discovered a massive, wormy growth that sprouted from the dead man's belly. No simple mugger or cutpurse, he was something unclean. The dead man had been a mutant! In a frenzied motion, Streng scraped the blood from his hands with the dead man's coat.

The mercenary gathered the bottle and the strange leather mask from the cobblestones and painfully lifted himself to his feet. Thulmann might even see fit to give him a bonus for his troubles. The thought cheered his dark mood somewhat. With one hand trailing along the wall of the alley to support him, Streng slowly made his way back to the street. Between the witch hunter's bonus, and what he had looted from the mutant's corpse, he'd have a grand time once he was back on his feet again.

Allowing, of course, that he was able to find a healer before he passed into the arms of Morr from loss of blood.

MATHIAS THULMANN PAUSED outside the door of the wizard's dwelling. The stench of magic was in the air, the noxious taint of unnatural power. Even the most untutored of men could have sensed it. The unseen aura of sorcery was what made even the lowliest animal loth to approach the domicile of a wizard. Thulmann stared up at the looming façade of the house, watching the flicker of a streetlamp cast eerie shadows upon a plaster gargoyle. His expectations were uncertain, but he looked for some outward sign of the corruption that raked its spectral claws against his nerve endings. It was more than the foulness and decay that characterised the magic of Amethyst wizards. An older, darker energy seemed to crawl from the very walls of the house. Thulmann had wondered if his fears were correct, if Wolfram Kohl had been fool enough to dabble into the forbidden power that had been entrusted to him. Now it seemed he had his answer.

The witch hunter did not have long to ponder his fears, before Meisser's swaggering frame squirmed his way past him. The captain's hand gripped the brass knocker that sprouted from the front door and delivered a sharp, imperious report. Meisser called out sharply, 'Wolfram Kohl. By the authority of the Temple of Sigmar, you are commanded to open this door.'

An animalistic snarl of frustration hissed from Thulmann as he shoved the meddler aside. Any chance of taking the wizard unawares was now completely lost. 'Idiot!' he spat at Meisser, drawing one of his pistols from its holster. Without hesitation, Thulmann fired the weapon into the lock, his boot smashing into the ruined mechanism. The door crashed inward. Thulmann stepped inside, shouting back to the startled men who had been following him.

'Three of you.' he snapped. 'Around to the sides and back. Make certain he doesn't slip away.' Without waiting to see who would execute his commands, Thulmann raced into the shadowy hallway.

THE HALLWAY OPENED upon a large parlour, its wooden floors furnished with heavy rugs, its walls concealed behind shroud-like drapes of black cloth. A small fire slowly smouldered within the fireplace that separated the drapes, a claw-footed couch and a cluster of chairs arranged about the hearth. The witch hunter's eyes darted across the chamber. He noted the crystal decanter standing upon a small table, and the glass goblet shattered on the floor beside it, a pool of Estalian brandy slowly seeping into the rug. A richly upholstered footstool had been kicked onto its side, and the rugs around it were clearly disordered. Someone had quit his habitat in a most reckless fashion.

Thulmann took another step into the parlour, fingers wrapped about the grip of his pistol. His eyes studied the room, his ears keen for any sound. But only the soft crackle of the fire competed with his breathing. Thulmann's eyes narrowed as he observed the flicker of the flames. The sound of footsteps intruded upon him. Meisser and Silja appeared at the parlour's entrance, each with an underling hovering behind them like a shadow. Thulmann lifted his hand, motioning for them to keep silent.

Removing his calfskin glove, he reached toward the draped wall. He could feel the faint touch of cold air caressing his palm, confirming his observation that the fire was reacting to a draught. Thulmann gripped the drape, pulling it toward him, exposing the doorway it concealed. He had known, of course, that the hidden walls would hide a number of doorways, a simple measure by the wizard to disorient any unwelcome visitors without calling upon sorcery. The wizard also would have known that a draught from an open door would make a secret portal much easier to find. It was either careless or maliciously deliberate. Did the wizard intend for his unwanted guests to follow after him?

'Two of Meisser's men are watching the sides of the house,' Silja whispered. 'One of mine is watching the back.' Thulmann tugged the black drape from its fastening, letting the heavy fabric crumple to the floor. The witch hunter glanced down at his pistol, assuring himself the hammer was still primed, the flashpan secure. He bestowed a grim smile upon Silja.

'I don't think our sorcerous friend intends to escape,' he told her. The words brought a nervous sweat beading onto Meisser's forehead.

'What – what does the swine hope to accomplish then?' Meisser asked. It was one thing to stalk a wizard when the roles of hunter and prey were clearly established. For all his political machinations, Meisser was uncomfortable when things became too complicated.

'There is only one way to find out,' Thulmann observed. He placed his hand upon the half-shut portal. The door creaked inward. Finding no sorcerous flame in the darkness, the witch hunter ducked into the opening. He found himself in a narrow hallway, with doors spaced across its length. Ahead of him he saw another chamber, the dim flicker of firelight dancing across its walls. Thulmann's gloves creaked as his grip on his pistol tightened and his steps grew hurried. In the flickering light he could see bookcases, their shelves bulging with leather-bound tomes. Behind him, he could hear the others follow.

It was Wolfram Kohl's library, of that he had no doubt. It reached upward for two storeys, every inch of wall space consumed. A wrought iron staircase wound its way upward from the centre of the room to merge with the narrow walkway that provided access to the upper tier. Against one wall, a bronze brazier, its bed of coals covered by a crystal hood, provided intermittent illumination. Thulmann stepped inside, eyes prowling amidst the shadows.

His gaze fell upon the broken, ragged thing lying upon the walnut desk that reposed near the room's north wall. Its sombre robes were in keeping with the grim raiment of an amethyst wizard, its pallid skin and weak frame the marks of a scholar. Its face resembled that of Ivar Kohl. The man Thulmann had been so anxious to subdue before he could unleash the profane lore of *Das Buch die Unholden*. Kohl's back was snapped like a twig, his neck twisted like that of a slaughtered hen.

Thulmann stared at the body, for once in sympathy with Meisser. Things were becoming complicated again, and he did not like it. Like an arrow hurled by Sigmar himself, Meisser's records had pointed the way to Wolfram Kohl. But now, the arrow was broken.

From the corner of his eye, Thulmann saw a withered apparition appear from the shadows around the bookcase. The gaunt, unspeakable form lunged at him with impossible speed. Talons, black and hard like the backs of beetles, reached for Thulmann's throat. Instinct saved the witch hunter's life, as he threw himself over the desk, spilling the ruined corpse of Wolfram Kohl onto the floor. In his wake, claw-like hands splintered the wood of the desk, shredding it as though it were paper.

Thulmann rolled onto his back, aiming and firing his pistol in one smooth motion. But the instincts of his attacker were just as keen, the silver bullet passing within inches of its skull-face as the monster dodged aside. Torn paper exploded from the far side of the room as the shot burrowed into a bookcase.

'Again you place yourself between me and what is mine!' the vampire snarled, eyes blazing from the pits of its face. 'You shall not do so a third time, witch finder!' it spat.

Sibbechai! By what dark and unholy arts had the creature been led to Wolfram Kohl's door? It removed even the faintest doubt that *Das Buch die Unholden* had been entrusted to the late wizard. But such logical reasoning would mean little if Thulmann was to allow his throat to be torn out. He ripped his sword from its sheath, glaring defiantly at the undead abomination. A wary quality entered Sibbechai's expression, for the necrarch remembered the weapon well. Vampire and witch hunter glared at each other, each waiting for the other to make the first move and the first mistake.

'Shoot!' Silja's quivering voice cried out. 'Kill it!' Thulmann looked past the vampire to see her standing just inside the room. Behind her, Meisser and his two witch hunters were dragging pistols from their holsters. Their movements may as well have been those of men wading through a bog. To the vampire, they might as well have been standing still.

The monster spun around, a snarl ripping through its withered lips, its shroud-like robe whipping the air. Sibbechai prepared to lunge at its new foes when Father Kunz's elderly face appeared behind the witch hunters. A small, silver twin-tailed comet icon flew from his hand as his mouth moved in prayer. The holy symbol was swatted aside with disgust by the vampire, but Sibbechai hissed in pain, acrid smoke sizzling from its dried flesh where it had touched. A deeper malice blazed from the vampire's eyes.

With a roar and a crack, the bullet from Meisser's pistol slammed into Sibbechai's chest, knocking the vampire back. The other witch hunters added their fire to the small fusillade, both shots smashing into the vampire's withered frame. Sibbechai curled its torso toward its midsection. A wracking, malevolent laugh oozed from the vampire. Straightening, it smiled at the men who were shocked by the vampire's vitality.

'Think your common pig iron is enough?' Sibbechai spat. Before the vampire could demonstrate its undiminished strength, Thulmann leapt upon it from behind the desk. The templar's momentum drove the steel of his sword deep into the necrarch's body, impaling its midsection. Sibbechai roared in agony, clawed hands grabbing Thulmann's shoulders and flinging him across the room. The witch hunter crashed against one of the bookcases, head ringing from his violent impact.

The vampire staggered away from the desk, twisting its body in a desperate effort to release the sword embedded in its flesh. Seeing the monster's weakened condition, Silja and her bodyguard charged forward, blades gleaming in the flickering light. The back of one hand smashed into the woman's chest, hurling her backward as though kicked by a horse. Claws ripped the face of her guard, his sword falling as he tried to push his ruined eyes back into his skull. The two witch hunters hurrying to support Silja's attack met similar resistance. One man lay in a pile of limbs and gore, his belly ripped open by the vampire's supernatural strength, the other was fortunate to escape with a fractured collarbone.

Empowered by the scent of blood in the air, Sibbechai's claws closed about the weapon trapped in its flesh. With a savage growl, the vampire ripped it free, pulling its length from the side of its body. Smoke rose from the wound as Thulmann's blessed sword clattered to the floor. The vampire's smouldering gaze burned as the witch hunter slowly rose. Then Sibbechai's eyes darted toward the hallway.

'Don't let it escape!' Thulmann shouted, but the vampire was already in motion. Like a thunderbolt of darkness, Sibbechai swept into the corridor, swatting Meisser aside like an irritating insect as the captain fumbled to reload his pistol. Father Kunz, striking at the monster with his staff, was rewarded with a torn throat. From deeper in the house came the sound of shattering glass, punctuated by a short scream from outside. As Thulmann staggered across the library to recover his sword, he knew it was already too late. Once more, Sibbechai had disappeared into the night.

Thulmann looked at the carnage all around him. Silja Markoff had crawled over to her injured guard, doing her best to help bind his mutilated face. One of Meisser's men was dead, the other a groaning heap of pain. Father Kunz lay in the hallway, dying noisily as he choked upon his own blood.

Meisser was struggling to bind a gash running along his leg, a clumsy operation with one arm still bound in a sling. Thulmann took a step toward the injured man, pausing to lift Meisser's pistol from the floor.

'That... a vampire!' Meisser gibbered. He had been an apprentice when last he encountered the foul undead in a tomb outside Carroburg. He had thought, or hoped, that he need never encounter such a being again. Politicking and scheming had become his vocations, in prosperous villages and great cities, not unhallowed tombs and ruined castles. But it seemed the undead were not content to remain in their own grisly habitat.

'Yes, a vampire!' Thulmann agreed, venom filling his words. He angrily tossed the lead bullet Meisser had been ramming into his pistol at the wounded man. 'Congratulations, captain, you've learned something this day! There is good reason for the Order of Sigmar to instruct its servants to use bullets crafted of silver, blessed by a priest!' Thulmann pulled Meisser to his feet, forcing a cry of pain from the older man. He could practically read Meisser's mind – silver bullets were an expensive piece of ostentation, why arm his men in so costly a fashion when the money might be better spent buying favours at court?

'I am of a mind to finish what Sibbechai started,' Thulmann spoke, his voice cold and murderous. The witch hunter turned his head, feeling eyes upon him. Silja Markoff's expression was perhaps even more horrified than before. He released his grip, letting Meisser crash back to the floor. 'I need your men, captain. All of them. If you found hunting down a witch an entertaining distraction, I'm certain you will find tracking a vampire's grave even more stimulating!'

Thulmann strode from the library, not trusting himself to remain near Meisser. Already he could hear the surviving guards from outside rushing into the wizard's parlour. He would need them to carry the wounded and the dead from the library. Then they would help him burn every scrap of paper in the room. There was no time to search it thoroughly. Even now Sibbechai would be gathering its strength to return. If *Das Buch die Unholden* was there, it would be consumed with the rest.

Either way, Thulmann knew, the vampire would soon be hunting him. Sibbechai would demand revenge for the events of this night.

But one thought troubled him even more than the vampire's ire. If it hadn't been able to retrieve *Das Buch die Unholden* from Wolfram Kohl's library, then exactly where was the book?

FURCHTEGOTT LOOKED UP from the mouldering pages he had been consulting. The wizard was happy that he hadn't eaten a large supper. The very substance of *Das Buch die Unholden* was abhorrent enough – bound in what looked like tanned human skin, the skull of some horned reptile fixed upon its cover, its parchment of human flesh written upon in blood – but the spells he had been deciphering were enough to sicken the most jaded murderer. They were designed to combat disease and plague, but it seemed to Furchtegott the cure was even more abominable than the sickness. Still, the wizard was taking the pragmatic view of a healthy man. Somebody with Stir blight coursing through his body would no doubt see things differently. Still, it was probably better if Baron von Gotz didn't know the secrets of the magic that his court wizard would employ on his behalf.

The wizard stared again at the ugly symbol that festered upon the page. It was like a crumbling scab, three intertwined circles each pierced by an arrow. Furchtegott knew enough about the proscribed gods of Chaos to recognise the symbol of one of the most dreaded: Nurgle, the god of plague. The ugly blemish seemed to writhe upon the page as he said the name of the lord of pestilence. The wizard dismissed the impression. There were no real gods, dark or otherwise. Chaos was simply a force, a power that men clothed in superstition because they did not understand it. Were not the winds of magic simply a manifestation of this energy? All magic owed its power to what men called Chaos.

No, there were no Dark Gods. Only petty men who used their dark imaginings as an excuse to oppress others. *Das Buch die*

Unholden was only one more grimoire, the spells he had deciphered not so different from those he had been taught in Altdorf, once they were stripped of references to the Dark Powers. Its spells would help him to cure the baron, placing his patron deeply in Furchtegott's debt. Which was exactly where he wanted him.

The wizard searched the list of material components he would need to work the spell. Many of them he could find easily enough. Others would be more difficult. He was especially nervous about the 'maggots from a sick man's belly'. Those, he realised, he would need to collect himself.

Furchtegott also realised it would be a long time before he could face anything approaching a large supper.

CHAPTER FIVE

THE EARLY MORNING sun peeked through the clouds that hung over Wurtbad. Slowly, like some wounded beast, the city began to stir. Doors made fast against the hours of darkness were unbolted, shutters swung open to admit the fragile grey light of morning. Bleary-eyed men emerged from their homes to face whatever labours the day held for them. The sound of traders carting their wares from storehouses to places that could yet afford their goods rattled from the main streets of the city. There was feed and straw to be taken from warehouses to the stables scattered across Wurtbad, wine and beer to be doled out to the taverns. The world of commerce had yet to be consumed by the disease that infested the city. Only the prices had changed, thus far. It would be weeks before most merchants became bold enough to raise their prices extortionately, before their greed devoured their decency.

Mathias Thulmann walked the early morning streets with a heavy tread. Twice he nearly spilled himself into the gutter, his tired boots keeping poor purchase on the dew-slick cobblestones. After the battle in Wolfram Kohl's library, Thulmann had gathered the rest of Meisser's witch hunters, telling them what needed to be done. Little more than an hour later, the wizard's home had been reduced to a mound of smoking rubble. He wanted to believe that the Klausner book had been destroyed along with the wizard's other possessions, but a grim foreboding warned him against it.

Beside him strode the slender form of Silja Markoff, her stately gait impaired by the limp that betrayed the injury dealt by Sibbechai. Thulmann had tried to induce the woman to return to her father, to nurse her bruises, but she brushed away his concerns.

'Your ambition is showing,' Thulmann commented, as they turned the corner onto the thoroughfare that led to the Seven Candles inn. 'You needn't worry about any influence Meisser has with me. I can assure you that the fool has none.' A harsher quality entered the witch hunter's voice. 'I can also assure you that I am not easily manipulated.'

'Forgive me, Herr Thulmann,' said Silja. 'I am better acquainted with Captain Meisser and his creatures. I had assumed that all witch hunters were spineless cowards content to allow others to do their fighting. Unfortunately, that presumption is rather at odds with your own character. I have much pondering to do before I can make further assessment.'

'You speak candidly,' Thulmann said. 'But spend not too much time taking my measure. I am just a humble servant of Lord Sigmar, nothing more. And don't be too hard on your templars, many of them are good and honest men. If they seem less, the blame lies in their leadership.'

The witch hunter stumbled, his fatigue overcoming his balance. Silja grabbed his waist, steadying the tottering templar. Thulmann gave his companion a weak smile. Silja removed her grip as she found him steady once more.

'You need your rest, Brother Mathias,' she stated. 'You'll do no one any good if you are dead on your feet. And believe me, you *are* dead on your feet.' The witch hunter turned to face the young woman. Her remaining bodyguard, several steps behind them, also came to a halt, making no move to close the distance between himself and his charge.

'Two things, Lady Markoff,' Thulmann's silky voice snapped. 'First, there is much to be done and no one else to do it. The day will not last forever. Only an idiot would attempt what we need to do after the sun has set. Second, you should call me Mathias.

Saving my bruised hide from a vampire entitles you to at least that much. Leave "Brother Mathias" to simpering cretins like Meisser.'

'Very well, Mathias,' Silja replied. 'But tell me why you take so much responsibility onto your shoulders? Surely you are not so conceited as to believe yourself the only one in Wurtbad capable of that which needs to be done?' Thulmann shook his head.

'I've seen enough to know there's a brain inside that pretty noggin of yours, even if it doesn't have the good sense to keep out of a vampire's reach,' Thulmann told her. 'But you are not of the Order of Sigmar. You are an agent of the secular authority, not a representative of the temple. The only men trained to find the vampire's hiding place are the witch hunters, and they will not follow you. Besides, you are just as tired and bruised as I am.' He lifted his hand, forestalling Silja's protest. 'Don't let Meisser fool you, there are decent, intelligent men under his command. It is a cruel jest that they must be subordinate to such a scheming toad, but the gods will have their amusements.'

'If there are such men,' Silja insisted, 'then put one of them in charge.'

Thulmann sighed, shaking his head. 'Meisser will let me run things because I'm an outsider. Frankly, the swine is afraid of me. If I put one of his own in charge, Meisser will undermine him and take command himself.' His voice grew sombre. 'Four men will be buried today because of that parasite, another will probably be crippled for the rest of his days. I'd say Captain Meisser has already made a great enough contribution, would you not?'

Thulmann began to walk away. Silja hurried to keep pace. 'Last night, after the vampire escaped... ' She stared into her face. 'You wouldn't really have... '

'Killed him?' Thulmann let a humourless sound rumble from his throat. 'By Sigmar I wanted to. But that would have been purely selfish. It would have been on account of my hate, not justice for the men who died for his stupidity.'

'Different motives, but the same end,' said Silja.

'No,' he corrected her. 'The reason that a man acts is as important as the deed itself. Nobility of purpose may excuse the blackest deeds, hate and greed may foul the proudest accomplishments.' Thulmann smiled as he saw the sign of the Seven Candles inn at the end of the street.

'My rooms are here,' he told Silja. 'We'll gather up Streng and hurry back to the chapter house.'

'This man of yours has some skill in these matters?' Silja enquired.

'Perhaps not skill, but certainly experience,' Thulmann said. 'We have faced these monsters together. I can trust him to stand his ground. Not everyone has the courage to confront the undead, much less go searching in cemeteries for their hiding places. I want Streng with me.' He paused to consider his words. 'That is, if his hangover hasn't left him in a state even less fit than my own.'

'You make him sound very gallant,' Silja observed. Thulmann paused again, casting an appraising eye over Silja Markoff's figure.

'When you meet him,' he warned her, 'watch his hands.'

EVEN IF THE threat of plague did not hover over the dockyards, Carandini suspected the foul reek of the fishmonger's shop would have kept inquisitive souls at bay. The Tilean was, he had to admit, rather impressed by his undead associate's choice of hiding place. Vampires did not see the world the way living creatures did. Only in places where the aura of death was great did they find any degree of comfort. Graves and mausoleums were more 'real' to such beings than the cities and towns of the living. It was only among such surroundings that they could find even the shadow of comfort and ease.

And Sibbechai was cunning. The necrarch knew it might become the hunted rather than the hunter, and had prepared for that possibility. Certainly, a rundown fishmonger's hut was the last place Carandini would expect to find a dread lord of the night, sleeping away the daylight hours.

The necromancer slipped into the hut, a single-room hovel filled with debris and rubbish. He navigated his way twixt the heaps of fish bones, cracked masonry and splintered wood. When the business had failed, it seemed its neighbours had adopted the building as a dumping ground. Of course, thanks to the plague, there was no one left in the vicinity to continue the practice. At the back of the room, Carandini found the small trapdoor. In the past, he supposed, the little cellar had been used to smoke fish. Certainly the smell rising from below seemed to bear out his theory.

The vampire's coffin filled most of the small cellar, pushed close against one of the walls. It was locked from the inside, another precaution Sibbechai had adopted of late. Carandini was more than a little irritated by the monster's fear and distrust. That it was well founded only made the necromancer's annoyance greater.

Sibbechai had failed to secure *Das Buch die Unholden*, Carandini knew. The vampire had fled the wizard's house in haste, not triumph. If the book had been there, then the witch hunters had destroyed it. Carandini had considered confronting them, but common sense had prevailed. The necromancer had lingered outside long enough to see the witch hunters set fire to the place. He had also seen them remove a body that had all the appearance of a wizard. He wasn't sure if it was they or Sibbechai who killed the sorcerer, nor did he much care.

Carandini unfolded a large sheet of leathery skin, setting it down upon the dank cellar floor. From a pocket he produced a bottle of ink, with more than a little dead man's blood in its substance. He set the withered claw of the mummy Nehb-ka-Menthu upon the sheet, dipping each of its fingers in the ink. The necromancer looked at Sibbechai's coffin. If Wolfram Kohl had told the vampire anything before he died, the sorcerer would soon know it. The spirit of the dead wizard would tell him – as he would anything else that he had neglected to disclose to the vampire.

Knowledge was power, and Carandini had every intention of regaining the upper footing in his alliance with Sibbechai.

At least until he found a safe way to dispose of the vampire.

THULMANN HAD BEEN given one of the topmost rooms by the proprietor of the Seven Candles, the very best in the house. The innkeeper had not been entirely pleased by the witch hunter's return, but, with plague abroad, his rooms were already empty. At least custom could not suffer any further.

They found Streng sprawled upon a massive canopied bed. Thulmann was not unduly surprised. It was not the first time his underling had appropriated his master's lodgings to impress some buxom tavern wench. A few sharp words would serve to reprimand the thug, at least until the next time he became drunk enough to forget his place. Silja sensed his irritation.

'If there is a reason you've commandeered my room,' Thulmann snarled acidly, 'then I would hear it.' The sound of his employer's voice caused Streng to stir. As he disturbed the sheets drawn about

him, Thulmann could see the ex-soldier's side was covered in
bloodied bandages.

'It would seem your drunken carousing has caught up with you,'
the witch hunter snapped. Streng reached for the wine bottle on
the floor beside the bed. Angrily, Thulmann kicked the bottle,
sending it rolling across the room. 'You look as though you've
had more than sufficient,' he declared. 'I warned you that I'd have
need of you soon, and here I find you in a drunken stupor, broken up in some tavern brawl!'

'Have a care, Mathias!' Streng protested. 'You know it takes
longer to knock me off my feet than a few hours, even if they were
serving Bugman's best!' With a groan, the mercenary sat up,
blinking his eyes to clear his vision. He blinked again when he
spotted Silja Markoff just inside the doorway. 'Well, now I see why
you're so cross!' he grunted. 'And here I was thinking you were all
prayers and sermons! Nice eye, Mathias,' he added with a lewd
wink, bringing colour to Silja's face.

'Mind your tongue, you misbegotten mongrel.' Thulmann
ordered. 'And get that filthy carcass of yours moving, if you expect
to get paid. Sibbechai is already here in Wurtbad and we're going
to find his lair.'

'You maybe, but not me,' Streng grinned back. 'Doktor says I
should stay off my feet for a few days – maybe even a couple of
weeks.' The mercenary coughed dramatically. 'Much as I'd like to risk
my neck fighting that gruesome blood worm again.' Streng's face
pulled back into a proud and arrogant smile. 'Besides, I've already
had a run-in with some nastiness,' he boasted, pointing to the far
corner of the room. Thulmann's brow furrowed as he saw the
strange leather object lying where Streng indicated. Looking closer,
he found it to be a curious, bird-like mask, the bill of its beak stuffed
with a pomander that reeked of lilac. Beneath the mask was something even more interesting – a small, dark glass bottle. Thulmann
picked the bottle up carefully, sensing the fell energies gathered
about it. It was empty save for a crusty residue on its bottom and
sides. A sickly reek, like old vomit, rose from within.

'It wasn't a bar brawl,' Streng explained. 'I saw this sinister character creeping around the back alleys. I knew there was something
wrong about him so I followed to see what mischief he was up to.'
The mercenary had decided Thulmann didn't need to know the
particulars of the encounter.

'That looks like the masks worn by the plague doktors,' said Silja moving up to examine the garment.

'Plague doktor?' Thulmann asked.

'They're healers, or so they claim. They haunt the plague-ridden districts, offering to cure those who've contracted the Stir blight,' she elaborated. 'Charlatans mostly, preying upon the poor and the sick, taking what little they can offer in exchange for water potions and quack remedies. My father would have had them imprisoned but feels the public outcry would be too great. They may offer the sick false hope, but they are the only ones to offer them any kind of hope.'

'Hmmph,' grunted Streng. 'That's all well and good, lady, but the one that knifed me was more than some quack healer.' He looked over at Thulmann. 'He was a mutant. And if that bottle he was carrying don't stink of black magic, I'm a Solkanite monk!'

Thulmann stared at the dark bottle, relieved to release it from his grip and set it back on the floor. 'A mutant masquerading as a healer,' he reflected. 'Carrying a bottle of... ' he hesitated. What had been in the bottle, leaving behind it so hideous a taint? Poison? Something worse than poison?

Streng lurched forward on the bed, pain and fatigue forgotten for the moment. 'You're not thinking... '

'We lost track of Weichs in Wurtbad,' Thulmann said. 'There's no reason to believe he's moved on. If this is really what it appears to be, it stinks to the Chaos Wastes of Herr Doktor Freiherr Weichs.'

'Who is this Doktor Weichs?' asked Silja. Thulmann removed his cloak, bundling the noxious black bottle within its folds.

'I'll explain that to you on the way.' Thulmann pushed Silja toward the door. Behind them, Streng rolled to the side of the bed, reaching for his boots.

'Give me a few minutes Mathias, and I'll be with you,' the mercenary said. He looked around the room for where he had thrown his breeches.

'Go over to the chapter house and keep an eye on Meisser,' Thulmann told him. 'Don't worry, if I learn anything I'll send for you.' It was a promise the witch hunter intended to keep. As much as anyone, Streng deserved to be there when Weichs was finally brought to justice.

'Where are we going?' Silja demanded as Thulmann ushered her back down the main stairway of the Seven Candles.

'Where we may be able to learn more about these plague doktors of yours,' Thulmann told her. 'Something I've learned is that when you want to find out about a healer, you don't ask the healthy, you speak with the sick.' The witch hunter extended his arm for Silja to precede him. 'I am still something of a stranger to Wurtbad, Lady Markoff. If you would please lead the way.'

'But where am I leading you?' Silja asked again.

'To meet some of your plague victims. The hospice of Shallya. But if I am correct in my readings, then your city is beset by something more terrible than any plague.'

A WILD-EYED, half-human thing grinned from behind the bars of its iron cage. Sometimes it would laugh, other times it called out random words in a shrill, sing-song voice. Mostly it moaned and cried. Doktor Weichs took it as a sign, perhaps, that the man's senses had not completely deserted him when the skaven fell upon the wretch. An insane subject was of very limited value to Weichs, enabling him to study only the physical effects of his experiments. But he was as interested in the mind as in the body. The ideal subject was one whose mind was strong enough to accept what was happening to it and still manage to endure. Naturally, such men were rare.

The doktor's laboratory was a network of caves, old warrens that the skaven no longer used. Skilk had said something about a conflict between two local warlords that resulted in a decrease in the population beneath Wurtbad. As with everything else the skaven priest said, Weichs accepted the story as a half-truth. In any event, Skilk had given the abandoned warrens to his human confederate. The grey seer had propounded it was much safer for Weichs to labour down below, where none of his fellow men might accidentally stumble onto his work. Again, it was nothing more than a half-truth. Weichs was more convinced that Skilk wanted him where the skaven could closely monitor his experiments. For all their bestial appearance, he had to keep reminding himself that the mind of a skaven was as sharp as that of a man, and more devious and conniving than the most degenerate Tilean robber-prince.

The old warren was hundreds of yards in length, but narrow, with a low ceiling that sagged in places to within six feet of the floor. Crude wooden pilings had been erected in places to support the weakened roof, while in some corners the cavern had been allowed to collapse, a jumble of broken stone and shattered earth. Dozens of small tunnels opened onto the warren.

In his exposure to them, Weichs had learned that perhaps the only sensation that ruled the skaven more than hunger was fear. The vermin were loth to linger in any place that was without at least half-a-dozen boltholes and escape routes. Many of the tunnels led into dead ends or hideously ingenious traps, others twisted and turned until the traveller found himself back where he had started. But the majority connected back to the main network that burrowed beneath Wurtbad. Weichs had navigated only a few of these, and there were only two or three he could follow without becoming hopelessly lost. It was yet another tactic by which Skilk kept him isolated and under his control.

A large number of the openings in the walls were shallow, only a few feet deep at most. These had been the individual dens where the skaven had made their nests. Now they served Weichs as cells in which to contain his subjects, each blocked by a framework of wooden bars. Flickering torches were set in sconces before each of the cells, their inmates visible at all times. Weichs doubted any of the wretched creatures would possess either the strength or drive to attempt an escape, given the mixture of debilitating herbs and meagre rations he provided them with. But he didn't believe in taking undue chances.

The central section of the cave was dominated by a maze of wooden tables, upon which were assembled every piece of alchemical apparatus Weichs had been able to describe for his skaven assistants. The skaven had displayed fiendish cleverness, covering their thefts by setting fire to the workshops of their victims. Alchemists were forever dabbling with materials of a dangerous nature, so no one was truly surprised when their homes suddenly burst into flame in the dead of night. A quiet chill crawled down Weichs's spine when he considered how many other 'accidents' were actually the fruit of mankind's ancient rivals.

Weichs strode past the bubbling alembics, the smoking clay vessels arranged about the brick athenor that the skaven had dragged down stone-by-stone from the surface. One of his less intelligent human assistants was engaged in working the bellows that supplied heat to the brick furnace. Weichs paused to assure himself the man was not too enthusiastic in his labours. Too much heat might spoil the mixtures slowly boiling away in the clay bottles.

The plague doktor paused at intervals to inspect the glass pelicans whose narrow beaks fed into one another, refining and distilling the substances boiling within them. A grizzled skaven snout leered at him from above the heavy iron press. Small green-black stones were placed beneath the press and ground by the ratman into fine black powder.

Such a small thing, yet the warpstone dust formed the very life-blood of his experiments. It could be combined with other substances, the mixtures refined until their disparate parts became a single whole. Given the right combination and conditions, the noxious properties of the warpstone could be controlled. Negated. Reversed. Or so Weichs was convinced. The ancient alchemists and warlocks had experimented with what they had called wyrdstone, and written much about its curative abilities. But they had guarded their secrets too well, neglecting to pass on the vital knowledge of how they conquered the corrupting influence of the stones.

Weichs turned, feeling eyes upon him. A leprous visage quickly shuffled back into the darkness of its cell, a shapeless tendril that might once have been an arm covering what could only mockingly be called a face. The doktor shook his head solemnly. The combination he had used on that woman had not worked, the mutating effects of the warpstone had not been conquered. She was degenerating more each day, like a worm shrivelling under the hot summer sun. Still, even her dissolution might teach him something. There was always something to learn, if one but had the wisdom to observe.

His theory was sound, no power on earth would convince Weichs otherwise. If an Arabyan fakir could render himself immune to the poison of an asp by controlled exposure to the same poison, then why could not men be made immune to a much greater poison by similar means? The power that men called 'Chaos' was not some daemonic malevolence, as superstitious idiots continued to preach, but a natural force which man had not yet been able to adapt to. Were the high mountains evil because their snows caused frostbite, or the deserts evil because their sun burned the skin? Men had simply been forced to adapt, to cover their feet in fur boots or their bodies in silken robes. And

men would learn to adapt to the mutating force of Chaos, to protect their bodies from its power just as they had from the frost and
the sun.

Weichs drew near the ironbound table upon which his newest
subject lay strapped. The old man's pinched face twisted into a
scowl of disapproval. He'd expected the conniving raconteur to be
made of sterner stuff, but the wretch hadn't even been able to
withstand the shock of abduction by the skaven. After a minor
application of a warpdust ointment to his skin, the baker's wits
had deserted him entirely. Weichs stared at the lustreless eyes that
gazed blindly at the roof of the cavern, listened as infantile mut-
terings dribbled from his mouth. The plague doktor uttered a
black curse and turned away.

What good would it serve if he at last unlocked the secret he
sought, found a way to render men immune to mutation, if the
cure left them drooling idiots. Weichs snapped his fingers. Lobo
leapt up from the small wicker chair in which he had been resting. The misshapen halfling scurried forward at his master's
summons, changing direction as Weichs stabbed a finger at the
cabinet that housed his equipment. Lobo hurried, swiftly removing a crystal decanter and a glass.

Weichs took the halfling's burden silently, charging his glass
from the decanter. Estalian brandy, looted from the cellars of a
baronet in Ostland, was one of the few vices the doktor allowed
himself. The rich liquor helped him to think, to ease his anxieties
and doubts. Idly, he wondered if he might not relocate to the arid
hill country of Estalia one day and thereby ensure a plentiful supply of the spirit.

A foul smell disturbed Weichs's repose. The plague doktor
looked up, noting with dismay the quivering, cringing shapes of
his skaven assistants. The ratmen were cowering behind their
apparatus, rodent faces hidden behind glass tubing and lead vessels. The foul smell had come from them, an instinctive
by-product of the fear that gnawed at their greasy hearts. Weichs
suspected there were many things that could cause the skaven to
vent their glands of noxious musk, for they were a slinking, skulking people, but he knew of only one such thing that would visit
his workshop.

A trio of skaven stalked through the maze of cages, tables and
alchemical machinery. Two of them, the largest skaven Weichs

had yet seen, muscles rippling beneath their sleek black fur, wore crude armour about their bodies, the metal plates pitted by rust, and on their backs they wore coarse black cloaks. A saw-edged sword hung from a rope tied about each of their waists, the steel so rotten with filth that Weichs suspected any man struck by it would die from infection long before he expired from his wounds.

Between the two black-furred killers strode a third skaven. The ratman hobbled forward on a gnarled staff, the crown of which was tipped by an ugly triangular iron icon representing the loathsome god of the ratmen. The ratman's frame was crook-backed, crushed by the weight of age. A black robe clothed its body and about its neck was a vibrant collar crafted from scraps of multi-coloured fur. Weichs knew the morbid story behind that garment – each scrap was a trophy, torn from the throat of a rival or enemy. The skaven's fur was grey speckled with black, fading into pure black upon his paws, as though the ratman wore fur gloves.

Grey Seer Skilk lifted his face, whiskers twitching as he inhaled the pungent odours of the workshop. Weichs felt a tremor of fear stab through him, thankful he did not have any musk glands to vent. The skaven were unsettling enough, but the grey seer was even more grotesque. Great horns erupted from the sides of his head, two curling tusks that framed the sides of his skull like that of a ram. Weichs had understood the skaven to be free from the more extreme forms of mutation – a remarkable thing for creatures exposed to raw warpstone on an almost continual basis – yet the first time he had laid eyes upon Skilk he had been forced to reconsider his belief.

The sorcerer-prophet halted only a few feet from Weichs, the bleary red eyes glaring at the human physician. 'Not rest!' Skilk's thin voice hissed. 'Work-work! Find-learn, yes?' The grey seer's nose twitched again, at the decanter still gripped in Weichs's hand. The doktor smiled weakly, arresting the motion before he accidentally displayed any teeth – a gesture the skaven used among themselves as a sign of aggression.

'Estalian brandy, grey seer,' Weichs explained. 'Perhaps you might forgive a man his humble vices?' Skilk bobbed his head up and down, the closest the creature ever came to displaying excitement. Weichs realised woefully that, before much longer, the ratman would deplete his dwindling reserves. Sighing regretfully,

Weichs proffered the decanter. The grey seer did not bother to take the glass offered with it, thrusting his pale pink tongue down the neck of the bottle like a fleshy cork. Wriggling his tongue, Skilk let the fiery liquor trickle down his throat. When a quarter of the bottle had been drained, Skilk withdrew, handing it back to Weichs. The doktor fought to keep the disgust from his face. 'No, I want you to have it, grey seer. Take it with you back to your burrow.' Skilk stared at Weichs, suspicion glowing in his eyes, but then made the sharp chittering that passed for laughter among his kind. Weichs wasn't stupid enough to try to poison Skilk.

'Progress?' Skilk hissed as he handed the decanter to a body-guard. 'Make-find potion to cure-heal?' The grey seer looked pointedly to a huge iron cage at one end of the workshop. Its inmate was a huge, malformed thing. It could have passed for a troll. No one would imagine it had been a cooper only a few weeks before. It was the most glaring of Weichs's failures.

'Not yet, grey seer,' Weichs admitted. 'Great discoveries are not made overnight. There is progress, but we must not expect miracles.' Skilk's eyes narrowed as it digested the words. Weichs understood the skaven were just as eager to harness the healing properties of warp-stone as he was, to eliminate disease and infirmity among their kind. A part of him shuddered to consider the horror of a skaven race not regularly culled by pestilence and plague. Even if he succeeded in his experiments, he might be eliminating one threat to mankind only to replace it with an even more terrible one.

'Time,' Skilk snarled. 'Always doktor-man want-take time!' The skaven bared his teeth, his naked tail lashing against the earthen floor. 'Skilk tired-sick, doktor-man. Progress. Now-soon.'

'I'll need more warpstone,' Weichs retorted as the grey seer turned to leave. 'More test subjects, better than those with which your people have been providing me.' Skilk continued to shuffle toward the tunnels, his bodyguards following behind him.

'Doktor-man get all-much need-want,' Skilk asserted. 'Take-fetch more man-people, take-fetch all man-people. Progress, doktor-man. Now-soon, Skilk need-want progress.'

Skilk's threat lingered long after the skaven priest's departure, like a black cloud filling the cavern. The skaven's demands were increasingly persistent and impatient. Weichs suffered no illusions as to what his fate would be when the grey seer's equanimity reached its fragile limits.

Shuddering, he lifted the glass of Estalian brandy and downed its contents in one quick swallow. Somehow, the expensive spirit was less satisfying than it had been only moments ago.

THE FAT FORM on the bed stretched his arms, a deep, throaty laugh rumbling from his immense frame as he felt strength and vigour flowing through his limbs. Only last night he was so weak that he'd been reduced to allowing a servant to feed him. Now he felt rejuvenated, restored.

He wrinkled his nose at the pungent reek of the salve that the wizard had smeared over his body. Vile muck, but it had done the trick. He'd been too tired and weak to protest the wizard's methods in the small hours of the morning; now he was jubilant that he had not. There was no denying that Furchtegott knew his business. Baron von Gotz swung his head around, smiling broadly as he met the gaze of his court wizard.

'By Sigmar, Taal and Manann, you've done it!' the baron roared. 'I can feel the health thundering through my veins!' He turned his eyes to the ashen faces of his doktors. The three men looked at the floor, the ceiling, anywhere that did not force them to meet that stern gaze. 'Hex-mongers! Take your damn leeches and get the hell out of my city!' The physicians quivered in their boots, turning their hats in their hands. Furchtegott felt triumph surge through him. These men had tried to humiliate him, now it was they who were feeling the sting of scorn.

'But your excellency,' Doktor Kleist spoke, his tone timid. 'The city is under quarantine. We cannot leave.'

'Then rot in the dungeons with the other traitorous vermin!' the fat baron snarled. 'You'd have had me weak as a kitten and dead within a fortnight! Science! Doktors! Bah!' The baron waved his bloated hand, motioning for the guards scattered about his chamber to lead the physicians away and for one of them to come near.

'Lord Markoff is waiting in the other room,' von Gotz said. 'Tell him I would see him now.' The baron waved the soldier away, turning his attention back to Furchtegott.

'You are a wizard's wizard,' the baron chortled. 'A wizard among wizards! I am going to have you knighted. No, a lordship! You deserve it more than half of those simpering maggots at court!'

'That is very kind, excellency,' Furchtegott replied. The wizard's earlier sense of victory was beginning to fade. He didn't like the look in the baron's eyes. They were bleary, unfocused. The boils had not receded, still visible beneath the layer of reeking salve the wizard administered a few hours earlier. There was no denying that the baron seemed healthier, but he certainly looked no better. Furchtegott decided he'd better consult *Das Buch die Unholden* as soon as he was able to detach himself.

The door to the baron's chamber opened once more, admitting the wizened figure of Wurtbad's Lord High Justice, Igor Markoff. The magistrate wore his crimson robes of state, the golden griffin of the Ministry of Justice displayed proudly upon his breast. Markoff bowed his head respectfully to his sovereign.

'I understand that you are feeling better, excellency,' Markoff said. There was doubt in the magistrate's voice. He could see the sickness marking the baron's exposed chest and arms, smell the disgusting stench wafting from his body. These were not the traits of good health.

'Quite well, Igor,' von Gotz replied with a smile. He waved a hand to a trembling servant boy. The youth stepped forward, retreating as soon as the baron had removed the silver platter from his hands. Von Gotz tore into the roast squab with savage gusto, wiping grease from his jowls as he paused to continue his conversation. 'You can help me to feel even better,' the baron said.

'Whatever I can do to serve,' responded Markoff. Von Gotz chuckled as he heard the servile reply, but then grew serious, peering into Markoff's eyes.

'You will clear out one of the keeps. The one on Muellerstrasse would probably serve best,' he pronounced. 'Clear it out and then gather up every one of these plague stricken dregs you can find. Herd them there and keep them there.' The baron smiled even as Furchtegott and Markoff opened their mouths in horror. 'We'll lock this sickness under one roof, contain it there. That's how we'll best this plague. There'll be no one left loose to spread it.'

It made a brutal kind of sense, but the barbaric cruelty of the baron's plan stunned the sensibilities of those who heard him speak.

'And you will do one more thing,' he declared. 'There is a brothel with a tavern's name, the Hound and Hare. You will round up everyone there and remove them to the Muellerstrasse keep. Then you will burn the brothel to the ground.' Von Gotz ground his teeth together as he imagined his revenge against the place that nearly killed him. 'I don't want two pieces of wood left nailed together or a single brick left intact.' He waved his hand, dismissing the Lord High Justice.

Furchtegott glanced nervously at the bloated figure of his patron. 'Excellency, I must be retiring also.' Von Gotz nodded.

'Yes, by all means.' he laughed. 'You've had a very busy morning and no doubt need your rest.' Von Gotz waved again, dismissing his wizard. He watched as the golden robed mystic hastily withdrew through the door, hurrying back to his tower to begin his next sorcerous enterprise. As well he should, for the wizard would not find the gratitude of Baron Friedo von Gotz either lacking or transitory.

Von Gotz's smile faded as the buzzing of a fly disturbed his thoughts. The baron looked askance, watching with revulsion as the insect crawled across his shoulder. Drawn from its pesthole by the pungent smell of Furchtegott's salve, the baron decided. His fat hand slapped against his shoulder with a sharp crack. Von Gotz stared at the smeared ruin of the fly staining his palm.

Looking aside to ensure that his servants were not watching, the baron lifted his hand to his face and licked the remains of the fly from his polluted skin.

THE TEMPLE OF the Lonely Sacrament had existed since the earliest days of Wurtbad, founded by pilgrim priestesses from the great temple in Couronne. The structure was long and low, filling a broad expanse of Wurtbad's old city district with its surrounding groves and gardens. Its outer façade was largely devoid of ornamentation, only the marble doves that topped the buttresses supporting the temple walls proclaimed the deity that was worshipped within. It was not the way of those who followed Shallya, goddess of healing and mercy, to announce their faith with garish displays and raised voices. Like the dove that was their emblem, they were quiet and content, secure in their faith. Those who had need of the goddess would find their way to her temples without expensive statues and cyclopean architecture.

There were many in Wurtbad who had need of the goddess now. The Stir blight had ravaged entire districts, devouring entire households. The secular doktors and healers had thrown up their hands in frustration, unable to combat the sinister malady. Most now refused to even try, fearful that they themselves might fall prey to the pestilence. For those who had been abandoned to the plague, there was only one place to turn to, one place that would not turn them away.

The halls of the temple were now filled with the sick. Wretched bodies had been crammed into every available space. An air of misery and disease hung about its interior, an aura of hopelessness utterly at odds with the white walls and alabaster floors. In times of plague, even the grace of a goddess was taxed to its limit.

Mathias Thulmann made his way through the crowded halls, keeping his eyes fixed upon the corridor itself, blind to the sorry figures, deaf to the moans and cries that echoed through the temple. He was no healer. There was nothing he could do to help these people. He was a warrior, for that was his calling. If he could make a stand with sword and courage, he would never abandon an innocent soul. But against something as nebulous and spectral as a plague the witch hunter felt the sting of his helplessness.

Silja Markoff and her bodyguard followed him. Thulmann was impressed by the woman's courage in following him to this place of disease and death. He knew it must be even worse for her to prowl these halls of misery. To him, these were pitiable unfortunates. To her, they were her people.

The high priestess of the temple was conducting services in the main chapel, a simple ceremony culminating in the release of a white dove from a small cage. The bird fluttered upwards, vanishing through the open window at the top of the chapel's lofty ceiling. With the ritual completed, the other sisters departed to continue their ministrations to the sick. Sister Josepha nodded solemnly to the templar and his companions.

'Your faith in the protection of Lord Sigmar does you credit,' Sister Josepha told Thulmann, her old face suggesting an owl as she peered from under her white hood. 'Or else your need is great. I was told there were questions you would ask of my supplicants.' A hardness entered the woman's eyes. 'I should warn you that I will not have these people abused any further than they have been already, not even by one of Sigmar's witch hunters. These people have begged the mercy of Shallya and such protection as her temple can provide.'

'Then how do we proceed, sister?' Thulmann asked. Sister Josepha smiled back at him.

'Your Captain Meisser would have made demands, you ask questions,' she said. 'That impresses me perhaps more than it should, but I am all too familiar with demands of late. The aristocrats demand that we turn away the poor; the nobles demand that we turn away those with the plague. Everyone seems to want the blessing of the goddess, but no one wants to share that blessing with those who need it most.' The priestess grew thoughtful for a moment, then looked back at Thulmann. 'How do we proceed?' she repeated. 'I shall hear these questions you would ask. Then I shall decide if others can hear them.'

Thulmann removed the garish leather mask he had been carrying in a linen sack. He held the bird-like mask upward so that Sister Josepha might see it better. The priestess nodded her head sadly.

'So, these plague doktors have finally come to the attention of the Order of Sigmar,' she mused. 'I hoped that they would. I have heard much about them, and little of it good. They are like vultures, preying on the dying, feeding off their desperate need for hope. Shallya venerates all life, but I must confess to believing men like that have no right to live.'

Thulmann nodded in sympathy, understanding well how she must feel.

Suddenly, a great commotion sounded from the entrance of the temple. Thulmann could hear harsh voices barking orders above the cries and shrieks of the sick. Sister Josepha hurried to find the source of the disturbance, her recent guests following after her. Soon, they found themselves fighting their way through a press of panicked, fleeing bodies.

The source of the disturbance was a body of soldiers dressed in the livery of the Ministry of Justice, supported by an even greater body of troops wearing the green uniform of the city guard. The soldiers were brutally herding every person they could out of the temple. Thulmann could see a large number of wagons strewn across the gardens into which the soldiers were loading the sick.

'What is the meaning of this outrage?' demanded Sister Josepha to a soldier wearing the bronze pectoral insignia of a captain. The officer forced himself to meet her withering gaze.

'Order of the Lord High Justice,' he said, pulling a sheet of parchment from his belt. 'All those who have been infected by the Stir blight are to be taken to Otwin Keep. Those orders encompass all those within the temple.' The high priestess staggered back, shaken by this violation of her temple's sanctity. Mathias Thulmann stalked forward.

'Surely those orders do not include the sisters?' It was not a question but a challenge. Before the captain could respond to Thulmann's words, they were answered by Sister Josepha.

'We will go with them,' the old priestess stated. 'These people are supplicants of the Temple. If they are not allowed to remain here, then what grace and solace the temple can provide shall go with them.' The captain nodded reluctantly, shouting an order to his men to allow the sisters to board any wagon that still had room. For a moment, Thulmann could see deep self-loathing in the captain. A man bound by oath and duty to execute orders he found contemptible.

'I can assure you that my father will hear of this,' Silja snarled, demanding the captain's attention for the first time. The officer's face turned ashen as he saw her.

'Begging your pardon, ladyship, but these orders *are* from Lord Markoff,' the captain repeated.

'Then you may be doubly certain that he will hear of this,' Silja hissed, pushing her way past, daring any of his soldiers to even think of stopping her.

Thulmann followed after her. There were a great many matters unfolding in Wurtbad that he was uncertain about, but one of which he was as sure as the Ulricsberg.

He was glad that Silja Markoff was on his side.

CHAPTER SIX

THE WITCH HUNTER stormed through the doorway of the Wurtbad chapter house like a thing possessed. The hideous cruelty he had witnessed at the Temple of Shallya gnawed at his brain, worrying at his thoughts like a dog chewing on an old bone. Mingled with feelings of frustration, anger and impotence was another emotion that disgusted him more. A deep and profound guilt.

Ruthless, merciless as the baron's edict had been, Thulmann understood it. It was as if a battlefield chirurgeon were cutting away an infected arm from a wounded man, killing the part to save the whole. Baron von Gotz had decided to sacrifice those already infected by the plague in an attempt to save those who were not. There was no question that relocation to the chill darkness of Otwin Keep was anything but a death sentence, but, the colder, more pragmatic part of Thulmann's mind told him the sick supplicants of the Temple were as good as dead already. But still, the decision to brush aside the lives of so many people who did nothing to warrant their destruction was one Thulmann believed he could never make. He secretly hoped there would have been enough humanity left in him to reject such a course of action.

Thulmann canvassed the entry hall of the chapter house. All at
once his distemper found something other than his guilt to direct
itself toward. A dozen men dressed in black were standing about
the hall, armed for battle. They cast surly looks at the pale figure
slumped in a chair near the door. This bearded warrior held a
loaded crossbow across his lap, beads of sweat dripping from his
forehead. Streng turned his head as Thulmann entered, nodding
weakly at his employer.

'By all the daemons!' Thulmann snarled. 'What is going on
here? Why aren't you looking for the vampire's grave?' His eyes
burned into the face of every witch hunter, causing some to look
away with shame burning on their cheeks. 'One of you shall
answer me!' he demanded.

'Unless someone has appointed you witch hunter captain of
Wurtbad,' a voice snarled back, 'then I don't believe you have any
right to abuse my men.' Thulmann turned his head to see Meisser
stalking forward. A bandolier of pistols now crossed the templar's
chest. Meisser had changed his apparel, adopting a uniform as
dark and nondescript as that of his men save for the pectoral
medal that hung from a chain about his neck, a twin-tailed comet
engraved upon it.

'You are a guest here, Brother Mathias,' Meisser went on. 'I suggest you start behaving like one.'

Thulmann gritted his teeth. He should have expected something like this. He'd made it clear to Meisser the previous night
that he wasn't going to help him in his power struggle with the
Ministry of Justice, told him in no uncertain terms he considered
him a dangerous incompetent and a disgrace to the holy name of
Sigmar. True, he'd lost control of himself following the fight with
Sibbechai, assaulting and abusing Meisser in front of his own
men. That was the kind of mistake that could make the scheming
witch hunter captain show his teeth – an assault on his distorted
ego. Thulmann had compounded his mistake by giving Meisser
time to brood over his injured pride, to allow the reptile to muster
the vitriolic venom that substituted for courage in his character.

'Why are these men not looking for Sibbechai?' Thulmann
growled through his clenched teeth. Meisser set his good hand on
his hip and snorted a contemptuous laugh

'Why should they?' he replied, defensive. 'It is not our task. The
Order of Sigmar is concerned with protecting the lives and souls

of the Empire's citizens. When a citizen has been corrupted by dabbling in proscribed magic or communion with profane deities, it is also our duty to seek them out and make them repent their crimes.' A smile spread across Meisser's swinish face. 'Sigmar is the benevolent god of our glorious Empire, watching over every living subject that walks our land. This creature, this vampire, is one of the restless dead. Therefore it is not our problem. Sigmar is a god of the living. Morr is the god of the dead. I have informed the temple of Morr about this creature and they are thus compelled to investigate the matter. It is their jurisdiction, after all.'

'*Scum.*' Thulmann spat. 'You filthy, conniving vermin. You cower behind words twisted beyond their meaning, like some snail slinking behind its shell! It is the duty of any servant of Sigmar to combat every menace to his Empire and his people, whatever form or shape it might take. How have you the gall to say the vampire is not our concern?'

Meisser retreated from the violence of Thulmann's outburst, until there was half a room between them. 'You must not try to involve the entire order in this personal vendetta of yours,' Meisser declared. 'The Raven Decree of 2345 made the clear distinction that the temple of Morr is to handle such matters.'

Thulmann shook his head in disbelief. How long had the filthy maggot burrowed through his books to dig up that piece of history? 'The Raven Decree states that no templar is to violate the sanctity of any field of Morr without first notifying his priesthood,' the witch hunter snarled. 'It was never intended to place the responsibility for hunting and destroying the undead under the sole authority of the priests of Morr.'

'Be that as it may,' Meisser said, not wanting to continue an argument he could not win, 'the priests of Morr are looking for your vampire now. This chapter house has more pressing matters with which to concern itself.'

A sharp stab of suspicion cut its way through Thulmann's anger. What was the purpose of Meisser's game? Clearly he had lost all taste for riding Thulmann's coattails after he beheld the grotesque monster that the templar was hunting, but what scheme had he put in its place? Thulmann found himself wishing that Silja had accompanied him back to the chapter house. With her knowledge of Wurtbad's politics, she would surely recognise what Meisser was plotting.

Meisser smiled again, mistaking silence for a submissive retreat. 'We are to help the baron's men clear out the ghetto. Round up every plague-stricken dreg and send them to Otwin Keep,' he added with a touch of pride. 'That is, if you will tell your man to stand down and let us get about our work.'

Streng looked up at Thulmann. 'I don't have your way with words,' the thug grunted. 'Had to find a way to keep them here until you showed yourself.' The witch hunter relieved his hench-man of his crossbow. Meisser's smile broadened, but it died when Thulmann swung the crossbow in his direction.

'I've had a taste of the baron's edict, captain,' he said. 'The Order of Sigmar will smell better for staying clear of it. I'd expect a true officer to recognise that fact.' Thulmann directed his words at Meisser, but his gaze swept the faces of the other witch hunters. He'd read the situation correctly – none of them had any taste for Baron von Gotz's draconian command. Now he'd give them an alternative. 'I believe last night's ordeal has taxed you greatly, captain, and under such strain and fatigue you are not yourself. Since that is the case, I must temporarily assume your duties as my own.'

'Khaine's blood, you will!' cursed Meisser, his face livid. The witch hunter captain reached for one of the pistols hanging from his chest. The other Wurtbad templars sprang into motion, pistols and hand crossbows appearing from beneath cloaks or inside leather holsters. None of them was pointed at Mathias Thul-mann. Face twisted into a scowl, Meisser let his hand fall away from his weapon.

'It seems I already have,' Thulmann pronounced, looking across the room at the men who pointed weapons at their former com-mander.

'Traitors! Heretics!' Meisser roared.

'Brother Mathias is right, captain,' a white-headed witch hunter named Tuomas stated. 'You are not yourself. You need a reprieve from the burden of command.' The consoling words did nothing to soothe Meisser's ire.

'You are all apostates!' he snarled. 'Sigmar's grace has deserted Wurtbad, Chaos walks the land and we are all damned to the Pit.' Meisser spun about on his heel, stalking back to his study.

'He took that rather well.' Streng grinned weakly as he watched him leave.

Thulmann paid no attention to his underling. He had read the feelings of the men correctly – pious, zealous men who chafed under the leadership of an inept scoundrel like Meisser, who had been ready to abandon ship as soon as an alternative presented itself. Thulmann gave the witch hunters their orders. Enough time had already been wasted, Sibbechai's lair had to be found before darkness descended upon Wurtbad once more.

But there was another concern just as pivotal. Six of the witch hunters would coordinate with the priests of Morr and help them in the hunt for Sibbechai, but he needed the other half-dozen for something perhaps even more important for the city. The second group were to enter the ghetto, not to aid the baron's soldiers but to look for any sign of the plague doktors, and to capture one if at all possible. If what he suspected about them was correct, what he asked of the second group might prove no less dangerous than the vampire hunt.

One last task had been saved for himself. The bottle Streng found would have to be examined. Thulmann had a grim premonition that he already knew what he would learn from it.

WITHIN THE CONFINES of his study, Witch Hunter Captain Meisser sat and brooded. His authority had been usurped, as good as stripped from him. He'd been a fool to think he'd be able to use someone like Thulmann. He'd seen his kind before, self-righteous lunatics so certain in their own beliefs that they hurl aside all worldly concerns. What did such men know of the balance of power? What did they understand of the constant struggle to maintain the authority of the Temple in the face of secular greed and manipulation?

Apostates and fanatics. The late lord protector had seen his worth, known the value of his appreciation for politics. Of course, there were ugly rumours circulating about Lord Gamow now, rumours of heresy and worse. The witch hunter rose from his seat and nervously poured himself a glass of wine. He almost jumped out of his skin when he turned around and saw a messenger boy standing in the doorway.

'How did you get in here?' Meisser demanded.

'The man in the red shirt was giving orders to everybody,' the boy explained. 'Nobody paid any attention to me.' He stepped toward Meisser, extending the letter he carried. The captain took it cautiously, as though it were a live serpent rather than a sheet of parchment. The wax seal upon the letter stared back at him.

Meisser broke the seal and hastily read the letter's contents. A smile spread its way across his features as he quickly finished the last of his wine. A summons. From Baron von Gotz himself. Requested by name, in fact.

'Play your games, Thulmann,' Meisser thought. 'You will find I'm much better at them than you are.'

'WE CAN'T LET the vermin live.' The murderous words were spoken in the softest whisper, yet sounded loud as thunder in Gregor's ears. His hearing had been improving, to such a degree that every moment was a tiny piece of suffering, like a hot knife stabbed into his brain. He could hear everything. The rustle of grass as he stepped upon it, the click of termite legs as they burrowed through the walls. He could hear the steady pulse of the men's hearts. He could hear the blood as it pounded through their veins.

They were smugglers, these men. Gregor had found the city of Wurtbad under quarantine, surrounded by a ring of soldiers with orders to let no one in and no one out. But the eyes of mortal men are weak in the night. Gregor's eyes were no longer those of a man. He had seen the bright red glow of the warmth exuded by the smugglers as they prepared to break the cordon. They were skilled villains, old hands at deceiving the servants of the law and the elector count, and this was not their first excursion into the forbidden city. But Gregor was something less than a man now. He had become a very part of the darkness itself, in a way even the blackest outlaw would never be. He'd confronted them as they prepared to scuttle along the old drainage ditch that would conceal them for the first leg of their journey.

Skorzeney, the half-Kislevite who led the small group had been alarmed, naturally, but shrewd enough to know that a fight was the last thing he could afford. The soldiers of the elector count were everywhere and the sound of conflict would be sure to bring them running. He had smiled, a cunning, faithless smile, and agreed to Gregor's compromise, his demand to be taken into the city. Shrewd to the last, Skorzeney had handed Gregor some of the grain sacks he and his men were smuggling into Wurtbad. The ditch would not conceal horses or mules, the only goods the smugglers could carry was what they themselves bore. Skorzeney was happy to put his unexpected and unwanted visitor to work.

Gregor had expected the men to turn on him. In truth, they could do nothing less. The money he had promised to pay them was a lie, and the peasant rags he wore betrayed that fact. But more importantly, Gregor would now know the smuggler's secret route into the city. He could betray it to the authorities. Worse still, he could go into the smuggling business for himself. Skorzeney had the look of a killer about him. Perhaps he would decide to murder Gregor even without good reason.

Gregor stood in the shadow of the old tannery the smugglers had converted into a storehouse. He had to acknowledge that the men knew their business – crawling along ditches and culverts, a sack of grain lashed to each man's back, until they reached a small storm drain set in Wurtbad's outer wall, a metal grill far less sound than it appeared. The tannery stood only a few blocks from the wall, the tall tower of the horse trader's guild obscuring all view of the tannery from the nearest gatehouse.

'A quick stab, just under the ribs,' Skorzeney was telling one of his subordinates. 'Something a bit extra for the butcher. Won't be too long before even long pig becomes a delicacy around here.'

The other smuggler laughed nervously, then turned, regarding the spot where Gregor leaned against the wall. He approached the stranger, trying to maintain an air of casual ease.

'Come along, old beggar,' the smuggler said. 'You can help me sort the goods we just brought in. Get it ready for distribution. Boss says that's part of the deal too.'

He was a man who had killed before with no taint of remorse or regret. The same look of casual indifference was on his face now. But Gregor could hear the quickening of his pulse, the soft slither of steel against leather as he drew his dagger from its sheath. Before the smuggler could even blink, Gregor's cold hand grabbed his, twisting it upward and snapping his wrist. The smuggler fell, screaming in agony and horror, scurrying away from him.

'You'll not find me so easy to murder,' Gregor stated in an almost aloof tone. He still leaned against the wall. Except for the broken, screaming thief crawling away from him, he might never have moved at all. The half-dozen other smugglers drew swords, but their show of force was half-hearted. Skorzeney took a step forward. Gregor could see the thoughts behind the man's cold, vicious eyes. If he let Gregor go, his gang would break apart, his men no longer respecting and fearing their leader. Fear was pounding in his veins, just as it was in those of his men, but he could not allow it to rule him.

'A fair trick,' Skorzeney conceded. 'A little elf in you, perhaps?' He feigned a thoughtful look, then spoke once more. 'I was rash in my decision. You're more than you appear, friend. I might be able to use a man like you.'

Gregor stepped away from the wall. 'No, *friend*, I've business in this city that presses upon me. Step aside and pray our paths cross no more.' Indecision flickered on Skorzeney's face, then passed as he noted his adversary's unarmed state.

'I can't allow that. You've seen too much,' Skorzeney said. 'And I don't think you'll be able to repeat that little trick against a proper sword.'

There was no further warning. The smuggler sprang forward, slashing at Gregor's belly. Too fast for the eye to see, Gregor dodged aside, the smuggler's sword cutting only through air. Disbelieving, Skorzeney attacked again, chopping at Gregor's neck. This time, his enemy did not leap aside. Cold hands caught the flashing blade in a grip of steel. Skorzeney's eyes were wide with horror as he heard his sword snap under the pressure of Gregor's unnatural strength. The look was frozen on his features as Gregor drove the broken tip of the blade into Skorzeney's throat.

He staggered away as Skorzeney fell. Stared at his hands in shock, horrified by the inhuman power they held. He'd seen only one creature with such strength, the power to break steel with its bare hands. How much longer, Gregor wondered, before he became what Sibbechai was? He looked back on the man he had killed, as the bright, glowing crimson drained from his body, beckoning to him with its promise of warmth and life.

The young man fell upon his hands and knees beside the body, his face inching toward the filthy floor of the alley. Gregor stopped himself, self-disgust and revulsion beating down the obscene compulsion. Like a human crab, Gregor scurried backwards from the expanding pool of blood. He looked into the dying face of Skorzeney and groaned in horror. As life fled the body it was becoming more distinct, clearer to Gregor's twisted sight. It was as if a veil had been pulled away, exposing that which lay beneath. The body became more real to Gregor in death than it had been in life.

The other smugglers had fled into the night as soon as their leader had fallen. Yet even as they hurried through blackened streets and dark alleyways, they could hear the long, anguished, inhuman howl from outside the tannery. It was the cry of the lost and the damned.

THE SUN HAD barely disappeared beneath the horizon when a chill imposed itself on the small cellar. A coldness that had nothing to do with the onset of night. A shadow rose from the heavy wooden casket. Another shadow greeted it, detaching itself from the gloom gathered about the walls.

'Good evening, mighty necrarch lord,' the sardonic voice of the necromancer broke the silence of the improvised crypt. 'I trust this night shall be more productive than last.'

Sibbechai's burning gaze fell upon Carandini. It had had enough of this conniving little mortal, and his usefulness was at an end. The vampire would find some less truculent wretch to serve it now. Shrivelled flesh fell away from its grotesque fangs as the vampire snarled at its deceitful ally.

'I grow weary of your baiting, little man,' Sibbechai growled. Its fingers cracked as it spread its hand into a claw. But almost at once, it relented, folding its arms back around its body. The necromancer was baiting it because he believed he had the upper hand. It might be dangerous to kill Carandini before learning why.

'You failed to secure the book,' the necromancer stated. 'And you let that witch hunter live. Not what I expected when I proposed this alliance of ours.'

'I will deal with the witch hunter in my own time,' Sibbechai hissed. 'Twice he has dared to interfere. Every breath he takes now is borrowed from Morr.' The vampire snapped its fangs, as though crushing its enemy's throat between its jaws. Sibbechai turned its eyes again upon Carandini. 'The book shall be mine again. I know where it has been taken. And by whom.' The vampire suddenly smiled. There had been a faint smell in the cellar, a subtle taint to the air. Sibbechai had been trying to remember where it had smelled it before. Now it knew – it was the strange ink Carandini used when consulting the mummy claw he carried. Sibbechai could readily guess what the necromancer had asked of the orac- ular talisman. 'But this is already known to you.'

Carandini nodded his head. 'Castle von Gotz,' he said with a note of pride. 'Taken there by a wizard named Furchtegott.'

'The wizard will not stand in my way,' Sibbechai snarled, moving toward the cellar's trapdoor. Suddenly it turned – springing on Carandini before the necromancer could react, pouncing on him like a wolf upon an unsuspecting lamb. Sibbechai could read the minds of most mortals, plucking their thoughts from thin air if it concen- trated hard. But Carandini was too well versed in the black arts, his mind guarded from the vampire's intrusion. Yet such protection was not complete. Sibbechai could still sense the emotions oozing from the necromancer's grimy soul. And as the vampire gave voice to its intention to kill the wizard, an intense joy gripped Carandini.

'What else do you know?' Sibbechai hissed into Carandini's face. The vampire held the sorcerer pinned against the wall, one talon gripping his neck, the other closed about the arm in which sleeve he kept a vial of holy water. 'What else did that daemon's paw show you?'

Carandini struggled to sneak air into his lungs. 'It… you will… the castle…' Carandini forced himself to make the words before Sibbechai crushed his neck. 'You'll die… if you go.' Sibbechai let the necromancer slide to the floor, the vampire's horrible gaze burning into his body.

'The castle is protected,' Carandini gasped as he sucked in huge lungfuls of air. 'Almost as potent as what the Klausners were using. Try to climb the castle's walls or fly up to its roof and the magic protecting it will destroy you.'

Sibbechai's skeletal features contorted into rage. Its withered claws smashed into the wall, crumbling the old brickwork as though it were sand. Carandini watched the vampire vent its anger. The vial of holy water had shattered when Sibbechai dropped him, removing his best defence. Now he was desperately trying to remember a spell that might work against such an undead horror.

'If the book is not mine, then neither shall it be yours,' Sibbechai snarled, fangs bared. The vampire advanced upon the cringing necromancer. Death was at hand.

'Wait!' Carandini cried out. 'There is a way! Listen to me!' The vampire halted, suspicion in its eyes. 'The wards are not infallible,'

Carandini continued. 'There is a way to elude them, something their creators never accounted for.'

'You say it is protected from without and from above,' Sibbechai said. Carandini nodded in hasty agreement.

'Yes, but not from below,' the necromancer declared. 'It would be possible to dig into the castle's dungeons and bypass the wards.' Sibbechai grinned at the Tilean.

'A clever plan,' the vampire conceded. 'It is almost a pity that you won't be around to see it employed.' The vampire closed in upon him.

'You still need me,' Carandini insisted. 'It will take an army to dig up into the castle. I can raise that army for you.' Sibbechai shook its head in amusement.

'I am a necromancer too, remember?' the vampire laughed. 'I am very capable of raising a few zombies.'

'But the magic will be much more potent, faster, with my help,' Carandini pointed out. 'The witch hunter is looking for the book too. If he finds it before we do, then it belongs to neither of us. Are you willing to gamble that you have enough time to deal with this alone?'

Sibbechai stepped back. It nodded its head and folded its arms once more. 'Well spoken, necromancer. It seems your usefulness to me is not at its end after all.'

'THE GREAT AND good of Wurtbad,' Baron von Gotz scoffed between swallows of wine. 'The leaders of the Empire's greatest city besides Altdorf.' He tore a scrap of mutton from the plate set before him, stuffing it into his swollen face. The meeting he had called was held in the smaller of the castle's three dining halls. With the baron's return to health had come a vigorous appetite. The nobleman felt it would be unseemly to appease that appetite during the meeting if it were conducted in any other environment.

Not that any of his prestigious guests displayed any trace of hunger. Choice wines from the cellars, plates of expertly prepared meats, mutton, veal and venison, sat untouched. The baron was oblivious to the fact that it was he who diminished their appetites. He was no longer able to smell the loathsome stench of the salve Furchtegott applied to his skin, so accustomed to it had his senses become. He did not seem to appreciate the ugliness of the boils that peppered his face and hands, grateful only that they were not those of the deadly Stir blight. But the man sitting beside him did. Had the baron condescended to look in his direction, he would have seen his trusted Furchtegott grow pale.

The assembled, abstemious diners represented the ruling elite of the city. The richest merchants, the most powerful nobles, the masters of the largest guilds. Commanders of the river guard, the city watch, and Wurtbad's standing army regiments. Even the Lord High Justice, Igor Markoff, who made a show of moving peas around his plate whenever von Gotz's gaze drifted toward him. They had been discussing for the better part of two hours how to destroy the plague before winter set in. If the quarantine was not lifted by then, if more supplies of food were not brought in, then the famine that would result would claim far more than the pestilence itself.

None of them had any answer. Indeed, several of them had openly decried the measures von Gotz had already taken, herding those infected into Otwin Keep. The heads of the different temples were particularly vocal on that point, furious that von Gotz had ordered the sanctity of the Temple of Shallya violated. The baron grumbled as he lifted a steaming bowl to his lips and began draining it of soup. Miserable, pious zealots, they'd all stand around waiting for their precious gods to save them while the entire city rotted away beneath their feet!

'A pack of pampered idiots,' von Gotz snarled, slamming his fist against the table. Several of his more timid guests jumped in surprise. 'Not a single one of you has any ideas? Not one? Maybe the Stir Blight isn't the only rot that I should confine to Otwin Keep.'

'Begging your pardon, excellency,' a tremulous voice called from the end of the table. 'But I may have a solution.' All heads turned to see the swinish countenance of Witch Hunter Captain Meisser. Many of those present had complained about the templar's inclusion in the meeting, the Lector of Sigmar among them. Fortunately, the witch hunter had kept silent, nursing some private trouble of his own. Until now.

'You spoke...' von Gotz hesitated a moment, trying to recall the witch hunter's name, '...brother templar. There is something you'd like to propose?'

Meisser stood, trying to look dignified despite his bandaged arm. He had the attention of every person in the room. 'We must convince the elector count that the plague has been exterminated,' he said, redundantly repeating the entire premise of the meeting. 'Now that we have most of those infected locked up in one place, why do we not exterminate the plague? It would be an easy thing to seal the doors and set fire to the keep.'

Gasps of horror and disbelief swept the room, along with muttered oaths of outrage. 'That's his solution to everything,' one elderly guildmaster called out. 'Put somebody to the torch!' It brought a round of laughter from the table.

One man was not laughing. Baron von Gotz hurled his wine glass to the floor, drawing all attention back to himself. The nobleman's face was turned toward the witch hunter. 'An inspired suggestion, brother templar,' von Gotz declared. More gasps and oaths greeted the baron's statement. 'Tell me what you will need to accomplish this.' Incredulous voices fell silent as the hideous reality of the situation became apparent.

'I'll need a goodly supply of oil and timber,' Meisser replied. 'And some men. My own are… otherwise occupied for the moment.'

'You shall have them,' von Gotz declared, stabbing his knife into a loaf of bread. The fat nobleman grinned at his shocked guests. 'Eat up gentlemen,' he laughed. 'No need to be timid now. Once the quarantine is lifted there will be plenty more where this came from!'

CHAPTER SEVEN

MATHIAS THULMANN FOUND Streng waiting for him just outside the alchemist's shop. The bearded thug had even less of a taste for magic than the witch hunter. Thulmann supposed that it might be another reason why the man had entered his employ. The foremost, of course, being the Temple's gold. There was a keen look in Streng's eyes that Thulmann recognised as agitated excitement. Clearly Streng believed he had found a worthy subject for his barbarous talents.

'You have the demeanour of the orc that swallowed the halfling,' Thulmann commented. The mercenary detached himself from the wall he leant on. He still moved stiffly, Thulmann noted, but at least the colour had returned to his face. Either he was somewhat improved or had managed to slither his way into a tavern on his way from the chapter house. Either possibility was equally likely.

'They caught one of my plague doktors,' Streng grinned. 'That young templar, Emil. Had a bit of trouble bringing him in, but they got him.' Thulmann digested the report.

'Has he said anything?' he asked. 'We don't know that this fellow is one of those we want. There might be any number of thieves and charlatans posing as plague doktors as well as Weichs and his scum.'

Streng gripped Thulmann's shoulder, forcing the witch hunter to stop. 'You're certain it's Weichs then?' he demanded. Thulmann gave a solemn nod.

'The alchemist found traces of warpstone burned into the glass of that bottle you found. We followed Weichs's trail to Wurtbad and now we find men posing as healers using warpstone. It does not take an overly analytical mind to accept that two and two make four.'

'Makes sense at that,' Streng agreed. He hurried to match pace with the witch hunter as Thulmann walked down the street. What little traffic there was parted before the templar. Thulmann wondered if it was the natural trepidation people felt in the presence of such grim agents of justice, or testament to the contempt and fear they felt towards Meisser's methods. He realised sadly that it was most likely the latter.

'Captain Meisser,' Thulmann said, 'has he caused any more trouble?' Streng shook his head.

'No,' the mercenary laughed. 'Hasn't showed his face. Still skulking in his room. Don't suppose you could ask old Sigmar to make that weasel stay there until after we leave?'

Thulmann chose to ignore his associate's casual blasphemy. 'This plague doktor Brother Emil apprehended, has he said anything?' he returned to the topic at hand.

'Just the usual nonsense about being innocent,' Streng replied. 'We've got the wrong man and all that. Never mind the fact that he tried to gut Emil with a fair-sized pigsticker, or that he's got pasty green stuff oozing out of the bullet hole Emil put in his shoulder.' Streng grinned again. 'Fair number of pint-sized tentacles, too, wriggling round his armpits. Be a bit of fun pulling those out.'

Thulmann sighed. His henchman's enthusiasm for the more violent aspects of his employment often troubled him, perhaps more so than the deeds themselves. Still, they were a necessary evil. This man was, by Streng's account, an obvious mutant and would need to be destroyed lest his corruption spread to others. But before that, Streng would need to extract the information Thulmann required from the wretch. By whatever means necessary.

'I don't care a damn for your vile amusements, Streng,' Thulmann stated. 'As long as you can make this animal talk, that is all I care about. If his information leads me to Weichs, there will be a bonus in it for you.'

Streng spat into the gutter, causing a mangy cur to flinch away. 'If we find Weichs, you can let me have a go at that bastard scum,' the mercenary swore. 'I don't know if I can think of anything horrible enough for him, but I'll enjoy trying to find out.'

FATHER SCHOENBECK HAD been a servant of the Temple of Morr for most of his forty years. He had seen much death in that time and buried many. But in the last few weeks, he considered he had seen more death than in all the years preceding, more bodies consigned to the plague pit than he had ever interred in Wurtbad's cemeteries. He shook his head at the massive pit, filled almost to the brim with a tangle of arms and legs. Soon they would need to dig a bigger one, the priest observed. The plague showed no sign of satisfaction with the toll already taken on the city.

Father Schoenbeck turned away from the morbid vista of the pit, shuffling over to the small fire where his fellow servants of the Temple warmed themselves. Three of these were lesser acolytes, initiates who wore the same black robes as the elder priests. There had been many new converts to the Temple, men whose lives had been destroyed as they consigned their families to the plague pit. There was great need of them, for the rituals and prayers required to sanctify the dead were important. The dead had suffered enough indignity by being cast into a mass grave; if they were not properly consecrated the corpses could become a terrible threat. Sylvania was not so far away, and the sinister tales of that cursed country were well known in Wurtbad – legends of the restless dead rising from their tombs to avenge themselves upon the living. Among the duties of Morr's priesthood was to ensure that such an abomination never occur.

Not all of his companions were priests, however. Two sombre black giants stood near the fire, their bodies similarly covered by the hooded habit of Morr's servants. But beneath their black robes they wore armour, plates of blackened steel as strong as obsidian. These were the dour templars of Morr, the fearsome Black Guard. These terrifying warriors were charged to ensure the sanctity of the pit was not violated by grieving relations, desperately trying to steal back their loved ones.

Father Schoenbeck clapped his hands together above the little fire, trying to force warmth back into his numbed fingers. The priest's attention was pulled away from the flames as the sound of a creaking cart grumbled out from the darkness. It was a sound he had heard far too many times, a plague cart emerging from the city to deposit its cargo. He walked away from the fire, motioning for the acolytes to remain where they were. There were rites to perform before a body could be consigned to the ground, but the priest felt fully capable of performing them on his own. It would help break up the tedium of another night camped beside the pit.

The plague cart was as dilapidated as the others Father Schoenbeck had seen, drawn by a sorry-looking mule that might have been lying inside the death wagon rather than pulling it. The man who drove it was similarly repulsive, scrawny and sickly. The priest nodded in greeting to the carter, circling toward the back of the wagon to begin removing its cargo of corpses. The sickly man dropped from the seat of the cart, brushing a ratty lock of hair from his face as he followed the priest.

Father Schoenbeck stopped, puzzled, when he reached the rear of the cart. The bed of the wagon was empty. 'Where are they?' he asked aloud. His mouth dropped open in a gargled scream as the pallid man cast a handful of dust into his face. The foul powder sizzled where it struck, its unholy energies withering the life from his flesh.

'I am afraid I came here to collect, not deposit,' Carandini said as the priest withered and writhed at his feet. The necromancer spun around, eyes glowing as terrible energies gathered within his corrupted soul. One of the acolytes rushed forward, a shovel gripped in his hands as though it were a battleaxe. Carandini smiled and uttered a word that was obscene centuries before even Sigmar was born. The dark energies responded. The acolyte crumpled into a screaming pile of rags, steam rising from his skin as the blood boiled within his veins.

The two templars of Morr reacted no less quickly than the shovel-wielding acolyte, but, weighed down by their armour, they were several paces behind. Carandini conceded they were a fearsome sight, black giants with cloaks billowing, the naked steel of their swords gleaming in the starlight. But there were far more fearsome things at large this night than mere mortal man.

From the darkness, a gaunt shape emerged, interposing itself between Carandini and the templars. The Black Guardsmen came to a hasty stop, hesitating to consider this new foe. Sibbechai's eyes burned from the pits of its face. Even the most ignorant peasant could not fail to recognise the vampire for what it was. Carandini was mildly impressed when the templars pressed their attack, instead of fleeing into the night as the surviving acolytes had done. Not that their bravery would count for anything.

The knight to Sibbechai's right slashed at the vampire with the edge of his massive broadsword. The undead creature did not so much evade the blow as shift position, the steel cleaving only through the edge of the vampire's shroud-like cloak. However, in avoiding the first knight's attack, Sibbechai left itself open to the assault of the second. It was a manoeuvre that the Black Guardsmen were very accomplished in, to allow their numbers to overwhelm the preternatural speed of the creatures they were called upon to destroy.

If the black helmets of the templars had left their faces exposed, perhaps they would have showed satisfaction as the second knight's sword crunched into Sibbechai's spine, as the force of the blow knocked the gaunt, cadaverous apparition back toward the first knight. The first Black Guardsman raised his sword upward, ready to deliver a decapitating blow to the vampire's neck.

Sibbechai had underestimated its adversaries. These were men who displayed no fear before it, whose wits and skills were not dulled by the clumsiness of terror. But they had underestimated Sibbechai as well. The simple tactics that allowed them to dispatch the debased, bestial strigoi vampires they discovered hiding in Wurtbad's Old Cemetery three years before were not enough to overcome a necrarch. Even as the first knight's sword slashed towards the vampire's neck, it was twisting around, claws gripping the blade lodged in its spine, spinning the second Black Guardsman around with it.

The first knight's reflexes were far quicker than those of most men. As the vampire used his comrade for a living shield, the knight changed the course of his blow, lowering the cutting edge. Instead of slashing into the other templar's neck, the blade glanced from his shoulder guard. However, even if the action preserved the life of his comrade, it left the guardsman momentarily defenceless. Sibbechai exploited the opening, hurling the overbalanced templar into the other who had thought to decapitate it. The two knights crashed against the earth in a pile of clattering steel. Sibbechai glared at them as it ripped the sword from its body and hurled the weapon away into the night.

'Servants of death,' the vampire hissed, extending its clawed hand. The templars struggled to regain their feet, dragging daggers from their boots as they rose. 'I send you to meet your master,' the vampire sneered. A hideous force seemed to erupt from its palm, a bolt of darkness that struck the armoured knights. The screams of the warriors echoed within their helmets as the necromantic force began to crush them, crumpling their armour as though crafted from paper, pulverising the bones within. Soon the screams stopped, leaving only two piles of twisted metal. Sibbechai regarded the sanguine pool slowly spreading from the mangled wreckage with satisfaction.

'You might have left them in some condition to be of use to us,' Carandini's whining voice complained from beside the corpse cart. Sibbechai gestured to the vast expanse of the plague pit.

'We have more than we can use already,' the vampire declared. 'It would be well if you got started. There is work to do here.'

Carandini glared at the vampire, then turned and dragged the boathook he had brought with him in anticipation of the night's labours. He might have expected the filthy coffin worm to leave all the dirty work to him. The necromancer moved toward the edge of the pit, sinking the boathook into one of the nearest bodies.

WINTER HAD ALREADY laid claim to the dungeons beneath the Wurtbad chapter house. Thulmann's breath turned to cloud as he stalked along the dark corridor. The water seepage that oozed from the brickwork had turned to frost, clinging to the walls like icy cobwebs. The chill of the dungeons matched the witch hunter's mood as his mind recollected the events of the past hours. Returning to the chapter house, he'd found that if the hunt for the plague doktors had gone well, then the search for Sibbechai's lair had not. Reports had come back from the templars with no favourable results. Thulmann was not surprised – in a city as large and old as Wurtbad, the cemeteries were both numerous and vast, offering an enormous amount of hiding places. He was certain that, given enough time, they would turn up whatever crypt Sibbechai had laid claim to. But the witch hunter did not know how much time they really had.

Neither had there been any word from Silja. Not that Thulmann expected anything favourable from that quarter. The Lord High Justice had impressed him as a man of resolve and determination; if he was set upon draconian measures, then not even the disapproval of his daughter would make him rethink his decision. Besides, Thulmann did not believe their origin lay with Igor Markoff. It had been decided upon by a still higher authority.

Thulmann dismissed his concerns about Silja and Sibbechai. Those had to be dealt with later. Now there was the plague doktor to consider. He was of the same ilk as the one Streng had fought against. The same ghastly leather mask, a lilac pomander stuffed into its beak. More importantly, he had carried a black bottle very similar to the one Streng had found. Only this time it was full. Thulmann had taken the vessel to the alchemist, though the scholar assured him it would take several days to make a definitive test of its vaporous contents. On one count, however, he had been ready to deliver a guarantee – there was, he assured, certainly more than a trace of warpstone within the bottle.

The plague doktor had spoken only little, giving Thulmann little choice but to leave the scoundrel in the capable hands of Streng. The professional torturer had been hard at work for the better part of the day. He had a particularly harsh system, tormenting the subject until he lost consciousness then awakening him minutes later. In the near-perfect darkness of the torture chamber, the prisoner had no idea of the passage of time. Streng had an amazing talent for making hours seem like days. Thulmann knew that the longer a man believed himself a captive, the weaker his resolve became.

Thulmann paused outside the door to the torture chamber, delivering his coded knock. Streng pulled the solid oak portal inward. The bare stone walls inside were lit by the diabolic glow of a brazier. A large wooden beam crossed the ceiling, chains dangling from rings set along its length. Within two of these manacles the wrists of the plague doktor had been bound. His back was red, raw, strips of ragged cloth dripping from his shredded body. Thulmann could see livid scars and burns running along the mutant's limbs. The witch hunter's gaze did not linger upon the plague doktor's visage. Unless Streng had spent an inordinate amount of time pounding the prisoner's features into their present lack of symmetry, the doktor had more than enough reason to hide behind a mask.

'Is the prisoner ready to confess his sins?' Thulmann demanded, his voice a theatrical snarl. Streng scowled at his master.

'Still as tight as a clam,' the mercenary spat. 'Might take another week or two to break this stubborn swine.' Thulmann could hear a soft moan of horror seep from the plague doktor's ruined mouth. Streng's acting ability wasn't exactly subtle, but given the right stage he could be as convincing as Detlef Sierck.

'M-mercy...' the thing that hung from the manacles groaned. Thulmann turned slowly toward the wretch, face twisted with scorn and contempt.

'Mercy? For a diseased, mutant heretic?' The witch hunter stooped to glare into the ruined face. 'For an unrepentant, murderous beast that revels yet in his misdeeds and blasphemies?'

'P-please...' the plague doktor whined, his voice cracking with the effort.

'What is your name, scum?' Thulmann demanded. This filth was desperate to make him stay, knowing full well that if Thulmann left, Streng would be set upon him again.

'Han... Hanzel... Gruber,' the prisoner said. 'I... I've done... nothing!'

'Nothing.' Thulmann growled back. 'Nothing. You carry a bottle of foul poison, telling unsuspecting innocents it will cure their ailments. You call that nothing?' He was guessing about their methods. But if Weichs was behind the plague doktors, such treachery was of a piece with his usual techniques. 'Your mind is as riddled with corruption as your filthy body, mutant cur!'

'Mercy... pity...' Hanzel implored. Thulmann started to pace the small chamber.

'Mercy? Pity?' the witch hunter repeated. 'Only a decent man warrants such favours, not murderous Chaos-spawn. A good man would have destroyed himself when he learned what he was becoming. A decent man would have given himself over to the Order of Sigmar, to be exterminated rather than continue his polluted existence, exposing those about him to the same abominable taint that defiled his own body. And you have allowed your villainy to plumb even greater depths. How long have you been a disciple of the Ruinous Powers? How long have you knelt before the Dark Gods and done their unholy bidding?' Thulmann gestured to indicate the malformations visible on the man's tortured body. 'Is this the mark of their favour? Tell me, mutant, which of the Lords of Chaos do you serve?'

Hanzel's body shook within the grip of the chains, trembling at Thulmann's accusations, his words carrying the sting of Streng's whip. Tortured, abused, and now condemned, the twisted creature began to weep, tears falling from his swollen eyes.

'I... am no worshipper,' Hanzel croaked. 'I serve no Dark Gods.'

'We know better, heretic,' Thulmann snarled. 'I shall hear the truth from your lips. Streng will extract the words from your rotten soul! If it takes a week, a month, even a year, I will have the truth from you, mutant.' Thulmann stopped pacing. He listened to the sob of horror from the bound Hanzel.

'Of course, if there is some spark of humanity left within that deformed carcass, if you have the courage to defy your dark masters, you may be spared such an ordeal.' Thulmann could hear the sudden spark of hope ignite in the prisoner, a spark he hastened to quell. 'You are a mutant, the seed of Chaos flows in your blood. Such corruption cannot be allowed to live. But if you will speak to me of what I wish to know, the end will be quick. Prayers shall be made that Sigmar might purify your soul when it has been expunged from its diseased shell.' The templar strode toward Hanzel. 'If you speak, Streng will not touch you again. You have my word. Now. Which of the Dark Gods do you serve?'

Hanzel sagged in the chains, weighed down by a despair his failing strength could not support. 'I do not serve the... Dark Gods,' he repeated with as much force as he could. 'It was a man who... who did this to me. Who made me a... thing.'

'Which man?' Thulmann demanded. 'What is his name?'

'The doktor,' Hanzel said, the words dripping from his mouth. 'Herr Doktor Weichs!'

Thulmann grinned. He had suspected as much, but now there was no longer any question. Weichs was in Wurtbad. Only this time, there was nowhere for him to run. The witch hunter stabbed a finger at Hanzel's miserable frame.

'You shall tell me everything you know about this man,' Thulmann ordered. 'You shall tell me how I can find him. That is how you will redeem your filthy existence. That is how you shall earn the mercy of a quick death.' In reply, Hanzel nodded his head weakly. He was resigned to the inevitability of death, now that the witch hunter offered him a chance to strike back at the man who had made him a monster.

Before Thulmann could continue his interrogation, there was a knock on the door. The witch hunter motioned for Streng to see who it was. He complied, peering through the narrow slit in the portal.

'Emil,' the mercenary reported. Thulmann gestured for Streng to admit the young templar. He stepped inside, his face eager and anxious.

'Begging your pardon, Brother Mathias,' Emil said. 'A messenger from Silja Markoff to see you.' The templar's voice became grave. 'He says she needs you to come right away.'

'Please inform the messenger I have other concerns that demand my attention here,' Thulmann replied. It cannot have been a trivial thing that caused Silja to send for him. But he was so close to finally setting a noose about the neck of Freiherr Weichs.

'Brother Mathias,' Emil continued, 'you had best come. The messenger says that Captain Meisser is burning down Otwin Keep!'

Thulmann cursed, stalking from the torture chamber like a thing possessed. He was unsure of the purpose of Meisser's game, but still the swine would have to be stopped. 'Streng, you'd better come along too. I may need every man.' Thulmann cast one last infuriated look back at Hanzel. 'Lock this door. I want no one disturbing our guest until I return.'

HANZEL GRUBER'S BODY grew slack as the witch hunters left, sealing the door behind him. Within the gloom of the torture chamber, the cumulative effects of terror and despair left the prisoner's mind and body fatigued. Now both seized the opportunity to rest.

The tired man ignored the soft scratching sound that gnawed at the edge of his senses. He did not see the trickle of dirt falling from between the stone blocks in the wall, as sharp claws began to penetrate the witch hunters' dungeon. If he had, Hanzel would have screamed out for Thulmann to return. For there were far worse things than torture in the dark, and one of those things was now coming for Hanzel Gruber.

CHAPTER EIGHT

OTWIN KEEP TOWERED above the half-timbered structures of the district around it. Although the houses, shops and tenements were clustered so closely that the lanes slithering between them scarcely allowed two men to walk abreast, the imposing stone tower stood alone. None had been bold enough to build close to the forbidding prison, unwilling for his home or business to lie within the keep's black shadow. A stretch of some fifty yards lay empty and vacant all around the keep, its expanse all the more unnatural and intimidating for the cramped cluster of the surrounding streets.

The tower itself was six floors of dank cells and dark corridors, encased within grey stone walls as thick as a man's arm was long. Narrow slits peppered the face of the structure, angling downward through the outer façade before reaching the chambers within. It had been no compassionate attempt to provide the keep's inmates with daylight, but a cruder one to improve the circulation of the air and eliminate the stench of unwashed bodies and human filth. The little windows failed in both respects, acting only to funnel the cold grip of winter into the dungeons.

A crowd had gathered around the gruesome structure as Thulmann led his retinue of witch hunters towards the keep. Most of them wore the livery of Baron von Gotz's personal guard, although there were others in the colours of the city watch. As Thulmann watched, the soldiers busied themselves by adding to the pile of kindling that surrounded the keep, hurling broken furniture and splintered beams. Others prowled the edges of the heap, massive stone jars held in their hands, sloshing thick black oil onto the kindling. Some distance away a large bonfire burned, its flames illuminating the brutal tableau. Even through the thick walls, Thulmann's ears could detect the shrieks and pleas for mercy rising from those confined within the keep.

Meisser was standing near the bonfire, dressed in the same dark mantle he had worn when Thulmann relieved him of command. The deposed witch hunter captain barked orders to the soldiers constructing the pyre, waving his hands and gesturing wildly to punctuate his commands. The image of a maestro conducting his orchestra in one of Altdorf's elegant opera houses flickered through Thulmann's thoughts.

Thulmann approached the swine-faced Meisser. Some of the soldiers working on the pyre turned to watch. Meisser started when he saw Thulmann. But a smug look of superiority spread across his face.

'Come to help me in my holy work, Brother Mathias?' Meisser grinned. Thulmann paused, the flickering light of the bonfire casting his profile in sharp relief. He studied Meisser for a moment. Then his hand released its hold upon his sword, curling into a fist as it bridged the distance and smashed into Meisser's nose. Meisser staggered backward, a stream of blood oozing from his nostril, gawking as it stained his fingers, stunned that anyone should have the temerity to strike him. Dimly, Thulmann was aware of movement to his right. He spun around, ready to defend himself. Some of the tension eased as he saw that the men closing upon him wore the gold of the Ministry of Justice, and Silja Markoff was at their head.

'Mathias!' Silja cried out. 'He means to burn down the keep with all the inmates locked inside!' Thulmann nodded grimly, turning back to regard Meisser. The witch hunter captain was still nursing his injured nose. His lip trembled as he saw his nemesis approach him. A quick glance at the soldiers standing by the pyre informed him he could expect no help from that quarter. The oaths they had sworn to Baron von Gotz bound them to their orders, it seemed, but not to their overseer. Thulmann might beat him to a pulp and the soldiers would be content to do nothing more than watch.

Meisser's hand dropped away from his nose toward his tunic. At once he snarled in pain, as strong hands closed about his own and pulled his good arm behind his back. Meisser struggled in Streng's powerful grip, spitting invective at the brutish mercenary.

'Can't have you shooting the gaffer now, can I?' Streng growled, giving a tug on Meisser's arm that sent a fresh stab of pain through his body.

'Damn you...' Meisser hissed. 'I have a proclamation... orders... in my pocket.' He groaned again as Streng fumbled inside his tunic, his hand emerging with a folded sheet of parchment.

'This looks to be what he's whining about,' Streng said, proffering the document to Thulmann. The witch hunter unfolded it and began to read. As he did so, the greasy smile returned to Meisser's face.

'Release him,' Thulmann ordered. Streng stared at his employer, wondering if he had taken leave of his senses. 'He has orders from Baron von Gotz himself. The baron is very concerned about the concentration of disease in this keep. This, it seems, is the solution.' With a sigh of disappointment and a last savage twist of his arm, Streng pushed Meisser away. He fell to the ground, another cry of pain escaping as he landed on his bad arm.

'But Baron von Gotz was the one who ordered the sick to be brought here,' protested Silja. Thulmann handed the document over to her, allowing her to examine the seal and satisfy herself as to its authenticity. For his part, there was no need for further inquiry. A scheming rat like Meisser would never have been brazen enough for so bold a deception.

'No doubt he had this second order already in mind when he gave the first,' Thulmann commented. Which, he wondered, was the worst monster at large in the city now: Sibbechai, Weichs, or His Excellency the Baron von Gotz?

'It was decided at a meeting of all the great and good of the city,' Meisser spat as he regained his feet. He stabbed an accusing finger at Silja. 'Your father was the one who proposed this action to the baron.' Silja's face turned white. The Ministry soldiers to either side of her stepped forward to support her suddenly weakened legs. Thulmann glowered at the conniving captain, sorely tempted to finish the job of breaking his nose.

'I don't care who the orders come from,' Silja insisted. 'You can't do this! For Sigmar's sake, the Sisters of Shallya are still inside!'

'You would consign the holy servants of the goddess of mercy to a hideous death?' Thulmann demanded. His words were intended not only for Meisser's jaded ears. The soldiers around the walls of the keep began to back away, eyes downcast as an intense shame welled up within them.

'They refused to leave,' Meisser protested. 'They insisted on defying the baron's order.'

'Because they were foolish enough to think that even you would not set fire to the keep with them still inside,' Thulmann snapped back. He turned his gaze toward the soldiers. 'You men have honoured your oaths and displayed your willingness to obey your masters, no matter how distasteful the task they give you. But this order is an evil!' He leaned toward the bonfire, holding the baron's proclamation against the flames. 'Lords and masters may demand many things from the men whose loyalty they command, but no man has the right to ask another to damn his immortal soul!' Thulmann held the parchment high so that the soldiers could watch it burn. Their faces betrayed the uncertainty they felt. Not one of them had been without his doubts, but now each saw he was responsible for his actions to powers far greater than that of Baron von Gotz.

As Thulmann was beginning to think the baron's hideous intentions had been thwarted, there was a sudden movement close beside him. Meisser had seized his chance, lunging at the bonfire, ripping a burning brand from the flames. He had allowed Thulmann to usurp his authority once before, but not this time. Before anyone could react, Meisser hurled the burning stick into the oil-soaked pile surrounding the keep. The kindling burst into an upsurge of flames, swiftly racing away to spread across the rest of the pile.

Thulmann ripped the cloak from his shoulders, the witch hunters from the chapter house following his lead. A large number of the soldiers grabbed spears, swords and whatever else was at hand to attack the blaze. The screams from inside the keep rose into an ear-splitting din, distinct and terrible, despite the thick stone walls and the roar of the flames.

'Keep it from reaching the door!' a soldier wearing a sergeant's pectoral cried out, a look of horror on his face. The witch hunter threw down the smouldering cloak in his hands. The sergeant's voice was a piteous moan. 'Captain Meisser had my men cover the floors in straw soaked with pitch!' he declared. Thulmann's eyes mirrored the horror as he looked to the keep's ironbound doors, the tiny serpents of flame slithering toward them from the piled kindling. Even as he called out for the men to redirect their efforts, he knew it was too late. The screams from the keep rose in intensity as the fire raced inside. A group of soldiers fought to force the massive doors open, trying to hack through the portal with axes until the heat of the conflagration drove them back. By degree, the men abandoned their efforts, retreating from the fire as it became obvious that their fight was in vain.

Thulmann stalked back toward the bonfire, trying to ignore the chorus of screams shrieking into the night. He looked for Silja Markoff, but could find no trace of her. Meisser's words had done their work well, penetrating her strength and determination, wounding the woman inside. Silja seemed to have few weaknesses, but her devotion to her father was beyond question. Thulmann hoped she would not do anything rash.

Nearby, Thulmann found Streng, grinning at him from above the crumpled form of Meisser. The witch hunter captain had been relieved of his weapons, presumably after Streng's fist had knocked the wind from his stomach.

'Keep your animal off of me!' Meisser demanded. The witch hunter glared back, ripping his pistol from its holster. The captain cringed away, eyes wide with horror.

'You should be begging *him* to keep *me* away from you,' Thulmann snarled. His thumb pulled back the hammer of his pistol.

'I was only following orders!' pleaded Meisser, pressing his face against the cobblestones so that he might not see the coming shot. Slowly, with an effort of will, Thulmann released the hammer, slamming the pistol back into its holster.

'Gunning you down in the gutter like a dog is not disgraceful enough an end, Captain Meisser,' Thulmann declared, his voice dripping with disgust. He glanced aside at his henchman. 'Streng, take this parasite back to the chapter house. Get him out of my sight.'

Streng pulled Meisser back to his feet, shoving him across the plaza. 'Count yourself lucky he's the gaffer,' he hissed in Meisser's ear. 'I'd have no qualms about putting a bullet in that slimy brain of yours.'

Thulmann did not watch his henchman leave, turning instead toward the blazing Otwin Keep. Its flames rose into the night sky like some infernal hellfire. Some soldiers were still harrying the edges of the conflagration, but most of them had withdrawn. The witch hunter looked in the direction of the distant Castle von Gotz, wondering if the baron had a good view of the atrocity.

CROUCHED UPON THE tile roof of a three-floor riverside slum like some withered gargoyle, the grotesque shadow twisted, its undead eyes regarding the distant flicker of light as Otwin Keep burned. Sibbechai's corpse-face remained impassive. Fires were a common enough hazard in the cramped, overpopulated confines of the Empire's cities, common enough that they held little interest for a vampire after five hundred years of pseudo-life. The fire was too distant to interfere with the necrarch's plans.

Sibbechai turned its attention back to the looming grey walls of the Schloss von Gotz. So near, the vampire thought, that it could almost reach out and touch them. Though to do so would be unwise. Sibbechai had not endured five centuries to end its existence in a trap set for a pack of long-dead von Carstein butchers. Carandini had been telling the truth about the wards, of that it was certain. The necromancer had been far too pleased at the prospect of ridding himself of his undead partner to lie.

A chill slithered across the vampire's withered skin. Its gaze settled upon the dark, indistinct shape that had joined it upon the rooftop, nestled within the shadow cast by the building's chimney.

'You have come so very far,' Sibbechai sneered. 'Does your courage fail you now that you are so close to your desire?'

'No, monster. I merely wish to savour the moment.' The shape emerged into the starlight, revealing itself as a man. Gregor Klausner's pale hand held the sword he had liberated from Skorzeney's corpse, its naked steel gleaming. The youth's eyes were no less rigid, drinking in the corpse-like form of the vampire with an almost emotionless regard. Before, this monster had filled his heart with terror, now it failed to even make his palms sweat.

Gregor wondered if it was because he was no longer human enough to know fear.

Sibbechai spread its arms wide, its shroud-like robes billowing about its lean frame. 'Strike me then,' it hissed. 'If you can.' Gregor needed no further invitation. He rushed at the vampire with a speed that would not shame a prize Arabyan stallion. Yet it seemed an eternity to Gregor's mind, as he sprinted across the slick clay tiles, as the gleaming point of his sword drew close to the vampire's putrid form. And in that eternity, Gregor learned that he was still human enough to know horror. Thrusting his sword at Sibbechai's heart, he felt his hand tremble, his arm hesitate. The vampire's leprous claws closed about his wrist, ripping the sword from him as easily as if he were a swaddling babe. Gregor's eyes filled with anguish as he glared into Sibbechai's rotten face. The monster's skull was distinct and vivid in a manner that the faces of the living no longer were.

'Your brother was a thuggish animal,' Sibbechai spat. The vampire's clawed hand smashed into Gregor's face, hurling the young noble across the rooftop. He landed on his back, feeling the tiles beneath him shatter as he fell. Gregor scrabbled at the broken shards as his body began to slide down the slope, arresting his fall only with a frantic effort. Looking up, he saw the burning eyes of Sibbechai glaring at him.

Sibbechai reached down, swatting aside Gregor's arm to grip his tunic. With an impossible strength, the vampire's withered arm lifted him into the air. Gregor tried to break the monster's grip, lashing out with his fists and feet. He knew prodigious strength was now his, equal to even the fiercest Kurgan warlord, yet the withered vampire did not so much as flinch under his blows.

'Your father was a doddering old coward,' Sibbechai snarled. Like a bundle of rags, the vampire hurled Gregor a dozen feet, across the expanse of the street and onto the roof of a neighbouring building. He landed hard. His hand groped at his surroundings to arrest his fall, finding purchase on an iron weather vane. Slowly, his every movement sending broken tiles crashing to the street below, Gregor crawled up the slope of the roof onto the narrow ledge that formed its peak. He was not surprised to see a thin shadow waiting for him. Gregor roared at the monster, ripping a tile from the ledge and flinging it. Sibbechai's

claw effortlessly swatted the improvised projectile aside. Shrivelled lips pulled back in a contemptuous grin.

'I will kill you!' Gregor screamed, charging across the rooftop,
intent on sending the vampire's withered form to the street below.
Yet his desperate attack never connected with his intended victim.
Displaying a still greater dexterity, and an agility that seemed
impossible for a creature so frail, Sibbechai dashed ahead of Gregor, catching the youth's throat in its cadaverous claws.

'And you,' the vampire laughed, like the rustling of dead leaves,
'are a fool.' Sibbechai tightened its grip upon his neck, a clutch
that would have broken the vertebra of any normal man. 'I had
thought you could be of use to me. To aid me against the necromancer. But you are nothing.' Once again, Sibbechai tossed
Gregor aside like a piece of garbage. This time, no rooftop
stopped his fall.

The last son of the Klausners hurtled out over the street, plummeting down like a thunderbolt hurled from the heavens.
Gregor's body slammed into the edge of the stone quay that overlooked the river, cracking the stonework as it pitched over the
side. The dark waters of the Stir closed greedily about his lifeless
form as it sank, only a few ripples marking his descent.

Sibbechai turned away, already dismissing the violent interlude.
The thrall had been a disappointment, weak and impetuous. Gregor Klausner tried to fight against the curse, deny it sustenance. It
bespoke a tremendous will, something that Sibbechai would
once have found impressive. But in denying the curse the nourishment it craved, Klausner made himself weak, little more than
a paper dragon. His defeat had therefore been contemptuously
easy.

The vampire looked again at the Schloss von Gotz. It would
deal with Carandini by some other means, when the time was
right. For now, it had more important needs to satisfy.

'You ARE so very good to me, Furchtegott,' the baron's words bubbled and gurgled like waters from a slimy pond. The wizard
nodded at his patron, a forced smile frozen on his face. 'Smile,'
Furchtegott thought, 'smile so he can't see the horror.'

'There is still a chance of infection,' Furchtegott advised. 'With
your body expelling the remnants of the plague, we must be very
cautious about allowing lesser afflictions to gain a foothold.' The

wizard had no idea of that which he spoke of, but if it persuaded the baron to remain isolated in his room, allowing no one but Furchtegott to see him, then the falsehood would do its work.

The wizard wound bandages around the baron's body, trying not to picture the abomination they concealed. 'Your skin will be very sensitive for some time, excellency,' Furchtegott said. 'We must ensure that it is protected.' The baron nodded his bloated head, already becoming bored with his wizard's explanations. He reached over with a bandaged hand, ripping a chunk of flesh from the platter resting beside him on the bed. The carcass of an entire pig had lain on that platter when Furchtegott received it from the kitchen servant at the baron's door. Better than half of that now resided in the baron's swollen belly, and the nobleman showed no signs of being unable to finish the remainder. The smile faded from Furchtegott's features as he watched the baron cram the meat into his mouth, seemingly oblivious to the sickly pus seeping through his bandages and tainting his meal.

'You should perhaps watch your diet,' the wizard advised. He tried to tell himself that the baron's face was not undergoing changes, that his mouth did not somehow seem wider than it should, that the bruises over his eyes were just large boils, not some unnatural growth. Baron von Gotz grinned at his physician-mage, displaying the rotten brown stumps inside his face.

'Didn't you say a good appetite was healthy?' the baron chuckled. Furchtegott tried not to wince as the nobleman's obscene breath washed over him.

'Yes, quite so,' Furchtegott agreed, nodding submissively. He hurried to finish wrapping the baron's leg, wishing there was some way he could convince the nobleman to let him cover his face. The wizard had no idea what was happening to his patient. He had followed the rites laid out in *Das Buch die Unholden*, the spell that would preserve its recipient against the ravages of disease. But something had gone wrong, it had not worked as it was supposed to. True, the baron was certainly no longer in danger of his life, but he was sicker than ever. Furchtegott couldn't even begin to name the disease rampaging through the baron's body, much less its legion of symptoms. It was more like an army of sicknesses than a single ailment. How von Gotz could remain so oblivious to his deteriorating condition, the wizard could not understand, but it chilled him to the bone.

He would need to scour the book again, Furchtegott decided. There had to be an answer in there, a clue to what he had done wrong. If he could correct it; he could still salvage the situation. If not, he would need to find some way of disposing of the baron, destroying him before his condition became any worse, before he became something *unnatural*. There might not be any reward waiting for him if that came to pass, but at least he could avoid the attentions of the witch hunters and charges of sorcery. Furchtegott looked back at his patron as the baron shoved the better part of the pig's leg into his mouth, his ruined teeth crunching away at its bones.

He had to do something soon, but first he had to make sure that the baron did as the wizard told him and stayed in his room. If anyone were to witness the state of him now, Furchtegott was certain the witch hunters would not be long behind.

MATHIAS THULMANN STORMED into the Wurtbad chapter house. The old servant who moved to take the witch hunter's hat retreated before that merciless gaze, a judgmental ferocity that would have given the most courageous man pause. Thulmann's mood was dark, his thoughts murderous. During the long walk from Otwin Keep, he had struggled betwixt the lust for vengeance and his respect for justice. There was a set procedure to follow, chains of command to be adhered to. Certainly no official within the order could be executed without the permission of Altdorf. But would they see things as Thulmann saw them? Could they understand how Meisser had befouled the Temple of Sigmar, if they had not witnessed the atrocity of hundreds of men, women and children burning to death? Creatures like Arch-Lector Esmer and Witch Hunter General South Sforza Zerndorff might even sympathise with Meisser's attempt to ingratiate himself with the temporal ruler of Wurtbad.

'Mathias.' Streng emerged from one of the corridors that connected with the vestibule, Emil and the veteran witch hunter Tuomas close behind him. The bearded mercenary jabbed a finger over his shoulder. 'Some visitors to see you.'

Thulmann sighed with fatigue, rubbing his temples with his fingers. 'Anyone we know?' the witch hunter asked. The best scenario would be Silja, or perhaps her father, come to explain the madness Thulmann had tried to stop. The worst would be a delegation from Baron von Gotz intent on arresting him for interfering with the baron's edict.

'Actually, they came to see Captain Meisser,' Tuomas said.

'I reckoned that might be a bad idea under the circumstances,' Streng elaborated. 'Meisser's mouth kept flapping on the way back here. I had to shut it for him. It'll be a few days before he's presentable.'

'How fares the captain?' he inquired. Streng smiled back.

'In his study licking his wounds,' the mercenary said. 'Don't worry, this time I made sure he's locked in.' His grin widened. 'For his own good, of course.'

Thulmann did not share in the jest, his mind on more important problems. 'Our other guest?'

'Still in the dungeons, Brother Mathias,' Tuomas answered. 'Missing you terribly, judging by the way he's been carrying on. I don't think he screamed that much when your man was tickling his ribs with hot irons.'

'Reckon I'll have to try harder when I get my hands on him again,' Streng mused. He looked over to his employer. 'We pick up where we left off with Hanzel?' Thulmann closed his eyes for a moment, then shook his head.

'No. We'll leave him be for a time. If he's so eager to talk now, he'll be doubly keen to speak if we let him wait a little longer. I'll see these visitors of yours first.'

Streng led his employer to a garishly appointed chamber that had once been a training hall for Wurtbad's witch hunters before Meisser had transformed it into a reception hall for his many guests. The furnishings were sparse, but expensive, claw-footed chairs from the reign of Emperor Boris Goldgather reposing beneath tapestries woven in the time of Talebecland's Ottilia. Thulmann found the gaudy collection of antiques from disparate cultures as tasteless as it was flamboyant. It added another crime to Meisser's misdeeds. He wondered what kind of spineless sycophants Meisser had been courting that they were so easily impressed.

The two men now standing in the reception hall were clearly cut from a different cloth. Or perhaps shroud was a more appropriate word. The first was a stoop-shouldered wraith, his elderly frame cloaked in the heavy black robes of Morr's sombre priesthood, a silver pendent depicting an archway hanging from his wrinkled neck. The shaven-headed cleric's face was pinched and wizened, his eyes cold and dark. His companion towered behind him, a giant of a man with his body encased in a suit of obsidian plates and a heavy black mantle, a raven embroidered across the chest, his face concealed behind the enigma of his helmet. Thulmann could feel the menace exuding from the warrior, the aura of death that hovered around him. Here was an engine of death, a killing machine as near to perfection as any Tilean assassin or Norse berserker. The witch hunter nodded his head respectfully toward the unmoving Black Guardsman of Morr.

'Father Kreutzberg,' Tuomas announced, indicating the bald priest, 'and Captain-Justicar Ehrhardt of Morr's holy Black Guard.' The priest blinked as his name was spoken. The hulking shadow that was Ehrhardt did not so much as twitch a muscle.

'I am Mathias Thulmann,' the witch hunter announced as he stepped into the room. 'Captain Meisser is indisposed at the moment. I am acting as his surrogate.' A strained smile creased the ancient face of Father Kreutzberg.

'I care not for whatever games you people play among your-selves,' the priest said, taking Thulmann by surprise. Obviously Kreutzberg was more informed about Meisser's situation than he had expected. 'I have come here because there is a matter that mandates a more integrated cooperation between our temples.' The priest's voice dropped into a subdued whisper. 'Your vampire has been found.' The words brought gasps from the Sigmarite templars.

'You've discovered the vampire's lair?' Thulmann asked, hardly daring to believe it.

'No, but the monster was seen. Only a few hours ago, outside the city. It attacked the plague pits.'

'The plague pits?' Thulmann tried to imagine what the vampire had wanted there, what relevance it had to its hunt for Helmuth Klausner's grimoire. Even for a necrarch, it seemed a strange thing to do.

'Two priests from my order were killed,' Father Kreutzberg elab-orated. He gestured toward Ehrhardt. 'Also two Black Guardsmen, crushed within their own armour.'

'But what would Sibbechai want at the plague pits?' Thulmann pondered aloud.

'It stole bodies, Brother Mathias,' Kreutzberg said. 'The corpses of my priests were taken, as well as an indeterminable number from the pit itself. The acolytes who escaped the massacre say the creature was not alone. It was helped by a heretic blasphemer, a necromancer.'

The priest's words did little to encourage Thulmann. The vampire alone was formidable enough, but if Sibbechai was working with a necromancer, the threat was doubled. The peculiar limitations imposed on the vampire by its profane state would not apply to a living sorcerer.

'The wheel marks of a cart were present,' Ehrhardt stated. 'It was heavier when it left than when it came.'

'Necromancers often profane the solemnity of Morr's realm by forcing the semblance of life back into dead bodies,' Kreutzberg explained. Gustl, one of the chapter house's templars, rushed into the room, his young face flushed with excitement.

'You'd better come quickly,' Gustl said as he tried to catch his breath. 'It sounds like your prisoner has got loose and is tearing apart his cell!' As if to punctuate the templar's report, a horrendous scream welled up from the depths of the chapter house, penetrating the thick stone floors. Even Streng was impressed by the violence of the act that could wrench such agony from a human throat.

'That was a cry of death,' Ehrhardt declared, his voice emotionless. Thulmann's hand fell to the hilt of his sword. He raced toward the stone stairway that descended into the depths. The other templars hurried after him, the metal-encased bulk of Ehrhardt easily keeping pace with the lightly armoured witch hunters.

The screams grew silent as Thulmann sprinted down the narrow dungeon corridor. A pair of templars stood outside the door to Hanzel's cell, drawn swords clutched in their white-knuckled hands. From behind the doors came the wet, visceral noises of a body being torn apart.

'Get that door open!' Thulmann snapped. Hanzel still offered his best chance to track down Weichs. He cursed himself. He should have done as Streng suggested, simply beating Hanzel until he spat out whatever they wanted to hear. Instead he had chosen the cleaner, more sophisticated approach of breaking the man psychologically. Sometimes, he considered, he was too timid for his kind of work.

'Out of the way!' barked Streng, pushing a rusty key into the iron lock. The mercenary ensured that he had a good grip on the dagger in his other hand, then flung the door inward.

Something leapt from the torture chamber, something spat out of a nightmare. The guards cringed, their minds refusing to accept the hideous apparition. The twisted shape moved with incredible speed, a blur of reeking rags and brown fur, its mangy hair caked in fresh blood. The thing hissed at Streng, filthy claws scratching at his face. The mercenary pulled away, the talons raking the heavy leather guarding his chest. The thing's muzzle snapped open, baring its chisel-like fangs, ropes of saliva drooling from its mouth. The abomination hissed again and lunged for Streng's throat.

Thulmann acted at once. He stabbed the point of his blade into the ratman's neck, tearing the steel out of its flesh with a savage sidewise motion. Putrid black blood exploded from the wound. With a pitiful mewing, the monster fell to the icy floor, its scabby tail quivering as life retreated from its malformed carcass.

'Skaven,' Thulmann pronounced. He could not blame the men for their shock and disgust. To most men in the Empire, the rat-men were a legend, a story told to frighten small children. But Thulmann knew better, he had seen their kind before, the inhuman patrons of his uncle, the sorcerer, Erasmus Kleib. The witch hunter jumped over the shivering corpse and into the cell.

Hanzel Gruber's death was more ugly than anything Streng could have inflicted on him. The remains of the plague doktor's arms still hung from the manacles, but the rest of him was strewn across the floor. Thulmann had heard men describe bodies being 'hacked to pieces', but this was the first time that he found the phrase appropriate. The sound of scrabbling claws snapped Thulmann's attention to the far wall where a jagged hole gaped, dislodged stones and earth scattered about its opening. A naked pink tail swiftly disappeared into the darkness of the tunnel.

'They're getting away!' Gustl cried out, sprinting for the tunnel, a pistol gripped in his hand. Ehrhardt and two of the other witch hunters were right behind him. Thulmann cried out a warning, but they were already disappearing. The templar hurried after them, cursing under his breath. He had just reached the mouth of the opening when a terrible groaning sound rumbled through the tunnel. In an instant, the roof of the crudely burrowed passageway came crashing down, sending a cloud of thick grey dust billowing back into the torture chamber.

Thulmann retreated, trying to blink the dirt from his eyes. When he could see again, he found Tuomas and one of the guards, swords drawn, eyes filled with terror. Thulmann could appreciate their distress. It was a horrible moment when myth became reality, when the underfolk of childhood stepped out from the shadows. Their minds were probably trying to find a sane explanation for the ghastly body lying in the corridor. Perhaps they might even find one they could believe in.

'You can relax,' Thulmann said, slamming his sword back into its scabbard. 'They are gone – for now anyway.' He could see the men were unconvinced, eyes fixed on the blocked mouth of the tunnel. Thulmann pointed to Tuomas. 'Fetch shovels, picks, whatever you can find to dig with. If luck is with us, we may be able to excavate the hole and find their tunnels.' It was a forlorn hope, but it would give the men something to do. Thulmann could already hear more of the chapter house's denizens rushing along the corridor outside. 'Take a few of them to help you,' he commanded as Tuomas headed back to the hallway, striving to avoid nearing the ratman's carcass.

'Phew! Somebody didn't want him to talk.' Streng inspected the carnage, turning over what may have been a part of Hanzel's face with his dagger.

'The skaven are quite accomplished at covering their tracks,' Thulmann agreed. It seemed that Sibbechai wasn't the only evil at large in Wurtbad that had found powerful allies. Weichs and the skaven was a combination that churned the witch hunter's stomach – the inhuman and the unhuman.

Other witch hunters openly marvelled at the horror that had been done to Hanzel Gruber, many of them making the sign of the hammer as they studied his scattered remains. Thulmann was about to give orders when the man watching the imploded tunnel called out.

'Brother Mathias! They return!'

His sword leapt from its scabbard. Dirt began to fall away from the hole, spilling into the cell. The witch hunter considered evacuating the room. If the skaven were returning it would be in far greater numbers. Or perhaps only a few had been trapped and managed to survive the collapse of their tunnel. If they could capture one of the monsters alive, Thulmann might yet be able to uncover Weichs's hideout. He motioned for the other men to make ready, noting the glowing iron Streng held in his left hand to augment the dagger in his right.

'I want one alive,' Thulmann declared, giving Streng a sharp look who gave a noncommittal shrug of his shoulders.

The dirt continued to spill into the room. Suddenly something black emerged from the earth, clawing at the open air. Thulmann eyed the flailing fingers, then advised his men to stand down. It was no skaven paw, but an armoured gauntlet. Thulmann hurried to the hole, helping the man to dig his way free. Captain-Justicar Ehrhardt emerged, his plate armour caked in dust, his sombre raiment torn and ragged. As the huge Black Guardsman fought his way free, he dragged the insensible shape of Emil with him, tossing the stunned witch hunter to the nearest of his fellows. Ehrhardt lifted the steel helmet from his head, exposing a harsh, weathered countenance that would not have been out of place on a seasoned veteran of the Reiksguard.

'We had the vermin in sight all the time,' Ehrhardt snarled. 'But there must have been others deeper in the tunnel. The scum collapsed their run on top of their own.'

'Courage and honour are not trademarks of the rat-kin,' Thulmann said. 'They will happily kill dozens of their own to eliminate a single enemy.' The Black Guardsman nodded in understanding.

'When we have finished with this vampire,' Ehrhardt growled, 'then this vermin will wish they had made a better job of it.'

'I was unaware that the underfolk were the concern of Morr's Black Guard,' Thulmann observed. Ehrhardt turned his penetrating blue eyes on the witch hunter, shaking a pile of dirt from his armoured shoulder.

'They are now,' the knight said.

'Then I shouldn't worry about losing the ones in the tunnel,' Thulmann said. 'Because where one skaven is found, there are always others.'

FILTHY PAWS SCRABBLED in the murky water beneath the docks, struggling to wash the odour from their fur. The pungent lilac scent was chosen by Grey Seer Skilk because his minions could track it easily across great distances. In truth, the skaven found the smell unpleasant, even more intolerable than the odour of the man-things they were sent to collect for the grey seer.

The leader of the small pack of ratmen looked over at the bound form they had abducted from the little fishing boat he called home. The skaven's teeth gleamed as it snarled at the fisherman, punctuating its displeasure by nipping at the man's arm. Skilk's doktor-man wanted his subjects alive, but 'alive' did not mean 'unharmed'. The fisherman screamed into the linen his abductors had crammed down his throat. The creatures chittered with amusement as the wretch struggled against his bonds. His days of dreaming about a big catch were over, his nightmare as the big catch itself was about to begin.

The skaven leader resumed its fastidious cleaning. The vermin paused as it noticed a shape floating upon the water nearby. Its whiskers twitched as it tried to pick up the object's scent, the lilac stench making it more difficult.

'Man-person,' it declared in a whispered hiss. In reply, the belly of the skaven beside it rumbled with hunger. The leader lashed its tail in agreement. They were forbidden to nibble at the subjects they secured for Weichs, but there was no reason they shouldn't avail themselves of other man-flesh. The body floating beside the dock was almost like a gift from the Horned Rat. The skaven leader looked about it nervously, afraid that it would see the eyes of its god watching from the shadows.

'Fetch-bring,' the ratman snarled, shoving the skaven with the growling belly toward the body. The creature glanced about cautiously, then slithered into the water, swimming slowly and silently. Soon it was back under the concealment of the dock, dragging the corpse with it. Five sets of hungry eyes glared at the body. The leader snapped at its subordinates with a display of teeth and the pitted sword it held in one claw. It wouldn't do for them to snatch the most succulent meat until after the leader had eaten its fill.

The ratman jumped back, tripping over one of its subdued minions. The leader picked itself up, gesturing with a claw at the corpse they had dragged from the river. 'Man-thing live-move,' it squeaked. The other skaven cast suspicious looks at the body, drawing their own weapons. Life was a problem they could solve quickly enough.

'No!' their leader hissed, lashing its tail through the mud. 'Tie-bind, quick-quick! Fetch-bring for doktor-man!' The ratman paid little notice to the ugly looks its underlings cast as they sullenly complied with its orders. Their leader was already lost in thoughts of the reward for bringing two subjects to Skilk's doktor-man. Of course, it wouldn't be big enough to share with its fellow skaven. Rewards never were.

CHAPTER NINE

THE SITTING ROOM was dark, the dying fire insufficient to banish the shadows that devoured swan-legged tables, upholstered chairs and fur-strewn divans. The room's sole occupant did not stir to replenish the flame, content to sit and study the darkening wall as he drained the contents of the crystal goblet in his hand. The intensifying gloom was a perfect companion to the pall covering his heart.

Lord High Justice Igor Markoff did not stir as the door to his sanctuary opened. Dancing candlelight fought against the darkness threatening to engulf him. He did not care who this midnight violator of his tranquillity might be. It was much too late for that. He had devoted his life to making his name respected and feared throughout Wurtbad, in the murky dens of petty thieves and the polished halls of the nobility. It was only now that he truly understood how tenuous and fleeting such strength and power were. With their parting they had left little but the shell of a tired, frightened old man. Markoff took another swallow from his glass. It might not be possible to restore his strength from a bottle, but he knew he could find oblivion within one.

Dimly, words began to filter through the darkening haze. Harsh, angry words, accusatory words. How could he have let such an atrocity come to pass? How could he have engineered such a hideous scheme? Once he had been a man worthy of respect, even emulation. Now, the self he had shown to the world was revealed as naught but a sham, unmasking the murderous coward within.

'Enough, girl.' Markoff lifted his hand, begging his daughter to cease her tirade. He forced his eyes to remain fixed upon the wall. She had been there, at Otwin Keep, when Meisser carried out his orders. She would not be silenced. Markoff smiled thinly, a tiny ember of pride flickering in the gloom. There was so very much strength in her, so much more than the gods had seen fit to bestow upon her father.

'How?' Silja's words cut at Markoff like a dull knife. 'How could you have conceived such a horror? How could you allow such wanton murder to be perpetrated in the name of the baron?'

'What good would it do to deny your accusations?' Markoff sighed. 'Oh, I am not pleading my innocence. Far from it! I am as guilty as any of the others, those great and noble lords so very concerned with the welfare of their mighty city.' He drained the last dregs of schnapps from his goblet.

'It was the baron's great vision,' Markoff stated. 'It was Meisser who gave it form and substance, the rest of us who gave it life. I've always had a good head for logistics, for efficiency,' the magistrate said. 'The baron has always appreciated that. Left on his own, Meisser would still be wondering which direction the keep is in. *Was* in,' he corrected himself.

'Then it was your idea, your plan,' Silja hissed back at him. The fire in her gaze had little to do with her reddened face and the salty trails staining her cheeks. Her knuckles whitened as Silja's anger drained into them. 'All these years I've admired you, tried to follow your example. What a fool I was to be so blind!'

Markoff rose from his chair, turning to glare at his daughter. 'You would have me play the fool then?' he snapped. 'Stand aside and refuse to have anything to do with the baron's mad schemes, just let Meisser ooze his way ever deeper into his good grace? Would that please you? Would that make you proud?'

'But you are the Lord High Justice–' Silja began to object. Markoff shook his head, scoffing at his daughter's protest.

'Simply another instrument of the baron's will. What power I have, what authority I have, is because the baron allows it. A snap of his fingers, a stroke of his pen, and I am no more powerful than the rankest ratcatcher in the sewers.'

'There must have been someone you could turn to.' Silja's voice had lost some of its venom, her father's pain, frustration and disgrace touching her heart. Markoff shook his head.

'Who? The Grand Theogonist? The Emperor, perhaps? Or maybe our gracious elector count, who has set a ring of steel around this city and is perfectly content to sit back and watch it die? No, Silja, there is no authority I can appeal to.' Markoff's hand began to tremble. 'Baron von Gotz is the only law in Wurtbad. While the quarantine is in effect, he may as well be Sigmar returned.'

'Then madness rules Wurtbad!' Silja swore. Her anger flared as she looked upon her father's trembling frame. She had come here to confront a traitor, an archfiend who had engineered the deaths of thousands. Instead she had found only a broken, defeated old man. She turned, striding from the chamber until she stood once more upon the threshold.

'Tell me, father,' she said, her voice a withering snarl. 'When the baron next calls for his sycophants to endorse whatever insanity stirs his rotten mind, will you crawl to him on your belly like a dog, or will you have enough dignity to stand before him like a man?'

Silja did not wait for an answer, disappearing into the maze of hallways that formed the Ministry of Justice. Markoff stared at the empty doorway for a time, then contemplated the empty goblet in his hand. It would be so easy to ignore her words, to sit out the storm. But she was right. The baron was dangerously mad, more of a threat to the city than the plague he was obsessed with destroying. But Markoff's days of boldness and bravery were behind him, all he wanted now was to live his few remaining years in peace, to enjoy the rewards of his labours in the time left to him. Someone else could try to counter the influence of the baron.

He tried to forget the contempt in his daughter's words. But, even with the schnapps dulling his mind, Markoff couldn't banish her accusations. With a deep growl, the magistrate hurled the goblet into the fading fire, watching as it shattered into a hundred shards of starlight. He grabbed up his cloak from where he had thrown it across one of the divans.

If he was unable to forget, then the time may have come to act in such a way that he would not be ashamed to remember.

FURCHTEGOTT SLAMMED THE book closed, too furious to experience the repugnance that crawled up his spine whenever he touched the binding of the mouldy old grimoire. The mystic wiped his hands on his golden robes. *Das Buch die Unholden* seemed to grin back at him with a mocking smile. He had consulted many tomes of magic since taking up the mantle of wizard, and learned many disquieting, profane secrets in his studies. Knowledge that some insisted man had never been meant to know.

But the ponderous volume compiled by the witch hunter Helmuth Klausner, from the writings of warlocks and sorcerers he had condemned during his career, was another matter. The book almost seemed to be alive, possessed by a malicious intelligence. Pages would turn of their own volition, even when weighted down by lead ingots. The book would never remain where Furchtegott remembered leaving it, always manifesting itself in some unusual spot within his laboratory, some place it had no right to be. Most frustrating of all, though, was the way in which it seemed to guard its secrets; the way text seemed to slither from one page to another, as though evading the prying eye that sought to decipher it.

At one hour of the clock, an ancient fertility rite of the Old Faith might be found beside the foul practices of the Arabyan snake cults. At the next, it might have moved much deeper within the book, lurking between a necromancer's spell for instilling vigour in undead automatons, or a Norse shaman's ritual for bestowing the curse of the werekin upon a warrior. The words themselves were cryptic, written in a dazzling array of languages, every sentence ridden with double-meanings and deliberate contradictions. Some of the ciphers the long-dead witches and enchanters had used to guard their spells were among the most complex Furchtegott had ever seen. Even without the book's malevolent trickery, dredging anything useful from its pages was a study in frustration.

He should have destroyed the damned thing, reduced it to slag with his own spells. But he allowed its power to seep back into the air around him. No, anger would not help him now. He had to keep his mind clear, to consider his best course of action.

Baron von Gotz was deteriorating at a faster pace than Furchtegott had imagined possible. Whatever the spell had been, it was working its unholy sorcery swiftly. The wizard reflected on how easily that first spell had revealed itself to him, that ritual said to preserve a man against the ravages of disease and plague. It had been almost as if *Das Buch die Unholden* had abandoned its usual tricks and misdirection in order to ensure Furchtegott's ruin.

Furchtegott looked over at the heavy beechwood shelves that loomed against the walls of his workshop. The accursed grimoire would not help him, but he had other resources to draw upon. A wizard of the gold order was an alchemist as well as a conjurer, and the array of chemicals, powders and elixirs resting upon those shelves represented the tools of his art. Among them were compounds and concoctions so deadly that even the most murderous Tilean poisoner would hesitate to employ them.

It had become a choice of life or death – the baron's life or his own. Furchtegott realised that there was really no choice at all. He walked to the shelf and removed an iron bottle. The way the baron was gorging himself, Furchetgott was certain that there would be ample opportunity for the contents to find their way into his stomach.

HERR DOKTOR FREIHERR Weichs sucked at his finger as he studied the prone figure lying on the floor of the cage. Quite an interesting specimen, he concluded, ignoring the unease that flickered deep within his subconscious. The skaven had dragged him from the river, so the claw leader that brought the man to Weichs had claimed. Not the most healthy of environments in the best of times, and with his manufactured plague still ravaging the city, these certainly were not the best of times. Still, mere sickness seemed an inadequate explanation of the man's many abnormalities. His temperature was far colder than it should have been. Respiration and pulse were so faint as to be almost imperceptible. And, of course, there was that thick treacle that oozed from the man's forearm when Weichs had cut him. The doktor had seen much blood in his life, but he would swear that the filth slopping through the specimen's veins was not blood. Even the black pollutant that coursed through the bodies of the skaven had more in

common with human blood than what he had drawn from the
man's wound.

A mutant, Weichs decided, but not like any he had studied, or
even created. It was unfortunate that the specimen seemed to
have lapsed into some form of coma. The sharp smell of rat musk
drew Weichs from his thoughts. The scientist turned around to
observe Skilk and his bodyguard scuttling through his laboratory,
causing the skaven working the larger furnaces and the presses to
abase themselves and squirt their pungent fear-scent.

'Doktor-man,' Skilk snickered as the horned skaven hobbled
toward Weichs. 'Progress? Like-hear much-much.'

'I am trying some new compounds,' Weichs explained, unable
to keep the fear from his voice. The words clearly did not appease
his inhuman patron. Grey Seer Skilk's face split in a menacing
smile, his fangs like daggers. Weichs took a step back, fearful that
Skilk's patience had finally reached its limit. Suddenly, the ratman's head cocked to one side, whiskers twitching.

'Man-thing die-die soon,' Skilk declared as he peered into the
cage. 'Doktor-man make bad-drink?' The grin was back on its verminous face.

'No.' Weichs protested. 'He was brought here in that condition
by your people. My potions will help him, make him strong
again.' Skilk chittered his laughter, shaking his head. Somehow,
watching the skaven make such a common human gesture was
more unsettling than his natural habits.

'Death-smell never false-speak,' Skilk stated, one claw tapping
the side of his snout. 'Die-die quick-soon. Food for doktor-man's
warren.' The colour drained from Weichs' face. Of all the disgusting habits of his skaven patrons, their penchant for human flesh
was the vilest. Any meat would appease their voracious appetites,
even that of their own kind. Man-flesh was no different. Weichs
had long ago been forced to allow his subjects to be consumed
when they expired from his experiments. The scientist averted his
eyes, trying not to think any more upon the gruesome subject.

'I have a few new preparations I will be trying on the latest
batch of subjects,' Weichs announced, gesturing for the skaven
priest-sorcerer to follow him. Skilk waited for the man to lead the
way. Skaven leaders were especially wary of allowing their underlings to linger behind them – at least those leaders who hoped to
live very long.

Skilk listened as Weichs prattled about his latest experiments, his black soul secretly mocking the man. Weichs was clever, for a human, but stupid too. He really did believe Skilk was interested in finding a way to unlock the healing properties of warpstone. The idiot. Skilk was not sick. What did he care about curing disease? The doktor-man was too foolish to see that Skilk was studying the effects of warpstone upon the human form, learning how much or how little was needed to corrupt it. Men were a violent, frightful breed, their minds moved by strange motivations and imaginings. They could not endure the taint of mutation among their own, unless that taint manifested in one of the nestlings produced by their own breeder. Then they would try to defend what they would otherwise destroy, forming strange alliances to protect their own from those they had formerly called protectors.

It was another of the many weaknesses that pervaded the human race, their curious affection toward others of their kind at the expense of their own well-being. It made little sense to Skilk, and the grey seer had spent his entire life studying humans after the example of his mentor, Grey Seer Kripsnik. But Skilk did not need to understand it to exploit it, any more than Kripsnik had truly understood the human lust for the yellow metal when he conceived of flooding the lands of men with poisoned coins. It was enough to know that the weakness was there, waiting to be used. The world of men would tear itself apart from within.

Skilk would be the instrument of that final triumph, polluting their cities in ways that the plague monks of Clan Pestilens and the warlock-engineers of Clan Skryre had never dared imagine. Then it would be his name, not that of Thanquol or Gnawdoom or Skrittar, that would be pre-eminent among the Order of the Grey Seers, he who would be acknowledged as the one true prophet of the Horned Rat.

The grey seer's paws scratched at his fur as he listened to Weichs' explanation, its own secret dreams and ambitions kept secret behind the skaven's beady eyes.

THE DANK STENCH of the sewers was overwhelming, overpowering even that of the shambling shapes that silently marched alongside him. Carandini would have preferred the noxious reek of his zombies. To him, the stench of death and decay was comforting. It smelled like power.

The necromancer exerted his will, compelling the two zombies carrying him through the effluent river beneath Wurtbad's streets to stop. The former priests of Morr complied, their ungainly husks swaying slightly as Carandini's weight shifted. The Tilean scowled as he considered how very close he had come to being dropped into the mire that soaked the zombies' feet.

'The mighty deathmaster fears getting his feet wet?' a hissing voice laughed from the shadows. Carandini could see Sibbechai's smouldering eyes in the darkness. The necromancer silently cursed the vampire. Let it laugh, he told himself, for the necromancer would laugh louder when he spat on Sibbechai's ashes and stamped them into the dust.

'Are we near the castle yet?' Carandini demanded. Wurtbad's sewers were not extensive, certainly not so all-encompassing as those of Altdorf or Nuln, where the entire city was served by a network of underground canals and channels. The sewers of Wurtbad extended only beneath the wealthier districts, allowing the elite of the city to enjoy the same comforts they enjoyed when travelling to the Empire's other great cities. The brick-lined tunnels conducted the waste out into the Stir, spoiling the riverfront even as the noses of the wealthy were spared.

The vampire's skeletal face leered. It had been Sibbechai's plan to use the sewers. It had returned to its lair after reconnoitring the area around the Schloss von Gotz, its travels taking it close to the river and the culverts that drained the sewers into the Stir. Carandini had to reluctantly admit that Sibbechai's plan was well plotted, if odious.

'Not so far now,' Sibbechai pronounced. 'We are beneath the royal quarter.' Carandini did not bother to ask the vampire how it could know such things. The supernatural senses of the undead were impossible for a mortal mind to comprehend.

Suddenly, the vampire snapped around. Carandini could see its lips pull away from its fangs. Sibbechai seemed to glide toward the wall, its feet causing not even a ripple upon the foul waters. Its clawed hand reached out, pulling one brick free. Carandini expected mud or dirt to spill from the wall, but instead there was only darkness. Sibbechai tossed the brick into the filth at its feet.

'It seems we are not the only sappers beneath Wurtbad,' Sibbechai mused.

'Some thief's strongbox,' Carandini postulated. The vampire shook its head.

'I can feel the air stirring here. It must open into a tunnel of some kind, not some ruffian's hiding place.' Carandini snapped his fingers, motioning for the zombies to advance. The rotting workers began to chip at the wall with picks and hammers.

'This tunnel of yours may be an old escape route from the castle,' Carandini observed. 'If it is, our work shall be much easier.'

'There are many fell powers in the night, necromancer,' Sibbechai declared. 'Some of them older and more merciless even than the houses of the vampires.' His eyes shone with a terrible intensity. 'If you still pray to any of the gods of men, pray that we find only dirt and stone and nothing more.'

Carandini watched as the opening in the sewer wall grew, finding Sibbechai's words of warning more frightful than the monster's threats. It was not wise to ponder what manner of creature could evoke caution in a powerful vampire.

A CURSE ECHOED about the old torture chamber, as Streng tossed aside his shovel to remove the large stone that disturbed his digging. Thulmann could not quite kill the smirk that grew on his face; his henchman never did have the heart for manual labour. The heaps of dirt set against the walls continued to rise. The witch hunters might not be experienced miners, but their enthusiasm was a worthy surrogate. Stripped to the waist, the templars attacked the blocked tunnel with vigour, hacking away at the earth and stone as though it were the neck of an enemy. Captain-Justicar Ehrhardt stood in reserve, powerful arms folded across his chest, waiting for the diggers to uncover any large stones that his immense strength could remove.

Thulmann could well understand the drive that motivated these men. The skaven had violated the sanctity of their chapter house, caused the ignoble death of their comrades. Already the diggers had uncovered one of their brethren, crushed and suffocated by the tunnel's collapse. The steady pace of the diggers had increased after that discovery, more eager than ever to come to grips with the loathsome underfolk.

It was not thoughts of retribution that stirred Thulmann's mind. Hanzel Gruber was dead; whatever the plague doktor could have told had died with him. His killers were now the only link to Weichs. The witch hunter looked at the hole his men were tearing into, almost wishing to see a rodent's snout, furry bodies and

clawed hands spill into the chapter house. Thulmann gripped the
pistols in his hands. He would need to be careful with his shots.
Some of the underfolk could speak and understand enough Reikspiel to converse with men. If Thulmann could capture such a
beast, it might have some very interesting things to tell him. He
looked at the two Wurtbader templars beside him, their pistols
held at the ready. He had given orders to shoot to maim, hoping
that they could master their emotions long enough to show
restraint.

Thulmann spun around as a foot struck the stone floor behind
him. It was not some rat-faced fiend, but one of the chapter
house's young page boys. The boy's eyes were on the filthy carcass
Streng had dragged from the corridor outside and thrown into a
corner of the chamber.

'You should not be here,' Thulmann stated. 'Go back upstairs.'

'There is a visitor to see you, sir,' the page reported. 'Silja
Markoff. Should I send her down?' The boy's eyes strayed back to
the unnatural carcass of the skaven. Silja had seen enough horror
for one night. The least that Thulmann could do was spare her the
sight of such an abomination.

'No,' he replied. 'I will see her in the reception hall. Please tell
her I will be come to her directly.' The page needed no further
encouragement, hurrying from the subterranean chamber. Thulmann gave orders to the men to maintain their vigilance while he
was gone, encouraging them to take one of the ratmen alive if at
all possible.

His thoughts turned to Silja, and the purpose of her arriving so
late. The witch hunter sighed as he mounted the steps. The last
thing he needed to hear this night was more bad news.

CHAPTER TEN

'WE SHOULD DO something about the slums.' The voice of Baron von Gotz was like the sound of a dog slobbering into its water dish, a nauseating, wet lapping noise. Furchtegott cringed as the baron spoke, struggling not to picture that grotesque parody of a mouth. The wizard had drawn the heavy curtains about the baron's bed, advising the nobleman to avoid drafts, yet, even with that ghastly bulk obscured, he could not vanquish the image from his mind.

'They are a breeding place for the plague,' the baron continued, noisily biting into the plate of mutton that rested in bed with him. 'The sooner they are removed, the sooner my city shall be free of the Stir blight. Besides, they obscure my view of the river.' The baron laughed, causing Furchtegott to think of swine wallowing in a pigpen.

'As you say, excellency,' Furchtegott replied, trying to keep his dinner down. Why by all the gods was he not dead? The wizard had chosen three of the deadliest substances known to his order, fairly drenched the nobleman's food in the stuff, and still he would not die. He didn't even seem to notice the poison, continuing to glut his insatiable hunger upon an unrelenting tide of dishes. He'd eaten enough to feed a battalion in the last few hours, and ingested enough poison to kill an entire army. And Furchtegott was becoming hard pressed to keep the servants out, to intercept the baron's meals at the door.

He shuddered, reaching for a bowl of soup the baron had yet to slurp down. The wizard removed the iron bottle from his bag, upending it and draining its contents into the soup. Troll vomit was one of the most caustic acids a man could find, capable of gnawing through just about anything if given enough time. Only magic kept it from eating through its bottle, but no magic would contain its deadly bite once it was resting in the baron's bloated belly. It would chew its way through the walls of his stomach, rip its way free of his flesh. It was the most horrible way to die that the wizard could imagine, aside from the loathsome metamorphosis already consuming the baron. But the troll acid simply had to work. It was his last hope.

The sound of angry voices outside the door turned the wizard's attention away from the baron's bed. Furchtegott had just risen to his feet when the door swung inward, a flush-faced Lord Markoff stalking inside like a rabid wolf, the guards hurrying behind him.

'What is the meaning of this outrage?' Furchtegott demanded. 'The baron is not receiving visitors.' The wizard lifted his hand, pointing imperiously at the open door. 'Get out of here.'

'Save your crooked words and twisted spells, sorcerer,' snarled Markoff, the fury in his voice causing Furchtegott to involuntarily flinch. 'My words are for the baron, not his simpering lapdog.' The two guards exchanged nervous glances, their halberds held at the ready. Furchtegott did not know what bribes or threats Markoff had used to force his way inside, but it was clear they were regretting their decision now. Two armed soldiers against the unarmed Lord High Justice might not be the one-sided affair they had imagined.

'Do I hear voices?' the baron slobbered. It was Markoff's turn to flinch, the colour draining from his face. Sigmar's grace, was that the baron's voice? 'Do I hear my dear Lord High Justice?'

'Yes, excellency,' replied Furchtegott. 'You must tell him to leave. He is disturbing your rest.' Sweat was streaming down the wizard's forehead. If Markoff threw aside those curtains, if he saw the thing lying upon the bed…

'I will not leave,' Markoff snapped. 'There are things I must discuss with your excellency. Crimes that must be addressed.' The magistrate's words dripped menace like the venom of an adder, his cold tone belying the terrible anger boiling just below the surface. Furchtegott could see the guards grow tense as Markoff spoke.

'Crimes?' The baron's swinish laugh grunted across the room. 'Crimes are your matter, Lord High Justice. Do not bother me with such petty details.' The baron continued to gorge himself, crunching bones as he broke them apart to suck the marrow within.

'I speak of the atrocity at Otwin Keep.' Markoff snarled. 'I speak of the massacre perpetrated on your orders, entire families slaughtered to appease your fear of the plague.'

'I rule Wurtbad,' the baron retorted, his voice like a boot sinking into mud. 'My word is law. My will governs the land. The city and all within it are mine. Mine. If they live to see the dawn it is because *I* have allowed it.'

Markoff took a step toward the bed. 'There are laws that are beyond those of any temporal ruler, baron. Laws even the Emperor himself must acknowledge and respect.' The magistrate gave no warning of his intentions. Even the soldiers, who had been watching Markoff closely, were unprepared when he ripped a dagger from beneath his clothing and leapt toward the bed. 'The thousands butchered in your name cry out for justice and by my hand they shall have it, monster.'

The curtains were torn aside. The sight they had concealed impacted upon Markoff like a brick wall. The dagger fell from his fingers, his knees crumpled as their strength withered. 'Monster,' he had called von Gotz – but in his darkest nightmares, Markoff could never have imagined how fitting the epithet truly was. A moan of horror surged from the magistrate's body as reason crumbled within his mind.

The soldiers rushed forward, eyes locked not upon the horror they called sovereign, but on the shuddering assassin. They drove the shafts of their halberds into the man's back, spilling him to the floor. Only then did they chance to gaze upon the source of Markoff's terror.

It surged forward, the thing sprawling across the bed like an enormous pustule. Arms that were twice the length of a man's reached forward, a clawed, scabrous hand closing about the neck of one of the guards like a hangman's noose. The soldier did not have time to utter the scream welling up inside him. As though it were killing a chicken, the thing twisted the soldier's neck, killing him with a sickening pop. His comrade shrieked, hurling his halberd into the thing's face and retreating back toward the door.

He might have escaped, for the thing baron von Gotz had become was not a thing of swiftness and grace. But Furchtegott could not allow the man to live, could not let him carry this episode of horror away with him before the wizard had a chance to correct the terrible mistake he had made. Furchtegott exerted his will and the door slammed close, held fast by invisible tendrils of irresistible force. The guard screamed again, smashing and clawing at the door, his nails digging deep scratches into the wood. The baron's corrupt bulk waddled slowly towards him, clawed hands outstretched.

'Traitors,' the baron spat. 'Murderers and assassins all!' The baron's obscene bulk loomed over the prone form of Igor Markoff. The once-feared Lord High Justice was mewing pathetically, his mind broken by the hideous thing he had dared to challenge. 'I am Baron Friedo von Gotz! Lord of Wurtbad, master of the Empire's most glorious city!' The baron's malformed claw drooped to the floor, snatching up Markoff's cringing form as though the man weighed no more than a doll. Furchtegott could hear the magistrate muttering and mumbling in his delirium, sobbing again and again the name 'Silja'. The baron pulled the magistrate toward the shapeless lump that served him as a face, the gigantic, gash-like mouth opening like the maw of a shark, displaying craggy, rotten teeth. Furchtegott closed his eyes as the baron's jaws snapped close and Markoff's muttering was silenced.

'This is a great day,' the baron said, when the sounds of flesh being ripped from bone had receded into Furchtegott's nightmares. Neither the guards nor Markoff would be telling anyone what they had seen. 'A terrible traitor to the Empire has been unmasked and destroyed. There must be celebration.' The grotesque mound resting atop the baron's shoulders shook up and down. 'Yes, all the city must celebrate. I shall make a proclamation and you shall record it for me, dear master wizard. I am going to declare a festival. The food stores shall be thrown open and distributed to the people as a reward for their loyalty. Anyone found not feasting shall be hanged as a traitor.'

The baron's voice trailed off into swinish laughter. 'I shall open the palace, too. It shall be a great festivity, such as Wurtbad has not seen since the last vampire count was destroyed at Hel Fenn.' A claw-like finger pointed at the wizard. 'You must make out the invitations, Furchtegott, I can trust no one else with such an honour.'

Furchtegott smiled uneasily at the hulking monster. The baron's mind was deteriorating even more swiftly than his body, but the wizard knew better than to challenge his insane notions. He obediently approached a writing table and readied quill and parchment. Out of one eye, Furchtegott could see the monster slurping down the bowl of soup the wizard had poisoned.

'One should always wash down meat with broth,' the baron burped, tossing the empty bowl aside. Furchtegott felt the last vestiges of hope curl up and die inside him. Even troll vomit seemed unable to kill the abomination! An even more horrible possibility presented itself as the baron began to dictate his decree. Perhaps the thing that von Gotz had become could not be killed.

IT HAD NOT taken long for their tireless workforce to excavate the compromised section of the wall. Beyond the broken brickwork, the zombies exposed a dank tunnel of earth, the walls uneven and crude, scratched as if by giant claws. The bricks they had torn down appeared to have been intended for removal, held by a simple clay that broke easily beneath the attention of an axe or a pick. Carandini did not like to think upon what sort of creatures had engineered such a tunnel and hidden it so cunningly. Goblins, perhaps, though they would have used tools more akin to those of men rather than the claw-like implements the diggers of this tunnel had employed.

'In that direction,' Sibbechai hissed, stepping into the tunnel beside Carandini. The vampire pointed to the north. 'The tunnel joins a crossroads ahead, we follow the left branch.' Carandini willed his zombies to lead the way. The passageway might be deserted, but the necromancer would not take any further chances. Sibbechai seemed to sense his fear, its skull-like face grinning at him from the darkness.

The tunnel continued for fifty feet before linking with the cross-roads. Carandini was quietly impressed by the vampire's vision, the monster penetrating the darkness as well as a mortal man could see in the sunlight. It was yet another disturbing detail to add to Sibbechai's list of strengths, another obstacle to overcome when the time came to break their tenuous alliance.

Carandini watched the zombies shuffle deeper into the tunnel, disturbed to hear the sound of their feet sloshing through water. It explained the persistent stench of the sewer, even in the tunnel. The filthy water was seeping through the earthen walls. The necromancer noted that the low ceiling of the tunnel would prevent his undead porters from carrying him as they had before. Whatever had dug these tunnels was not disturbed by confined spaces.

The zombies completed the intersection, waiting for the puppeteer to tug at their strings and give them new tasks to perform. Carandini watched Sibbechai's gaunt shadow disappear to the left. At least if anything was waiting for them, the vampire would discover it first. It brought a greasy smile to the necromancer's face, which faded when he discovered the extent of the seepage. The tunnel ahead of them was like a subterranean swamp, a stinking quagmire festering between the crudely excavated walls. The Tilean snarled a curse on the unknown builders of the passage, willing his slaves forward before Sibbechai's skeletal shape vanished completely from view.

The reeking filth of the sewer lapped about his knees as he walked. Side tunnels opened onto the passageway, dark, cave-like openings that sent a chill of unease up Carandini's spine as he passed, wondering what might be watching their intrusion with malevolent, inhuman eyes. Several times, he fancied that he heard a soft, scuttling sound, or the hiss of bestial voices. Nervously, the necromancer willed several of his zombie slaves to walk behind him and protect his back.

They had proceeded several hundred yards through the darkness when the fear gnawing at his spine finally manifested itself. The necromancer stumbled into his fifth pothole, spilling himself into the filthy water. He rose from the muck, his cassock dripping stagnant brown water. Then he saw Sibbechai turn from where it stood a dozen yards deeper into the tunnel, its fiery eyes blazing. At first the Tilean believed the monster was simply gloating at his discomfort, but then he recognised an intense wariness. Sibbechai's voice rasped from the darkness.

'We are not alone,' it hissed. 'The underfolk are coming.'

No sooner did the vampire speak, than Carandini detected the squirming, splashing sound of many bodies racing up the tunnel behind him, a squeaking noise growing from a faint murmur into a distinct roar. Sibbechai returned its attention to the tunnel ahead as dozens of eyes gleamed at the vampire from the darkness. Carandini willed his zombies to form a defensive line around him. The vampire could attend to its own welfare.

Then they were upon them, a snarling, squeaking mass of vermin. The tunnel crawled with the verminous shapes, the pungent stink of their fur overcoming even the stench of the sewer water. Carandini saw a riot of shapes and forms, small brown rats swimming through the water alongside vermin the size of dogs. Most hideous were those that scuttled forward on two legs, loathsome mockeries of men carrying rusty knives and driftwood spears. Some of the creatures wore tattered rags about their furry bodies, others went naked, their fur pitted and marred where ugly symbols had been branded into their hides. These were hurled against the defensive line of Carandini's zombies like a living wave. The ratmen slashed into his undead guards with knives and claws, their fangs gnashing together as they chittered their fury.

Carandini drew back, with the words of a spell on his lips. Even in Tilea tales were told of the underfolk, the foul skaven. His native Miragliano had been repeatedly attacked by the creatures, plagued by their corruption for countless generations. There was little Carandini held in common with the men of his homeland, his dark studies setting him as a breed apart. But the necromancer remembered the old hatred of his race, the ancient enemy of his people. It was a hate deeper than his contempt for the men of the Empire, a hate that dwelled in his blood. The necromancer stretched forth his hand, invoking the terrible name of the Power. Several of the skaven shrieked, steam rising from their mangy fur. The vermin turned to scurry back into the shadows, but found themselves blocked by the spears and swords of their own kind.

The necromancer exerted his will once more. The skaven squealed as their fur fell from their bodies, as the flesh beneath shrivelled into leather, the blood in their veins turning to dust. Before the horrified eyes of their comrades, the creatures toppled

C.L Werner

into the filthy water, their bodies reduced to mummified husks. The skaven attack faltered, the vermin chittering in fear, then surged forward once more. Carandini urged the remaining zombies to close ranks around him while he called upon the Power once more. But nearly half of his undead guards had been dragged down by the ratmen's savage assault.

Further down the tunnel, Sibbechai confronted the advance packs of the skaven. Dozens of chittering monsters clawed and hacked at the vampire with an inhuman swiftness nearly the equal of its own. But if the vermin were fast, they lacked the supernatural strength of the vampire. While their claws and knives ripped ineffectively into Sibbechai's withered flesh, its talons tore open their throats, snapped their limbs and crushed their skulls. The vampire snarled its own rage and fury, licking black skaven blood from its talons. With seven of their number strewn about it, the skaven cringed, squealing in fright. Sibbechai saw a large, white-furred warrior, its scarred face scowling at the vampire, barking furious orders at the cowardly soldiers. The vampire glared back at the skaven leader. It had not come so close to achieving its destiny in order to let a mob of subhuman scum cheat it of victory.

Large brown rats milled about the tunnel, squeaking in confusion. Urged to attack by the musk-scent of the skaven, the rats had followed their more advanced relations. But the object of their aggression had filled their tiny minds with fear. The mind of an animal could feel the profane energies that gave the vampire its pseudo-life, the power that exuded from the undead monster. The rats quivered and whined, goaded to attack by the musk-scent of the skaven but repulsed by the unnatural life-force of the vampire. Then, almost as a single creature, the rats grew still. Their confusion was at an end.

Sibbechai extended its clawed hand, stabbing a talon in the direction of the white-furred skaven. 'Kill,' it hissed, its smouldering eyes glowing like embers in the darkness. The rats surged forward, their beady red eyes mirroring the glow of the vampire's. The skaven chittered in terror as the swarm engulfed them, gnawing and tearing at their flesh. The leader was barking orders to its warriors as a tide of brown death swept over it, tiny bodies worrying at its furred limbs, clawing at its rodent face. The skaven tore desperately at the wriggling, gnawing beasts, but for every one it ripped free, ten more leapt upon it. Soon, the creature's white fur was blackened with blood and it plummeted into the water about its feet, writhing weakly as the rats continued to chew on its ravaged flesh.

With the death of their leader, the remaining ratmen scurried back down the tunnels, squealing in fright. Sibbechai watched them flee, annoyed that it could not expend the power to destroy them all. Perhaps once *Das Buch die Unholden* was in its hands, the vampire would return to settle with the vermin. But that was for a later time. The vampire turned, looking toward where Carandini had made his stand. Sibbechai still needed the necromancer. It would have been inconvenient if the skaven had managed to kill him.

Carandini stood at the centre of a circle of charred, withered bodies. Only a handful of the necromancer's zombies remained, their rotten flesh torn asunder, many of them lacking arms and hands where the skaven had hacked them from their bodies. The Tilean met the vampire's gaze. Sibbechai could see the fear and loathing behind the necromancer's eyes.

'What do we do now?' Carandini demanded.

'We proceed,' Sibbechai replied, its voice a cold whisper.

'We cannot,' protested Carandini. 'What if they return? Neither do we have enough zombies left to dig our way into the castle.' Sibbechai sneered at the necromancer's fear.

'Then make more,' it hissed back. 'There is no lack of material to work with.' It gestured with its clawed hands at the twisted, mangled remains of the skaven floating in the stagnant water all around them. 'The vermin have not diminished our workforce, they have added to it.'

SILJA'S TIDINGS HAD indeed been ill. She had confronted her father at the Ministry of Justice, admonishing him for his role in the destruction of Otwin Keep. Rather than refuting her accusations, the old magistrate had quietly accepted the blame, with no more justification than fear of Baron von Gotz, sovereign ruler of Wurtbad, and the nobleman's growing madness.

Mathias Thulmann had listened to Silja, hearing in her voice only the palest echo of the strength and conviction he had become accustomed to. The Lord High Justice's complicity in the baron's hideous edict had crushed her spirit, her father's failure to stand firm before such horrendous misuse of power had broken her. The witch hunter knew that no words he could speak would comfort the pain in her heart. She looked upon him in pained misery, a desperate pleading in her gaze.

Thulmann took her in his arms, holding her tightly, willing the pain to flow out of her and into him. Silja's body trembled as the tension slowly faded, eased by the simple solace of the touch of another human being. The witch hunter's hand kneaded the back of her neck, trying to soothe the stress he felt tight beneath the skin. Almost against his will, he found trite words of comfort, promises that all would turn out for the best. Silja did not seem to notice their vapidity, or the emptiness of their reassurances. Her only reaction had been to hold the witch hunter still more tightly, her breath hot upon his shoulder.

Thulmann slowly pulled away, uncomfortable with where this moment might lead. He had claimed the affection of a woman once, and that love had ended in a tragedy that nearly destroyed him. Such things were for other men. Men who walked beneath the clean light of the sun, men who did not skulk in the shadows of night, chasing the dread Dark Powers. Silja deserved better than Thulmann could ever offer her, even if he dared. As he released the woman, a regretful smile cast its pall upon his face. He saw a brief flicker of fresh pain flash cross Silja's features and felt a twinge of agony somewhere deep inside himself.

'You need rest,' Thulmann said. 'I will have the servants prepare a room for you, Fraulein Markoff. Please accept the humble hospitality of the Order of Sigmar.' The witch hunter bowed before his guest, then turned. 'If you will forgive me, there are pressing matters I must attend to which I dare not delay longer.'

'Perhaps you might allow me to help,' Silja offered. The need in her eyes touched Thulmann's heart. She wanted something to distract her from the black thoughts clouding her mind, until the pain she was feeling became dulled. Against this he weighed the twisted, grotesque thing lying in one corner of the old torture chamber, the terrible horror his men were even now breaking their backs to unearth. The image of soft white flesh being torn by the claws and fangs of malformed monsters.

Thulmann shook his head. 'No, this is a matter for my order to resolve. I must decline your gracious offer.' The witch hunter opened the door, stepping into the corridor. 'Get some rest, we shall talk more in the morning.'

Then he was gone, leaving Silja alone with her doubts and fears. With no observer to steel her nerves, Silja dropped down into one of the antique chairs, her pretence of strength dispelled like a magician's illusion. She thought again of her father, hidden away within his fortress, drinking his soul numb. He had always seemed such a good and honourable man. She thought again of the witch hunter. He too seemed a good and honourable man. But if she had been so wrong about a man she had known all her life, how could she put any faith in a man she had met only days ago?

Doubt, distrust and fear clawed at Silja's thoughts as the hours of night wore on.

FREIHERR WEICHS RAN a cloth against his forehead, drenching it in sweat. Grey Seer Skilk was an unpleasant creature at the best of times, but the skaven sorcerer-priest was even more intimidating when angry. Weichs cringed every time the ratman's long, scaly tail slapped against the floor, writhing like some gigantic worm. Skilk ran one black-furred paw across the ghastly collection of trophies ringing his neck, the monster's teeth bared in a fearsome grin.

The source of the grey seer's ire grovelled on the floor before him, its belly resting on the bare earth. It mewed piteously at the horned ratman, chittering in its own shrill, piercing language. Whatever words were exchanged, they only seemed to add to the grey seer's fury and increased the creature's misery. Weichs could see that the skaven had already undergone some terrible ordeal, dozens of wounds marking its body, apparently bite marks, its foul black blood slowly dripping. Was there some disagreement among the ranks? From what Weichs had seen of the brutality that passed for society among the skaven, some schism among their own kind might explain both the messenger's wounds and the grey seer's ire.

'Dead-things?' Skilk suddenly snapped, turning his hostile gaze upon Weichs. 'Dead-things in tunnels?' he hissed. The grey seer reached down at the miserable wretch whimpering at his feet, grabbing the ratman by the scruff of its neck. With a savage shove, Skilk threw the messenger across Weichs's lab toward one of the iron specimen cages. 'Look-scent.' Skilk snarled, still glaring at Weichs. With horror, the scientist understood what Skilk was saying in his debased Reikspiel.

Something had invaded the skaven tunnels, something the messenger described as 'dead-things'. Skilk had connected this description to the strange comatose man lying in the cage, the one who had 'death-smell'. The grey seer was quick to suspect treachery, and now his distrust was focused upon Weichs. The scientist felt a wave of nausea as he contemplated what Skilk would do if he thought he had betrayed him.

'Same-same,' the messenger squeaked, scurrying away from the cage as though it held all the daemons of the Wastes within. Skilk's malevolent smile grew as he advanced on Weichs.

'Doktor-man plot-sneak,' the grey seer accused. 'Want-like Skilk kill-kill, yes?' Weichs could see the two armoured killers that always accompanied the priest slinking toward him from either side. The scientist glanced about his warren-like lab, searching for some means of escape. His own assistants were cowering behind their stations, even the malformed Lobo trying to hide behind one of the presses. The skaven that had been working with him were slowly creeping forward, their faithless hearts eager to see the drama play itself out. Guttural screams of excitement and glee roared from the cages, their twisted inmates rattling the bars at the prospect of seeing their tormentor destroyed.

'I've been loyal.' Weichs shrieked. 'I would not betray you.' He backed away from the snarling skaven, trying to place a worktable between himself and Skilk's guards. 'Someone is trying to trick you, trying to stop our work.' Weichs knew enough about the skaven mind to understand it was useless to try to appease its suspicious nature. If he was going to save his skin, he had to redirect its paranoia.

Skilk hesitated, almost visibly contemplating Weichs's desperate words. His bodyguards continued to stalk him, corroded swords clutched in their hands. Weichs began to scan the table for anything heavy enough to serve as a weapon. Suddenly Skilk lifted a black paw and uttered a sharp hiss. The two skaven warriors backed away, lashing their tails as they withdrew.

'Doktor-man true-speak, maybe,' Skilk said, his voice still dreadful in its uncertainty. 'Other grey seers like-want Skilk fail-fall,' the sorcerer considered. After what seemed an eternity Skilk turned

away. Weichs breathed a deep sigh of relief as the grey seer barked
orders to the other skaven.

'Take-fetch dead-thing,' Skilk snapped. 'Burn-burn,' he added,
pointing a clawed finger to the largest of the workshop's furnaces.
Weichs would regret losing the opportunity to study the strange
man, but the loss was more than balanced by the continuance of
his own life.

Three of the ratmen scurried toward the cage, one of them
snatching the key to the lock from Lobo as the malformed
halfling emerged from hiding. The furred monsters hesitated at
the unpleasant smell of the cage's occupant, but a glance over
their hunched shoulders at Skilk reminded the vermin who they
were more afraid of. The ratmen opened the lock, scuttling into
the small cell and dragging the unconscious man from his prison.
Weichs could see him move his arm slightly, a faint groan rasping
from his mouth. The man should have stayed in his coma longer,
Weichs considered. It was certainly no respite to wake up to discover the skaven's intentions toward him.

The ratmen dragged the man across the laboratory, toward the
fiery maw of the furnace. One of the ratmen was the mangled
specimen that had brought word to Skilk of the intruders in their
tunnels. Black blood continued to drip from its injuries, trickling
from the monster's fur onto the pale skin of the prisoner's arm.

The prisoner shuddered into motion almost faster than the eye
could perceive, throwing aside his captors as though they were
made of straw. One crashed into the side of a cage, its back snapping on the unyielding metal. The ratman's pitiful cries became
frantic, as limbs that had once been arms reached from inside the
cage and began to tear the rest of his bones from its skin. Another
of the skaven flew across a worktable, its body colliding with the
delicate glass apparatus as fiercely as if fired from a ballista. The
vessels exploded under the impact, bathing the hurtling skaven
with their volatile contents. The ratman struck the floor screaming, the corrosive mixture melting the flesh from its bones.

The wounded skaven was not cast aside by the prisoner, but
dragged close to the man's breast. Weichs saw the man throw back
his head, mouth opened wide, displaying a set of serpentine
fangs. The skaven held in his powerful grip shrieked as the fangs
buried themselves in its neck. Blood exploded from the wound.
Weichs was sickened to see even more of the foul liquid sucked

up by the prisoner's leech-like mouth. He had always discounted
the myths and legends that spoke of the Children of the Night,
the creatures known as vampires. Now he knew better.

GREGOR DRANK DEEPLY, the squirming skaven he held clawing inef-
fectually at his face. The world around him had become red, his
mind thundering with the unclean hunger that filled his entire
being. He had denied it too long, so long that even the putrid
smell of the ratman's corrupt blood was enough to make the
hunger explode inside him. It was an avalanche, a tidal wave. He
could no more resist it than an ant could resist the crushing tread
of a giant. Now the skaven's blood surged through him, feeding
the foulness he had tried to resist. Gregor could feel the strength
rippling through his body, feel the power coursing through his
ravaged frame. He howled in disgust as he tossed the dead skaven
aside, feeling the triumph of the corruption within him.

More of the ghastly underfolk were surging toward him, chittering their wrath, knives and swords flashing in their unclean
hands. Gregor knew them for the monsters they were, had heard
his own father wake up screaming in the night as his dreams
touched upon memories of the vile ratmen. But there was no
room for terror in the shrivelled, dying thing that had been his
heart. What were these noxious vermin beside the horror that he
himself had become? Gregor roared back at the scurrying ratmen,
not waiting to receive their charge but pouncing upon them, such
was the unholy lust burning in his veins. Like a lion among jack-
als Gregor lashed out at his inhuman attackers, each blow
crushing ribs or breaking limbs.

Above the cries and screams of the skaven, Gregor could hear a
sharp, shrill voice shrieking commands. He turned his red-
rimmed eyes, scowling at the verminous shape that barked orders
to its kin. The horned skaven priest withered before Gregor's terrible gaze. He saw the creature lift a shard of black stone to its
muzzle. As it gnawed the stone, profane energies gathered. The
sorcerer stretched forth its hand, a sizzling bolt of black lightning
leaping from its paw.

'The apparatus.' an elderly man hiding behind a cabinet
screamed. 'Be careful of the apparatus.'

A normal man would have been struck by that terrible lightning, his body burned to a crisp. But Gregor was no longer a

normal man. As swiftly as the priest's spell was unleashed, Gregor was faster still, diving aside an instant before it could strike him. The terrible energy struck like daemonic thunderbolts, smashing into the bars of the cage behind him, turning them into molten slag.

Gregor did not have the luxury of relief. Set upon by a pair of frantic men wielding heavy hammers, his unholy eyes could see the blood glowing inside them, a foul, corrupt purple. 'Mutants,' he decided as he broke the arm of one, and tore out the throat of the other, his filthy blood spraying across the cavern. Gregor grabbed the crumpled, shrieking shape of his wounded antagonist, pulling it toward him. Man or monster, blood or daemon ichor, Gregor would appease the hunger with the creature's life.

Across the workshop, Grey Seer Skilk gathered the terrible energies of the warpstone he had consumed, preparing to unleash another bolt of destruction. Then he watched the creature lift one of Weichs's human servants over his head and break the man's back like a twig, reconsidering the wisdom of drawing its attention.

Skilk backed away, promising his bodyguards a death far worse than anything the creature could do if they did not stop it. The armoured skaven hesitated, cautiously scuttling forward. Skilk watched them depart, then turned and scurried for the nearest tunnel, his infirmity forgotten in his flight. Skilk was dimly aware of others hurrying after him. The skaven was about to snarl his wrath at whichever of his kinfolk was endagering Skilk's life by deserting the fray. But his companions were not skaven.

'Follow-quick.' Skilk snapped at Weichs and his malformed halfling slave. They followed close behind the retreating skaven priest as he raced down the burrow-like passageway, leaving the carnage to unfold in the workshop.

As he fled, Skilk was already making new plans. Someone was concerned that Weichs's discovery might place great power in Skilk's paws. Skilk considered that the list of possibilities was almost endless, but only the plague priests of Clan Pestilens or another grey seer would be so bold as to strike in this manner. He had to keep Weichs safe, at least until the human had done what was required of him. And he had to find out who was unleashing these alive-dead man-people.

The resources of an entire warlord clan were at his disposal. Skilk would flood the tunnels with skaven warriors, bring down these horrible man-monsters, and unmask whatever foolish rival thought himself powerful enough to destroy Grey Seer Skilk.

'IT'S NO USE,' Streng protested. He hurled the shovel across the room, doubling his body over and sucking great gasps of breath back into his lungs. 'We've been working for hours and for every shovel we remove, three times as much dirt rolls back.'

Thulmann stared hard at his henchman, angered not by his words, but by the truth they held. The witch hunters had been working all night to excavate the skaven tunnel, yet their efforts had only exposed a few feet. At such a rate, the year would turn before they uncovered more than a few yards of the passageway.

'It is your decision, Brother Mathias,' old Tuomas advised, leaning on his pick to rest. 'You currently hold the authority of witch hunter captain.' Thulmann silently considered the problem.

'We serve no purpose here,' he finally relented. 'If we would find these creatures, we must do so in some other fashion. Though I confess that how we will do such a thing eludes me.'

'Sigmar provides,' Tuomas replied.

'And no debt owed to Morr is left unpaid,' Captain-Justicar Ehrhardt growled. The Black Guardsman stabbed his shovel into the earthen wall as though spearing the throat of an enemy and stalked from the chamber, pausing only to gather up the armour he removed when he started to dig.

'Friend Ehrhardt has the right idea,' Thulmann confessed. 'We all of us need rest. Then we shall plan our next move.' Days of searching for Sibbechai's lair had turned up nothing. Now he had lost his best chance of finding Weichs. All he had managed to accomplish in the last few days was an act that many within the Order of Sigmar would decry as mutiny, heresy and insubordination. His only hope to avoid censure was that perhaps Meisser was not entirely unknown to his superiors in Altdorf. His duplicitous character was Thulmann's best hope of exoneration.

He ascended the steps leading up from the dungeon, squinting as he emerged into daylight. It did nothing to diminish his grim mood. The witch hunter's mind turned over the many failures he had endured since returning to Wurtbad. He had failed to find *Das Buch die Unholden* and failed to destroy Sibbechai. He had spoiled his best chance at tracking down Doktor Weichs, the man who, his instinct told him, was responsible for the horrible plague ravaging the city. He had even failed to stop the atrocity at Otwin Keep, underestimating the lengths to which Meisser would go. The witch hunter shook his head. It was at such times that the power and grace of Sigmar were hard to perceive, when the might of the Dark Powers seemed unassailable.

The witch hunter saw Ehrhardt's huge figure filling the hallway. Beside him stood Tuomas and the old servant Eldred. There was an expectant air about the trio, as though they were waiting for him. As Thulmann approached, Eldred stepped away from his companions.

'A messenger from the baron left this in my care not five minutes ago,' Eldred announced. 'It is for the captain of witch hunters.' A conspiratorial smile spread on the old man's wrinkled features. 'Since Captain Meisser is unwell, I thought it would be prudent if I were to impart it to yourself.'

Thulmann took the scroll Eldred offered him. He broke its wax seal and slipped the ribbon that held the scroll from the document. His eyes raced over the precise, practised lettering that filled the page, outrage mounting within him as every word imprinted itself upon his mind.

'Brother Mathias?' Tuomas spoke, worried by his obvious distemper. The templar looked up, crumpling the scroll in his fist.

'It is an invitation from Baron von Gotz,' Thulmann declared. 'Herr Captain Meisser has been invited to a feast the baron is holding in his castle. Indeed, he has declared a city-wide celebration.'

'Celebrating what?' Ehrhardt dourly rumbled.

'The execution of Lord High Justice Markoff,' Thulmann spat, as though the words were poison. 'The baron names Markoff a traitor here, and says that he will not forget Meisser's noble and heroic action at the keep when he appoints a new Lord High Justice.' Thulmann slammed his fist against the wall, cracking the plaster with his fury.

'He can't do that.' protested Tuomas.

'He has the authority to do whatever he wants.' Thulmann scowled, then paused as a thought occurred. Silja had said her father was convinced that the baron was mad. If this could be proven, if someone was bold enough to level such charges against him in public, and had the power to enforce the baron's removal…

'Brother Tuomas,' Thulmann said, pointing a finger at the older witch hunter. 'Rouse Captain Meisser. Inform him that he has an engagement this evening and that he will be taking a number of guests with him.' Tuomas's brow knitted with puzzlement until he realised what Thulmann intended. The old witch hunter hurried to follow his orders.

'Whatever scheme is hatching in that crooked brain of yours,' Ehrhardt growled, 'make room in them for a Black Guardsman. The baron consigned all those poor wretches to the flames without allowing them the final grace of Morr. I would hear him answer for such sacrilege.'

Thulmann smiled and gripped Ehrhardt's hand. 'I am coming to believe that there isn't anyone the Black Guard of Morr doesn't have a grievance with.'

'Does the Order of Sigmar begrudge sharing its heretics with the templars of Morr?' Ehrhardt retorted.

The smile faded from Thulmann's face. There was one other person he would need to inform of Baron von Gotz's message.

Of all the trials he had endured in Wurtbad, telling Silja Markoff that her father had been executed as a traitor was going to be the hardest.

CHAPTER ELEVEN

AWARENESS BEGAN TO fight its way through the red mist that filled Gregor's mind. He looked at his surroundings, the subterranean laboratory of the plague doktor, Freiherr Weichs, seeing it clearly for the first time. The cavern was a shambles, fires burned unchecked where chemicals and volatile compounds had been scattered during the fray. Broken glass and splintered wood lay strewn all about.

Scattered amidst the debris were twisted, inhuman bodies, the corpses of Weichs's malformed human assistants, the hideous forms of his skaven patrons. Blood, black and foul, stained the earthen floor. Gregor felt an intense loathing turn his stomach, as he realised that it was on such filth that he had gorged himself. That it was upon such vermin that the hunger raging within him had satiated its thirst. If he had believed he could fight Sibbechai's curse, if he had thought he could remain a man, he knew better now. He recalled the cold, evil gaze of the vampire, and the life that he had been cheated of. Miranda, with her soft tresses and passionate kisses, his ancestral home with its ancient setting and noble history. He thought of his father and his brother, both slain by the vampire. Sibbechai would suffer for what it had done. Nothing would stop him from having his revenge.

Gregor abased himself upon the charnel house floor of the cavern, begging for Sigmar to hear his plea. To grant him the determination to pursue his revenge. To do what had to be done in order to redeem his soul from the darkness. As he opened his eyes again, he saw a shaft of splintered wood torn from one of the tables during the battle. He grabbed it with an almost tender embrace, holding it as though the crude spear were some holy relic.

He could sense the vampire lurking somewhere nearby. The hideous curse that bound Gregor to Sibbechai would also lead him to it. Gregor walked forward into one of the gaping tunnel openings. However crooked the burrows of the underfolk, he would not lose himself. The profane light of Sibbechai's foul existence would lead him on.

And when he found the vampire, he would drive his spear through its shrivelled heart. Only then could he allow his own corruption to be purged from him by stake and hammer and flame.

SILJA MARKOFF HAD returned to the garishly appointed reception hall. This time, however, the young woman's reserves of strength were depleted. She could not hold back the emotions raging within her. Tears flowed freely from her reddened eyes, her body trembling with terrible sobs. Thulmann's comforting hand rested on her shoulder. He knew that no empty words of comfort would provide solace now. It was much too late for platitudes. He found himself wishing that Father Kreutzberg had not returned to the Temple of Morr. The old priest was well versed in the ways of death and offering succour to the bereaved. But Kreutzberg did not seem to share Ehrhardt's opinion that skaven were of concern to the disciples of Morr. Indeed, he had left the chapter house in almost unseemly haste after the ghastly events in the torture chamber, preferring the hunt for vampires to a confrontation with the underfolk.

'I shamed him into it.' Silja wept. 'He tried to explain and I wouldn't hear him.' She looked up at the witch hunter. He winced as he saw the pain in her face. 'The things I said to him. The hideous things I said, the last words he ever heard from my lips! I may as well have put the sword to his throat myself.'

Thulmann remained silent, letting her anguish fill the air. What could he say? That because of her, Igor Markoff had remembered his duty and his honour? That he had died the death of a hero, striving against a maniacal tyrant? Later such words might be of help, now they would only feed the misery of her loss.

Thulmann's hand tightened about her shoulder. His voice spoke firm and grim. 'He will be avenged, Silja. Your father's murder will not go unpunished.' A faint shadow of hope tinged the pain in her eyes, her hand closing over his own. 'By Sigmar's holy name, I swear it,' the templar added, feeling the power behind his words. Thulmann was a devout Sigmarite, some might go so far as to call him a zealot. He did not make oaths in his god's name lightly.

There was a sharp knock at the door. Slowly the portal opened, revealing Streng's unkempt visage, dust from the aborted excavation still covering his clothes. Thulmann noted that the mercenary had found time to raid the chapter house's armoury, a brace of pistols hanging from his belt.

'We're ready, Mathias,' Streng said. 'If we're to go through with this, we'd better act now.'

Thulmann extracted his hand from Silja's grasp. She looked from Thulmann to Streng and back again. The old cunning and suspicion that had allowed her to act as her father's agent returned to her eyes.

'Go through with what?' she demanded.

'It would best if you did not know,' Thulmann replied, smiling weakly. Silja rose to her feet.

'That was the only answer I needed,' she said. 'I'm coming with you.' Seeing the disapproving light in the witch hunter's eyes, Silja's voice grew soft, at once stronger and more vulnerable. 'He killed my father, Mathias. Surely that gives me the right.'

'I don't think they'll let the daughter of a man the baron executed as a traitor anywhere near the castle,' Streng pointed out.

'And how are you planning to approach the baron?' she asked.

'We have an invitation,' Thulmann admitted. 'Captain Meisser has been invited to attend a social gathering. Naturally a man of such importance is not going to attend such an event without his own functionaries to hand.'

'Then I'm coming with you,' she repeated. 'You can furnish me with one of those oversized cloaks and horrible hats you people always wear. Even the baron's own guard don't like witch hunters. They make them uneasy. They won't look too close at the face beneath the hat.'

Thulmann realised there was to be only one resolution. He nodded at Silja. 'Streng, have Eldred provide Fraulein Markoff with an appropriate raiment and see that she doesn't lack in the area of armaments.' He didn't like the lewd wink Streng gave as he loped off to implement his employer's commands, nor the way it brought colour to his own face. He was allowing Silja Markoff to accompany their expedition because it was the right thing to do. There was no other reason.

'I should warn you that Captain Meisser will be accompanying our excursion,' he said. 'You might say he's our walking invitation.' He raised an admonishing hand. 'Tempting as it might be, try not to kill him. At least not until after we're safely inside the Schloss von Gotz.'

'I REALLY MUST advise against such exertion after such a trying recovery, excellency.' It had been some time since the wizard Furchtegott had known stark, utter terror, but now he was fully reacquainted. He trembled with a helpless fear far beyond the child watching the shadows in its room assume monstrous shapes, or the woodsman who hears the scratching of a wolf at his door in the dead of night.

When the baron's proclamation had been made, Furchtegott had been too overwhelmed by the aftermath of Markoff's death to consider the consequences of such a whim. The food stores of the city were to be thrown open, the rabble allowed to plunder them to their hearts' content. If Graf Alberich Haupt-Anderssen did not lift the quarantine soon, if he could not be satisfied that the plague had been eradicated, Wurtbad would starve. There had been little chance of making it through the winter before, now von Gotz had ensured that there was none at all.

However, there was something of more immediate concern to Furchtegott. Something he cursed himself for not realising when he wrote down the baron's edict and hastily passed it on to his steward. Von Gotz was hosting a grand feast to celebrate the destruction of the plague, a great festivity to which all the notables of the city had been commanded to attend. The wizard should have realised that the baron would hardly host such an event without attending it himself.

The wizard regarded the abomination rummaging about its wardrobe, trying to find some piece of finery that would still fit its bloated bulk. Furchtegott pondered the horror of the baron's mind: how could he not see what he had become, not realise what was happening to him? Yet he carried on as though he were still as he once had been. Was it madness, Furchtegott wondered, or something even more unnatural?

'You take good care of my welfare, dear Furchtegott,' the baron's voice bubbled. 'But I am a robust man, a man who needs to be active and vital. I have been too long locked away in these rooms, my mind craves diversion. Do not trouble yourself, my friend, I shall not expire from overexertion, I promise you.'

Furchtegott could readily agree with that sentiment. He had tried every poison known to him, and quite a few deadly improvisations with the chemicals in his workshop, and still the baron lived. His constitution was not even remotely human now, his appearance even less so. Perhaps clean steel or a little battle magic might still destroy the monster, but after witnessing what the baron had done to Markoff and his own guards, the wizard knew it would take a heart much stouter than his own to put such a theory to the test.

'Why so glum, magician?' The sound that slopped from the baron's mass more resembled the gagging of a cat than human laughter. 'If I suffer a relapse, you will simply have to doctor me back to health once more. It would prove beyond a doubt your prowess in the arcane arts.'

The wizard forced himself to look on the baron, at the pools of black bile that had replaced the nobleman's eyes. 'I will take no responsibility for your health if you dismiss my admonition,' Furchtegott said, with all the disapproval he could muster. 'You have recently recovered from a most virulent pestilence and your body is still weak, even if you do not feel it. In your present state, you are highly sensitive to the ill humours of others. That is why you must keep to your room and allow no one in.' The wizard threw up his hands. 'Yet now, you seem intent on undoing all of my work, attending a feast where there will be hundreds of people from all over the city, each of them bringing with them who knows what diseases and foul airs!'

Baron von Gotz, or the creature that used to be him, wore an almost childlike look of contrition. The thing nodded its head almost sheepishly. 'I apologise, magister,' the baron croaked. 'You know best, of course.' The thing shuffled toward its bed, letting the ermine cloak it had been fondling trail behind it like the tail of a slug.

'Stay here and rest,' Furchtegott replied, all conviviality now. 'I shall be back in a few moments with a restorative for you to drink.' The wizard retreated, pleased to see von Gotz draw back the curtains of his bed to keep any foul airs from lighting upon him when the door was opened. More importantly, it kept anyone in the corridor from accidentally catching a glimpse of him.

The baron was becoming more and more unpredictable, more unstable. Furchtegott could not be certain how much longer he would be able to control the thing. The time had come to escape, before he found his way onto the gallows or the witch hunter's pyre. He would gather up his most precious paraphernalia and slip from the castle while the feast was taking place. The guards would be too intent on checking the people flooding into the castle to pay much heed to someone leaving.

In the baron's bedchamber, an obscene puddle of rotting flesh and protruding bones waddled the floor once more. The baron's clawed hands fondled the soft, rich fur of his ermine cloak. He always looked so splendid in this pristine garment. He turned his viscous eyes toward the floor, imagining the gathering in the halls beneath his feet. It was his celebration, after all. It would be the height of impropriety for the host not to show himself to his guests.

The baron's talons fumbled at the clasp of his cloak, trying to fasten it about his swollen neck. He wanted to look his best when he made his entrance.

'WELL, COLLECTING THESE was a waste of time.' Carandini hefted the pick he had taken from a zombie, hurling the tool back down the tunnel. He wrinkled his nose at the ragged fur that hung from the reanimated skaven's shoulders, where the fangs of Sibbechai's rats had done their work. Removing a dagger from his cassock, Carandini began to cut away the flapping length of fur-covered flesh.

The necromancer and his living dead attendants had followed Sibbechai for hours through the wandering network of tunnels and passages. They had not been troubled again by the skaven, but Carandini was certain that the hideous underfolk had not forgotten the invaders. The hairs of his neck prickled every time he considered inhuman eyes watching their every movement, waiting for the opportune moment to strike.

They faced a stone wall, already breached long ago and resealed in a hasty fashion. Like the bricks in the sewer wall, the stones were intended for easy removal to afford access from the skaven tunnels. It made sense for the ratmen to extend their network to include the castle itself, allowing their spies to creep into the halls of power to observe the world above their own shadow kingdom.

'Do not complain, necromancer,' Sibbechai's sardonic voice intoned. 'The mutants have done our work for us. We need only remove a few stone blocks and the prize shall be in my grasp.' The vampire pointed a clawed finger at the wall. 'Set your creatures to work. I grow impatient.'

Carandini was chilled by the fanatical tone in its words. For centuries the monster had striven to recover the book compiled five hundred years ago by its brother, the witch hunter Helmuth Klausner, bound in the skin he had flayed from Sibbechai's undead husk. Now the flames of its desire glowed beneath the vampire's withered hide, even greater than the bloodthirst of its kind. Sibbechai would tolerate no more failures.

The zombies shambled forward, clutching and groping at the stone blocks. Carandini could sense the vampire's frustration and impatience mounting by the moment. The necromancer retrieved the claw of Nehb-ka-Menthu from his bag, crouching in the filthy earth that covered the tunnel floor. He drew signs and symbols in the dirt, the words of ancient Nehekhara slipping from his tongue. The already damp air of the tunnel suddenly became colder, the mud clinging to the fur and rags of the zombies crackling as frost appeared upon it. In response to the necromancer's invocation, they jerked and twitched with new life, attacking their labours with increased speed and strength. A cold sweat peppered Carandini's brow as he struggled to complete the complicated litany of words and gestures. Calling upon the malevolent spirit of the dead tomb king to bolster the strength of his own spells was not without its cost, or its dangers.

If Sibbechai noticed the necromancer's ordeal, it gave no indication. As still as the skeleton of a blackened tree, the vampire's unclean anticipation grew as each block was pulled away. Often the grip of dead fingers would prove insufficient for the task at hand, the huge stones tumbling free, crushing bones and breaking limbs. Those still able would rise again, limping back to their labour with the same silent obedience with which they endured mutilation. Others remained trapped beneath the stones, feebly trying to wriggle free and continue their work with broken spines and shattered skulls.

It was not long before the opening was large enough to admit a man's body. The vampire stepped forward, gesturing with its claw for Carandini to cease his spell. The zombies were instantly still as the necromancer's voice stopped, standing like grisly statues. Carandini rose slowly to his feet, breathing deeply as he tried to replenish the air in his starved lungs. Even with so potent a talisman as the hand of Nehb-ka-menthu, Tomb King of lost Khareops, drawing on the dark magic of necromancy had its price.

Sibbechai regarded the recovering sorcerer, its eyes smouldering in the darkness. The creature lifted its skeletal hand and gestured at the opening. 'You first, deathmaster,' it hissed. Carandini heaved himself upright, stumbling toward the hole as his weakened body recalled the mechanical exercise of moving his legs. Carandini stepped through the hole in the wall, into the darkness below the Schloss von Gotz.

His sensitive eyes pierced the shadows. The skaven had chosen their entry point well. The room was large, with only a single iron-bound door leading from it. Much of it was empty, the rest occupied by stacks of wooden planking, bricks and clay roof tiles. Clearly it was some manner of storeroom, but the layer of dust showed it had not been entered for some time.

Sibbechai had made a terrible mistake in allowing the Tilean to precede it. Carandini was a black sorcerer versed in the magic of death and undeath, but he was still a man, living blood still flowed through his veins. Sibbechai was one of the undead, a child of the night. Strange were the limitations placed upon its unholy kind. The castle was a human abode, and no vampire could gain entry to such a residence without being invited across the threshold. Carandini smiled at this flaw in Sibbechai's plan. The vampire would still be scratching at the door when Carandini retrieved *Das Buch die Unholden* from whatever fool now possessed it.

Sibbechai's eyes glowed in the dark like dancing flames. Even as Carandini opened his mouth to hurl a parting jibe, he realised his mistake. The vampire had helped Carandini turn the corpses from the plague pit into zombies, but had lent no aid in restoring their ranks after the skaven attack. It had not helped Carandini control the automatons, nor lent its own dreadful power to the creatures' penetration of the castle wall. It had conserved its power while letting the necromancer expend his. Now, Sibbechai turned its hypnotic eyes upon the Tilean, forcing its thoughts into his weakened mind.

Like a puppet, Carandini drew closer to the hole. Words came unbidden to his lips, words that did not originate in his own mind. In truth, any living, human being could gain entry for a vampire to a human dwelling. It was for this reason that the dread vampire counts had kept living slaves among their undead households, to steal into places their masters could not go, to unlock doors a vampire could not open. It was for this reason that Sibbechai had allowed Carandini to come so close to the prize.

'Enter, master,' Carandini heard himself say. Sibbechai's malevolent laughter crackled about the underworld like lightning. With a flourish of its shroud-like robes, the vampire swept forward, its gaunt shadow falling upon the sorcerer. As its fiery eyes burned into his own, he knew he gazed upon his death. Sibbechai had spared him only so that he might invite the monster across the threshold. Now his usefulness was at an end. Raw terror threatened to explode his heart as he realised there was nothing he could do to stop it.

'No, deathmaster,' Sibbechai laughed. 'You will live a short time yet. You will be granted the privilege of seeing Sibbechai in all his magnificence. You shall see the treasure you thought to cheat me of before I allow death to still your screams.' The vampire laughed, gliding away from the necromancer as though it were nothing more than mist and shadow. Carandini watched as the ranks of zombies followed the vanishing fiend toward the storeroom's only door. But Sibbechai had not finished with its treacherous confederate, placing another obligation upon Carandini's weakened mind.

'Remain here, necromancer,' it hissed. Carandini watched the vampire's claw close about the heavy door, tearing it from its hinges as though it were crafted of paper. 'Do not fear,' it said as its shadow drifted away into the cellars beyond the storeroom, 'I shall not be long.'

THE CASTLE VON GOTZ was alive with activity. Servants dressed in their garish livery bustled about, seeing to the care and comfort of the small army of guests that filled the castle's halls. They represented the very best the city had to offer – the scions of the ancient families of the nobility, the wealthiest of the river merchants who brought trade and prosperity to the city, guildmasters representing virtually every lawful vocation in Wurtbad, and several that existed upon the grey fringes of the law. Foppish aristocrats in powdered wigs rubbed shoulders with grizzled army officers who wore their scars as proudly as their medals.

Young baronets dressed in silk shirts hobnobbed with ageing countesses, their wrinkles buried beneath layers of powder and perfume. Above them all the marble walls of the castle gleamed, alabaster cherubim frolicked, and the faces of barons long dead and forgotten glowered from massive canvases. But above all else there hung that intangible pall of dread and foreboding that reached out and clutched at every soul. Among the gathering, conversation was either idle or far too desperate, the laughter nervous or raucous. The music of the orchestra assembled in the castle's grand ballroom was too precise, too dispassionate, as though even the notes felt subdued by the weight of the atmosphere.

There was no one who did not submit to that tension hovering in the air. The baron claimed that the plague had been vanquished, but few would verify his boast. The baron said that Graf Alberich would soon lift the quarantine, and that food from all across Stirland and the Empire would be brought into their city, but most were sceptical of such assurances. The assembly was perhaps the largest the castle had ever paid host to, but it was not from jubilation or gratitude that the throng had manifested. Each had received the note asking them to the castle. The baron had not invited his guests, he had commanded them. Now each nervously waited for whatever misery would unfold next, or else gave way to reckless abandon, to deny the dread numbing their hearts.

Like the music, the festivities were hollow and lifeless, a moth heeding the call of the flame and knowing it to be its death knell.

'For a city on the brink of winter, plague and starvation, they certainly know how to suffer in grand style,' Streng said, tearing into a goose leg appropriated from one of a dozen long dining tables in the castle's cyclopean ballroom. The mercenary patted his belly, letting a loud belch rumble.

'If the quarantine isn't lifted soon,' Thulmann stated, 'these people will be boiling boot leather and tree bark in a month.' Streng shrugged his shoulders, taking no interest in what befell the populace of Wurtbad. 'You might do well to remember that we are in this together, friend Streng. Until the quarantine is lifted, what happens to the city, happens to us.' Streng shot a sour look at his employer, then set the plate down on a nearby divan. The witch hunter's words went far toward ruining his appetite.

'I could do without remembering that sort of thing,' he grunted. 'Now I have to go and find enough ale to let me forget.'

'Keep your wits about you and your eyes open,' Thulmann warned. 'Don't forget why we are here.' The mercenary gave Thulmann a sour glance, but he understood.

It was a mad plan. If Thulmann was completely honest with himself, it was akin to bearding a dragon in its lair – arresting Baron von Gotz in his own castle, stealing him from the midst of a veritable army of guards, retainers and sycophants. The witch hunter's only hope was that the baron's madness was just as obvious to his guests as it was to him. From the few snatches of subdued conversation he had heard, he felt that perhaps his hopes were not idle ones. The great and the good of Wurtbad might be perfectly happy to see von Gotz deposed, so long as someone else risked his neck to do so.

There were seven of them in the group Thulmann had led into the castle. No, eight, the witch hunter corrected himself, though he wasn't counting on any help from Meisser. True to Silja's prediction, the baron's guards had barely even looked at them, passing them on after only the most perfunctory examination of Meisser's invitation. Thulmann was mildly surprised that the delegation from the Order of Sigmar had not been asked to relinquish the weapons they so openly wore, but then, nobody would expect the pious templars, sworn servants of Sigmar and the Empire he founded, to raise arms against its highest representative in Wurtbad. Besides, with the execution of Markoff, Thulmann suspected that Baron von Gotz might be expecting

Meisser to protect him from other elements within the Ministry of Justice.

If the sentries at the gate had been anxious not to offend the witch hunters, they had been even more careful not to disturb the imposing black giant, Captain-Justicar Ehrhardt. Morr was a god who was worshipped not out of devotion, but fear. That fear encompassed the god of death's morbid servants, the Black Guard of Morr. The baron's soldiers had not been courageous enough to ask Ehrhardt for the massive sword hanging from his belt. Even now, with the castle's ballroom playing host to such a crowd as it had never seen before, the Black Guardsman was given a wide berth, afforded a level of fearful respect Thulmann doubted even the Emperor himself would be able to evoke. Ehrhardt stood poised against a fluted column, his hard eyes surveying the crowd like a wolf studying a flock of sheep.

'I still say this plan of yours cannot work.' Meisser had not left Thulmann's side since leaving the chapter house, perhaps sensing that the witch hunter was the only one preventing Streng from smashing in his skull and Silja from slitting his throat. Of course, Meisser was hardly thrilled by the prospect of challenging Baron von Gotz, especially after all the pains he had suffered to ingratiate himself to the nobleman. He found Thulmann's notion akin to the dangerous ravings of a lunatic. It gave him no joy to share in that danger. It had taken a few overt threats from Streng to close his mouth, but Meisser would not forsake one last attempt to sway Thulmann. 'Arresting the ruler of Wurtbad in his own castle? Maybe you should rethink which of you is the insane one.'

'Your concern is duly noted, Brother Meisser,' Thulmann replied in a low hiss. 'You might, however, consider that if anything runs afoul, there are certain members of our group who will make sure you are in no condition to gloat about it afterwards.' The smug look that had flashed across Meisser's face every time he observed a soldier wearing the baron's colours now evaporated. Thulmann decided to drive the point deeper. 'Besides, if my plan does fail, the baron will not take any chances. He will execute anyone who played a role in trying to depose him. And it was your invitation that opened the door for us.' Meisser's eyes widened with horror at the truth of it. When the time came, he would have even more to fear from von Gotz than he did from Thulmann and his associates.

'You... you may be right,' Meisser admitted, sweat trickling down his face. 'You should allow me to aid you. If von Gotz is the monster you think him to be, you will need all the help you can get.'

Thulmann gave the witch hunter captain an incredulous stare. Did Meisser really believe him so stupid as to misplace his trust, or was the man simply so desperate that he would switch loyalties at the eleventh hour? 'I take comfort in your conviction,' he sighed. Meisser nodded his head like an excited vulture.

'Oh, you will not regret your confidence in me,' Meisser assured him. 'All my skills are at the disposal of this bold enterprise.' He held his hand out to the witch hunter. 'But of course I should be much more helpful with a weapon.' Thulmann rolled his eyes.

'I'm afraid I'll feel better for not looking over my shoulder,' he observed. He looked past Meisser, at the slender, black-clad figure close behind. 'Though I'm certain that Silja Markoff would happily give you one of her blades.' Meisser almost jumped out of his skin at the woman's presence, and the violent hatred burning within her eyes.

'Worry not, toad,' Silja spat. 'I desire the baron's head more than I do yours.' Her gloved hand patted the sword hanging from her belt. 'But his is the only head I want more than your own.'

Thulmann looked across the crowd of burghers and aristocrats, seeking out the dark-garbed figures of the other witch hunters. They were scattered about the fringes of the room, as Thulmann had instructed them. From their vantage points, they should have been able to observe anyone entering or leaving the room, as well as maintaining eye contact with at least one of the other conspirators. When the baron made his entrance, one of them would give the signal to the others. Events such as the feast were coordinated to a strict regime dictated by centuries of tradition. Tradition held that the first waltz would be reserved for the baron and the baroness. Thus far, the musicians had busied themselves with less elegant melodies, awaiting the appearance of their patron. The baroness was a handsome woman entering the borderland of middle-age, despite her elaborate wig and the low neckline of her sapphire-hued dress. She had remained seated on a throne-like chair upon a dais at the centre of the north wall, engaged in idle chatter with courtiers and casting sullen glances at the empty chair beside her.

Then the screams began. Sharp and piercing, they were the cries
of men and women who felt the chill of Old Night clawing at
their souls. The cacophony of terror sounded from the main hall,
rising in pitch and volume as more voices joined the chorus of
dread. Soldiers sprinted from the ballroom, hastening down the
marble corridors to the extravagant great hall. Thulmann shouted
sharp commands to his own men, signalling them to follow his
lead.

Death and decay filled his nostrils as the witch hunter raced
toward the great hall, the reek of profane and unclean powers. It
evoked the filth and perversion of the most obscene cults he had
uncovered, the horror of men who grovelled before a god that was
nothing but foulness and corruption. Thulmann felt the writhing
of invisible worms upon his skin, the air grow heavy with spectral
filth. As he ran, he could see less stalwart men doubled over, emptying their bellies onto the marble floor as the atmosphere of
disgust overwhelmed them. He prayed that he was wrong, that
the horror his mind told him was loose within the castle was only
a nightmare conjured by his macabre recollections.

He forced his way through the shrieking, fleeing mass of perfumed finery into the main hall and lifted his eyes to the grand
stairway, upon the visage of Baron Friedo von Gotz, and knew
that his worst fears paled beside the reality.

The hand of Nurgle was upon Wurtbad.

WITHIN THE DARKNESS of the cellar, Carandini shivered, pulling his
heavy cassock tight about his body, though he knew the chill that
gripped him was not of the flesh, but of the soul. Somewhere in
the castle above his head, Sibbechai was even now moving toward
its desire, the abhorrent *Das Buch die Unholden*. Once the vampire
had the dread tome in its undead claws, it would return for him.
Then the death Carandini had hoped to cheat forever would
reach out and claim him.

A sound from the yawning mouth of the tunnel opened his eyes
wide with fear. So intent had he been upon the impending triumph of Sibbechai, he had neglected to remember an enemy just
as horrible, and just as near. Carandini's eyes searched for any
sign that the underfolk had returned. He breathed a sigh of relief
when the object of his fear showed himself, not a twisted figure
covered in fur and filth, but the shape of a man like himself.

'Stand aside,' the cold voice rasped from out of the darkness. As he came closer Carandini was surprised to find that the man's face was not unknown to him. The necromancer smiled at the pallor of Gregor Klausner's skin, the lustreless quality in his eyes. So, Sibbechai had chosen to let both of Wilhelm's sons share in the necrarch's curse? How very thoughtful. But why had the vampire waited so long to summon its thrall to its side?

'I know the vampire is here,' Gregor snarled as he continued to advance. Carandini was startled by the crude wooden shaft clutched in his hand. 'Don't try to stop me.'

Understanding suddenly dawned in the necromancer's mind. The vampire did not have complete control over its creation. Gregor had not been reborn as some dutiful slave, but as a vengeful revenant, determined to destroy the monster that had damned him. Spectral cords bound the two together, allowing Gregor to sense the presence of the elder vampire.

'Stop you?' Carandini laughed, making an elaborate show of stepping from Gregor's path. 'What makes you think I'd even try?' Gregor eyed the necromancer suspiciously as he stalked past. Carandini was amused by the irony of it all.

'Good hunting,' he shouted, as Gregor vanished into the corridor beyond the storeroom. It would be terribly fitting if Sibbechai were to be destroyed by one of its own creations, if all its foul dreams were foiled by its own twisted schemes. There were few thralls with the strength of will to rise against their masters. Carandini hoped that Gregor was one such man. If he were, the necromancer would know soon enough. The compulsion Sibbechai had placed upon him would die with the vampire.

But then, the necromancer's attention was arrested by the din of a vast host flooding through the tunnels. The Tilean shuddered at the chittering squeals of rats, the verminous speech of the under-folk. He slid back into the shadows of the storeroom as the squeaking horde drew closer, the clatter of swords and spears became distinct. The necromancer called the darkness to him, wrapping the shadows about him like a cloak, willing himself to become one with the night.

The skaven spilled from the tunnel, a tide of rancid fur, ragged leather armour and rusted steel. Rodent muzzles sniffed at the air, red eyes scoured the darkness, eager for any sign of life. More and more of the slouching beasts crept forward, urged on by the force of bodies behind them. Carandini watched in silent horror as the skaven began to fill the room, chisel-fangs bared as their sensitive noses discerned the scent of those whom they hunted.

Then a creature more horrible than a thousand of those that preceded it stole into the cellar. It was a grey furred ratman, wearing a dark robe and fur collar, an iron-tipped staff clutched in its paws. From the sides of the vermin's skull, great horns protruded. Carandini could sense the power of the hideous creature, could almost see the obscene energies swirling about him. The skaven wizard barked a command and the entire host surged forward, squeaking as they pushed and shoved their way into the corridor, following in the very footsteps of Gregor Klausner. The horned ratman turned its head, glaring directly at Carandini before scurrying after the horde it commanded. The necromancer cringed. Even a man used to the dead fires of Sibbechai's face was unsettled by the inhuman malevolence of the ratman.

A tremendous relief washed over Carandini as the rodent cacophony faded. He would never forget the hateful look the horned ratman had directed at him. Then the Tilean's eyes happened to look downward toward the floor. Hundreds of tiny red eyes looked back at him. The floor had become a living carpet of scrawny, furry bodies. Dozens of mouths snapped open hungrily, displaying sharp fangs.

Carandini wondered if Sibbechai would have at least inflicted a more dignified death upon him, as the army of rats swarmed forward and a living tide of vermin engulfed the necromancer.

CHAPTER TWELVE

THULMANN'S EYES WATERED at the stench of the walking putrescence. It may once have been a man, but it was such no longer. Dark Powers had been invited into the flesh and they had consumed it utterly. Perhaps the mind of a man, the tattered, broken fragments of a human soul, yet shrieked within the hulking heap of filth and corruption, the mass of bloated, shapeless flesh. Gangling arms, disproportionate to the body of a man, fell from what might be called shoulders, the green-tinged flesh of each broken by pus-dripping boils and livid red rashes. The abomination's body was like a pile of unformed meat, folds of fat rippling against each other, filth drooling from its sores and lesions filling the crevices between each ripple, making a wet, smacking sound as it moved. The daemon's belly was an open wound, devoured from within by some powerful acid, displaying its purple intestines with the pride of a general displaying his medals. The brown muck of partially digested food stained the monster's belly as it walked, its broken guts spurting more of the filth across its body. Peering from behind the monster's organs, tiny yellow eyes glistened. It seemed to Thulmann that small, daemonic things moved within the host.

Its head, if such the ghastly blob rising above its shoulders could be called, was swollen beyond any semblance of humanity. Features were stretched and distorted, the eyes askew and lacking symmetry, two pools of blue putrescence amidst the decayed green flesh. The mouth was a gigantic maw, stretching from ear to ear, ragged rows of rotten, brown tusks jutting from its jaws, a writhing yellow tongue wriggling between the fangs like a great maggot. Antlers, broken and decayed like the rest of the monster, sprouted from the sides of the beast's head, like some profane parody of a saint's halo.

The final ghastly touch was the ermine cloak that fluttered from the beast's neck. Thulmann recognised the emblem that the clasp bore, on the seal that had been fixed to Meisser's invitation, the seal of Baron Friedo von Gotz, ruler of Wurtbad, now a child of Nurgle.

The obscenity continued its descent, dribbling, babbling and oozing. Thulmann had no intention of listening to whatever blasphemies the daemonic horror might be struggling to give voice to. Disgust unseated the fear in his breast. With one fluid motion, the witch hunter drew one of his pistols. Almost screaming a litany from the *Deus Sigmar*, Thulmann aimed and fired, sending the bullet crunching into the monster's skull.

For a moment, the unclean one was still, its eyes rolling about as though unfixed within its head. Grimy black sludge spilled from the gaping wound at the centre of what was once its forehead, leaking across its face in a stream of filth. As the sludge dripped down into the beast's mouth, the maggot-tongue flickered outward, licking the muck from the daemon's diseased visage like some exotic delicacy. The daemon's corrupt flesh sizzled as the tongue passed over it, putrid smoke rising from its decay. Then the eyes became focused, the tongue retreated back into its cavern-like dwelling, and the monster continued to slither down the stairs.

Thulmann threw the spent pistol aside, drawing two more from the bandolier that crossed his chest. Perhaps the shambling monster could not be harmed by clean steel and lead, but the witch hunter was determined to put the possibility to the test. From the corners of his eyes, he saw movement all around him, as people raced back into the main hall. One of these he recognised as the old templar Tuomas, another was the huge shape of Ehrhardt, his enormous blade gripped firmly in his armoured hands.

There were many more who owed no particular allegiance or loyalty to Thulmann. Perhaps emboldened by the witch hunter's display of defiance before the monstrosity, perhaps feeling the strength and courage of Sigmar coursing through their blood, or trying to purchase time for their families and loved ones to escape, they all came. Thulmann saw halberdiers in the colours of von Gotz stand beside elegantly dressed noblemen, slender rapiers and longswords filling their perfumed hands. One man, his brown hair and beard wild and unkempt, his flowing robes a deep rust red, began to utter strange words, words that were old when mankind was young. Thulmann felt the temperature in the hall rise as the wizard drew power into himself, the fires of sorcery gathering about him. The bronze-hilted sword grasped in the wizard's leathery hand began to glow, lit by an internal fire. The sorcerer glanced respectfully at the stalwart templar, a gesture that was returned.

Wizards and witch hunters were uneasy allies, their mutual fear and loathing too great for either to ignore. But, standing before the obscenity that had once been Baron von Gotz, it was enough for Thulmann that the sorcerer was human.

The unclean one hesitated as its bilious eyes glowered at the armed men arrayed against it. The daemon's mouth dropped open as it slobbered a guttural noise that sounded too much like 'traitors' to be coincidental. It surged forward and, from its mutilated belly, tiny shapes burst forth, miniature horrors much like itself, spilling down the steps like a tide of slime, capering and squealing as they bounded across the stairs. Thulmann pointed a pistol at one of the gibbering imps, exultant when the bullet exploded it into a splatter of muck and excrement. A moment later, Tuomas fired his weapon and another nurgling exploded.

'Kill the small ones.' Thulmann shouted. 'One scratch from their claws will kill just as surely.' Thulmann fired his other pistol, then drew his sword as the creatures swept forward, slashing at them, hearing their pained squeal as their diseased limbs were cut away, as their pus-filled bellies were split open. All about him, the other men desperately hacked at the daemonic vermin, screaming out as diseased claws broke past their defences and tore into their flesh.

Above it all, the unclean one waddled forward, opening its gigantic maw to spew a stream of stinking liquid corruption into the armoured figure of a soldier. The halberdier shrieked as the steaming green filth sizzled upon his armour, gnawing through his flesh. He toppled forward, his weapon clattering across the floor as the unclean one's vomit hungrily dissolved his very substance. A foul liquid laughter rumbled from the daemon, its swollen head mocking the men desperately struggling to stave off the assault of its nurglings.

ALL WAS CARNAGE as Furchtegott emerged from his chambers. As the screams reached his ears, as he saw the fleeing crush of bodies filling the corridors of the castle, the wizard knew there could be only one cause. Baron von Gotz had decided to ignore the advice of his physician and meet his guests. Furchtegott cursed his own stupidity for waiting so long to escape. Even now, the abomination that von Gotz had become was prowling through his castle, killing Morr only knew how many. And, even worse, leaving others alive to bear witness to the obscene consequences of the wizard's spells. Furchtegott could almost feel the flames of a witch hunter's pyre slithering up his legs.

But they would have to catch him first, and Furchtegott was determined to make that as difficult as possible. He firmed his grip upon the heavy leather bag he carried, his spell books and the rarest of his material components safely concealed within. He had cast aside his golden mantle, assuming a silk tunic and leather breeches, polished black boots with silver buckles and a shapeless velveteen hat. Amidst the finery of the baron's shrieking guests, the wizard would become just another face in the mob.

Furchtegott stepped from the doorway, into the tide of panicking humanity. He could dimly hear the sounds of combat above the screams and cries. It seemed a few valiant foes were trying to make a stand against von Gotz in the main hall. Furchtegott silently wished them luck, he himself having done everything he could to kill the abomination. The wizard joined the exodus swirling around him, the mass of frightened men and women fleeing toward the servant's wing and the kitchens. It was as good a direction as any, and there was a small side entrance near the kitchens through which stores were brought into the castle. The little side door would make an undignified but useful exit.

Even as such cheering thoughts occurred, Furchtegott's hopes of escape were dashed. More screams sounded from up ahead. The fleeing mob became frozen as those at the front of the pack tried to turn back and those behind them tried to press forward. The wizard struggled to see beyond their bodies, to discover what was happening. There was no possibility it could be von Gotz, even if he had managed to overcome the forces fighting him in the main hall. Then the wizard saw an arm covered in fur and clutching a bloodied meat cleaver. One of the bodies obscuring his view was cut down. As she fell, her hideous killer stood revealed.

It was a giant rat. An enormous rodent standing upon its hind legs, wearing a ragged leather tunic and wielding a butcher's blade. As if the very existence of such a monster were not horror enough, the creature's furry hide was torn and mangled, ripped apart by fangs and blades. From its throat, a dagger protruded and its eyes were lifeless orbs of emptiness. The ratman was dead, its carcass animated by some abominable will. Beyond it, Furchtegott saw a fleeting glimpse of other zombie creatures, some as verminous as the first, others the mutilated husks of men. The walking dead slowly, emotionlessly and inexorably hacked their way through the crowd.

Furchtegott reached into his travelling bag, removing the *Das Buch die Unholden*. In scouring its pages for the spells that damned von Gotz with something more horrible than Stir blight, the wizard had seen many rites and incantations related to the living dead: spells to summon them from their graves, and spells to control them. The wizard's frantic hands flipped through the pages. As he did so, a terrible chill seemed to wash over him. The world seemed to grow darker, reality twisting into a soundless shadow.

The wizard looked up from the abhorrent tome and found himself staring into the eyes of ageless evil. Furchtegott could feel the malevolence emanating from the tall, gaunt shadow, feel the ancient hate of all things living burning in its eyes. The vampire exposed its fangs in a bestial snarl. A clawed hand rose, a talon pointed. In a moment of ultimate horror, Furchtegott realised the awful spectre had come to the castle for one purpose. It had come for *him*.

Furchtegott clutched the dread book to his chest, somehow sensing that the vampire would not risk using its unholy magic upon him while he still held the book. But that grace did not extend to the cowering masses between him and the necrarch.

Even as the zombies began to redouble their attack with frantic haste, Furchtegott could feel the winds of magic shifting as the vampire drew upon their darkest energies.

The wizard turned, his voice roaring, one hand clutching *Das Buch die Unholden* to his breast, the other gesturing madly as he wove the heavy substance of the sorcerous wind Chamon to his will. The crowd pressing upon him from behind suddenly fell, wilting to the floor as their limbs became as heavy as gold. Furchtegott dare not risk looking back to see what fell power the vampire was unleashing upon the mob, but sprinted back down the corridor, leaping from one prone, screaming victim of his magic to another as if they were a living carpet.

Sibbechai watched the wizard flee, snarling. With a gesture, the vampire unleashed the dark magic it had summoned to itself, sending a withering spectral wave into the mob. As the ghostly light struck living flesh, the victims screamed and fell, their hearts bursting within their chests. The vampire was heedless of the energy it now expended, restraint the farthest thing from its mind. It willed the ghastly force to grow, to hasten its harvest of shrieking souls. It had seen the mortal fool who dared violate the vampire's grimoire with his filthy touch. Sibbechai would pay him the price for such audacity, when it strangled the wizard with his own dripping entrails.

As the wall of screaming flesh withered before it, the vampire swept forward, gliding amidst the havoc like a hungry vulture. Its shadow-like form flitted across broken corpses and twitching bodies, its eyes fixed upon the fleeing wizard as Furchtegott fled back down the corridor. The vampire snarled a command to its zombies, ordering them to follow after it. But Sibbechai had little need of such miserable slaves. It had seen the terror in the wizard's face. There was little it had to fear from such a man. Sibbechai spread its arms wide, willing its body to change. The loathsome substance of its form twisted and contorted, bones snapping and remoulding themselves. Soon, where once the vampire's gaunt frame had stood, a great bat hovered. Its grotesque face spread in a shrill shriek and then it streaked down the hallway, a black blur of shadow and menace.

The wizard's flight carried him to the great hall, but no further. Furchtegott froze as he saw the carnage he had only heard before. Soldiers struggled against hideous, decaying imps, their rotting fangs and diseased claws caked in blood and filth. The immense hulk of von Gotz lashed out at a dozen adversaries, massive claws scraping the marble walls when his clumsy blows failed to connect. A wizard of the Bright College slashed at the horrible daemon with a burning blade, while a huge giant in the armour and surcoat of a Black Guardsman hacked at the monster's flank as though chopping into a tree trunk. But it was the sight of nearly a half dozen men in the dark cloaks and hats of the Order of Sigmar that caused him to freeze, to magnify his terror even beyond that evoked by the vampire. The private dread that lurked in the back of every wizard's mind had at last taken shape, the witch hunters had come.

Paralysed by fright, Furchtegott spilled to the floor as the gargantuan bat swooped upon him. Sibbechai's shape twisted and shuddered back into its corpse-like state, cruel talons closing upon the wizard's neck, forcing his head back, striving to expose the book crushed against the man's chest.

The vampire snarled in rage as cold steel raked its face. Burning eyes glared at the ashen-faced woman who had slashed at Sibbechai with her sword. The necrarch hissed at Silja. She returned the monster's glare with a defiant glower.

'Mathias,' she shouted, slashing at the vampire again. 'Sibbechai is here!' The woman's sword cut into its dead flesh once more, but no blood swelled from the wound. With a savage growl, the necrarch slammed Furchtegott's head into the stone floor and leapt toward Silja.

Sibbechai's leap was caught in mid-pounce, a heavy sword smashing into its body, severing its spine and flinging it across the hall like a sack of straw. It crumpled against the far wall of the room, limbs twisted about its broken carcass like the crooked legs of a spider. Captain-Justicar Ehrhardt strode toward the vampire's body. Thulmann's gloved hand restrained him.

Both men had heard Silja's cry. Ehrhardt had detached himself from the combat with von Gotz in time to rescue the woman from the vampire's attack. Thulmann gave thanks to Sigmar that Ehrhardt had been able to intervene, but now it was his duty to ensure Sibbechai's destruction.

'Help them against the daemon,' Thulmann ordered. Ehrhardt saw the determination in the witch hunter's eyes and did not argue. The Black Guardsman had a debt to settle with Sibbechai, but Thulmann staked an even greater claim. He pulled the vial of holy water hidden within his tunic and, oblivious to the melee swirling around him, stalked toward the vampire's body.

Silja moved to follow him, but, as she did so, her eyes fell upon the soiled and befouled cloak hanging from the daemon's neck, the gold clasp sparkling from between the folds of flesh. She felt a red rage blaze within her as she noted a ghastly familiarity in the creature's distorted features, a twisted echo of the face of Baron von Gotz, the man who murdered her father. All thoughts of Thulmann and the vampire vanished as Silja charged into the fray, slashing at the corrupt monstrosity with all the ferocity of an Arabyan dervish. One thought now filled her mind, one purpose moved her hand. Silja Markoff would be the one to still the diseased heart of the baron and send his soul shrieking into eternal night.

THE WITCH HUNTER closed upon Sibbechai's carcass, watching for any sign of movement. The swords of Morr's Black Guard were enchanted by the dark priesthood, enchanted to strike sure and certain against the undead. But Thulmann had seen for himself that vampires were hideously difficult to destroy, and would rise again so long as their profane spark endured. He would only be satisfied when the necrarch's body was ashes and its dust scattered into the fast-flowing waters of the Stir.

'Mathias.' Thulmann turned away from the vampire's corpse at the sound of his name. He turned to see Streng and a number of soldiers struggling against a ragged pack of shuffling, shambling figures. Zombies. Slaves of the vampire. Nor were all of them human, but a number of skaven were included among their ranks. Streng struck the head from the shoulders of one of the rat-man zombies with a huge axe. Even as the zombie tottered, its clawed hand lashed out, ripping the warrior's sleeve. The furred paw was cut away by the clean, deft stroke of a broadsword. Thulmann was startled to find Meisser's hand gripping the blade. Clearly Streng had not been the only one to liberate a weapon from the suits of armour ranged about the hall.

Meisser stabbed once more, ripping open the rotting chest of another zombie, spilling its festering blood across the floor. He attacked an undead creature that was menacing a flush-faced aristocrat with powdered wig dangling from his frilled collar. Enough of Wurtbad's great and good had lingered behind to confront the von Gotz daemon. They would witness Meisser's bravery and remember it in the years to come. The lust for power had won over the weasel's sense of self-preservation.

Suddenly, a grim, bloody figure tore its way into the hall, flinging soldiers and zombies aside with equal disregard. Thulmann felt his soul sicken as he saw the sanguine apparition, its once handsome features now contorted into the visage of a monster. Gregor Klausner glared back at him, his eyes already beginning to lose the last flicker of humanity within them.

'Get away from him, Thulmann,' Gregor growled, brandishing the jagged wooden spear he carried. 'Sibbechai is mine!'

Thulmann stood silent, sword in one hand, holy water in the other. What could he say to this creature, this thing that had once been a man? This abomination that he had permitted to exist? He had known such a thing might happen, had shuddered at its possibility on the long road back from Wurtbad. He should have killed Gregor while he had still been a man, while his soul remained untainted. Now it was too late. Thulmann begged Sigmar's forgiveness for the selfish timidity that allowed such a fate to befall Gregor Klausner. The witch hunter knew there could be but one way to atone for his failure.

Gregor watched Thulmann prepare to meet him. Watched the witch hunter lift his blade. He did not want to fight this man, but he could not allow Thulmann to stand between him and the creature that had polluted his very existence.

'Your fight is not with me, witch hunter,' Gregor said. 'Let me pass.'

'I cannot suffer you to live,' Thulmann replied. 'I should never have allowed this to happen.' The guilt tore at him. Gregor cocked his head, listening intently to something. A wicked smile spread across his face.

'You have more pressing concerns than myself,' he stated. Thulmann believed the vampire's words merely a trick to lower his guard. Then he heard it, a low murmur beneath the sounds of battle. The scratching of claws on stone, the chittering voices of inhuman throats. Its source grew nearer. Cold dread filled the witch hunter as a horde of furry bodies and gleaming fangs burst into the great hall.

The skaven had come.

* * *

THE HORDE OF vermin spilled into the great hall, a living flood of inhuman evil. Rusty, crooked swords slashed out, hacking into living and undead flesh with equal disregard. Caught between the soldiers and the skaven, Sibbechai's zombies had their rotting bodies crushed beneath the tide of frenzied ratmen, cut to ribbons until no sign of unnatural life remained. Their living foes proved more difficult, mustering a hasty defence to meet the assault. Halberds impaled squealing skaven bodies as the creatures threw themselves at their human enemy, sizzling black blood mixing with the filth streaming across the floor.

Streng hacked into one ratman's collar, splitting the creature almost to its belly, losing his axe as the corpse toppled away and ripped the weapon from his hands. The mercenary cursed as more of the vermin surged forward to take the place of their slain comrade. He snarled defiance at the hideous creatures, throwing himself at them, letting his larger mass crush the small ratmen to the ground. Streng's fingers closed around a furry throat. The ratman clawed at him, frantically trying to push his weight from its body. Before life could completely fade from the creature, Streng's world was hurled into darkness as the blade of another ratman struck his head, pitching him across the floor.

Grey Seer Skilk scurried behind the horde of clanrats, the warriors he brought to destroy the undead forces he believed were created by his enemies and rivals. Madness was engulfing the great hall of Castle von Gotz. Man struggled against skaven, even as capering, imp-like daemons slashed and gnawed at their legs. At the foot of the stairs, a number of human warriors struggled to combat a greater, even more obscene form. Some of the ratmen drew too near this hulking monster. Skilk saw a pair of them disembowelled by a single sweep of the daemon's claw. He cringed as he sensed the hideous energies emanating from the monster, an aura of such vileness that he had felt only in the presence of the diseased plague priests of Clan Pestilens. Skilk watched as a huge black knight chopped into the monster with his sword, only to have the wound close upon itself as he withdrew his steel. Only the burning blade of a wild-haired human magician seemed to inflict any lasting hurt upon the behemoth.

Skilk snapped commands to his bodyguards. The sooner he destroyed the creatures he pursued, the sooner he could scurry back into the safety of the tunnels. A half-dozen black-furred warriors snarled back, spears gripped in their paws. One pair of skaven scuttled forward from behind the protection of the larger black ratmen. Both of the ratmen wore heavy leather cloaks, the garments glistening with moisture. One of them had a large wooden cask lashed to his back, the other carried a massive, wide-mouthed instrument of iron and copper like an oversized blunderbuss. Heavy tubes of insulated ratskin connected the barrel carried by one to the weapon wielded by the other. Skilk gleamed with feral glee as they scurried forward. There was no quicker way to clear a path to one's prey than the employment of a warpfire-thrower, one of the most ghastly products of skaven technosorcery.

The grey seer snarled for the fury of the weapon to be unleashed. The leather-clad ratmen hissed and squeaked in response, swinging the wide mouth of the weapon towards the combat raging before them. With a wild roar it was loosed, a gout of liquid fire rushed from the mouth of the weapon, spraying flaming ruin across a wide stretch of the hall. The black, viscous fire clung and burned, charring flesh and fur, blackening steel and melting skin. Soldiers, zombies, nurglings and ratmen alike were consumed by the horrific discharge, for the skaven cared little for their fellows caught in the flame. It was enough that the enemy perished alongside their own.

Skilk chittered happily as he watched the warpfire-thrower do its ghastly work. But the sorcerer's glee turned to horror as his eyes darted back to the huge, plague-ridden monstrosity that slobbered and roared at the foot of the stairs. The hulking monster had been surrounded by dozens of enemies, both human and ratman, the blades of both sides doing little more than scratch its polluted surface. Only the burning sword of the man-thing wizard seemed to deal the daemon any harm, and that threat was ended when a sweep of the monster's claw lifted his head from his shoulders. With that single threat destroyed, the unclean one's diseased gaze fixed upon the black flames spewing from the warpfire-thrower. Uttering an inarticulate, slobbering bellow, the bloated daemon barrelled through the ring of foes that surrounded it, smashing aside those too slow to react to its charge, ignoring the half-dozen blades that sank into its body as it thundered across the hall.

The skaven sorcerer shrieked to the warpfire holders to turn it upon the bellowing daemon. The gunner dutifully turned, fear of

Skilk overwhelming the urge to flee, but the skaven carrying the fuel tank wanted no part of it. Desperately, the ratman struggled to free itself of the wooden cask strapped to its back, succeeding only in snagging the fuel tube. As the gunner pulled back the lever that would bathe the unclean one in devouring flame, only a pitiful trickle dribbled from the nozzle. The ratman stared incredulously at its weapon, then squeaked in terror as the massive paw of the daemon smashed into it, throwing its broken body a dozen feet across the hall. Still connected to the gunner by the thick ratskin tubes, the fuel carrier hurtled after it, landing with a sickening crunch as the heavy cask crushed the ratman's spine.

Skilk snarled at the daemon, his sorcerous energies gathering in his black paw. Warpfire-throwers were difficult and expensive to obtain, and could only be had from the warlock-engineers of Clan Skryre. Monster, man or preternatural abomination, Skilk was determined that the daemon would suffer for this inconvenience. The grey seer unleashed the crackling energy, sending a bolt of swirling black lightning stabbing into von Gotz, scorching a hole clean through its chest, shocking the gibbering horror's heart into a crusty cinder. Smoke and steaming filth rose from the crater in the daemon's chest, Skilk admiring his own marksmanship when his glands suddenly spurted the scent of fear into the air. The abomination was still moving, still alive, even with its heart cooked! Worse, the formerly wavering, vacant gaze of the daemon was now focused on the skaven sorcerer-priest.

Awed by the power and strength the monster had shown, Skilk backed away from the monstrosity, barking orders at the mob of black-furred warriors to defend him. The armoured ratmen demurred, cringing alongside their master. Skilk hissed angrily, unleashing another charge of black lightning, directing its baleful energies not at the daemon but at the nearest cowering warrior. The ratman squealed in agony as a gaping hole the size of its own head was blasted through its torso, tearing through flesh, bone and armour as easily as wet paper. Their terror of the grey seer restored, the black skaven firmed their grips on spears and shields and surged forward, attacking the hulking monster in frantic desperation.

Skilk hid behind the protective wall of steel and fur, lips writhing as he muttered spells to bolster the flagging courage of his defenders, filling their minds with a reckless bloodlust that would swiftly burn out their brains. But the loss of a few dozen warriors mattered little, especially if it kept his own hide intact.

THULMANN FOUND HIMSELF swept up in the skaven assault, desperately slashing and thrusting at the inhuman warriors of the underfolk. Rodent muzzles snapped and chittered inches from his face as the vermin pushed deeper and deeper into the hall. Beside him, valiant soldiers screamed and died, noble aristocrats spilled their blue blood upon the floor as curved skaven blades gnawed hungrily into their bellies. For every man that fell, two furry corpses littered the ground, but still it was not enough. They could not fight a battle of attrition with the skaven, for the vermin might lose ten of their own for every man they killed and still carry the day.

Then the witch hunter saw the warpfire-thrower brought forward. Alone amongst the men who struggled against the monsters, Thulmann recognised the weapon for what it was. He threw himself to the floor as the skaven fired, as a blast of sizzling fire incinerated those around him. The screams of dying men and ratmen filled his ears, as the incredible heat, the stench of singed fur and burnt flesh filled his other senses. Thulmann felt the dripping mass of a charred skaven topple onto his prone body. He rolled away, ripping his cloak from his shoulders as some of the liquid flame from the ratman's corpse began to devour it. Only the mind of an inhuman monster could have conceived so ghastly an invention, could have imagined fire that clung to its victims like paste and would consume flesh down to the bone.

Even as Thulmann recovered, he was borne down to the ground, his sword flying from his fingers. A shrieking, clawing, rodent shape straddled him, slashing him and snapping at him with its fangs. By luck or cunning, the skaven warrior had survived the fratricidal blast of the warpfire-thrower, but the nearness of such a death had unhinged the creature's mind. Like a mad beast, it clawed at the witch hunter, frenziedly trying to bury its fangs in his neck. Thulmann tried to hold the snapping jaws away, pressing upward on the underside of the ratman's muzzle. His other hand groped across the marble floor, struggling to reach the sword just beyond his reach. The skaven's frenzied strength was starting to win, despite the creature's slighter mass.

Thulmann struggled to shift his attacker's weight and stretched once more for his sword.

GREGOR KLAUSNER STOOD above the withered ruin of Sibbechai's body, glaring down upon it with a cold, lifeless hate. He held the crude wooden spear in his hands, poised for the final, lethal stroke that would impale the vampire's heart and end its profane existence forever. But he found that his limbs would not obey him, that his body would not heed his command. A terrible will beyond his own held him frozen in its grip, a force just as powerful as the vile thirst that coursed through him, just as alien to the mortal being he had once been.

Sibbechai's wilted form began to shift and move, leathery lids rolling back from smouldering eyes. The Black Guardsman's blow had been a killing stroke, even for a vampire. But the foul breed of the necrarchs were more than mere vampires. They were powerful sorcerers, versed in all the black arts. Where another of its kind might have perished, Sibbechai had merely retreated until it could call its shadowy energies back into its body, could magically repair the damage done to its dead husk. A cruel smile spread across Sibbechai's skeletal visage as it saw Gregor standing above it. Like an expanding shadow, the vampire rose from the floor, its gaunt frame looming before him.

'Now you understand,' it laughed. 'Few there are among men with the will to resist that of an immortal. Fewer still are those thralls with the strength to harm their masters!' Sibbechai's cruel laughter grew as it saw despair fill Gregor's features. 'Perhaps in a few hundred years you may be strong enough to try again. If you are still human enough to care, that is.' The vampire ripped the wooden shaft from Gregor's frozen hands, hurling it against the wall with such force that it shattered into a shower of splinters.

Sibbechai's gaze scoured the chaotic battle for the man it sought. It found him staggering toward one of the corridors connecting with the great hall, blood streaming from a gash in his forehead. Furchtegott moved awkwardly, his wits rattled by the blow to his head inflicted by the vampire. He had somehow escaped the notice of the opportunistic skaven. But the only thing that mattered to the vampire was the forbidding tome still clutched in the wizard's arms.

* * *

THE WRITHING SKAVEN pressed itself downward, fangs designed to gnaw through wood, to chew solid earth asunder, now eager to worry the witch hunter's throat. Thulmann's fingers groped at the hilt of his sword, his fingertips brushing against the cold metal pommel. Desperately he tried to close even a single finger around the sword, to pull it back towards him. The ratman's efforts were growing more desperate too, more frenzied and frantic with each passing breath. The monster understood the deadly game it played with the man pinned beneath it and was just as determined to survive. Claws raked through the templar's chest, digging deep furrows in his skin. Blood welled up from the wounds, spilling across the skaven's paws. Thulmann could feel his strength fading, could feel the arm that held the rodent muzzle away from him begin to falter.

Abruptly, the contest was decided. Steel erupted from the ratman's forehead as a sword was thrust through the back of his skull. The twisted, inhuman corpse flopped to the floor, twitching as death spasms racked its nerves. Thulmann breathed deep, staring up into the face of his rescuer. Gregor Klausner glared down at him, kicking the witch hunter's sword within reach of his grasping hand.

'It is time to finish this farce,' Gregor snarled. He waited for Thulmann to gain his feet, then thrust at the witch hunter's throat. Thulmann swatted the stroke aside with his own blade. Gregor gave him little time to recover, thrusting at him with inhuman speed. The battle unfolding all around them no longer existed for Thulmann and Gregor, their world narrowed to the clash of steel, thrust and parry, attack and counterattack. Gregor's strength was tremendous, his speed incredible. Thulmann had been hard pressed in his duel with the vampiric monster that Sibbechai had made from his brother Anton, now he discovered Gregor had been far better with the blade than his sibling. The witch hunter found himself increasingly on the defence, giving ground to his foe, retreating before his strikes. He knew that retreat was death, that there was no chance of survival unless he could mount his own assault and put his enemy on the defensive. But his struggle against the von Gotz daemon, against the nurglings and the skaven, had already tried his strength and endurance. Soon he would tire, his guard would falter and Gregor's sword would spill his life onto the floor. Thulmann was experienced enough a swordsman to be under no illusion that there was any other outcome.

Then, as Gregor overextended his thrusting sword, Thulmann saw an opening. There was no time for thought, no time to ponder the providential moment. The witch hunter's sword stabbed into Gregor's chest, crunching through ribs to transfix his heart. Thulmann pressed his weight into the attack, forcing the point of his weapon deeper until it emerged from his enemy's back. It was only then, as he heard Gregor's sword fall from his dying fingers, that the templar considered the amateurish sloppiness of the manoeuvre that left his enemy exposed for the attack.

'Why?' he asked as darkness began to creep into Gregor's eyes.

'I could not... destroy Sibbechai... could not destroy myself,' Gregor's voice rasped. A faint tinge of respect briefly flickered in his eyes, a last gleam of friendship and admiration for the man who had killed him. 'Could not... could not give you time... for pity...' Gregor's body trembled. Thulmann watched it topple to the floor.

The witch hunter shook his head sadly, bending down to retrieve Gregor's sword. With a savage thrust, he stabbed the dead man's blade into his chest, then withdrew his own sword from Gregor's heart. Without the penetrating steel transfixing it, there was the possibility that unholy life might return to the vampire. Thulmann would leave no chance for that to happen. Gregor Klausner had earned the peace of the grave.

The templar looked to the wall where Sibbechai's body had lain, not surprised to see it gone. His fist tightened about the grip of his sword, fatigue vanquished from his body as a fresh surge of fury filled him. This time the necrarch would not escape him.

FURCHTEGOTT STAGGERED across the great hall, his bleary senses regarding the battle with cold detachment. The wizard tried to focus, to clear the clouds from his mind, but the discordant din within his skull would not be silenced. Even the pain pulsating from his shattered nose seemed numb and unreal, as though he were remembering rather than experiencing the injury.

The wizard's mouth suddenly dropped open, a dry rattle sounding from deep within his body. Furchtegott's limbs grew slack, his head lolled downward. Only the thin, skeletal claw buried deep in his back held the conjurer upright. The gaunt shade of

Sibbechai twisted its hand, ripping still deeper, puncturing his lungs with its sharp talons. The vampire hissed a curse upon the dying wizard, tossing him away like rubbish. The wizard was of only minimal interest to the necrarch, it was the treasure he had thought to steal that blazed within its brain.

Almost reverently, Sibbechai crouched before the massive tome, gazing upon it with the same intense fascination as might shine from the eyes of a weirdroot addict. *Das Buch die Unholden*. Long centuries had passed since the grimoire had been stolen, and many had been the secrets Helmuth Klausner had added to its already copious store of profane knowledge. With those secrets, Sibbechai might become the most powerful of its sorcerous breed, its mind filled with arcane lore that few minds had ever known. The vampire's hand stretched forward to grasp the book, trembling. For the first time in centuries, Sibbechai felt nervous anticipation shudder through its veins. Flesh of its flesh, bound in skin flayed from the vampire's own body, now it would reclaim its own.

A piercing scream ripped from its withered lips as the necrarch's hand touched the evil binding. Crackling green light rippled up its arm, scorching and consuming the vampire's body. Even as Sibbechai tried to pull away, its arm crumbled into ashes, the charred corruption spreading to its chest as the fell sorcery worked its horrific magic. Long had the Klausners known the nature of their nemesis, and long had they prepared for Sibbechai's moment of triumph. Potent wards had guarded Klausner Keep from Sibbechai, but still more potent were they that protected *Das Buch die Unholden*.

The vampire slithered back, legs crumbling into dust as the green light devoured them. Sibbechai's skeletal jaws gnashed and cursed as its withered face cracked and crumbled. Its clawed hand fell apart, fingers dropping to the floor as the flesh burned away. Finally, its entire body seemed to collapse upon itself, into a pile of corpse dust from which the vampire's skull glared, before it too fell into ruin and ashes.

From behind the defence of his bestial warriors, Grey Seer Skilk observed Sibbechai's destruction with deep satisfaction, but also a keen malice. The skaven sorcerer had seen the magical tome the vampire had killed in order to claim. Had felt its power as its protective wards consumed Sibbechai. Feral greed gleamed in Skilk's beady eyes as the ratman considered to what purposes he might put such potent magic. He dragged one of his warriors from where it stood jabbing at the daemonic von Gotz abomination with an iron spear.

'Fetch-bring, quick-quick!' Skilk snarled, gesturing with his claw at the book of sorcery lying beside the ashes of the vampire. The black-furred warrior demurred, sensing the unnatural energies it exuded. Skilk lashed the ratman's face with his tail, repeating his command in a low growl of fury. The warrior scurried forward, recalling all too vividly the black lightning that devoured one of its comrades. The strange book might very well kill him, but the grey seer most definitely would.

Trickles of saliva fell from Skilk's muzzle as he watched the warrior pick up the book. The armoured skaven hesitated, as though waiting for a strange and ghastly death to fall upon it. Skilk snapped an impatient command and the warrior scurried back. The grey seer snatched the book from his slave, squeaking happily as his furry paws caressed the skin-binding. He could feel the fell energies trapped within the tome, taste the dark sorceries crying out to be released. Skilk had invaded the human fortress for revenge and had instead found power. Surely the Horned Rat was smiling upon his humble servant.

Many of his warriors still stood, forming a wall of shields to contain the bloated daemon's advance. Skilk could also see a number of humans waging desperate combat against the abomination. He watched as an older man with one arm bound against his chest slashed his sword into a skaven corpse still smouldering from the warp-fire attack. A length of burning rag from the corpse's tunic was cut away by the stroke as the blade swirled through the air, wrapping the burning cloth around his weapon. He returned to his attack, opening a sizzling wound in the monster's back. The daemon roared in anger, returning its attention to the humans.

Skilk had little interest in which side would win. It was enough that the foolish humans had diverted the daemon's attention. The grey seer barked another order, commanding his warriors to retreat back into the tunnels, an order the terrified ratmen lost no time in obeying. Skilk hastened to slip into their midst, scurrying along as they raced back along toward the castle's cellars. One of the oldest axioms of skaven wisdom was that of safety in numbers. Skilk wanted plenty of bodies between himself and any lingering foes they might encounter as he made good his escape.

THULMANN WATCHED WITH impotent rage as the skaven scurried back to whence they had emerged. He had seen the horned grey seer retrieve *Das Buch die Unholden* from its resting place beside Sibbechai's ashes. The witch hunter did not like to ponder what purpose so loathsome a being might put the tome to, but there was nothing he could do to thwart the monster's escape. The unclean one stood between him and the skaven. There seemed little hope of destroying the daemon before the ratmen disappeared back into their subterranean world.

The thing that had been Baron von Gotz showed no sign of tiring. Liquid filth that might have been its internal organs drooled from the gashes in its diseased hide. Still it clawed and slashed at its foes. Only the touch of flame seemed to pain the beast, and it lashed out at all who threatened it with purifying fire. The pyromancer who had joined the attack was dead, his head ripped from his shoulders by the daemon's claws. The skaven warpfire-thrower had been similarly dispatched. Now, it was the crude expedient of burning cloth wrapped around steel that troubled the monster as it lashed out with enraged, if clumsy, swipes of its enormous hands.

Meisser's courage had not broken, doubtless because a few of Wurtbad's notables had not yet fled or been killed. Thulmann had to reluctantly credit the scheming Meisser for improvising his fiery weapon, a tactic many of the remaining defenders were quick to emulate. Yet the stabbing flames could do little more than annoy the bloated monster. If they would destroy the beast they had to find a way to engulf it in fire.

The skaven with the fuel cask lashed to its back was writhing upon the floor, trying to crawl away. Inspiration suddenly gripped Thulmann. He reached a gloved hand out, pulling the fighter beside him away from the battle.

'We've got to try and work that damnable machine!' he yelled, pointing at the skaven weapon. The witch hunter dashed toward the crippled ratman, smashing his foot into the creature's neck and stilling its mangled form. He cut the rat-gut straps binding the cask to the ratman's body. Beside him, the other warrior removed the wide-mouthed fire-thrower from the creature's companion. Thulmann was surprised to find that his helper was Silja. She nodded grimly to him, handing the witch hunter the arcane device.

'Do you have any idea how to work it?' she asked as he made a hurried study of the weapon.

A grim smile flashed upon his face as he hefted the heavy metal cylinder and directed its nozzle toward the rampaging beast. 'None at all,' the witch finder admitted. 'It may be wise to step back.' Whispering a final prayer to Sigmar, Thulmann's fingers tightened around the brass lever protruding from the underside of the weapon and pulled it back.

The unclean one's gaping mouth twisted in a burbling moan of agony, as liquid fire bathed its gruesome bulk in flame. The abomination staggered and swayed, slithering about the great hall as the flames greedily devoured its obscene flesh. In its agonies, the creature's fiery touch set tapestries and carpets burning, its pain-maddened tread grinding corpses into cinder beneath its splayed feet.

Thulmann dropped the unclean skaven weapon, appalled by its horrific power. A daemon beast that had slain over a dozen men, whose unnatural flesh had resisted hundreds of blows from sword and axe, had been consumed in an instant by the tech-nosorcery of the ratmen. He watched the thing fall, shuddering upon the floor as its polluted hide blackened and blistered.

'Justice for my father.' Silja's words were as chill as ice. Thulmann acceded.

'Yes, and justice for Wurtbad,' he announced, as the thing that had been Baron Friedo von Gotz shrivelled and died.

WITCH HUNTER CAPTAIN Meisser advanced on the daemon as it burned, intending to bury his sword in its dying bulk. It was as good as dead already, a fact even the grim Black Guardian seemed to accept as he stepped back, but Messier was determined to impress the handful of soldiers and noblemen still able to bear witness. When Meisser cut the head from the dying abomination, it would be he, not Thulmann, who was named slayer of the beast. In the weeks to come, it would be important for Meisser's name to be held in higher regard than that of Mathias Thulmann, if he were to wrest back control of the Wurtbad chapter house.

But, as Meisser stepped forward, thunder roared across the room and the witch hunter captain's schemes exploded from the back of his skull. A shock of disbelief contorted Meisser's face as his body crashed forward into the burning carcass of the daemon.

'Shit! I missed.' Streng snarled, from where he lay crumpled upon the marble tiles. The mercenary let the smoking pistol fall from his fingers, reaching up to dab his hand against the gash that the skaven had torn across his scalp. Thulmann hurried to his henchman's side, Silja following close behind him. The witch hunter removed linen bandages from a pouch on his belt, kneeling to treat Streng's injury.

'Very slovenly marksmanship,' Thulmann reprimanded him. 'I don't think you'll ever master the pistol.'

THE FIRES FROM the dying daemon had spread from the main hall, racing through the castle as though possessed of a malevolent intelligence of their own. Or perhaps a benevolent intelligence, Thulmann considered. Everything the daemon horror had touched might have become tainted by contact with it. The fires would consume the taint as certainly as they had consumed the walking pestilence that had been Baron von Gotz.

Thulmann wondered how the baron had come to such an end, how he had so swiftly changed from a mortal man into a living effigy of the Lord of Decay. Doubtless the answer lay with *Das Buch die Unholden*. He shuddered to think what awful uses the underfolk might find for such a work of arcane knowledge.

Beside him, Silja turned her eyes from the inferno. 'Is it over?' she asked. Thulmann shook his head sadly.

'It is a beginning, not an end,' he replied. 'We've won the battle, but the war rages on. The skaven have retreated back into their tunnels, but the threat they pose is more terrible than before. And Doktor Weichs is still out there, somewhere. While he lives, sickness and plague could run rampant at any time.' Thulmann sighed deeply, returning his gaze to the castle.

'Small victories are sometimes hard to accept, Fraulein Markoff, but sometimes they are the only ones the gods see fit to offer us.'

WITCH KILLER

PROLOGUE

THE MAN'S BREATH came short and sharp, his pulse quickening as he heard the scratching of verminous claws upon naked earth. There is no shame in fear, he thought, only in how you confront that fear. He reached into his shirt, his hand closing around an icon set upon a silver chain. He smiled as he felt the hammer-shape press upon his palm. Whatever haunted the darkness, he did not face it alone.

Alone, once again Mathias Thulmann cursed himself for being such a fool. Nearly a hundred men had entered the gloom beneath the Schloss von Gotz, invading the black underworld below Wurtbad. Soldiers from the Ministry of Justice, veteran witch hunters from the Wurtbad chapter house, elite troops from the palace guard of Baroness von Gotz, even half a dozen templar knights of Morr, the forbidding Black Guard, had placed themselves under Thulmann's command, following his lead into a grotesque labyrinth of nightmare and horror: nearly a hundred men, the most disciplined fighters Wurtbad could offer.

Thulmann uttered a hollow laugh. A thousand would have been too few to explore the insane network of tunnels under the city. Passageways snaked and writhed through the dripping, stagnant earth without pattern or scheme. After a half hour traversing the madhouse corridors, Thulmann had been unable to decide if he was a few feet beneath the surface or a few hundred.

Their foe had struck, erupting from numberless openings in the walls, floor and ceiling of the tunnel. A living tide of snapping fangs and slashing claws, the ratmen had set upon them in feral savagery. Only with blood and steel had the vermin been driven back squealing into the darkness, leaving their dead littering the floor. The victorious men had given pursuit, hounding the fleeing monsters through their burrows.

It was then that the tunnel began to shake and quiver. Thulmann recognised the sound and the sensation all too well. Looking over to the hulking armoured form of Captain-Justicar Ehrhardt, he saw that the grim templar recognised it too. Both men shouted a frantic warning and the entire company took to its heels, fleeing the passageway as the skaven collapsed it in upon them.

THULMANN SHOOK HIS head at his own audacity. His newly-lit torch had revealed something else to him – he was alone. None of his soldiers had reached the safety of the side tunnel he had sheltered in. Lost and alone, with only the feeble light of his torch to guide him, he had enough to worry about without wishing for a confrontation with the skaven sorcerer who had drawn him down into the darkness.

The scratching of claws on bare earth came more distinctly, with a suggestion of whispered hisses. Thulmann pulled his sword from its sheath. They'd found him at last, the scuttling horrors of this black underworld. With their inhumanly sharp senses, he had known it would only be a matter of time before the skaven tracked him down. The possibility of running passed through the witch hunter's mind, quickly subdued and killed by his iron resolve. If he were fated to die in the skaven warren, he would do so with honour, with his wounds to the front.

Chittering laughter crawled through the darkness. A loathsome shape crept forward, its scrawny body covered in lice-ridden fur. The face that snarled at him from beneath a rusted steel helmet was that of a monstrous rodent, chiselled fangs jutting from the lips of its muzzle. In an extremity that was more paw than hand, the ratman held a crooked sword crusted with decay. A long, scaly tail lashed the floor behind the creature as it squinted at him with hungry red eyes. Thulmann felt disgust fill him as he watched the skaven creep forward. He prepared himself for the monster's attack, knowing only too well with what frenzy the ratkin could fight.

The shrill, inhuman laughter was repeated. More of the under-folk emerged, their fanged faces slavering at the lone human they had cornered. Thulmann's hopes of survival withered before him as more and more rodents emerged from the darkness. They stood there for a moment, squinting against the light of Thul-mann's torch, squealing and hissing to each other in hungry anticipation. The witch hunter knew it would only be a matter of time before the skaven overcame their trepidation and pounced upon their prey. Thulmann firmed his grip upon his blade. Whichever monster was first to dare his steel, that one at least would accompany him into the kingdom of Morr.

A furry body slammed into Thulmann from behind, clawed feet digging into his legs as they scrambled for purchase, a wiry arm wrapping around his throat while sharp fangs snapped beside his ear. Only the witch hunter's heavy cloak prevented the would-be killer from ending his life, turning the murderous knife gripped in its paw so that it merely slashed along the flesh. Thulmann cried out in pain and outrage. Even as the skaven clinging to his back pulled its knife back to make another strike, the witch hunter's arm was swinging upward, thrusting his burning torch into the ratman's face. The skaven dropped away from him, its shrill screams deafening as it writhed across the floor.

There was no time to savour the cringing killer's agony. As soon as the ambusher had attacked, the other skaven were in motion, lunging forward like a pack of starving mongrels. Thulmann's sword licked out into the darkness, bisecting the snout of one attacker as it scurried towards him, gashing the shoulder of a sec-ond. Then they were on him, a burly black-furred monster crushing him to the ground as its powerful arms closed around his midsection. A clawed hand ripped his sword from his fingers as he struck the ground while furred feet kicked dirt upon his dropped torch, causing its light to flicker and dim. Ravenous eyes glared down at him, ropes of drool dripping from fanged muz-zles. Mathias Thulmann had always expected his service to the Order of Sigmar would end in a hideous death, but being eaten

alive by the skaven was a more ghastly end than his worst nightmare.

Suddenly the shrill scream of a skaven rattled through the passageway. The monsters turned around in fright, noses twitching.
Thulmann saw the body of a ratman fly through the air, filthy
blood streaming from an enormous gash in its chest, a hulking
shape beyond it. The witch hunter laughed aloud as he renewed
his struggle against the ratmen holding him down. The monsters
had been so intent upon tormenting their prey they had failed to
notice their new adversary.

It was not a battle but a massacre, and one the skaven quickly
decided they wanted no part in. Thulmann could hear the meaty
impact of his saviour's massive sword as it cleaved apart the bodies
of the ratmen. The feral courage of the skaven swiftly crumbled,
squeals of fright and the acrid reek of fear replacing their hungry
snarls and mocking laughter. The monsters holding the witch hunter
broke and ran, leaving only the black-furred warrior straddling his
midsection. The ratman snapped its fangs in fury at its craven comrades, and transfixed Thulmann with its malicious gaze. Before the
monster could bring its crooked sword stabbing down, an immense
length of steel flashed through the darkness, sweeping through the
ratman's body, bisecting the creature at the waist. The spurting wreckage of the skaven's lower half crumpled to the floor.

Thulmann painfully lifted himself to his feet, accepting the
gauntleted hand that reached down to him. The witch hunter
wiped the reeking filth of the slain ratman from his clothes. Gazing around him, he recovered his sword and hat.

His rescuer leaned upon his mighty zweihander, the point of
the giant sword stabbed into the bloodied floor. Covered from
head to toe in black plate armour, the warrior did not seem even
slightly fatigued by the brutal battle that he had fought. The only
concession to comfort he made was to lift the rounded cylinder
of his helmet from his head, exposing his hard features and bald
pate. Captain-Justicar Ehrhardt of the Black Guard of Morr
watched Thulmann while the witch hunter recovered his gear.

'It seems I am not the only one who escaped the trap these
thrice-damned fiends set for us,' Thulmann observed as he
restored the wide-brimmed hat to his head.

'Indeed, Brother Mathias,' the knight growled. 'These creatures
seem determined to increase the retribution I owe them.' Looking

at the carnage Ehrhardt's sword had visited upon the underfolk, Thulmann almost felt pity for the vile creatures.

'I have seen some sign that others made it clear,' Ehrhardt continued. 'You are the first I have actually found, however.'

'It is well that you came when you did,' Thulmann said.

The Black Guardsman shrugged off the witch hunter's gratitude. Thulmann could understand the sentiment: Ehrhardt did what he did out of duty, not for recognition.

The witch hunter took stock of his injuries. Most were little more than scrapes and bruises; only the dampness along his back worried him. He winced as his fingers probed where the skaven's dagger had cut him. The wound was shallow, for all its painfulness, and seemed to have stopped bleeding. Infection was a more pressing concern than bleeding to death, but there was little he could do about this at the moment.

'You are injured?' Ehrhardt enquired.

Thulmann nodded his head as he set a linen handkerchief against the dripping wound. If it was infected it would prove every bit as lethal as the mutilating strokes of Ehrhardt's zweihander.

'Nothing that will prevent me from doing Sigmar's work,' Thulmann said. He studied the black openings that peppered the passageway before them. 'Shall we see if we can't find more survivors?'

'And if we do?' the knight asked as he fell into step beside Thulmann.

'We pursue our original purpose,' the witch hunter replied after a pause. 'We track down this skaven sorcerer and visit the justice of Sigmar upon it.'

CHAPTER ONE

THE CHAPTER HOUSE of the Order of Sigmar in Wurtbad stood on a winding street some small distance from Wurtbad's temple district. The building was a squat, two-storey affair, its gabled roofs pointing towards the north, a plaster icon of the twin-tailed comet fixed above its entrance. The chapter house was not immune from the caprices of change that had settled on Wurtbad. One of the dungeons beneath the structure had partially collapsed after being penetrated by the inhuman skaven, damaging the foundations themselves. More far-reaching, however, would be the death of the chapter house's master, Witch Hunter Captain Meisser, a final casualty in the fierce fighting that had raged within the Schloss von Gotz. It would be months before Meisser's successor was appointed and installed in Wurtbad.

A more immediate change, however, was what interested the man who had devoted himself to watching the chapter house since dawn. From the window of the house of a petty Sigmarite official, he had watched the comings and goings associated with the brooding structure across the cobbled street, with keen interest. With a quill, he carefully made a note of every person arriving and leaving. As darkness settled, he at last turned his eyes from the chapter house door, consulting the notes he had scratched into a sheet of vellum. A smile twisted his features.

By his calculations, there should only be two or three men left in the chapter house, one of them wounded. He considered the rather numerous household of the owner of the home, patiently waiting for him in the parlour below. Eight against two and a half were the sort of odds he was willing to entertain, especially since his eight would be a bit more durable than the denizens of the chapter house.

Yes, he decided, the risk was slight, and the potential reward, promising.

ELDRED HURRIED THROUGH the lonely halls of the chapter house. He had been long in the service of the witch hunters and knew well the priceless value of speed. With such dark powers at work in Wurtbad, even the slightest delay might mean damnation and death. Certainly the relentless, steady pounding upon the oak doors of the chapter house bespoke urgency.

The pounding on the door continued unabated as Eldred rushed towards it. Had something gone wrong? Did the witch hunters need help? And if they did, what sort of aid could Eldred possibly render them? With a sense of grim foreboding he placed his hand on the thick steel bolt that held the door shut and peered through the narrow grate set into the portal.

The man who stood outside the chapter house was not one of the templars, although he was not unknown to Eldred. Constantin Trauer was a clerk for the temple of Sigmar, maintaining the many accounting ledgers that monitored the temple treasury. He was a small, nondescript man, with an almost effete demeanour. In the light brown cloak of his office, his thinning hair plastered against one side of his forehead, there was certainly nothing about the man that suggested menace. Yet Eldred found himself instinctively recoiling. The clerk seemed oblivious to his alarm, barely registering the fact that the door had swung open, his right hand half-raised as if to strike upon it once again.

Eldred's fingers tightened around the slim dagger he wore upon his belt. Ever since the attack in the dungeons, Thulmann had ordered all the servants to go about armed. Eldred was thankful for this edict as he watched Constantin stagger forwards, his steps clumsy and awkward. The clerk's head swayed brokenly upon his neck and Eldred gasped as the blind, lifeless chill of Constantin's eyes met his gaze. The servant rushed forwards, dagger clenched in his fist, determined to slam the door shut before the clerk could stagger into the room.

Eldred barked a command for the clerk to withdraw, and threatened him with the dagger, but Constantin continued to shuffle forwards. His bleary eyes did not even react to the sound of the servant's voice. The eerie lack of response from the clerk sent a shiver of fear wriggling down Eldred's spine, but what he saw beyond the clerk caused him to gasp. More figures were stepping out from the darkness, moving with shuffling, swaying steps. Whatever was wrong with Constantin, he was not alone in his affliction. Too late, Eldred realised he had allowed the intruder to stand between himself and the warning bell set beside the door.

The old servant cried out, screaming an alarm to the other occupants of the chapter house. There were two other servants in the building and Franz Graef, a witch hunter who had been injured in the battle with Baron von Gotz. He only prayed that his warning came in time.

Eldred flung himself at Constantin. For all his ungainliness, the clerk was immovable, and held his ground against the charge. Eldred's fingers stabbed his dagger into the thing's shoulder. For the first time, the zombie seemed to take notice of him, lifting its cadaverous fist and smashing it into Eldred's skull, spilling the servant to the floor. Head swimming, Eldred struggled to rise to his feet and face the monster once more.

'I need one of you alive,' a sneering voice hissed from the doorway. Eldred turned towards the sound, seeing a man who was almost as corpse-like as his undead followers. He wore a grey cassock around his lean body, trimmed in thick brown fur. The exposed skin of his hands and face was pallid and sickly, his black hair stringy and unkempt. But there was a malevolent life in the eyes that stared from the man's thin, hungry face, exuding an almost tangible sensation of the profane and the evil. Here, then, stood the master of the corpse-puppets.

The necromancer waved his leprous hand and the zombie of Constantin shuffled back towards Eldred. 'If you behave, you can be my prisoner,' the sorcerer said as he strode into the building.

With arcane gestures, the necromancer ordered the zombies into the chapter house, and watched them march silently into the building.

It was not long before screams banished the eerie silence. The necromancer's pale features pulled back in an appreciative smile as the sound reached his ears. Eldred groaned in horror as he heard his comrades murdered.

The sorcerer glared down at his captive. 'Do the sounds of death disturb you?' The necromancer laughed. 'This is but the prelude to the symphony!' He crouched down to stare into Eldred's eyes.

'If there was one thing I learned from the tedious operas of my homeland, it is that every instrument has its part to play.' Impossibly, the smile on the sorcerer's face became even more menacing. 'Now it is time for you to play yours. I will ask a question, you will provide an answer. Where did they put the vampires?'

Eldred moaned in renewed horror as he heard the necromancer's words, but a fresh string of screams from deeper within the chapter house killed any thoughts of refusal. The sorcerer rose to his feet again, motioning for the zombie of Constantin to lift their captive from the floor. With an extravagant flourish, the necromancer motioned for Eldred to lead the way. The servant complied with shocked subservience, moving almost as lifelessly as the zombies.

You may have thought yourself finished with me, Sibbechai, the necromancer thought as he followed behind Eldred, *but Carandini has not yet finished with you*.

'LIE DOWN AND die!'

Streng's boot smashed into the ratman's face, spattering the earthen wall with blood and fangs. The mercenary delivered another brutal kick to the creature's throat, crushing its windpipe. The body continued to shudder and twitch, but the brute was good and dead. Streng wiped a hand caked in dirt and blood across his forehead to stem the trickle of sweat seeping into his eyes. He cleaned his gory blade on the ratman's body, not allowing himself to think about how it had nearly been him lying on the floor of the cavern. Even a moment's distraction meant the difference between life and death in the creeping dark of the skaven warren.

The mercenary turned away from the dead monster, eyes narrowed as he looked for any other sign of opposition. The floor of the cavern was strewn with furry carcasses. Some were old, others were much more recent. Streng saw human bodies mixed in with those of the vermin. Some of these, too, had been present before the ambush. Only one of them wore the livery of the von Gotz palace guard, and there did not seem to be any other soldiers or witch hunters among the dead. Streng breathed easier, but did not fully relax his guard.

'I don't think they planned that ambush,' a scar-faced soldier in the griffon-tabard of the Ministry of Justice said. 'I think they were trying to hide in here and we surprised them.'

Streng spat on the corpse nearest him. 'That evens things a bit. They damn well surprised us with that cave-in of theirs.' The warrior could see the expressions of the men around him darken as he mentioned their recent escape. Only a dozen of them had gained the safety of the side tunnel before the entire passage had collapsed. Since then two emotions had struggled to control every man: terror and rage. Streng had been careful to cultivate the fury every man felt, bringing it to the fore. Fear would do nothing to help their chances of survival, but savage hate might.

'Rather peculiar hole, even for underfolk,' one of the palace guards commented, tapping the side of what looked like a large iron stove with the flat of his sword. Streng looked at the strange objects scattered around the cavern: tables strewn with stoppered jars and foul-smelling bottles, a brick kiln, several iron furnaces and some sort of immense press. The hair on the back of his neck began to rise. Since taking service with Thulmann, he'd seen the laboratories of more than a few alchemists, and this apparatus looked disturbingly similar.

A thought flared through his mind and he strode towards one of the human corpses. Turning it over with his foot, he found himself looking into a villainous face, frozen in an expression of horror. But more interesting was the leather mask that he found in a pocket of the man's tunic, a leather mask with a long, bird-like beak and crystal lenses over the eyes: the mask of a plague doktor.

The inarticulate howl of frustration that exploded from Streng turned every eye on him. The soldiers watched, puzzled, as the mercenary hurled the leather mask across the cavern with a savage gesture. He'd been here, the foul scum Thulmann had hunted across half the Empire, the bastard physician who experimented upon his fellow man, filling the veins of his victims with the filth of Chaos. Freiherr Weichs had been here. This was his lab, the fountainhead of Stir Blight and the plague in Wurtbad.

Streng snarled, sweeping his arm across one of the tables, knocking jars and bottles to the floor, and then gripped the edge of the table and upended it, sending it crashing to the floor. He turned away from his vandalism to find the soldiers watching him warily.

'Come on,' he barked. 'There's nothing here, let's get moving!'

'Where?' protested on of the palace guards. 'Where are we supposed to go? Where?'

Streng's eyes were like ice as he turned on the man. 'We'll take one of these tunnels and find our way back to the surface.' The mercenary stabbed a finger at one of the black tunnel mouths, a decisive gesture that gave no hint of the randomness with which he had chosen it. 'We kill any rat bastard unlucky enough to come across our path!' he added with a venomous oath.

THE THREAT OF plague had kept the waterfront of Wurtbad abandoned, even the most desperate of the city's denizens forsaking the area where the disease had done such brutal work. With the quarantine in effect, the steady stream of ships plying the river had vanished, the river patrol keeping ships from the port.

Even so, two men stood upon the wooden pier in the early hours of dawn. The taller of the pair wore the heavy black robe of a priest of Morr. Beside him stood a thin figure garbed in grey, his lank black hair hanging in his eyes, his features displaying a trace of foreign blood. In his hands, the Tilean held a glass vessel filled with black ash.

Carandini watched the sun rise into the sky, the shadows of night retreating before it. He smiled as the warm rays bathed his face. A necromancer was not the sort to cultivate an intimate relationship with the sun, their loathsome activities best conducted under the shroud of night, but today, today he could think of no more glorious a sight. His fingers stroked the surface of the bottle – it would not be long now.

'I will not do this thing,' the priest groaned. 'It is an affront to Morr! I will not do it.'

Carandini took a step towards the man, shaking his head sadly. 'I worry that you are looking at this the wrong way, father. While it may be true that my chosen vocation is at odds with the puerile superstitions of your morbid little cult, that doesn't mean we can't be friends. Why, I am doing you a great boon! I'm giving you the opportunity to do a favour for your god, to be of noble service to him. You are being given the chance to right an affront to the divinity of your god, to reclaim something stolen from his domain.'

'You are a monster!' the priest spat, horrified by Carandini's words. 'You are a profaner of Morr, a violator of graves. Corpse-stealing monster!'

The necromancer tapped a forefinger against the bottle he held. 'Hardly as monstrous as what is in this bottle, father.' He thrust it towards the priest, laughing as the robed man shrank back from the vessel. 'See, even reduced to ash and dust, the dread Sibbechai still has the power to frighten you! How can you say what I ask of you is some crime against your god? Why, I am only doing what the witch hunters would have done had I left the vampire's cinders in their possession.'

'Then why steal them at all! Why this profane farce?'

The necromancer's face lost its air of humour and condescension. 'Because I owe this thing a debt. I have to see for myself that it has been destroyed, that its remains have been removed from any possibility of resurrection. I have to make sure that none of its filthy kind will learn of Sibbechai's death and seek to restore their fellow fiend.'

Carandini smiled once more as he looked back to the rising sun. The long game of trick and trap he had played with the necrarch was over, and it was Carandini, not Sibbechai, who had emerged as the victor. The vampire had almost triumphed, leaving the necromancer in the cellars beneath the castle, compelled to stay behind while the necrarch tried to claim *Das Buch die Unholden*. The arrival of the skaven had nearly been the death of him, the filthy magics of the horned skaven sorcerer sending an army of ravenous rats to consume the necromancer. It had taken every trace of his willpower and skill to conceal himself from the rats, to weave such a cloak of black magic around himself so that even their keen senses could not find him. The effort of focusing and maintaining such power had nearly killed him. Even now, the memory caused his heart to thunder within his breast.

But the spell had held, and Carandini had not died. He'd sensed the destruction of Sibbechai when the enchantment the vampire had placed upon him was broken. Before Carandini could rush into the castle above to look for the grimoire, however, he'd seen the skaven return, fleeing back into their burrows. Once again he had locked eyes with the horned sorcerer, but this time the ratman held *Das Buch die Unholden* in its foul paws. Had the creature been alone, Carandini might have dared to confront it, despite its tremendous power. The ratman had not been alone though, nearly a score of its fellows still hurried after it. The necromancer had remained hidden, his sense of self-preservation overcoming his lust for the book. Now he knew who had it, he would be able to find it again, and when he did, it would be under circumstances that favoured him, not the skaven.

'Are we ready, father?' Carandini asked. The cleric did not speak, merely bowed his head in submission. He joined the necromancer on the edge of the dock, a silver talisman clutched in his hands, arcane words whispering past his lips. Carandini tapped the glass bottle one last time, and held it out over the river, popping the cork from its neck. As the priest continued to invoke the rite of exorcism, Carandini turned the bottle over, scattering the vampire's ashes into the swift moving River Stir.

'*Repast en pace*,' Carandini echoed the priest as he watched the last dregs of ash tumble from the bottle. He hoped that wherever Morr deposited the souls of vanquished vampires, it was unpleasant

'Sɪʀ, I ᴛʜɪɴᴋ I see light ahead!' The words were spoken by a young, blond-haired soldier from the Ministry of Justice. He was one of only three survivors Thulmann and Ehrhardt had encountered in the tunnels.

'Do you think there might be more survivors?' Ehrhardt asked the witch hunter.

'Possibly, or it may be our ratty friends trying to draw us into a trap,' Thulmann replied, his voice heavy with fatigue. 'Either way, we can't afford to avoid it. If it is some of our comrades, we cannot abandon them. If it is a trap, it shows more intelligence and organisation than these running battles we've been fighting. Something will be in charge, one of their noxious leaders. If we can capture it alive, we may be able to get information from it, find a way out of here, or perhaps find the creature we came here to kill.'

One by one, Thulmann's group extinguished their torches, crawling through the darkness as they followed the witch hunter towards the light. Soon they were close enough to see shadows moving in the tunnel ahead, and hear voices whispering from the darkness.

'I still say we are heading the wrong way,' a man's voice snarled.

'Do as you like,' came the growled reply, 'but I'm sticking to this tunnel. The way the mangy curs have been thick along it, it has to lead somewhere!'

The second voice was terribly familiar to the witch hunter. He was pleased to find that his henchman Streng had also been lucky enough to escape the skaven trap.

'You've been saying that for the last half hour!' snapped another of the soldiers, busily tying a bandage around his left arm.

'And he is no doubt correct.'

The men all spun around, blades at the ready as Thulmann spoke, eyes narrowed as they peered into the darkness. The witch hunter strode boldly into the ring of light, his fatigue forgotten in his joy at finding more of his men alive. To Streng and the men with him, the witch hunter's sudden emergence from the gloom was almost supernatural, some divine sending of holy Sigmar himself. The effect lessened somewhat when Ehrhardt and the three Ministry of Justice troopers followed Thulmann into the light. The miracle was somehow cheapened for being shared.

'We thought you was dead,' Streng observed when he managed to recover from his shock. The mercenary scratched a filthy hand through his scraggly beard. 'I shoulda known it would take more than a few tons of earth falling on your head to finish you, Mathias.'

Thulmann clapped a hand on Streng's shoulder, causing a puff of dust to rise from his leather hauberk. 'I'm not so surprised to see you either. You've crawled your way out of more miserable holes than this in the aftermath of one of your drunken revels.'

The stocky mercenary smiled at the remark; his employer never had approved of the impiety of his ways.

'Now that you've decided to put in an appearance, I'll let you lead this rabble,' Streng said, gesturing at the men around him. 'You've fought the skaven in the past, maybe they'll believe you when you say the best chance we've got of getting back is to go where the rats are thickest.'

Thulmann stared at his henchman, noting the curious look in Streng's eyes. He was not sure exactly what the warrior was playing at, but he would follow his lead, for the time at least. 'My assistant is indeed correct,' the witch hunter said in a quiet, controlled voice. 'If there have been more skaven in these passages, then they are most likely trying to keep us from reaching a path to the surface and escaping this pit. Stick to this passage and before long we'll be feeling the sun driving the dampness of these burrows from our bones.'

The encouraging words had their effect. Thulmann saw many of the soldiers smile grimly at the prospect of regaining the surface. Streng had driven them as far as he could with nothing more than simple hate. Thulmann offered them something that would take them still further: hope.

He felt remorse that his hopeful words were untrue, but knew that only by keeping the men moving would they stand any chance. Ehrhardt seemed to be the only one who detected the hollowness of Thulmann's words. He said nothing, however, simply resting his enormous sword against his shoulder and taking a torch from one of the soldiers. Holding the brand aloft, the giant knight marched deeper into the passage. The survivors lost little time in following after the imposing Ehrhardt. Streng and Thulmann lingered behind to form a rear guard.

'Mind explaining what is going on?' Thulmann asked, his voice low so that only his henchman would hear his words. 'You know as well as I that whatever organised defence these monsters had has collapsed as surely as that tunnel back there. They aren't trying to keep us from some path back to the city. These are frightened, disorganised packs of animals falling back to their innermost lair, instinctively protecting the most vital areas of the warren – the breeding pits and the burrows of their ruling elite. I'm not leading these men towards the surface; I'm leading them deeper into the warren. Why?'

A harsh intensity was on Streng's face when he turned to answer the witch hunter.

'We found a room back there,' the mercenary said. 'A big cave with lots of strange equipment in it. The sort of stuff an alchemist might have... or a physician. We found a lot of bodies too, and not all of them were rats. Most of them, man and rat alike, had masks like that plague doktor was using.'

'Weichs,' Thulmann hissed, spitting the name off his tongue as if it was poison.

Streng nodded grimly. 'He was here, Mathias, working with the skaven. Looked like he might have fallen out with his hosts, but if he did, his body wasn't among the dead.'

Thulmann looked away, his eyes fixed upon the shadows of the passage. A hundred bitter memories swarmed inside his skull, snarling their anger in his mind. Of all the heretic scum he'd hunted over the years, he could think of only one worse than the renegade doktor.

'You think he might still be here?' Thulmann asked through clenched teeth.

'If he isn't, whatever rat is boss of this nest might know where he's gone,' Streng answered. 'That's why I wanted to press deeper into this maze, try to get my hands on one of their leaders.'

The witch hunter nodded his head. He knew that Streng did much of what he did for money. No higher purpose motivated him, but catching Freiherr Weichs had become as much of an obsession to the callous mercenary as it had to himself.

'Our first priority must remain finding the horned skaven and recovering the book,' Thulmann cautioned. The black knowledge contained within *Das Buch die Unholden* had been enough to transform the ruler of Wurtbad into a living avatar of the Unclean One. Who could say what even greater horrors the tome might unleash upon the world if it was allowed to remain in evil hands? As much as he wanted Weichs, he was forced to recognise that the book represented the greater threat.

'I'll remember that,' Streng replied, favouring Thulmann with a murderous grin. 'But if I have a chance at Weichs, all the black secrets in Sylvania won't keep me from taking it!'

CARANDINI WATCHED WITH eager anticipation as the sun began to sink from the sky, casting long shadows into the dilapidated fish-monger's shop. There had been a great deal to make ready before the onset of night, yet even so Carandini had spent the last few hours in impatient expectancy. The ritual he was preparing was an ancient one, from a time when the spires of ghoul-haunted Lahmia still stood proud and tall beside the Crystal Sea. It had been in his possession for a long time, but he'd never before had the opportunity to test its efficacy.

Thanks to the witch hunters, however, that opportunity had finally presented itself.

Carandini retreated back into the building, treading cautiously so as not to disturb the chalk sigils he had drawn on the floor. He could feel the mystical energy being pulled into the ancient symbols, the sorcerous power growing even as the sun's light became more feeble. Soon, the light of the thirteen candles he had placed around the room would be the only thing contesting the darkness. The flames that rose from them glowed with a haunting blue light. They were true corpse candles, necromantic talismans crafted from the fat of murdered men.

Carandini was careful to avoid staring at the flames directly. The black arts were dangerous to evoke, even to necromancers. The flame of the corpse candle formed a bridge between the domain of life and that of death. The incautious might find themselves mesmerised by the haunting light, helpless to prevent their souls from being drawn into the flame, or to prevent something from the other side from slipping through and investing itself within their flesh.

The necromancer fixed his attention instead upon the object that was the focus of his ritual. Lying in the centre of the room, at the very nexus of the symbols and designs drawn on the floor, was a large black wooden box, the coffin lately inhabited by the necrarch Sibbechai. Carandini could almost see the dark energies gathering around the casket, permeating its wooden surface and iron fittings, suffusing the thing lying within. The ritual required one more component... human blood.

Carandini snapped his fingers, exerting his will. There was a gap between the circles and pentagrams on the floor, a narrow walkway leading from the outer ring of the chamber towards the casket lying at its centre. The necromancer exerted his will and two shuffling, tattered shapes began to approach the coffin. Between them, the two zombies bore the struggling, whimpering figure of the priest of Morr. The captive's cries were little more than inarticulate gargles, the necromancer having removed the man's tongue. Gods sometimes answered the prayers of priests, and Carandini was not of a mind to take any chances.

The zombies carried their charge to the casket, forcing the man to bend at the waist and lean over the open coffin. The priest's inarticulate screams rose in pitch as he saw what lay inside, and he suddenly understood the necromancer's purpose and his own role. The cadaverous claw of a zombie ripped into the priest's throat, tearing though his flesh and slashing his windpipe. The dying man struggled in the remorseless grip of the zombies as a cataract of blood exploded from his neck, spraying a wash of gore into the casket.

Carandini exerted his will once more and his undead servants withdrew, bearing the remains of the priest with them. The necromancer paid them no further notice, his attention riveted to the casket. Would it work, he wondered?

The necromancer dismissed his doubts. The ritual would succeed; it would succeed because he willed it so. He would not be denied. His enemies would not keep him from his destiny. *Das Buch die Unholden* would be his. He would make its secrets his own, and the thing inside the coffin would help him take it from those who stood in his way.

From his vantage point across the street, Carandini had seen Thulmann lead his witch hunters back to the chapter house. He had seen them bearing the ashes of his treacherous former partner Sibbechai and the more intact corpse of the vampire's minion, the vengeful creature Carandini had briefly encountered in the cellars of the castle. The ashes of his ally he had already attended to. Now he intended to put the remains of Sibbechai's errant thrall to use.

Carandini held his breath as he sensed a change in the air of the room. The light of the corpse candles dimmed, the atmosphere became colder. A black mist gathered around the casket, and was sucked down inside the coffin. Then the moment passed, warmth began to creep back into the room, and the candles returned to their former brilliance.

A pale hand rose from within the coffin, closing around the edge of the box. Carandini watched in fascinated triumph as a body slowly rose from the casket, a pallid shape that exuded an aura of strength and power despite its sickly hue. The creature turned a once handsome face in the necromancer's direction, the patrician features drawn and haggard, eyes at once both empty and hungry.

Slowly, awkwardly, the thing pulled itself up from the coffin, struggling to get out. The necromancer watched its efforts with pride, revelling in his own accomplishment. After a moment, the undead thing stood upon its own feet. It glared at Carandini and the necromancer could see a spark of awareness behind the vampire's hunger. He felt no fear, however. The wards he had placed on the floor would contain the vampire until he was ready to release it.

'Gregor Klausner, I believe,' Carandini laughed, the sound filled with all the mockery and scorn of Old Night and the Dark Gods.

CHAPTER TWO

THE GAPING BLACK cavern spread out before them, only partially illuminated by the torches and lanterns the soldiers bore. What that light revealed was every bit as noxious as the stench that assaulted their senses. The men stood upon a narrow lip that circled the cavern, the floor of the pit some twenty feet below. The floor was littered with bits of straw, fur and even strips of grimy cloth. Piles of immense rat pellets were scattered everywhere, punctuated by jumbles of gnawed bone. Several immense shapes covered in dirty brown fur lay amidst the squalor and excrement. Each was the size of an ox, but the form was that of a mammoth rodent. The beasts lounged on their sides, exposing the twin rows of furless teats that pimpled their upper bodies. The rat-like faces of the breeders stared up at the torchlight with wide-eyed, uncomprehending fear, recognising danger but incapable of understanding it. The pale, wrinkled things that clung to their teats did not react to the presence of the men at all: for the blind skaven pups, their entire existence consisted of drawing milk from their bloated mothers.

Thulmann stared coldly into the pit of horror and then turned, and gave the order to the soldiers to set it aflame. The loss of the breeders would effectively destroy the warren. Without their females, any remaining skaven would scatter, finding refuge or enslavement with other tribes of their kind.

When the orders were given, a great roar ripped through the cavern. Thulmann spun around as an immense form loomed up from the darkness of a side tunnel. Its beady red eyes gleamed as it strode into the light. The true magnitude of what they faced hit the men. The monster was not unlike the bloated breeders in the pit below, but was if anything larger, its body swollen with muscle. The rat-like head that jutted from its impossibly broad shoulders snapped and slavered with diseased ferocity, bloody froth drooling from its mouth.

Scurrying out of the shadows beside the hulking rat ogre was a smaller, black-furred skaven. The creature held a sickle-bladed halberd in its paws and its body was encased in steel, more armour than they had seen on any of the skaven they had encountered thus far. Strangely, the armoured skaven appeared to have been partially burnt. Even before the creature spoke, Thulmann knew they had found the master of the warren.

'Snagit!' the warlord hissed. 'Rip man-meat! Rip!'

Under its master's prodding, the rat ogre roared again and surged forwards with a speed Thulmann would not have believed possible for such a large creature. The foremost of the soldiers turned to run, but he had not reckoned upon the monster's speed. The rat ogre's claw crunched through the man's armour, nearly ripping him in two. The beast roared again as it shook its victim's entrails from its claws and swung around to resume its attack.

Captain-Justicar Ehrhardt held his ground as the immense brute charged forwards, his black garments melding with the shadows to make him almost as spectral as the chill hand of his sinister god. But Snagit did not need his eyes to find his prey. The Black Guardsman did not react as eight hundred pounds of slavering death rushed at him, standing his ground as solidly as a statue.

Snagit's murderous claw swept out at Ehrhardt with a powerful slash that should have knocked the knight's head from his shoulders. The instant the rat ogre closed, Ehrhardt was in motion, dropping beneath the powerful blow and lashing out double-handed with his massive zweihander. The huge blade crunched through both of Snagit's knees, all but severing the monster's legs.

The rat ogre toppled like a felled tree, and the creature howled in terror as its bulk tumbled down into the darkness. A moment later there was a sickening crunch as the rat ogre struck the unforgiving floor of the pit.

The black-furred skaven warlord's eyes were round with incredulous horror. Thulmann did not give the creature time to consider flight, dropping his sword and pulling his pistol. He tried to place his shot in the beast's knee, but the fever starting to burn in his body conspired to render his aim imprecise, shattering the warlord's hip instead. The skaven shrieked as its body spilled to the floor.

Thulmann wiped perspiration from his eyes and holstered his pistol. He waved Streng off as the bearded thug moved to help him. He'd come this far on his own and he would finish it on his own feet. The witch hunter carefully made his way towards the crippled skaven leader, leaving Streng and the remaining soldiers to inspect the breeding pit and assure themselves that the rat ogre was indeed dead. He found Ehrhardt's armoured foot planted firmly on the warlord's back, the creature struggling weakly beneath the knight's weight. Thulmann paused for a moment, trying to steady his breath before closing with his captive.

'Rather lively for a keep-sake, Brother Mathias,' Ehrhardt commented as Thulmann stood beside him. The creature pinned beneath his boot squirmed ever more desperately.

'No hurt! No kill!' the skaven croaked in shrill, pathetic tones.

'That depends upon how many of my questions you answer,' Thulmann snarled, his words punctuated by the increased pressure of Ehrhardt's foot upon the ratman's back. 'I want to know where your horned priest is and what has happened to a man named Doktor Freiherr Weichs!'

The pinned warlord chittered in twisted mirth, wrenching its neck around to fix its eyes on Thulmann. 'Gone,' the skaven hissed. 'Fled when templar-man hunt burrow! Take doktor-pet! Take stormvermin!' The warlord turned its head still further, displaying its burned cheek. 'Thrat try to slay grey seer. Grey seer magic strong.'

'There was a book the grey seer stole from the palace,' Thulmann told Thrat. 'What became of it?' The ratman's answer was the one he feared he would hear.

'Gone. Grey Seer Skilk stole words when they fled.' Thrat's lips curled in a savage snarl. 'Templar-man hunt Skilk? Rip grey seer?' Faced with its own extermination, the only thought that warmed Thrat's scheming heart was that through the witch hunter it might have its revenge on the treacherous grey seer.

'First you will lead us from this rat nest,' Thulmann said, rubbing at his eyes as fireflies began to dance through his vision. He only dimly heard the warlord's shrill assurances that it would show his men the way out. The last things he was aware of were his legs buckling beneath him and the bare earth floor rushing up to meet him.

CARANDINI'S EYES SWIFTLY adjusted to the darkness as he returned to his refuge. He could see the piles of refuse and rubble, and the silent figures of his zombies lined against one of the walls. But it was the thing squatting in the recesses of the small chamber that arrested his attention. As he entered, he saw it quickly throw something away, a gesture ridden with guilt and shame. The necromancer felt a small measure of triumph swell within his breast as he set the bag down and moved to light a candle.

The crouched figure rose to its feet as the light shone upon it. The man was taller than the necromancer, and more sturdily built. He wore coarse homespun breeches and a heavy wool vest, crude garments in contrast to the mouldering finery of Carandini's cassock. The man's fair hair and heavy, squared features were also far removed from the black hair and sharp, cunning face of the Tilean, but there was one quality that both men shared, the unhealthy pallor of their flesh.

'Dining in?' Carandini asked, voice laden with mockery. He gestured with his hand to the thing his guest had flung away, the tiny shrivelled carcass of a rat.

The other man turned his face towards the floor in shame. 'I didn't want to do it,' he said. 'I tried not to, but its life burned so bright, calling to me, tempting me.' The man clenched his fist in anger. 'Why did you do this to me! Why could you not leave me among the dead! Why did you make me come back as this unclean... thing!'

'As I have told you before, Gregor,' the necromancer replied, 'because you are useful to me.'

The vampire looked up, snarling in hate and disgust. Even in the grey, chill world his undead eyes now saw, Gregor could discern clearly the smirking features of the sorcerer. He glared at the necromancer, seeing the sickly light of Carandini's blood shining from within his body. Then his gaze shifted to the burlap sack the necromancer carried, a sack that writhed with an inner life and glowed with the bright, beckoning promise of blood. Soft blonde hairs poked from the mouth of the sack.

'What is in that bag?' Gregor asked.

'I thought you might be hungry,' Carandini said. The necromancer's smirk died as he found Gregor's hands coiled in the fabric of his cassock, lifting him savagely off the ground. Even in his weakened condition, the strength and speed of the vampire were far too easily underestimated.

'Take it away!' Gregor snarled into Carandini's face. 'I don't want it. Take it away!'

Carandini's moment of fright faded as he heard the pleading tone in Gregor's voice. 'Put me down, filth,' the necromancer ordered. The fury drained from Gregor's eyes and the vampire released his hold on the man.

Carandini brushed dirt from the front of his garment. 'Your ingratitude is becoming tedious, Gregor. Don't forget that just as I am the one who brought you back, I am the only one who can purge the taint from your body! I can make you whole again, Gregor! I can restore you to true life!'

Gregor turned away from the necromancer, wringing his hands in despair. 'I only want to die. I only want to die and to stay dead, to die before this curse takes complete control of me, to die before it makes me kill.'

'But you can't die, Gregor,' Carandini said, 'not a true, clean death. The touch of the vampire has removed that hope from you. Your spirit can never find rest. Only I can help you, but first you must help me.'

The vampire turned to face Carandini, his features a mask of misery and despair. 'I will do anything if you can drive this curse from my body!'

The wicked smile returned to Carandini's face. 'Then you must feed, you must not deny your urges. I will need you strong if you are to help me… and I you.' The necromancer gestured towards the squirming bag. Gregor shook his head, a moan of agony

ripping through his throat. The vampire retreated, hiding his face
in his hands. Carandini watched the wretch withdraw, lips curling
with amusement.

'Fight it all you like,' the Tilean muttered, 'but you can't fight
what you are forever, *vampire*.'

AN INARTICULATE CRY ripped its way past the witch hunter's lips as
his body surged upwards from the feather mattress. His hands
trembled as they wiped perspiration from his face. Thulmann
froze in mid-motion, wondering for a moment what had happened to the sword he had held in his nightmare, the sword he
had been thrusting into the neck of the Grand Theogonist. His
confusion only increased when a soft hand closed around his
own and a damp cloth was set against his forehead.

'You're alright, Mathias,' a soothing voice told him. Disbelief
flared within him as he heard the soft, comforting tones and he
tightened his grip around the hand he held. He looked up into
the woman's face, almost crying out in joy as the beautiful face
smiled back at him with all the old, patient understanding he
remembered. Memory struggled to rebel against his senses, but
Thulmann refused to allow it to affect him. He would not question a miracle.

'You are in the Schloss von Gotz,' the voice said, but there was
something troubling in its tone, something familiar yet different
at the same time. 'Streng brought you back to the surface.' The
more the voice spoke, the more it changed. Thulmann ground his
teeth against the wave of cold, unforgiving reason that killed his
fevered fantasy. The face he looked upon changed, blurring in
front of his eyes before resolving itself once more. It was still a
beautiful face, but it was no longer the face he had imagined, the
face he had been so desperate to see.

Thulmann knew this new face well. It belonged to Silja
Markoff, daughter and chief agent of the late Lord Igor Markoff,
the man who had been Wurtbad's Minister of Justice before the
madness of Baron von Gotz had seen him executed, and perhaps
the only person in Wurtbad he truly trusted.

'How… how long?' Thulmann's words forced themselves from
his dry throat in a rasping croak.

'Five days,' came the answer. Silja Markoff reached forward to
place another pillow beneath Thulmann's head. 'The Baroness

von Gotz has taken every effort to care for you. This is the bedroom of her major-domo, and you've been attended by no less than Sister Josepha of the Temple of the Lonely Sacrament.'

Mention of the Shallyan Sisterhood caused Thulmann to close his eyes and shake his head sadly. He had failed to prevent the late Baron von Gotz from removing plague victims from the Shallyan temple, confining them within Otwin Keep. Nor had he been able to prevent Meisser from setting the structure ablaze on orders from the possessed baron. Many of the Sisters had remained in the keep along with their doomed charges. Thulmann felt a profound sense of unworthiness that he should be attended by one of the few survivors.

'You stayed by me all this time?' It was strange that of all the thoughts swirling about in the turmoil of Thulmann's mind this should be the one to find voice.

Silja smiled at him and withdrew the damp cloth from his forehead. 'I didn't exactly have anything better to do,' she said with casual indifference.

Despite his fatigue and fever, the witch hunter managed to smile back at her. Silja Markoff had endured much in the past days, from the loss of her father to playing a part in the destruction of the daemonic horror that had infested the diseased body of Baron von Gotz. She gave no sign of the emotional ordeal she was going through, displaying a strength of will that even he found formidable. Only in her eyes could he detect some hint of pain.

Silja looked away as Thulmann studied her face, trying to conceal the emotion his scrutiny threatened to set loose. As she turned her face, Silja suddenly pulled her hands away and shot to her feet. Thulmann followed her redirected gaze. There was a man at the doorway.

'I can come back later if you're busy, Mathias.' There was an impertinent tone in Streng's voice and a smug suggestion in his smile. The thug punctuated his remark with a lewd wink at Silja, bringing colour to her pretty features.

'Make your report,' Thulmann snapped, putting as much strength in his voice as he could muster. 'I'll get no rest with you lurking at my threshold, trying to spy on me.' Streng's smile broadened and he swaggered into the room, ignoring the reproach in his employer's words and the glare Silja directed at him.

'The city guard's been busy clearing out the tunnels,' Streng said, 'though it seems they've had a damn easier time of it than we did! After you went cold on us, I had them put the breeding pit to the torch. You were right, Mathias, with the bitches and pups gone, all the fight went out of the vermin. Didn't so much as run across one of 'em when we made our way back up.'

'Did they find any more survivors?' Thulmann asked.

'A few,' Streng replied. 'Biggest group was a bunch led by some of Meisser's men who found their way back to the surface before us. All told, the skaven accounted for sixty-five men, most of them from the cave-in. No sign of Weichs though, and they've been over as much of the tunnels as it's safe to search. Looks like that animal you nabbed was telling the truth.'

Thulmann shook his head in regret. 'You've verified the creature's story?'

It was Streng's turn to look awkward and sheepish. The mercenary avoided Thulmann's gaze as he made his reply. 'I put the thing to the question back at the chapter house. It was already injured from your bullet, though. I don't think it could've lasted long in any event.'

Thulmann sighed: so much for any hope of getting more information from the ratman.

'There's more, Mathias.' Streng's voice became even more nervous, almost frightened. 'When we returned to the chapter house, it was a shambles. Everyone you left there was dead. Mathias, someone stole the vampire's body!'

Thulmann sat bolt upright in his bed. 'Gregor's body!' The witch hunter pounded his fist against the mattress. He had determined to see for himself that the body of Gregor Klausner was properly disposed of, that the destruction of his infected remains was carried out with all the ceremony and ritual necessary to ensure that his spirit would remain at peace in the gardens of Morr. Tracking down the book and the skaven sorcerer had been a more pressing concern, however. Now he cursed his decision to pursue the skaven. There were many reasons a vampire's body might be coveted by a practitioner of the black arts, none of them healthy.

'What about Sibbechai's ashes?' Thulmann demanded. The thought of Gregor's body falling into the hands of a sorcerer was sickening enough, but the theft of Sibbechai's remains was even more terrible. The essence of a vampire was bound to its carcass, a bond that could be severed only through extensive ritual and prayer. It was not unknown for a vampire's body to be restored through dark sorcery.

'Stolen as well,' Streng said. 'Ehrhardt has his templars scouring the cemeteries and plague pits looking for any sign of them.'

Thulmann sank back wearily into his pillows. 'If we couldn't find Sibbechai before, we won't find it now. Whatever human agency has been helping the vampire apparently continues to do so.'

'What will you do?' Silja asked. It was a question that Thulmann didn't want to answer. He wanted to stay in Wurtbad to find Gregor's body and make certain that his spirit had been allowed to stay at peace. He wanted to rip open every tomb and crypt in the city and see for himself that Sibbechai had not been restored to unholy life, but what he wanted and what he needed to do were two different things.

'This changes nothing,' Thulmann said. 'I must find Helmuth Klausner's grimoire and see it destroyed before anyone else can tap into its unholy powers. If what we fear has come to pass, if Sibbechai has been restored, then I think the same purpose will drive the vampire. It too will be hunting the book. If I find it, then the vampire will come to me.'

CARANDINI CROUCHED ON the floor of the fishmonger's hut, black candles flickering to either side of him. Resting on the ground was a ghastly sight – a great strip of flayed human skin spread out across the floor like a roll of parchment. Even if Gregor had refused Carandini's gift, the necromancer had found another use for what he had trapped inside his bag.

The strange words slithering past the necromancer's lips seemed heavy with the ancient past. Carandini carefully set a jar of ink on the edge of his morbid parchment, ink crafted in part from the blood of murderers. Beside it he set an even more repellent object, a withered human claw, its shrivelled shape bound in mouldering tomb wrappings. He carefully and deliberately dipped each of the claw's fingers into the ink.

There was a strange timidity in the necromancer's actions. The claw of Nehb-ka-Menthu, ancient tomb king of Khaerops, was the most potent of his sorcerous talismans, an object always to be treated with respect and caution, but there was something different about it this evening. Perhaps it was something to do with the change he perceived in the winds of magic, the growing strength in the ether and most particularly the baleful energies associated with dark magic and the black arts.

The necromancer brushed aside his doubts and fears, setting the claw down upon the skin. As he continued to chant the sibilant tones of the incantation, Carandini focused his will on the claw. He could feel the lingering strands of Nehb-ka-Menthu's spirit gathering around the claw. As he had done many times before, the necromancer bent his mind and soul towards subduing the spirit of the ancient tomb king and binding it to his power. As before, the residue of the mummy's essence struggled to resist him, to refuse his commands with all the malice the dead reserve for the living.

This time, however, the mummy's spirit did not relent as Carandini exerted his will upon it. The necromancer could feel Nehb-ka-Menthu drawing power from the swollen magical energy in the air. He could feel the spirit's resistance growing, fighting against him… and winning. Carandini's body doubled over in pain as the tomb king's wrath boiled over into the necromancer's flesh.

You will never be what I should have become.

In his mind's eye, Carandini could see the cadaverous face of the tomb king glaring at him with immeasurable hate. He fought to concentrate on his physical surroundings rather than his spectral vision, but even so slight an effort of will power was a struggle. He could feel his heart slowing and his lungs collapsing as the malevolent spirit began to drain the life from him. Carandini's body trembled like a sapling in a storm as he reached towards the black candles flanking him. The necromancer focused every scrap of his being into reaching out with his shaking hand and snuffing out the candle on his right.

The instant the dancing flame was extinguished, the invisible grip on his heart was gone, the smothering pressure on his lungs vanished. Carandini sank back, breathing heavily as he struggled to recover from his ordeal. He looked with disgust at the mummy's talon. The dismembered limb had crawled off the parchment, its lifeless fingers clinging to the hem of his cassock. What, he wondered, would it have done had he not ended the ritual when he did? Carandini shuddered and pried the dead fingers free, stuffing the talisman back into the leather satchel.

The claw was too dangerous to consult with the concentration of dark magic in the air. Just as Carandini's black arts were magnified by the sorcerous energies, so too was the undead spirit of Nehb-ka-Menthu. He had thought to use the claw to divine the whereabouts of *Das Buch die Unholden*. Now he would need to find it some other way... before someone else did.

The thought gave Carandini pause. The witch hunter would still be looking for the book, that much Carandini had gleaned from the servant Eldred before he decided the man was of no further use. If he was clever and careful, maybe he could let the witch hunter do some of the work for him? It would just be a matter of keeping track of the man's movements, and, when the time was right, extracting the information he needed.

Carandini wiped a greasy lock of hair from his face and smiled. After all the complications the witch hunter had caused him, first in Klausberg and now in Wurtbad, enticing him to reveal his secrets was something Carandini was certain to enjoy.

CHAPTER THREE

IT WAS TWILIGHT when Mathias Thulmann led his horse down the creaking wooden pier. His convalescence in the palace had forced him to delegate much of the work he would otherwise have taken upon himself. He could not quite shake himself free from guilt over his forced rest. He felt that perhaps with him leading the effort the templars would have found the hiding place of Sibbechai and its minions. Still, with men like Emil and Father Kreutzberg of the temple of Morr leading the hunt, the work rested in the hands of good and capable men. It was the only silver lining in the black cloud that had settled over him since the theft of Gregor's corpse and the vampire's ashes.

'Look at that,' Streng said from beside him. The unkempt mercenary gestured to the river. Even at such a late hour, the docks were a frenzy of activity with every manner of cargo vessel tied to the moorings and being hastily unloaded. On the water, the black bulks and flickering lights of other ships could be seen, ready to slide into position as soon as a space became free.

'The vultures gather,' Thulmann observed, voice dripping with contempt. News that the quarantine had been lifted had spread along the Stir even faster than news of the plague. In response, every merchant with stores of provisions and access to the river had descended upon the city. Greed, not concern for their fellow man, moved the merchants to such impassioned enterprise. The markets of Wurtbad were both desperate and frightened. These fresh goods would command prices five times what they would in the more stable towns and villages of Stirland and Talabecland.

Streng shook his head as he saw Thulmann glaring at the merchantmen and the frenzied activity surrounding them. He set his hand against his master's shoulder and redirected the witch hunter's attention. The *Arnhelm* stood apart from the other ships. Here the docks were deserted... deserted except for the massive armoured man who loomed beside the gangplank, his immense zweihander resting casually across his left shoulder. Thulmann nodded respectfully to the Black Guardsman as he approached the gangplank of the *Arnhelm*.

'Captain-Justicar Ehrhardt,' Thulmann said. 'How very nice of you to see me off. I wanted to thank you for your valiant assistance. But for your strength and courage I would've been rat food several times over. I think Wurtbad little appreciates the noble protector they have in you.'

The black-shrouded knight bowed in return. 'Wurtbad will have to do without its protector for a time. I have it in mind to accompany you, to see this affair through to its end.'

'Then you still believe skaven to be the concern of Morr's Black Guard?' Thulmann asked.

'Filling Morr's gardens with plague, digging them up to steal bodies, and raising those bodies as undead abominations. There have been enough affronts to Morr's authority and dominion to justify every templar in Wurtbad accompanying you,' Ehrhardt said. 'Father Kreutzberg and I reached a compromise.'

'You alone instead of all your Black Guardsmen?' Thulmann asked. Ehrhardt bowed his shaved head. Thulmann nodded in agreement. Unlike many of his order, he was not averse to working with elements from the other faiths of the Empire, not when they shared a common cause and a common purpose.

'It seems, then, captain-justicar, your city will need to do without you,' Thulmann said. 'Your aid has been considerable. I am certain it will continue to be so. What say you, Streng?'

The mercenary scratched his scraggly beard. 'So long as he shares in the work and not in the pay, I'm agreeable.'

'Then perhaps you won't mind more company.'

All three men turned at the soft, feminine voice. Thulmann had hoped to avoid any complications now that he was leaving Wurtbad, but as so often happened, his hopes were sadly at odds with reality. Standing on the pier, wearing a loose shirt, leather vest and tight riding breeches, was Silja Markoff. A flicker of joy flashed in the witch hunter as he saw her, but was quickly smothered by an even heavier cloud of gloom. Silja read the play of emotions in his eyes, her own look darkening.

'I asked myself why my good friend, my comrade in arms, Mathias, didn't stay around long enough to say goodbye.' Silja stalked forwards. At her approach, Ehrhardt and Streng stepped away from the witch hunter. Sticking by Thulmann's side in the face of daemons and rat ogres was one thing, but neither man wanted any part in the templar's current peril.

'You are a cultured, refined man,' Silja continued, 'surely considerate enough to treat me with more respect than some ten-shilling strumpet.' The accusation brought colour to Thulmann's face and a coarse laugh from Streng. 'Then I considered that maybe the reason you didn't say goodbye was that you wanted me to go with you, that your snubbing me was simply a backhanded call for my help.'

Thulmann swallowed. The truth of the matter was that he had avoided Silja after he had arranged the use of a ship with Baroness von Gotz. He didn't trust his feelings for the woman. It had been a long time since he had thought of someone the way he was beginning to think of Silja.

'Lady Markoff, I only thought to spare you the pain–'

'What? By slinking from the city like some thief in the night!' Silja's voice cracked with anger. 'Oh yes, that is much more compassionate. Now step aside and tell these idiots to let me board.'

Thulmann stepped into Silja's way, gripping her shoulders. He stared solemnly into her flustered features.

'This hunt will take me into danger...' he began.

Silja pulled away from him, storming past Thulmann and up the gangplank of the *Arnhelm*.

'Well, maybe there's some hot blood flowing in your veins after all,' Streng quipped as he watched Silja stalk away. Thulmann didn't seem to notice his henchman's jibe. His mind was elsewhere.

Streng shook his head as he observed the faraway look in his employer's eyes. 'Just remember, she ain't on the payroll either,' the mercenary warned, his tone less amused than before.

COLD EYES WATCHED as the *Arnhelm* pulled away from the dock back into the river. It had not been difficult to determine which ship the witch hunter would be leaving on. Other vessels had departed the waterfront as quickly as their cargoes were unloaded, eager to put Wurtbad and the lingering dread of plague behind them. The *Arnhelm*, however, had sat at her moorings for nearly the entire day. It had just been a question of waiting.

'And he's off,' Carandini hissed. 'Where are you off to in such a hurry, I wonder?' His chest heaved as he croaked a hoarse laugh. 'I'll be finding that out quite soon.' The necromancer moved away from the window of the ramshackle warehouse from which he had been observing the harbour. 'Time we were leaving too,' he said. The mob of slouching, slack-jawed shapes clustered around the room stiffened as their master spoke. Carandini turned his attention from the automatons to his other minion. Gregor was sitting on the floor, his back to the wall, and the shrivelled carcasses of half a dozen rats strewn around him. The vampire's pale face was a mixture of shame and hate as he looked up at Carandini.

'Now we simply procure passage on a ship and follow the witch hunter,' Carandini said. 'The Stir is quite wide and quite deep. Ships vanish without a trace all the time. No one will ever know what happened to Mathias Thulmann.'

Gregor felt the remains of his soul darken just a little more as he heard the necromancer's murderous plot.

THULMANN STARED OUT into the swift-moving river, watching the moons dance across the current. It was strange to think that they were the same moons as they had been all those years ago. So much had changed; so much had been destroyed, yet Mannsleib remained as it had ever been. As it had been that night when he had proposed to Anya.

The witch hunter closed his eyes, seeing her face again, imagining the fragrant smell of her hair, the cool softness of her skin, the curve of her lips as they smiled, and the shine of love in her eyes. Thulmann opened his eyes quickly, before the memories could blacken. Even the memory of love had been stolen from him, every happy moment they had shared consumed by that final, hideous horror.

'What were you thinking about?'

Thulmann was startled to find Silja standing beside him at the rail of the ship, her flaxen hair whipping around her shoulders in the cool autumn breeze. He looked back at the river, but now found his eyes drawn not to the reflections of the moons, but to that of the woman next to him.

'I was thinking about Altdorf, and the things I must do when I get there,' he said. It was not an untruth, in its way.

'It will probably sound strange to you, but I have never been to Altdorf,' Silja said. 'I understand it is many times the size of Wurtbad.'

'Forgive me, Lady Markoff,' the witch hunter said. 'River travel does not agree with me. I think I had best retire.' He did not give Silja the chance to respond, hastily retreating below decks, trying to outrun the dark memories swirling around him.

Silja watched Thulmann depart. For all that she felt for him, she knew very little about the man. Perhaps there was already a woman in his life, maybe even a wife.

She spotted Streng sitting on a coil of rope at the base of the mainmast. The witch hunter was a secretive, close-mouthed man, as his vocation demanded, but Streng was quite a different creature. The mercenary winked at Silja as she walked towards him. She could smell the ale on his breath.

'Finally had a bellyful of all that pious chapel-talk, eh?' Streng took another swig from the bottle gripped in his grimy fist. 'I'm not surprised. Red-blooded lass like you can only listen to so much o' that rot!' Streng slapped his knee. 'Come here and have a seat. I promise to share the booze.'

'You've been with Mathias for quite some time, haven't you?' Silja asked, keeping far enough from Streng to avoid the worst of the alcohol fumes.

The mercenary nodded. 'Several years,' he answered.

'He seemed very disturbed about returning to Altdorf,' Silja said. 'Do you know why?'

'There's someone he's going to see,' the mercenary said. 'Someone he should've killed and had done with a long time ago.'

Streng returned to his bottle and refused to elaborate on what he had told her.

* * *

THE WITCH HUNTER awoke with a start, his face dripping with perspiration. He rose from the bed, his limbs shaking as the nightmare slowly drained from him. He was just reaching for the small jug of water when a pounding knock sounded at the door of his cabin.

'Brother Mathias,' Ehrhardt's deep voice sounded from the other side of the door. 'Come on deck at once.' Thulmann pulled open the door, finding the knight's armoured bulk blotting out what little light flickered in the corridor.

'Sigmar's grace,' the witch hunter swore. 'Don't you ever sleep?'

'No,' the knight replied. 'There is a strange ship two hundred yards astern.'

'Probably another merchantman waiting for the sun to come up,' Thulmann said.

Ehrhardt shook his head. 'Not this one,' he said. 'Something doesn't feel right about it.'

Thulmann nodded, stalking back into his cabin to put on his boots and gather his weapons. He was not one to dismiss a man's misgivings out of hand; the supernatural often heralded itself with perceptions of unease and dread. The witch hunter followed the knight down the corridor and back on deck. Ehrhardt's misgivings seemed to be shared by no small number of the crew, the men clustering along the rail and pointing nervous fingers across the dark water.

What they pointed to was the dark silhouette of a ship, a fat-bodied merchantman not unlike the *Arnhelm*. There was no denying that there was something menacing about the vessel. Thulmann overheard one of the sailors give voice to the most obvious enigma the unnamed ship presented. There was no evidence of anyone on her decks and not a single running light gleamed from its hull. Any river trader at night, especially one at anchor, should be ablaze with lanterns and torches, proclaiming its presence and reducing the risk of a collision.

Noticing Thulmann among the growing crowd, Streng pushed his way from the rail and strode to his employer's side. 'Ill-favoured boat, I'll give 'em that,' the mercenary commented. 'Some of the crew are all for sendin' her to the bottom. They've a cannon positioned in one of the holds for stickin' holes in the hulls of river pirates.'

'A bit drastic for a ship that's done nothing but sit there and look sinister,' Silja commented, having followed after Streng as he pushed his way through the crowd of sailors. Thulmann felt an icy trickle along his spine as fragments of his nightmare returned to him, but managed to keep the feeling off his face.

'Even for a witch hunter, that would be extreme,' Thulmann agreed. 'Although there are some I've known who have done worse on even more nebulous grounds. Just the same, I think it might be wise if we lowered a longboat and I had a look at that hulk. At least then we might learn if our fears are justified.'

Concern filled Silja's eyes. 'You don't mean to go over there alone?'

Thulmann chuckled in amusement. 'I'm a faithful servant of Lord Sigmar, not a suicidal hero,' he said. 'I'll take Ehrhardt, Streng and whatever sailors have the stomach to face their–'

Thulmann's face contorted in disgust. Around him the crew's did likewise. Silja covered her nose with her hand, wincing at the terrible smell that assaulted them.

'What in the name of Manann is that reek?' Captain van Sloan's voice barked from the quarterdeck. Before anyone could answer the Marienburger, a scream rose from one of the sailors. Illuminated by the moonlight, a number of shambling shapes were pulling themselves over the portside rail, their clothes hanging from their bodies in dank, dripping folds. In less light, they might have been mistaken for men, but Mannsleib was full and there was no mistaking their lifeless state. Many of them sported ghastly wounds, and the flesh of others was split and decaying. Nor could there be any question about the stink rolling off them, the corruption of rotting meat.

Thulmann drew his sword. 'Steel yourselves!' he cried. 'If you would save your flesh and your souls, strike these abominations. Strike in the name of holy Sigmar!'

Ehrhardt was the first to close with the zombies, his immense blade crunching through the torso of something wearing the ragged remains of a priest's robe. The butchered carcass spilled across the deck, putrid organs flopping from the mutilating wound. The knight hacked the arm from a second zombie as it shuffled forwards. The undead monstrosity did not notice the injury and set the belaying pin clutched in its remaining hand cracking against Ehrhardt's helm.

Thulmann hurried to Ehrhardt's side, slashing the legs out from under his attacker, and then removing its head with a twist of his blade. Some of the crew were overcoming their terror and closing with the zombies with billhooks, daggers and even lengths of chain. Thulmann caught sight of Streng over his shoulder. 'Get some of the crew below and fire that cannon!' he snarled. He was certain their attackers had come from the strange ship. It was probable that whatever fiend was guiding them had remained behind, preferring to orchestrate the attack from afar.

The slack-jawed thing that slashed at Thulmann with a sword caused the witch hunter to recoil in disgust. Despite the decay gnawing away at it, there was no mistaking the face of old Eldred from the Wurtbad chapter house. Before Thulmann could react, the zombie's blade was slashing at him again. He flung himself back from the zombie's attack. The creature shuffled forwards after its prey, but found Silja's sword crunching into its breast-bone. Silja freed her weapon with a savage tug that sent Eldred's zombie falling to the deck. As the zombie awkwardly began to rise, she severed its spine, leaving it twitching on the planks.

Thulmann had no time to thank Silja for her help. The decks were swarming with zombies. At least two score of the things had pulled themselves from the river and a few stragglers were still climbing up the portside. Thulmann was thrown through the air, crashing against the side of the forecastle with such force that lights danced before his eyes. He groaned as he rolled onto his side, and then groaned again as he saw what had attacked him.

'Surprised to see me, Mathias?' the pale-faced creature snarled as he stalked towards the witch hunter. Gregor's face was twisted into an almost inhuman mask of rage. One of the crew tried to stop the vampire as he prowled across the deck. Gregor seized the man's sword arm, breaking it with a single twist of his wrist. 'Are you not pleased to see the fruit of your carelessness? The spawn of your timidity?' The vampire reached down to seize Thulmann by his tunic, lifting the witch hunter from the deck.

'Where is the book?' Gregor hissed.

'Don't do this, Gregor!' Thulmann pleaded, his heart cracking beneath the weight of the guilt swelling up within him. 'Let me help you find peace again!' Thulmann fumbled at his belt, struggling to drag one of his pistols from its holster.

'The peace of an uncertain grave?' Gregor snarled, shaking the witch hunter like a rag doll. 'The oblivion of the undead for all eternity!'

The pistol fell from Thulmann's fingers as the vampire shook him again. 'I've had a taste of your charity, Mathias. I will save myself my way! Where is the book?'

The deck of the *Arnhelm* trembled as the cannon roared from below decks. Shortly afterwards the crack of timber sounded from across the river. The cheers of Streng's gun crew rose through the planks. The vampire paid the turmoil no notice, tightening his grip on Thulmann, strangling the witch hunter with his own clothes.

'Alive or dead, he will find out what he wants to know from you!' Gregor snarled.

'You… will… be… damned…' Thulmann wheezed as the air began to burn within his lungs.

'I already am,' Gregor said. 'He will set me free!'

The vampire threw back his head and roared in agony, dropping Thulmann to the deck. The witch hunter sucked in deep lungfuls of air, clutching his injured neck. He saw Silja standing behind Gregor, Thulmann's silvered sword clenched in her hands. She had been paying attention during the fight with Sibbechai in Wolfram Kohl's home and knew that normal weapons would not harm a vampire, but blessed ones like Thulmann's would. The slimy treacle seeping from Gregor's side told the rest of the story.

'Stay out of this!' Gregor roared at her. 'Don't come between me and the templar!' Thulmann could see the terror in Silja's eyes as the vampire snarled at her, but felt proud to see her hold her ground, to see his sword still clenched in her hands. The vampire lunged at her with unholy speed. Gregor's flesh smoked as he swatted the sword from her grasp. With the back of his hand, Gregor split Silja's lip and spilled her to the deck. The vampire glared hungrily at the stunned woman, at the blood trickling from her wound.

'Keep away from her, Gregor!' Thulmann drew his remaining pistol, aiming it at the vampire's head. The man he had known was gone. All that was left of him was this abomination, this unholy slave of Sibbechai. He felt regret and guilt that he had not destroyed Gregor's remains when he had the chance. This time nothing would keep him from doing a proper job. The witch hunter pulled the trigger of his gun. The hammer fell, clicking noisily against the steel. Thulmann looked down in horror. Misfire! Over the course of the struggle the firing cap had come loose.

Gregor spun and pounced on him like a wild beast, crushing him to the deck. The vampire's fangs glistened inches from his face, his unclean breath washing across Thulmann's features.

'I don't want to kill you,' Gregor said. 'I only want the book!'

'No,' Thulmann retorted. 'It is the fiend who made you what you are that wants the book!'

Shouts of confusion rose from the melee beyond them and Thulmann could hear heavy bodies striking the water. A look of despair and confusion came over Gregor's face and he turned his head in the direction of the other ship.

The vampire looked back down at Thulmann. 'I'll come for it again,' Gregor warned, rising and stalking back towards the side of the ship. 'Next time there may not be enough of me left to care how I get it.'

Thulmann scrambled for his other pistol where it had fallen on the deck, but by the time he recovered it, the vampire was gone. The zombies were gone too, at least those that had not been destroyed by the crew.

'Damndest thing I've ever seen,' Ehrhardt said as he strode towards Thulmann. 'One minute they are full of fight, the next, they turn tail and rush back over the side.'

'There's your answer,' Thulmann said, pointing at the other ship. It was listing badly as water rushed into the two ragged holes the cannon fire had blasted into its hull. 'It seems I was right about the power behind this attack being on that ship. Clearly he's not terribly keen on the idea of sinking and called back his slaves to try and salvage the ship.'

'So what do we do now?' Silja asked, carefully rubbing her bruised jaw.

'We make certain that thing goes straight to the bottom and everything that goes down with her stays down with her,' Thulmann declared. But even as he said the words, the efforts of Captain van Sloan's orders began to bear fruit. The *Arnhelm* was under sail once more. It seemed the captain had reconsidered braving the narrows by night.

For the better part of ten minutes Thulmann argued, demanded, ordered and bullied the captain, trying to get him to bring his vessel about and go back to ensure that the sinister ship and its passengers were destroyed. But even the captain's fear of witch hunters and the Order of Sigmar could not overcome his fear of the undead. Unable to captain the ship himself, Thulmann had no choice but to watch in frustration as they sped upriver and the sinking hulk slowly slipped from view.

'You knew that monster?' Silja asked.

'He was Gregor Klausner once,' Thulmann replied, 'a valued friend and ally. Now he is a slave to the thing that killed him.

'It seems that we once again find a common purpose. I too would like to know where *Das Buch die Unholden* has gone.'

THE MUSTY STINK of fur and raw earth filled the narrow tunnel. They had been travelling for a week through the cavernous network of passages and burrows that connected the far-flung strongholds of the skaven realms. The journey had been one of gruelling monotony, punctuated by moments of absolute terror. They had endured attacks by packs of enormous rats, ambushes by crazed escaped slaves, tunnel collapses and horrifying swims through icy underground streams. They had even been attacked by some massive blind creature that resembled an enormous mole! After seeing what the creature had done to a pair of Skilk's stormvermin, Weichs found a new appreciation for the word 'mutilation'.

The scientist's fear was compounded by the attentions of his ally. The grey seer's command of written Reikspiel was poor, yet the sorcerer-priest had recognised exactly what the book was. Every time the skaven had stopped to rest, Skilk had demanded Weichs work on the book, only relenting when the former physician presented the grey seer with several translated rituals. The attrition rate of their warrior bodyguard climbed each time Skilk tested new spells from the book.

At last, just when Weichs was beginning to think the ordeal would never end, they reached their destination. The tunnel they had been following for the past day was narrower than any they had thus far travelled, barely wide enough to allow three skaven to pass through it side by side. The barren walls of the tunnel had begun to display the scratchy writing of the underfolk, and Weichs could sense the feverish excitement of his ally/captor as the symbols became more frequent. Some time later, the tunnel widened, opening into the gaping mouth of a barred gateway. Several black-furred guards stood poised around the gate, their whiskers twitching as they caught the scent of Skilk's entourage, their eyes gleaming weirdly in the green glow of the warpstone lamps around them.

Grey Seer Skilk strode towards the gate, his crook-backed figure deceptively frail in the eerie light. The skaven wore no armour, dressed instead in a ragged cloak of grey. Skilk's grey fur was speckled with black, and the horns on his head stabbed upwards, curling in on themselves. The grey seer barked commands to the guards. Several abased themselves, while others scrambled through a small door set into the gate. Weichs could feel the tension in the air as Skilk leaned on his staff and waited.

'Master, what it do?' The half-articulate question came from the slopping, disfigured vocal cords of Lobo, Weichs's mutant assistant. Some scholars held that halflings were immune to the forces of mutation, but Weichs had proved that with enough warpstone, anything was possible. The little, hunchbacked creature was the only one of his assistants to escape from the disaster in Wurtbad.

'Be still, Lobo,' Weichs ordered. 'Just wait and see, and be ready to make a run for it.'

It was not long before the gates opened and a procession of skaven emerged from what Weichs deduced must be another burrow stronghold. However, these were no warlords and petty chieftains, but a group of robed, horned priests not unlike Skilk himself.

'Skilk crawl home, yes?' one of the grey seers said, baring its teeth at Skilk. The other grey seers seemed to find great humour in their leader's scorn, chittering laughter echoing through the tunnel. 'Find place? Serve Gnatrik now!'

Skilk's lips pulled back, exposing his yellowed fangs. 'Skilk learn much. Now show all Skrittar-kin! Fester Gnatrik-meat!'

The sneering Gnatrik coiled himself into a bundle of hate-ridden fur and fangs. Weichs could see the unholy light glowing within Gnatrik's eyes as the sorcerer called magical energy into his body. The grey seer stretched his paw forwards, sending a blast of crackling green light sizzling towards Skilk.

Skilk responded by hissing one of the new words of power he had learned from *Das Buch die Unholden*. Skilk's body seemed to flicker and fade. Gnatrik's warp lightning passed harmlessly through Skilk's spectral body and incinerated three of the stormvermin behind him.

'Gnatrik-meat die now!' Skilk snarled as his body became once more a thing of flesh and bone. The ratman swept its paws in a complicated series of gestures, daemonic words burning Skilk's throat as it forced them into sound. Gnatrik had time for one ear-splitting scream as the scintillating light Skilk had called into being engulfed him. Then the cavern resounded with the sound of tearing flesh and cracking bone. When the light had faded, all that remained of Gnatrik was a puddle of gore and offal. It looked as if some incredible force had literally turned Gnatrik inside out.

Skilk stalked towards the gory ruin and rubbed his paws into the mess. The other grey seers bowed in obeisance, accepting Skilk as Gnatrik's successor by right of challenge. The triumphant Skilk turned away from his new minions, striding back towards Weichs.

'Now doktor-man learn more for Skilk!' the grey seer patted the skin-bound book where it reposed in a sling at its side. 'Teach Skilk make dead-things speak.' The skaven laughed as it swaggered back to take command of his new domain.

CHAPTER FOUR

A PALL HAD settled on the mightiest city in the Empire, a palpable sense of loss that hung heavy in the air. The snapping fangs of doubt and despair followed upon that sense of mourning. Grand Theogonist Volkmar the Grim was dead. The leading priest of Sigmar's holy temple was gone. More than ever, the future seemed dark and uncertain.

The streets of the city were far from deserted, although the throng was not quite the teeming morass of humanity that Thulmann had always encountered on his other visits. Their very numbers added to the unreal, spectral air that gripped Altdorf. Those who travelled the streets did so in silence. Not the slightest murmur rose from the crowd, and the few who did speak did so in soft whispers, as if measuring the value of every word. As Thulmann and his companions left the waterfront and passed through a dockyard marketplace, he was treated to the eerie spectacle of two men silently haggling over the price of fish.

It was not only the spires and towers of Altdorf that had been draped in mourning. Leading the way from the waterfront, Thulmann soon discovered that every window was draped in black, dark cloth hung from every street lamp and nearly every doorway sported a crude griffon image drawn on it in charcoal. The men and women they passed on the streets were similarly dressed, even the beggars displaying at least a black rag tied around their arms. Aristocratic nobleman, scruffy rag collector or fat-bellied banker, the faces of everyone they passed was downturned.

The despair was infectious and Thulmann felt his own dread taking new strength from the gloom all around him. He could see tears in Silja's eyes, her thoughts no doubt returning to her father. Even Streng's gait lacked its usual, careless swagger, his uncouth tongue for once still. Only Ehrhardt seemed unaffected, but the Black Guardsman was hardly an example of cheer and light in any surroundings.

Even as his mind turned over the troubles gnawing at it, Thulmann's senses were alert. His ears strained to listen to the hushed, whispered exchanges between the despondent citizens of the city. Time and again, he heard a name uttered – the name of the monster that had killed the grand theogonist, the name of the dark champion who would usher in a new age of Chaos. Archaon, they called him, and made the sign of the hammer as they did so.

Thulmann stopped his horse in the middle of the street and dismounted. He handed Streng the reins. 'Take the horses to the Parravon Stables, and get us lodging at the Blacktusk. See that Silja gets a nice room.' The remark brought a brief smile to the woman's face.

'And what about you?'

'I have to report to my superiors,' Thulmann replied. 'They will want to hear about my investigation in Klausberg and what happened in Wurtbad.' The witch hunter rested his gloved hand on Silja's shoulder. 'Before you ask, it is something I need to do alone. Besides, I need someone to keep an eye on Streng and make sure he gets everything done *before* he finds some bottle to crawl into.'

Silja's expression told Thulmann she was far from convinced, but she nodded. 'Will you be long?'

'I can't say,' Thulmann said. 'Zerndorff may ask me to expand upon my report. It could take some time.' The witch hunter smiled as a thought occurred to him. 'Why don't you have Streng show you some of the sights once you're settled in. Head to the Fist and Glove around dusk. If I can, I will meet you there for dinner.'

Silja watched Thulmann go, navigating his way through the crowds until his black hat and cloak vanished in the distance.

'I must part company here as well,' Ehrhardt's deep voice rumbled. 'Like Brother Mathias, I too have superiors I must report to.' The knight bowed, and then turned and marched off through the crowd, the pedestrians nervously stepping aside as the grim black templar strode past.

'That just leaves you and me then,' Silja sighed.

Streng smiled back at her, displaying yellow teeth behind his beard.

'You'd better lead the way,' she said.

Streng chuckled, adjusting his hold on the reins of the horses. 'Don't worry, you'll get your bearings soon enough. Upwind are all the good areas, downwind are the Morrwies and the slums.'

'I wasn't worried about getting lost,' Silja said. 'I just want you where I can see you. I haven't forgotten Mathias's warning about your hands.'

Streng grumbled, sullenly pulling the horses after him. 'Something else I have to thank Mathias for. And what was that crack about me crawling into a bottle? He knows as well as me we haven't been paid yet!'

THULMANN WAS LEFT alone with his thoughts for longer than he had expected. Sforza Zerndorff maintained a set of offices within the grim façade of the templar headquarters. The squat structure nestled in the shadow of the Great Cathedral of Sigmar. Its situation permitted daylight to reach it only for a few brief moments when the sun was directly overhead, the Cathedral and other buildings of the Domplatz acting to keep the structure in perpetual shadow. The symbolism had never been lost on Thulmann, for witch hunters forever lived their lives in the shadows. The templars of Sigmar were men who surrendered the clean life of their fellow man to prowl a world of limitless intrigue and darkness.

The waiting room was spartanly adorned, although Zerndorff's extravagant touch was still in evidence. A long carpet, its thread woven into the sinuous, writhing patterns of Araby, cushioned Thulmann's feet as he paced the small hallway. Velvet-backed cherry wood chairs lined the wall and tempted him away from his vigil.

If Zerndorff was trying to wrong-foot him by keeping him waiting there was no need. Before setting foot in Altdorf, Thulmann's

mind was already afire with doubts and fears. The news of Volkmar's death had only increased their strength and number. The
grand theogonist had been a great man, a man of faith and
courage, truly touched by the light of Sigmar. Not all who wore
the mantle of a Sigmarite could claim such virtues and grace. The
late Lord Protector Thaddeus Gamow was one such creature,
rumoured heretic and worse. Thulmann considered Sforza Zerndorff another, a man whose ruthless ambitions took second place
to nothing. While Volkmar had been alive, there had been a force
to keep such men in check, a power to which they would answer
should their ambitions grow too bold. Volkmar had been an
embodiment of hope, Thulmann realised, hope that the sickness
within the temple would be contained, would one day be cut out.

Thulmann continued to pace the small room. He feared
towards what purpose Zerndorff might put his report. There was
the ruin of the noble Klausner name, and what Zerndorff might
do with that information, discrediting and diminishing those
who had been close to the Klausners. Then there was *Das Buch die
Unholden* itself to consider. Thulmann knew that the potent tome
would excite his superior's interest. It was not that Zerndorff
would seek to actually use the book – he was no heretic – but the
capture of such an artefact would do much to impress the scions
of the temple, and to cause Zerndorff's name to circle within the
upper echelons.

The hall door of the small waiting room swung open. A short
man dressed in grey entered, a black cape billowing around his
shoulders and a shapeless black hat scrunched on his silver hair.
He clutched a gold-tipped cane in his gloved hand. There was
colour in his full features, the neatly trimmed beard drooping in
a smouldering scowl. Sforza Zerndorff's eyes narrowed as he saw
Thulmann, the scowl remaining fixed on his features.

'Brother Mathias, you were expected several weeks ago,' Zerndorff said, his words clipped. The Witch Hunter General did not
break his stride but continued to move towards the inner door of
the waiting room.

'There were complications, my lord,' Thulmann replied. 'I was
delayed.'

Zerndorff paused, his hand on the gilded doorknob. 'Delayed?'
he asked, in disgust. 'You are a servant of Sigmar's temple, on temple business. Would our Lord Sigmar allow petty considerations

to distract him from his duty? Did he tarry in Reikdorf while orcs sacked Astofen? Did he stay safe and secure in his golden halls while the Black One's lifeless horde stalked the land?'

'Wurtbad was struck down by plague,' Thulmann answered, chafing under Zerndorff's withering reprimand. 'It was impossible to leave.'

Some of the colour left Zerndorff's features and he took a step back from Thulmann, pulling the door open as he moved. He seemed momentarily at a loss for words. Another voice intruded into the silence, a deep imperious voice that Thulmann knew quite well.

'Plague did you say?'

Thulmann had been so intent on his superior that he had allowed his normally keen senses to slip. He had not paid attention to the second man who had entered the waiting room, dismissing him as one of Zerndorff's bodyguard. Now he found himself looking at someone who was far more imposing than the pair of silent, matched killers that served Zerndorff.

The man was tall and lean, with broad shoulders and long arms. The riding breeches and tunic he wore were of fine leather and cut in military fashion, but the black cloak draped around his shoulders, the ornamentation of his boots and the leather vambraces around his wrists could tell any observer that this was no officer of the militia. The golden ornaments were twin-tailed comets and the style of the cloak was of the kind that only one organisation in the Empire wore. The face of the other witch hunter was sharp and aristocratic, black hair swept back in a widow's peak, the eyes penetrating and commanding.

'I trust that Brother Mathias has not come here in too great haste?' There was a suggestion of actual amusement in the witch hunter's tone as he spoke, although Zerndorff did not share his companion's mirth.

Thulmann forced a strained smile on his face when he made his reply. 'No, Brother Kristoph, there is small cause for worry. I remained in Wurtbad until the disease was defeated. Graf Alberich lifted the quarantine. That is how I come to be here, tardy, but healthy.'

Thulmann's words displayed more confidence than he felt. Kristoph Krieger was far from a stranger to him, there had been several occasions in the past when the two had crossed paths.

Krieger was everything that Thulmann was not. Coming from a long line of templars, the Kriegers were almost an institution in Bogenhafen and Kristoph's star had risen quite quickly and effortlessly within the Order of Sigmar. Thulmann had been the son of a Bechafen priest, entering the Order of Sigmar with only his own determination and talents to recommend him. Krieger was something of a political animal, currying favours and debts where they would prove the most beneficial. By contrast, Thulmann refused to play the parasitic game of politics, working for everything he earned.

'Since we are all in good health then,' Zerndorff said, opening the door to his office, 'I would hear your report, Mathias.'

Thulmann followed Zerndorff through the gilded portal, Krieger close behind him. The time for doubt and fear was past. Now there was only duty and honour.

IT WAS WELL into the night before Thulmann was dismissed from Zerndorff's chambers. The witch hunter general had listened attentively to every facet of Thulmann's report, hanging on his every word as he related the corruption of the Klausner family, and their employment of the unholy *Das Buch die Unholden* to protect themselves from the vampire Sibbechai. When Thulmann described the book, and its gruesome history, he could almost see the greedy light burning in Zerndorff's eyes. The remainder of his report was continually interrupted with questions about the book and its fate and whereabouts. It did not ease Thulmann's conscience that Krieger seemed as keenly interested in the matter as Zerndorff was.

Given the turn his meeting had taken, it was small surprise to Thulmann that Zerndorff was agreeable to Thulmann's intention to track down the skaven sorcerer. Also not surprising, although exceedingly unpleasant, was Zerndorff's decision that the matter was too important for Thulmann to take on alone. Kristoph Krieger would help Thulmann in his hunt and ensure that the book was recovered and brought back to Altdorf.

Thulmann left the meeting feeling weary, but it was a fatigue of the soul not the body that sapped his strength. The long river journey had given him much time to think about what he would need to do. There had been time to desperately struggle to devise another plan, a way to proceed without going to the Reiksfang,

without seeing the creature confined there. There had been time
to remember all that had passed between them. It was the pain
that never left. He could feel it still, like a cold dead hand closing
around his heart. Thinking about the man in the Reiksfang had
caused that pain to stab into him with a vengeance. If there were
any other way, he wouldn't come within a league of the Reiksfang,
content to allow the man there to rot in his black cell, but he had
no choice. The prisoner was his best hope of tracking down the
skaven sorcerer.

As darkness settled on Altdorf, only the mourning bell of the
Great Cathedral of Sigmar continued to toll, leaving the rest of
the city to grieve in silence. Thulmann turned away from the dark
alleyways leading from the Order of Sigmar, striding out into the
wide plaza before the cathedral. The plaza was deserted, save for
a single line of black-robed monks, silently lashing themselves
with whips as they marched, lamenting with their blood the
death of Volkmar. Thulmann watched them for a moment,
impressed by their devotion, and then mounted the massive
stone steps leading up into the cathedral's cavernous chapel. The
fortress-like doors stood open, the hall within glowing with the
light of thousands of candles. Thulmann took a silver coin from
his belt, handing it to the shaven-headed initiate standing beside
the doors and bowing his head as the priest handed him a small
black candle.

The witch hunter walked through the nave, down past the aisles
of pews where even at so late an hour a small army of mourning
Altdorfers kept vigil. Ahead, Thulmann could see the sanctuary,
glowing with the brilliance of thousands of candles, their flickering light making the enormous golden hammer fixed above the
altar seem alive with molten flame. A bronze brazier fumed on
the altar, its sacred fire filling the sanctuary with foggy incense.
The sight was both spectacular and woeful, uplifting and despondent at once. The eerie beauty of the sanctuary could not erase the
reason it was so adorned: the loss of the grand theogonist.

As he reached the altar, Thulmann knelt, bowing his forehead
to the cold stone floor. He thought again of Volkmar, the stern,
uncompromising priest who had been the heart and conscience
of the Sigmarite faith for decades. He remembered the priest who
could bring hope to the miserable with a few soft words, and with
a single glance bring the mighty low with humility. Thulmann

had been fortunate enough to meet Volkmar several times, and the sword the witch hunter bore had been blessed by the grand theogonist's own hand. The Empire would mourn its grand theogonist formally, but to the teeming masses, Volkmar was a distant, unknowable figure. Thulmann knew exactly what sort of man they had lost, and knew how much diminished the Empire was without him.

The witch hunter began to retrace his passage between the aisles. He had nearly reached the nave when he heard a voice call his name. Out of habit, his gloved hand dropped to the hilt of his sword, but as he turned he saw that he would not need it. A man dressed in the white and red of a warrior priest of Sigmar hurried down the aisle. Thulmann smiled as he recognised the weathered features and rampaging grey beard that curled down to the priest's chest.

'Father Brendle,' Thulmann greeted the priest, keeping his voice low to avoid disturbing the mourners. 'Of all the people I expected to see in Altdorf, you certainly weren't one of them.'

'It has been a long time,' Brendle replied, 'but I could not fail to recognise Mathias Thulmann when he walked to the altar. It warms my heart to see you fit and well.'

'I could say the same, old friend,' Thulmann said, clapping the priest's shoulder. Despite his age, the body beneath Brendle's coarse robes was still muscular, retaining some of the strength his years as a mercenary had given him.

Brendle looked around him and shook his head. 'I fear that it might be disrespectful to catch up on old times here. I know a wine shop not too far away where we can sit down and talk like gentlemen, or at least reasonable facsimiles of gentlemen.'

'Are you certain I wouldn't be taking you from your duties?'

'Quite certain,' Brendle said, waving aside the question. 'I'll explain once we have a bottle between us.'

THE WINE SHOP Brendle led Thulmann to was a small, nondescript little building. Except for themselves, the only denizens of the shop were a bleary-eyed watchman deep in his cups and a pair of lamplighters trying to drive the night's chill from their bones. Brendle appropriated a bottle of Reikland Hoch from the wine seller, and settled down at the rearmost of the establishment's few tables.

'To Volkmar,' Brendle said as he poured a glass for himself and his guest. Thulmann returned the toast and sat down at the table.

'I must confess to being surprised to see you serving at the cathedral,' Thulmann said as Brendle poured another glass, 'quite an advancement from your old posting in Middenland.'

Brendle laughed and took another drink. 'You'd think so, but actually I had no more reason for being in the cathedral than you, just a faithful Sigmarite paying his respects to the grand theogonist. I think mentioning the name of Horst Brendle in connection with a position at the cathedral would cause a few arch-lectors to have heart attacks. I'm between postings, to be honest.' Brendle coloured as he made the confession and then laughed. 'Seems I was sent up there more as a liaison between the temples of Sigmar and Ulric. It probably made a bit of sense to some high-up, what with me being from Middenheim and all. Anyway, it didn't work out so well.'

'Why do I find that unsurprising?' Thulmann asked. 'Please tell me you didn't call Ar-Ulric a backwards heathen or some such?'

Brendle's colour grew a shade more crimson and he refused to meet Thulmann's gaze.

'Nothing that scandalous,' he replied. 'The fellow I had words with was several steps beneath Ar-Ulric. We had a pretty good scrap just the same.'

Thulmann almost choked on his wine. 'You... you got in a fist fight with a priest of Ulric?'

'Something like that,' Brendle admitted. 'He had an axe handle and I had a plucked chicken. You'd be surprised how hard you can hit a fellow with one of those. Cleared the street plenty quick when they heard that thing smacking against his arm.'

'You got into a street brawl with a priest of Ulric?' Thulmann's incredulity continued to grow. He knew Brendle could be hot-tempered, but brawling with another priest in the middle of a street was riotous even by Brendle's standards.

'We were in the street when it started. Everything on the Ulricsberg is a street of some sort or another.'

'The Ulricsberg! Middenheim?' Thulmann shook his head. Middenheim was the city-state fountainhead of the Ulrician faith, the centre of Ulric's worship. Brendle's brawl would have been bad enough in some Middenland backwater, but in Middenheim itself...

'Well, that's where Wolf-father Baegyr was.'

'Wolf-father Baegyr! Ar-Ulric Valgeir's cousin! Never mind, I don't want to hear any more.'

Brendle poured himself another glass of wine and smiled at his friend. 'So, what brings you to Altdorf? Last I heard you were down in Stirland someplace tracking a heretic physician. Don't tell me the news about Volkmar has reached Stirland already? They only found out about him here three days ago.'

'No, official business brought me back.' Thulmann related in the most general terms his reasons for returning to Altdorf, keeping from Brendle details such as the involvement of the skaven and the existence of *Das Buch die Unholden*. When Thulmann had finished, Brendle leaned back in his chair, nodding his head as he turned over the witch hunter's words.

'You are certainly in an unenviable position, my friend,' Brendle stated. 'Sforza Zerndorff isn't somebody I'd like to be reporting to. Now more than ever.'

'Why is now so inauspicious a time?' Thulmann knew he would like hearing whatever details lay behind Brendle's comment even less than he had the account of his brawl with Baegyr, but he also knew it would be wise to hear the information.

'The temple's in turmoil,' Brendle said. 'Volkmar's death has sent shock waves through the church. Worse, it has made the cult of Sigmar look vulnerable in the eyes of the commoners. They're already talking about this Kurgan filth Archaon as if he's the second coming of Asavar Kul. The temple needs to do something to reassure the people, and they need to do it soon. The lectors are already holding meetings behind locked doors. I think before the week is out, you'll find they've elected a new grand theogonist.'

'Any idea who?'

'Yes, from the information I've heard it's going to be Arch-lector Esmer.' Brendle nodded as he saw Thulmann's face drop. 'Yeah, that's how I felt too. He's a far cry from filling Volkmar's mantle.'

'But that should be better for Zerndorff, not worse,' Thulmann pointed out. 'There was never any love lost between Volkmar and Zerndorff, but I don't think he's ever crossed swords with Esmer.'

'However, Zerndorff is one of the witch hunter generals appointed by Volkmar after he abolished the position of lord protector.' Brendle tapped his finger on the table as he made his point. 'What is the one thing Esmer is absolutely infamous for? He's a miser, guards the temple treasury like it was his daughter's chastity belt. You take a man like that and make him grand theogonist, first thing he's going to do is start streamlining the church and seeing where he can save money. Then we have the witch hunter generals, three officers, each with their own staff and command, doing the job one man was doing only a few years ago; a man whose heresy was never even proved.'

'Esmer's going to restore the position of lord protector?' The thought was a troubling one, because if true, Thulmann knew Zerndorff would be doubly determined to claim it for his own, both to expand his power and to prevent him losing that which he had accumulated as Witch Hunter General South.

'That possibility is certainly the rumour of the moment within the Order of Sigmar,' Brendle replied. 'A few templars are even sending out feelers, trying to get their name where it might be noticed. Zerndorff is certainly sparing no effort in that regard and neither is Lord Bethe. I'm actually surprised that you hadn't heard any rumours. These days they are thick as flies at the Fist and Glove.'

Mention of the infamous tavern frequented by Altdorf's witch hunters caused Thulmann to rise from his seat. Silja! His mind had been so troubled that he'd forgotten he was to sup with her. He glanced out of the wine shop's small window, wincing as he saw how dark the night had grown. Small chance she would still be waiting.

'Forgive me, Horst, but I just remembered I was supposed to meet someone at the Fist and Glove.' Thulmann recovered his hat and turned from the table.

'If it was Streng, that lout has probably drunk himself under a table or into a cell by this time.' Brendle laughed as Thulmann made his retreat from the wine shop.

MATHIAS THULMANN SLOWLY mounted the stairway that wound upwards from the extravagant foyer of the Blacktusk. Like the Fist and Glove, the Blacktusk inn was an institution in Altdorf, serving as a luxurious alternative to the barracks of Altdorf's three chapter houses. The proprietors of the Blacktusk were retired witch hunters themselves, a tradition that stretched back almost to the time of Magnus, and were more than happy to turn over rooms to their brother templars in return for whatever small gratuity they saw fit to bestow. Such pious devotion never failed to touch the normally stern hearts of their patrons, so the gratuities were rarely inconsequential.

As he had expected, Silja was long gone from the Fist and Glove. Streng was present however, sharing cups with a scar-faced ruffian named Gunther whom Thulmann recognised as the underling of a witch hunter named Gottfried Verdammen. Streng managed to detach himself from his new drinking crony long enough to tell Thulmann that he had stabled the horses and secured rooms at the Blacktusk inn. Silja had waited until after sunset before leaving. Streng supposed she had gone to her room at the inn.

The oak boards of the inn's upper floor creaked beneath his feet as Thulmann made his way down the narrow hall to the numbered room the innkeeper had given him. The witch hunter entered the darkened room, removing his cloak and hat and draping them across the top of a small bureau. As he began to unbuckle his weapon belt, the sound of movement made him spin around, his hand dragging a pistol from its holster.

'Who's there?' he demanded, eyes striving to penetrate the shadows. A slender silhouette slowly resolved itself as it drew nearer.

'It's only me, Mathias,' Silja's voice purred from the darkness. The voice sent a thrill racing along Thulmann's spine and then the old gnawing fear began to creep back into his mind.

'My apologies, Lady Markoff,' Thulmann said, reaching for his hat and cloak. 'I was informed this was my room.'

'It is,' Silja said. Thulmann could see that she had swapped her travelling clothes for a loose gown of frilly lace and diaphanous silk. The sight dried his mouth on the instant. 'Please don't think me brazen. I've been quite patient and a woman should only wait so long, after all.'

Thulmann could feel the old fear struggling to find purchase within his mind, could feel every black and hideous recollection trying to force itself before his eyes, but Silja Markoff's warm, inviting smile held them at bay.

'You shouldn't be here, Silja,' Thulmann said. Silja's expression dropped as his words reached her.

'If that is the way you feel, Mathias…' she said in a quiet, fragile tone.

Thulmann set his cloak and hat down on the bureau again. 'You shouldn't be here, Silja,' he repeated, 'because tonight… tonight I don't have the strength to turn you away.'

CHAPTER FIVE

MATHIAS THULMANN SAT in a claw-footed chair and watched as the light slowly illuminated the sleeping woman. He felt a tinge of envy, watching Silja sleep. It had been a long time since he had slept so soundly. There were too many black deeds and fell memories to allow him the sleep of the just. Of late the problem had been made even worse by his feelings for Silja. The nightmares he suffered were not merely the horrors of the past, but fears for the future. If he closed his eyes too long he could see Anya's face, not the way it had looked when he had wed her but the way it had looked that last ghastly night in Bechafen. Reason told him it was impossible for the same thing to happen to Silja, but reason did not keep that dread from filling his heart and tormenting his mind.

The great witch hunter, Thulmann thought. The man of iron whose courage never wavers, whose resolve is as unshakeable as the Great Cathedral of Sigmar. Only he wasn't. He knew the fear of Old Night and the uncertainty of pity and mercy. He knew the despair of loneliness and the desperate longing for someone to fill the emptiness of his heart. He'd been unequal to the labour of holding his selfish desire in check, too weak to deny himself the solace and warmth Silja offered him.

Thulmann felt guilt well up within him. He should never have accepted Silja's love. He couldn't claim her, couldn't do justice by her. All he could do was bring her more pain, and she had already had enough of that in her life. Perhaps far worse than pain, he thought, considering the task he intended to accomplish before the day's end. Anya had been destroyed for loving him. He had no right to allow Silja to risk the same. He would tell her as much and force her to understand that their night had simply been a pleasant happenstance, nothing more.

It couldn't be allowed to be more.

Thulmann nearly jumped from his chair when a fist pounded against the chamber door. He saw Silja stir uneasily in the bed as the sound reverberated through the room. The witch hunter leapt to his feet and hurried to the door before the summons could be repeated.

'About time you was moving your arse, Mathias.' Streng's grimy countenance filled the doorway. The mercenary carried a pair of heavy leather coats over his arm. 'You still have a mind to go?' he asked. Then his gaze settled on the bed and a bawdy smile spread across his bearded face. 'Of course if you are too tired we could always go tomorrow.'

Thulmann snatched one of the coats from his henchman. 'Damn your tongue,' he snapped, joining the mercenary in the hallway and closing the door behind him. 'Is everything ready?'

'Just the way you wanted it,' Streng said. 'I hired a pair of horses for us from a stable near the south gate of the city. If anybody's waitin' for us to take our own mounts they're going to be disappointed.'

'As they should be,' Thulmann said. 'I'll have none of Zerndorff's dogs meddling in my business.' With the uncertain political climate in the temple of Sigmar and the upper echelons of its witch hunters, Thulmann knew there would be even more spies and informants abroad than usual, each eager to catch some morsel of information their masters might find of use. The change in horses, the early hour and the crude clothing both men had adopted by way of disguise should cause at least enough confusion to see them free of Altdorf without any undue interference.

When they reached the street, Thulmann cast one last look back at the Blacktusk and the window of his room. He thought again of Silja Markoff and how peacefully she slept. Then he thought of the monster he was going to see, the monster who had robbed him of so much in the past, and who now stole from him whatever happiness he might have claimed with Silja.

FIERY TWILIGHT SMOULDERED on the horizon before their destination rose up before them. They had followed a cautious, circuitous route, leaving by Altdorf's most southerly gate, and riding a winding path that turned in upon itself several times, circling their way past the numerous small towns and villages scattered beyond the walls of the city. The witch hunter showed extreme care while they travelled, constantly watching for any sign that they were being followed.

Their destination was an island, a jagged fang of rock rising from the middle of the River Reik. The rough grey rocks were capped by an immense structure, its fang-like towers apparently stabbing vindictively at the starlit sky. A palpable atmosphere of suffering and misery drifted down to them from the island fortress as they drew near.

The ferryman was not hard to find in the encroaching gloom, the light from his house the only sign of life along the desolate shore. A scrawny boy led their horses into a large stable building while the ferryman lit a lantern and led the way to the large flat-bottomed skiff. Thulmann hesitated as he saw the boat, and his hand unconsciously closed around the small hammer icon hanging from his neck, the holy symbol of Sigmar.

The river was shallow along a narrow expanse, stretching from the shore to the rocky island. The ferryman propelled his skiff through the water with a long pole, pushing them ever closer to their goal. The feeling of misery grew as the craggy grey rocks and crushing architecture of the fortress drew nearer. Streng blanched as the grim influence washed over him, retrieving a small flask from his boot and taking a liberal pull on its contents.

A small wood jetty projected from the base of the rocky cliff, a long winding stair snaking its way up towards the fortress perched on the island's summit. Two soldiers watched them with keen interest as the skiff drew near. Streng recognised the funnel-mouthed contraption one of the pair held as a blunderbuss, a murderous weapon infamous for its ability to butcher multiple foes with a single shot. The man trained the weapon on them, his face as expressionless as a stone mask.

'I have business with the castellan,' Thulmann told the soldiers as the skiff came to a rest beside the jetty. The two guards remained silent, studying the coarse, ox-hide coat and scruffy clothing Thulmann had adopted. 'Tell him that Herr Grübel is here,' he added. It was an old alias. He didn't want anyone knowing of his visits to the Reiksfang. The soldier without the blunderbuss turned, stalking into the small shack nestled between the jetty and the stairs. A moment later he reappeared, a slip of parchment in his fingers. He placed it in a small clay jar, its rim attached to a slender rope that rose up into the darkness. The soldier glanced at Thulmann, and then struck a large brass bell. The jar began to rise as the rope was pulled up.

Long minutes passed. The guards remained immobile, the blunderbuss still fixed in the direction of the skiff. The ferryman sat at the far end of his little boat, ready to drop into the river if the soldier started to fire.

Thulmann closed his eyes and thought about what he had come to do. Perhaps the castellan would not admit him? Perhaps the man he had come to see had finally died? The witch hunter dismissed both possibilities, refusing to deceive himself with such desperate and foundless hope. The castellan would admit him. Thulmann knew too much about the man for him to do anything else. The prisoner would still be here, alive, because Morr would not admit such scum into his kingdom.

At last, the clay jar reappeared, dropping from the darkness as if by magic. The guard withdrew a slip of parchment from the vessel. He read it for a moment and nodded to his companion. Streng gasped in relief as he saw the soldier turn his blunderbuss away.

'Herr Grübel,' the first guard was saying as Thulmann stepped up onto the jetty, 'welcome to Reiksfang prison.'

THE SPRAWLING BULK of the prison fortress loomed above their heads as Thulmann and Streng made their way deeper into the heart of the Reiksfang. Streng had drained his flask of schnapps, yet still he could not keep the hairs on the back of his neck from crawling. The Reiksfang was perhaps the most infamous structure in Reikland, if not the Empire. Once consigned to the black depths of the Reiksfang, few would ever see the light of day again. Disease, malnourishment and despair were the great killers within the prison, running rampant through its close, confined labyrinth of halls. With the onset of winter, hundreds of the miserable wretches would perish from the frosty chill that would sink into the cramped, lightless cells.

The castellan's meeting with Thulmann had been brief. The aged officer had been quick to hand over a set of keys to his unwelcome visitor, and then hurried back to the upper reaches of the Reiksfang's central tower. One of the keys served to unlock a heavy iron-bound door, exposing a narrow stairway that wound its way deep into the bedrock. With only a small torch to light their way, the two men had descended. The eerie silence of their passage was broken only by the occasional muffled moan, reaching to them through the stone from the network of cells and dungeons just beyond the walls of the stairwell.

In years past, the lord and master of the Reiksfang had been the notorious Judge Vaulkberg, a power-mad magistrate who had terrorised the Reikland for decades with his sadistic and brutal brand of justice. Vaulkberg had ordered special dungeons excavated far beneath the main prison, so deep within the roots of the rock that they were below even the level of the river. It was here that Vaulkberg confined his choicest prisoners, those who had in some way earned his personal enmity.

Down, ever down the stairs wound, until at last the chill of the river began to turn their breath to frost. Streng stifled a sneeze with the sleeve of his tunic. The stair twisted around one final corner and stopped before a massive steel door. Thulmann hesitated a moment, and then fumbled among the keys the castellan had given him before selecting the one that would open the portal.

Beyond was a long corridor, stretching away into the gloom beneath the Reiksfang. Heavy steel doors were interspersed along the stone walls of the passage. A few torches sputtered and crackled in sconces set into the walls, their light illuminating the condensation seeping through the walls and dripping from the roof.

Streng tried to stifle another sneeze and failed, and the sound of his affliction rolled down the silent corridor like thunder. Thulmann cast an annoyed look at his companion and then returned his attention to the passageway. One of the steel doors creaked open, slapping against the wall with a metallic ring. An immense hand gripped the edge of the doorframe. A gigantic arm followed it and then a huge bulk pushed its way through the opening, bent nearly double to fit through the doorway. Streng fingered his sword nervously, and then realised that the weapon would be about as much use as a letter opener when the creature emerged fully into the corridor and straightened to its full height. It had been many years, and he'd forgotten the gruesome aspect of the secret dungeon's special gaoler.

The monster was immense, easily twice the height of either of the men and as broad as an ox. Two complete bearskins had been stitched together to form the long fur coat it wore. One foot was shod in a leather boot, the other nothing more than a steel-capped peg fixed to the iron rod that had replaced the creature's right leg from the knee down. Yellowed tusks jutted from its enormous mouth, a deep scar bisected the side of its broad nose and a scabby black burn pitted the left side of its face from cheekbone to scalp. In his years serving with the Count of Ostland's army, Streng had seen many ogres, but none as hideous as Ghunder.

The ogre stared at the men, his nostrils flaring wildly as he snorted down their scent. Streng found himself backing away towards the stairs as the ogre rumbled forwards but Thulmann held his ground, meeting Ghunder's formidable stare. The ogre's peg clapped against the floor as he strode towards the men, the sound stretching away into the unseen limits of the dungeon. Streng could see the powerful muscles rippling beneath the ogre's fur coat and shuddered as he recalled some of the stories that were still told about Ghunder in Reikland taverns when the hour was late. Ghunder had served Judge Vaulkberg as his chief executioner, lopping off heads with such violence that they shot away from their bodies like corks from a bottle.

'Key,' Ghunder growled, his deep voice vibrating through the passageway. The ogre extended his enormous hand to Thulmann. The witch hunter nodded, placing the ring of keys in the monster's palm. Ghunder turned, hobbling across the passage towards one of the cells. Thulmann found his eyes locked on the door, the only thing still remaining between him and the thing that haunted his darkest nightmares.

The door swung open and Ghunder stepped away, exposing the inky darkness of the cell. Thulmann felt his body shudder as he found himself staring into the darkness, visualising what it contained in his mind's eye. 'Come along Streng,' he said, still staring into the darkened cell.

The witch hunter's words startled his henchman. In their past visits to the Reiksfang, Thulmann had always left his associate in the corridor while he had gone into the cell alone. Streng wondered at how uneasy Thulmann must be to require the mercenary's company to give him the strength to face whatever was in the cell.

IT WAS A small room, scarcely ten feet square, with a low, dripping ceiling. The walls were bare, fungus-ridden stone. Scraps of straw and muck littered the uneven floor.

An iron cage hung from a chain set into a hook in the ceiling at the centre of the room. Streng wrinkled his nose at the stink emanating from the tattered shape crushed inside the iron box, and even more at the wooden slop bucket resting on the floor beneath the cage, filled to the brim with the inmate's filth.

The man in the cage turned his head ever so slightly, blinking milk-white eyes as the light from Thulmann's torch intruded upon his universe of darkness. A raw pink tongue licked at scabby lips as the prisoner's ragged breath became rapid with excitement. The man's arms were folded awkwardly against his chest; palms turned outward so that his fingers were able to grip the bars of his cage. In his agitation, the prisoner tried to move them, succeeding only in a sickly, fluttering motion. The mercenary recognised the brutal residue of extreme torture and long years of confinement – the man's bones had been broken before he had been imprisoned in his cage. The bones had reset, but they had healed in the crooked manner dictated by his contorted position inside the cage.

The prisoner continued to blink at the light, his empty mouth snapping open and closed as slow, dry croaks wheezed their way up his throat. It was with a start that Streng realised the croaks were actually words.

'Nephew,' the inmate wheezed. 'Nephew...' There was a hate beyond hate in the croaking voice, a limitless malice. As the word rasped across the cell, Streng took a harder look at the crushed, malformed thing inside the cage. Beneath the dirt, beneath the filth and the scabs, beneath the liver-spotted skin and the wrinkled flesh, there was the faintest suggestion of a resemblance, the echo of a face that had once, perhaps, not been very much unlike that of Mathias Thulmann.

'I see you remember me, Erasmus,' Thulmann said, every word coming as an effort.

The thing in the cage began to cough, choking on his sickly laughter. 'See? See? I see nothing, nephew.' Erasmus Kleib twitched one of his broken fingers, trying to point at his milky eyes. 'Too many years in this tomb you made for me. Only your light, just a yellow glow, that's all. That's all there is, just a yellow glow.'

Thulmann handed the torch to Streng and took a step closer to the cage. 'You had sight enough to know it was me when I came here, sorcerer.' Erasmus Kleib's festering laughter hissed again from his wasted frame.

'In ten years, who else has come here? Only the ogre to feed and water me like some potted plant.' The captive closed his blind eyes, tears crawling down his face. 'Doesn't bring a light with him! No, not that one! Just sniffs his way over here, like a great big cat. No light. No warmth. Never ever, only the dark and the cold. Always the dark and the cold.'

The witch hunter was without pity as his uncle's mind fell into half-mad babble. Erasmus Kleib could not suffer enough to pay for the crimes he had committed against humanity and the Empire, the crimes he had committed against his own family. Instead, a deep satisfaction throbbed through Thulmann's chest. Perhaps it was the same sort of sadistic pleasure creatures like the late Captain Meisser or Sforza Zerndorff took when they watched suspects being tortured, the perverse enjoyment they experienced that had nothing to do with justice or retribution. If it was, Thulmann did not care, giving himself over to it completely. He knew the feeling was as fragile as a desert flower. As he watched the monster that had destroyed his life weep, he remembered everything his uncle had done. Other faces filled his mind, faces Kleib had destroyed. The moment was gone, replaced by the deep sorrow of all that he had lost, all that Kleib had taken from him.

Thulmann's hand closed around his sword, pulling it a hand's-breadth from its scabbard. Kleib cocked his head at the sound of steel sliding against leather, an obscene light of hope filling his blind face. Disgust overwhelmed Thulmann's rage and he slammed the blade back down. 'I have questions, heretic,' he snarled. 'Questions you will answer.'

'All that I hear, all that fills my endless night is the dripping water,' Kleib's voice wheezed from the cage. 'Drip, drip, splash. Drip, drip, splash.'

'Listen to me sorcerer, I will not be ignored.'

Kleib's nearly empty mouth spread into a mocking smile. 'Drip, splash, drip. Drip, drip, drip.' Thulmann glared into the heretic's sightless eyes.

'Douse the torch, Streng, we are done here,' Thulmann growled, turning his back on the cage. Kleib's body shuddered as he wailed in horror.

'No! No! For all pity's sake don't take the light away!'

Thulmann waved his hand stopping Streng as the mercenary moved to extinguish it against the damp stone floor. Slowly the witch hunter turned back towards his uncle. 'You are still sane enough to know fear, Erasmus, aren't you? Perhaps coming here wasn't a complete waste of time after all.'

The relief in Kleib's face faded, and even in his milk-white eyes a vindictive hate could be seen. The caged sorcerer spat into the shadows, his lips curled in a sneer. 'It has been a long time, nephew. Tell me, is your family well?'

An inarticulate growl exploded from Thulmann's chest and the witch hunter lunged forwards, gloved hands closing around the bars of the cage. With savage fury Thulmann shook the hanging prison. Kleib cried out in agony as his crushed body was thrown about within his cramped container.

'I ask the questions, filth!' Thulmann roared. 'The only things I want to hear from that crooked tongue of yours are answers!'

'Or what?' Kleib challenged. 'What more can you do to me, nephew? Kill me?'

Thulmann leaned forwards, so close that he could smell the sickly breath gasping from the sorcerer's lungs. 'Believe me, Erasmus, I have spent many sleepless nights thinking of things that could still be done to you. Every time I hear a child laugh, every time I see a face that reminds me of Anya, every time I feel alone and forgotten, I think of you and I think what more can be done to increase your suffering. Do you really want to discover how inventive my imagination has become?'

As much as he was able within the confines of his cage, Kleib slumped in defeat, all the defiance draining out of him. He shook his head, weakly. 'Speak your piece, nephew.'

Thulmann stepped back from the cage, wiping his hands on his trouser leg in an effort to remove the filthy grime from his fingers. 'I need information about your old friends, the ones who used to help you so very much. The ones you helped so very much.'

'The underfolk will gnaw your bones yet, nephew,' Kleib swore, 'but this time Erasmus Kleib will not be there to stop them. Strange you should be so ungrateful to your uncle for sparing your life.'

'I trust in Sigmar's protection, not yours, heretic!' Thulmann spat. 'I have returned the "familial courtesy" you showed me beneath the streets of Marienburg. I did not burn you at the stake, Erasmus. You spared my life, I spared yours.'

'You call this life!' Kleib moaned.

'I call it revenge,' Thulmann retorted, his tone more venomous than an Arabyan viper's kiss, 'but you have not answered my question. I am looking for a particular skaven, one of the horned sorcerer-priests who command their verminous breed. The creature stole something, and I will have it back.'

Kleib's coughing laughter returned, causing the cage to shake once more. 'A grey seer? You are hunting a grey seer? Your bones will line the nest of skaven pups and your soul will be a chew toy for the Horned Rat!'

'I will find this creature,' Thulmann said, 'and you will help me. Your dealings with the underfolk were extensive, there is no man in all the Empire who knows more about their pestilential kind.'

'There are thousands upon thousands of the rat-kin!' Kleib continued to laugh. 'Their tunnels stretch from the Wastes to the jungles beyond Araby, from the hills of Estalia to the mists of Cathay! Better to ask me where to find a particular leaf in the Forest of Loren, the chance of success would be much higher!'

'Then you cannot help me,' Thulmann said. 'I am sorry to have wasted your time, Erasmus. Streng, we are done here.'

Kleib could sense the yellow glow of the torch withdrawing as Streng moved to the cell door. The sorcerer cried out in panic, desperate to keep himself from being plunged back into complete oblivion. Thulmann motioned with his hand again and Streng stepped back into the cell.

'Yes, Erasmus? You have perhaps thought of something?'

'Maybe, maybe I can help you.' The sorcerer's words were rapid, fawning, and eager to please the witch hunter's demands. 'I have had dealings with the grey seers; they are not so numerous as the rest of their kind. Perhaps if you described the creature you are looking for, I might recognise it.'

'The creature I am hunting is an older specimen of its kind, crook-backed by the weight of its years. Its fur is grey speckled with black, the fur of its hands completely dark. Two great ram horns grow from the sides of its head. When I saw it, the creature wore black robes and a curious patchwork fur collar.' Thulmann studied Kleib's face as he described the monster, watching for any sign that might betray the sorcerer's thoughts. He saw Kleib's eyes narrow as the witch hunter described the fur collar. Something about that detail had touched upon Kleib's memories.

'You know something, Erasmus,' Thulmann stated. 'I will hear it.'

Kleib shook his head. 'Only if you promise me something. Promise me that you will kill me when you leave here.'

'I will not,' Thulmann replied. 'I suffer for your crimes every day I draw breath. So should you. No, Erasmus, I will not kill you. It would sit ill with me to execute the heretic who spared my life.'

'Then promise me you will leave the torch,' Kleib pleaded. 'Promise me you will leave me the light.'

Thulmann was silent for a moment, and then slowly nodded his head. 'I will leave the torch for you if you can tell me something useful.'

'The rat-kin you hunt is indeed a grey seer,' Kleib said, 'one that belongs to a particular sect of their kind called the Skrittar. Their talisman is that unusual collar you described. It is the custom of the Skrittar to rip the fur from the throats of vanquished rivals and stitch their trophies into a garment they wear around their necks. This grey seer you saw was one of the Skrittar.'

'The warren the creature was operating from has been destroyed,' Thulmann told the captive. 'We captured the warlord of the nest and before it died it claimed the grey seer had escaped to some other lair. Where would it have escaped to?'

'I have your promise about the torch, nephew? Then I shall speak. My dealings with the Skrittar were extensive; I came to know them quite well. They are more interested in mankind than

most of their breed. They think it might be possible to domesti-
cate us one day.' Kleib's coughing laughter wracked his crumpled
body once more. 'For centuries they have maintained a stronghold in the western reaches of the Reikland, a few days' journey
from the foot of the Grey Mountains. I visited that lair once, if
you were to release me I am certain I could guide you to the place.'

'The years have not rendered me an idiot, Erasmus,' Thulmann
snarled. 'It cost many good men to put you into that cage and in
that cage you will stay until Sigmar returns and cleanses the land
of all its evils. If you can show me how to find this stronghold,
you can tell me how to do so.'

'You will need to travel into the south-west corner of the Reikland,' Kleib said, his voice subdued after his desperate gamble for
release had been firmly rejected. 'Find the old Silver Road that
once ran through the province into the dwarf holds of the Grey
Mountains. Follow this into the west until the mountains blot out
the twilight and then turn south until you find the township of
Wyrmvater. The stronghold is somewhat near Wyrmvater. With
diligence and care, you should find it easily enough. If the skaven
don't find you first, that is.'

The witch hunter was silent again as he considered Kleib's directions. The Order of Sigmar maintained one of the best collections
of maps outside the Imperial Cartographer's Guild. It should be
easy enough to verify the existence of Wyrmvater and its situation
in Reikland. It was not much to go on, but it was a start and somehow, despite the vile nature of its source, Thulmann could not
shake the conviction that by following Kleib's directions he
would indeed track down both the grey seer and *Das Buch die
Unholden*. Perhaps even a despicable wretch like Erasmus Kleib
could be made into an instrument of Sigmar's will.

'That will be enough, Erasmus,' Thulmann said, turning away
from the cage. 'You have given me a place to start.' The witch
hunter walked to Streng, relieving him of the torch and then
stepped back to the cage. The warm glow of the torch washed over
Kleib's face and it twisted with ecstatic pleasure.

'Farewell then, nephew,' Kleib said. 'Remember me to your family, won't you?'

Thulmann felt the sorcerer's words plunge through him like a
knife through his vitals. Pain flooded his face. The witch hunter's
voice was a low hiss as he snarled at the cage. 'Here is your torch,

Erasmus.' The light vanished as Thulmann plunged the brand into the over flowing slop bucket beneath the sorcerer's cage. The witch hunter turned and stalked through the darkness out of the cell. Behind him, Kleib shrieked his despair and outrage.

'Liar! Liar!' Kleib cried. 'Kill me, Mathias! Kill me, you spineless cringing cur! Your wife was a harlot and your child was an idiot brat! The best thing for them was to die! Kill me, you bastard! Kill me!'

The cell door swung shut behind Thulmann, drowning out the obscene cries of the sorcerer. Streng stood beside the witch hunter, watching as he tried to force back the pain tearing through his body. At last, Thulmann seemed to regain some of his composure, enough to accept the ring of keys from the hulking Ghunder.

'Come, Streng,' Thulmann growled, marching off towards the stairway. 'We have work to do.'

Streng lingered behind, watching as the witch hunter mounted the stone steps and disappeared beyond the first spiral of the stairwell. The mercenary dug into his pouch belt and removed a few coins he had yet to squander on cheap drink and tavern doxies. He turned towards the ogre, placing the coins in Ghunder's callused grip.

'That thing in there,' Streng said, pointing his thumb to Kleib's cell door, 'has too many teeth. I'd appreciate if you'd take care of that.'

CHAPTER SIX

THULMANN STOOD IN the centre of the courtyard and watched as the packhorses were loaded with everything from hard tack to casks of fresh water and canvas tents. He turned away, regarding the curious faces watching them from beyond the stone walls of the courtyard. The Nag and Mare was the only inn in the village of Reikwald, and as such was the centre of the community. For all that it was situated only a few hours outside the walls of Altdorf, it was still a sleepy little village where the appearance of a witch hunter and his entourage was certain to be noticed. Every villager who wasn't at work had swarmed around the inn to watch as Thulmann's party sorted out its supplies and prepared to leave.

Thulmann turned his attention away from the villagers as a hulking black-armoured shape appeared in the doorway of the inn. Captain-Justicar Ehrhardt strode across the courtyard, stable boys and mule skinners hurrying out of his way. The Black Guardsman seemed indifferent to their frightened deference, striding directly to the witch hunter's side.

'We leave soon, Brother Mathias?' Ehrhardt asked. 'I confess that I grow impatient to send more of these creatures to stand before Morr's final judgement.'

C.L Werner

'Very soon now,' Thulmann replied. 'We wait only for Streng
to get back from the city. If Krieger hasn't seen fit to grace us
with his presence by then... well, he can just catch up with us
later.' Without providing Zerndorff with too much detail, Thulmann had reported to his superior that he would be pursuing
a new line of enquiry that he hoped would lead him to *Das
Buch die Unholden*. The witch hunter general had informed
Thulmann that Kristoph Krieger would be accompanying him,
in the event that his wild goose chase turned out to be something more. Thulmann told Zerndorff about his intention to
set out from Reikwald, and Zerndorff agreed that Krieger
would meet him there so as not to draw even more attention
to their departure from the city. Zerndorff seemed even more
concerned about watchful eyes than Thulmann was, and especially concerned about Sister Karin and some of Lord Bethe's
more proactive supporters. He agreed with Thulmann that the
hunt for *Das Buch die Unholden* should be conducted with as
much secrecy as possible.

The crowd of villagers at the gate of the courtyard slowly began
to part. Thulmann turned to see Streng riding up to the inn,
another rider following close behind him. The other rider was a
plump, pop-eyed little man, his swarthy hands clenched around
the reins of the mule he rode, a stream of invective dripping from
his tongue as he cursed his mount. Upon laying eyes on Thulmann, however, the target of his wrath shifted. With a muttered
curse, the man pulled hard on the reins of his mount, and awkwardly scrambled his way free of its saddle.

'I see you had no trouble finding him,' Thulmann congratulated
Streng.

'I'll show you trouble!' the little man snarled at Thulmann. He
was dressed in a set of thin linen hose and an extravagantly
sleeved tunic, its deep blue fabric accented by scrolling vines of
gold thread. A frilly hat of identical hue was crushed down
around his ears. 'You send this... this maniac to drag me out of
my own house... in the middle of breakfast... halfway across the
province.' He stabbed ringed fingers at Thulmann as the words
sputtered past his enraged lips.

'Would you have preferred I sent the city watch?' Thulmann
asked. 'I don't think the years have changed you so very much that
you'd care to have them poking through your home.'

The little man pulled himself straight, holding his head high. 'Let them look all they want. I am a respectable dealer of tinwares.'

Thulmann shook his gloved hand at the man. 'It isn't nice to lie to servants of Sigmar, Lajos. Some people even call it sacrilegious.'

Lajos Dozsa's face became pale as the witch hunter made his thinly veiled threat. 'I... I didn't mean it like that. You know that! Just a little joke between two old friends!'

'Since we are such good friends, Lajos, perhaps you can help me out?' The way Thulmann said it Lajos had the feeling it wasn't really a question. He simply sighed and removed his hat, sullenly waiting to hear what Thulmann had to say.

'You used to peddle all across Reikland, especially in the south,' Thulmann said. Lajos shrugged his shoulders, acknowledging that he might have done something of the sort. 'I imagine you knew the area quite well, given your penchant for hasty departures when people's property started vanishing.' Again Lajos shrugged his shoulders, but this time there was an expression of guilty embarrassment on his face. 'Excellent! I need the services of a guide familiar with that area for a few weeks.'

'A few weeks!' Lajos gasped, twisting his hat in his hands. 'I can't go gallivanting all across the province and just abandon my business. Besides, I know you, Mathias. Wherever it is you want a guide to isn't the sort of place I want to be within a hundred leagues of! Where are we going, Castle Drachenfels?'

'Your business will survive without you,' Thulmann told the irritated little man. 'It might even turn a legitimate coin for a change in your absence. As for where my final destination is, that is something that needn't concern you. All I need you to do is lead us near enough for me to find it on my own, to a town called Wyrmvater, and perhaps smooth things with the locals. Unless of course you robbed them too badly the last time you were there.'

'Oh I don't think they'd still remember that,' Lajos muttered, his face reddening when he realised he'd made the comment out loud. 'No, no, Mathias, I simply can't do it. I'm much too busy.'

'Think of this as your chance to perform a noble service to Lord Sigmar,' Streng suggested.

'Actually, friend Lajos here is no great patron of our temple,' Thulmann explained. 'He prefers his heathen strigany godlings to a decent, civilised faith.' The witch hunter's eyes narrowed as he stared hard into the merchant's nervous face. 'But you will help us all the same.'

'My wife will be worrying about me,' Lajos whimpered in a final effort to change Thulmann's mind.

'Which one? Last time we met it seemed to me you had one in Nuln, one in Altdorf, two in Marienburg...'

'Three in Marienburg,' Lajos piped in before thinking. Thulmann cocked an eyebrow at the strigany's comment. Streng's harsh laughter rolled across the courtyard. 'I was married last Mitherbst.'

'Congratulations,' Thulmann said. 'But it doesn't change things. You are coming. The pay is ten silver shillings.'

Lajos looked down at his hat, which he had twisted almost into a knot. He made an effort to smooth it out on his leg. 'I suppose I have no choice,' he grumbled. 'Can I at least get a change of clothes?'

Thulmann grinned at the plump thief. 'Of course. I am sure there are some children in Reikwald who would be willing to donate some of their cast-offs. Captain Ehrhardt, would you accompany Herr Dozsa and see that he finds something a bit more suitable for travel?' Lajos's eyes threatened to burst from his head as the hulking armoured knight stepped towards him. Ehrhardt closed his gauntlet around the little man's shoulder.

'I'll check with the local shrine of Morr,' the Black Guardsman said as he led Lajos away. 'I am sure the priest will be able to dig something up for your friend.'

Thulmann was still chuckling when the templar and his charge disappeared into the village. Lajos Dozsa was far from the most dependable or trustworthy of men, but he had a yellow streak as wide as the Sea of Claws. Thulmann could be certain the strigany wouldn't try to run, not with someone like Ehrhardt acting as his chaperone.

The witch hunter's good humour drained away when he saw someone else emerge from the Nag and Mare. He'd tried to delay the moment as long as possible, praying that somehow the right words would come to him, that time might make what he had to do easier. The right moment should have been when they had relocated from the Blacktusk to Reikwald, but he hadn't been able to do it then. It was ridiculous, a man who had stared unflinchingly into the eyes of vampires and daemons was afraid to look into the eyes of a mere woman and speak a few simple words.

It did not help that Silja Markoff looked so damnably appealing in the cool morning light, her blonde hair ablaze with the vibrant rays of the sun. She wore the tight-fitting riding breeches and loose blouse she had worn on their departure from Wurtbad, a slender longsword sheathed at her side. She smiled across the courtyard at him, a smile Thulmann hastily returned even as he tried to find the strength to confront her.

Thulmann felt needles of agony stabbing into his heart. He could see the desperate plea in Silja's eyes; the terror of being left behind lost and alone as she had been when her father had died. But in his mind he saw very different things. He saw the shambles of a nursery, bloody strips of a child's nightshirt strewn about like so much litter. He saw the misshapen thing crouching amid the ruin, jaws worrying a tiny bone. He saw Erasmus Kleib's mocking face, supreme in his hideous triumph.

'I have to ask again, Silja,' the witch hunter said, his tone solemn. 'Will you stay? It won't be safe where I am going.'

'Old ground, Mathias,' the woman replied, a warning tone in her voice. 'We've discussed this before.'

'I still have to try,' Thulmann said, but there was defeat in his voice. He knew when a battle was lost before it was begun.

STRENG WATCHED THE exchange between Thulmann and Silja, trying to decide if there was something he could do to intervene. The wry amusement with which he had regarded Thulmann's tryst was gone, killed in the black pit beneath the Reiksfang. In its place was a deep concern for Thulmann. Streng had briefly glimpsed an ugly memory from the witch hunter's past, something that had made the ex-soldier's own turbulent history seem as idyllic as a summer daydream. It had given him some inkling of just how much Thulmann needed Silja to overcome that past, to finally shake free the spectres of blackened memories.

The crowd at the gates of the courtyard parted and Streng saw several riders approaching the inn, the foremost draped in the black of the Order of Sigmar. It seemed that Thulmann's hope that Krieger would fail to show had been in vain.

The arrival of Krieger and his entourage put an end to the emotional debate between Thulmann and Silja. The witch hunter saluted the new arrivals, forcing a strained smile onto his face. Silja simply glowered at the men, furious that they had interrupted just when she had sensed Thulmann giving ground before her.

'Brother Kristoph,' Thulmann greeted the mounted witch hunter. 'I was beginning to worry we would be forced to leave without you,' he added in a tone clearly devoid of anxiety.

Krieger removed his leather hat, running through his disordered hair. 'Have no fear, Brother Mathias,' he said, 'we would have crossed paths soon enough had I missed you here.' The witch hunter turned his attention to Streng and then to Silja Markoff. Krieger nodded his head in deference to the attractive woman. 'It seems your retinue has expanded somewhat from what Lord Zerndorff described.'

'I might say the same for your entourage,' Thulmann retorted. He'd paid scant attention to Krieger, instead fixing his attention on the other riders. Two of them were rough-looking villains that might not have been out of place in one of the seedy dives Streng liked to call home. One of these was a large, bull-necked man with a scarred head who had a large, ripple-bladed sword lashed against the saddle of his mount. The swordsman's companion was much smaller. A slender-necked firearm rested on the saddle of this man's steed and leather ammunition pouches swung from the belts that criss-crossed the marksman's chest.

It was the third of Krieger's associates that truly drew Thulmann's attention. Like Krieger, this man was dressed in the black of a witch hunter, his tricorn hat sporting a hatband displaying a silver icon of the twin-tailed comet. The cut of the man's clothes was more severe than the more refined style of Krieger's tunic and breeches, almost suggesting the robes of a full priest. His face was withered and drawn, high cheekbones and deep-set eyes conspiring to create a cadaverous air. Peder Haussner, for all the frailty of his frame, was infamous within the ranks of the witch hunters, having earned a reputation as a religious fanatic in an organisation where such qualities were normally regarded as virtues.

With Haussner's foreboding presence, Thulmann was expecting the mob of tattered, unkempt men who sprinted into the courtyard a few minutes after the riders. 'Haussner's Wolf-hounds' as they were often deridingly labelled were half a dozen wild-eyed, ratty-haired zealots, perhaps even madder than the witch hunter they served. The men were dressed in dull robes of coarse cloth, eschewing the comforts of footwear, their feet swollen and bloodied by their hurried sprint from Altdorf. As the men came panting to a halt, they gripped the rope belts that circled their waists, pulling free the long leather lashes tucked there, and began to lash themselves fiercely with their barbed whips. The sight of the flagellants seemed to finally satisfy the curiosity of the Reikwald crowd and the people began to slink back to their homes. Silja regarded the ugly display with obvious shock.

'You know Brother Peder and his assistants?' Krieger asked.

'Only by reputation,' Thulmann replied, his tone making it clear that Haussner's reputation was anything but a good one. 'The other two are your own, I assume?'

'Anton Driest,' Krieger said, indicating the wiry marksman, 'one of the best shots in Hochland. The ugly fellow is Udo Gernheim, lately detached from the Carroburg militia. Given the nature of our hunt, and what we are apt to find, I thought it would be prudent to bolster our forces.' Thulmann considered that Krieger was less concerned about *their* forces than he was about *his*. Apparently, Krieger was trying to take the upper hand in their alliance.

'This... this female is tagging along?' Haussner interjected, his nose raised in pious disapproval.

'Her name is Lady Silja Markoff,' Thulmann informed the zealot, turning towards Silja.

'I had understood this expedition was to be conducted with some discretion,' Haussner said.

'Lady Markoff can be trusted to be discreet,' Thulmann said. There was a tone in Haussner's voice he didn't like and he was reminded again that the man was a delusional fanatic, fully capable of almost anything.

'The wagging tongue of a woman has ever been the swiftest messenger of corruption and heresy,' Haussner stated. Thulmann could hear the twisted gears turning inside the fanatic's withered head. 'A woman has no place in temple business,' Haussner stated. 'I must protest this decision, Brother Mathias.'

Krieger smiled snidely at Thulmann and then shifted his attention to Haussner. 'I think that Brother Mathias is quite right. Lady Markoff may be of some help to us.'

'The female mind is too feeble to withstand the temptations of the ruinous powers,' Haussner persisted. 'Its innate iniquity is the

breeding ground for doubt and confusion. Allowing this woman
to accompany us is like inviting a viper into the fold.' Haussner
snapped his fingers and the mob of flagellants took a step forward. Thulmann found his hand closing around the hilt of his
sword in response.

'I have made my decision, Brother Peder,' Krieger's voice, loud
and imperious boomed. The smouldering light behind Haussner's eyes dimmed, something approaching reason struggled to
the fore. He snapped his fingers again and the flagellants came to
a halt. 'Come along, Brother Peder, let us leave Brother Mathias to
attend to the baggage train. We will ride ahead and discuss… matters.' As the mixed entourage of Krieger and Haussner began to file
back out of the courtyard, Krieger glanced back at Thulmann.
There was no mistaking the meaning behind that look. *Now you
owe me*, it said.

Thulmann let out a breath he hadn't realised he had been holding when he saw the last of Haussner's lunatics disappear around
the wall of the courtyard. He wrapped a hand around Silja's waist,
crushing her against his side. He could feel her pulse hammering
through her body. He could sympathise with her, a witch hunter
was a menacing figure in his own right, but someone like Haussner was a different story entirely.

'So that's the infamous Peder Haussner,' Streng commented,
joining them beside the gate. The mercenary's crossbow had
somehow found its way into his hands during the tense exchange.
'Rather pleasant chap. Would have been a shame to stick a bolt
between his eyes.'

EERIE GREEN LIGHT flickered from the iron lamps fastened to the
rough rock walls, casting a ghostly illumination around the room.
It was little more than a cave, a cavity chiselled out of the bedrock
by arcane technology and inhuman diggers. A few ramshackle
tables were scattered around the place, their surfaces littered with
such apparatus as Weichs had been able to salvage from his laboratory in Wurtbad. Iron baskets were heaped against one wall of
the dingy cavern, each holding a snarling rat the size of a lamb,
the only subjects Grey Seer Skilk had seen fit to provide the scientist with for his experiments. The skaven sorcerer-priest had lost
much of his interest in Weichs's work, concerned now only with
the man's translation of the unholy grimoire.

The scientist rubbed at his eyes, trying to force the weariness from them. He'd been scouring the pages of *Das Buch die Unholden* for weeks, resting only when he was too fatigued to continue. The devilish tome was taxing his scholarship to its limits, the antiquated language and curious jargon of many sections making them as impenetrable as the scratch-slash script of the skaven. Then there were the assorted ciphers and enigmatic codes the original authors had employed to further obscure their words. Under the best of conditions, with an entire library to consult and a dozen or so capable assistants, it might have taken years just to translate a small portion of the volume. But Weichs had no library to consult, his only assistant was the twisted mutant halfling Lobo, and his aid was limited to ensuring that his master did not forget to eat from time to time. As for the conditions…

For the first time, Weichs fully understood the grave mistake he had made. His alliance with Skilk and the skaven had been one born of necessity, the lure of a limitless source of wyrdstone too great to resist. But he had entered into the agreement thinking he would be an ally, a partner. He had believed Skilk's claims that the skaven were truly interested in his experiments, that they were eager to share in the fruits of his research. Now Weichs understood his inhuman patrons better. They did not make allies, they did not share accomplishments. He was not their partner, he was their vassal, their serf, their slave. Skilk's insane obsession with unlocking the secrets of the book had stripped away the thin veil of deception, exposing the naked truth of their relationship. Weichs lived in constant terror of the grey seer's visits, grovelling before the impatient Skilk, begging for more time. He was under no illusion that each time he was begging for his own life.

The damnable book! It seemed to mock him, revealing no more than tantalising hints and clues that he might be close to unlocking its secrets. Pages would appear to move within the tome, scuttling between its skin-bound covers like crawling lice, resisting his efforts to catalogue them, to pin them down. Bookmarks would change position, dancing about like carnival acrobats. Sometimes the words themselves would change before his very eyes. But always, just when he was on the verge of giving up, some new hint would catch his gaze and he would be drawn back to his quest to unravel the tome's dark secrets.

Finally, after many long weeks, the book gave up the black secret that Weichs had been trying so desperately to find. It had happened just after one of Skilk's visits, when the grey seer had seemed at his most impatient, when a gruesome death seemed only hours away. Weichs tried to resist the mad idea that somehow the book had been toying with him, that it had somehow known Skilk's patience was at an end and that it could no longer torment the scientist by keeping from him what he needed to find.

Weichs stared in a mix of horror and relief at the translation he had composed for Skilk. The original had been transposed on two pages, in such an old dialect of Estalian that it was a miracle he'd been able to make sense of it at all. Yet he was uncannily certain of the translation's accuracy.

What he had written nauseated him. It smacked of necromancy, the most loathsome of all the black arts. Yet the spell promised what Skilk wanted most – to call up the spirit of one who had crossed the threshold to Morr's realm, thus enabling the caster to summon the shades of the dead.

How strange, Weichs thought, that a man who had devoted himself to science, who had given his life to unlocking the secret contagion of mutation, should find his life dependent upon a scrap of centuries-old magic. The irony might have made him laugh, had not the sour scent of the guards outside his subterranean grotto suddenly impacted against his senses. He knew only too well what the fear musk of the skaven sentinels portended.

'Doktor-man find spell, yes?' Grey Seer Skilk stalked into the chamber, his staff clicking against the uneven rock floor with its every step. There was a hungry, feral light in the sorcerer's beady eyes, the sort of gleam Weichs had grown accustomed to seeing when the grey seer had overindulged in its consumption of warpstone. Lobo crawled under one of the tables and hid his misshapen head beneath his arms.

'Yes, grey seer, I have made significant progress!' Weichs said, his words hurried and frantic.

'Doktor-man speak truth?' Skilk threatened, black paws snatching the translation from Weichs's hands. The skaven's hungry eyes scoured the pages of Reikspiel, his twitching nose hovering above the paper as if trying to sniff the ink. 'Nice,' Skilk squeaked. 'Doktor-man learn words nice.'

'I live to serve,' Weichs said, bowing his head to the exultant grey seer. Skilk seemed to like the sound of that sentiment, and Weichs knew his life depended on remaining in his good graces. The skaven priest continued to read the translation eagerly and Weichs decided there would be no better time to try and exploit the ratman's goodwill. 'Now that I have translated the spell for you, perhaps you will allow me to resume my experiments. I am very eager to return to my studies and I must confess that I've learned more about the dark arts than I ever wanted combing through that insufferable tome.'

The scientist's words caused Skilk's eyes to narrow and the grey seer looked away from the papers in its hands. The ratman's eyes first focused on Weichs and then shifted to *Das Buch die Unholden*. The ratman scurried towards the grimoire and lifted it from the table, setting it in the crook of its arm. Weichs felt a thrill of horror as he read the thoughts squirming through Skilk's mind – the skaven was worried about what else Weichs had translated from the book, what spells the man might have kept to himself.

'Maybe doktor-man catch much,' Skilk hissed. Weichs felt the colour drain from his features. He decided to misinterpret the grey seer's meaning.

'No, there is still much my experiments can tell us,' he insisted. 'There is still a great deal to learn. Before we left Wurtbad I was certain I was on the verge of a great discovery, one that would hold enormous benefit for both our peoples.' Weichs held his breath as Skilk digested his words, as the grey seer considered his next decision. At length the grey seer uttered a chittering laugh, turning and stalking out of the cave.

'Doktor-man make experiment. Learn to make sick,' Skilk told him as he left the makeshift laboratory. At the entrance, Skilk turned, patting the book. 'Maybe let doktor-man find words again.' The grey seer laughed and vanished into the blackness of the tunnel.

Weichs breathed a deep sigh of relief. Let Skilk think he was an idiot. It would make the skaven underestimate him, hopefully relax his guard. Somehow Weichs knew he would have to escape the ratman, preferably before Skilk decided to enact the obscene ritual he had translated for him.

* * *

DISGUSTED, DESPISING HIMSELF, the vampire crept back through the shadows, back to the small woodsman's shack that had become his refuge. The blood of the deer he had killed had done little to satisfy the hunger pounding inside him, but it was all the sustenance he would allow himself. Gregor had grudgingly allowed himself to claim birds, rats and squirrels when the unholy lust became too hideous to endure. Carandini took a sardonic amusement from Gregor's desperate determination to resist the urge to graduate to higher forms of life.

Gregor was coming to despise the necromancer as much as Sibbechai. The attack on Thulmann's ship would have succeeded had it not been for the Tilean's cowardice, his panic when his own ship began to take on water. Gregor should have left Carandini to drown like the rat he was, but the vampire knew he could not allow the necromancer to die. Carandini was the only man who promised him any measure of hope, who claimed there was a way to purge the evil from Gregor's soul.

After dragging themselves from the river, any chance of picking up Thulmann's trail was quickly lost, but Carandini had said that there were other ways to find someone. All they needed to do was be patient and wait for the moons to become amenable. So they moved from the river to the woods, keeping to the shadows like a pair of wraiths, waiting for Carandini's moons to align.

As Gregor drew near the shack, he could feel the fell energies gathered around it. His undead eyes could see wisps of black mist swirling around the structure, slithering between the logs that formed its walls and seeping down through the thatch roof. The necromancer's voice echoed on the night wind, raised in some profane invocation to the unholy forces of the night. Gregor felt his flesh crawl as he heard the ancient names Carandini cried out. Strangely the vampire found the sensation reassuring – it meant he hadn't completely forsaken his humanity yet.

Suddenly the invocation was cut short, silenced by a loud gasp and then a low, hideous gargle. Gregor rushed through the trees with all the supernatural speed his altered body could command. In an instant he was at the door, tearing the heavy oak portal from its hinges and tossing it aside as if it was nothing. Inside the tiny confines of the shack he could see the sheets of flayed skin the necromancer used in his rituals scattered on the floor, black candles shining in the darkness. Carandini himself was writhing on the floor, hands clasped around his throat.

There was a third hand at Carandini's throat, closed around it like a python. It was the tattered, withered mummy claw he used in his rituals, the dismembered hand of Nehb-ka-Menthu. Some dreadful power beyond the necromancer's control animated it, giving it a terrible and malevolent life of its own. Carandini's face purpled as he fought to suck breath down into his collapsing throat.

Gregor lunged at the necromancer, seizing the mummy claw. Even with his unnatural strength, Gregor found it hard to pry the claw from Carandini's throat. At last the foul thing came free. The claw twisted in his grip, its talons ripping into his flesh. Disgusted, Gregor dropped the vile thing to the floor. The hand landed on its back, fingers flailing at the empty air. Then, with a powerful twist of its small finger, the claw flipped onto its palm. Like some mammoth spider, it scurried across the floor.

Something sharp and silver flashed in the dim light within the shack, stabbing down into the animated claw and pinning it to the floor.

'The... the winds... blow strongly,' Carandini rasped, releasing his grip on the dagger he'd used to impale the mummy's hand. He began to massage his torn and bloody neck. 'Too... much. It slipped from my control.'

Gregor looked at the necromancer, and then back to the still struggling claw. Some sign of his horror must have shown on his face, because Carandini laughed.

'Don't worry, my friend,' he said. 'I am quite all right.'

Gregor chafed under the necromancer's grim amusement. 'You should be more careful, sorcerer. I can't have you dying on me. I am lost without you.'

Carandini's face spilt into a weasel's smile. 'Yes, I am quite aware of that fact,' the necromancer said, 'but this evening's experiment proved most useful, for all of its hazards.' He turned his eyes again to the squirming mummy claw and some of the bravado slipped from his demeanour.

'I was granted a vision before Nehb-ka-Menthu's spirit became strong enough to prove uncooperative,' Carandini stated. 'I saw a clearing with three huge grey stones, perhaps the ruin of one of the standing circles your barbarian ancestors used to build.'

'The book you need is there?' Gregor asked. Carandini shook his head.

'No,' he said. 'Wherever the book is being kept, it is in a place where the spirits will not go. Instead, I asked how we might find the witch hunter again. In answer I was shown the clearing and the stones.'

'Where is this place?' Gregor demanded after considering the necromancer's words.

'I will be able to find it, do not trouble yourself on that account,' Carandini replied. 'The vision would have been of little merit otherwise. Perhaps it is a force kindred to what drew you after Sibbechai, or perhaps something as simple as what moves the birds south when Ulric's bite is in the air, but I will be able to lead us to the place. The only thing I do not know is how long we might need to wait there for our quarry to show himself.'

'Whatever it takes,' Gregor said.

Carandini stepped towards the struggling claw, pulling it from the floor and dropping both claw and dagger into a large leather satchel. There was an evil glint in his eyes when he turned back to Gregor. 'You know we'll have to kill the witch hunter when we catch up with him again.'

Gregor stared hard at the grey shadow world around him, at the beckoning glow of Carandini's blood shining within his veins. He thought of the unliving claw of Nehb-ka-Menthu, still bound to the earth aeons after its death. He wouldn't allow himself to exist like this, in the obscene world of the undead.

'Whatever it takes,' Gregor repeated.

CHAPTER SEVEN

THE JOURNEY SOUTH through the Reikland was a forlorn, forbidding one. With winter's chill in the air, there was far less traffic on the roads, and the landscape was a desolate shadow of its green exuberance and golden abundance. Brown fields stood barren after the harvest. The lush greenery of the woods was gone, smothered by the clinging frost that lingered long into the afternoon. The few travellers they encountered had their forms and voices muffled beneath heavy layers of fur and wool. At night, the haunting howls of wolves pierced the darkness, the savage cries replacing the whistle of night birds and the clatter of crickets as less hardy creatures abandoned the land to the coming cold.

It was not only the surroundings that made the travel tense and uneasy. The expedition was anything but a homogenous enterprise, but rather a group cast together by the politicking of Sforza Zerndorff and his lofty ambitions. There was little enough love lost between Thulmann and Krieger, he and his henchmen keeping themselves to themselves both on the road and in camp. Haussner's flagellants followed a similar example, sprinting behind the riders during the day, and then lashing their exhausted bodies with their whips until they collapsed from fatigue every night when the witch hunters made camp. Thulmann marvelled that the fanatics could maintain such a gruelling, brutal regime day after day, but as his respect for their devotion to Sigmar grew, his apprehension about their twisted vision of reality grew as well.

Silja remarked that it was as well that Krieger could maintain control of Haussner and his men. Thulmann found the observation of little comfort. He was far too familiar with Krieger's methods. Krieger might control Haussner, but who would control Krieger?

NESTLED ALONG THE slopes of several rolling hills, flanked on two sides by the lush growth of the Thrungiwald forest, the town of Wyrmvater basked in the late afternoon sun. It was a small clutch of half-timbered structures, surrounded by fields of grain and bisected at its centre by a swift-moving stream. Even from a distance, Thulmann could see that the buildings in the town were very old, displaying a style of architecture that had fallen out of fashion centuries before. Thulmann could feel the weight of the town's antiquity pressing upon him the nearer they drew to it. He could see squat little grubenhauses scattered between the fields of crops beyond the town, simple structures of thatch and clay no different in any respect from those that men had dwelt in before even Sigmar had walked the land.

'Doesn't look like they're too happy to see us.' Streng gestured with his crossbow towards the town beyond. Thulmann could see people rushing from the fields, abandoning their labours and racing back to the safety of the town's timber walls. Some manner of bell or gong could be heard ringing and at the town gates a small group of armed figures was assembling.

'I rather see your point, friend Streng,' Thulmann said.

'Perhaps they think we're bandits,' Silja suggested.

The remark brought a withering sneer to Haussner's lips. 'We are holy servants of Sigmar, as any fool can see!' Haussner glared at Silja, his anger only swelling when she did not back down from his gaze. 'Bandits indeed!' he finally snarled.

'However preposterous it might seem,' Krieger said, 'we had better make allowances if we can't convince these people who we are.' He snapped his fingers and both Driest and Gernheim dismounted. The sharpshooter Driest pulled the elegant Hochlander rifle from its saddle holster and settled into position behind a small rock pile beside the road. Gernheim, the scarred swordsman, removed his own weapon from his saddle. Nearly the height of a man, the lightning-shaped zweihander was hardly the weapon of a mounted fighter. Gernheim stalked ahead of the witch hunters several yards down the road and took up position. Captain-Justicar Ehrhardt dropped down from his own horse and joined Krieger's man on the road. Looking on the two massive warriors and their deadly weapons, Thulmann hoped the people of Wyrmvater would see reason.

It would cost them much blood to wrest their road back from two such fighters.

'Silja, stay close to Streng and keep an eye on our flank,' Thulmann said. 'I don't want any surprises popping up from those fields.' He really didn't think they were in any danger of a flanking action, but Thulmann knew giving Silja a task would be more effective than another concerned injunction for her to keep back and keep safe. 'Lajos, I want you up here with me.'

The little strigany stopped scratching at his uncomfortable garments. 'Couldn't... wouldn't it be better if I...'

'With me, Lajos,' Thulmann said. 'You've dealt with these people before. You can talk to them.'

Lajos began to wring his much abused hat through his hands again. 'That... it might be better... I should stay here and make sure our line of retreat is open.'

'Lajos, up here,' Thulmann repeated. 'These people know you. They see you and they will know we aren't bandits.'

Lajos rolled his eyes and slowly walked his mule forwards. 'They spot me and they'll *know* we're bandits,' he muttered under his breath.

The armed group at the gates of the city had grown to nearly two score men. Thulmann saw the afternoon sun gleaming off a surprising number of weapons. He'd expected whatever force the town could muster to be armed mostly with farming implements and hunting spears. More men were standing behind the timber walls on a palisade, an assortment of bows and crossbows clutched in their hands. Perhaps his disdain for the warcraft of Wyrmvater's leadership had been erroneous. He only hoped it was not fatally so.

Wyrmvater's militia parted as a mounted figure emerged from the gate and then the iron-banded timber doors swung shut, sealing off the town. The group advanced slowly, warily, down the road towards them.

'Hold your ground,' Krieger ordered, his words directed mainly at Haussner and his mendicant fanatics. 'We're past the range of their archers here. Whatever happens, don't let them draw you closer.' The witch hunter turned his head and called over to the rock pile. 'Driest, can you hit the walls from here?'

'Just say the word and I'll start carving notches,' the sharpshooter responded, his head cocked above the length of his rifle, his eye almost resting against the smooth metal as he sighted his weapon.

'Let us pray it does not come to that,' Thulmann said.

'Keep faith in Sigmar, but hobble your horse,' Krieger replied, repeating an old adage that warned against bothering the gods with the petty concerns that a man should see to himself. The almost flippant tone in Krieger's voice sickened Thulmann. The lives of the innocent, frightened townfolk didn't matter to Krieger, to him they were simply an obstacle to be overcome. If they had to butcher half the town, it would be of little consequence to the man.

Thulmann turned from Krieger in disgust, watching instead the slow advance of the militia. The distance between them and the witch hunters diminished steadily. Thulmann could make out greater details now. While they wore no armour, the men bore weapons that might have been the envy of most state regiments: sharp-bladed halberds and poleaxes, leaf-headed spears and steel-tipped bills. However, for all the sophistication of their weapons, the militia approached in a disordered fashion, lacking in precision and drill. Still, they were disciplined enough to stop well before reaching Ehrhardt and Gernheim, and well before leaving the range of their own archers on the town walls.

'Skaranorak's black bones!' Krieger swore. 'Now we'll have to do it the hard way. Driest...'

Thulmann grabbed Krieger's arm before the other witch hunter could give the order to his man. 'They are just being cautious, trying to protect their lands and their families,' he said. 'Let me go forward and speak with them.'

'You'll be within range of their bowfire,' Krieger stated, shaking his head. 'If they don't listen to you, you'll never make it back before they are all over you. And don't think I'd risk any of my people becoming pincushions trying to get to you. Better to sit tight and get them to make the first move. If they know we can hit them even from here, they may prove more cooperative.'

'At least let me try and reason with them,' Thulmann persisted. 'Besides, I'd think you'd be rather eager to get rid of me; no one to share Zerndorff's appreciation.' Krieger smiled as Thulmann made the remark and then extended his hand towards the road-way in a gesture that seemed to say 'be my guest'.

Thulmann walked his horse slowly forwards. 'Come along, Lajos,' he called back when he noticed the merchant's mule was not beside him.

'I can see things perfectly well from here,' Lajos said. 'Good luck, Herr Thulmann. My best wishes go with you!'

Thulmann brought his horse to a halt, turning in his saddle to look back at Lajos. The fat little man withered under his stern gaze, trying to muster a friendly wave of his fingers to appease the angry witch hunter. 'Brother Peder, if that fat strigany trash isn't at my side in the next few seconds, you have my leave to execute him.'

'You're certain we're in no danger?' Lajos asked for what seemed the fiftieth time since they had ridden past Gernheim and Ehrhardt. Thick streams of nervous sweat plastered the merchant's hair to his forehead, while the hat in his hands was contorted into a rumpled coil of fabric.

'No,' Thulmann said, deigning at last to answer his companion. 'If they are certain we're bandits, they'll attack us before we can even say "Good morning". But that's a risk I'm willing to take.'

'Well I'm not,' Lajos hissed, turning his mule's head.

'I wouldn't do that,' Thulmann said. 'We're within bow range now. Turn tail and run back and your back will sprout more feathers than a goblin headdress.' The words had their desired effect. Lajos fell into a terrified silence and followed meekly beside the witch hunter. The armed militia were only a dozen yards from them now. They were grim-faced, weather-beaten men, farmers and woodsmen, their hard, lean bodies wrapped in wool breeches, fur tunics and leather boots. The weapons they bore shone murderously beneath the sun.

The mounted figure in the midst of the militia was dressed in a fur cloak and a massive silver pectoral rested against his chest, fastened around his neck by a thick silver chain. The rider was different from his fellow townsfolk, his skin paler, his features a bit fuller and less hungry. The clothes beneath his cloak did not have the stamp of crude utilitarianism of his fellows and the rings on his fingers gleamed with gold. The rider watched Thulmann approach and when he judged the strangers had come close enough he raised his hand. At once the witch hunter and his reluctant companion brought their steeds to a halt.

'Who are you and what is your purpose in Wyrmvater?' the mounted leader called out, his voice heavy with authority. 'If you think to do mischief here, it will not go unopposed.'

Thulmann lifted his own hand in greeting. 'I am Mathias Thulmann, templar knight of the most holy Order of Sigmar,' he said. He noticed that the pronouncement did not seem to diminish the wary hostility that exuded from the militiamen. 'Who do I address?'

'I am Bruno Reinheckel,' the leader said, 'duly appointed burgomeister of Wyrmvater township these past twelve winters,' he added, patting the silver pectoral. 'But you have answered only one of my questions, sir. What business do you have here in Wyrmvater? We are a decent, Sigmar-fearing community, why should we interest a witch hunter?'

Thulmann could hear the anxiety in the burgomeister's voice. Far from relieving the man's unease, Thulmann had the impression Reinheckel would almost have preferred a gang of brigands than a visit from witch hunters. The grim servants of the Order of Sigmar were hardly popular beyond the confines of their own temple, their fearsome reputations well known in even the most remote corners of the Empire. No man's conscience was so clean that he felt entirely at ease in the presence of a witch hunter, be he burgomeister or baron. The question was: how far would Reinheckel allow his reservations to take him? There were a good many witch hunters who vanished without trace in remote towns and backwoods villages, and only a naïve fool would believe all had been the victims of the ruinous powers.

'He's not interested in your town,' Lajos offered. Thulmann wasn't the only one who had appreciated the lingering suspicion in Reinheckel's expression. 'The templars are on the trail of some heretics who are supposed to have taken refuge in the forest near here.' The merchant looked towards Thulmann as he spoke, repeating the story they had decided to tell were they challenged about their mission. It would hardly have helped matters telling Reinheckel they were hunting for a nest of the mythical under-folk. The burgomeister was uneasy enough entertaining a witch hunter; he would be even more so if he thought Thulmann was mad.

Lajos was largely unconvinced by Thulmann's tales of scheming ratmen, although he was certain the story was meant to conceal an even more horrible truth he was better off not knowing.

'Yes, the men we are looking for are hiding in the woods around your town,' Thulmann said. 'They could cause you any measure of hurt if allowed to linger here.'

The burgomeister listened to Thulmann's words, but kept looking at Lajos, eyes narrowed as he scrutinised the little man. 'No, brother templar, things have been very quiet in Wyrm-vater. We've seen no strangers since Mittherbst, either in the woods or in the streets. You are the first guests our town has seen in some time.'

'Perhaps my information was erroneous,' Thulmann said, adding a ring of disappointment to his voice. It was much too early to tell if what Kleib had told him was actually false. 'Just the same, I would be remiss in my duty if we did not make a search of the woods.' Thulmann noted that he still enjoyed only a part of Reinheckel's attention. The burgomeister continued to stare at Lajos. The merchant squirmed nervously in his saddle. It was just possible somebody did remember him.

'It is my intention to use your town as a base of operations while we search the woods,' Thulmann continued, hoping at least some of what he said was being heard by the burgomeister. 'Perhaps you have a building we could employ as a headquarters?'

Reinheckel nodded. 'The Splintered Shield, Wyrmvater's only inn. It's empty just now, only Schieller and his family in residence there. I'm certain he would give you the run of the place if I ask him.'

'I'm certain he would,' Thulmann agreed. 'I should also like to consult your town records. If there are any ruins or old mine works in the area they might prove a good place to start looking for my fugitives.'

'I'll have them ready for you by the time you are settled at the inn,' Reinheckel said. He turned in his saddle, waving to the town behind him. Slowly the archers began to withdraw and the gates swung open. The militiamen began to disperse, filing off towards a squat stone building that Thulmann assumed must be the town armoury.

The witch hunter followed the burgomeister's example, waving his hat over his head, giving the sign to the watching Krieger that all was well.

When Thulmann turned back around he could see peasants already heading back into the fields. The last of the militia had vanished into the town, but Reinheckel remained on the road, still staring at Lajos.

'I shall leave you then to gather the town records,' Reinheckel said, turning his horse back towards the gates of Wyrmvater. 'Believe me when I say I will do everything I can to ensure a quick hunt, brother templar.'

Lajos crumpled into his saddle as the burgomeister rode off, muttering to himself in his singsong strigany dialect. Thulmann had heard enough prayers of thanksgiving over the years to recognise the gist of Lajos's whispers.

THE WITCH HUNTERS rode through the narrow streets of Wyrmvater, their arrival watched with keen interest from behind shuttered windows and cracked doors. Frightening and forbidding even in the cosmopolitan environs of Altdorf or Nuln, in a backwater village the arrival of such men was viewed in equal parts fascination and dread. Hushed voices whispered half remembered travellers' tales of witch hunters and their doings. Not in living memory had men such as these descended upon Wyrmvater and its people could only wonder at what their arrival might mean. The burgomeister would be busy the rest of the day, not in securing the records Thulmann wished to consult, but in addressing and alleviating the fears of his citizens.

Thulmann's expedition marched through the cramped streets until at last the timber and plaster walls of the Splintered Shield rose before them. Testament to the prosperity Wyrmvater had once enjoyed, the inn was a large, three storeyed structure with glass windows and a cluster of brick chimneys.

The witch hunters unloaded their gear from their horses, leaving Streng and Gernheim to settle the animals in the stables.

When the last of Thulmann's group had entered the inn, a lurking figure rose to his feet in the alleyway from which he had observed their arrival. The tall, gaunt man dusted the grime from his long brown coat, and scowled at the building. With a stifled oath, the old man slipped deeper into the back alleys of the town, putting distance between himself and the witch hunters. Freiherr Weichs had enough to trouble his mind without the accursed witch hunter intruding upon his affairs.

Thulmann, always Thulmann. The man's tenacity was matched only by his lack of vision. Superstitious prayer-mongers like him would never be able to grasp the noble work, the great experiment upon which Weichs was engaged. Through his studies, mankind might one day be free from the taint of mutation, immune to the baleful energies the theologians dismissed with the word 'Chaos'. What did it matter if a few hundred, or even a few thousand, had to be sacrificed to bring about such a noble end? But no, instead of acclaim and recognition, Weichs had been pursued and hunted across the Empire by zealot lunatics like Thulmann, forced to hide like a hunted animal and seek refuge with creatures straight from a nightmare.

Weichs was not sure how Thulmann had tracked him from Wurtbad. Nor did he care. That the witch hunter had chosen to turn up just as Skilk had finally allowed him to resume his experiments, to venture beyond the caverns of the skaven to collect test subjects, this was more than Weichs could endure. It was unjust for the witch hunter to interrupt his great experiment again.

The scientist hesitated, allowing his thoughts to turn down roads they had not travelled before. Always he had run before the witch hunter, always he had allowed Thulmann to set the pace. He had accepted the role of prey and allowed Thulmann the guise of predator. No more: now it would be the witch hunter who would be the victim, the witch hunter who would be the hunted. Weichs thought of the Splintered Shield, of the room Thulmann had no doubt secured there. The templar might still be looking for his quarry, but Weichs had already found his.

FOR ALL THAT it was virtually unused, Schieller and his family maintained the sprawling inn in admirable condition. The rooms were somewhat musty, thick layers of dust on the windowsills, but otherwise were exceedingly spacious and comfortable. In Thulmann's opinion, the Splintered Shield's rooms put a number of better-known establishments to shame. The vacancy of the building allowed nearly all in his group to secure separate rooms, only Haussner's fanatics eschewing the comfort of the establishment, opting to sleep in the loft above the stables instead to avoid 'the pitfalls of hedonistic indulgence'.

After dinner, the witch hunters discussed their plans, Thulmann illuminating once again where they should be concentrating their search. They would scour the town records for any mention of old ruins, abandoned mines, troll caves, fissures in the earth, or any other place that might easily conceal a tunnel. They would keep a keen watch for any mention of beastmen, mutants, goblins or fey folk – anything that might be a disguised reference to the skaven or their activities.

It was long into the night by the time they broke away from their consultation. Thulmann mounted the stairs leading to his room with a leaden step, fully appreciating the ungodliness of such a late hour.

As he climbed the stairs, his soul felt again the echoes of that long ago dread, of the terror that had so filled him. He'd raced home from the temple, from his betrayal of Erasmus Kleib's vile scheme. As soon as he'd thrown open the door of his home, he'd known he was too late. Some instinct, some sense of wrongness told him Kleib was gone. The witch hunters had searched the lower floor anyway, leaving Thulmann to make that long, terrible climb upwards. His steps were no longer hurried. He knew that he was too late, knew that he didn't want to see whatever had been done, what terrible revenge Kleib had visited upon him. He wanted to delay the moment for as long as he could, the moment when he would see his fears realised, when he would know his wife and child were no more.

Thulmann paused at the door of his room, his mind still fixated upon the past. He'd paused then too, forcing his arm to rise with an effort that dredged every speck of courage from his pounding breast. The bedroom door swung inward beneath his hand. It took long, tortuous moments for his eyes to adjust, for him to see that the room was empty. Strangely, Thulmann felt an intense wave of relief rush through him – his illusion of hope had been preserved for another fleeting moment. Then he discerned the sounds coming from further down the hall. Grotesque, hideous gnawing, slobbering sounds that sickened his sensibilities and ignited his terror to still greater depths of misery. He trembled with fright, his body shaking as with an ague, yet somehow he forced himself to follow those sounds, to find his way to the closed door of the nursery.

Thulmann shuddered again, forcing his mind away from its morbid reverie. The past was the past, and there was nothing even the gods could do to change it. It was the present that he needed to focus on, the real horrors that plagued the land and would work their evil upon it. He needed to let the dead rest.

He pushed open the door to his room. His eyes had grown sharper since he'd left Bechafen all those years ago. Thulmann saw at once the slender figure waiting for him in the darkness. His eyes told him he looked into the pretty face and shining eyes of Silja, but the waking nightmare still lingered at the edges of his consciousness. In his mind he saw not Silja but a thing of dripping hideousness, its gaping mouth ghastly with blood, its cyclopean eye glowing like a pool of rancid pus. He thought he could smell its pestilent stench, the reek of excrement, thought he could hear it gnawing, gnawing on the tiny bones clasped in its wizened claws. Thulmann cried out in horror, recoiling against the door.

Silja rushed forward, her stern expression draining away into a look of concern. The nightmare's grip lessened as she reached out to him, the evidence of his eyes and not his fears finally prevailing within Thulmann's mind. The witch hunter sank to the floor as he tried to collect himself and recover from the ghastly phantasm he had imagined.

'Mathias! Mathias, it's me, Silja,' her soft voice told him over and over again. Slowly, gradually, the hammering in his chest lessened and his breathing resumed its normal steadiness.

'I am… I apologise, Lady Markoff,' Thulmann said. 'I was… my mind was… elsewhere. I'm afraid you gave me a fright.' He smiled weakly at her. 'I wasn't expecting to see you.'

Silja helped him to his feet. A trace of the old severity worked its way back onto her face. 'I wanted to talk to you.'

'Please, Silja, not now,' Thulmann said. 'Tomorrow will be a very busy day.' He laid his hand on the woman's shoulder, moving her towards the door.

'Who is Anya?' Silja asked. The question caused Thulmann to freeze. He looked at her in disbelief. 'When you came in just now you cried out "No, Anya! No!". Who is she, Mathias?'

The witch hunter let his hand fall to his side. He paced deeper into his room, sitting down at the side of his bed. His words were hollow, rasping echoes devoid of their usual strength and command. 'Anya was my wife,' he said, almost in a whisper. 'She... she died, our daughter with her. It was a long time ago, but sometimes it seems like only yesterday.'

Silja closed the door and walked across the room, sitting down beside Thulmann, taking his hand in hers.

'I'm sorry, Mathias,' she said. 'I really do know how you feel. Sometimes I imagine I can still hear my father's voice calling to me. Someone once told me that the pain never goes away, but it does get better.' Thulmann nodded as she spoke to him. Those had been his exact words when he had broken the news of her father's execution to her in Wurtbad.

'For me, it doesn't,' Thulmann said. 'There are some wounds that never heal.'

'Maybe you haven't let them,' Silja replied. Thulmann shook his head.

'I failed her. I should be the one who is dead, not Anya,' he said. 'It was because of me that she was... destroyed. I was forced to make a choice. I knew what I was doing when I made it, knew that she would pay for my "duty", but I did it anyway. I thought I could have things both ways, but the world is never so kind.'

Silja was silent, uncertain what she could say, what she should say. Thulmann stared at the darkened walls of the room, his eyes lost in some horrible past. Silja held him, trying to soothe the turmoil in his mind. At length, the witch hunter turned his face towards her.

'That is why we can never be,' he said. 'I failed her. I would fail you. I cannot let that happen.'

'You wouldn't,' Silja insisted, rubbing his hand. It was so cold, as if all the life inside Thulmann was retreating from her touch.

'Silja, I can't let anything happen to you because of me,' Thulmann said, rising to his feet. 'You should ride back to Altdorf. I'll see to Haussner and Krieger.'

'If that's what you really want, Mathias,' Silja replied, 'but I want to hear you say it. I want you to say you don't want me. Tell me you don't love me.'

Silence filled the room as Thulmann stared down into Silja's face. He knew what he needed to say, but he could not force the words to his lips. Silja waited for him to speak and then rose, embracing him, crushing her lips to his.

A tremor of fear crawled its way along the templar's spine. After so many years, after all he had suffered and lost, he hadn't learned anything.

He still thought he could have things both ways.

CHAPTER EIGHT

THE TOWN HALL of Wyrmvater was a large, timbered structure that dominated two corners of the town square. The lower walls had been reinforced with stone, and a quick inspection verified Thulmann's suspicion that the precisely cut blocks had been exhumed from the old dwarf road rather than hacked from any local quarry. The interior of the building, at least those rooms Burgomeister Reinheckel led them through, was spacious, with high ceilings, panelled walls and tiled floors. The witch hunter was reminded again of Wyrmvater's lost prosperity as he encountered the unexpected finery of its town hall. He broached the subject with Reinheckel as the official led him up a flight of stairs towards the record room.

'Ah yes,' Reinheckel said. 'Wyrmvater was once a most lively place. It used to be called "Zwergdorf", after our little friends from the mountains. We were an important stopping point on the way to Altdorf and Nuln, and more than a little of the dwarfs' gold and silver found its way into the town coffers.'

'What happened?' Silja asked. She had decided to help Thulmann go over the town records. Examining old documents was something she'd had a great deal of practice at in her function as

Igor Markoff's chief investigator and agent. Thulmann had readily agreed; two pairs of eyes would do the work faster than one
and the quicker they made their study, the sooner they might fer-
ret out the location of Kleib's skaven lair.

'The dwarfs decided they could get a better price in Bretonnia?'
Lajos suggested, drawing a scowl from Reinheckel and a stern
look from Thulmann. Like Silja, the strigany had decided to
accompany the witch hunter, mostly because he found the
prospect of spending time with any of his other travelling companions rather unhealthy.

Reinheckel paced across the record room. It was a long, narrow
chamber, its walls filled with shelves, its floor littered with piles of
books and rolls of parchment. A few long tables stretched across
the centre of the room, their surfaces strewn with a scattering of
dusty volumes. An old, thin man in black robes turned away from
one of the tables as they entered, bowing deferentially to Reinheckel. The old man went to one of the tables, retrieving a large,
leather-bound book.

'May I present Curate Andein,' Reinheckel said. 'In addition to
his duties at our small chapel to Lord Sigmar, he also helps to
maintain the histories of Wyrmvater.'

Thulmann fixed Andein with a fierce look. 'I trust he keeps his
books better than he keeps his chapel.'

The first place Thulmann had paid a visit to had been Wyrmvater's chapel. He had been incensed to find the icons within the
sanctuary dusty and cobwebs clinging to the wooden beams
above the nave.

The old man cowered before Thulmann's smouldering anger.
'Forgive me, templar, I am but acting curate here. Our priest was
taken from us by a sickness six months ago and the holy temple
has not seen fit to send someone to replace him yet. I helped
Father Schmidt in his services so it was decided that I should minister until his replacement arrives.'

Lajos raised his eyebrow as he heard the old man address Thulmann, but kept silent. The last thing he needed was to get
involved. Besides, the old man's story had caused some of the
templar's anger to pass.

'That is worthy of you, but the temple should be maintained to
a nobler standard,' Thulmann said. 'It is the house of Sigmar. It
should be kept as such.'

Reinheckel coughed loudly, trying to draw attention back to himself and defuse the tense situation. He took the volume Andein had selected, opening it and displaying it for Thulmann's inspection. 'This book was commissioned near-on six hundred years ago by one of my predecessors,' Reinheckel said. 'It is a detailed history of our town, at least until that point.' He extended his hand, indicating the other books strewn across the tables. 'All of these are histories of the town. Some are official records, others are diaries and journals. Wyrmvater was quite well versed in the craft of letters at one time,' he added with a note of pride. 'The rest are accounting ledgers, figures on harvest yields, expenditures from the town treasury. I rather thought such mercantile concerns would be of little interest to a witch hunter.'

THE BURGOMEISTER BEGAN to flip through the book he had retrieved, smiling as he reached the page he sought. He set the book down on the table, standing back for the witch hunter and his companion to examine the open page. Snarling back at them was an old woodcut of a fanged reptilian face, horns ringing its brow.

'The dragon Skorn,' Reinheckel pronounced. 'It never was agreed upon why the old wyrm emerged from his mountain. Some said it was the dwarfs, who dug their mines too near the dragon's lair and that the smell of raw gold caused him to stir. Others claimed it was the will of the gods, that the dragon was set loose to punish the land for its greed and avarice. There were even rumours it was the work of the Great Enchanter, that it was his fell magics that broke its slumber. Whatever the reason, he came with wrath and ruin, laying waste to the countryside. The dwarfs retreated into their strongholds, trying to wait out the wyrm, leaving men to fend for themselves. Skorn wiped many towns and villages from the map, for none it seemed could stand against the dragon. Then, one day, there came a warrior, a knight from Altdorf. People tried not to laugh when he said he would kill the dragon, for how could he prevail where so many others had found death? Yet the knight's intention was sincere and he left Wyrmvater to find his way into Skorn's mountain and bring doom to the monster.'

'None can say what powers guarded the knight,' Reinheckel continued, turning the page, exposing another woodcut. This one showed a riot of images, from a jagged, craggy mountain peak to a lone warrior striking at a writhing dragon with his sword. The largest and centremost figure was the same knight standing beside a well, washing blood from his armour. 'But surely more than skill and luck were needed to accomplish what he did that day. Into Skorn's lair he went, one man against a beast that had killed thousands. That it was the man who would walk away from that mighty battle was a miracle none would have dared hope. The knight staggered back into our town, weary from his great ordeal, weak from his wounds. His armour steamed with Skorn's searing blood and the townsfolk rushed to wash it from him. But as they drew bucket after bucket from the well, casting the water across the knight's battered body, the dragon's blood was splashed across the town square, draining back down into the well. It was found later that the dragon's blood had polluted the water, rendering it unfit to drink. It was sealed and a statue of Skorn and the knight was placed above it.'

Thulmann had wondered at the strange brickwork base that supported the statue Reinheckel described. It had struck him as peculiar that a piece of sculpture that was fine enough to be a Caliosto or even a von Geier should endure such a crude and unsightly pedestal. Now he had his answer.

'The knight took the name of von Drakenburg for his great feat and was awarded lands to the north by the Count of Reikland for his heroism. Zwergdorf honoured that day too, rechristening itself Wyrmvater after the knight's valour and courage.' Reinheckel sighed, closing the book. 'Sadly, even with the dragon gone, the land still suffered. It took many years for men to resettle the places Skorn had destroyed. The dwarfs stayed in their mountains, their shame at hiding in their holes while men fought their terrible foe outweighing even their lust for trade and profit. Without the dwarfs, the old trade road fell into disuse and Wyrmvater was slowly forgotten.'

'The dragon's mountain,' Thulmann said, tapping the drawing. 'Do you know where it is?'

'Of course,' the burgomeister replied. 'It is a place shunned and avoided by my people even unto this day. A day's travel to the north. Really more a pile of rock than a proper mountain.'

'You think what we are after might be in the dragon's mountain?' Silja asked.

'It is possible,' Thulmann replied. 'A dragon's hole would be quite large, just the sort of place,' he looked at Reinheckel and paused. 'Just the sort of place that might serve a rabble of heretic scum as a refuge; save them the bother of digging their own.' Thulmann glanced at the other books scattered across the table. 'Still, we are ill served pouncing upon the first thing we see. We still need to peruse the histories Herr Reinheckel was so kind to prepare for us. There may be something even more promising in their pages.' Thulmann settled into a chair and pulled one of the books towards him, fishing in his pocket for a pair of pince nez glasses before beginning what promised to be a long day. Silja sat across the table from the witch hunter and began consulting the book Reinheckel had shown to them.

'I shall leave you to your studies,' Reinheckel said as he withdrew from the room. 'Good hunting.'

'INNKEEPER! ANOTHER STEIN all around!' Streng's voice roared across the Splintered Shield's taproom. He made a show of draining the last dregs from the lead stein clutched in his fist and set the vessel down on the table with a sharp bang.

'Keep that up and I'll be winning our wager,' the ferret-faced Driest said from across the table, taking a measured swallow from his own stein. 'Their ale is strong for a backwoods piss-pit like this.'

'I've had stronger,' Streng grunted. 'Got a good kick to it, I'll allow that. They probably got a taste for this stuff from the dwarfs. Not that it matters, I'll still drink you under the table.' The mercenary laughed appreciatively as Schieller's young daughter came walking to their table, a wooden platter supporting three steins held in her hands. Streng snatched all three vessels from her, sliding two across the table to his companions and taking a long pull from the other. The girl retreated back across the taproom.

'Keep them coming, innkeeper!' Streng bellowed, 'and hire some older barmaids!' The mercenary laughed again. At the far end of the table, Gernheim shook his scarred head. Streng fixed the Carroburger with a sullen stare. 'Something bothering you?'

Gernheim scowled back at Streng, clenching his fist. The Carroburger had been captured by goblins during the rampage of Azhag the Slaughterer's horde in the northern reaches of the Empire. In addition to his facial mutilations, the goblins had cut out the man's tongue, a disability that Streng seemed to find amusing.

'He doesn't think you'll win our little wager either,' Driest answered.

'Then the gobbos butchered his wits as well as his face,' Streng said, taking another pull from his tankard. The rich dark ale slopped down his face, dripping from his beard. Driest smiled and carefully took another measured sip from his own. The only one with befuddled senses at their table was Thulmann's man. He seemed oblivious to the fact that he was already three steins ahead of Driest and working on a fourth.

'So… so… so.' Streng blinked his eyes as if trying to capture an errant thought. 'What's the deal with yer gaffer, ole Krieger there? Seems a hard bastard.'

'He pays well enough,' Driest answered, 'and the work isn't exactly unenjoyable.' A sadistic smirk worked its way onto Driest's face. 'But I don't have to tell you about that.'

'Krieger's thick with Zerndoff, ain't 'e?' Streng grumbled. 'Can't see where that'd leave much time for field work.'

Driest took another measured swallow from his drink, scratching at his narrow nose. 'Oh, you'd be surprised the sorts of things we get up to sometimes.'

'Would I now?'

Gernheim reached a huge paw to his comrade's shoulder, but Driest shook him off. The sharpshooter leaned forwards across the table, his face only inches from Streng's, his ale-laced breath washing over the mercenary's features, oblivious to the clarity and attentiveness in Streng's eyes.

'YOU DO FINE work.' Krieger's gloved hand stroked the black wolfskin hanging on the wooden wall. It was a large specimen of its breed, expertly skinned and cured. He could understand why the tanner would have chosen to keep such an example of his trade for himself.

The tanner remained seated in his chair, his wife standing behind him, her arms resting protectively on his shoulders. 'Th-thank you, your lordship.'

Krieger stepped away from the wall and paced slowly around the small common room of the tanner's home. 'Tell me, Herr Kipps, perhaps you have even more impressive examples of your trade to show me?'

'You mean like bears?' the tanner asked.

The gaunt face of Haussner turned from his inspection of an oak cabinet to glare at Kipps. 'No, not like bears, you fool. It is unwise to be insolent to the servants of Lord Sigmar's sacred will.' The witch hunter stalked towards Kipps, stabbing a finger at him as if it was a dagger. 'We are interested in anything out of the ordinary that might have been brought to you by one of the hunters or foresters of this village; something foul and obscene, the shape of a beast granted the unholy semblance of a man.'

'We don't have anything like that in these parts,' Kipps declared, a tremor in his voice.

'Are you certain?' Krieger demanded. 'Sometimes unwise, unlearned men encounter such abominations and prevail against them, but not understanding the true nature of what they have slain they think it to be like any other beast. Sometimes such men may try to keep a trophy of their victory.'

Haussner stalked back across the room, this time descending on a large trunk resting against the wall. Kipps watched nervously as the witch hunter flipped the trunk open and began pawing through its contents.

'I tell you I've seen no such thing as you describe,' Kipps insisted, 'and if it please the gods, I never shall. No one in these parts has seen such things.'

'Indeed?' sneered Krieger, drawing closer to the tanner and his wife. 'Across the length and breadth of our glorious Empire the deep woods are infested with such monstrosities, their envy of man drawing them time and again to plague the remote outposts of civilisation. I have seen such creatures many times, from the woods of Middenland to the forests of Sylvania. Yet you tell me there are none here? That no one in all Wyrmvater has told stories of mutant beasts in the dark woods?'

At the word 'mutant', Kipps's wife gave a weak moan of fright, clutching her husband's shoulders still more tightly. The tanner tried to keep his expression neutral, but Krieger did not fail to notice the flicker of apprehension he had seen there. The tanner did know something, something he preferred not to tell a witch hunter. Peasants, Krieger thought, their superstitious dread of the creatures of Old Night befuddling what passed for reason in their simple minds. Even in the presence of men experienced and skilled in combating such monsters, the peasant would let his fear of them keep his tongue still. It had been Krieger's experience that the quickest way to get a peasant talking was to show him that there were things much more fearsome than the ghoulish denizens of darkness.

'I am a reasonable man, Herr Kipps,' Krieger said, 'but I fear that you begin to try my patie…'

Krieger was interrupted by the harsh, snarled oath of Haussner. Even Ehrhardt, his armoured bulk looming against the door of the tanner's home, was startled by Haussner's invective. The gaunt witch hunter rose from the trunk he'd been pawing through, a jumble of blue fabric clenched in his claw-like hand.

'Lying gutter swine!' Haussner snarled. 'You dare spit your blasphemies into the ears of Sigmar! But no deceit can prevail against Him! Behold the evidence of your perfidy!' Haussner waved the bundle of fabric beneath the noses of Kipps and his wife. Ehrhardt could see that it was a pair of dresses, the dresses of a young girl. Haussner crushed them between his fingers as if strangling a viper.

'You informed us you were alone here, Herr Kipps,' Krieger said, his voice cold and unforgiving. 'Just yourself and your wife. I don't think these are quite her size. Tell me, who else lives here?'

The tanner and his wife were pale with horror, unable to take their eyes from the tiny garments Haussner held. When Kipps could speak, it was in a dry croak. 'I don't know what those are,' he said. 'I told the truth, my lord, there is no one else here.'

'More lies!' Haussner roared. The back of his thin hand cracked against Kipps's face with such force that the man was spilled to the floor. The man's wife wailed in panic, launching herself at Haussner. The witch hunter planted his fist in her midsection, doubling her over in a coughing, wheezing wreck. He took a step towards Kipps as the man started to rise, but found himself suddenly lifted from the floor when a cold steel hand closed around his arm.

'That's enough, Haussner,' Ehrhardt growled at the man. Haussner tried to twist out of the knight's grasp even as his hands tried to tear the axe from his belt.

'Get your hands off me, you heathen trash!' Haussner snarled. 'These swine have dared speak false to an appointed instrument of Lord Sigmar and I will have the truth from their lying lips! Release me, you scum!'

With a twist of his powerful frame, the Black Guardsman slammed Haussner face-first into the floor. The sharp slap of Haussner's head bouncing against the floorboards echoed through the room. Krieger watched the awesome display of strength in shocked silence, Kipps and his wife similarly awed. Ehrhardt rose from the stunned, insensible fanatic, walking slowly towards the door.

'Slip your dog back on his leash, Krieger,' Ehrhardt's deep voice rumbled. 'For today at least, your "investigation" is over.'

THAT NIGHT, AROUND the largest table the dining room of the Splintered Shield could offer, Thulmann conferred with his associates. It was a heated exchange that soon had the innkeeper and his family keeping as far from the diners as they could. Haussner angrily related the incident at the tanner's, demanding that Ehrhardt be restrained and confined until charges could be brought against him. The skeletal witch hunter was convinced that the knight was nothing less than an agent of the ruinous powers, inflicted upon them to undermine their holy work. Silja was the first to rise to the Black Guardsman's defence, causing Haussner to shift the focus of his verbal attack on her. Under his venomous tongue, an infuriated Silja left the table, storming upstairs to her own rooms.

With the patience of an Arabyan sphinx, Ehrhardt bore Haussner's lashing tongue and then slowly explained why he had acted in such extreme terms. He reminded Thulmann that he wanted to retain as much as possible the goodwill of both the people of Wyrmvater and his fellow witch hunters. As a result of this injunction, Ehrhardt had perhaps allowed Krieger and Haussner to press too far with their overbearing questioning of the town's citizens, but when intimidation had crossed into brutality, he had drawn the line. A few choice observations on Haussner's unbalanced state of mind brought a fresh stream of fury spitting past the gaunt witch hunter's lips, a tirade that ended only when the fuming Haussner quit the table, marching off to the stables to enjoy the 'pious company of true believers' and be rid of the odious presence of heathen heretics.

Throughout the scene, Krieger had remained largely silent, not speaking a word to either defend or support Haussner. Thulmann demanded an accounting of Krieger's overbearing tactics. Krieger's reply that fear was the fastest way to get the townsfolk to talk, that they had no time to waste soft-stepping around dull-witted peasants, rang false in Thulmann's ears. Krieger was deliberately trying to undermine Thulmann's efforts to generate goodwill in the town. What puzzled him was why his fellow witch hunter should be set upon such a course.

Thulmann and Silja's study of the town records had yielded better fruit. The histories and legends of the region suggested quite a few likely locations. The underfolk were a lazy race, never forsaking the opportunity to spare themselves hard work if it could be avoided. If there was a skaven lair in the area, then it was more than likely it had started out life as something else before the ratkin claimed it for their own. The town records had contained references to goblin caves, ruined watchtowers, troll holes and more than a scattering of deserted villages. Above all, there was the prospect of the old dragon lair, a cavernous pit clawed in the belly of a mountain, just the sort of place a skaven would happily make into a stronghold. Krieger digested this information carefully, making suggestions about one avenue of investigation or another. At length it was decided that they would make further, more restrained, inquiries on the morrow and then make preparations to check out whatever location seemed the most promising.

After the discussion broke apart, Thulmann tracked down Streng, finding the mercenary lounging at one of the tables in the taproom.

The witch hunter sat down beside his henchman. 'Tell me everything you were able to learn,' Thulmann said, his voice lowered.

Streng leaned back in his chair, a lead stein clenched in his fist. 'I'm afraid it isn't much,' Streng replied. 'That Driest can't hold his ale too good, and that dummy Gernheim holds it a bit too well. Kept trying to get Driest to shut up every time he started to say something too interesting.' Streng sucked at his teeth, spitting a bit of gristle from his dinner onto the floor. 'I did manage to learn that your pal Krieger might not be quite the loyal son Zerndorff thinks he is. Seems he's been doing the odd favour for some of the other big-wigs in the temple now and again, strictly under the table and without Zerndorff knowing anything.'

'Krieger's an opportunist,' Thulmann stated. 'I already knew as much. His only loyalty is to his own ambition.'

'But did you know he met with Arch-lector Esmer just before we left Altdorf?'

'Now that is interesting,' Thulmann agreed, wondering what Krieger and the soon-to-be grand theogonist had discussed. 'Did Driest say anything else?'

'Not about Krieger, anyway. Gernheim got a bit too intrusive. Seems he could see I wasn't as drunk as I let on, even if Driest was oblivious.' Streng took a swallow from his stein and laughed. 'I'll have to play our little game again, for real next time. That reminds me, you owe me five silver shillings.' The mercenary extended his hand towards Thulmann, waiting while the witch hunter dug the coins from his purse and set them in his palm. The witch hunter rose to leave, but Streng motioned for him to stay.

'Learned a few things about your other playmate as well,' the thug stated. 'When Driest stopped talking about Krieger, I thought it might be smart to turn things around and see what he knew about Haussner.'

'I am well acquainted with that fanatic's career,' Thulmann said.

Streng nodded his head. 'Yes, but do you know anything about his past? Did you know for instance that his name used to be *von* Haussner, as in Count von Haussner? Used to have a big estate somewhere up near the Middle Mountains. Then, one day, he learned where the countess was spending her free time. He had his servants accuse her and her lover of witchcraft, took it so far that both were burned in fact. It was only after they were dead that his sister-in-law finally confessed that it was she, not the countess who had been sleeping around on her husband. Haussner's wife was guilty only of helping her sister cover up the affair. Seems that bit of information really rattled Haussner's cage. The sister-in-law had a little accident coming down a flight of stairs and afterwards the count denounced his title and donated all of his lands and wealth to your temple. As a reward for his piety, the temple elders appointed Haussner a templar in the Order of Sigmar.'

Thulmann sat in silence for a moment, absorbing Haussner's sordid history. That Haussner was a deranged fanatic he already knew, but Streng now raised the very likely possibility that the man was insane as well. It also went a long way to explaining the unreasoning hatred Haussner exhibited towards women. 'We'll have to keep a closer eye on Brother Peder,' Thulmann said. 'It sounds as if his mind walks a very fine line. I don't want it falling off while Silja's around.'

The witch hunter rose to his feet, heading upstairs to retire, leaving Streng to his alcoholic indulgences. Tonight, at least, he was in no mind to reprimand the mercenary for his vices.

AN HOUR LATER, a restless Streng was pacing across the hallway, nursing a bottle of port. He lifted his head when he heard a door creak open on the landing above and smiled as he saw Silja Markoff emerge from her room. The mercenary gave her a lewd wink when she looked in his direction. The woman ignored him, turning and pacing down the hall to Thulmann's room. Streng laughed and shook his head, taking another swallow from his bottle as he slowly made his way back towards the taproom. He seemed to recall a small keg of beer Schieller had left out in the open, and was rather keen to see if his memory was sound. Thulmann would be too occupied to reprimand him for taking advantage of their host's hospitality.

The mercenary had just reached the stairs when a scream wailed down the hallway, a cry of shock and horror. Streng spun around, running down the corridor. The voice had been Silja's and the scream had come from Thulmann's room.

CHAPTER NINE

SHADOW FILLED THE witch hunter's room as Silja opened the door and slipped inside. She could hear Thulmann's heavy breathing rising from the bed, worn out by the dual toils of scouring Wyrmvater's records and of restraining the excesses of his fellow templars. Dealing with the likes of Haussner might wear anybody out.

Silja felt a moment of guilt as she listened to the sound of Thulmann sleeping. The witch hunter did not rest easily. He must be wholly exhausted. She reached behind her for the door, intending to steal back into the hallway. Her hand froze on the brass latch.

Something moved inside the room, and scurried across the floor. The sound caused her eyes to stray towards the window. There was a shape perched there, something small and grotesque, with a fat body and a grossly swollen head. She could not see its face, but she had the impression it was snarling. The creature clutched a large sack. As Silja watched, the creature shook the bag, forcing something to fall from it to the floor with a sharp slap. Whatever it was squeaked in agitation, beady red eyes glaring in the darkness.

The sight of the strange shape had stunned Silja for a moment, but she soon found her voice, and screamed a warning she hoped would be heard in every room in the Splintered Shield. The apparition withdrew, dropping down from its perch on the sill. At the same time, Silja heard Thulmann rolling over in his bed, looking for the weapons she knew he'd have set on the sideboard. The scurrying sound intensified as the echoes of her scream died away.

'Mathias! There's something here!' Silja cried out and then cursed herself. In diverting her attention to her lover, she'd lost sight of whatever menace the strange creature at the window had left behind. Her eyes scoured the darkness, trying to find some sign of it again. She thought she saw black shapes hurrying about the room, scrambling under the legs of chairs and along the bases of the walls.

'Up here. Get off the floor!' Thulmann shouted. The witch hunter was standing at the edge of the bed, a pistol in his hand. With his other he reached towards Silja. Silja did not hesitate, springing towards Thulmann's outstretched hand. As she leapt to safety, she felt something flash past her leg, and fancied she could hear the snap of jaws closing around the empty air behind her. Thulmann pulled her up beside him, wrapping his arm around her in a protective gesture.

The scurrying claws scratched across the floor all around them, sometimes punctuated by shrill squeaks and whines. Silja felt her fear mounting. It was certain from the sound that the prowler had set more than one of the things loose in the room.

'What are they?' Silja whispered into Thulmann's ear, realising now that any noise might draw the attention of the unseen lurkers.

Thulmann continued to scan the darkness, head turning at every sound, his pistol at the ready. 'Rats,' he whispered back. 'I saw one as I grabbed the guns.'

'Rats?' Silja almost laughed at the ridiculousness of the thought. They had stood side by side against the daemonic filth of Baron von Gotz, against the undead wrath of Sibbechai, now they cowered like frightened children before simple rats.

The witch hunter's grip only tightened around her waist as he heard the incredulous note in her voice. 'These are not like any rats you have ever seen before,' Thulmann whispered, and the concern in his voice removed any doubt in Silja's mind that the things scurrying around the room were anything to underestimate.

Silja hurriedly pulled one of the heavy blankets from Thulmann's bed and hurled it in the direction of the scurrying sounds. Angry squeals told her that at least some of the rats had fallen foul of her improvised weapon. Then something large and hairy flung itself onto the bed, hissing and spitting at them, red eyes gleaming in the dark. Thulmann dived upon the thing, pinning it beneath his hand and smashing it with the butt of a pistol.

Silja could see the struggling shapes pinned beneath the blanket she had thrown. Nearer at hand, however, was the mangled thing struggling beneath Thulmann's grip. It was nearly the size of a fox, yet its shape was certainly that of a rat. Much of its fur had sloughed away, exposing a pale, blistered skin and ropes of green pulsating veins. An evil black froth bubbled from its fanged jaws, while trickles of pus dripped from its eyes. With the light to guide him, Thulmann set the butt of his pistol smashing down into the over-sized vermin's skull, crushing it like an egg. The witch hunter rose from his grisly labour and then flung himself at the trapped vermin on the floor, stomping them within their prison of wool and thread.

Thulmann was breathing hard before the struggling rats grew still. One of the crippled vermin tried to scuttle away. The witch hunter turned on it, kicking the mangled carcass across the room. He spun around, hurrying back to Silja. 'Did they touch you?' he demanded, despair in his voice, his eyes scanning her for any trace of injury.

'I'm fine,' Silja protested, trying to pull away.

'You are certain you are all right?' Thulmann whispered. When Silja nodded, Thulmann stepped down from his perch, turning over the carcass of the rat he had killed with the barrel of his pistol. 'I think you should find that even a small bite from these diseased fangs would prove as deadly as a dragon's kiss.' The witch hunter flopped the thing onto its back, exposing its wasted belly. A long scar ran down its length, the injury sealed by a crude cross-stitch of what looked like sinew. 'And I think they were designed that way.'

Silja dropped down beside him, careful to keep her feet clear of any of the rat blood spattered on the floor. 'When I came in, I saw someone – something – at the window. It had a large sack in its hands. I saw it drop one of the rats into the room, that was when I screamed.'

The rattle of armour caused them to turn back towards the doorway. Still tightening the straps on his chest plate, Captain-Justicar Ehrhardt lumbered into the room, his intense gaze sweeping the chamber. 'What did I miss?' the Black Guardsman demanded.

'Only a bit of pest extermination,' Thulmann said and then returned his attention to Silja. 'This creature you saw, was it a skaven?'

Silja was quiet for a moment, conjuring up the image of the strange shape she had seen at the window. That weird apparition still seemed somehow unreal, even with its handiwork scattered all around her. 'No,' she said at last. 'I don't think so. It was smaller and fatter. Its head was malformed in some way, but I'm certain it had a face.'

'Goblins?' Ehrhardt asked. Thulmann shook his head.

'I don't think so,' the witch hunter said. 'Surgically altered giant rats infested with a nice cocktail of disease seems a bit sophisticated for goblin-work.' He stepped around the bed, pulling clothes from the chair he had thrown them onto before retiring. 'Disease. Malformed mutants. A keen interest in seeing me dead.' Thulmann ticked off each point by raising a finger as he made it. 'Sounds as if we might be getting close, close enough to worry an old acquaintance of mine.' Thulmann shook his head, gesturing at the splattered rats. 'Although I had thought Dr Weichs had a higher opinion of me than this.'

'You think Weichs is here?' Ehrhardt demanded, a growl in his voice. The infamous plague doktor had unleashed the Stir blight on Wurtbad, slaughtering thousands, forcing the priests of Morr to dig vast plague pits outside the city. As a Black Guardsman, Ehrhardt took such ruthless trespass in the domain of Morr quite personally.

'It is a very distinct possibility,' Thulmann said. 'I suggest we go outside and see if we can't pick up my late caller's trail and see where that takes us.'

A FEW MINUTES later found armour donned and weapons readied. There was just a chance that the would-be assassin's trail might lead back to Weichs, and Thulmann had no intention of letting that chance slip through his fingers.

Rushing down the stairs, the witch hunter found his path impeded by a strange tableau. Streng, arms folded across his chest, was sitting on Lajos Dozsa's back. As he saw his employer descending, the mercenary rose, grabbing the back of Lajos's nightshirt and hauling the merchant to his feet.

'I heard someone scream,' Streng said. 'Is everything well?'

'Well enough,' Thulmann replied. 'No thanks to your besotted carcass.'

'I was on my way up to help,' Streng protested, 'but I tripped over this scum tearing down the stairs as if Khaine was on his heels.' The mercenary gave the nightshirt a savage tug, forcing a whine of protest from Lajos. 'I knew you'd want words with him, so I thought I'd make sure he didn't go anywhere.'

'Did you now?' Thulmann asked.

'There weren't any more screams, so one way or another I figured you were past my help.' Streng tightened his hold on Lajos's shirt, bringing a yelp of pain from the man.

'Is that necessary?' Lajos hissed. Streng only grinned back at him.

'Where did you think you were going, strigany?' Thulmann demanded. 'Let me answer that for you,' he continued before Lajos could reply. 'You heard the scream as well and saw an opportunity to separate us from your dubious company.'

'I was afraid something had happened to you,' Lajos protested. Thulmann looked unconvinced, so the merchant hurried to explain. 'Do I honestly look like I planned an escape?' Lajos pulled at the waist of his nightshirt, indicating his lack of preparation. 'You are the only one protecting me from that lunatic you brought with you from Altdorf. I'm sure he'd have me dancing from a tree as quick as say "good morrow" given half a chance.'

Mention of Haussner caused Thulmann's eyes to narrow with a sudden realisation. He'd been too wrapped up in the moment, too focused on the recent attempt on his life. He hadn't considered the absence of Haussner and Krieger until Lajos reminded him of it. Surely his fellow witch hunters could not have failed to hear Silja scream, or miss the commotion that followed? Thulmann had even seen Schieller peering inquisitively from behind his cracked door, frightened curiosity on his face. There might be no love lost between them, but the other templars would at least have sent one of their minions to see what had happened.

That is, if they were still in the Splintered Shield.

'Where are Brother Kristoph and Brother Peder?' Streng wondered aloud.

'The tanner!' Ehrhardt cursed, smashing his gauntlet into an armoured palm.

'I fear Brother Ehrhardt has the right of it,' Thulmann said. 'I should have realised Krieger gave ground a bit too easily on that front.' He was silent for a moment, weighing the trouble Krieger and Haussner might cause against his hopes for picking up the assassin's trail. It did not take him long to reach the uncomfortable decision that his fellow witch hunters were the more immediate danger. 'Streng, my would-be killer came and went by means of the window. See if you can't find some sort of track for us to follow later. Brother Ehrhardt, please lead the way to the tanner's. Lets see if we can't put an end to whatever misery those two are stirring up before it goes too far.'

'What about me?' Lajos asked. Five sets of unsympathetic eyes turned on him. 'Surely you don't expect me to go gallivanting around town dressed like this?'

'Unless you want someone to carry you,' Thulmann stated, pushing past the merchant.

As SOON AS they set foot outside the inn, Thulmann knew it was too late. Any hopes he might have had that he could contain Haussner's overzealous fanaticism were dashed the moment he heard the man's raised voice shouting into the night. He wasn't the only one, either. Every window in the town was lit up, anxious faces filling many, all eyes turned in the direction of Wyrmvater's square. Thulmann cursed again and set off at a run towards the square.

The scene unfolding in the square confirmed all of Thulmann's fears. Ropes had been flung across the wings of the dragon statue at the centre of the square and the nooses that dangled from the end of each rope had been tied around the necks of two battered and bleeding figures. Thulmann decided that they could only be the tanner Kipps and his wife. But his eyes did not linger too long on the sorry sight, drawn instead to the heap of broken furniture and straw that had been assembled a few yards from the statue. Two of Haussner's flagellants stood beside the makeshift pyre while two others were tying a small, struggling shape to the framework of a ladder. Orchestrating the entire scene, fairly shrieking a litany from the *Deus Sigmar* into the night, was Haussner. It took Thulmann a few moments to spot Krieger and his henchmen. Unlike the fanatic Haussner, they seemed to be avoiding the limelight, keeping to the shadows cast by the town hall.

'What in the name of Sigmar are you doing?' Thulmann growled as he stormed towards Haussner. The fanatic turned on him, the *Deus Sigmar* clutched in his clawed hands, the fires of his zeal filling his eyes.

'Not all of us are so remiss as to forget our duties and our oaths simply because their execution seems distasteful,' Haussner declared. He closed the *Deus Sigmar* and stabbed a talon at the wretched figures of Kipps and his wife. 'These heretics dared to lie to holy servants of Sigmar today. I would not allow such a slight against the temple to stand. From their forked tongues, I harvested the truth!' Haussner spun around, swiping his hand in the direction of the flagellants with the ladder. Thulmann could see that the tiny shape they were binding was a terrified little girl, no more than eight summers old. Haussner gestured and he saw more. One of the flagellants pulled up the hem of the girl's dress, exposing the black, gleaming hoof that replaced one of her feet. Thulmann heard Silja gasp in horror as the child's mutation was exposed. His own feelings were no less sickened.

'These heretics will hang for sheltering such filth! But first their lying tongues will be cut from their miserable heads that they may speak no further blasphemies against Lord Sigmar.' One of Haussner's minions stalked towards Kipps, a pair of brutal-looking metal tongs gripped in his hands. 'And we will purge this village of its mutant taint!' Haussner roared. 'By the method proscribed by Sigmar's holy law. By burning them!' At Haussner's gesture, the men with the torches set the pyre ablaze. Thulmann realised the jumble of wood must have been treated with oil or pitch, as the flames quickly took hold. The girl, lashed to the wooden ladder began to scream as the flagellants lifted her and started to carry her towards the fire.

'Stop this, Haussner,' Thulmann snarled, grabbing the fanatic's shoulder. Ahead of him, Ehrhardt interposed his imposing armoured bulk between the ladder carriers and the flames. Even the crazed mendicant-monks realised that the sword clutched in the Black Guardsman's hands was not an idle threat.

'Those are strange words coming from a witch hunter.' Thulmann turned his head to see that Krieger had emerged from the shadows to lend his support to Haussner's brutality. 'Brother Peder is engaged in one of our order's most important duties – the extermination of mutants and those who would offer them sanctuary. A witch hunter of your reputation, Brother Mathias, has instituted such executions many times over, surely.'

Thulmann could feel Silja's shock like a knife twisting in his guts. It was one thing for her to accept the things he had been forced to do on an abstract, intellectual level. It was another to be there, to see the horror and monstrosity of it.

'Not like this,' Thulmann growled. He thought again of that small child in Silbermund, the one who had been treated for a leg injury by Weichs and his abominable medicines. She too had been young and innocent, yet the taint of Chaos had infested her flesh. Thulmann had ordered her destruction, knowing that there was no other way. But he'd ordered the child rendered insensible first, ensuring she would not know what happened. It was a far cry from the calculated brutality of Haussner's methods. 'Never like this.'

'The creature is a mutant and must be destroyed.' Haussner spat. 'You know this! Call off that heathen thug and let the will of Lord Sigmar be done.'

'Mathias, don't let him!' It pained Thulmann to hear the agony in Silja's voice, the terror that edged her words. It was not the horror of the situation, but the horror that the man she loved would stand aside and let it happen.

'And the others will be found!' Haussner shrieked. 'In whatever hole they have hidden themselves, in whatever pit they have buried their abominable flesh, they will be found.'

Thulmann shook his head. 'I can't talk to this fanatic,' he said. 'Krieger, I would have words with you.'

'If you think that would serve any purpose,' Krieger replied, 'but I warn you that I place a higher price on my soul than the charms of a…' the witch hunter looked in Silja's direction, his face twisting into a sneer, '…lady.'

Thulmann bit down on his anger. Krieger was baiting him, trying to force him to lose control. He would not allow Krieger to take over the situation, to let him start playing the tune. Thulmann led Krieger some distance from the others.

'We can't let Brother Peder do this,' Thulmann said, his voice lowered so that his words would not carry to Haussner. 'He jeopardises our entire investigation with his fanaticism. There is more at stake here than burning one wretched mutant.'

'He is only doing his duty,' Krieger replied. 'I thought you would be able to appreciate that. Besides, it is hardly one mutant. Brother Peder was most thorough in his interrogation of the heretics. He has discovered that there are several families in Wyrmvater hiding mutants in their attics and cellars.'

Thulmann quickly digested the information, drawing from it a possibility he hoped would make Krieger at least see reason. 'Don't you see what that means? It means that something around here is polluting these people. It could be warpstone poisoning. Even a small trace of warpstone in the ground or water might work its way into the crops, and if there is warpstone…'

'Then our skaven lair might be nearby as well,' Krieger concluded. 'A viable theory, Brother Mathias.'

'Zerndorff sent us here to find *Das Buch die Unholden*,' Thulmann reminded Krieger, 'not to scour some Reikland backwater of mutants. I don't think our next Lord Protector will be terribly pleased if we let his prize escape.'

Krieger smiled at Thulmann, nodding his head. 'Well played, Brother Mathias. You do indeed put things in their proper order.' The smile broadened. 'In truth, I couldn't care less about Brother Peder's mutants. I encouraged him only because I felt you were becoming a good deal too friendly with the peasants. It occurred to me that you might use that influence–'

'Ridiculous,' Thulmann snapped. Krieger's mind might be a morass of treachery and intrigue, but Thulmann found the suggestion that his own methods were similarly duplicitous revolting.

'It is now,' Krieger admitted. 'Now we will all be in the same boat. After Brother Peder's display tonight, the peasants won't care who wears the black, they will all be afraid. Just as they should be.'

'What about Brother Peder?' Thulmann demanded.

'He will do as I ask,' Krieger said confidently. 'I helped him with his… domestic… concerns once. He'll do as I say. We can have the mutant and its parents locked away and burn them after we've found the book and have no further use for Wyrmvater or the "goodwill" of its people.'

Thulmann watched in disgust as Krieger stalked back towards Haussner to give the fanatic his orders. He wondered if deep down Krieger cared about anything or anyone beyond their ability to further his ambitions. He also wondered just how far Krieger would allow those ambitions to take him.

'IDIOT!' THE OLD man snarled, his scrawny hand swatting across the brow of the misshapen creature beside him in the darkened alleyway. The mutated halfling cringed from the blow, slinking away from his furious master. Doktor Weichs turned his attention back to the town square and the black-garbed figure that was the focus of his wrath. The witch hunter should have been dead. The rats Lobo had set loose in Thulmann's room were infested with one of the most virulent strains of plague that Weichs had ever come across in his studies. Yet there he stood, consulting his fanatical brethren.

Perhaps they were even talking about him. The thought chilled Weichs to the bone, but he couldn't dismiss the possibility. Now that he had tipped his hand and tried to kill the witch hunter, Thulmann would be even more determined to hunt him down. He was already much too close for comfort and Weichs didn't want to think of Thulmann getting any closer.

It was time to convince Skilk to take a paw in matters. Thulmann might have escaped the trap Weichs had set for him, but the plague doctor didn't think he would fare so well against the skaven.

CHAPTER TEN

THULMANN WATCHED THE dawn slowly gather beyond the frosted glass of the window. He felt a wave of sudden fatigue grip him, as his restless body registered the passing of night and any chance for slumber. The witch hunter yawned, rubbing at his eyes. There had been many sleepless nights. He would suffer no worse for adding another to their number. There was much his mind still needed to sort through.

Without Krieger, he was certain the standoff in the plaza could only have ended in blood. Haussner was beyond appreciating that by engaging in his crusade to purge Wyrmvater of whatever mutants it might harbour, he had put the more important mission to uncover the skaven warren and recover *Das Buch die Unholden* in jeopardy.

If Haussner's unreasoning fanaticism was a dark omen on their chances for success, then Krieger's calculating ambition was an even blacker one. He could have stopped Haussner at any time, but hadn't, more troubled by what he perceived as Thulmann's growing influence with the townspeople than he was by the prospect of losing their aid. Krieger would brook no rival and Thulmann wondered just how much of the credit if they succeeded in capturing *Das Buch die Unholden* would be shared.

Shared? The realisation suddenly hit Thulmann, the true rationale behind Krieger's gambit. He wouldn't share anything. By interfering with Haussner, by stopping the fanatic's brutal and untimely execution of his duty, Thulmann had played right into Krieger's hands. Thulmann could almost hear Krieger making his report to Zerndorff, giving voice to carefully worded accusations and insinuations. There were few charges so damning to a witch hunter as those of heresy.

Of more immediate concern, however, was the effect the violent scene had had on the people of Wyrmvater. Nearly the entire town had watched, drawn from their beds by Haussner's strident voice. Thulmann had seen the anxious, fearful look Reinheckel and his militiamen had given the witch hunters as they led Kipps and his family to the cells. He had seen the hate boiling in the eyes of the townsfolk, the unspoken curses on their lips, as they watched the witch hunters slowly make their way back to the Splintered Shield.

The witch hunter rose from his chair, walking across the room to where his weapons belt hung from a nail in the wall. Thulmann wrapped it around his waist, drawing it tight. He cast an envious look towards the bed. If he could find sleep as easily as the woman did, perhaps he might be a contented man. With everything that had happened, there had been no question of letting Silja stay alone in her room. Who could say that their misshapen visitor might not return? No, he wanted Silja somewhere he could watch her and make sure she would come to no harm.

Thulmann carefully opened the door, closing it softly behind him. He stalked down the stairs, towards the common room of the inn to greet the figure he had seen through the window. He heard the heavy oak door below open and close and boots stamping against the wood floor as their owner tried to coerce warmth back into his limbs. Streng's grizzled frame loomed just within the entryway.

'Well?' Thulmann demanded. Streng stopped blowing on his cold hands to regard his master.

'Found the tracks right enough,' the mercenary stated. 'Little things, not quite like a child's and too wide for a goblin's.

Possibly a halfling. Round and round the town, down just about every alley and pig-run this muck-hole has to offer. Got me turned around so often I can't tell you where he started from, much less where he went.'

Thulmann sighed, rubbing again at his tired eyes. 'Hardly the best of tidings, friend Streng. I had hoped that murderous mongrel might lead us back to its master. Fortunately, I think Herr Doktor Weichs will present us with another opportunity when he tries again.'

'Unless he tucks his tail between his legs and runs off again,' Streng replied, his voice a low growl. 'If we lose that bastard I'm going to carve Haussner like a Pflugzeit goose. If it wasn't for that idiot we might have caught this scum and tracked it back to Weichs!'

The witch hunter placed a gloved hand on Streng's shoulder. 'Be at ease. There will be another opportunity. Weichs will try again, all we have to do is be ready for him when he does.'

'How can you be so sure?' Streng challenged. 'We've been one step behind that filth for nearly a year. How can you be certain he'll stick around this time?'

Thulmann's voice grew grave as he answered. 'Because I think things have changed. The good doktor can't run any more. We've got him cornered at last... and that makes him more dangerous than ever.'

WEICHS CAUTIOUSLY WALKED through the vast, subterranean cavern. The ragged, gnawed walls of the cave curved upwards into the gloom. Small iron cages hung from the walls at intervals, a sickly green glow spilling through their bars and illuminating the cavern. The scientist could see the diabolical shine of warpstone in the walls of the pit and could feel the malevolent power of the substance in the air. Scattered about the cavern were picks and hammers, and a few larger tools for stripping the warpstone from the earth, huge devices with drills and claws, like monstrous beasts of steel and bronze.

Small gangs of scrawny skaven, wretched slaves of the Skrittar, were hacking away at the walls, mining the warpstone for their masters. The scientist kept his distance from these half-mad dregs. Starved and crazed, Weichs knew such creatures might dash past the whips of their masters to gorge themselves on his flesh. The thought caused him to shudder: the most brilliant mind among all humanity reduced to a meal for the detritus of skaven society.

Given a choice, he would never have descended into the mines, but Grey Seer Skilk had ignored Weichs's plea to see it. After his failure to kill the witch hunter in Wyrmvater, Weichs knew that he didn't have time to waste waiting for Skilk. He had to have the help of the skaven now, not when it suited the grey seer.

Weichs found Skilk near the very centre of the cavern, where a large crevasse bisected the cave floor, creating a narrow crack that stabbed its way into the black depths of the earth. A stone altar had been erected on the flattest section of the floor. Eight massive iron spikes, as tall as a man and pounded deep into the rock were arrayed around the altar. A riotous array of bones, an assortment of animal, human and inhuman remains hung from the spikes. Weichs recognised the ugly characters that had been daubed onto each bone, it was the same ancient picture-script that figured in much of the profane lore contained within *Das Buch die Unholden*. The scientist knew these characters only too well, for they were the very ones revealed to him in the ritual he had translated for Skilk. He tried not to think upon what else the ritual required.

Skilk was standing behind the altar, overseeing a pair of lesser Skrittar as the under-priests painted characters onto still more bones. Skilk turned his horned head as he smelled Weichs approaching. He gestured, motioning for one of the half a dozen armoured stormvermin surrounding him to fetch the human.

'All smell like books,' Skilk chittered. The skin-covered *Das Buch die Unholden* rested atop the altar and Skilk patted it with a black paw. 'Kripsnik say soon,' the grey seer hissed, avarice dripping from his muzzle. 'Skilk like Kripsnik speak much!'

Weichs found himself shuddering. The skaven, and the grey seers in particular, were horrible things, abominations that offended the senses of a man at the deepest, most primal level. How much more hideous then, to contemplate the prospect of evoking the loathsome spectre of one of their breed decades in the grave?

Weichs forced himself to set aside his disgust at what Skilk intended to do and forced his mind back to the more immediate problem of Thulmann and the witch hunters. 'Grey Seer, we have a problem,' he said. 'The witch hunter from Wurtbad has followed us here. He's in Wyrmvater!'

Skilk lashed his tail in amusement, one of the under-seers join-ing in with a chittering laugh. 'Doktor-man thinks Skilk a fool? Skilk know hunter-man near long time. Hunter-man not stay long.' The skaven laughed again, this time the scratchy, inhuman mirth spreading even to the armoured bodyguard.

'Don't underestimate him!' Weichs protested. 'I know this man. He is dangerous!'

Skilk's lips parted in a bestial snarl. Before Weichs could react, the grey seer lunged forward and a black paw closed around his throat. The skaven priest pressed Weichs's body against the altar, his back arching over its pitted, stained surface. He could see the crazed, feral light in Skilk's eyes; the ugly twinkle of madness and obsession.

'Doktor-man thinks Skilk not dangerous?' Skilk hissed. 'Not fear hunter-man! Fear Skilk! Fear not Kripsnik! Doktor-man fears much!'

The grey seer released his hold on Weichs, almost flinging the terrified scientist from him. Skilk hobbled his way back towards the under-seers. 'Hunter-man die soon,' Skilk promised. 'Hunter-man not found doktor-man.' Skilk turned his attention from Weichs, returning to his supervision of the other grey seers.

Weichs rubbed at his throat, trying to massage the pain away. Skilk's talons had torn the skin, causing tiny rivulets of blood to trickle down his neck. The old man pulled himself away from the altar, hurriedly making his way back across the cavern.

He had been too fixated on the witch hunter to consider whether Thulmann might be the least of his worries. What if the ritual he had translated for Skilk failed? What if he had made a mistake? What if the damnable book had deceived him? Worse, what if it did everything Skilk wanted it to do?

Perhaps Weichs had been a bit hasty in trying to get rid of the witch hunter. Perhaps the greater danger hanging over his head was not Thulmann but Skilk.

'OF COURSE THE people are upset, but it will pass. Give them time and they will understand how Kipps put them all in danger by hiding his unfortunate progeny among them. The taint of muta-tion simply cannot be abided.'

Burgomeister Reinheckel paused to take another sip from the beer stein Schieller had set before him on the table. The man

smiled appreciatively as he finished, wiping foam from his moustache. Thulmann sat across the table from the burgomeister, not
entirely reassured by his words.

On Thulmann's left, Kristoph Krieger seemed unmoved by anything the burgomeister said. As far as he was concerned, these
were peasants, and nothing they had to say was worthy of deep
consideration. Thulmann could see that Reinheckel was growing
more and more irritated by Krieger's indifference, but at least
Krieger hadn't made things worse by inviting Haussner to the sit-
down.

'It is a sorry fact that the forces of Chaos so often afflict the most
innocent,' Thulmann replied. 'The corruption takes sanctuary in
the love and pity of good, decent men. That is one of the greatest
strengths of the Dark Gods.' The witch hunter shook his head.
'The duty of a templar is to protect the people of Sigmar's holy
empire, and our duty is never more onerous than in situations
such as this, when we must stand against our own wishes. Mercy
is a temptation that has loosed many a daemon upon the land.'

Reinheckel nodded his head grimly. 'Believe me, Brother Mathias, I do understand. I understand you have no choice in the
matter. You must do what is good for us all.'

'Knowing why something must be done does not make it any
easier,' Thulmann cautioned, 'but the ruinous powers must be
opposed, wherever they might manifest.'

The burgomeister took another sip from his stein. 'One of our
woodsmen, a fellow named Naschy, says he saw some strange
things near an old ruined shrine about a half-day's ride from
town, and thought you should be told.'

'Why the deuce do you bother us with this prattle about
mutant-whelps and heretic tanners when you've more important
news?' Krieger snapped, causing Reinheckel to recoil from him.
'What sort of "things" did this peasant-wretch claim to see?'

'He heard them before he saw anything,' Reinheckel said, 'shrill,
scratching noises, like the hissing of beasts but somehow different, as if there was something of speech within all the chirps and
squeaks. Then he saw them, four or five ghastly things creeping
around the old ruins. He says they were covered in fur, but walked
upright like men: gruesome mixtures of man and animal. Naschy
was frozen to the spot in horror but fortunately, the monsters did
not see him.'

'What happened then?' Krieger asked.

'Naschy watched them for a while. They seemed to be collecting something, gathering weeds from around the stones. After a time, the monsters withdrew, retreating into a big hole in the ground. Naschy said it looked like a big badger burrow.'

'An interesting account to be certain,' Thulmann said. 'It might be worth looking into. You know where this place is?'

'No, at least I have never been there myself,' Reinheckel said, 'but I can fetch Naschy and have him guide you to the spot.'

'Then do so,' Krieger said, 'before we lose any more of the day to empty chatter.'

'Please, burgomeister, if you would send for Naschy,' Thulmann said. 'If there is anything behind his story, we should look into it without delay.'

'Of course, Brother Mathias,' Reinheckel said, rising from his chair. 'I will have Naschy waiting for you at the town hall within the hour. Good day, Brother Mathias, Brother Kristoph.' Thulmann watched the town official withdraw from the inn and turned to regard Krieger.

'You might try to be at least somewhat pleasant to these people,' he said. 'After Haussner's display last night we hardly need to do anything else to antagonise them.'

'I leave grovelling to peasants to those with the stomach for it,' Krieger retorted. 'These backwater pigsties are a blight on the Empire, a breeding ground for the sort of ignorance and superstition that keeps our land under the influence of Old Night.'

'They are people,' Thulmann protested, 'citizens of the Empire, no different from those in Altdorf or Nuln or any of the great cities.'

'You think so?' Krieger shook his head. 'I know different. My family has a very long history, a very long and proud tradition of serving the temple. For many generations my forefathers pursued Dieter Heydrich, the necromancer. That fiend's shadow still haunts parts of the Empire. He was born in such a backwoods as Wyrmvater.'

Thulmann was silent for a moment, fixing Krieger with an intense look. 'I am well aware of Dieter Heydrich's atrocities. I also know that the great cities can produce monsters every bit as terrible.' He found his mind returning to the streets of Bechafen, turning up the little lane leading to his house where Erasmus Kleib waited for him with his wife and daughter.

Krieger chose to say nothing, sipping instead at his wine. 'Does it strike you as terribly convenient? The burgomeister's little story I mean?'

'On that, at least, we can agree,' Thulmann replied. 'It's suspicious that this Naschy should only come forward the morning after Brother Peder's little display. One might say the timing is a bit off to be entirely coincidence.'

'A trap then?'

'Possibly,' Thulmann said, considering the possibility, 'but the question is, a trap set by whom?'

'You suspect Weichs?'

'Or his skaven masters,' Thulmann added. 'If their lair is near here, they would have agents keeping tabs on Wyrmvater. Naschy may be one of them.'

'So what do you propose we do, Brother Mathias?' Krieger took a final sip from his glass, turning it upside down and setting it on the table. 'It would be a pity to ignore so obvious an invitation.'

Thulmann smiled at his fellow witch hunter. 'Then we agree upon something else,' he said.

THE WITCH HUNTERS left Wyrmvater's town hall, arranging to meet with Naschy at the town gate once they had gathered their gear and mobilised their followers. As soon as they were back at the Splintered Shield, Thulmann began making his own arrangements. With Krieger and Haussner bellowing out orders to their men, Thulmann discussed preparations with his own entourage, meeting with them in the new room he had been given by Schieller.

'We've had a bit of luck,' Thulmann told them. 'One of the locals claims to have seen strange creatures lurking around some old ruins in the woods. From his description, they sound very much like skaven.'

'Rather fortuitous,' Ehrhardt commented.

'Brother Kristoph and myself feel it is,' Thulmann agreed. 'Too much so, but it is also an opportunity we can't pass up.'

'What if it is a trap, Mathias?' Silja protested. Thulmann felt the concern in her voice. It gave him pause for a moment. He never gave much thought to his own welfare when riding out to confront Sigmar's foes. Now, for the first time he did. Not for himself, but for how his fate might affect Silja. The witch hunter waved aside the distraction. This was a chance to track down Weichs and the grey seer, to recover *Das Buch die Unholden* before it could be used to plunge the countryside into plague and madness. There were more important things at risk than himself. More important even than Silja.

'If it is a trap, we go into it expecting deceit,' Thulmann said. 'That might be enough to turn the tables on anyone waiting to work any mischief.'

'You don't make that sound terribly convincing,' Lajos observed. The fat merchant had his hat in his hand again, torturing it out of shape as his nervousness increased.

'It is our best chance to find Weichs,' Thulmann repeated. 'He's close, I can sense it, and if he's here, the grey seer and the book will be too.'

'Besides, strigany, if anything happens to you, I've watched the priests enough to plant you decently.' Everyone in the room stared at Ehrhardt. Had the Black Guardsman actually made a joke?

It was Streng who finally broke the awkward silence. 'Well, if it gets us closer to that mutilating bastard Weichs, you can count me in,' the mercenary swore.

'Actually, I have something more important to occupy your time,' Thulmann said. 'If we really do find a skaven lair in the woods, it will take more men than we have here to attend to it, even if we can count upon the aid of the townsfolk. I need you to ride south to Falkenstein. There is a garrison there. Present these orders to the commander and then lead him back here.' Thulmann reached into his tunic and produced a scroll. He handed the document to Streng, who stared at it with distaste. 'It is a hard ride and there is no one I trust better to make it in good time,' Thulmann stated. Streng scowled as he accepted the scroll.

'You just remember to save a piece of that maggot-bait for me,' Streng snarled. 'No burning Weichs 'til I have a chance at him.' The mercenary pushed past Thulmann. They could hear him stomping his way down the stairs as he made for the stables.

'Well, I suppose we should be on our way too,' Silja announced, rising from her seat at the edge of the bed. Thulmann shook his head.

'Not this time,' he said. 'This time you will do as I say and stay put. Lajos will stay behind and look after you.'

'I hardly need looking after,' Silja retorted. 'I can hold my own, Mathias. I don't need to be treated like some fragile waif.'

'This is apt to be quite dangerous, like bearding a wyvern in its cave, if my suspicions are correct,' Thulmann said. 'I'll have a hard enough time trying to keep my neck safe. If I'm distracted by trying to keep you safe as well, it is quite likely I'll get us both killed. I know you are a capable and courageous woman, but if you think that would keep me from worrying about you, then you must think me a very shallow rogue indeed.' He took a step towards her, closing his hands over hers. 'Please, Silja, I need you to stay here. I need to know you are safe.'

Silja looked into Thulmann's desperate, pleading eyes and slowly nodded her head. She knew he was right. If it really was a trap then the witch hunter would be too concerned with her safety to guard his own.

'I leave her in your care, Lajos,' Thulmann said. 'Make certain nothing happens to her.' The witch hunter turned, embracing Silja. 'Don't worry, Sigmar will watch over us. We will not fail.' He kissed her passionately and then slowly pulled away.

'He'll be back,' she said, more to herself than anyone. 'He has to come back.' She cast a sidewise look at Lajos. 'Come along, I want to watch them go.' When Lajos made no move to follow her, she frowned down at the little man. 'Mathias told you to keep an eye on me. I don't think you should disappoint him.'

The strigany grumbled to himself as he followed Silja from the room. 'Mathias said a good many things,' he muttered. 'Feh! A pox on all witch hunters and their women!'

THE STREETS OF Wyrmvater were crowded with townsfolk watching as Thulmann led his small group of riders from the settlement, Haussner's dismounted flagellants bringing up the rear. Their mood was sombre – no shouts of encouragement or wishes of good fortune and no garlands tossed to the departing heroes. No, the faces of those who watched the witch hunters go were as stern as stone, rigid and unmoving. There was an air of unspoken resentment around the onlookers, a suggestion of slowly smouldering hostility. Silja shook her head. That was Haussner's work, poisoning the town against Thulmann with his unreasoning fanaticism. Without Haussner's draconian tactics, Silja was certain Thulmann would have made the people see that what he was doing was as much to protect them as anyone. Thulmann would have made them see that he was on their side.

As Silja searched the faces of the crowd for some sign of under-standing or sympathy, she found her eyes drawn to a particular countenance. An old man, almost rail-thin with a wild shock of white hair had emerged from a particularly dark alleyway just as the last of Haussner's flagellants passed through Wyrmvater's timber gate. There was something about the old man that instantly struck her as familiar, a furtive quality that awoke her suspicion at once. She turned away from the gate and began to move her way through the crowd, trying to keep sight of the old man as she wended her way through the press of bodies. She could hear Lajos grumbling behind her as the little merchant tried to keep up with her.

The old man took notice of her approach when she was only halfway to him. He pulled his heavy brown coat tighter around his shoulders and began to stalk away. As he turned, Silja had a good look at his profile and knew, knew without question, she had seen that face before. Years spent in the service of her father, the Lord High Justice of Wurtbad, had given Silja an eye for detail and a bear-trap mind that seldom let any of those details slip from her memory. She had seen this man before, and in Wurtbad. Silja felt a wave of red hate pulse through her body as the realisation set in. There was only one person they might expect to find in Wyrmvater who had lately been in Wurtbad.

'Herr Doktor Weichs!' Silja called out. Instinctively the old man turned around as his name was called. His narrow eyes grew wide with alarm as he realised what he had done. Abandoning all pre-tence at discreet escape, the plague doktor spun around and took to his heels, shoving shepherds and farmers from his path.

'It is Weichs!' Silja shouted, drawing the sword from her belt and tearing after the fleeing physician. A string of thick strigany curses sounded behind her as Lajos huffed along after her. 'Hurry! We have to catch him!' If they could capture Weichs, there might be no need for Thulmann to risk riding out into a possible trap. The plague doktor would be able to give the witch hunters all the information they needed. There was more than simply bringing justice to the infamous fiend; there was a chance to save the life of the man she loved.

Silja was just behind Weichs when the old man turned a corner, dashing down a wide stone path that wound its way towards the northern edge of the town.

Silja smiled. Weichs had made a wrong move; there was no gate in Wyrmvater's north wall.

'Come on Lajos!' she called. 'We have him now!' The cry seemed to lend speed to the old man's legs, the plague doktor sprinting several yards ahead as he heard Silja shout. The woman redoubled her efforts, determined not to lose sight of the villain.

Panting, his insides feeling as if they were on fire, Lajos Dozsa turned the corner, clutching at the stonework for support. He could see Silja running down the path, her elderly quarry a short distance beyond her. The merchant sucked down several deep breaths, bracing himself for another huge effort.

'Lajos! We nearly have him!' Silja called again.

'How nice,' Lajos wheezed as he pushed away from the stonework and staggered after the woman. 'Just what I always wanted, a psychotic heretic of my very own.'

CHAPTER ELEVEN

THE STONE PATH twisted its way past the hovels and storehouses of Wyrmvater, winding its way towards the timber walls, where the buildings dwindled, giving way to animal pens and vegetable gardens. Weichs darted into one of them, scattering swine before him as he struggled to keep his lead on Silja. The woman smiled at the useless effort. The plague doktor was far from physically fit, there was no chance he could outlast his pursuer. All he was doing was dragging out the inevitable.

Or perhaps not. As Silja leapt into the swine yard, she saw the old man turn yet again, and this time she could see there was definite purpose in his direction. Weichs was trying to reach a ramshackle-looking mill. Silja's lip curled into a snarl. After all this man had done to her city, after the hideous deeds Thulmann and Streng said he had done, she wasn't going to let anything stand between the scum and the justice he so deserved.

Silja sprinted after the fleeing man, trying to intercept him. Cabbages were crushed under her boots, squawking chickens kicked into the air as she scrambled across gardens and crashed through fences. Weichs dragged on his last reserves of strength and lunged towards the timber door of the mill.

Silja saw the villain's desperate gambit, smiling as she judged
the distance between the old man and the door. She would reach
it first, and then Weichs would be hers. She lunged through the
slop of another pigpen, the last obstacle between herself and the
windmill. As she did so, one of the panicking swine charged into
her legs. A coloured curse that would have reddened the face of a
Sartosan pirate spilled from Silja's mouth as she toppled headfirst
into the stinking mud.

The woman scrambled back to her feet, not even hesitating to
wipe the mire dripping from her hair down into her face. She
could see how dearly the accident had cost her. What had been
certain moments ago was certain no more. Weichs might very well
reach the sanctuary of the mill.

Weichs gasped in terror as the muddy figure of Silja Markoff
rose from the pigpen and lunged over the waist-high stockade of
sticks that formed the wall of the pen. He felt the fear hammering
against his heart, the breath burning in his throat. Even as the
woman charged across the small radish patch that grew in the
very shadow of the mill, the scientist felt a surge of victory. The
door was close. He sneered at his pursuer and dived the last few
feet that separated him from safety. The old man's weight pushed
the portal open. His lean hands closed around the frame of the
door and he leaned into it as he drove the timber panel shut
behind him.

He was unable to close the door, however, the toe of a black
boot was wedged between the frame and the jamb. Weichs put his
full weight against the door, trying to force it closed, but found it
being pushed back. Slowly, steadily, the door was opening. The
plague doktor abandoned the uneven contest, leaping back and
allowing the door to crash inward. He cringed at the awful apparition that stood in the doorway. Silja's countenance was caked in
black, dripping mud, her features hidden behind clumps of damp
earth, but he could see her eyes, smouldering hateful embers
shining from beneath the mask of mud.

Weichs backed away, dragging a small dagger from his belt. It
was Silja's turn to sneer as she tightened her hold on the sword in
her hand. Youth, strength, reach and skill, all of these were
staunchly stacked in her favour. The plague doktor was out-
matched, and she could see in his eyes that he knew it. She
watched him look around for some avenue of escape, but there

was nothing. Sacks of grain and processed flour, the immense mass of the mill wheel, a frightened donkey lashed to its turn post, and a large wooden sifter were the only things within the mill beyond Weichs and his adversary.

'This is intolerable!' Weichs declared, trying to force a note of authority into his voice. 'Why do you pursue me? I am a respected elder of this community. I shall report this outrage to the burgomeister!'

Silja's voice was equally cold. 'You are a human maggot, Weichs, and you will burn in hell!' She took a step towards the old man, causing him to retreat deeper into the gloom of the mill. 'Fortunately for you Mathias needs you alive. Otherwise I'd sink this blade in your gut here and now!'

Weichs continued to back away, eyes darting into every corner of the mill, still hunting a way to escape. The plague doktor stopped when he found himself backed against the immense millstone. He glowered defiantly at the woman. 'So you are the witch hunter's slut? What makes you think I'm going anywhere with you?'

The point of Silja's sword twinkled in the gloom as she pointed it at the man's throat. 'Because I say you are,' she hissed.

'We'll see about that,' Weichs sneered back, a sardonic smile tugging at the corners of his mouth. 'Lobo! Kill the bitch!'

Before Silja could react, something sprang at her from the shadows. The impact bashed the woman into the wall of the mill, rattling the wood frame and knocking the sword from her grip. She felt powerful fingers clawing at her body and could smell the diseased breath of the creature fouling the air. A grotesque face leered at her with manic ferocity. Here, Silja knew, was the disgusting assassin Weichs had sent to kill Thulmann. Now the creature was determined to do the same to her.

Weichs stepped hurriedly away from the millstone as the heavy rollers began to turn. Already agitated by the raised, angry voices, the eruption of violence had completely disordered the little donkey. Braying and snorting, the animal tried to flee the fight, running rapidly in the clockwise path allowed it by its tether. The scientist wiped flour dust from his clothes as the residue of grain on the stone was crushed beneath the rollers. Then his gaze fell to the floor, settling upon Silja's abandoned sword. A malevolent gleam came into his eyes as he stooped and retrieved the weapon.

Weichs stepped towards the struggle. Silja strove to keep Lobo's clutching fingers from her throat, even as the mutant halfling's flailing feet smashed into her midsection and the idiot mouth snapped at her with crooked teeth. The plague doktor smiled down at her, raising the sword.

'Such hate when all I want to do is make the world a better place for my fellow man,' he sighed. 'I suppose that has ever been the price of genius.'

'You are no genius!' Silja spat. 'You are a monster!'

Weichs shook his head. 'No, that thing trying so very hard to strangle you,' he gestured at Lobo's twisted form. 'That is a monster. I... I am a visionary!'

The plague doktor thrust down at Silja with his blade, but as he did so the woman finally managed to gain a firm grip on Lobo's shirt, twisting the fabric in her fist until the garment was tight around the mutated body. With a savage snarl, she ripped the halfling off her, kicking him away and sending him crashing into a pile of grain sacks. At the same time, the sword stabbed downward, but Weichs was no swordsman, and he'd failed to anticipate his target rolling from the path of his blade.

Weichs pulled his arm back, slashing with the edge of the sword as Silja rolled into a crouch. The murderous steel swept through the air just above her head, dragging strands of hair away with it. Silja did not allow him a second chance. Her hand scraped across the floor and in one fluid motion sent a cloud of dust and flour rushing into his face.

Silja rushed the blinded physician, smashing her fist into his face before he could recover, her other hand closing around the hilt of the sword, trying to pry it from Weichs's fingers. The scientist struggled in Silja's grip, but he could feel his hold on the weapon slipping. The contest had shifted once again, this time against him.

Silja had just succeeded in wresting the sword from Weichs's hand when a noxious weight smashed into her back, tiny arms wrapping around her throat. She could feel the creature's full weight strangling her as it hung against her back, its idiot, drooling mouth biting her scalp.

'No hurt the master!' Lobo shrieked into her ear. Silja could feel the mutant's weight crushing her windpipe. Reluctantly she released her hold on Weichs, trying to clutch at the murderous halfling, hoping to relieve some of the pressure on her throat.

This time Weichs did not gloat and did not try to lend a hand to his rescuer. The scientist dabbed at the blood trickling from his mouth where Silja had struck him and dashed out of the door of the mill. Silja thought she heard someone cry out in pain a moment later, but with Lobo growling in her ear, she could not be certain.

Silja staggered across the mill, trying to smash Lobo into the walls and the support beams, anything that might dislodge the strangler. Black dots began to dance before her eyes, every gasp of breath being drawn down into her lungs becoming a battle in its own right. Then, suddenly, amazingly, Lobo screamed in pain, the pressure on her throat vanishing at once as the halfling released her and crashed to the floor. Silja fell to her knees, sucking in great breaths as she tried to recover from the assault. Almost in a daze, she saw Lobo writhing on the floor, a huge gash ripped from his shoulder. She lifted her gaze to the beam she had last been trying to batter the murderous fiend against. An iron hook, perhaps for holding the tether of the mill's donkey, jutted from the beam. She could see blood and a ragged strip of flesh dripping from it.

Silja forced herself to her feet, looking around for her weapon. There was still a chance that she could catch Weichs. As she reached down to recover her weapon, however, the misshapen halfling lunged at her for a third time. The edge of her blade raked Lobo's body, nearly severing one of the mutant's legs, but the murderous weight of the halfling slammed into her without losing its impetus, knocking her back. Silja crashed against the millstone, the snarling halfling atop her.

'Kill! The master says kill!' Lobo crawled up Silja's body, spitting blood as he groped for her neck. Silja drove the hilt of her sword into the lumpy face, crushing the already concave cheekbone. Fragments of tooth dripped from Lobo's mouth, but still the clutching hands reached for her throat. Silja twisted her head, trying to keep away from the ruined, slobbering mouth. As she did so, her eyes grew wide with a new horror.

The frightened donkey still raced around the millstone, turning the heavy rollers as it did so. Now Silja found herself staring at one of the oncoming rollers, watching as it swiftly made another circuit of the millstone. With a strength born of stark terror, she rolled her body, forcing the halfling beneath her. She smashed Lobo's bulbous head against the stone, almost cracking his skull as she tried to force the monster to release his grip. At last the clutching hands slackened and Silja was able to pull away. She held the still struggling mutant against the millstone as the rollers completed their circuit, ducking as the drive shaft passed over her. Lobo gave voice to a shrill shriek before the roller crushed his skull like an egg. Silja turned when she felt his body go limp, having no desire to see what the roller had left behind.

Silja put her hand to the back of her head, feeling the damp ooze of blood seep through her fingers where Lobo's teeth had worried at her scalp. She staggered towards the entrance of the mill, thoughts of pursuing Weichs quickly diminishing. After her battle with the mutant, even Weichs would be able to get the best of her in a fair fight, and now she knew that the plague doktor was not likely to fight fair.

Outside the mill, Silja found Lajos leaning against a water trough, a makeshift bandage wrapped around his forearm. The merchant looked up from tending his wound, not quite able to hide his shock when he saw Silja's miserable condition.

'He got away,' Lajos said. 'I tried to stop him but he had a knife. He cut me, see?' He held up his bandaged arm to be certain Silja could see it.

Silja shook her head and then started to laugh.

THE RUINS OF the old shrine were scattered amidst a stand of ancient trees. 'Shrine' seemed a bit too grand a word to encompass the broken suggestions of walls and the toppled debris of columns that lurched up from the undergrowth at every side.

Naschy came to a halt beside the cracked stump of a granite column. The woodsman turned around, bowing deferentially to the mounted templars. 'This is the place,' he said. 'I saw the monsters over there.' He pointed with his finger, indicating a jumble of stone blocks and the fragmentary remains of a stairway that rose into the nothingness of the collapsed upper floors of the temple.

Krieger turned in his saddle, addressing his men. 'Dismount and spread out. Look for any sign of them, and keep your wits about you.' Driest and Gernheim dropped from their horses, drawing their weapons as they gained their feet. Ehrhardt followed their example, while Haussner's flagellant monks began to tear at the overgrowth clothing some of the fallen stonework, looking for any clues that might be hidden in the weeds.

'The area doesn't look despoiled enough for there to be any skaven about,' Thulmann observed. 'If there was a warren of any size near here, most of the foliage would have been stripped bare to keep the vermin fed.'

'It may be a side entrance, an escape route from the main complex,' Krieger replied. 'The ratkin are quite careful to leave no sign of themselves when they need to.' The witch hunter tapped the side of his nose. 'Besides, something doesn't smell right about this place.'

Thulmann swept his gaze across the piles of stone and weed-choked debris. 'Perhaps the lingering influence of whatever god was once worshipped here. In the old days, men paid homage to many curious things. We have no evidence that what we seek is here.'

A sharp, wailing cry reverberated through the ruins. One of the flagellants was writhing on the ground, clutching the bleeding stump of his left arm. Snarling above him, crouched on the side of a fallen column, blood dripping from the notched sword in its paws, was a shape of madness and nightmare. Lean and wiry, its furry body clothed in a crude armoured harness, the skaven pounced on the maimed man, burying its chisel-like fangs in the flagellant's throat. A moment later the monster's head snapped back and its body was thrown to the ground, a smoking hole punched through its forehead.

'You wanted evidence?' Krieger roared as he holstered the spent pistol. 'There is your evidence!' Thulmann drew his own pistols, watching as skaven poured from concealed holes hidden among the rubble. 'Abide not the filth of Chaos!' Haussner shouted, axe gripped tightly in his hands. 'Suffer it not to defile your land! Tolerate it not, whatever guise it might wear.' The fanatic urged his horse forward, charging into the swarming monsters at full gallop, swinging his axe in a red arc through the slavering, snarling ratmen. The remaining flagellants hurried after their leader, roaring their devotion to Sigmar as they fearlessly charged into the press of inhuman beasts.

The sounds of battle crashed through the ruins. Everywhere Thulmann turned he could see the loathsome skaven. Gernheim had his back to the remains of a wall, the ex-soldier's sword dark with foul skaven blood and the ground littered with twitching bodies. Ehrhardt stood alone atop the stump of a pillar, chopping down with his sword as the ratmen scrambled to reach him.

Thulmann drew his sword, but as he tried to turn his horse towards the thickest of the fighting, he found Krieger's hand closing around the reins.

'Leave them! We'll come back with the soldiers you sent for!' Krieger shouted. Thulmann turned his head back to the melee, watching in disgust as Driest, his ammunition spent, was dragged down and hacked to pieces by a dozen chittering ratmen.

Thulmann stared in disbelief at his fellow templar. Did Krieger really mean to abandon his comrades, to slink from the field of battle like some frightened cur? 'Let me go, Krieger,' Thulmann snarled.

'Leave them!' Krieger repeated. 'It is more important that we escape and guide the army back here! Use your head, man!'

'You go,' Thulmann growled, ripping the reins free from Krieger's hand. 'I'll be certain to mention your bravery to Zerndorff if I survive.' Without another word, Thulmann dug his spurs into his steed and charged into battle.

Squealing ratmen were crushed beneath the impact of his horse, their scrawny bodies cracked beneath its hooves. The silvered edge of his sword was soon black with skaven blood as he lashed out again and again. The chittering monsters slashed at him with crooked swords and stabbed at him with rusty spears. Thulmann struggled to control his screaming horse as a skaven spear thrust into its flank, narrowly missing Thulmann's leg. The animal reared up, its flailing hooves cracking skaven skulls as the monsters pressed their advantage.

Then, suddenly, the assault seemed to falter. Thulmann could see skaven being thrown back, pummelled by the impact of another charge. It was with shock that he saw Krieger appear at his side, the templar's sword stabbing downward into the verminous throng. The unexpected attack seemed to break the fragile spirit of the ratmen. They began to scramble back towards the ruins and their concealed burrows, shrieking and chittering as they ran.

'I shouldn't like unkind stories being told about me in Altdorf,' Krieger said, wiping blood from his sabre. Thulmann opened his mouth to reply, but an abrupt change in the air stilled his words. There was a perceptible chill in the atmosphere, and a nauseating sensation, like spectral insects crawling across bare flesh. Even the light filtering down through the trees seemed to dim as if repulsed by some unholy force.

The skaven sensed the crawling change in the air too, stopping their frantic retreat. They turned in a savage, slavering mob, gathering around one of the broken walls. Thulmann could see another figure there, a pallid shape standing atop the remnant stairs. Great horns spread from the sides of the creature's skull, massive ram-like tusks that framed its snarling, rat-like face. Ragged grey robes clothed it, and around the creature's neck, Thulmann could see a patchwork collar of fur, the talisman of the Skrittar. The white-furred monster was not the same as the sorcerer-priest he had encountered in Wurtbad, but it was certainly of the same breed. If it was here, then the creature Thulmann hunted would not be far away.

The grey seer glared at the pack of skaven gathered at the base of the stairway and turned its smouldering gaze towards their foes. The monster chittered something in its own ghastly language and gestured with the long wooden staff it carried. The stench of ozone scratched through the air as a crackling tendril of black lightning leapt from the tip of the staff and smashed into the bloodied figure of a flagellant. The mendicant cried out in mortal agony as the sorcerous power seared his flesh, boiling his innards with the intensity of its fury. After a moment, the black lightning vanished and the smoking carcass of the flagellant toppled to the ground.

'We don't have the men to fight that thing!' Krieger shouted. 'We need to retreat while we can.'

Thulmann nodded in agreement, struggling to turn the head of his protesting horse. The maimed animal resisted his urges to move it, sinking down on its knees as blood gushed from its wounds. The witch hunter pulled himself from his saddle before the expiring animal collapsed on its side.

The dying animal must have drawn the grey seer's attention. Thulmann could hear it spit-squeaking in its language as it shouted down to its minions. Thulmann could well imagine the substance of its hisses as he saw black lightning gather around its staff once more. 'Behold the might of the Horned Rat,' it was saying. Thulmann braced himself for the annihilating touch of the skaven's sorcery. The smell of ozone grew in the air.

Then there was a crack like the groaning of a mountain, echoing through the forest. Thulmann opened his eyes, shocked to still be alive. Atop the stairway, the grey seer was chittering and spitting in its obscene language, gesturing madly with its claws. Something had disrupted its spellcraft.

That something stood only a few feet in front of Thulmann. Hands clasped across his chest, head bowed, Thulmann thought he could see a faint golden aura shining around Peder Haussner. Thulmann could hear the solemn, repetitive words of a prayer from the *Deus Sigmar* emerging from the fanatic's lips. Had it been Sigmar's divine grace that had broken the grey seer's magic?

'My devotion is my shield. My faith is my hammer. The light of Sigmar shines through me and before me no darkness will prevail.' Haussner began to walk slowly towards the broken wall and the stairway. There was something unreal, almost trance-like about the way he moved, the unfaltering regularity of his steps. The rekindled courage of the ratkin railed against this display and the pack began to give voice to all manner of craven squeals.

The grey seer atop the steps swung around, snarling at the reticent mob. Then it turned its attention back to Haussner, screaming its rage at the defiant templar. The tip of the monster's staff began to crackle with black lightning again. With a roar, the grey seer thrust the staff forward, sending a crackling blast of warp-lightning searing down at Haussner. This time Thulmann could see the deadly sorcery break, shredded to the four winds as it seemed to smash against some invisible barrier surrounding Haussner. As the black lightning crashed against this unseen barrier, Haussner came to a halt. For a moment, the fanatic was silent and then the words of his prayer rose once more, louder and more strident than before.

'He is the rock upon which the unclean will be broken. He is the tempest…'

The grey seer's bullying valour faltered before this second display of Haussner's faith. The skaven massed below it sensed their leader's doubt, fear spreading like wildfire through them. The frightened squeals grew into a maddening din and the monsters began to scatter, scurrying back towards their boltholes and burrows. The grey seer shouted and shrieked at its minions, furiously demanding their return. The sorcerer raised his staff in one hand and sent it smashing against the edge of the step upon which it stood. The horned ratman started to scramble back down the steps, intent on joining the flight of its kin, but the tremulous spell it had evoked had done more than it had anticipated; the fell energy had also weakened the remains of the wall. As the grey seer's hurried steps rattled the unsteady ruins further, they came tumbling down around him. The skaven gave voice to a single shriek of terror before it was crushed beneath the heavy stone blocks.

Thulmann could see Ehrhardt and one of Haussner's flagellants running towards one of the burrows as squealing skaven scurried down them. Before they could reach it, the ground shook and a cloud of dust erupted from the hole. Moments later, the other burrows vomited brown clouds of dirt and soil. It was scant consolation to know that the skaven had probably killed many of their own when they had collapsed their tunnels.

The witch hunter rose, surveying the carnage all around him. Four of Haussner's men were dead, as was the sharpshooter Driest. Gernheim was sporting a deep gash in his leg and arm, but otherwise seemed to have suffered no injuries. Captain-Justicar Ehrhardt appeared unharmed, his black armour proving invulnerable to the crude, rusted blades and rude swordsmanship of the ratkin.

'Shall we pursue those abominations, Brother Mathias?' Haussner asked as he approached Thulmann, apparently oblivious to the miraculous energies that had passed through his body only moments before.

'No,' Thulmann replied, trying to keep any trace of awe from his voice. 'It would take us days to clear enough rubble to get into their tunnels.' He turned his head, looking directly at Krieger. 'From past experience I can say we will need more men if we are going to scour an entire warren.'

'Then what do you propose we do?' Krieger asked.

'We go back to Wyrmvater,' Thulmann answered, 'but first I want a search made of these bodies. Unless I miss my guess, I don't think we will find our friend Naschy among them.'

'You still think he was a part of this?' Ehrhardt's voice was a deep, forbidding growl.

'It would be an interesting question to pose to him,' Thulmann said, 'especially if we find him in Wyrmvater instead of here.'

STRENG WAS JOLTED by the agonised shriek of his horse as he galloped through the fields beyond Wyrmvater. The animal reared back and crashed to its side. Streng felt the wind knocked out of him as he struck the ground, the impact stunning him. When he was able to suck breath back into his body, the first thing he observed was the dull throbbing pain in his leg. The second was the arrow sticking from his horse's throat.

Streng's mind raced as his eyes scoured the landscape. The arrow had certainly come from the woods on his left; it was the only cover from which an archer could have concealed himself and still struck his horse from that direction. He turned his attention to the right, scanning the terrain for something that might afford him shelter. The thug smiled as he sighted a jumbled pile of boulders a few yards from the edge of the woods. Next to the walls of Brass Keep, it was the best he could ask for.

Slowly, painfully, Streng dragged his leg from beneath his dead horse. The real pain didn't set in until his foot was free and then a shockwave of throbbing misery exploded through his body. A quick inspection confirmed his fear – his ankle was broken. Streng rolled onto his side, reaching towards his saddle and then cursed again. His ankle hadn't been the only thing crushed beneath his horse, his crossbow had been as well. He shook his head in disgust.

Loud voices rose from the woods. Streng peered over the carcass of his dead mount, watching as three figures emerged from the treeline, bows clutched in their hands.

'I THOUGHT YOU were going to clean up?' Lajos sat in the chair in Silja's room, changing the bandage wrapped around his arm.

'Not with you watching,' Silja said. She checked her pistol again and slid it into the holster fastened to her belt. The little merchant seemed to wilt with disappointment, returning his attention to the ugly gash running down his forearm.

'Hurry up,' Silja said. 'Don't you want to catch that scum?'

'Me?' A shocked expression filled the merchant's face. 'I'm no warrior. I am perfectly content to leave that sort of stupidity to people like you and Thulmann.'

'I noticed,' Silja growled. 'At least you could help us look.' Their first stop after losing Weichs at the mill had been Wyrmvater's town hall to report the skirmish to Reinheckel. The burgomeister had listened with grave concern as Silja described the fight and the escape of the heretic physician. Reinheckel had promised to round up the town militia and help Silja uncover the dangerous outlaw. He would check with the gate guards whether the fugitive had passed through their posts and report his findings to Silja. He suggested that Silja might use the time to get clean and rest before the hunt. She would have welcomed the chance, but in truth she found the delay insufferable. She needed to be active, needed to be out there trying to find this madman. After coming so close and having him slip through her fingers, she felt a gnawing guilt chewing at her gut. How was Thulmann able to endure this for so long?

'I'm quite happy to stay right here,' Lajos said. 'That maniac already had some of my blood, and that's all he's going to get. Besides, I don't get along too well with your burgomeister.'

'Are you a man or a m–' Silja stopped in mid-sentence, her words arrested by the sharp click that had sounded from the hallway. She thought at first that she had been hearing things, but Lajos had turned his head towards the door too. Silja walked over to the door, and tested it. Someone had locked them in.

'I guess you are staying too,' Lajos said, but there was a troubled note in his voice. Silja walked to the window and stared out at the streets of Wyrmvater.

'Something is going on out there,' she said. There was a steady stream of people making their way through the streets, all in the same direction. The only place of any importance in that quarter of the town was the Sigmarite chapel. 'It looks like they are all going to temple. There isn't any sort of Reiklander holy day today, is there?'

'It wouldn't matter anyway,' Lajos quipped, walking away from the window. 'They don't have a priest here.' The strigany dropped back down into his chair. Silja followed him across the room.

'What do you mean they don't have a priest?' she demanded. Lajos frowned, realising that he might have said too much. He tried to shrug off the question but Silja would not be put off.

'All right,' he at last relented. 'When I was here years ago they said their priest had died, they had an altar boy or something filling in for him. Well, the altar boy is still filling in.'

Silja stood staring at the merchant, digesting what he had just told him. She turned and walked towards the door, drawing her pistol. Lajos leapt from his chair, darting over and grabbing her hand before she could fire.

'What do you think you are doing!' he gasped.

'Something strange is going on here,' Silja replied. 'I intend to find out what.'

Lajos raised his hands, urging Silja to remain calm. 'All the more reason to stay put. Thulmann's the witch hunter, let him figure out what's going on.'

'I might have expected a strigany to say something like that,' Silja hissed. Lajos glared back at her, colour filling his cheeks.

'Oh, that's right!' he snarled. 'All strigany are thieves and liars! We grovel before daemon idols and help vampires steal babies in the night! We're all money-grubbing villains who would sell our own mothers to a goblin's harem and wouldn't give a crust of bread to a starving child unless we saw a way to profit from it!' Lajos stormed back to his chair, his body trembling with fury.

Silja walked over to the seated merchant, setting her hand on his shoulder. 'I'm sorry for what I said,' she told him. Lajos smiled sadly, patting her hand.

'You go through your whole life with people hating you and despising you not because of who you are, but who they have decided you are,' Lajos said. 'They call you thief and idolater, the lapdog of monsters and the helpmate of daemons. You'd think eventually you'd get used to it, but you never do.'

Lajos sighed and turned his head back to the door. 'You still want to get out of here?'

'I have to,' Silja said. 'I have to do something.' Lajos nodded his understanding, pushing himself back out of his chair.

'Well, let's see about getting that door open,' he said, 'but put away that hand cannon. Somebody wants to keep us here and if they hear that thing go off, they'll know we're loose.' The merchant reached into his sleeve, his hand returning with a slender piece of twisted metal. Silja had seen enough lockpicks in her time to recognise one when she saw it. Lajos saw the recognition in her eyes. 'Sometimes, when people tell you that you are something long enough, you decide that you are.' He made his way to the door, thrusting the pick into the lock of the door. After a few moments of fiddling, Silja heard the mechanism click.

Lajos gripped the knob, slowly pulling the door open. A quick inspection of the hallway determined that there was no guard. He closed the door again and turned to face Silja. 'Now that it's open, where are we going?'

Silja walked over to the door, opening it and stepping into the hall. 'I want to see what's so interesting at the chapel,' she said. She turned and began to creep her way towards the stairs.

Lajos rolled his eyes. 'I should have left it locked,' he grumbled.

CHAPTER TWELVE

'I STILL SAY we should get out of here.' Lajos cast another apprehensive look in the direction of Wyrmvater's small chapel. A steady stream of people was still filing into the building. Old and young, women and children, it seemed the entire town was heading into the house of worship.

Well, except for the two militiamen haunting the Splintered Shield's taproom, Silja reflected. After Lajos had opened the door, the two had cautiously made their way downstairs. Not knowing who had locked them in, or why, Silja decided that the best idea might be to slip out the side entrance of the inn rather than the front. Their route had very nearly caused them to walk straight into the two swordsmen, only Silja's quick reaction allowing them to drop back behind the corridor wall before one of the guards saw them.

They were guards; the turn of the conversation Silja overheard removed any doubt of that. They'd been left behind to ensure that Lajos didn't go anywhere while the witch hunter was gone. It seemed the burgomeister was quite concerned that he wouldn't get his chance at the plump strigany merchant. The gruesome speculation about what Reinheckel would do to Lajos caused all the colour to drain from his face. Lajos had scurried along the corridor, finding a shuttered window he decided that he could squeeze through. Silja hurried to keep up with the man as he made his escape.

'We should go someplace safe and wait for Thulmann to get back,' Lajos stated. Only threats had kept him from deserting Silja and leaving Wyrmvater on his own. Silja felt a pang of guilt as she reminded him how angry Mathias would be if Lajos let anything happen to her, deliberately pitting his fear of the witch hunter against his terror of Reinheckel's revenge.

'I want a look inside,' Silja said. 'I have to know what is going on.' She watched as the last people on the street withdrew into the chapel. There was something unsettling about the way they had lurched and stumbled their way up the chapel steps. She could not dismiss their gaits as the ravages of injury or old age. 'Come on. Every Sigmarite temple I've ever seen has had a separate priest's entrance. We'll try that.'

'And then what? We go in and find the entire town howling prayers to the Prince of Pleasure? What will you do then, arrest everybody?' Lajos shook his head. 'I would have been better off sticking with that fanatic fruitcake Haussner!'

'I just want to see what's going on,' Silja insisted. 'We find out what these people are doing, then we go find Mathias and tell him and let him decide what to do.'

Lajos twisted his hat in his hands, staring at his feet. At last he sighed and nodded. 'All right, I know I'll regret it, but we'll try it your way.'

THE PRIEST'S ENTRANCE was a small oak door set into the side of the stone-walled chapel, almost directly opposite the main entrance. With the entire mass of the chapel lying between themselves and any last-minute arrivals, Silja felt there was little risk of being spotted. The door was locked, but once again Lajos displayed the skill that common folk belief endowed every strigany.

As the merchant pushed the door inwards, voices emerged from the shadowy interior of the chapel. Silja felt her skin crawl as the sound reached her ears. The voices were raised in some manner of song, but it wasn't any that Silja had ever heard. The intonations didn't even sound human, and the words of the hymn certainly did not belong to even the most ancient and debased forms of Reikspiel.

'I suppose that explains why the walls are so thick,' Lajos commented. Despite the flippancy of his words, Silja could see that his hands were trembling. Seeing the merchant's anxiety firmed Silja's own resolve.

'Come along,' Silja ordered, stepping into the narrow hallway, sword in hand. There was a heavy, almost animal smell to the hallway. The doors of storerooms, the vestry and the priest's cell opened into the hallway. The hissing, snarling voices of the congregation emanated from around the turn of the corridor. The volume intensified as Lajos closed the door and joined Silja in the hallway.

'Where do we...?' The strigany's question died on his lips as heavy footsteps sounded from beneath their very feet. Silja and Lajos stared at the floor as the steps continued, following their unseen path. They could hear what sounded like a trapdoor creaking open from behind the door of the priest's cell. The heavy footsteps continued. This time there was no question that they came from the priest's cell.

Silja grabbed Lajos by the arm, pulling him to the vestry. She pushed the strigany into the room and scrambled in behind him, closing the door after her so that only the most slender crack remained. She peered through it into the hallway, waiting for whoever was in the priest's cell to emerge.

'Lady Markoff.' Silja tried to ignore Lajos's whisper, focusing her attention on the hallway. She could hear the occupants of the cell moving around. It was hard to judge exactly how many there were. What was more puzzling however was her conviction that they had heard the steps begin underneath the chapel. It was not impossible that a Sigmarite chapel might have a crypt or a reliquary vault beneath it, but why would such a chamber emerge into a side room rather than near the altar?

'Lady Markoff!' Lajos's voice was louder and more insistent. Silja turned her head to snap at him and quiet the merchant. As she did so, she was struck by an even more pungent sample of the bestial musk that permeated the chapel. Lajos was standing near the rows of wooden racks that held the vestments and priestly robes. There was a look of horror on his face. Silja quickly saw why.

The robes were not the white and black of ordained Sigmarites. They were not woven from cloth. Instead the racks held row upon

row of mangy, ill-smelling furs. Silja cast one last look into the
hallway and closed the door completely. Her interest aroused, she
walked across the vestry, joining Lajos beside the reeking garments. Conquering her disgust, she reached out and lifted one of
the furs.

Her loathing was rekindled as the garment flopped open in her
hands and its shape was revealed to her. She dropped the disgusting thing to the floor, but was still unable to tear her eyes
away from it. It was crafted from the furs of dozens, perhaps even
hundreds of rats, the verminous hides stitched together to form a
vile approximation of an immense rodent shape. From the back,
a rope of dried pig intestine curled, ghastly in its semblance to a
giant rat tail.

Silja looked back at the racks horrified by what she was seeing.
The furs were all like the one she had examined, hundreds of
grotesque vermin vestments. She almost leapt out of her skin
when Lajos grabbed her arm.

'Can... can we go now?' Lajos asked, his voice cracking. Silja
nodded, struck mute by the sheer scope of the weirdness they had
discovered. It was insane. What possible reason could there be to
craft one such hideous raiment, much less hundreds of them?
And why hide such a loathsome secret in the vestry of a chapel?

'Yes,' Silja finally said. 'We'll go get Mathias. He'll know what to
do.'

'I am afraid that we can't have you leaving us so soon.'

A man stood in the doorway of the vestry, a big brutal looking
man with a bushy beard and smouldering eyes. He had managed
to slip into the vestry while Silja and Lajos's attention was fixed
on the grotesque rat-cloaks. He held a broad-bladed axe in his
hairy hands, looking as if he dearly wanted to put it to use. But
what struck Silja the most was the fact that she recognised him.
Only hours before she had seen this man in the streets of Wyrmvater. He was Naschy, the man who had ridden out to guide
Thulmann to the ruined shrine.

'Try to stop us,' Silja snarled at the axeman, gesturing at him
with her sword. 'I promise to leave enough of you in one piece to
tell me what happened to Mathias.'

Naschy grinned back at her. For a moment Silja thought the
woodsman was going to meet her challenge, but he simply put a
hand against the door behind him. 'I'd stop worrying about the

templar and start worrying about yourself.' Naschy pushed the door open, revealing what was outside in the hallway. Lajos cried out in terror and Silja felt her grip on her sword falter.

'And we meet again, my dear.' Doktor Freiherr Weichs touched his bruised face before allowing his visage to twist into a triumphant sneer. He looked down at the feral shapes surrounding him. 'I was quite excited when my friends caught your scent in here, but, alas, it seems they have their own plans for you.' Weichs's expression became grave and even his voice seemed to tremble as he spoke. 'If that doesn't frighten you, let me assure you that it should.'

THE NIGHT WAS well along when the remnants of the witch hunters' entourage limped back behind the timber walls of Wyrmvater. 'Limped' was a precise term, Thulmann reflected. Following the skaven attack in the ruins, the only horse that had not run off or been killed was Kristoph Krieger's, and the rival witch hunter had resolutely resisted all attempts to share his steed. Thulmann felt his already not inconsiderable dislike for the man swell with every mile that scarred the soles of his boots.

Reinheckel greeted them at the gates of the town, and Thulmann quickly told the burgomeister about the fight in the ruins. Leaving Reinheckel to organise his men to track down Naschy, if the man was stupid enough to return, Thulmann's weary party returned to the Splintered Shield.

The witch hunter made his way slowly up the stairs, his mind turning over everything that had happened. There was something wrong, something that worried at the edge of his mind, dancing from his grasp every time he tried to seize it and make sense of it.

Thulmann paused outside Silja's room. The woman must be sound asleep not to have stirred at the noise of their return. He considered leaving her alone, but decided that Silja would be slow in forgiving him if he delayed in letting her know he was all right. He rapped against the portal, waited for a response and then tried again.

After receiving no reply, Thulmann tried the door. He was surprised to find it open, but even more surprised to find the room empty. Out of habit, he stepped inside, eyes scouring the room for any hint of something amiss. They soon settled on the faint ruddy stains on the bedding and floor.

'Silja!' Thulmann called out. He tore open the wardrobe, half expecting more plague rats to spill out and set upon him with their diseased fangs, but there was nothing inside except for Silja's riding clothes.

'Silja!' he roared. He'd been a fool to let her out of his sight. He should have known Weichs would not give up. It was like Anya all over again. He could almost feel his heart wither as that long ago tragedy stabbed through him.

'Silja!' Thulmann cried tearing through the woman's room and rushing into the hallway. He found Ehrhardt, his armoured breastplate still fastened around his hulking chest running towards him.

'Brother Mathias, what is ill?'

'Lady Markoff, have you seen her?' Thulmann demanded, grabbing the Black Guardsman's arm with a grip that whitened his knuckles. The witch hunter turned his head as he heard bodies rushing up the stairs. Krieger and Haussner stared at him, drawn by his cry of alarm.

'We have bigger problems. Take a look outside,' Krieger said. Thulmann released Ehrhardt and turned towards the window. The Black Guardsman followed his gaze.

'It looks like the entire town is out there,' Ehrhardt muttered, 'and they don't look happy.'

Mobs of townsfolk, armed with everything from farm tools to old dwarf axes and swords, were prowling through the streets, closing on the inn from all sides. As Thulmann watched, a voice called out and the mob came to a halt. Two figures emerged from the ragged masses.

'Looks like we found Naschy faster than you expected,' Thulmann commented, drawing a scowl from Krieger.

'Why don't you go out and collect him for me?' Krieger retorted. It was obvious that Naschy was far more than a lone renegade, that the skaven had more than a single traitor among the populace of Wyrmvater.

The treacherous guide poised arrogantly, hands on his hips. There was a smirk beneath his beard. He shouted at the men inside the inn. 'I don't know how you escaped, but you won't do so again.' Naschy pointed to the angry mob of townsfolk. 'We have you surrounded, outlanders. Surrender or be destroyed!'

The guide's body suddenly shuddered as thunder sounded from the inn. A smoking hole erupted from his breast. Even before the echo of the shot could register, a second bullet slammed into Naschy's face. The guide howled in agony, dropping to the cobbles as his body spasmed and life oozed from his frame.

Thulmann glanced at Krieger across the barrel of his smoking pistol. 'Mine struck first.'

Krieger holstered his own smoking weapon. 'Mine was a head shot.'

Outside, Naschy's sudden and brutal death had caused townsmen armed with crossbows to stalk to the front of the mob. Krieger slammed the inn door shut an instant before several bolts slammed into it.

'Any ideas?' he asked Thulmann. 'I don't think a brace of pistols is going to keep them off for long.'

'The first ones through that door won't live to boast about it,' Ehrhardt swore. The knight had recovered his sword and his helmet from the room above. He might have presented an amusing sight, his torso and head encased in steel, his limbs clothed in his quilted surcoat, but Thulmann knew there was nothing amusing about a Black Guardsman preparing for battle. A look through the inn's window, however, dimmed some of his confidence.

'They won't need to,' Thulmann warned. Outside many of the townspeople had started lighting torches. They had no intention of assaulting the inn. They would simply burn them out.

'Let them get their fire started,' Krieger advised. 'Once the smoke gets going it'll provide us some cover from their archers. At least a few of us might stand a chance of getting away.'

Thulmann nodded sombrely. It was a thin chance, but better than throwing their lives away in a reckless, headlong charge, or staying put and getting roasted. He drew his unspent pistol and recovered his sword.

The torch-bearing peasants were beginning to gather. Thulmann could hear them shouting and yelling as they tried to work up their courage for the attack. Then they fell silent. Thulmann could see a dark, spindly figure emerge from the shadows beside the town bakery. There was something repulsively familiar about that shape. The figure spoke with the torch men and then indicated a wheelbarrow being rolled out from the alleyway. The torch carriers handed their brands to others in the mob and converged on the wheelbarrow, fetching up what looked to be small pots or bottles.

Then the spindly figure turned towards the inn and Thulmann saw his face. Hate flooded the witch hunter's body. He fired his unspent pistol, but the distance was too great, the shot striking one of the townsmen in the shoulder instead of the lean, elderly visage of his intended target. The stricken man cried out, dropping the pot he held. The vessel shattered on the stone road, spilling a thin grey vapour into the air. The mob parted to either side of the vapour. The man who had dropped the pot was unable to escape the fumes, crumpling soundlessly to the road.

'Weichs!' Thulmann screamed, pulling powder and shot from his belt in a frenzy to re-arm his weapons. After so many months, after all the horror and the atrocities he had witnessed this man perpetrate, he finally laid eyes on the monster once more. The plague doktor was just beyond his reach, but Thulmann wouldn't let him slip away again. He couldn't, not after everything he had done, not after...

Silja was dead. The possibility he had refused to even consider now seared through his soul as hideous, abominable truth. The blood traces in her room, the treachery of Wyrmvater, it all added up to the same thing. Silja was dead and Weichs was responsible.

Ehrhardt grabbed Thulmann's arm as the witch hunter dashed towards the door. He struggled to restrain Thulmann, to keep him from the suicidal charge he was planning. The witch hunter tried to pull away, turning to strike the knight with the butt of his pistol. At the last instant he realised what he was doing and arrested the blow.

'You can't get him that way, Mathias,' Ehrhardt said.

'I have to try,' Thulmann growled, struggling to pull away.

'Here they come!' Krieger shouted. Thulmann freed himself from Ehrhardt's grip, but the knight's words had soothed some of the red fury in his soul.

Thulmann watched as the pot carriers sprinted towards the inn. He aimed one of his hastily reloaded pistols and brought one of the runners down. As before, the pot disintegrated as it struck the ground, spilling a grey fume from its ruptured frame. One of the other runners was caught in the vapour, dropping as he inhaled the grey wisps. Two men were down, but there were many more, too many to stop.

'I think we were better off when they just wanted to burn us alive,' Thulmann said.

DOKTOR FREIHERR WEICHS watched as the pot carriers converged on the Splintered Shield. Pistol shots from within the inn had claimed a few of them, but they were casualties Wyrmvater could easily afford. There were more than enough left to deliver their noxious cargo. The inn would soon be filled with the grey fumes, a concoction Weichs had spent many months perfecting. He used it to subdue unruly subjects when he needed them compliant and pliable. He'd never considered that his sleep-inducing vapour might have any sort of military application.

Weichs grinned as he watched the pot carriers hurl their weapons at the inn. As he had instructed them, each man tried for a different window, so the saturation of the fumes within the structure would be maximised. Five, then ten, then still more of the clay pots went crashing through the windows of the inn. Soon grey mist was billowing behind the windows, obscuring any hint of what might be within.

The plague doktor began to tick away the seconds, mentally, as they passed. A full grown man might take perhaps a minute to succumb, depending on how much of the fume he had inhaled. He'd give the witch hunters at least five times that long. It didn't pay to underestimate such men. Skilk had learned that in Wurtbad.

Thinking of the grey seer soured Weichs's sense of triumph. The skaven sorcerer-priest was growing more deranged and erratic with every passing day. As the time for its great ritual drew closer, Skilk seemed to withdraw ever further into a paranoid realm of its own imagination. And what if that great ritual failed? What if after all it had put him through, the damnable *Das Buch die Unholden* had deceived him after all?

Weichs looked back at the inn. There was an Arabyan proverb about making use of an enemy's enemy. It was dangerous to contemplate, but not considering it might be more dangerous still.

The plague doktor watched in amazement as the front door of the inn crashed open. A huge figure, his chest enclosed in black armour, staggered from the Splintered Shield. In one arm he carried a massive sword, under the other he bore the insensible body of a man Weichs knew only too well. Blind panic swelled up within him. It was impossible for anyone still to be mobile after such a lengthy exposure to the fumes. Then he paid closer attention to the slow, clumsy steps of the armoured giant. Weichs bellowed an order to the crossbowmen.

'Hold your fire!' Weichs screeched. The bowmen cast questioning looks at him, but obeyed just the same. Weichs had taken pains to take these men alive; he didn't want all that work undone at so late an hour. He felt the mob release a sigh of relief as the huge warrior at last stumbled and fell, admitting defeat at last.

'Now, Mathias Thulmann,' Weichs hissed. 'You are mine.'

CHAPTER THIRTEEN

AWARENESS SLOWLY STRUGGLED to overcome the blackness swirling inside Thulmann's mind. His head felt as if a goblin was inside it pounding on a drum. And why did it sound like someone kept calling his name? He found he was unable to move his arms or legs. Something was restraining him, something that felt uncomfortably like ropes drawn tight around his body. He tried to open his eyes but found them heavy. It was an effort to force them to obey.

'Mathias?'

Thulmann finally forced his eyes open. The first thing he saw was Silja's face. It was filthy with dirt and grime, her hair caked with dried blood, eyes bloodshot either from emotion or fatigue. She had never looked more beautiful to him. He groaned with relief as he saw her, feeling a great darkness lift from his soul. He forced a reassuring smile onto his face, trying to hide the concern that had been tormenting him.

'Well, at least you're in one piece,' he said, looking Silja up and down. Her clothing was torn, her body bruised and battered. Heavy ropes bound her legs together, more ropes lashed her arms to her sides, and still more fastened her to the straight-backed chair in which she sat. Thulmann tried to move again and concluded that he was similarly restrained.

'I told you I'd look out for her.'

Thulmann shifted his gaze, finding Lajos tied in a chair beside Silja. The strigany sported a black eye but otherwise looked none the worse for wear.

'You're doing a great job, Lajos,' Thulmann said. 'I'll be sure to have you do it again.' The attempt at humour brought a faint smile to Silja's face.

'Are you all right?' she asked. 'When they brought you in we thought you were dead.'

Thulmann considered the question. His lungs felt odd, as if they were coated in fuzz and there was a coppery taste in his mouth. He'd taken more than a few breaths of the plague doktor's concoction, they all had. He tried not to think about the many examples of Weichs's diabolic craft that he had seen during his long hunt, tried not to consider the changes the madman's gas might be causing inside him. 'I'm fine,' he said. 'Best sleep I've had in years. I really should thank Weichs. Right before I light his pyre.'

Thulmann glanced around him. Now that most of the drowsiness had drained from him, he took a more interested look at their surroundings. The room they were in was quite familiar; they were inside Wyrmvater's town hall. He found that Krieger, Haussner and the flagellants were tied to chairs in a row behind him. To either side he found the still slumbering figures of Gernheim and Ehrhardt. Their captors had used chains instead of ropes on the Black Guardsman. It seemed they were taking no chances with the knight.

Thulmann turned to face Silja again. 'Weichs got you too?' he asked. Silja nodded her head.

'After you left, I spotted Weichs in the crowd. We chased him but he got away. When we got back to the inn, someone locked us in the room. Lajos made short work of the lock,' the comment caused the strigany to stare sheepishly at his feet, 'and we noticed something strange going on at the chapel. Matthais... it wasn't just Weichs! There were... things... monsters!'

'Skaven?' Thulmann's voice was sharp, a sick feeling growing inside him. 'Underfolk?'

Before Silja could answer, the door to the room opened. Thulmann twisted his head around to see who had entered. He saw a grinning Reinheckel, his robes of state swirling around him.

Several militia men and Curate Andein, now wearing the white robes of a Sigmarite priest, milled around behind the burgomeister. The strange headpiece he wore, looking like a fur hat with ram horns fastened to its sides, was anything but a talisman of ordained Sigmar worship.

'That would be telling, now, wouldn't it?' Reinheckel said. The burgomeister walked around the rows of chairs, resting his hand on Thulmann's chair. 'Tell me, witch-smeller, how do you find the hospitality of Wyrmvater now? Is everything satisfactory, m'lord?' Reinheckel laughed at his own joke, provoking awkward chuckles from his men. 'We even held onto your woman and this strigany weasel for you. Wasn't that considerate?' Reinheckel began to pace once more, coming up behind Silja's chair. She shuddered as the burgomeister leaned over her shoulder, still facing Thulmann. 'Though I must admit I'm rather tempted to keep her for myself.' He patted her cheek, laughing as Silja jerked away from his touch. Reinheckel stepped back and sighed.

'You realise of course that assaulting a templar is a crime against the Temple of Sigmar,' Thulmann said. 'That makes it heresy, punishable by several forms of death. All of them unpleasant.'

Reinheckel laughed again and this time the amusement of his soldiers wasn't forced. Even the old priest with the sinister headdress laughed.

'I think you will find, Herr Thulmann, that we are most religious here in Wyrmvater.' Reinheckel walked slowly back towards the door. 'Most religious indeed. In fact, we were about to renew our sacrament to our lord. You might find it interesting.' He snapped his fingers, causing the militia men to fix their attention on him.

'Take them to the temple.'

COLD, LIFELESS EYES stared at Streng, frozen in an expression of surprise and accusation. The knife wound running across the corpse's belly had bled the life from the man some time ago, but all the same he had been a long time in dying. Streng had no regrets; he didn't care a jot for what the dead bastard had thought about him during his lingering death. He only wished the scum hadn't been able to crawl so far after Streng had gutted him. He was out past the rocks and well within sight of his friends, and their arrows.

The attack had come shortly after the onset of night. The ambushers had been quiet for several hours, only firing if it looked like Streng might try to break from cover. Then, without warning or reason, the bowmen had set a sustained volley clattering against the rocks. Streng knew that they were trying to keep his head down for some reason. He also knew that if they had a friend creeping up to flush him out, he would hardly do so with arrows whistling around his ears. The ex-soldier took note of the direction of the bowfire and braced himself for the coming assault.

For all their murderous intentions, the men who had ambushed him were amateurs. Streng was ready for the backstabbing assassin, springing upon him before he even rounded the boulder. A bit of gory knife-work and Streng dropped back into cover before the lurking archers could recover from their surprise.

Streng listened while the man he had killed cried out in agony, begging the archers to carry word back to his wife and children. *Too bad, you murderous shit,* Streng thought. *If things had played out your way, it'd be my blood soaking into the ground.*

The archers maintained their vigil through the night. With just two of them, though, Streng guessed they wouldn't try sneaking up on him again. Still, he wished he'd been able to strip the hunting bow from the dead one's body just to make sure. Exactly what they would try, Streng wasn't sure, and as the hours stretched, his anxiety began to increase. It seemed almost as if they were playing for time.

A few hours after dawn, Streng had his answer. A group of scruffy-looking men appeared on the road, heading towards Streng's dead horse. The remaining ambushers hailed the trio, waving them over to their position in the meadow. Streng swore loudly. Even if they were amateurs, now there were enough of them to do the job properly.

Streng rubbed at his eyes, trying to fight the sleep tugging at him. The bastards in the meadow had probably slept in turns during the night. The mercenary spat into the dirt and turned his attention back to the dead man. The body was close, so damnably close. He could see the tightly strung hunting bow looped over the body's shoulder, the quiver of arrows hanging from his back. With that weapon in his hands, he might just be able to make his enemies pay a heavy price if they thought to storm his refuge.

The thug looked back across the meadow at his attackers. For the moment they were busy explaining the situation to the newcomers. He looked back at the corpse, judging the distance.

'Why the hell not?' he grunted, launching himself from his refuge and towards the corpse. He heard the ambushers cry out in alarm as he broke cover; another instant and their arrows would be flying. Streng's flesh crawled in anticipation of an arrow striking home. The mercenary dived before reaching the dead man, rolling him onto his side, using the corpse as a gruesome shield. He felt the body shudder as an arrow struck it. He held it fast, wrapping his arms around its waist and began to crawl backward towards his refuge, taking it slowly to keep the body between himself and the archers.

Streng heard his attackers cry out again. He gritted his teeth and swore. If they decided to charge him now, there wasn't a thing he could do about it.

After half a minute of desperate, agonising effort, Streng dragged himself and his shield back behind the boulders. The mercenary breathed a sigh of relief, hurriedly pulling the quiver from the corpse. Then he froze. Why were those bastards still shouting?

No, they weren't shouting. They were screaming, screaming like the damned.

Streng risked peering from behind the boulders. Someone, no something, was attacking the assassins. Something Streng hoped never to set eyes on again.

It might have borne more resemblance to Gregor Klausner if there had been any suggestion of life in the ghostly pallor of its flesh, if the feral expression spread across its face had borne the faintest suggestion of humanity, if it hadn't torn the arm off one of the attackers clean from the socket and wasn't now using it to cudgel the others. The fingers of its lean, almost skeletal hands ended in claws, black talons that were swiftly painted crimson as they tore the throat out of one of the hunters.

Vampire. It was a word that struck terror on an almost primal level, offending the very core of the human psyche. Yet it was the merest echo of the true horror evoked by the appearance of one of their fell kind. Streng felt it fully as he watched Gregor butcher his way through Kipps and his friends. He broke from his cover, running for the woods, injury and fatigue replaced by stark terror.

He'd faced vampires before, but never alone. Streng prided himself on being a man who placed his trust in no one, be they god or man. Now, for the first time, he appreciated just how much confidence and faith he invested in Thulmann, how much fortitude he drew from the man. Somehow, Thulmann seemed the equal to whatever nightmare the ruinous powers spat from the abyss. There was something about the witch hunter that seemed to assure the triumph of light over darkness.

Streng knew he had no such quality. Alone, before such unholy evil, all he could do was run.

Run, and perhaps pray. If he could remember any of the words.

GREGOR STARED IN disgust at the carnage strewn across the meadow, the debris of five human beings. He looked down at his hands, the fingers splayed like talons, the skin caked in wet, dripping blood. A hideous urge swelled up inside him. He bent his head towards his hands, mouth open, his tongue licking expectantly at his lips.

With a shudder, Gregor recovered himself, hastily wiping his bloody hands on his clothes, furiously trying to get the residue of the massacre from his flesh. The hunger pounded inside his veins, urging him to fall on the wet, ragged corpses scattered about his feet. He sobbed in despair. How could the gods allow such an abomination to walk the land? How could they suffer such a thing to live?

The sound of slow, condescending applause caused the vampire to turn his head. He could see the amused, mocking look on Carandini's face as the necromancer walked towards him. The sorcerer paused to cast an appraising glance at Gregor's victims. 'Nicely done, and in daylight no less. I must say I'm impressed. You really are full of surprises, Herr Klausner.'

'I care nothing for your praise,' Gregor snarled. 'I only want to die.'

The necromancer wiped a stray lock of his greasy hair from his face. 'So you have said. It is a rather tired refrain. Well, if you've had a nice rest, I suggest you get back to work.'

Gregor crossed his arms, glaring at the necromancer. 'No.'

Carandini regarded the vampire with a look of exaggerated disbelief. 'I don't believe I heard that correctly.'

'I said no,' Gregor repeated. 'I won't be a part of this any more. I won't take any more lives.'

Carandini smiled and shrugged his shoulders. 'Have it your way,' he said. He turned his face upwards, shielding his eyes with his hand. 'Tell me, how are you enjoying the sun this bright morning? Does it burn? Does it make your skin itch? It will do far worse to you as time goes on, as your humanity withers away and the taint of the vampire consumes everything that is left. Eventually the sun will wither your flesh like salt on a slug. You'll be a thing of the night, body and soul.'

Gregor looked down, feeling a great weight pressing down upon him. Carandini always knew just what to say, what to do to crush his spirit, to cow his defiance. 'I only want to die.'

'As you are?' Carandini scoffed, 'as an unholy blood-worm, feeding on the living to maintain the semblance of life in your unclean shell? You already know how fleeting such a "death" may be.' The necromancer shifted his gaze to the distant tree line. Something flew out from the darkness of the woods, something black and winged, cawing and croaking as it flew. The reek of rot and decay impacted against Gregor's senses as the thing circled the necromancer.

The horrible thing landed on Carandini's shoulder. It had been a crow… once. Its black feathers were crusted with decay, and the eyes in its skull were tiny, blind dots oozing pus. Carandini called the horrible carrion crow his 'eyes'. He'd created several of the hideous things since they had left the banks of the River Reik, employing a spell he had 'borrowed' from the grimoire of a necromancer named Simius Gantt, the infamous Crow Master of Mordheim. Now the abominable corpse-thing pressed its beak to Carandini's ear, as if trading words with its master.

'Our friend tells me there is still no sign of the witch hunter,' Carandini reported with a sigh. 'It seems we must content ourselves with his lackey.' They had come upon the standoff between Streng and his ambushers during the night, driven to the place by the vision Carandini had evoked from Nehb-ka-Menthu's spirit. Carandini had decided to wait, to see if Streng's master would arrive to rescue his henchman. Only when it looked as if things would favour the men from Wyrmvater had he at last given Gregor the order to intervene.

Gregor looked at the dark, brooding treeline into which Streng had retreated. To his unclean vision, the darkness seemed warm and inviting. He struggled to resist its lure, just as he had fought back the unholy thirst and every other filthy abnormality the poison in his body sent screaming through his mind.

'The sooner you go and fetch him, the sooner we can start seeing about curing you,' Carandini said, prodding the vampire with his oily words. Gregor faced the necromancer, nodding his head slowly and then turned and stalked off into the forest's inviting shadows.

With every step, he could feel a little more of him rotting away, oozing from him like the corrupt fluids from the carrion crow.

Gregor wondered how much of himself there was left to save.

THEY WERE LAID out in a row, thrown into the first line of pews facing the sanctuary of the chapel. Bound hand and foot, the witch hunters and their associates had been carried into the temple like sacks of grain. After depositing their burdens, their captors had withdrawn, busying themselves with the ghastly transformation that was occurring all through the chapel. A large group of Wyrmvater's citizens were hurrying around the chapel, strange burdens in their hands. As Thulmann watched, they began setting their burdens against the walls, fixing them in place on small hooks. Thulmann felt sick as he saw the things – stretched skins upon which the scratch-dash script and icons of the underfolk had been daubed in crimson ink. The fact that some of the hides still bore hair or displayed facial features left the witch hunter no illusions what had served the degenerates as parchment.

Thulmann felt his revulsion increase as Andein emerged from the rear of the chapel, a ghastly idol held reverently to his breast. The witch hunter didn't like to consider from what the vile thing had been cobbled together, it was revolting enough for him to realise what it was meant to represent. The devotion with which the curate bore his burden became all the more abominable. Thulmann had uncovered many a cult of perverted, diseased madmen, but he had never expected to see this, never dreamed that men could allow their minds and souls to decay so far.

How could any human being bow his knee before the infernal horror of the vermin god? How could any man make obeisance to the corrupt father of the skaven? What sane mind gave their soul to the gnawing hunger of the Horned Rat?

Isolated madmen, driven by their own greed and lust for power, tempted to betray their own race by the promises of the scheming underfolk, this was something Thulmann could accept, something he had seen before. But here was an entire community, an entire society that had given itself to the cult of the Horned Rat.

As Thulmann watched, Andein set the ghastly effigy of his daemon god on the altar, prostrating himself before it. Such was their contempt for Sigmar, the cultists hadn't even bothered to remove any of the talismans of his worship, content to let the holy hammer rest in its customary place even as the fanged eidolon grinned across the sanctuary.

The congregation of heretics finished dressing the temple to suit their profane sacrament, paying no heed to the enraged shouts of Haussner and his flagellants. They were certain of the power and providence of their scurrying god, having long ago abandoned any fear of Lord Sigmar, much less his devoted servants. As the townsfolk strode back towards the pews, they retrieved hideous furred garments, loathsome rat-skin cloaks. When they put them on, Thulmann felt his revulsion rise. They looked like shabby, horrible imitations of skaven, men transforming themselves into parodies of rats even as the skaven race was a twisted shadow of man himself. Each garment sported strange cuts, cuts that exposed the sickly, diseased malformations that infested nearly every one of the town-folk, the corrupt taint of mutation. The mutants flaunted their abnormalities, revelling in the horror of their flesh. Many put the mutations of the little girl Haussner had tried to burn to shame in their repugnance.

Bruno Reinheckel forced his way through the congregation, one of the rat-hide cloaks draped around his shoulders. The burgomeister sneered down at his prisoners.

'You should feel privileged,' Reinheckel said. 'We've given you the place of honour, right up front near the altar. Normally my family and I sit here.'

'Heretic filth!' Haussner spat. 'You dare defile a shrine of Lord Sigmar with this abomination? Sigmar will rot your flesh for this blasphemy!'

Reinheckel smiled at the fanatic's outburst, turning to display his back to his prisoners. A long cut in the rat-hide cloak displayed the lumpy, bubo-ridden skin that clothed Reinheckel's body. 'The Horned One already has,' the burgomeister declared, 'but in Wyrmvater we do not revile the touch of the gods, we do not cringe at the gifts they see fit to bestow upon the flesh. We accept them. We honour them.'

'You honour madness,' Krieger hissed. 'By Sigmar's hammer, I've uncovered the most diseased, depraved madmen in my day, seen the most unholy of cults, but you've managed to distinguish yourself. Your town outshines even the lowest of them.'

The burgomeister shook his head, laughing. Then he straightened, striking Krieger across the mouth. 'I think I've borne enough of your insults, Altdorfer. I know that my community has.'

Krieger glared at the smirking Reinheckel, hate smouldering in his eyes. Somehow, someway, he'd pay the peasant back for his temerity.

Thulmann's gaze was drawn back to the altar. The curate had returned, bearing with him a large bronze bell. Horrible designs and symbols were engraved into its surface and from its midsection, the sculpted visage of a rat with antler-like horns stared at him.

'How, Reinheckel?' Thulmann asked. 'How does an entire community become so debased as to worship such obscenity?'

The burgomeister moved away from Krieger, looking down at Thulmann. 'Wyrmvater has a long and distinguished history,' he began. 'You read some of it for yourself in those books I allowed you to see, but you didn't find all of Wyrmvater's history there. No, not all of our history. You didn't read about what it was like when civil war gripped the Empire, when Imperial crowns graced the heads of nobility in Altdorf and Marienburg and Middenheim. In those days it was not the depredation of the orc or the wolf we had to fear, it was the hand of our fellow man that threatened Wyrmvater. Companies of soldiers would set upon Wyrmvater, taking what they wanted, killing what they did not. It mattered little to them whether they wore the colours of Reikland and the emperor in Altdorf. They came with sword and pike, to steal food for their bellies, blankets for their steeds and leather for their feet. Year after year, this town was despoiled, forced to toil all year in the fields only to starve in the winter. Cries for help did nothing, none would raise their hand against the soldiers. The baron who exacted a tithe from this town stayed behind his castle walls, content to ignore our plight so long as there was enough left for him to claim as tribute. The people turned to the gods, praying to them for mercy.'

Reinheckel spun, stabbing a finger at the fanged idol resting on the altar. 'One of the gods answered the prayers of my forefathers, witch hunter. The Horned One sent his holy children to strike down the pillagers, to deliver our town from its misery and suffering, to free us from the corrupt tyranny of a corrupt land. All that was asked of the town was its devotion and tribute to feed his sacred children. Wyrmvater had given both before, but never to its own benefit. The Horned One was not the baron, not your petty Sigmar. He did not promise things with words, but with deeds. The Horned One would protect us from orc and wolf, and those men foolish enough to think us easy prey. The Horned One has never strayed from his compact with us.'

'All it cost you was your souls,' Thulmann said, 'your souls and your humanity.' Reinheckel laughed.

'More wisdom from your weakling god, templar? Where is Sigmar now? Why does he not brave this temple that was once his to deliver his servants? I shall tell you: because he dares not, because he cowers before the might and glory of the Horned One!'

'The Horned Rat cares little for its "sacred children". How much less must it regard men stupid enough to offer it their prayers? It has promised the skaven will inherit the world, not the deluded madmen of some Reikland backwater!'

Reinheckel snarled in outrage, drawing the knife from his belt. He moved to lunge at Thulmann, but was kept from his attack by Andein's restraining hand.

'It is not for us to destroy these infidels,' the fallen curate admonished Reinheckel. 'Their fate is the prophet's to decide.'

The curate turned away, retrieving the heavy bell he had brought into the sanctuary. Thulmann felt his mind cringe as the curate struck it, sending a noxious, brassy note reverberating through the chapel. Andein allowed the last echoes of the note to fade and then struck it again, still harder than before. Twelve times, the priest struck the bell, each time the notes sounding louder and more strident. Thulmann thought his skull would crack by the time the curate finally struck the twelfth note. By then Lajos was already moaning in agony, one of the flagellants had started to froth at the mouth and Haussner had lost consciousness. Then, as the echoes of the twelfth note began to fade, a thirteenth note sounded. Not from the curate or his bell, but from deep beneath the sanctuary. Thulmann saw a section of the floor sink, vanishing into darkness. The verminous reek flooded into the chapel, threatening to smother him with its overwhelming stench. The people of Wyrmvater began to hiss and squeal in excitement and adoration, attempting a perverse rendition of the skaven language. Thulmann shook his head at their delusion. The ringing of the bell was no sacred ritual, it was a warning to their inhuman masters, a sign that all was safe in the sanctuary and that the underfolk might emerge from their burrows.

A black, furry head poked its way from the hole in the floor, sniffing the air with its rodent-like snout. The ratman crawled its way into the chapel. Half a dozen of its kin followed, spears and halberds gripped in hand-like paws. They adopted wary, guarded poses, casting nervous glances not only at the congregation and their prisoners, but also at the hole from which they had emerged. After a moment, something else followed the stormvermin into the chapel, something with horns curling from the sides of its rat-like skull. The grey seer's eyes actually glowed with a greenish light, one black furred paw stroking the hairy collar worn around the thing's neck.

Thulmann cursed as he recognised the creature and realised what a fool he had been. It was the grey seer from Wurtbad, the monster named Skilk. Erasmus Kleib had told his nephew where the monster might be found, only too happy to set Thulmann on its trail. But the sorcerer had neglected to tell him one very important detail. The skaven warren wasn't near Wyrmvater. It was *under* it.

The grey seer hobbled from the hole, supporting himself on a wooden staff tipped by an iron icon. The cultists began to howl in adoration as their 'prophet' stepped down from the sanctuary. Skilk paid them no notice, his eyes fixed in the direction of the prisoners. Even with the energies of refined warpstone racing through his body, enflaming his mind, Skilk remembered the witch hunter. A skaven never forgot an enemy, no matter how briefly their paths crossed.

The ratman grinned hungrily, lashing its tail as it drank in Thulmann's scent. 'Hunter-man find much?' Skilk chittered, hobbling forward. There was spittle dripping from its chisel-like fangs, an air of ravenous menace on its rancid breath. Silja cried out in loathing as the monster came close. 'Hunter-meat find words?' The grey seer chittered again, its inhuman laughter crawling across the prisoners. Thulmann felt the full extent of his defeat when the skaven pulled a skin-bound object from beneath his tattered robe. *Das Buch die Unholden*, the tome they had come so far and risked so much to find. Skilk drank in the smell of the witch hunter's defeat, savouring the sensation.

'Words tell much,' it chittered again. 'Make Skilk master-Skrittar.' The grey seer stroked the fur collar around his neck again. 'Soon make Skilk master-seerlord! Make Skilk master-skaven! ' Skilk's body trembled as he announced his insane ambition, as the maniacal emotion flooded through him. The grey seer turned, squeaking commands to his stormvermin guards. The muscular ratkin scurried forward.

'Feast much when Skilk made seerlord. Hunter-meat taste nice!'

Thulmann struggled as skaven paws closed around the ropes binding him, pulling him from the pew. Other skaven grabbed Krieger and Silja, dragging them towards the dark hole in the chapel floor.

Reinheckel sneered as the witch hunters were dragged away. The burgomeister emerged from the congregation, walking towards Grey Seer Skilk. The skaven's lips curled back as the man's scent filled his senses, displaying his sharp fangs.

'Revered and holy one, your most unworthy servant prays you find this humble offering satisfactory…' the burgomeister said.

Reinheckel got no further in his explanation. The grey seer had grown weary of his slave's temerity, of his audacity in daring to speak to his master. Almost faster than Thulmann's eyes could follow, Skilk lunged at Reinheckel, sinking his jaws into the man's throat. Skilk shook his head furiously as he worried the wound, the burgomeister gagging and choking beneath the skaven's fangs. The cult howled in horror, but made no move to aid their dying leader. After a moment, the crazed grey seer released his grip, letting Reinheckel crash to the floor, his body sputtering as life fled from it. Skilk raised his bloodied paws to his muzzle, licking the black fur with his pink tongue.

'Take hunter-meat to larder,' the grey seer hissed, savouring the taste of Reinheckel's blood. 'Soon feast much.' The warpstone-laced insanity in Skilk's eyes appeared to intensify. 'Feast much after making ritual. After Skilk make seerlord!'

CHAPTER FOURTEEN

HOT, CLAMMY DARKNESS enveloped them, the stink of decaying meat and the perpetual reek of skaven fur all but smothering them. In the past, Thulmann had invaded the lairs of daemons and the feeding grounds of ghouls. The skaven larder was worse than any of them. A dank burrow had been chewed from the earth deep below Wyrmvater, the cave littered with the mouldering provisions of the underfolk. Barrels and sacks of grain were strewn about in chaotic disarray, some of them sporting growths of white fungus. Carcasses in varying states of decay and dismemberment hung from iron hooks set into the ceiling. Beast, man and even their fellow ratkin, the skaven seemed indifferent to what source they claimed their meat from, at least, usually.

Thulmann looked up as the hulking stormvermin who had been set as guard over them prowled amongst the provisions, taking the opportunity to steal the odd handful of rotting corn or to nibble on one of the hanging carcasses. The ratman's master, Grey Seer Skilk, appeared to have a special end in mind for the witch hunter and his companions, something he prayed to Sigmar would be quick at least, although he knew any mercy from them would be unlikely.

'Do you think we have a chance?' The voice was soft, barely a whisper. Thulmann could only just make out Silja's outline in the darkness, but he could see that her body was trembling.

'Have faith in Lord Sigmar,' Thulmann replied. 'Faith and courage are what separate us from these vermin. If it is our hour, then at least we can deny this scum the satisfaction of seeing our fear.'

The skaven guard was suddenly looming over Thulmann in the darkness. The monster's paw slashed across the witch hunter's face. 'Hunter-meat be quiet!'

Long hours passed in the pit of horror, slowly wearing away at them all. Lajos Dozsa, never the bravest of individuals had started sobbing and moaning, much to the amusement of their captor. The incessant prayers of Haussner and his men were less entertaining for the guard, but even after repeated abuse, Haussner persisted. At last the vindictive ratman let the fanatics alone, trying his best to ignore them. Beside him, Silja contrived to squirm closer to Thulmann, at last managing to touch his side with her fingers. They both found even so slight a contact comforting.

When the heavy iron door to the larder was opened, the cave was suddenly engulfed in the green glow of the warpstone braziers that lit the tunnel outside. After the darkness, even the weird green light was blinding. Thulmann could hear footsteps entering the larder. It seemed their hour had come. He braced himself to hear the scratchy, gnawing voice of Skilk.

Instead, he was surprised to hear a human voice speaking. The tones were too hatefully familiar to him, however, to draw any hope from it. He should have expected as much. Theirs had been a long game of cat-and-rat. Now that the game was at an end, why shouldn't the winner come to gloat?

'I see you have managed to hold onto them all,' the snide voice of Doktor Freiherr Weichs stated as he paced through the larder. As his eyes grew used to the green light of the corridor, Thulmann could see that the physician had a scented pomander crushed to his nose.

'Doktor-man bad,' the skaven guard hissed. 'Leave! Skaven meat! Not doktor-man meat!'

Weichs smiled indulgently at the guard, trying to hide the fear the ratkin made him feel. 'That is not quite true,' he said. 'In recognition of my great contribution, Skilk... Grey Seer Skilk... has been kind enough to make a gift to me of one of the prisoners.' Weichs turned away from the guard, letting his gaze sweep across the bound figures strewn across the floor. His eyes settled on Thulmann. 'I need more subjects for my experiments, after all.'

The guard whined, but Weichs had evoked the dreaded name of Grey Seer Skilk and it was not about to risk provoking its master. Weichs walked towards Thulmann, the guard creeping along beside him, as if suspicious that Weichs might try to steal some of the provisions while he was in the larder.

'Well, well, well,' Weichs laughed as he stared down at Thulmann. 'We come to the finale at last. Tell me, did you think it would end this way all those months ago when you started your senseless persecution of my work?'

Thulmann glared up at the smirking plague doktor. 'Your work is an abomination, and you are worse.'

Weichs shrugged his shoulders. 'Still, there are worse things than Doktor Weichs in this world,' he said, shifting his gaze towards the guard beside him.

'You'll forgive me if I don't share that sentiment,' Thulmann spat. Weichs sighed and shook his head.

'All I am doing is trying to better mankind, to make the body of man stronger, more resistant to the inimical forces that pollute our world. There are some who dream much nastier dreams, I assure you.' There was something strange in the plague doktor's tone, something that fought its way through Thulmann's disgust and loathing. Almost against his will, he found himself considering what Weichs was saying, the meaning he was trying to convey. Weichs looked down at him, and there was something expectant, almost desperate in his eyes. It was not the look of a man basking in the glow of victory but one cringing in the shadow of fear.

Weichs shook his head again as Thulmann remained silent. 'That was always the problem with witch hunters,' he said. 'They never know when to prioritise.' Thulmann nodded his head ever so slightly. They were all dead anyway, what was there left to lose.

'Doktor-man talked enough.' the skaven guard snapped. It had struggled to follow the conversation, but its command of Reikspiel had not been up to the task. 'Doktor-man fetch subject. Leave!' Weichs turned and smiled at the monster.

'Oh, I am quite finished here,' he said. He dropped the pomander from his hand, the skaven's attention shifting as its eyes were

drawn to the sudden movement. In that instant, the plague doktor's other hand was driving a dagger into the ratman's side,
stabbing deep into its heart. The skaven squeaked in pain and
crumpled into a twitching pile on the floor. Weichs turned to
Thulmann.

'You'll forgive me if I don't applaud,' Thulmann said, displaying
his bound hands. 'I was rooting for the skaven anyway.'

Weichs knelt beside the witch hunter, holding his bloodied
knife to the ropes. 'I find your lack of trust disconcerting. Perhaps
I should leave you to enjoy Skilk's dinner table.'

'Which you would have no problems doing,' Thulmann said, 'if
you didn't need us for something.' He stared hard into Weichs's
elderly visage. 'What is it you want of me, heretic?'

The strength seemed to drain out of the plague doktor. When
he spoke, it was with a voice as timid as that of a child. 'I want you
to kill him for me, templar. I want you to kill Skilk.'

Thulmann's mind raced. Weichs was turning on his patron, on
this inhuman beast that had protected and supported him. 'Why?'

'Skilk is preparing for his great ritual, the spell I translated for
him from that abominable book he took with him from Wurtbad. Tonight he will try to work the magic, try to summon the
spirit of his dead mentor. Through that communion Skilk hopes
to learn the secrets of beyond and use them to gain mastery over
the entire skaven race. If the spell fails, I will pay the price for that
failure. Somehow, I am even more frightened that it will succeed.'

'We'll need weapons,' said Ehrhardt who, like everyone else, had
been listening to the conversation with undivided attention.

'Just outside, in the corridor,' Weichs said. 'I told the skaven I
wanted to examine them. They were all too occupied with preparing Skilk's ritual to question me too closely.'

'All right,' Thulmann agreed. 'We'll kill your rat for you.' Weichs
made no move to cut the ropes.

'One other thing,' the scientist said. 'I am not fool enough to
save myself from Skilk only to die on a witch hunter's pyre. I want
your oath, your solemn oath, that I will go free. Neither you nor
any of your witch hunter friends will seek to restrain me, bring me
to trial or cause me harm. You kill Skilk and then we all go our
own ways.'

Thulmann glared at the plague doktor. The words tasted like
wormwood, but he knew he must say them. It was their only

chance. 'On my honour, Weichs, when this is settled I will not try to stop you.' The words brought a roar of protest from Haussner, a protest that was quickly silenced by Krieger's harsh reprimand.

'Swear it, by Sigmar,' Weichs insisted. Thulmann ground his teeth. He really hadn't wanted to draw his god's attention to his humiliation. Spitting the words from his mouth, he told Weichs what he wanted to hear. Grinning, Weichs cut away the ropes from Thulmann's hands and then rose and crept back towards the door.

'What about my feet?' the witch hunter demanded as he massaged feeling back into his limbs.

'I leave you to attend to those,' Weichs said. 'It is not that I do not trust you, but I'll feel better knowing you are busy freeing your friends rather than haunting my trail. I've left a map with your gear. Follow it precisely and it will lead you to the cavern where Skilk is conducting his ritual. Don't be late.'

With that, the plague doktor slipped away into the green light of the corridor. Thulmann began pulling at the ropes binding his legs, cursing under his breath.

'A devil's bargain, but it had to be done,' Krieger said. 'I will not speak ill of this to Zerndorff.'

'I have graver considerations to occupy me, Brother Kristoph,' Thulmann said, managing to free one of his feet. 'You put whatever you like in your report to Zerndorff... if any of us are still alive to take it to him.'

MONOLITHIC WALLS OF stone encompassed the cavern that sprawled before them, surfaces pitted and scarred where they had been gnawed by pick and hammer over countless centuries. Iron cages were set into the walls, smouldering chunks of warpstone casting their sickly green glow across the underworld. Smaller lights gleamed from the faces of the walls, warpstone deposits the skaven had yet to plunder exuding their corrupt radiance.

'What was that Weichs said about being late?' Krieger pointed into the cavern with the barrel of his pistol. Thulmann followed his fellow templar's lead. They had seen no sign of life since entering the cavern. Even the bloated rats that normally infested any lair of the skaven were not to be found. Picks and hammers were strewn haphazardly around the diggings, forges and smelters standing silent and cold. There was a crawling, malignant force

about the place, something different even from the stifling stink
of the skaven warren, something that seemed to repulse him on
the most primitive, primal level, urging him to keep away just as
it had the rats.

Ahead, illuminated by the glowing fumes billowing from a
dozen iron braziers, Thulmann could make out a large gathering of figures. Most were skaven, their naked tails lashing
nervously behind their slouched bodies. Strewn around them,
transfixed on pikes of steel, were human figures. Perhaps Wyrmvater had earned such a massacre for their diseased worship
of the Horned Rat, but their butchered ruins were dreadful to
behold. They had learned the true nature of their inhuman
'benefactors', too late.

Beyond the mob of ratkin, the black expanse of the crevasse
snaked its way through the centre of the cavern. Great digging
machines stood on one side of the crack, neglected and forlorn.
On the near side of the crevasse stood a great stone altar, pitted
and scarred by the passage of time. Around this was an array of
tall iron stakes, a jumble of painted bones hanging from them by
ropes of sinew and chains of steel. Thulmann could see more
bones stacked on the altar, a hideously malformed skull with
great ram horns grinning from atop the pile. Surrounding the
altar were a dozen robed skaven, each of them sporting the
grotesque horns that marked them as disciples of the Horned Rat,
a collar of fur surrounding their necks marking them as members
of the Skrittar. These chanted and hissed, banging the ground
with their staffs.

Skilk stood behind the altar. Even across the distance that separated them, Thulmann could feel the grey seer's aura of triumph
and exultation. The skaven's eyes were afire with expectation,
ambition drooling from his muzzle. Skilk held *Das Buch die
Unholden* in his paws, gripping it as if it was some sacred talisman.
Weichs stood to one side of the grey seer, his face even paler than
it had been during his visit to the larder. The plague doktor's
mouth was moving as he read from a bundle of papers he held,
but what he read was smothered by the sound of the chanting
Skrittar priests.

'Looks like they persuaded the good doktor to participate after
all,' Silja observed, venom in her voice. Thulmann looked over at
her and nodded.

'Just be thankful he didn't tell them about us,' the witch hunter said. 'Skilk must have almost every skaven in the warren down here.'

'And you honestly expect to kill them all?' asked Captain-Justicar Ehrhardt. The Black Guardsman was again fully armoured, the steel of his helm making his voice sound cold and inhuman.

'Not all of them,' Thulmann confessed, 'just Skilk. We kill him, we can at least hold our heads high when we get to the gardens of Morr.' There had been some discussion about trying to escape the skaven warren after Weichs had released them, to get to the surface and come back with an entire garrison of Reiksguard. Krieger had been a rather vocal proponent of such a tactic, finding heartfelt support from Lajos. He wished he could have shared such optimism, for Silja's sake, but he could not allow the illusion to linger. Thulmann and Ehrhardt were under no illusion as to how slim any chance at gaining the surface was. The memory of Wurtbad and the warren beneath its streets was too fresh in their memories to forget the confusing labyrinth even a small skaven stronghold made.

Thulmann turned from the other witch hunters, placing a hand on Silja's shoulder. Driest's Hochland rifle was among the weapons recovered by Weichs. Thulmann had appropriated the weapon for Silja's use. With Streng gone, the woman was the best marksman among them. They had both heard the extravagant claims Driest made about the range his weapon could cover, but now was not the time to put such claims to the test. 'We will distract them. If you get a decent shot at him, take it. You may not get a second chance. I am counting on you.' Silja started to reply but Thulmann put his fingers to her lips. Leaving her side on what would soon be a battlefield was hard enough. 'I know you will try your best.'

Thulmann unlimbered his pistols, handing them to Lajos. He looked down at the strigany merchant. 'I am putting her in your care again, Lajos. Keep the vermin off her as long as you can.' The witch hunter glared at Lajos. The man seemed to be only half listening to him. Thulmann cuffed the man's ear. 'Did you hear me?'

Lajos rubbed at his bruise, staring meekly up at the witch hunter. 'I... I'm sorry but I could have sworn I heard someone shouting over there. Shouting in strigany!'

Thulmann grabbed the merchant's arm. 'What were they saying?' he demanded.

'Something about making an offering. Offering the "blood of corruption", whatever that might be.'

Screams rose from the centre of the cavern, sharp, shrill and human. Two of the grey seers had stopped chanting, scurrying forward to seize a human cultist who had not yet been slain. Even across the distance, Thulmann could tell it was the mutant daughter of Kipps.

BREATH CAME TO Streng in hot, stinging gasps. The mercenary's leg throbbed with stabbing pain, protesting in no uncertain terms his fear-fuelled flight from his refuge among the rocks. Streng ground his teeth together, trying to keep his agony silent, trying to keep it from betraying his position.

Crouching among the brambles of a half-dead stand of bushes, Streng tried to collect his thoughts, tried to fight past the fear flooding his mind. If he could not control his panic, he would die. He had to think, had to figure out how he was going to escape, how he was going to elude the inhuman thing stalking him through the shadowy woods.

Every plan he started to formulate quickly collapsed as his mind recalled the ferocity and power of the vampire, as his mind's eye saw Gregor Klaussner standing triumphant above the mangled bodies of the Wyrmvater assassins. Streng chided himself for his terror. Thulmann would not have allowed his fear to control him. The witch hunter would have found a way to prevail against the vampire, to turn panicked retreat into victory, but Streng was not Thulmann.

The mercenary tightened his grip on his knife. There was an uncanny silence in the woods; no bird song, no scurrying of squirrels through the brush, not even the soft rustle of a winter breeze. It was as if the entire world was holding its breath, trying like Streng to remain silent, waiting for some awful thing to pass.

Then the silence was shattered by the harsh, ugly croak of a crow in the branches of a nearby birch tree. Streng fell onto his rump as the sound pounded against his strained senses. He picked himself up angrily, staring murder at the stupid bird that had so unnerved him. Fury turned to fright as the dead, rotting thing stared back at him with white, lifeless eyes. The thrill of terror raced through his veins.

He had been found.

Streng turned to run, to force his battered frame to new effort. If the filthy carrion crow had found him, how much longer before the horror that it served would too? He certainly didn't want to linger and find out. He pushed his way back through the brambles, fighting his way clear of their clawing, clutching thorns. Then he froze, colour draining from his body. It was already too late.

'Gregor,' Streng rasped through lips gone numb with fright. The vampire stared back at him, eyes the colour of old blood, talon-like hands still crusted with gore from his massacre of the assassins. Gregor's pale visage pulled back in a toothy smile, the oversized fangs of the vampire gleaming in the sparse light beneath the trees.

'Come with me,' the vampire said, the stink of the grave in his voice. Gregor extended one of his pallid hands towards Streng, beckoning to him. Streng felt the vampire's will reaching out, clouding his thoughts and smothering his defiance. It would be so easy to just obey.

With a roar, Streng launched himself at the vampire, slamming his knife into Gregor's chest. He'd never allowed himself to be dominated by anyone, not his drunkard father, not the bullying road wardens in his native Stirland, not even the officers in the Count of Ostland's army. Even the gods didn't command his life. He was his own man and he wasn't going to submit to some grave-cheating parasite. The thug's knife dug deep into Gregor's breast, tearing the vampire's unclean flesh, crunching through its rancid ribs.

Gregor snarled, flinging Streng aside with a swipe of his hand. The mercenary slammed into the ground, stunned as all the air fled his body on impact. It was like being kicked by an ox, such was the impossible power within the vampire's withered limbs.

The vampire reached into his chest, pulling Streng's blade from the deep wound the mercenary had dug there. Streng groaned in disgust – he'd missed the monster's heart by mere inches. Gregor lifted the weapon to his face, studying it for a moment before hurling it away in anger. The wound in the vampire's chest wept a sickly thick liquid that was unlike the blood of a mortal man. If the injury impaired the vampire, there was no sign of his pain as he strode towards Streng.

'I don't want to hurt you, Streng,' Gregor said. 'I need you to help me. I need Thulmann to help me.'

Streng struggled to rise from the ground. It felt as if a rib might have cracked when he'd landed, filling his entire side with burning pain. 'Sure,' he wheezed, 'let me get my knife back and I'll help you.' The vampire snarled, pouncing on the injured man, smashing him back to the earth. Streng gagged as Gregor's decayed breath smothered him.

'Sell-sword scum!' Gregor hissed. 'You owe me! You and your master allowed me to become this... this... obscenity. Now you will help me. You will redeem me.'

The mercenary smashed his fist into the vampire's face, breaking Gregor's nose. 'Piss off!' he growled, bringing his other fist cracking against Gregor's cheek. The vampire roared back, seizing Streng's wrist and wrenching it with a savage twist of his hand. The vampire's other hand smacked against Streng's face, breaking teeth and tearing skin. The thug cried out in pain, rolling his head and spitting blood and bone into the grass.

Gregor stared down at his prone victim, watching as the bright glowing warmth trickled from Streng's torn face and bleeding mouth, throwing rich vibrant light into the cold, chill grey of his vision. The vampire could feel the hunger thundering through his veins, the primal urge clawing at his mind. In response to the hunger, he could feel the fangs in his mouth shifting, elongating, and anticipating the swift strike to come. The vampire reared back, opening his mouth in a hungry hiss.

Streng saw Gregor's mouth open, the dagger-like fangs pointing down at him, ready to rip and tear at his throat, ready to drain the life from him. The mercenary struggled to free himself from Gregor's grip, but it was like a rabbit struggling in the jaws of a wolf. Desperately, his good hand groped along the grass, trying to find a stone, a rock, anything that he might use to defend himself. Eyes locked on the murderous, bloody orbs burning within Gregor's face, Streng's questing fingers at last closed around something slender, round and wooden. When he had struck the ground, the quiver he had stolen from the dead assassin had ruptured, spilling broken arrow shafts all around him.

Even as Streng's fingers closed around the arrow, the vampire's head shot downward with the speed of a striking cobra. Streng shuddered, expecting the sharp, diseased bite of the vampire as his throat was torn open and the living corpse drained his life away.

Streng froze as the vampire paused, its deadly fangs only inches from his skin. Suddenly, Gregor recoiled, a look of mortal horror and disgust on the vampire's pale features. A groan of terror rasped from the vampire's body at what he had nearly done, at what he had almost let himself do. He was a man. His mind was his own. He was not Sibbechai. He was not some foul thing of the night. So long as he maintained control, so long as he denied the unclean urges of the corruption within him, he was still Gregor Klausner, not the vampiric fiend the necrarch had damned him to become.

STRENG SAW THE guilt and confusion on Gregor's face. He did not know what strange thoughts tortured the vampire, nor why the monster had relented at the last instant. Nor did he care. He was an old soldier, a veteran of many battles. He knew a prize opportunity when he saw one, and he seized it before it had a chance to escape from him. With a bestial roar, Streng forced himself upwards, using every muscle in his body to drive the arrow into Gregor's chest. He sank the wooden shaft into the still dripping knife wound, twisting his improvised weapon so that it dug deep into the vampire's left breast, skewering the unclean heart.

A wail of anguish shrieked from the vampire's lips as Streng's weapon was driven home. The wracking death rattle trembled through Gregor's body as he collapsed to the ground. Streng pushed the suddenly weak and powerless monster aside, leaving it to thrash out its death agonies on the grass beside him. Streng delivered a savage knee to Gregor's skull when he had struggled back to his feet, the arm the vampire had twisted cradled gingerly against his chest.

'Consider yourself helped,' Streng spat at the expiring abomination. He watched Gregor writhe in agony a few moments longer and then started to hobble back through the woods. He still needed to reach the baron and get Thulmann the troops he would need to purge the skaven lair.

More importantly, after coming inches from death, after being tossed about like a rag doll by an undead horror fresh from the grave, Streng needed a drink, perhaps even two.

* * *

SKILK WAS POISED behind the altar, daubing his black paws into the tiny body strewn across the ground before him. Red droplets fell from the monster's hands as he reached to the bones lying on the altar, gingerly painting the symbols Skilk saw depicted in *Das Buch die Unholden* on them.

Thulmann whispered a prayer to Sigmar and charged towards the skaven. If they could strike while the grey seers were occupied, while they were unable to call upon the hellish sorceries of their daemon god, they might have a chance. But it was a forlorn hope, even if the skaven did not hear the witch hunters approaching, their keen noses caught the scent of their new foes.

The first ratman to close upon Thulmann found itself slashed from shoulder to groin. The witch hunter pushed the shrieking thing from his path, engaging the second as it leapt towards him, opening its throat. He saw a pair of armoured stormvermin hurled back, their bodies broken and twisted as they flew through the air. He was not surprised to see Ehrhardt's armoured bulk beside him, skaven blood already drenching his blade. Haussner and his fanatics crashed into the main body of the melee, striking out wildly with axe and flail. Krieger and Gernheim were closer at hand, fighting to repel the onslaught of skaven warriors swarming towards them.

Thulmann judged the distance between him and the altar, judged how many skaven were between himself and Skilk. It was not a comforting estimate, not the sort of chances any but a follower of Ranald would care to entertain. Silja and the rifle were their only real hope.

SCREAMS AND SQUEALS of agony scratched at the edge of his hearing, the smell of blood, excrement and death pawed at his nose, but Skilk refused to lose his focus. None of it mattered. The ritual was nearly complete. That was what mattered. The door would soon open. Kripsnik's spirit would be forced back into the world: a creature that had crossed the barrier, stood in the presence of the Horned Rat and been privy to a god's secret councils. Such a being would be Skilk's to use, to bend to his will.

The world would change; the skaven would rise from their burrows and consume the weak meat-races of the surface. The underfolk would inherit the dominion promised to them by their god, led not by the squabbling lords of decay, but by one divine underlord, by Grey Seer Skilk, the Prophet of the Horned Rat.

Skilk could feel the power swirling around him; feel the dark energies of the ritual being drawn down from the beyond. He could feel the cavern being infused with power, could see the glyphs it had painted onto the bones glowing with black energy. Skilk could almost hear the barrier between worlds being torn open as the line between life and death was breached.

Then sharp, hot pain exploded within Skilk's brain. The grey seer struggled to remain standing, but strength was draining from him too quickly. Skilk's muzzle snapped open to snarl his protest to the heavens, but all that emerged was a froth of black blood. The skaven crumpled and fell, toppling against the side of the altar, scattering the bones of his long-dead mentor.

THE REPORT FROM the Hochland rifle echoed above the roar of battle thundering from the walls. It seemed to resonate forever, creating an unworldly din. The swirling melee faltered as alarm and confusion filled the combatants. Beady skaven eyes looked around the cavern, trying to find the source of the clamour. Then every eye was drawn towards the altar. Skilk's form lay crumpled against the stone surface, apparently struck down by the gods themselves. The skaven squealed in dismay, stunned that their dread leader should be dead.

Thulmann saw their nervous hesitance, offering up a prayer of gratitude to Sigmar. Silja's aim had been true. The evil of Grey Seer Skilk was no more. Whatever else happened, they would know that they had won. The witch hunter raised his sword above his head, glaring at the skaven that only moments before had been so eager to spill his blood.

'No quarter! No mercy!' he cried, leaping back into the attack. 'For Sigmar!' He heard the cry repeated across the cavern as Haussner returned to the fray and as Krieger split the skull of a snaggle-toothed brute still looking in the direction of its slain master.

Thunder roared from nearby and one of the skaven was hurled back, a hole blasted through its face. Thunder roared again and then Silja was at Thulmann's side, smashing the butt of a pistol into the snout of a stormvermin.

'You should have stayed put,' Thulmann gasped as he parried the blade of a slavering ratman.

'I thought you might be thankful for the help,' Silja replied, slashing open the belly of a mace-wielding skaven with her sword.

'I am more thankful for your aim,' Thulmann said. 'We die well knowing that scum precedes us.'

Silja might have replied, but at that instant a thrill of horror swept through the skaven. For the second time, the monsters abandoned the attack. This time, however, the cause was not one to celebrate.

'But he's dead,' she shuddered. 'I killed him!'

THE SKAVEN WHINED in abject terror, dropping to their bellies, their every muscle twitching in fright. They had smelled the death scent, the scent that never lied. Grey Seer Skilk was dead. Yet now, Grey Seer Skilk stood beside the altar, lip curled in a snarl. In his forehead, a smoking hole still drooled a greasy mixture of blood and brain. It was impossible for Skilk still to be alive.

Part of Skilk marvelled at his survival, but why should he? Had Skilk not been exalted by the Horned Rat himself? Was Skilk not its favoured prophet and apostle? Why should Skilk be surprised when the Horned Rat interceded to preserve its own?

The grey seer turned his eyes towards the melee, searching for the one who had thought to slay him. There were agonies beyond contemplation for that creature, the breeder human with the jez-zail. She had thought to destroy the greatest mind the Horned Rat had ever vested into one of his children. Worse, she had disrupted the ritual, denying Skilk the secrets it could have torn from the spirit of Kripsnik.

Skilk's eyes narrowed as he spotted Silja. The sorcerer-priest began to draw the heavy winds of magic into its verminous frame, weaving the ethereal forces into an extension of its murderous will.

The grey seer's body was wracked by violent spasms as the sorcer-ous energies flowed into it. Skilk felt a mind that was not his own hissing within his brain. The skaven could feel its evil, malicious presence, mocking Skilk as it consumed the energies the ratman gathered. Skilk tried to cut off his conjuration, tried to stop the flow of magic, but it was too late. Something else was in control.

Skilk cast his eyes down, meeting the empty grinning stare of Kripsnik's painted skull. Understanding thundered through the skaven's brain. The ritual had not been a failure. The ritual had been a success, but the soul of Kripsnik had not been content to infest the tired old bones it had worn in life. Kripsnik had demanded a fresher vessel to inhabit.

The presence within Skilk's mind exploded into scratching laughter as the grave mistake Skilk had made was finally realised. Kripsnik had been more powerful than Skilk in life. In death, the lord of Skrittar's power had grown even greater.

Skilk opened his jaws, shrieking his defiance into the uncaring darkness at the fickle favour of his capricious deity.

THULMANN WATCHED IN amazement as Skilk began to draw sorcerous energy into his wretched body. The witch hunter slashed at the nearest skaven, trying to fight his way through them, trying vainly to reach the resurrected grey seer before he could unleash his deadly magic. Even as he stabbed and slashed at his foes, Thulmann knew he would be too late.

Then Skilk started to scream, a sound so filled with agony and horror and the despair of the damned, that even Thulmann felt himself go numb as he heard it. He saw the screaming grey seer's body wracked by spasms, his bones twisting and writhing beneath his skin. Then a jagged, bleeding crack began to spread from the bullet wound in his forehead, snaking down across the grey seer's face, widening as it descended towards its toes. Black stinking blood sprayed from the ghastly stigmata as it widened. Skilk's scream ended in a wet gurgle as his jaws fell apart, hanging limp and ruined from the debris of his face.

Blacker than sin and midnight, two great horns began to rise from the gory ruin of Skilk's head. Straight as lances and twisted like unicorn ivory, the horns rose and rose, until they were nearly as tall as a man. Beneath the horns, a mammoth head thrust its way from the disintegrating rubble of Skilk's body. It was a great rotting visage, mangy fur strung taut across the long-snouted face of an enormous rat. Chiselled fangs the size of swords hung from the abomination's muzzle, while cold, merciless eyes twinkled within the depths of its skull.

Shoulders as broad as the length of a draught horse followed the diabolic head, powerful arms reaching upwards in exultation as they emerged from the puddled refuse of Skilk's carcass. Strange glowing runes were scratched into the pox-ridden skin, large chunks of radiant warpstone pounded deep into its flesh. Torcs and amulets swung from black chains sunk into the beast's chest, exuding their own malefic energies. From the waist down, the apparition was covered in coarse grey fur, its crooked legs ending in monstrous cloven hooves. A scaly tail, yards long and thick as a python, squirmed behind the brute as it howled its malevolence across the cavern.

Vermin lord! A daemon of the great dark, an emissary of the obscene Horned Rat himself! Such things had been recorded seldom by scholars, and even then passed on as perverse myths. Even in his sickest nightmares, Thulmann had never allowed himself to imagine such a malignity. He wondered if even Skilk had imagined the horror he was summoning into the world.

The daemon howled again, stepping out of the gory husk of Skilk as a lothario might step from his discarded breeches. As its cloven hoof crunched against the rock floor, the stone steamed and slithering, rat-like shadows scattered from where it stepped, vanishing into grey vapour as they scurried away from the vermin lord. All within the cavern stood transfixed by the awful presence the daemon exuded, unable to move or even cry out before its aura of dread. The skaven seemed caught between abject terror and grovelling devotion, recognising in this horror the handiwork of their terrible god.

The choice between flight and slavery was decided for them when the hulking beast stretched its clawed hand and closed its talons around the spindly shape of one of the Skrittar. It lifted the squeaking grey seer from the ground and, like a child cracking nuts in his fist, crushed the horned ratman into a black paste.

The shrieking, whining skaven gave no thought to Thulmann and his comrades, scrambling around them as they fled before the malign power of the daemon. The witch hunters were of no mind to stop them. It was all they could do to control their own terror, to stand their ground before the towering daemon. The vermin lord's laughter scratched and echoed through the cavern as it watched the skaven flee before it. Consigned to the darkness beyond, betrayed into death by the paws of its own kind, Kripsnik exulted in his brutal dominion over the ratmen.

Thulmann looked around. The only ones still standing within the cavern were himself and the survivors of his group. Haussner's flagellants were down, victims of the struggle against the skaven.

Lajos was nowhere to be seen, lost in the tide of battle. Haussner sported a grievous wound that split one side of his face and carried on into the remains of his shoulder. Krieger favoured his left leg, the other wrapped tightly in a hastily improvised bandage. Of their group, only himself, Silja and the indefatigable Ehrhardt seemed largely without impairment.

Kripsnik cocked his head in their direction, staring down at them, eyes gleaming with horrific intelligence and wicked mirth. Thulmann was struck again by the size of the daemon, easily three times as tall as any man. The vermin lord seemed to sense their despair, its mammoth jaws opening in a sneer. It spoke, its words clawing the minds of those who heard it, profaning the very souls that endured its susurrations. 'Nice meat not flee. Kripsnik rend filth for Horned One.'

Thulmann felt what valour lingered within him wither as the vermin lord strode towards them, its every step sending tiny ghost rats scurrying into nothingness. There was nothing he could do, nothing any man could do before such horror.

'The voice of the daemon is heard in our land!' The outburst rose from Haussner's ruined lips. The zealot held the *Deus Sigmar* in his mangled left hand, his axe in his right. The crazed light of fanaticism shone in his wild-eyed stare. 'It shall not be allowed to endure. It shall not profane the dominion of Lord Sigmar with its obscenity.'

Haussner charged towards the daemon, armed with nothing more than his axe and his determination. The vermin lord regarded the witch hunter with something that might have been disbelief and lashed out at him with its claw. Haussner was ripped open by the massive talon, split from belly to breast. The fanatic crashed to the ground, wallowing in his own gore.

Somehow, Haussner's crazed charge electrified Thulmann. If a deluded fanatic's faith could be so great, how could he demand less of his own resolve? Better to die a martyr, fighting to the last breath against the ruinous powers, than to flee before them and shame Sigmar with his cowardice. Thulmann tightened his grip on his sword and with an inarticulate roar, charged towards the slavering daemon. Still contemplating the wreck it had made of Haussner, the daemon did not react to Thulmann's attack until the witch hunter's sword slashed into its furry leg, digging deep through its unclean substance. Before his blessed blade, Kripsnik's skin bubbled and smoked, the stink of sulphur adding to the cavern's reek.

The vermin lord snarled in pain, turning its massive body towards Thulmann. The witch hunter braced himself for death as he saw the daemon fix him with its eyes. He imagined the ripping talons of the monster tearing him to ribbons, but the blow never came. Thulmann had not been the only one to be shamed into action by Haussner's death. He saw Ehrhardt's armoured form, dwarfed by the mass of the daemon, chopping at the horror with his enormous sword. Gernheim, too, slashed and cut at the daemon, ignoring the spear-shaft a skaven had thrust into his side as he unleashed his mute fury on the monster.

The witch hunter felt his pride in the heroism of his comrades wither when he saw Silja jabbing at the daemon's flank with a spear she had recovered from one of the dead skaven. He'd been so wrapped up in his own guilt and shame that he hadn't considered that Silja too was menaced by this abomination. He felt his stomach sicken when he saw Kripsnik reach down once more, seizing Gernheim in its claws. The daemon lifted the struggling man to its jaws, snapping its enormous fangs closed around him, biting off the man's head and a massive portion of his torso in one bone-breaking chomp. How easily that could have been Silja's fate.

Thulmann attacked the daemon with renewed ferocity, slashing it savagely with his blade. Unlike the brutal blows of Ehrhardt and Gernheim, the cuts Thulmann dealt seemed to pain the creature, but any hope Thulmann had drained from him as he saw the steaming wounds slowly closing behind his sword. There were few mortal weapons that could do any lasting harm to a daemon's ethereal substance. Even a blade blessed by the late grand theogonist himself was little more than a penknife against a thing like the vermin lord.

Kripsnik swung his massive body around, focusing on the little human slicing away at its leg. The daemon snarled at the impudent little maggot. The daemon leaned down, sweeping its enormous hand along the ground. Silja dodged aside as the daemon's claws flashed past her, but Thulmann, intent on his attack, was too slow in reacting. The back of Kripsnik's hand threw Thulmann, sending him rolling across the ground. The witch hunter stopped himself just as he rolled near the edge of the crevasse, eyes staring into the limitless gloom that stretched away beneath him.

'Templar,' a shrill, terrified voice called out to him. At first Thulmann thought the daemon's blow had rattled his senses, but as he painfully regained his feet, it came to him again. 'Templar, you can't beat him that way.'

'Then I'll die trying, Weichs,' Thulmann hissed. He watched in agony as the vermin lord tried to stomp Silja with its hoof, the woman narrowly avoiding the daemon's pounding step. He searched the ground near him for his sword, settling for a rusty skaven blade when he didn't see his own.

'It will kill her,' the plague doktor said. 'It will kill us all if you don't listen to me!'

This time Thulmann turned to face the heretic. At some point during the melee, Weichs had sought shelter beneath the huge skaven mining machines, cowering beneath their steel frames like a cringing cur. 'Why should I believe you?' Thulmann demanded.

'Because I have read this,' Weichs said. The plague doktor reached beneath his coat, removing the bloodstained bulk of *Das Buch die Unholden*. His own hide hadn't been the only thing Weichs had tried to escape with during the battle. 'I didn't tell Skilk everything. I kept a little back, like how to deal with this horror should it actually respond to his ritual!'

Thulmann glared at the physician. 'Then do so, you scum!' Weichs shook his head.

'I don't have the stomach for that sort of thing. I am quite content to leave that to fools like you.' Weichs returned his hand to the inside of his coat, removing something else from the pockets within. He tossed a small sackcloth bag to Thulmann. 'According to the book, the thing Skilk called into being exists only partially in our world. The rest of it is in whatever hell it came from. Cast the powder in that bag into its face, and it will materialise fully within our reality.'

Thulmann fought down the impulse to hurl the packet into the crevasse. He could feel its cool, clammy evil, the unclean touch of sorcery about it. He glared back at Weichs, fingering the edge of the sword he held.

'Don't you understand! If you make it real, then it will act like any normal beast. It will bleed, templar. Steel will make it bleed!'

Thulmann stared again at the little bag in his hand. It was vile, the foul product of sorcery, the handiwork of a murderous heretic. He couldn't use such filth. There had to be another way, but he knew there was no time to find one. He had to act. The sorcerer's filth was his only chance, their only chance. If he acted now, he could use it to send this abomination back to the abyss. He could force its evil to do good. Briefly, the image of Wilhelm Klausner and the evil he had embraced in the name of good flashed through his mind. The laughing faces of Freiherr Weichs and Erasmus Kleib danced before his eyes, men who had become monsters because they thought they could bring good from evil.

The last of his doubts faded as he saw the vermin lord turn towards Silja. With a howl of savage fury, Thulmann charged back towards the daemon. He tore open the sackcloth, hurling the black powder within into the rat-like face of Kripsnik. The daemon shielded its eyes with its claws, recoiling from the cloud of dust. Thulmann grabbed Silja, pushing her away from the daemon's lashing tail. He waited, watching, expecting something to happen. The daemon did not so much as cry out, instead sneering down at him as the cloud dissipated and it unshielded its eyes. The powder had done nothing. Weichs had lied to him. He'd trusted the word of a heretic and he would die for it.

Then Kripsnik threw back its head, bellowing in pain as Ehrhardt's blade slashed into its leg once more. This time the wound did not close behind the steel. This time thick black blood jetted from the wound. This time tendons parted before the steel, bone splintered and flesh tore. The vermin lord howled as its maimed foot crumpled beneath its weight and it crashed to the ground with a thunderous impact.

Kripsnik reared its head, glaring straight into Thulmann's eyes. It knew what had happened and who had caused it. Thulmann turned and fled as the daemon scurried after him, crawling on all fours like some titanic rat. The witch hunter leapt across the crevasse, joining Weichs on the far side. The vermin lord followed him, lunging across the pit, crashing on the far side with an impact that set the digging machines rattling. Weichs retreated before the enraged daemon, but Thulmann turned and slashed at its face, cutting deep into its muzzle.

With a bellowing roar, Kripsnik lunged for Thulmann, smashing into the mining machines head on. Thulmann was thrown back by the daemon's impact, knocked from his feet as the mining machines shuddered across the floor. The world exploded into a whining, shrieking clamour. Thulmann risked a look back at the enraged daemon. It was only a few yards behind him, but pursuing the witch hunter had become the least of its concerns. In its headlong charge, the daemon's massive bulk had struck the line of machines with the force of a thunderbolt. That impact had driven Kripsnik's body hard against a pointed drill, the fury of its velocity impaling the monster's chest on the device. The violence of its attempt to free itself had somehow caused the machine to become active, the churning drill slowly digging its way deeper and deeper into Kripsnik's struggling bulk.

Thulmann watched as the shrieking, wailing monster tried to pull itself free, oblivious to the path its struggles were leading it. There was almost something human about the expression that came over the vermin lord's features as it suddenly felt its hindquarters hanging over empty space, but Kripsnik's surprise had come too late to aid him. Unbalanced, the hulking daemon fell into the crevasse, the immense weight of the digging machine hurtling after it into oblivion.

As the daemon disappeared from sight, Thulmann could feel the oppression in the air vanish and the chill stink of sorcery fade. However they had been brought about, the powers of Old Night had been driven back.

'Masterful, absolutely masterful.' Thulmann turned his eyes from the crevasse to see Weichs creeping towards him. The witch hunter stalked towards the old man, causing him to recoil in terror. 'Your promise! You swore an oath!' Thulmann glared at the plague doktor, seizing the tome the old man cradled in his arms. Weichs resisted for a second before deciding to relinquish his claim on the tome. The book was a small price to pay for his liberty. Thulmann studied the human-skin binding for a moment and then stuffed it under his arm, trying to contain his disgust. He stared again at Weichs, regretting the desperation that had made him agree to the villain's bargain. Weichs smiled back at him, recognising the frustrated outrage in his expression.

'You aren't going to let him go,' Silja exclaimed. Thulmann turned, discovering with some surprise that Silja and Ehrhardt had crossed the crevasse to join him. The witch hunter shook his head sadly.

'I swore an oath,' he said sadly. Silja gave him an incredulous look, as if doubting his sanity.

'Given to a maggot, a murdering parasite,' she swore. 'Such an oath counts for nothing!' Weichs trembled as the woman turned on him. 'I didn't swear any oath.' Thulmann grabbed her by the arm, pulling her back to him.

'I spoke for you as well as myself,' Thulmann said. 'My oath may not mean anything to you, but it does to me.'

Weichs grinned at the two lovers, smoothing out his coat. He flicked a snide salute to Thulmann and turned to leave. He found his way blocked by Ehrhardt's armoured bulk.

'A templar of Sigmar does not speak for a knight of Morr,' Ehrhardt's sepulchral voice intoned. The knight's armoured gauntlet closed around Weichs's shoulder, lifting him from the ground. The plague doktor turned ashen with terror.

'Stop him, Thulmann! Call him off!' he screamed. Thulmann smiled as Ehrhardt carried Weichs towards the crevasse.

'You heard the man, Herr Doktor,' the witch hunter said. 'The Order of Sigmar has no right to speak for the Black Guard of Morr.'

A litany of curses and pleas rolled from Weichs as he struggled in Ehrhardt's grip. At last the knight stood beside the crevasse. He extended his arm, holding Weichs above the black pit's depths. 'I think I'll let you go after all,' the knight said. 'Morr can be most merciful.'

Weichs's last scream seemed to linger after him as he plummeted into the abyss.

THULMANN HELD SILJA close to him as they made their way back through the carnage. She found his sword lying near the altar and he found one of his pistols lying beneath a mangled ratman's corpse. Ehrhardt made his way over to Krieger, helping the injured man back to his feet. Whatever the Black Guardsman felt about the man, he was not going to abandon him in the black depths of the skaven lair.

As they made their way back towards the tunnels, Thulmann paused beside one of the smouldering warpstone lanterns. He watched its eerie green flames dance and shimmer. Silja sensed the change that came over him.

'What is it?' she asked. He looked at her and then down at the book cradled under his arm. *Das Buch die Unholden* glistened in the unholy light.

'So much suffering, so much death over this abhorrent thing,' Thulmann said, 'so much evil unleashed in the world because of one book, one madman's collection of corruption. It would be so easy to destroy it, here, now.'

'Why don't you?' Silja asked. 'Tell Zerndorff you didn't find it. Tell him you couldn't stop it from being destroyed.'

Thulmann sighed. 'It is a lie that would sit ill with me. For better or worse, Sforza Zerndorff is my superior, his order is my command.' He held Silja tighter. 'He is also a man who has a habit of seeing through deception. He is most zealous in pursuing those who offend him. No place in the Empire would be safe for us if I did that.'

Thulmann felt the warmth of Silja Markoff against him. He felt the clammy chill of *Das Buch die Unholden* under his arm. He watched the green flames flicker and dance.

Even after all these years, he still wanted things both ways.

EPILOGUE

OBLIVION. GREGOR KLAUSNER embraced it eagerly, desperately as his corrupt body slipped back into the death it had perverted. His every waking moment had become a struggle, a battle against the unclean filth within him and the obscenity he had become. How much longer could he have continued that struggle, that hopeless fight to remain human? How much longer before he was a thing like Sibbechai, before in mind as well as body he became one of the accursed undead, a vampire? It was better to die while he was still a man and not a monster.

Harsh grey light banished the darkness of oblivion, the tangy odour of blood exciting his senses, setting the abomination within him on fire. Gregor's tongue licked his lips, finding them coated in warm, wet blood. The vampire could not subdue the hunger, licking his face clean before he could even begin to resist. When the compulsion faded, he reached to his chest, shocked to find that the arrow that had pierced his heart was gone. He turned his head, finding a body lying only a few feet away. For a moment he wondered if against all odds he had managed to overcome Streng even after having his heart skewered, but a closer look showed him the body was not that of Streng, but some poor shepherd. Gregor saw the dead man's youthful face, his features twisted in terror, his life stripped from him in a moment of crimson horror. Gregor hung his head, gripped by misery. He couldn't even remember killing the boy. Somehow that made the murder even more terrible.

'Don't carry on so,' a condescending voice said. 'You didn't do anything to him.' Gregor looked up, finding the necromancer Carandini standing nearby, one of his cadaverous crows perched on his shoulder. 'The poor lad simply had the misfortune to fall on somebody's knife.' The Tilean made a show of replacing his bloody dagger in its sheath.

'Why?' Gregor demanded. The necromancer smiled at him.

'We needed his blood,' Carandini replied. Gregor shook his head.

'No, why did you bring me back?' he asked. 'Why couldn't you let me stay dead?'

'I was tempted,' Carandini warned. 'I must say you disappointed me terribly. That man was injured and unarmed, yet somehow you conspired to let him kill you. One might think you have some kind of death wish.'

Gregor glared at the sneering sorcerer. 'I only want to die. You had no right to bring me back.'

'I thought you might still be useful to me,' Carandini said. 'That was all the reason I needed.' The necromancer removed a small silver icon from his pocket. Gregor cringed when he saw it, feeling it sting his eyes. The Tilean laughed at his discomfort. 'You see, I know you will try harder next time, because you know now that I can bring you back any time I choose. Every time you are restored a little bit less of what was once you comes back. The vampire becomes even stronger.'

Gregor tried to force himself to look at the icon Carandini held, but knew he could not. The light of Sigmar had abandoned him, now he was a profane thing and the talismans of his god were anathema to him. Even the simple silver hammer Carandini held reviled him.

'There is only one way you will find peace, vampire,' Carandini said. 'You will help me gain possession of *Das Buch die Unholden*. Only then will I free you from the curse of the undead.'

'Streng escaped,' Gregor said, feeling the full weight of his defeat crushing his spirit. 'He can't lead us to Thulmann and the book now.'

Carandini laughed, patting the decaying head of the carrion crow. 'You lost him,' he said. 'I did not. Even now, one of my little pretties is following him, shadowing his every move. When he returns to the witch hunter, we will know it.'

ABOUT THE AUTHOR

C. L. Werner has written a number of Lovecraftian pastiches and pulp-style horror stories for assorted small press publications and *Inferno!* magazine. Currently living in the American south-west, he continues to write stories of mayhem and madness set in the Warhammer World.

NAGASH THE SORCERER

The undead will rise...

⟨ MIKE LEE ⟩

UK ISBN 978-1-84416-660-2 US ISBN 978-1-84416-556-8

MALEKITH

A Tale of the Sundering

GAV THORPE

UK ISBN 978-1-84416-673-2   US ISBN 978-1-84416-610-7

WARHAMMER

Bloodthirsty action from the battlefields of the Old World

BLACKHEARTS
THE OMNIBUS

Nathan Long

UK ISBN 978-1-84416-510-0

WARHAMMER

Bloody tales of heroism from the
dark and gothic world of Warhammer
Featuring fiction from

Graham McNeill
Robert Earl
Sandy Mitchell
Nathan Long

Buy this
anthology or read
a free extract at
www.blacklibrary.com

TALES OF THE
OLD WORLD

Edited by Marc Gascoigne & Christian Dunn

ISBN 978-1-84416-452-3